HOPE IN THE FOREST OF DESPAIR

Also by Goldeen Ogawa

THE ADVENTURES OF BOURAGNER FELPZ
Volume I: A Study of Magic
Volume II: Anatomy of a Magician
Volume III: The Aubergine Spellbook

PROFESSOR ODD
The Complete Season One (Episodes 1-6)
The Complete Season Two (Episodes 7-12)

DRIVING ARCANA
By Moon and Star (Wheel 1)
Paving the Road to Hell (Wheel 2)

LUCENA IN THE HOUSE OF MADGRIN

For a complete catalog of titles, please visit us online at
HELIOPAUSEWEB.COM/FICTION

GOLDEEN OGAWA

HOPE IN
THE FOREST
OF DESPAIR

DRIVING
WHEEL 3
ARCANA

a HELIOPAUSE PRODUCTION

For Orion—hidden hero

ON RAMP

What do you do when your drastic measures to save your own life result in you becoming a strange, half-undead creature that even other monsters are afraid of? If you?re Jill Hamilton, you start a company dedicated to the study of those monsters?and anything else that looks remotely magical.

What do you do when you lose your best friend when she falls off a bridge in Purgatory? If you?re Clara Nordstern, you try to find the next thing that needs doing. Even if it means confronting your worst fears and your deepest guilt.

What do you do when you get sucked into Hell by the demon Lilith? If you?re Selene Shields, you start walking. One foot in front of the other. Even if it means going right through the center of Hell.

CONTENTS

1. LIGHTNING DOES STRIKE TWICE   1

2. MOONRISE OVER HADES   61

3. THE HOUR I FIRST BELIEVED   112

4. HOPE IN THE FOREST OF DESPAIR   170

5. CLOTH OF MAN   220

6. BLOOD AND FURY   279

7. FEAR NOT   328

8. A COLD DAY IN HELL   389

9. THE GREAT GATE   433

   THE LADY IN THE GRAY SUIT   508

Three sights incredible to see:
A white stag leaping through the trees
An eagle diving to the sea
The new moon rising
over Hades

1.
LIGHTNING DOES STRIKE TWICE

Lafayette, IN
December

IT WAS CHRISTMAS EVE, and it was snowing. Big, fluffy flakes that piled on the sidewalks and choked the window above Mantha Fulgeroiu's bed. It would have been exciting, except this was the fourth night in a row that the cloudy skies had opened and shed piles of cold white stuff all over the city, and at this point it looked like Christmas was going to be whited right out.

It was cold, too. Bună had piled her bed with all the blankets in the house and put their one working space heater in her room, but Mantha had reached over and switched it off as soon as she heard her grandmother settle down in the kitchen (where it was "warmer, *minunăție*, don't worry, we had much colder winters back home, when I was your age—and we didn't even have a house back then—only a shed!") because she knew how much Bună worried about covering their electric bill. She curled herself into a tight ball and watched the snow collecting on her windowsill until holding her eyes open became too much trouble and she went to sleep.

Other children might have stayed up hoping to hear a sign of Santa Claus, but Mantha had never found that story very convincing. Neither did her bună, who had instead told her the story of Saint Nicholas, and it was their tradition to open such presents as they received in time on his day, December 6th, and any presents afterward as soon as they arrived. Christmas Day was reserved for celebrating the Birth of Christ with a morning service at St. Mary's Cathedral and a lot of singing. After which they would volunteer in the soup kitchen, dispensing food for the needy—which sometimes included themselves. Bună would scrape the bottom of the pot and pour the leftover contents into neat Tupperware containers, which they would put in the freezer for those weeks when food money ran short. But for Christmas dinner Bună always roasted a ham with cloves pressed into it, and allowed Mantha to select from the local Saveway a cream-covered pumpkin pie. It was the ham and the pie that Mantha really looked forward to, and when her stomach woke her, growling angrily, she rushed out of bed, hoping to get the day over with so they could get on to dinner.

She had slept in, which was surprising. Usually Bună came and got her up before sunrise to help clean the house before church, even on Christmas. Mornings for Mantha usually meant gray, achey feelings and tired eyes, but that morning, with a credible amount of sleep under her belt, she felt positively bright and sharp.

Thrusting her feet into her ragged bunny slippers and keeping the thickest blanket wrapped around her shoulders Mantha padded out of her little room and poked her head into Bună's. As expected, the bed there was neatly made and unoccupied.

Mantha went downstairs and found Bună sitting in her favorite armchair next to the stove, right where she'd left her the night before.

She was cold to the touch and didn't respond to Mantha's greeting.

So Mantha made her warm again, and presently Bună got up and together they cleaned the kitchen and dusted the seldom-used living room. Mantha made herself a slice of toast with jam, but Bună didn't eat anything.

"I don't need the same kind of nourishment that you do," she said, kindly.

Secretly, Mantha thought she did. Her face was so thin and wrinkled, and had grown hollow in recent months, like something had come in and sucked the filling out of it. But she knew better than to argue with her bună, so she got out the shovel and started clearing them a path to the street.

Bună kept tipping over all through the morning, and Mantha had to keep a hand on her side to make her sing properly. It was exhausting, but she knew it was wrong for Bună to keel over in the middle of the Christmas service, and so she kept them going. All through the morning and through the afternoon dispensing soup and buying the pie.

But it was too much work for Bună make dinner, and so Mantha got Lady Bibbit to help.

Lady Bibbit was the stuffed plush bunny with silver-gray fur, a white belly, a pink nose, and bright blue glass eyes that Bună had given Mantha on her third birthday. And she might have stayed that way but for the fact that Mantha had been introduced to *Calvin and Hobbes* and *The Velveteen Rabbit* in quick succession soon afterward, and thereafter had sworn never to abandon Lady Bibbit or let her be thrown away. Lady Bibbit slept in her bed and, when not playing with Mantha or bouncing along in her backpack, spent her days propped up in Bună's room, reading her extensive collection of romance novels.

Lady Bibbit had never cooked a ham before, but she helpfully kept Mantha company while she dutifully read out the recipe and chopped the potatoes.

Mantha laid the potatoes on a sheet under the ham and put it in the oven. She propped Bună in her favorite chair and the three of them had a very pleasant dinner and all agreed the pie was excellent—though Bună was sick afterward and threw up everything she had swallowed. It didn't matter. Mantha put on a pair of rubber gloves and cleaned it up. Mantha decided it had been, all in all, a good Christmas, and as a special treat, left her electric heater on that night.

Bună was cold again in the morning, and this time when Mantha went to make her warm the old woman snapped at her:

"No one should lose their bună on Christmas morning, so I gave you that! But this is too much, minunăție! Too much! You must call my priest now and get on with it."

"Get on with what?" Mantha asked, drawing back, afraid. Bună rarely used that tone of voice, but when she did things were serious indeed.

Bună's face softened a little, but she just shook her head and laid it back against her chair. Her mouth was open slightly, and her eyes stared up at the ceiling, unblinking.

This time, when Mantha made her warm again, all she did was begin to smell faintly.

"No," said Mantha, shaking her grandmother by the shoulder. Then, louder and louder: "No, no, no! No! NO!"

The final "no" came out as a long, piercing scream that lifted the dishes from the drying rack, rattled the silverware in the drawer, and temporarily caused Bună's hair to stand up on end.

Then Mantha's lungs ran out of air and everything fell back into place as her voice cut off in a choke.

The crash made her jump. She looked around the kitchen, and found Lady Bibbit had come down the stairs and was standing in the doorway.

Only it was not Lady Bibbit. It was a four-foot tall rabbit with little hand-paws and a wet, twitching nose and limpid blue eyes. Her fur was silver-gray but for a white splash across her belly, which rose and fell with the breath going in and out of her warm, living body.

It was exactly the person Mantha had always imagined Lady Bibbit to be, except she was no longer confined to Mantha's imagination.

She was real and standing there and looking sadly from Mantha to Bună and back again, her narrow shoulders slumped.

"Oh, oh Mantha," she said, and her voice spoke, not in the back of Mantha's head, where it had always done in the past, but rang in her ears. She had a faint lisp, but otherwise sounded just the same.

Mantha screamed and ran out the door.

Behind her there was a faint *flump* sound, as of a small stuffed animal falling onto the floor.

Bloomington, IN
January

It was not snowing in Bloomington, but only just. Instead, what the forecast called a "wintry mix" and what Julianna called "winter is a bitch in a pissing contest" was sleeting down hard against the windows of the rambling house. Work had been understandably suspended, which sent Julianna into fit of vocal anxietizing over money.

"I never shouldda married a Jew!" Tyleo shouted over his shoulder as he went to take refuge in the playroom.

"If you hadn't you'd be homeless!" Julianna screamed, and Tyleo shut the door in a hurry and then leaned his back against it, breathing a mock sigh of relief for the benefit of Brodi, who was constructing a maze of train tracks across the playroom floor.

"Are you in trouble?" Brodi asked gravely.

"Not yet," Tyleo told her with a bright grin, and sat down to help with the maze.

The playroom was a den-like room at the front of the house with a wide window (curtained) which looked out onto the road. As such Tyleo and Brodi were the first to hear the motorcycle as it turned onto their street and came chugging slowly down it.

"Jesus-ass-christ," Tyleo said, twitching back the shades to get a better look at the intrepid rider. They were big, dressed all in black, and their bike was similarly bulky and muscular. It had a prong of metal welded above the headlamp. "There's balls, and then there's bein' an idiot."

"Are *they* in trouble?" Brodi asked.

"Maybe," said Tyleo. "But it's not our fault if they get hypothermic."

The motorcycle passed. At the end of the street it turned around and came slowly back.

"What the hell?" said Tyleo, when he heard the engine cut off in their very driveway.

He heard the wet smack of boots climbing up onto the porch. The confused silence while the rider realized the doorbell didn't work, and then a sharp, but polite, knock.

No one answered for a long time. Tyleo sure as hell wasn't going to.

The rider knocked again.

That got Julianna out of the kitchen. He heard her open the door and ask "What do you want?" in a tight voice.

The rider answered, too low for the words to be made out, but Tyleo was surprised to hear they sounded like a woman.

He knew then what this was about. Knew, but didn't understand why he knew and so pretended he didn't. He kept right on pretending while Julianna told the woman to wait, shut the door in her face, and came around to the playroom.

"Ty, it's for you," she said. "Some dyke on a bike."

Still firmly telling himself he had no idea what this was about, Tyleo got up and followed his wife out of the playroom. Brodi trotted behind him, but Julianna grabbed her hand and took her safely into the kitchen while he unlatched the door.

The woman standing outside was very tall, very white, very wet, and very, very bald. Seriously. Tyleo thought she might not even have eyebrows, unless her hair was just naturally so pale it was invisible.

She must also have been very cold. The wet air that blasted him in the face when he opened the door was frigid. The drops were as big and thick as they could be without actually being snow, and she'd been *biking* in that weather. Granted, she was wearing a leather jacket and pants and big boots, but everything was shiny with wet and there was a puddle slowly spreading under her feet.

Tyleo's instinctive thought was neo-Nazi skinhead, but he couldn't see any tattoos and he wasn't sure if women were even allowed in that group. She didn't have any gang symbols visible either: everything was plain black leather and a few silver buckles here and there. She was wearing a rather complicated harness which held a sword strapped to her back, but it was wedged firmly in its sheath and her hands were folded neatly in front of her.

"Tyleo Jordan?" she asked, her voice soft and small.

"Who wants to know?" Tyleo asked. He'd been clean for years, but before that there had been enough lost time he was sure he'd never be rid of weirdos from his past showing up at his door asking for money. Strangely, that was a much more comforting prospect than what he really knew this was about.

Except he didn't know, he reminded himself.

"I am Clara Nordstern," said the woman in black leather. "I am very sorry, but I am here to inform you that your sister is dead."

"Ah," said Tyleo, and nodded. As if he'd already known. Which he had, ever since he'd heard that woman's voice. Not because of some precognitive bullcrap like Aunt Elsa would have called it, but because—even more than a female neo-Nazi skinhead biker, this Clara Nordstern seemed exactly the sort of person Selene would hang out with. And why else would one of *her* lot be here?

"I have a death certificate," Clara said, taking his muted response as disbelief.

"No, no," said Tyleo, raising a hand to stop her reaching into the breast pocket of her jacket. "I believe you. And you don't need to tell me how. I can imagine it just fine."

Clara gave him a strange, pained look. She had remarkable eyes: pure blue, pale as ice, and heart-wrenchingly tragic.

Suddenly Tyleo got a whole other idea of who this person might be.

"Sorry," he said. "Were you two, uh," he waved a hand between them suggestively, "like . . . ? 'Cause she mighta told you some things about me, which, let's be real, we haven't talked since she joined the army—and I . . . uh . . . I was an idiot back then and . . . uh . . . look I'm just real sorry, okay?"

Clara blinked at him, slowly.

"We were partners," she said quietly. "Not romantically. We worked together."

"Oh," said Tyleo, suddenly feeling very small.

"She did not speak of her family much," Clara went on. "But this seemed necessary." She continued rooting around in the pocket of her jacket, eventually drawing out a bulging envelope. "Her assets did not amount to much, but you are legally entitled to this, as one of her surviving relatives."

She handed him the envelope. It had a white label on it with his mother's name and address, crossed out, and his own written beside it in his mother's angriest handwriting. It hadn't been opened.

Well, that explained how Clara had found him. He sighed.

"Sorry about Annabee," he said.

Clara lowered and raised her shoulders. A shrug.

Suddenly it seemed important that she understand.

"Our dad, he'd barely gotten back on the wagon when she came out. Fell right off again after she left. Now, I told Mama it was the bottle that killed him, but she always blamed Selene."

Clara nodded stoically. "We are not always rational in our grief."

"Yeah," said Tyleo. There was nothing else to say, really. He opened the envelope. Counted the bills inside. At the back there was a small white card. Tyleo fished it out and read what was printed on it, and frowned.

"The *Moonshield Center for Supernatural Investigation and Research?*" he said, incredulous.

Clara nodded again, gravely. "The work we were engaged in . . . if you find yourself in any unnatural trouble . . . please call. There won't be a fee."

Tyleo stuffed the card back into the envelope, shaking his head.

"Well, thanks, I guess," he said, trying not to sound too sarcastic.

Clara inclined her head: a stiff sort of bow.

"Farewell," she said, then turned to go.

"Okay, hold on," Tyleo said, causing her to pause in the action of putting on her helmet. He waved the envelope. "Now I do gotta ask . . . how did it—what happened?"

Clara gave him a baleful look. She seemed torn by some internal conflict, and then her expression cleared and she said, with frightening sincerity:

"She died saving my life."

Then she put on her helmet and walked away into the sleeting rain.

Tyleo stood there, dumbstruck, and watched until she'd mounted her bike and ridden off down the street: a black shadow sliced to pieces by the hard, slanting streaks of gray and white.

Detroit, MI

The building was impressive. Big and tall with square supporting rectangles, like shoulders, on each side. The face was riddled with narrow, deep-set windows and below the towering body was a relatively low outcropping of building with a slanted roof, arches and columns.

Even more impressive were the masses of rigging and construction gear which mobbed the north half of it, currently swarming with workers taking advantage of the first clear day in over a week. Their work was already evident on the south side: stone and brickwork gleamed, even under the gray sky, and the windows glittered with new glass—some with the manufacturer's stickers still on.

The young man with dark brown skin and bright orange hair picked his way carefully under the scaffolding. Someone had been hard at work bagging the refuse which had collected over the course of the building's half-century of abandonment, and these bags—big, bulging and black—had been piled against the columns which supported the vainglorious façade. Bits of faded graffiti were still visible in places, but for the most part they were succumbing to the attention of a group of workers in gray overalls.

Once under the arches, the man found himself inside the building's cavernous front hall—which had once been its waiting room and was still furnished with the double-fronted benches arranged in columns up its center. The arched ceiling above was a patchwork of old stone tiling and new plaster bandages, with some scaffolding down at the end to his left where someone was erecting a sign that said LIGHTFAST over the door to a room beyond.

The place was lit by crude floodlights aimed at sheets of white canvas, and the man understood why when he glanced at the windows and saw they were all covered with blackout cloth.

Beyond the waiting room was a complex of cubicles and offices that had once housed such important things as the telegraph, the barber shop, drug store, cafeteria, a newsstand, and chiefly of all: the ticket office. The man with orange hair made for that as his most likely point of contact and was not disappointed.

A small Asian woman in a neat black suit with short black hair was sitting behind the window, writing industriously on a battered laptop.

The man frowned. He only had vague memories of the woman named Jill Hamilton, but he was pretty sure she'd had brown hair. And glasses. But she had been small, and she had said she would be here.

The woman behind the laptop looked up sharply when he cleared his throat.

"Do you have an appointment?" she asked.

"I think . . . not really," the man admitted. "I . . . I'm Marcus Bowerman. I—we spoke on the phone last week. That is, we did if you're Jill Hamilton."

The woman shook her head. She had very pale skin. Almost translucent, and a little green in the corners.

"Marcus Bowerman . . . " she repeated, scanning something on her screen. "Bowerman, Bowerman—oh, here you are." She seemed surprised. "2:30, Friday." She checked the time. "You're early." She sounded approving. Marcus swallowed. Flammard had said they would be happy to have him, but even so Marcus had gotten the distinct impression that some force had been fighting him every inch of the way from Chicago to Detroit. Canceled flights (they *were* in the middle of a snowstorm, granted), late buses, and finally the cab he'd hired had gotten a flat right outside the city limits. In the end he'd walked from his hotel to the station, leaving well in advance in case of complications, but for once the trip had gone smoothly.

The woman was giving him an appraising look. "Here for a job interview," she stated.

Marcus nodded, trying not to show how nervous he was. "Nothing specific. Just, wherever you could use the help."

"That's very generous of you," said the woman. She didn't make it sound like a good thing. Then she shrugged. "Come around then," she said, and indicated a little door to the side.

Marcus went as directed and found himself in the gutted ticket office, where two folding chairs had been set up on either side of a rickety light stand. The center of the room was occupied by a large, dusty-looking vault with paper laid out over the floor. It smelled strongly of vinegar and bleach.

Marcus sat in the nearest chair while the woman moved her laptop from the ticket counter to the light stand. She did this one-handed, thumbing something into her smart phone as she went.

"All right," she said, scooting forward so she could continue typing on her laptop. "You are Marcus Bowerman, 4947 S Calumet Avenue, Chicago?"

"That's right," said Marcus, uncertainly.

"Okay," said the woman, turning the laptop around so he could see the screen. "Could I have you confirm your telephone and email for me?"

Marcus did. When he had finished, the woman took the computer back and typed something in. She raised her head and looked at him sharply over the top of her screen.

Marcus thought her eyes flashed red for a moment.

"All right, Marcus, what's your race?"

Marcus stared at her, not sure whether to be offended. White people usually read him as black—which was correct—despite the orange hair, but something in this woman's tone led him to believe that she meant the question in a different way than most people did.

"I'm . . . sorry?" he said.

The woman pursed her lips impatiently.

"I can tell you're not full human. You smell of something, but it's faint and I can't place it. Jill wants you, which means it's probably unusual. Do you know how many applications we get each day?"

"I . . . I don't know," Marcus admitted.

"We've had a hundred and thirty so far," she said. "Most of them spelled very badly and only a dozen through the proper channels. My junk folder is *full* of people wanting jobs with mixer who think they can get one on the basis that their great-grandmother told a really good ghost story. Once. But you, Jill says, you, we want. Even though we're not fully operational. Even though we don't yet know what sort of work we'll have for people. Even though we don't even have *payroll* set up yet. So what's your deal, Marcus? Are you a witch? Scholar? Lumenite? Got leprechaun ancestry?"

"No, no, no," said Marcus, finally realizing what this was about. He shook his head. "Look, can I talk to Jill? Jill was the one I was told to talk to."

"By who?" asked the woman.

"Flammard Nordstern," said Marcus, almost defiantly.

He thought the woman's eyes would pop right out of her skull the way she stared at him. She looked down at her laptop, then she looked back up at him, then she frowned and typed at her keyboard some more.

"Okay," she said, in a very different tone. "I see. I didn't have access to your full file. I'm sorry." She shut her laptop and extended a pallid, bony hand. Marcus shook it gingerly. Her skin was cold.

"I'm Lansing Ise," said the woman. "Formerly of the Great Northern Conference of United Vampires, now Chief Counsel for Jill Hamilton and Assistant Director of mixer. Welcome to mixer, Marcus. It'll be good to have a son of Loki working with us."

"I—thank you—does that mean I—what is *mixer?*" Marcus asked, feeling confused. "And I'm not actually a *son* of Loki. More like a great, great, great, great grandson, by Flammard's reckoning."

"Whatever. We're happy to have you," said Lansing Ise. "And it's not 'mixer', it's MCSIR: the Moonshield Center for Supernatural Investigation and Research. Can you start . . . oh . . . now? Animal Control just brought in a stray dog they say is a werewolf but Jill isn't convinced. Maybe you can help?"

"Can't you tell?" Marcus asked, slowly getting to his feet.

Lansing snorted. "Sure. But then we'd never get payroll set up." She pointed to the door. "They have him in the carriage entrance. Just head out into the concourse and take a right."

In something of a daze Marcus followed her instructions and found himself in another hall, this one filled with scaffolding and people working away plastering the ceiling. A small arch had been left open at the righthand end, and when he ducked through this he emerged into a covered parking lot of sorts, open to the air by a wide, gently sloping driveway. Sure enough, a white van with ANIMAL CONTROL stamped on the side was backed up next to the loading dock, and two people in white coveralls were standing beside its open rear doors.

As he drew closer, Marcus saw that only one of them was in coveralls, really: the man with scruffy blond hair and a potbelly. The woman, tiny by comparison, was in fact wearing a white lab coat with a hood (up) and a dirty gray apron that came down to her knees. A pair of thick, black rubber gloves were tucked through the strings of the apron, which wrapped double around her waist, and she was fingering her phone as if trying to take a picture of whatever was in the back of the van.

Marcus cleared his throat, and Jill Hamilton looked over at him, a few stray wisps of brown hair escaping from under her hood. She pushed her glasses up her nose and blinked at him.

"Um . . . hi," said Marcus, waving awkwardly. "Lansing, uh . . . Lansing sent me over. Something about a werewolf?"

"Marcus Bowerman," said Jill Hamilton, as though confirming this fact. Marcus nodded.

"Great," said the small woman. She beckoned him closer. "This is Pete Boskin, Wayne County Animal Control." A jerk of her hooded head at the potbellied man, who acknowledged Marcus's presence with a shrug of his shoulders. "I've been trying to tell him that just because it's a weird dog doesn't automatically make it a werewolf."

"But he's *weird*," said Pete Boskin. "Ain't a normal dog. Too smart. Look, there he goes at the latch again!"

There was a jangling and clanking from the van, and drawing up next to them Marcus peered inside to see a dirty white dog attempting to unlatch its cage with its teeth.

"If he was a werewolf," Jill said, in the tired tones of one who had explained this before, "he could turn into a human and get out that way. Which he would do," Jill added, apparently for Marcus's benefit, "since I've been going on about how we *know* about werewolves and we'll happily release him to his pack leader if he'd just turn human and *explain* things."

"Lady, I don't know what you want me to do," said Pete Boskin. "We can't keep him, I'm telling ya. He's weirding out the staff down at the pound."

"If he's not a supernatural or otherwise paranormal entity," Jill said tightly, "then MCSIR can't do anything with him. Unless Marcus wants a dog. Do you want a dog, Marcus?"

Marcus gazed at her, appalled. He loved dogs. He would like, in the future, to have a dog of his own. But not when he was financially and locationally uncertain, and probably not a ghost-like dog with creepy yellow eyes and ears that looked like they were stained with blood.

Jill sighed. She did it very deliberately: air went in, then out.

"Fine," she said. "Can you at least tell me if he's got anything supernatural about him? Ordinarily I'd ask Clara but she's out on business."

Marcus didn't ask about her other bodyguard, the black sister with the guns. Flammard had already told him why she wasn't around anymore.

"I'll try," he said. "I'm not as sensitive as Flammard."

The dog had stopped chewing on the latch. It was sitting on its haunches and looking at Marcus perceptively. Too perceptively. It felt more like being sized up by a tiger. Marcus got the feeling that this dog knew exactly how long it would take it to run Marcus down and rip out his throat. And that the answer was: not very.

Nevertheless, and with the rationale that there was a sturdy wall of cage between them, he walked up to the back of the van and bent over to take a better look at it.

At first all he saw was a rather funny-looking but otherwise perfectly ordinary dog. A dog who was actually a bitch, he was pretty sure. The state of her teats suggested she'd had puppies in the past, and on closer inspection there were several old scars marking her face. She was lean, but not thin, and growled low in her throat when he got his face too close to the wire.

He smelled a faint stink of urine and dog musk and pulled back a few inches. The dog glared at him. She really did seem to have human emotions and expressions—maybe she was a werewolf after all? Marcus had never met a werewolf, but Flammard had told him they were real. These days, he trusted Flammard's word over just about any other evidence. Flammard had a way of looking at the world where anything that was at all magical or supernatural became immediately obvious. He'd been teaching Marcus how to do it himself, as a measure of self-defense against people who tried to exploit his extraordinary heritage, but Marcus still felt woefully inept at it.

Nevertheless, now seemed like a good time to put what he had learned into practice. So he squeezed his eyes shut, held his breath, and tried shifting his point of view—not outside his head, just pushing his mind into that bigger, scarier space where it could do things like open portals or conjure fire or see things that other people couldn't.

When he opened his eyes there was no longer a dog in the back of the van. Instead there was a tight, bright knot of wild energy, and it was staring at him with eyes like holes torn in the fabric of reality, through which he could just glimpse a vast, black, unknowable world.

He jerked back, letting out a surprised, inarticulate sound. The dog snapped back into focus, but still Marcus felt it more like a sharp twist of energy in space and time. An ancient, wild energy which was presently pleasing itself to look and act like a dog.

"Th-that's not a dog," he said, hearing his voice shake.

"I knew it," said Pete Boskin, triumphantly.

"Then what is it?" Jill asked, coming to stand beside him.

"I told you," Pete Boskin said, "it's a *werewolf.*"

"That ain't no werewolf," Marcus said. Even having never met a werewolf in his life, he knew this wasn't one. "That's a . . . well I think it's a *she*. And she's . . . oh, man, Ms. Hamilton, I don't know what she is."

"Call me Jill," said the woman. She put on her gloves. "All right then. She's dog *shaped*, so I guess we'd better set up a kennel."

Indianapolis, IN

Riding counterclockwise around the state capital through a haze of fresh rain and spatter from the other motorists, tired and depressed and so cold it was almost problematic, Clara got lost inside her own head.

It was not the most pleasant place to be. She'd had another dream last night, which had been troubling in and of itself. Clara didn't, as a rule, allow herself to dream, because her dreams had an uncanny habit of coming true. But this one had snuck in under all her guards and against all expectation had been a perfectly nice dream.

She'd been living in a big house with a lot of roses in the front yard and a white picket fence. It was sunny and hot and she'd taken off her jacket. And there had been someone else. Someone kind and golden in among the roses, pruning them. They had made a joke, and Clara had laughed.

Clara in the waking world couldn't remember laughing like that, and had clung to the feeling even as she'd felt herself being dragged from sleep. She'd woken up in a moldy hotel room outside Atlanta, halfway between Selene's last two living relations, on her way back from a brusque exchange with her late partner's mother.

That had stung. From what she knew of Selene's past, Clara hadn't been expecting a warm reception. Still, to hear the bitter old woman talk, one would have thought she was *glad* that her daughter was dead. Clara had wanted to shake her. Instead she'd gotten back on her bike and ridden north until the sun came up. She'd slept through the day and then kept riding, right into the teeth of the storm that was only now abating, until she'd reached Bloomington.

She'd considered resting after the meeting with Selene's brother and before the final push back to home base, but resting meant she might dream again, and Clara dreaded what would come next. It turned out pleasant dreams were even worse than ominous ones. Now she had something to lose.

She already felt lost, adrift in a cold sea. It was as bad as when Schiavona had left. Worse, almost. Schiavona was, in all likelihood, still alive— or at least, liable to come back from the dead—while Selene . . .

For all Selene was one of the most remarkable women Clara had ever met, she was still purely human. That had been part of why she was so remarkable. But it also meant her body couldn't survive long outside its native dimension, even in the more friendly environs.

And she had fallen into Hell.

Because Clara had dropped her.

She was lost. Literally. She'd missed her exit. 465 was turning into 865 and she was seeing signs for 65 N, Lebanon, Lafayette, instead of 69 N and Fort Wayne. That exit was behind her now, somewhere in the spray of a semitruck.

She looked for a convenient escape, but it appeared she'd reached a stretch of highway that was determined to channel her onto 65 N, and the next suitable stopping point wasn't until the neighborhood of Zionsville.

She coasted onto 65 and felt something tug, just under her breastbone. It was sharp and sudden and gone almost as soon as it happened, but it left a nagging, itching ache in her bones.

Clara knew that feeling. It had been the same feeling that had led her west, almost two years ago now, west to the very edge of the continent, pursuing a hive of bloodthirsty chimeras. She'd felt it again, in Georgia, during the advent of Fury-Joy. It was not as strong as when Vjor had come through the Gateway Arch in St. Louis, but then, it was hard to tell at this distance.

Clara got off the freeway and pulled into the parking lot of a strip mall, but she did not get out her phone and start plotting a route back to Detroit. Instead she stood astride her motorcycle, letting it idle under her, while the rain pattered down on her shoulders and helmet.

It was lightening up, even as the temperature was dropping. In a little while, it would probably be snow.

Clara ignored it. She focused on the itching ache, trying to draw out its source.

North. That was all she had. North, in the direction that 65 would take her.

And why not? It wasn't so terribly out of her way. And what was waiting for her in Detroit? Construction work and whatever project Jill was presently working on. While this . . .

Frankly Clara had no idea what *this* was. But following these feelings had been what she had done for the better part of her life. Before Jill and Selene; then as now, when she had been alone.

In a strange, abrasive way, it felt comforting going back to that. Retreating into the cold.

But Clara had changed in the intervening years. Which was why she did get out her phone at last and, holding one glove in her mouth so she could operate the touch screen, texted Jill to tell her she was taking a short detour.

someting in lafayette

She didn't bother to correct the typo. Jill would understand. She sent the message and stuffed the phone back into her pocket. She pulled out of the parking lot and got back on the highway, heading north.

The itching ache grew stronger with every mile.

Lafayette, IN

Samantha Folger woke up in the dark of the winter morning, feeling like something was wrong. But when she turned on her light and examined her room, everything was exactly as she'd left it the night before. There was her My Little Pony backpack with the rolling wheels, ready for her first day back at school after Christmas break. Her purple-and-pink polka-dot comforter was pulled up under her chin, and Mr. Bun, the stuffed yellow bunny in a red blazer, was sitting protectively at her feet. Across the mint-colored carpet was her bookshelf with all her favorite books on it, starting with the four omnibus volumes of *Calvin and Hobbes*, and going on to include weathered hardback copies of *The Hobbit*, *The Sword in the Stone*, *Matilda*, *Momo*, and *Tehanu*—which was, to her parents' bewilderment, the only Earthsea novel she considered worth owning. With Christmas had come the optimistic addition of a bright, shiny, paperback edition of *The Lion, the Witch, and the Wardrobe*, the first *Harry Potter* book, and a used hardback of something called *Archer's Goon*, which had such a terrible cover that Samantha had pushed it right to the back and tried to forget about it. She could just see a corner of it now, peeking out from behind *Harry Potter and the Sorcerer's Stone*.

She could also see her alarm clock, which said it was half an hour before it was due to go off. Too early to get up, but not early enough to go back to sleep. So she lay in bed and stared at the ceiling, trying to think of what had woken her up in the first place.

There had been a dream, she was pretty sure. Not frightening, but still upsetting. She felt desperately sad for some reason: as if she'd lost someone precious. But upon taking stock of her important people she remembered that both her parents were in perfectly good health, and excluding her dad's dad, who had died in a car crash before he was born, so were all her grandparents.

No one should lose their grandmother on Christmas day . . .

Now where had that come from? It felt like someone had said that to her recently, but she couldn't think where or when.

Or she didn't want to.

Suddenly it was like she'd been thrust out over thin ice on a dark lake. She was skating along, sliding toward a bright shore, but it was far, far away. And the lake was deep. And there was something in it, reaching out to her . . .

Samantha got up. She put on the clothes that had been laid out for her and went downstairs. The kitchen was dark and cold and she was not allowed to use the electric stove unsupervised, but she made herself a cup of hot, instant cocoa in the microwave and a bowl of cold cereal with sliced banana. She was eating the cereal and drinking the cocoa when her father came down, still rubbing the sleep out of his eyes, and began making coffee. He was so focused on the activity that he mistook her for Mom and asked, "Do you want a cup, Margie?" and when Samantha answered, "No, thanks Dad," he jumped so hard he nearly dropped the jar of beans.

"Sweet jeezus, Sammy," he gasped, blinking at her. "What are you doing up so early?"

Samantha shrugged. She didn't like being called Sammy, but she'd given up correcting Dad. Truth was, she didn't like being called Samantha, either, but she wasn't sure what she *did* want to be called. Something shorter than Samantha—but not Sammy.

"Bad dream," she said at length. "And I didn't want to be late on my first day."

"You've only been gone two weeks," Dad said, pouring the beans into the coffee grinder. "And so has everyone else!" He chuckled as the grinder buzzed to life.

Mom came down eventually, and was less surprised to find Samantha already awake and dressed. She was mostly relieved.

"It'll be slow going, with the roads the way they are," she pointed out.

It had precipitated in the night, but not snow this time. The roads were full of slick slush and ice and Mom crept along at 30 mph in the Land Rover all the way to school. Samantha had offered to walk, but Mom wouldn't hear of it.

"It's freezing out there, Samantha!"

Not as cold as the winters when I was your age, and we didn't even have a house then—

Samantha shook her head, trying to clear it.

School was a big, square brick of a building with echoing halls. Samantha felt momentarily at a loss for where to go upon entering, but once she checked her sheet it all came back. She settled down in Mrs. Douglas's 6th-grade class and got out her notebook with a supreme sense of relief.

This was her life, after all. Two loving parents in a big, warm house and an ordinary teacher at an ordinary school. Everything was fine.

The blissful mundanity was shattered midway through the afternoon when something went *splat* against the classroom window, and then slowly oozed down the pane. Maintenance was called, and the man who came up on a ladder to scrape the thing off informed the inquiring minds within that it had been a dove.

"Birds do that all the time," said Ricky Stevens, knowledgeably. "They don't see the glass and *splat!*" He mimed a bird smacking into the glass with his hands.

The girls around him gasped and squealed in disgust. The other boys nodded knowingly, and began offering up similar anecdotes.

Samantha remained in her seat, hardly hearing a word.

Part of the bird had traveled clean through the window and lay in a crumpled lump on the floor by Ricky Stevens's desk.

No one else seemed to be able to see it, but now as the class was shooed back to their seats it picked itself up and came flailing over to Samantha's desk.

It looked like a dove that had been squashed, but was somehow still alive. It shed blobs of blood and guts as it moved, which evaporated as soon as they hit the ground. It flopped over and, with a momentous effort, managed to flutter up on broken wings to sprawl over her notebook.

There was something in its beak: a sprig of ivy. It was dark green and glossy, and remained even after the shade of the dove had faded away to nothing.

Samantha ignored it for the rest of the day, hoping it, like the dove, would fade. But it was still there when the bell rang; had even sprouted tiny roots that were wriggling their way into the fiberboard of her desk.

She walked out quickly, before Mrs. Douglas could ask her about it.

She got outside. It was snowing again, but lightly, and the fragile flakes melted as soon as they touched the ground. All around her, kids were being bundled into minivans and suburbans by harried-looking parents.

Without thinking, Samantha began to walk, heading east.

A Land Rover detached itself from the crowd and came careening up to the sidewalk. Its passenger window rolled down and Mom shouted through it:

"Samantha Vanessa Folger, what are you *thinking*? Get *in!* We'll be late for gymnastics!"

That jerked Samantha out of her daze in a hurry. Of course! She got to do gymnastics three times a week now. Samantha had always yearned to do gymnastics, ever since she'd learned about Nadia Comăneci, but they hadn't had the money for it until recently.

She puzzled over this all the way to the gym. How could she have forgotten? And why was Comăneci so important? The Folgers weren't Romanian. But Samantha had specific memories of watching old clips of Nadia Comăneci on uneven bars, and when she couldn't take gymnastics lessons, had contrived to get her bangs cut just the way Nadia's had been in the 1970s. With her hair up in a ponytail she thought she looked very much like Nadia that way; they had the same olive-peach skin, dark brown eyes and hair, and their faces were a similar shape—though Samantha's eyebrows weren't as good, she felt.

Sitting in the back of the Land Rover, looking at the back of Mom's blond head, she wondered how she had come out looking so different from her freckly, blue-eyed parents.

"It's the Italian on my side of the family," Dad used to joke. "It always finds a way to come out!"

Mom went grocery shopping while Samantha was in gymnastics, and it was dark by the time they were driving home. Dad had beaten them to it and left the porch light on, so Samantha could see the rabbit sitting on their front step perfectly well as soon as she got out of the car.

It was not Mr. Bun. This rabbit was silver, which a white patch down her front, and two huge, limpid blue eyes.

She was also a living, breathing, and—as soon as Samantha approached—*talking* rabbit. She was about four feet tall, not counting her ears, and stood on her hind legs, rubbing her front paws together nervously.

"Mantha," she said, in an eerily familiar voice. "Mantha, won't you please come back. Bună needs taking care of . . . I can't do it by myself. I don't last."

Samantha froze. So did Mom, coming out of the car laden with groceries. There was a moment where she saw what Samantha saw: a four foot tall, breathing, talking rabbit with blue eyes.

Samantha shouted something. It felt like "*No!*" And then there was a scurry of paws in wet snow and a dark shape hurrying off into the night.

"Samantha, come help with the groceries," Mom said. "We can't do anything for the poor bunny. You'll never catch it."

To her relief, Samantha did not insist on "rescuing" the animal, and helped bring in the bags without complaint.

It was a cold night and a slow one for the Maumee Bar and Grill, and yet the big, bald woman who'd come in out of the snow, shedding slush off her shoulders and hanging her jacket up to drip in the entryway, somehow managed to disappear into the booth near the back of the dining area. She'd gazed at the menu with a desolate expression before ordering an entire grilled chicken with an extra side of vegetables, and eaten it quietly with a tall cup of water (no ice) while she spun a little silver top again and again on the table next to her plate.

Angie had forgotten she was still there—a tired family of six had come in and made themselves distracting, plus there were the regulars at the bar who needed a lot of watering. It was the January blues. She got it. If only they tipped proportionately to the amount they drank. Angie was counting down the minutes to 10:00, when she could close the bar, when something struck the front window with a crunching sort of *thwack*.

It was loud enough to stop the petulant conversation at the family-of-six's table for a brief minute, but then the toddler began to cry, and they paid it no more attention. Neither did Angie, until it happened again. And again.

The fourth time the window broke, and something bloody and feathery came hurtling into the restaurant and slid across an empty table before exhausting its kinetic energy on the floor, where it fetched up against the quickly evacuated chair of the family's mom.

A lot of screaming followed. Angie rushed over with a broom and a dustpan, ready for damage control, only to stop dead in her tracks at what she saw.

The bloody mess of feathers on the floor—it looked like it was some kind of owl—had split open and there was a tall, lanky, dark body rising out of it. Something black and gooey dripped off its skin, splattering the table and the hastily retreating family.

The thing was roughly human shaped, with a big, lolling head and two weeping red eyes, like raw holes in its skull. It turned to look at Angie, whose body had frozen up, her heart in her throat and the breath gone clean out of her.

Run, run, run! screamed a voice inside her head. Which she knew she should, but it felt like all her limbs had been filled with live insects; her body was alive with energy and yet weak as water.

Something split along the bottom of the face. A mouth. A gaping, raw mouth with mismatched teeth sticking out through the bloody gums at odd angles. And the creature began to howl.

Not angry, not threatening, but *sad*. It was so sad Angie felt it in her bones, and suddenly her mind was filled with all her saddest memories: the baby bird she'd rescued as a kid which had died before they'd gotten it to a nursery; her aunt, who'd gotten cancer; and just the year before, the stray cat she'd adopted, run over by a truck in front of her very eyes.

She was crying, gasping, choking. The grief felt fresh and raw and it was strangling her.

"*Run!*" screamed a voice. Not inside her head this time; in her ear.

The bald woman had left her table and come storming up the aisle. She'd pulled a sword out of somewhere and it flashed in the dark.

Angie took a step backward, tripped, caught herself on a nearby table, and scrambled away, dragging the family's young son—who was similarly petrified, tears streaming down his face—with her.

"Harry, Harry, *do* something!" the mom was shouting between great, gulping sobs.

Chris and Johnny had come over from the bar, obviously ready to take on anyone who made Angie unhappy, but stopped when they saw the monster rising up out of the dead bird.

Poor bird! Angie thought, and found herself overcome by another wave of grief. It grated on her nerves, like a physical pain.

She *was* in physical pain. She had fallen over a chair and landed hard on the floor. She was staring up at the ceiling, where the creature's head was having to bend in order not to ram into it.

Long black legs stepped over her, and then she was looking at the bald woman's back as she put herself between Angie and the monster. She spoke, her voice steady, but with a throaty huskiness that suggested she was also fighting back tears.

"You do not belong here," she said. "Please return whence you came."

The creature roared at her. Stick-like arms lashed out, knocking over more tables. There was a crash of breaking glass.

"I am sorry," said the bald woman, and she sounded like she meant it. "I cannot give you what you need."

Angie saw the woman's arm come up holding the sword—it was huge, with a big, orb-like pommel and little decorations, like four-leafed clovers, at the ends of its cross guard—and then down.

Something went *snap* inside her mind. Like the white-hot blaze of sensation when you've hurt yourself very badly but the pain hasn't hit yet. It knocked Angie silly for what must have been several moments, because when she was able to raise her head and look around, the monster was gone, and the woman was kneeling beside the eviscerated bird, gently wrapping it up in a napkin. Her sword was in its sheath, strapped across her back, and though her eyes were wet and red-rimmed, she wasn't crying.

Angie was. She couldn't stop the sobs now they had started, even though the overwhelming sense of grief had abated somewhat. Now it just felt like an ordinary attack of melancholy.

At her feet the boy had curled into a ball and was whimpering faintly, while the rest of his family were sprawled nearby, all in similar positions. Chris and Johnny, disconcertingly, were flopped in the doorway to the bar, crying like babies. The actual baby, meanwhile, was wailing like a siren, and his mother was too overcome to do anything but hug him and drip tears and snot into his hair.

The bald woman finished making a neat, if rather soggy, bundle of the owl. She picked it up gently, then transferred it to one hand so she could grope around in the pocket of her trousers. This action produced a damp-looking wallet, which she held open with her teeth while she teased a bill out of it.

Another step of her long legs brought her over to Angie. Pocketing the wallet, she handed the bill to her. It was a fifty.

"I'm sorry about this," she said, as if the mess was somehow her fault. She seemed about to leave when she shook her head and made a sort of shrug—drawing her shoulders down, then up—and put the wallet back into her mouth so she could slide a small white rectangle out of its card pocket. She set it on the table next to Angie and pushed it toward her meaningfully.

"In case you need help," she said. Then she was striding toward the door, the bloody bundle held carefully in front of her.

Where the monster had been there was now nothing more than a red stain, a few stray feathers, and a faint smell of saltwater and dust.

Clara had booked a room at a budget motel on the outskirts of the city, and now she returned there, carefully rolling out a damp oilcloth over the bathroom floor before setting the bloody bundle down on top of it. She went and got a small flashlight and two disposable nitrile gloves from a pouch on her saddlebag. She got the gloves on with some difficulty (her hands had gotten wet on the ride home), and with caution akin to one excavating a priceless artifact, she gently loosened the knot of the cloth and drew it away.

She considered what this revealed for a moment, then she stuck the flashlight in her mouth and began carefully rearranging the pieces of bird until they somewhat resembled the small owl it had once been. In doing so she discovered a tiny, shiny black seed—like an acorn, but rounder—in the chest cavity where the heart should have been. When she removed this, the whole bird—feathers, flesh, blood and bone—shriveled up like mud under a hot desert sun, turning gray and ashen until there was only the dusty mummy of an owl, and even this soon crumbled away, collapsing under its own weight.

Clara considered the seed. It felt both hot and cold through the nitrile of her gloved palm, and when she unfocused her eyes she thought she could see live tendrils creeping out of it, poking around as if looking for cracks to take root in.

Returning to her saddlebag she removed a small glass bottle with a few flakes of silver leaf (sterling, not imitation) at the bottom. Removing the cork she dropped the seed inside, replacing the cork and rolling it around so the silver stuck to its surface. Then she dug around until she found a stump of a candle and her lighter. She melted the candle over the bathroom sink, creating a wax seal over the seam of cork and bottle.

She put the bottle in her bag, but she left the ruined napkin and the ashen remains of the owl out on the bathroom floor, inside a light dusting of black powder.

Then she stripped out of her sodden clothes, rolled them up in a towel and pressed as much water out of them as she could in the bathtub, before hanging them up to dry over the curtain rod. From her other saddlebag she produced the sealed plastic bag that contained a clean change of underwear and a dry, thin woolen shirt. Putting these on she picked up her boots and laid them beside the radiator, where they had at least a small chance of drying over the remainder of the night.

Then she went and sat crosslegged in the middle of the bed, her sword laid across her lap, facing the window. She felt raw inside; drained and wrung out, like the clothes she had just hung up to dry.

The grief that had been brought on by the apparition had not been her own, but it had felt real. It was the grief of loss, the same as the breed that was currently tormenting her, but it was not *her* grief.

Being inhabited by someone else's grief, grief that was strong enough to cause physical manifestations, was enough to leave anyone exhausted. For Clara, it had compounded what she already felt, and now she barely had the energy to imagine what could have caused it. In the end, after entertaining the idle notion that it was a particularly vivacious ghost, she gave up cogitating altogether and just stared blankly out the window until the street lights flicked off and a hesitant, almost apologetic dawn broke over the snow-covered city. Then she finally allowed herself to lie down and take what rest she could before the events of the day demanded her attention.

Detroit, MI

Jill's sneakers squeaked on the freshly polished floor of the concourse as she led Marcus around his new workplace, and her voice echoed as she explained the renovations currently preventing them from accessing most of it.

"We're restoring as much of the ground floor as possible," she explained. "We got a grant from the Friends of the Michigan Central Station, and since most of the functional offices are on the upper floors it basically means we get this for free."

"This" was a breathtaking space of high, vaulted ceilings with herringbone brickwork, palatial columns, and marble walls.

"We're adapting most of the space to different uses, of course," Jill went on. "The ticket office is now my office . . . or Lansing's office, really. We can use the vault as a light safe if necessary. Lunch counter will be the main lab, restaurant and café will be a break room. Reading room is for staging. Women's room will be partitioned into bedrooms; so will the smoking room. Newsstand will become a visitor's orientation center. Not sure about the cigar store and the barber shop. Really, we've got too much space—and we haven't even finished clearing out the basement or the under-station."

"Under-station?" Marcus asked.

For answer Jill turned them off the concourse, heading along a wide corridor which sloped gently down. The ticketing blockade had been torn out, and they passed into a low, dark area lined with doors. Yellow light flooded out of one of these, and there was the sound of shoveling and grunting from within.

"This used to be the train access system," Jill explained. "It's got a post office, customs office, baggage room, even elevators up to the tracks . . . according to the plans. Realistically, it's been abandoned so long half of it's filled with dirt, and the other half needs a complete overhaul. For now, we're just getting the unclaimed baggage room cleared out so I can have a light-safe bedroom."

This was the second time Jill had referenced a "light-safe" but Marcus resisted the temptation to ask. Lansing he knew was a vampire. Jill, Flammard had told him, was . . . something else. Marcus had to admit he didn't get the same cold, dead feeling off of Jill that he did Lansing, but she *was* cold—her body didn't give off any heat—and he noticed that when she wasn't talking she had a tendency to stop breathing for minutes on end.

"Basement proper is a parking garage," Jill was saying, turning and leading them back up to the concourse. "Also there's a kitchen, but it needs massive remodeling. Especially considering we're probably going to have people with really peculiar dietary needs. Speaking of which, do you think she'll need to eat? The magical-vortex dog, I mean?"

Marcus sighed. He had no idea. They'd made up a sort of den in what had been the drugstore where the dog seemed content to sit and stare at anyone who passed by. She had not urinated or defecated, nor had she touched the water bowl Marcus had filled and left by the door.

"Pete gave us a bag of kibble," Jill said, almost to herself. "It couldn't hurt if we offered her some of that . . ."

They were walking back up to the concourse as she spoke, from which Jill led him up a flight of stairs hidden in a corner to the B level, which contained the old employee break room, a few offices—currently receiving new coats of paint—and a bathroom.

"Above is C level, and then floors one through thirteen," Jill explained. "Plenty of office space that we'll probably never use. Not until we can get the ventilation overhauled and the elevators working, anyway."

"Thirteen?" asked Marcus. "I thought buildings didn't *have* thirteenth floors."

Jill rolled her eyes. "Well, technically, if you count levels A, B, and C, it's the sixteenth floor anyway. Also, buildings don't label the thirteenth floor *as* thirteen because of a superstition."

"I know that," Marcus said. "It was a bad joke . . . "

"Well, we're a center for supernatural investigation and research," Jill went on, as if she hadn't heard him. "One of the things we'll test is whether there is demonstrably more unfortunate coincidences on the thirteenth floor, by clearly labeling it as such. We'll also monitor floor ten, since that's the thirteenth floor if you start at ground level, with floor one for control."

Marcus stared at her.

"Now you're joking," he said.

Jill glanced at him, her glasses flashing in the electric light. "Not at all," she said. "That is exactly the sort of thing I'm interested in. Filtering out which superstitions are based on actual empirical phenomena, and which are purely imagined. And, as an aside, if those that are purely imagined can influence the tangible world."

"I'm sorry?" said Marcus, feeling lost. Partly because the hall they were in looked like a movie set made to look bigger by putting a mirror at one end, and he'd forgotten where the stairs were.

Jill led him unerringly, however, talking as she went.

"I'm interested to see what effect concentrated human belief has on the physical world," she said. "Beyond the, 'people who believe *this* are more likely to behave in *that* way,' et cetera."

"You mean like making dreams come true? Like, literally?" Marcus asked, striving for the wildest possible interpretation in an effort to get ahead of Jill's strange ideas.

"That's one possible result," Jill said, sounding pleased. "I'm also talking about imbuing inanimate objects with energy and cognizance, or creating sentient metaphysical beings out of pure belief."

"You mean, like ghosts?" Marcus said. They were at the head of the stairs now, which were dimly lit by a flashlight someone had aimed against the wall.

"Ghosts," said Jill. "Spirits, demons, gods . . . that sort of thing. Yeah."

Marcus nearly missed his step.

"Did you say *gods?*" he choked out.

"Sure," said Jill, as if this was a perfectly reasonable assertion.

Marcus thought of his fiercely Catholic grandmother; of his own distant heritage.

"You're saying you think gods might be figments of human imagination?" he said, just to be sure.

Jill stopped on the stairs and looked up at him. In her white lab coat she stood out remarkably well in the dim light, and under her glasses her eyes looked momentarily red.

"I'm interested to learn if they are," she said. "And if not, if they are derived from some other source, what that source is, and how it relates to our world."

She blinked, and her eyes were normal again. She smiled. "Or, if it is some combination of the two. Or something we haven't even thought of." She rubbed her hands. "It's exciting work."

She turned to continue down the stairs, took one step, and stopped dead. Rounding the landing Marcus saw immediately what had caused this and had to brace himself against the wall to keep from falling down in surprise.

Magic-vortex dog was standing at the foot of the stairs. In the dimness—the sun had set and the only light came from around the corner, where the last workman was in the process of packing up his toolkit—her creamy fur seemed to glow white, as if illuminated from within. Her red ears were perked in slightly floppy triangles, and her yellow eyes shone like stars.

There was a faint shimmer in the air around her, which Marcus realized was his second sight bleeding over. He blinked and rubbed his eyes, and when he looked again the dog's eyes had ceased to blaze, and she was only as pale as a cream-colored dog would be in a dark stairwell.

"Hi," said Jill, a little uncertainly.

The dog, ears still perked, sat down and yawned.

Once Marcus got over her strange appearance and tendency to bring out his own odd powers, he realized she was behaving like a perfectly happy, if expectant, dog.

"Good girl," he tried.

The dog lay down. Animal Control had put a temporary collar on her, which sat oddly amidst her gleaming fur.

"Um . . . okay," said Jill. She finished descending the stairs, and when the dog did nothing but follow her with expectant yellow eyes, she reached down and tugged at the collar gently. "Come on," she said. "You're not supposed to be out."

Leading the dog half bent over, Jill walked her around to the barbershop, where the makeshift gate was still closed and latched—and the water bowl untouched.

"Huh," was all Jill said, opening the gate and leading the dog inside. She went agreeably enough, but when Jill left she came right back to the gate and sat there, gazing at Jill imploringly.

"How did she do that?" Marcus wondered aloud.

Jill was examining the gate.

"Either she's got opposable thumbs hidden somewhere on her forelegs," Jill said. "Or she can go incorporeal enough to pass through solid objects." She stood up and shrugged. "We'll find out, I suppose. Can I give you a ride back to your hotel? It's dark now, so I can drive."

Marcus hesitated. He didn't want to put Jill to any more trouble, but at the same time, the dog had unnerved him considerably and he much preferred a quick car ride to the twenty-minute walk through the cold, dark night.

Jill seemed to read his mind. "I'll give you a ride. Arcana needs the exercise, anyway. Where are you staying?"

Arcana, it turned out, was a huge Dodge Ram truck with double wheels on his back end, the color of a ripe strawberry. He gleamed, even under the yellowish floodlight which illuminated the streetcar entrance, though Marcus could see a few scratches and dings decorating his bumper.

Jill's phone beeped at her as they were climbing into the cab, and she swore violently.

Marcus remained diplomatically silent.

Jill sat in the driver's seat, fiercely thumbing out a text reply, and then groaned as she put the phone away and started the engine.

"That building is full of dead spots," she explained. "I think it might be the steel frame. So I only just now got Clara's message."

"Oh?" said Marcus.

"She's not coming back tonight. She's in *Lafayette* for some reason," Jill said, putting the truck in gear and nudging her way out toward Michigan Avenue. "Said she found 'someting.'"

"Did she say how long she'll be there?" Marcus asked.

Jill shrugged. "No. Look, how soon can you start, really? I can front you your first payment, cash, so you don't have to wait for Lansing to set up payroll. We can put you up in the women's room, so you won't have to worry about renting a place. Free room, though you're responsible for your own food."

Dawn. Sunlight crept across the sky, first touching the tips of the trees on the west shore of the lake, painting a broad stripe of gold across their green-and-brown faces, then creeping down to ignite ripples stirred by the early morning wind. The surface reflected a vast blue sky, empty but for the pale ghost of a waning moon in its last quarter, almost directly above her. Clara could pick out its tenuous reflection on the surface of the lake: a tiny, pale crescent in an otherwise vivid cyan sheen over the murky waters below.

The air smelled sweetly of pine and earth. It was rather dry, but in a pleasant, clean sort of way, and though the shadows were still chilled from the night, the sunlight, now stalking along the bank, was quickly warming the air above it.

Clara sat on an open face of granite which ran down from the forest behind her, legs folded neatly under her, and knew that she was dreaming. Yet she didn't do anything to stop it. She felt peaceful here, content in a way she never did while awake.

With the sun came the sound of footsteps, crunching through the pine needles off to her left, where the rock ended and the forest began. Clara didn't have to turn her head to know who it was; she felt the presence, like a second sun, come up onto the rock and sit down beside her.

"This is a pleasant surprise," said Ariel Freeman, unlacing his boots and kicking them off with relief.

He was smiling at her. Clara was still staring off across the lake, but she could feel it, like a patch of sunlight on her cheek. She nodded agreement.

They sat together in silence as the sun rose over the lake, and in the distance birdsong rang across the water.

"I've always wanted to go swimming in a lake like this," Ariel said after a while. "I wonder how deep it is."

He was sitting sprawled next to her, his legs stuck out in front of him and his pale feet sticking out the ends of his black trousers. He'd unbuttoned his jacket but still wore his priest's collar, a little snip of white at his throat. Looking down at him, Clara found all but his angular, scruffy chin hidden beneath a white felt cowboy hat. It was decorated with a black band of suede, fastened on the nearer side with an eight-pointed brass star inside a circle. The star flashed in the sun, like it was winking at her.

Frowning, Clara reached over and lifted it gently off his head.

Ariel Freeman blinked hazel eyes up at her, squinting a little into the morning light. His face was crinkled in a warm smile; laughing at her, out of surprise and . . . was that joy? Clara peered at him, curiously.

He took the hat out of her hands and, reaching up to the full extent of his arms, set it on her head.

"There," he said, proudly. "Shade for both of us."

"I'm not a white hat," Clara said, out of habit more than anything else.

"Maybe not," said Ariel. "But it looks good on you." He nudged her gently in the side with his elbow.

The touch came as a relief. Like the spread of an anesthetic over an open wound. Or the reassuring shape of a weapon in the dark. Clara didn't fully understand it, but she didn't pull away.

Loss of contact felt like a cold draft from an open window.

Clara stared out at the lake, finding the moon's reflection and staring at it as though it would steady her against the strange feeling slowing unrolling in her chest.

It wasn't grief this time, but something similar. Like sadness mixed with regret and yearning, but for what she didn't know.

Ariel must have followed her stare, but misinterpreted it.

"I heard about Selene," he said. "I'm sorry."

And he meant it, that was the thing. Clara felt a little staggered by the sincerity of his feelings. Ariel wasn't just sorry in the general way; he was specifically sorry that Selene was gone, and he was sorry that her death was causing Clara pain.

Clara didn't know how she knew this. It was a certainty, just as she was certain that, in this little golden fantasy, nothing bad was going to happen. Ariel could go swimming in the lake if he liked; there was nothing in it that could harm him.

That thought uncovered another certainty, something Clara had known for months but hadn't carefully examined: whatever else happened, Ariel Freeman, the world's second sun, should not be harmed.

Ariel was like the sun to her: distant, untouchable, but bright and warm and reassuring. As long as the sun would rise, as long as Ariel was swaggering around out there in his fake priest costume, she could endure anything, keeping this tiny portion of her mind free of whatever disasters assaulted her.

As long as the white stag ran, uncaught, uncatchable, through the limitless forest . . .

Yet at the same time he was sitting next to her, wiggling his toes in the morning light. Her mind had spun a fantasy where the sun had come down to sit with her; the stag had come out of the forest. Not caught, not tamed, but simply seeing no reason to run from her.

Experimentally she leaned into him, felt the contact of his shoulder against her upper arm. The relief was immediate, and when he did nothing but put out his opposite hand to steady himself under her weight, Clara remained that way.

"I wish this was real," she whispered.

A hand, calloused and tan and a little hairy, found hers. Squeezed.

She felt him shift under her; turn his face to hers. She felt his breath on her cheek.

"For now, it is." His voice was low, golden thunder in her ear.

Lafayette, IN

The warmth did not dissipate all at once. It caressed and held her until she became aware of her body, curled sideways on top of the covers, her skin cool. The afternoon sun was shining on her back, but for a few transient moments Clara thought she could still smell the clean, dry, pine-scented air, and could pretend the form of the bed beneath her was actually reassuring pressure from another living body.

She opened her eyes and found herself blearily staring down over her hands, across the bed, to the wall of the motel room with a faded watercolor of an iris hung in the center. At the same time she held the vision of the lake at sunrise at the forefront of her mind, working it into her waking consciousness. She wasn't sure of the particulars, but she knew if she could just fix that image the rest would come back to her in time.

For the moment her head was surprisingly clear. The grief and loneliness which assailed her had banked, ready to pour in, but Clara felt like her foundations had been shored up, the cracked parts of her outer armor replaced with new, strong plates.

In essence, she felt well rested, and gliding on the high of this feeling the puzzling occurrence from the previous night made a lot more sense.

Grief manifested in many ways. If you were human—or functionally human—it remained within you. But if you were something else—specifically, the *right sort* of something else—your grief could manifest physically. The number of beings who could do that were limited, but they were all easy enough to find—if you knew what you were looking for.

Clara got up with purpose. She went into the bathroom where, not entirely to her surprise, the ashen remains of the owl had vaporized. The black powder was untouched. She checked her bag: the little stone had tarnished the silver, but it was stable. She got dressed in her damp clothes and slipped the bottle into her pocket. She restocked her emergency kit with supplies from her pannier, put the napkin into the trash, and packed everything she owned back into her saddlebags. She left a dollar bill on the pillow and headed out the door.

Something dark came hurtling out of the sky toward her face and she ducked, leaving the animal to slam into the lintel of the door behind her—which she closed quickly.

It was a pigeon, and it flopped pathetically at her feet for a few seconds before expiring. Even as she bent to examine it the bird's breast split asunder and a black, dripping limb reached up out of it.

This time it looked more like a spider's leg, and Clara lost no time in skewering it with her knife. Then she cut open the bird, and with little difficulty—now she knew what to look for—teased out the little stone from under its breastbone.

It felt hot in her palm, even through her gloves. Like tears burning trails over her cheek.

She put it in the bottle with the other, jamming the cork in tight to make up for breaking the wax seal, and looked around.

The parking lot of the motel was quiet. A few mounds of melting snow indicated where cars had been entombed, and on the far side a lone woman was engaged in excavating her vehicle.

Clara went over to Unicorn, who had weathered the night safe under her throw cover, and began packing it away. She moved quickly, but without rushing. Yet she was all too aware of how the darkness in the skies above was not from clouds this time, but a growing flock of birds.

There was a ghost in Samantha's room. That was the only reasonable explanation. After a night ill-spent burying herself under the covers trying to ignore the plaintive whispers coming from the closet she awoke to find the ghost had gotten out and torn through her room like a whirlwind. It had gotten into the magic markers and written GIVE THEM BACK on the wall below her window. Samantha took the disturbance gamely, however.

She had snuck into the bathroom and gotten the cleaning kit and been at the wall for an hour getting the stuff off. She could not—*could not*—let her parents see that. She'd only just got back from putting the kit away when her mom came in to check on her and gave her a lecture about keeping her room tidy.

Samantha had been obliged to sit through it penitently, trying not to glance nervously at the closet, whose door would jiggle now and then.

On Saturday, in an effort to placate the ghost, she had brought it toasted pop tarts with jam and a glass of milk. The pop tarts had been the last in a box pushed all the way to the back of the cupboard. Dad had looked at her strangely when he saw her toasting them. Everyone knew Samantha didn't like pop tarts.

The ghost did, it appeared, and gobbled them up with audible delight as soon as Samantha had shut the closet door. Encouraged, she'd also made it a peanut butter and jelly sandwich—with the crusts cut off!—for lunch, which had been similarly appreciated. It meant she had some peace and quiet in which to do her homework, and had managed to get most of it done before it was time to go to Anise's birthday party.

Samantha was a little confused as to why they were going. Ostensibly it was because she was friends with Anise, but Samantha couldn't imagine why. Anise was . . . well, she was difficult. Her room was packed with My Little Ponies, all arranged in a particular order, and Samantha had to ask specifically before she played with any of them. And when they did play, it was always the same story: some little pony had a house, and had to keep it clean and cook food and mow the lawn. Samantha always felt that there was enough of that sort of stuff in real life. She didn't want to play at it too.

"But my dad cooks, and my mom hires people to clean and mow the lawn," Anise had pointed out.

And Samantha had opened her mouth to say that they were too poor to hire someone, when she realized this was wrong. They did have someone come and mow the lawn once a week in summer, and a woman named Elise to vacuum and clean the bathrooms, and though neither of her parents were big cooks, they were always buying bread rolls and hotdogs and bringing home takeout, so Samantha never had to cook.

It was part of the strange way her mind seemed to contain two levels. On top was where she knew who she was and where she lived and who her parents were, but underneath was a basement mind where she knew all sorts of other things. Frightening things. She didn't want to examine them, so she kept herself firmly in the top part of her mind, and shoved whatever annoyed feelings she had about Anise to the back of it.

It helped also that Anise had twelve other friends at her party as well, and so after leaving her present (bought and wrapped by Mom) on the table, Samantha barely had to speak to the birthday girl before she could hide herself in a quiet corner until the cake was cut.

The wait was interminable. Anise's mom was determined that the girls should play party games—games which each girl had different ideas about how they should be played—and in the meantime Samantha got hungrier and hungrier. As if she'd split her lunch with the girl trapped in her closet.

At long last the discordant sound of "Happy Birthday" signaled the cutting of the cake, and Samantha got politely in line between two girls from their shared class. Girls whose birthdays she'd also attended, but her memories of those parties were happier, washed out by a sunny haze. As if they'd come from another life.

The cake was exactly the kind of birthday cake Samantha had always wanted: big and fluffy and sweet with bright blue icing. It tasted of almonds and vanilla, but mostly of sugar. One part of her—the upper half—reminded her that this was the same cake she'd had for her own birthday last summer. But she felt a niggle of doubt creeping up from below; the feeling that her birthday was in the fall, and her bună had made baked apples stuffed with raisins and nuts: twelve of them, one for each of Samantha's years, with a little candle in each. They'd had to pick wax out of the filling, but they were delicious in their own way. Not as sweet as the cake presently melting in her mouth, but spicy and flavorful and filling in a way the cake was not.

In fact, if she ignored how sweet it was, the cake was practically like ash—collapsing under its own weight and dissolving in her mouth.

Ash that tasted of saltwater and bitter misery.

It had been a sunny day, but now the light from the broad windows illuminating Anise's living room was abruptly blacked out by a cloud of feathery bodies slamming into them so hard they ruptured, sliding down the glass in red streaks, while one window shattered under the impact of a falcon, which dove in and landed in the cake, sending clumps of frosting and screaming girls scattering.

Samantha stared into one orange eye, which was glaring at her accusingly.

Then the bird rolled over as something exploded out of its chest, rearing up with a scream that split her ears.

It was like a horse, but it had no skin, and it was shedding blood and fluids all over the table. The cake was completely destroyed and Anise's mom was already on the phone to the police.

The skinless horse looked at her, and Samantha felt something deep inside her stir. Something from her lower mind awakened and struggled desperately to get out.

"No!" she shouted. Then clapped her hands over her ears, jammed her eyes shut, and shouted again and again, "No, no, *no!*"

"All right, Samantha, you don't have to play Master Go with us if you don't want to," said Anise's aunt.

Samantha opened her eyes and took her hands off her ears.

The monstrous horse was gone. So was the dead falcon and the rest of the birds which had smashed themselves against the windows. The windows themselves were intact and clean, and clear winter sunlight was streaming in through them. The cake had been partly demolished, but one corner with DAY! in yellow icing was still intact.

Anise and her friends had retreated to the far end of the room and were fighting over who got to throw a bright yellow ball at the wall. Her aunt was holding another ball and hurrying over to settle the dispute.

Only Anise's mother remained where she had been. She had the phone in her hand, and from the other end Samantha could just hear a concerned operator's voice saying, "Ms. Laurens? Are you still with me? Hello?"

"I'm here," said Anise's mom, still staring at the cake. Where a moment before there had been a horrendous bloody monster getting ready to massacre the lot of them.

"No," Samantha whispered, letting the word out in a faint hiss.

"I'm sorry, everything is fine," said Anise's mom, blinking fiercely. "Sorry. False alarm. I think I need to go lie down. Yes, yes I have people here with me. I'll be fine."

The operator let the call go without another thought. The lines were full of similar calls, and since those did not spontaneously resolve themselves, she couldn't bother herself with hounding after a woman who sounded as though she'd suffered from a brief hallucination.

The others, as far as she'd been able to ascertain, were not hallucinations. If the steady stream of reports from the front desk were anything to go by.

All over the city birds were falling from the sky, striking roads, sidewalks, windows and roofs. They were tangling in power lines and upsetting traffic.

Worse, once they hit a solid object they burst open, and all manner of unpleasant things came pouring out. Disfigured animals like dogs and cows were most common, but there had been a few spiders and Cheryl had fielded a call from a school janitor who'd discovered a mess of vines overtaking a classroom. The vines had been black and oozing puss which attracted flies, and the man had been in tears.

Most of the people had been, actually. Natalie listened to their anguished voices and couldn't help feeling a pang of grief herself—though for what reason she had no idea. As far as she could tell, no one had *actually* died. Yet.

But it was only a matter of time, the way things were progressing.

"Someone really oughta call that chick in Detroit," Cheryl said after dispatching another team to a caller in Wallace Triangle.

"The what?" asked Natalie.

"That one who's squatting in their old train station," said Cheryl, even as she took another call. "Isn't this supposed to be her thing?"

And that was when the talking rabbit showed up.

Lightning Does Strike Twice

Detroit, MI

The administrative tasks associated with getting the Center up and running had so far consumed Jill's existence that she hadn't been able to do hardly any of the research that had impelled her to establish a permanent base in the first place. The only time she had was during the wee hours of the morning, after she'd gone through the paperwork shunted to her by Lansing, when no one from the diurnal world would bother her.

She was waist high in research for a contraption to accurately sense and measure magical activity—tentatively called the Ambient Magical Energy Detector—when Lansing put her head in through the ticket window.

"Hey," she said. "It's twenty minutes to sunrise. I'm going under for a while."

"Sounds good," said Jill, not looking up. She was compiling a list of needed materials, and didn't continue her response for another minute. "I'll try to get some sleep too," she said, raising her head at last. But Lansing had gone.

Jill walked tiredly, dragging her feet over the newly swept floor of the concourse, down to the underground complex, and into the little room she had set aside for herself—furnished mostly with the contents of their camper trailer. It had everything a pseudo-vampire could want: a soft bed and no windows. There was also a power drop for Jill's computer and a lamp, but she could see so well in the dark that she didn't turn it on.

Besides, the dog on her bed was glowing. Her pale, creamy fur gleaming like the moon glimpsed through clouds.

She was lying right in the middle of the pillows, her head laid pleadingly on her paws, and her glowing yellow eyes looking at Jill imploringly.

Jill was too tired to be upset. She didn't become physically tired the way she used to, but mentally she was exhausted.

"Fine," she said. She put her laptop on the charger and changed into her pajamas. The dog thumped her tail once, hopefully, when Jill approached the bed.

"No," she said. "Move. Off."

The dog didn't budge, but Jill dragged at the blankets, rolling the dog down to the foot of the bed. She climbed in, swept dog hair and grit off the pillows, and had barely pulled the blankets up when she felt the sharp press of paws on her leg, and then the weight of the dog settled along her side with a contented groan.

The body was cool beside her, and it wasn't merely her vampiric vision—the dog really did *glow* in the dark.

Jill sighed. "I suppose you'll need a name," she mumbled, already half asleep.

The dog stretched beside her, luxuriantly, and made a sound like *"Urrp."*

What felt like a moment later—but was really six hours when Jill checked—her phone rang. On the other end was a voice which would have been brisk and professional except it sounded like its owner was on the brink of hysterics.

"What?" said Jill. Then, "Yes, yes this is Jill Hamilton. No, no it's not a joke. We are a center for researching supernatural and paranormal— what? How many? Wait, they're coming out of *birds?* Where . . . um . . . I'm sorry, where are you located, again? Lafayette? Lafayette *Indiana?* Uh . . . actually. Yes, yes, I can have an agent there, um . . . immediately, actually. Assuming she can get through the rain of birds."

Lafayette, IN

Clara was riding cautiously through downtown Lafayette, stopping now and then to walk her bike around upset trucks and other cars which had been left turned around or skewed sideways in the wake of a wildly thrashing serpent. Clara could just see its tail, disappearing around the courthouse, leaving a wide smear of something gooey and black that began to steam in the wan winter sun. It had left her with a relatively clear trail, and she accelerated up 4th Street in its wake.

She had entertained the idea of following the serpent to see where it went, in the hopes that this apparition would eventually return to its maker, but her plans were upended when she turned onto Main and found it trying to eat a truck. It had most of the cab in its mouth when Clara arrived.

Leaving Unicorn safely propped against the curb, she took no preliminary steps but ran up beside the snake-creature's body and rammed her sword into its neck, just below the base of its skull.

As with the manifestation in the restaurant the night before, the creature's flesh gave way to Bellatrix's cold steel in an instant, ballooning up around the blade before ripping apart like a bubble bursting in slow motion. Clara didn't stop, however, until she'd contrived to separate the head from the body, at which point whatever forces were holding the thing together gave up entirely, and she had to somersault backward in order to avoid being hit by the discharge. She caught a strong blast of sadness as it was, flavored with a sour spit of rage, and had to spend a moment regaining her emotional balance while around her the air filled with acrid steam.

She fought her way through it to the truck and wrenched open the passenger door.

The driver was a balding man with a paunch, and he was slumped against the steering wheel, sobbing like a baby. From what Clara could see he was otherwise unharmed.

Her phone rang.

The remains of the serpent had mixed with the slush on the road and congealed into slime that clung to her boots as she stomped back to Unicorn, pulling off a glove with her teeth in order to tease her phone out of its pocket with her bare hand.

"This is Nordstern," she said.

"Clara!" Jill's voice sounded in her ear, so loud she had to pull the phone away. "We've got something *big* going down in Lafayette!"

Clara looked around at the mess and wreckage in the street. The serpent in its flailing had smashed a storefront, and there was the distant sound of sirens. Above her, on a rooftop, pigeons were gathering ominously.

"Yes," Clara agreed, even as Jill carried on:

"And I just got a rather frantic call from the Tippecanoe County Nine-One-One dispatch. Lafayette PD wants MCSIR's help, and they'd like it *now*."

"The police," Clara repeated, heavily. "It would be better if they kept out of—"

"They have a walking, talking, four-foot rabbit which may or may not also be a stuffed animal in their lobby," Jill went on.

Clara came to a stop next to her bike and stared across it to the intersection of Main Street and North 5th, where two cars had just collided as they both tried to avoid the giant, white bird which had swooped low over the street before correcting itself and gone flailing off into the sky again.

It did not look like a bird that belonged in Lafayette, Indiana. It did not look like it belonged anywhere in the middle of the North American continent.

It didn't fit. Then again, neither did the talking rabbit. Clara glanced back at the truck and saw the driver had recovered sufficiently to get out and begin looking around for someone to blame. The bird had vanished.

"Where is the police station?" Clara asked, tiredly.

"You're . . . what . . . on Main and 5th?" Jill asked, clearly tracking her location via their phones.

"Yes," said Clara.

"Just around the corner, actually," said Jill. "On 6th, between Columbia and South."

"Understood," said Clara, throwing a leg over Unicorn's back and walking the bike around to point away from the crash. "Tell them I will be there momentarily."

It had been a trying day for Sergeant Canning. Roland had called in sick and so she was double-shifting on what was possibly the worst day to be a public servant in Lafayette.

The phone would not stop ringing. Not in dispatch, not at the front desk—even the captain had barely managed to make it out of his office before the cry of the phone called him back. And they were all, with practically no exceptions, the same sort of call.

Someone had found a dead bird. Or a bird had splattered itself against their window, their roof, or dining room table. And now there was a monstrous spider, or dog, or giant cat—or a tree—climbing, clawing, or growing out of their window, roof, or dining room table. The officers sent to handle such calls had either gone off radio and required backup, or returned shaken and tear-streaked with no rational explanation of what they'd seen. Backup usually suffered the same. Paramedics were having similar problems, which made it difficult to estimate the number and severity of the injuries. A fire had broken out in Hedgewood, and the response team was apparently sitting on the sidewalk outside, crying into their fire-retardant clothing. The only thing that had stopped the blaze jumping to neighboring buildings was the blanket of slushy snow still coating the city.

And all that was before the rabbit walked in.

Well, flopped in, more like. She made it through the front doors and then collapsed in the middle of the floor, going limp and lifeless as a worn-out stuffed animal. Which was what she was, Canning now saw. About the right size for a six-year-old to use as a body pillow, her fur was silver-gray and she was wearing patched denim overalls. She was just the sort of toy Canning had loved to death as a small child—only hers had been a badger.

At the same time Canning was also certain she'd seen the same rabbit, standing on her hind legs and pushing the swinging door open, four feet tall with real fur and real, wet, scared blue eyes. Like something out of a damn kid's movie!

And now, even as she watched, a little shudder passed through the limp toy on the ground, and then the surface of its plush body rippled and it stood up, arms and legs filling out and body enlarging until it was once again a living, breathing, four-foot-tall gray-and-white rabbit in denim overalls.

Its blue eyes saw Canning, and it made for her in a determined, hopping kind of gait. Its paws grasped the edge of Canning's desk, and it pulled its head up to gaze imploringly at her.

"Help," it had wheezed in a lisping, feminine voice. "My name is Lady Bibbit. There's been a death in my family. Mantha needs help!"

Then it had turned back into a stuffed animal again, falling to the floor with a faint, anguished cry.

Canning hadn't known what to do with that, so she'd taken the rabbit into the captain's office, where she'd almost been fired before the rabbit came back to life and repeated her plea into the captain's astonished face.

Which was when the captain had picked up the phone and called, as he put it, "The pros."

Canning had then spent the next half hour playing host to an intermittently living, breathing, talking stuffed rabbit.

"You want anything? Coffee? Tea? Um . . . a carrot?" she'd asked when the rabbit had been sapient for almost five minutes, sitting on a stool behind her counter.

She'd looked up at Canning with those big blue eyes—very deep and sad for a stuffed bunny, Sergeant Canning thought—and said quietly that some tea would be nice.

So Canning had gotten them both tea—coffee was really the last thing her over-stressed body needed right now—and as they sat together sipping gingerly from the steaming styrofoam cups, she was suddenly struck by the sheer insanity of it all and burst out laughing.

"I'm sorry," she said, when the rabbit looked at her in confusion. "It's just, I used to have a stuffed badger when I was a kid. Named Matilda, after the character from the Roald Dahl novel. And we would—oh, I'm sorry—we would have *tea* together! Just like this!"

She was still laughing. This was incredible. Her head must have cracked somewhere.

Lady Bibbit looked at her over the rim of her cup and blinked several times.

"That's . . . nice," she said uncertainly.

"No, no, you gotta understand," said Canning. "She was a *stuffed* badger. A *toy*. It was all make-believe!"

"So?" said Lady Bibbit. "You made-believed she was real, right?"

"Well, yeah, maybe," said Canning. "But only . . . not? Like, it was only real in that moment . . . and she certainly wasn't real to anyone else."

Lady Bibbit did not answer, but sipped her tea thoughtfully. She really was *drinking* it, Canning saw with amazement.

When they had both finished she took the cups and walked them around the corner to the trash can. When she returned, Lady Bibbit was an ordinary stuffed bunny again, precariously balanced on her stool.

The phone rang. Canning fielded more calls. Then, in the middle of the afternoon, in walked a woman with *trouble* written all over her.

Canning came from a family of tall women. She had played volleyball in high school. Her sister was a junior varsity basketball player. This woman would have made both their teams look like . . . well, like normal people.

This woman had a sword strapped to her back, wore black leather head to toe, and was bald as a newborn baby. She was also blindingly white, with eyes of such a pale blue they made Canning feel cold just to look at.

She walked right up to the counter and laid her gloved hands along the edge.

"My name is Clara Nordstern," she said in a stiff, formal way. "I'm here to help with your—" She cast about for the right word. "Trouble."

The ghost had made a mess of Samantha's room by the time they returned from the party. It had been slow driving. Two birds had struck the windshield of their car, and Samantha had spent the following twenty minutes firmly ignoring the great beasts, like spindly legged elephants, that had grown out of their corpses and trudged morosely alongside them. It had taken even more energy to keep Mom ignoring them as well, and a great burst of effort when they turned down their street to find it blocked by the putrefying corpse of what might have once been a giant boar. Its ribs, pale cream and streaked with dark red, extended up from the mess of brown and black glop of its body, yet its sightless eyes remained, staring reproachfully at Samantha.

Samantha, who had turned her face to the door of the car and whispered "No," through clenched teeth.

"What a *day* to be doing roadwork!" Mom exclaimed, driving up onto the curb to get around the corpse. "You'd think they'd have something better to do than ripping up perfectly good streets."

Samantha nodded and kept her head down as they piled out of the car and shuffled up the icy path to the front door. The bottom half of her mind was roiling, like an upset stomach getting ready to vomit, but she kept stomping it down as she climbed the stairs to her room.

That was when she had discovered that the ghost had emptied her bookshelf and scattered the contents across the floor. Books lay haphazardly this way and that, some open face down, others splattered sideways with their pages bent out of shape.

The ghost had been at her bed as well, ruffling the pillows and blankets up into a nest, and in the middle of that nest, its hideous cover facing the sky, was her copy of *Archer's Goon*.

With a sigh Samantha went back downstairs and heated up some leftover casserole for the ghost. She shoved this into the closet and then got to work putting the books away, carefully smoothing their pages out as she did so.

She left *Archer's Goon* for last. She had a bad feeling about that book. When she got to it she saw that the ghost had stuck her library card about three-quarters of the way through, to act as a bookmark.

The cover was really quite atrocious. Three giant people, viewed partly from above, crouched around what looked like a doll's house. The artist, Samantha thought, had not been very good. One of the people had an abnormally small head, and there was something that was probably supposed to be a trench dug around the house, but because of the coloring looked like a lumpy worm.

Out of a perverse curiosity, Samantha peeled back the cover to find that it was a used copy, formerly the property of the Lafayette Public Library. Right in the front was a statement to the effect that the story contained would prove the following . . . and then a list of humorous facts which Samantha thought were obviously true in their own right. One in particular struck her as especially adroit:

Power corrupts, but we need electricity.

She stared at that line for almost a minute, trying to figure out why it resonated with her the way it did. It was like the words sent a ripple through her mind, temporarily unifying the two layers.

"Power corrupts," she repeated, out loud. "But we need electricity."

She realized that, though she remembered reading the book, she could not actually remember what it was about. Out of curiosity she turned the page and started the first chapter.

Twenty pages on she settled herself more comfortably amongst the pillows, drawing the blankets up around her shoulders and putting a cushion across her lap, to support her hands as she continued to read.

Once it became clear that Clara was there to mitigate the disaster, rather than compound it, she found herself dragged in several directions at once by people wanting her help right then and there.

"I told you: cut off the apparition's head and remove the source stone from the bird's body. You'll find it where the heart should be," she explained to a tearstained officer with a trembling lip.

"But I can't get near it without—without—" The officer broke off to blow his nose.

Clara gazed at the ceiling, trying to restrain her frustration. When she lowered her eyes again she caught sight of the sergeant who had met her when she first arrived. Making eye contact, she strode purposely over to the woman and leaned on the counter.

"I was told you had a talking rabbit here," she said.

"Sort of," said the sergeant, with a fragile grin, and pointed behind the divider to where a small plush bunny in denim overalls was propped on a stool. It looked worn out and sad, like a toy once loved but now abandoned.

"May I?" Clara asked, extending her hand.

The sergeant looked uncertainly at the rabbit, reluctant, it seemed, to pick it up. Clara understood why a moment later when the rabbit shuddered, shimmered, and then grew into a living, breathing, softly furry animal about four feet tall. The denim overalls grew with it, and its glass eyes turned into real ones, its nose was wet and twitched, and its ears stood up alertly. Its fur was silver-gray except for a white patch on its belly, soft and thick.

"Ms. Nordstern," the sergeant said drily, "meet Lady Bibbit." She flipped up the divider so Clara could come behind the counter, and then went to go "make some more tea. Unless you'd like coffee? We don't have decaf. No? Tea good? Okay."

Clara stared at the rabbit as she walked around behind the counter and drew up a spare chair. She could still see a shadow of the stuffed rabbit at the center of the apparition, but right now this warm, furry rabbit was in the foreground. She was as real as the stuffed toy, but she seemed to be having difficulty maintaining that form.

Clara took off her glove and offered the rabbit her bare hand. When she felt the soft, furry paw close gently around her fingers she concentrated on the sensation, on the size and shape of the rabbit, who was not really a proper bunny shape anymore: elongated, with recognizable fingers and a flatter face. Essentially, a rabbit infused with just enough humanlike characteristics to get her upright and talking. Clara fixed the image in her mind, solidifying it with the firm belief that *this* was the rabbit's true form, and that the limp, stuffed, worn-out toy was the ghost; the illusion.

"Oh, *thank* you," said Lady Bibbit, her eyes much brighter and focused now. "I needed that."

"I do not know how long it will last," Clara admitted. "But I hope you can help me. There is a person of power here, perhaps a young mage or even a small god, who is projecting their grief onto the physical world, and it is causing . . . " She paused, searching for the right word. In her lapse there was a muffled crash from the street and a terrible cry, like an elephant had just been run into by a police van. " . . . difficulties," Clara finished.

Lady Bibbit looked down at her lap despondently.

"It's Mantha," she said, the weight of the name hanging heavy in the air. As if in response, somewhere from above something that sounded a little like a wolf howled its misery into the sky. Then there was a gunshot.

Clara waited patiently, never taking her eyes off Lady Bibbit.

The rabbit's ears drooped, but she went on.

"Our bună died on Christmas morning," she said quietly. "But Mantha didn't believe it, so Bună got up and had Christmas with us. I mean, I could tell she was dead, but she was also alive sort of in the way I am alive. Because Mantha believed in us."

"And the things Mantha believes in . . . come true?" Clara asked.

That didn't sound to her like a mage—similar, but not at all the way Faraday had described it.

"They *become* true," said Lady Bibbit. "For a while, anyway. You understand, I'm one of her creations, so I only see one side of it."

Clara nodded acknowledgement, though she thought the rabbit seemed very perceptive for a realized figment. Mantha, whoever she was, hadn't just believed in her *realness*, she had believed in her *life*, and that life had developed into something much larger and more complex than anything Mantha probably imagined.

Mages could be diverse, she supposed. Perhaps Mantha was just an incredibly strong one.

"What happened then?" she asked.

Lady Bibbit sniffed.

"Mantha went through the day in, like, a haze. She was working so hard at *not* believing her bună was dead that she didn't even notice that I'd become corporeal to help her make dinner. It wasn't until the next morning, when Bună flat out refused to keep playing along, that she realized what had happened. Then she . . . well, she was very upset. I lost hold of myself, and when I was able to move again she had run away."

"Run away?" Clara prompted.

"She's gone and forgotten all about us," Lady Bibbit said, tears welling up in her enormous blue eyes. "She's convinced this other family to take her in. She's pretending she's *their* daughter, and since it's Mantha, everyone is going along with it! Meanwhile, Bună's still in the kitchen, only she's properly dead now. And I'm just . . . oh, I don't know what to *do!*"

And with that the rabbit broke down in tears. Not the forced, debilitating sobs of the excess grief, but of her own anguish and fear.

The sergeant came back in the middle of it, carrying three steaming styrofoam cups on a tray. She seemed unfazed by the sobbing bunny and set two cups down next to them and took the other back to her seat behind the counter. Clara ignored them in favor of teasing out her least-dirty rag from the sleeve of her jacket and offering it to Lady Bibbit.

She leaned forward, elbows on her knees, and peered closely at the rabbit as she wiped large, glittering tears out of her eyes and blew misty spray out of her nose.

"Can you take me to Mantha's house?" she asked.

"Of course," sniffed Lady Bibbit. "But Mantha's not there anymore. Just Bună, and she's . . . "

"She still needs to be taken care of," said Clara. And, at three weeks dead, would probably need more attention than what Clara was capable of giving. She turned to the sergeant.

"There is a woman dead of natural causes in her house. Her body must be cared for."

The sergeant stared at her incredulously.

"Lady," she said. "We've got more important things right now—"

"This is one of those important things," Clara said, standing up. She picked up her tea and drank it down, knowing she would welcome the warmth inside her later on. "I only need a pair of first responders."

"We don't *have* any first responders available," said the sergeant scathingly. "They're busy helping the people who are *still alive.*"

Clara was not dissuaded. After taking the matter to the police captain, it was eventually ascertained that the coroner himself wasn't presently detained—no one had, it appeared, actually *died* yet—and he was persuaded to follow Clara, guided by Lady Bibbit, through the chaotic streets of Lafayette to where Mantha and her bună used to live.

It wasn't far, all things considered, though they had to detour around the library in order to avoid the intersection of South and 8th, where a garbage truck had been overturned and there was an octopoid creature rolling in the wreckage.

Mantha and her bună had lived in a tall, narrow, fiercely tidy house on a quiet street with patched pavement. The slush lay thick in the gutters and the state of the steps leading up to the front door indicated no one had been in or out since the last snowstorm.

The coroner, who was an agreeable, bearded man with bushy brown hair and a prominent nose, offered to go in first.

"If this lady's been dead as long as your friend says, it might not be a pretty sight," he said.

Clara stared at him blankly, utterly at a loss for words, then declined the offer by marching up to the front door and opening it.

It hadn't been locked.

Mantha's bună was slumped in a chair in the little kitchen, relatively intact for all the time that had passed—the heat had been turned off and the interim temperature had discouraged all but the most determined bacteria from going to work, and the house itself protected her from the larger members of nature's waste-disposal team.

She was a small, withered woman with thin gray hair, wearing a wool skirt and a paisley shawl draped loosely over her shoulders. Clara imagined she must have been the perfect sort of grandmother: all crinkly smiles and stern affection.

Lady Bibbit was clinging to her leg, which made moving about the tiny kitchen awkward. The coroner caught up to them and let out an exclamation of disappointment at the sight.

"Aw, so *that's* what happened to Mrs. Fulgeroiu," he sighed, stepping around Clara and prying the woman's head back to get a better look at her face.

"You know her?" Clara asked.

"Used to see her every Sunday in church," he explained, now moving on to her hands. "Nice lady. Very Romanian. *Yee*up, looks like heart failure, probably. Can't be surprised—she must've been pushing ninety. What's she doing here, though? Her granddaughter shoulda phoned ... us ..." He trailed off, looking around the kitchen sharply.

"I told you," said Lady Bibbit in a small, unhappy voice. "Mantha didn't want to believe it, so she ran away."

The coroner didn't seem to hear. Apparently he didn't want to believe that there was a four-foot tall walking talking rabbit in the room.

"Where is Mantha's room?" Clara asked.

"Upstairs," said Lady Bibbit, and pointed to a doorway leading into a dusty living room.

Through this and up a flight of stairs covered in worn carpet brought Clara to a pair of bedrooms on either side of a tiny bathroom. The right-hand one clearly had belonged to the grandmother. It had a queen-sized bed, bureau, reading chair and nightstand. The lefthand one had a single twin, a low table, rocking chair, space heater, and a battered wardrobe. Everything was very stark, very clean, and forlorn in a way that made Clara feel hollow inside.

Something flitted at the edge of her vision. Lady Bibbit was standing in the doorway, clutching the frame. Clara could see a bit of her seams showing through her fur, and went over and picked her up.

"Do you know where Mantha is now?" she asked.

Lady Bibbit nodded. "But she keeps blocking me. I can't get to her."

"We'll go together," Clara said, "after we take care of her bunặ."

Eternal Light Funeral Home was technically closed on account of the shadowy apelike creature rampaging through the street, but the owner's mother went to the same church as Vasilica Fulgeroiu, and the coroner knew them both. They were let in the back door by a shaken-looking man in his forties, who nevertheless took charge of the deceased woman.

"Not to argue," he said as they wheeled her into the prep room. "But why am I doing this *now?*"

"For the good of the city," said Clara gravely.

"I don't see how embalming Mrs. Fulgeroiu is going to help matters," said the undertaker.

"It will," Clara assured him. "In the long run it will make all the difference."

There she left the two men and the dead woman, ducked an incoming bird which splattered itself on the mortuary's wall, and mounted Unicorn.

Lady Bibbit had gone downright floppy, so Clara set the rabbit in her lap as they rode slowly through downtown Lafayette.

It was getting to be, as her sister might have called it, a Biblical Mess. Shadowy grief monsters were lolling in the street, hanging off of storefronts, or sprawling over roofs. People caught unawares were immobilized by sudden violent bursts of weeping; they passed one woman slumped in the middle of the sidewalk, hugging her knees and crying so hard she could barely breathe.

Clara wanted to stop, to at least help the woman inside; it was beginning to snow again, softly, and she knew it was only a matter of time before they started accruing casualties. The monsters might not kill anyone directly, but they could bring death about in other ways.

"How far to Mantha's new house?" she asked Lady Bibbit.

"N-not far," stuttered the rabbit. "C-corner of Perrin and Herbert. You c-can get to it from Main S-street."

But she hardly needed to give Clara any directions. The sky had darkened, not just from the snow-bearing clouds, but also from the streaming flock of birds that was congregating overhead. They were flying in an ever-tightening circle—a spiral—centered over some place a little north and east of downtown.

Clara made for it. She wasn't certain what streets she took—in many cases, the signs had been knocked down or otherwise obscured by the plague of corporeal sadness that was swarming over the city. They passed broken shop fronts, downed power lines, and edged around overturned cars. At one intersection two cars had had a head-on collision, and the drivers were still slumped, sobbing, over their deflated air bags. The cause of the accident was a thing like a whale with long, spindly legs. It was presently tearing the bulbs out of the intersection's stoplights.

Clara ducked and wove her bike between the legs, Lady Bibbit clutched safely against her chest. The rabbit was noticeably smaller now, and felt less like a living animal and more like a sack of stuffing.

They missed Perrin Ave. in the confusion, and Clara had to take 18th up to Herbert St. But by that point it was obvious where they needed to go.

The vortex of birds had let down a funnel over a house near the corner of Perrin and Herbert, and around them howled a fierce wind. Or they were also the wind. It was difficult to tell. They weren't proper birds, that much was obvious. Some of them were more than a little insubstantial, and one passed through Clara's shoulder as she parked Unicorn a safe distance from the house. It felt like something sharp had just torn through her chest, but when she checked herself, there was no physical injury.

"Has Mantha done anything like this before?" Clara asked as she made her way, leaning into the wind, across the street.

"Nothing this big," gasped Lady Bibbit. She'd rejuvenated a little, but was still unable to walk. "Little things; food not going bad, spare change when she needed it. Bună called her *minunăție*, her 'miracle' because things would—oh, *duck!*—sorry, things would always work out when Mantha was involved. What's wrong?"

Clara had stopped. The rabbit's entreaty to duck had been caused by a white bird, far larger than any of the others, which had swooped in at an odd angle—against the wind—cutting across their path before disappearing into the maelstrom.

And it was a real storm now. Lifting her hand to shield her face, Clara could feel the wind slicing against her arm, even through her leather armor. Resuming her progress she had to tack against it, like a ship sailing across the wind, walking in zigzags toward the big, peach-colored house behind the white picket fence.

Strangely enough, the house itself seemed unaffected by the storm raging just beyond its yard. Clara could see the bare tree in front, perfectly still and serene behind a sheen of whipping wind filled with bird feathers and sharp rain. An empty soda can hit her in the head as they mounted the curb, and she had to drop to her hands and knees and crawl the last two feet, head turned aside from the ripping gale.

It was more than wind now. It was furious, ferocious denial. They were in the seam where the displaced grief met the force which was causing it to manifest outwardly, and the result was something akin to a waterfall.

Clara felt flattened by it, pressed into a thin, filmy version of herself that was barely able to clutch at the gatepost and, after an endless minute to gather what passed for her strength, to haul herself and the rabbit over the threshold and onto the house's front lawn.

There was one harshly disorienting moment when her rear half remained in the rushing torrent of wind, birds and emotion, while her head and shoulders fell forward into comparatively balmy air and a stifling silence. Then she kicked herself the rest of the way in and sat up in the front yard of the comfortable, peach-colored house with the white picket fence.

Someone had shoveled the driveway not too long ago, and there was a string of Christmas lights hung over the railing of the front porch. A light was on inside, casting a warm glow over the snow-covered lawn—for the storm of birds above them was so thick it appeared evening had come early.

From here, this felt more like a heavy storm cloud. Clara would have mistaken them for such if she hadn't known better. If she hadn't just fought her way through it, with the scratches to show for her efforts.

Lady Bibbit shuddered at her side and picked herself up. She looked more herself now: sleek and furry with soft, moist blue eyes. She straightened her overalls and offered a paw to Clara, who was still getting her breath back.

Whatever was in that house, it was stronger and sadder and more lonely than anything she'd ever encountered. She wasn't sure if it was the overbearing presence that made her muscles turn to water, or just that it scared her.

Strangely, once she admitted this, she felt better, and was able to climb shakily to her feet and approach the front door. Lady Bibbit hop-walked behind her, careful to stay in the safety of her shadow.

The doorbell chimed agreeably under her thumb, but after a whole minute with no response, Clara let herself in. This was a simple matter of pushing the door off its hinges, stepping through the aperture provided, and then setting it back in place. Clara's body was still stronger than most of the world, if she bothered to concentrate.

Lady Bibbit hopped around behind her, and they found themselves in a tasteful entryway with an elaborate light fixture dangling above their heads. Three sets of coats, scarves and hats hung on pegs opposite the door, with matching pairs of boots beneath them. Two were of adult size, a man and woman each, while the third must have belonged to a child. A girl, Clara guessed, if the prevalence of flowers and colorful ponies were anything to go by.

Music was playing, a soft, crooning song that set Clara's nerves on edge. She moved further into the house with cautious steps, but did not unsheathe her sword.

It was, by anyone's estimation, a nice house. Freshly vacuumed carpets and framed pictures, the floor in the kitchen was tile and there was a big oak table dominating the dining room.

A man was sitting at that table. He was in his mid forties, white, of average height and build, wearing a pinstriped button-down shirt and a tie which hung loose from his neck. There was a magazine open on the table in front of him, and in one hand he clasped the handle of a mug. As Clara watched he raised the vessel and appeared to take a drink—but she did not see him swallow anything. After watching him for a minute she saw him repeat the motion twice—and make no other move.

Cautiously she moved around the table until she was in his line of sight. He made no sign that he had noticed her, but took another fake sip from his cup. Leaning forward Clara saw why he had to mime the action: the mug was empty, with only the dried dregs of coffee in the bottom.

His other hand, lying on the magazine, twitched, and Clara saw two scared eyes staring at her from under a fringe of gray-blond hair. But he did not alter his pattern of movement.

"She's keeping them still," Lady Bibbit whispered. "So they don't ruin things."

The man's eyes rolled sideways toward the rabbit's voice, but he did not turn his head.

Clara frowned. She'd heard of magic users with this level of influence over the behavior of others, but they were rare—and those rare few had been specialists in their field. For a child, presumably untrained, to do so. . . .

Clara began to suspect a demigod. Except not even Flammard in his worst tempers had done anything like this.

She reached into her pocket and fished out her charm pouch. Pulling the set out on its leather string, she unhooked a silver ring and held it up so the man could get a good look at it.

"Put this in your mouth, but do not swallow. Whatever you do, don't scream."

With these words she dropped the ring into his cup, then watched as he raised it, tipped it back much further than he'd done before, and then worked his jaw as he maneuvered the ring under his tongue.

He set the mug down slowly, his mouth puckering uncomfortably. Then he looked up sharply at Clara, at Lady Bibbit, and then glanced at the ceiling.

"She is upstairs?" Clara asked.

The man nodded, got the ring into his cheek so he could speak.

"Susan—my wife—she's . . . " he pointed limply toward the living room.

"I'll take care of her," Clara promised. "Make no sudden moves."

She left the man at the table and went into the next room, another silver ring already between her fingers.

Susan was a tall, sandy-haired woman sitting in a forcibly relaxed attitude on an overstuffed sofa with a book in her lap. Her eyes rolled in Clara's direction as she came and knelt beside her, but that was all she did.

Clara repeated the process with the ring, along with her warning not to scream or make sudden moves. It was complicated by the fact that the woman didn't have an excuse to open her mouth, so Clara held the ring against her forehead until the woman let out a relieved gasp and slumped forward.

"Sarah," she whispered frantically. "Where's Sarah? I haven't seen her in *weeks*."

"Who is Sarah?" Clara asked.

"Why didn't I report her missing?" the woman gasped, raising her hands to clutch her face. "What's *wrong* with me?"

"I think Sarah must be their daughter," Lady Bibbit said, sadly. "She's probably hidden somewhere."

The woman's head snapped up so fast she jerked out from under Clara's hand. Immediately her eyes glazed over, and Clara quickly slipped the ring into the palm of her hand, closing her fingers around it.

"*Don't* let go of this," she ordered.

The woman nodded, more frightened than ever now.

"Who is Samantha?" she whispered, her eyes wide and bulging.

Clara blinked, and turned to Lady Bibbit.

"Samantha?" she repeated.

The rabbit shrugged. "Samantha is her full name. She never liked it. Didn't like Sam or Sammy either, so we called her Mantha."

The woman—Susan—seemed to see Lady Bibbit for the first time, and her mouth opened in horror. Clara closed her free hand over it.

"Susan," she said, quiet and serious. "I am going to find Sarah. I'll find your daughter and bring her back. But you must keep yourself safe. You husband is in the dining room. I want you to go sit with him. Speak only in low voices; do not sound alarmed."

The woman's eyes continued to bulge, but she nodded, and when Clara slowly removed her hand she got up from the couch and walked, a little unsteadily, into the dining room.

Looking around, Clara quickly found the stairs and started up them.

"When we find Sarah," she said to Bibbit. "I want you to take her down to her parents."

"I don't know if I'll be able to do that," Lady Bibbit said with a worried frown. "But I'll try."

Clara nodded in acknowledgement, and led the way up to the second floor. Here there was another hallway and another set of doors. This time Samantha's room was immediately obvious: it had a big, red, S made of lacquered wood hung in the center, and there was light streaming out from under the door.

Clara slipped the string of charms around her wrist, tucking it under her glove so the silver was flush against her bare skin. Then she took a breath, focusing herself, and opened the door.

Samantha Fulgeroiu was a small, dark-haired girl—older than ten but not yet into her teens—sitting on an unkempt bed in the middle of a sea of upended books scattered over the floor. She had one in her lap as well, open nearly at the last page, and her head was bent over it in concentration.

The air felt heavy with that concentration, and Clara found she was compelled to stop and wait until the girl had finished reading, slowly closed the book, and then looked up at her with brown eyes like doors into a deep and dangerous place. Her face reminded Clara of a barn owl: beautiful, but haunting and eerie at the same time. Or perhaps that was because she could not move. Could barely breathe, come to that.

"You must be a sort of Goon, aren't you?" the girl said. "You've come to remind me of who I am."

Clara swallowed, but did not speak. She could not. Not with Samantha staring at her with those deep, limitless eyes. A greater will than hers was controlling her body, and right then it wanted her to be still and quiet. So she was.

The girl rubbed her face with a hand and looked sadly down at the book.

"You don't have to tell me. I'm like Venturus. From this book. I just wanted . . . I just wanted to have a proper childhood. With parents and birthday parties and . . . and store-bought cake . . . and . . ."

Clara found the words creeping out of her mouth on a swell of sympathy:

"Grandmothers who don't die," she croaked.

Samantha looked up at her sharply, and there was fire in the depths of her eyes for a moment. Real fire that lit them a dull red, and something unseen, like smoky wings, began gathering around her shoulders. But her attention wavered, and Clara found she still had a voice.

"But . . . this isn't your life, Samantha. You really must . . . let them go."

Samantha was pursing her lips, shaking her head, tears welling up and quenching the fire in her eyes.

"No, no, no," she cried. "I won't go back, I *won't* go back!" And Clara felt reality try to shift around them.

It wanted to hurl her and Lady Bibbit away, back out into the storm of grief. Samantha's grief, which she had redirected away from herself. It spoke volumes for how deep her soul was that it had taken over an entire city, but Clara didn't have the energy to examine the implications just then.

Growing up with two demigods as her older siblings had taught Clara a thing or two about asserting her presence in the face of overwhelming personalities. The first, and this was a lesson which Mother had hammered home to her again and again, was that you must believe in yourself as a person. That you exist, apart from anyone else's opinions or desires or beliefs. And Clara had taken that lesson to heart, cultivated an unshakable belief in her own being—of herself, Claymore—that sustained her even when the world around her was coming to pieces.

What Samantha did to reality then did not overcome it, but Clara felt the foundations shudder. She bent her head, clenched her fists, and felt her skin begin to burn along the lines of her marks. The pain grounded her, and she remained where she was. She remained who she was.

"You . . . don't have to go back," she whispered. "But you . . . cannot . . . stay . . . here . . ."

She wasn't sure if Samantha heard her. The girl gripped her head in her hands, curling herself into a ball, and continued to shout, "No, no, *no!*"

Outside the window the darkness had condensed into a storm of whirling, feathery shapes. One of them scraped across the glass, leaving a long, pale scratch.

Lady Bibbit took a hesitant step forward.

"Mantha," she began, and then came up against the expanding wall of fear and sadness and rage. It, which had forced Clara to a standstill, shredded Lady Bibbit into strips of fur and denim and a long, shrill scream that warbled and echoed around the little room. Pieces of cloth and clumps of stuffing formed a brief vortex around Samantha, and then abruptly dropped to the floor, lifeless and cold.

Samantha's hair was steaming even as tears flowed freely from her eyes. She seemed not to see Clara anymore, but stared at the wreckage of the stuffed animal with growing horror.

Clara herself was on her knees, it being too much energy to keep her balance on two feet. Across the floor she could see a piece of Lady Bibbit's face—a patch of silver velveteen with a blue glass eye stitched to it. And at the same time she saw a butchered rabbit which stared sadly at the girl on the bed, before slowly fading into the material remains of what she had originally been.

Clara could barely raise her head, but she did, and she found Samantha's face across the wreckage of the room.

"Samantha," she whispered. "I am so, so sorry."

Samantha looked at her, and it was like getting blasted in the face with heat from an open oven. Only instead of burning her, it pressed her back, flattening her against the wall. She felt Bellatrix digging into her back, her head hitting the wall, but even the associated pain was dulled, distanced by the overwhelming sensation of being the focus of such terrible attention.

She couldn't breathe.

"What's to be sorry about?" Samantha asked, her voice like a brittle piece of ice over a swiftly warming lake. "It was only a toy bunny."

The pressure broke, and Clara collapsed to the floor with a gasp.

"You should not deny death," she wheezed, dragging herself across the carpet toward the girl, who had gotten up off the bed to stand in front of it. Clara could see her feet, in fluffy pink socks with white unicorns printed on them, planted in front of her face.

"I can if I want," said Samantha, but she sounded more petulant than angry.

"Of course you *can*," said Clara, not raising her face. It was easier to resist the assumption that she was not there if she didn't meet those bottomless eyes. "Anyone can. Lots of people . . . do." She took a breath. It was painful, but necessary. Her vision was blurring, this time because of the thick, pearly tears collecting in her eyes. "When . . . when someone we care about dies . . . it is better . . . it is better to be sad. To grieve."

And it was her own grief this time, she could tell. There was a taste of bitterness in the back of her mouth, of harrowing disappointment, and a sour lump where her heart should have been, and behind it all, the memory of a woman—an incredible, brave, *kind*, human woman, who fell away into nothing, leaving Clara holding the barrel of a shotgun.

She shook her head, trying to keep herself present. It was more important now than ever, in the face of whatever Samantha was, that she remember *where* she was.

"We all grieve in our own way," she went on hoarsely, fumbling for the bottle in her pocket. It felt hot, even to her gloved fingers. "We should not deny death, but we can accept it on our own terms."

She got the bottle between two fingers and teased it out of her pocket. The silver had all but deteriorated into a fine black powder, and the two stones inside were bleeding profusely.

Unable to get any closer to the girl, Clara rolled the bottle across the carpet, so it came up against her stocking feet.

For a long while Samantha didn't move. It was difficult to tell, but Clara was fairly certain that the conventional flow of time stopped, leaving them in a temporary bubble. An eye within the eye of the storm.

Then Samantha stooped and picked up the bottle. She didn't uncork it, but looked at the two stones inside, like someone seeing a picture of a loved-one, long gone.

Behind her, against the window, something white was beating itself against the glass. Within the room, however, a stifling peace had settled.

At last Clara looked up, and saw that Samantha had uncorked the bottle and rolled the two stones out onto her palm. They glistened faintly in her hand, but appeared no more threatening than two lumps of wet coal. She closed her fingers around them and shut her eyes.

The window exploded, sending a wave of broken glass cascading into the room. Smokey shadows streamed in after it, tearing around the room in an ever-tightening circle until they concentrated on the small, dark-haired girl in the fluffy pink socks. Then they condensed into a solid line of black which pierced her in the chest and was promptly sucked inside.

On and on the grief came, streaming in from where it had been spread over the city. Clara thought she glimpsed owls, foxes, wolves and giant cats. She was pretty sure she saw the spindly legged elephant and something like a human with too many hands. They came pouring into the girl in a howling torrent, on and on with a sound like a million voices crying in despair.

Clara knew the sound. It had been ringing in her ears ever since Selene had taken that fatal plunge. Always in the background, carefully controlled—Clara accepted death as a natural part of life, but her terms were strict and demanding—but now she could not keep her own feelings safely battened down, and she collapsed face-first on the carpet, wailing in empathy.

At last something came through the window that was large and white and flapped awkwardly around the room until it settled on Samantha's shoulders, where it vanished as soon as Clara tried to look directly at it.

Samantha was standing in the exact same place and pose as she had been when the window broke. Pieces of glass glittered in her hair, but there were no visible wounds upon her body. Her eyes and nose were streaming with tears, but her breathing was steady and easy.

She looked at Clara, and for once it felt no different than if any other person had done so. Clara found she could sit up and take a full breath at last.

"Bună is dead," the girl said in a dry, hollow voice.

Clara nodded. "She will be buried tomorrow, in consecrated ground."

"She died on Christmas morning," Samantha continued. She looked down at her hand, still clenched. When she opened it, there was nothing inside.

"This is not my house," she said. She didn't sound sad or angry now, only tired and empty. "This is not . . . my life."

Something creaked behind Clara, and she turned to discover the closet door had been pried open. A scared-looking girl in rumpled, dirty clothes with matted yellow hair poked her head fearfully into the room. Her face was drawn and pinched, like someone who hadn't been eating well. Her hand on the door was shaking.

Samantha sighed.

"Your parents are downstairs," she told the girl. "I didn't hurt them."

The girl—Sarah Folger, Clara assumed—nearly tripped in her hurry to get out of the closet and scramble out the door. She heard the sound of feet on the stairs and stifled gasps from the dining room.

Samantha was looking at her accusingly.

"Now what?" she asked.

Clara shrugged. "That is up to you."

Samantha pinched her mouth in unhappily. She looked around at the mess of the room, at the remains of Lady Bibbit, and the overturned books. She hugged her arms around herself and shivered.

"I don't want to be here anymore," she whispered.

And then she was gone, with a faint inrushing of air and the sound of the final heaving gasp of a sob.

Clara sat in the abandoned room for some time, feeling herself slowly recover. Eventually she got up, tidied the books into a corner, and picked up every piece of Lady Bibbit she could find. She took a plastic bag from the collection in the bathroom and put the pieces in it, then went downstairs to where the Folger family was huddling in the dining room.

Clara didn't know how she appeared to them, disheveled and tear-streaked as she was, and profoundly didn't care.

"I am sorry about the mess," she said, her voice sounding hollow even to her own ears. "But it won't get any worse."

She left them staring after her, letting herself out the front door and into a dark, silent, and increasingly frigid night.

Clara felt like a plastic water bottle that had been emptied out, then crushed and tossed in a gutter. There was a heaviness in her bones and a lightness in her head that told her she was exhausted, but for all the world she couldn't sleep. Her brain refused to slow down; kept spinning over the events of the day. Most of all she kept thinking of Samantha Fulgeroiu.

Her grandmother might have had some witchiness about her, but that house hadn't struck Clara as one belonging to an active practitioner. Clara wasn't even certain a mage was what Samantha was. A lot could change in a generation, as Clara well knew.

People of power cropped up everywhere, for all sorts of reasons. Maybe they had a god somewhere in their lineage. Maybe they *were* a god and didn't know it yet. Maybe they were a sleeping angel. Or a sleeping demon.

It was that last possibility that kept Clara awake. The Earth was liberally sprinkled with sleeping angels—people going about their lives oblivious to the divine aspect of their soul, an aspect which would be reborn time and again. The Nameless God's perennial messengers in the mortal realm.

There was only one sleeping demon at a time, and if that one awoke it would mean a world full of trouble for everyone in it. Even Jill Hamilton, Clara suspected, would not enjoy being witness to an apocalypse.

But Clara had made a careful study of the antichrists, and Samantha did not feel like one. Nothing she had done reeked of infernal influence; the only outright aggressive action she had taken had been the destruction of Lady Bibbit—and that had been an accident.

No, what she felt like to Clara was an ordinary girl saddled with extraordinary powers that she could not understand or control. In that regard the situation was a painfully familiar one, and Clara's entire body ached in sympathy.

Eventually she stopped trying to rest and got up. She pulled out her first-aid kit and the bag with Lady Bibbit's remains and set them on the little table by the hotel bed. Turning the light on she began to lay out the pieces, sorting them until she had a more-or-less rabbit-shaped pile. Then she began, with the needle and thread which had previously stitched living flesh, to sew the pieces back together.

The work was strangely relaxing, and around four in the morning Clara could not keep her eyes open any longer. She was physically and emotionally drained, and she had just the presence of mind to push her sewing project out of the way before slumping forward on the desk and going to sleep with her face in her arms.

The dream lapped at Clara's consciousness like the gentle waves of a sun-warmed lake, and she was too tired to resist.

She was floating face down in the lake, but in the manner of dreams, could breathe through the water. The bottom was golden in the sunlight, silt-coated logs and stones stretching off into a blue-green mist. Little fish flickered back and forth, their bodies reflecting the gold and green and blues of the water, visible only when their gleaming scales caught the light and flashed.

Someone was calling her name . . .

It was a distant, golden voice, and mingled with the gold of the light reflecting off the silt at the bottom of the lake.

A shadow fell across her back, and something pudgy and insistent, like an animal's snout, pushed at her shoulder.

Clara flailed out of the water, putting her feet down in a cloud of billowing silt as she stood up, water cascading off her jacket and dragging at her arms. Her ungloved hand brushed something furry and solid, and she blinked dream-water out of her eyes to find herself face to face with a brilliant white stag.

The animal gazed at her with eyes bright and black, and blew a wet, concerned breath in her face.

Clara stared back, unmoving, hardly daring to breathe. The animal was huge—as tall as she was at his withers—with majestic, seven-pronged antlers reaching like arms up to catch the sky. These too were white, but the tips flashed in the sun, as if capped with bronze.

Then the eyes closed in a slow blink, and the huge head turned away. With a shrug and a heave the stag got his front hooves up onto the surface of the water, which shuddered but took his weight as he pulled his hindquarters up behind him. Then he was trotting off across the surface of the lake, leaving faint ripples in his wake. The sun, high overhead and reflecting blindingly off the water, washed him out so Clara did not see whether he reached the trees on the far bank, or if he disappeared into the light itself.

Someone was calling her name, but laughing at the same time.

She turned around. Ariel Freeman was coming down across the big, bare rock which sloped to meet the lake. He was barefoot with his trousers rolled up, and in one hand he was carrying his shoes; in the other, Clara's giant motorcycling boots. He was smiling, laughing, like he was happy to see her.

"I dunno if that jacket can take that sort of treatment," he chided her. "It's only mortal, after all."

Clara set off wading toward the shore, but she took off her leather jacket once she got there and hung it on a nearby tree to dry.

The sunlight felt surprisingly pleasant on her bare arms, and she realized with a jolt that she'd forgotten to be embarrassed about them.

Ariel was looking—and he looked interested—but he had a pleased expression on his face, as if what he saw reminded him of something good.

"S'nice," he said, gesturing at Clara's bicep. "I should show you mine some time."

Automatically Clara glanced down at her arm. She'd forgotten just how vivid the marks were, the black outlined in a thin seam of red. A water droplet running down from her shoulder hit the first band and evaporated in a hiss of steam. She covered it by reflex, realized this just exposed her other arm even more, and gave up. She wiggled her hands into the sodden pockets of her trousers, and shrugged.

"I always liked the way you shrugged," Ariel said, conversationally. He imitated her, pulling his shoulders down, then up again. "It's less like saying, 'I don't know?'"—he pulled he shoulders almost up to his ears and made an exaggerated clueless expression, raising his eyebrows and sticking out his lower lip—"and more like, 'I don't know.'" He dropped his shoulders, stretched his neck out, then allowed them to rise back to their normal position.

He shook his head, suddenly embarrassed. "Sorry," he said. "Maybe it only works when you're tall."

"You're tall enough," Clara told him.

"Really?" Ariel looked surprisingly gratified. His chest puffed out and he stood up straight. "That means a lot, coming from you."

Clara began to shrug again, but she stopped herself; looked down at her feet. She was wearing socks. The sight reminded her of another pair of feet, smaller, in pink socks with unicorns on them. She felt her whole frame sag.

"Something wrong?" Ariel asked.

"I don't know what to do about Samantha,"

Another pair of feet, bare and a little hairy, came into view.

"Who's Samantha?" Ariel asked.

Clara raised her gaze to his face. His eyes were waiting, steady and hazel. There were the faintest traces of freckles across his cheeks. Why hadn't she noticed that before?

Because she hadn't dared look. Not in the waking world. And this wasn't the real Ariel, she reminded herself. Just an agreeable facsimile dreamed up by her overwrought brain. It was probably fleshing out the pieces of him she didn't know with memories from other important people in her life. Schiavona had gotten freckles just like that, the summer they had spent at Tesla's forge. And of course Flammard's face was a mess of them . . .

"Claymore?"

"Sorry," she replied automatically, shifting her gaze to the lake, the forest on the far bank, the sky overhead. Anywhere but the golden, earnest man standing in front of her.

But the dream remained, vivid and surprisingly solid. So Clara began to tell Ariel about Samantha, about the grief monsters, Lady Bibbit—the whole lot.

They went wading in the shallow end of the lake while she talked, and Ariel listened with his hands in his pockets and his chin on his chest, nodding understandingly and waiting patiently whenever Clara trailed off.

"And I don't know what I should do now," she finished helplessly as they climbed out of the lake and began putting their shoes back on. "She shouldn't be alone, but there's nothing out there for a person like her. The state won't know what to do with her. She'll terrorize a string of foster families—like Joy King—until she comes of age angry, lost and confused, and with powers like she has, I'll probably end up having to fight her sooner rather than later."

Ariel nodded understandingly.

"It's tough," he agreed. "I mean, the scary thing about kids like that is that they're so vulnerable, you know? They'll latch on to whatever's nearest—whatever is there *for them*—and if whatever that is isn't so good . . . well, then they don't turn out so good."

Clara nodded.

"But I mean, really," Ariel said. He was looking at her again, direct and focused. "They're like plants. Whatever dirt is *there*, they'll grow in it."

Clara looked down at him.

"You are trying to tell me something indirectly," she observed.

"Hey, it's your life," he said, raising his hands. "It's not my place to dictate. I'm just saying . . . that's my experience. I'll understand, whatever decision you make. You have to look out for yourself, too."

His last words tipped Clara's world sideways. As if her life was a diorama, and someone had turned the stage around so that suddenly new angles and shapes were visible.

"Myself?" she repeated dumbly.

"'Course," said Ariel. "It's good to take care of people, but firstly, you gotta take care of *you.*"

He gave her a friendly nudge, just like the stag had done.

"Though, sometimes other people can help with that," he said, almost invitingly.

Clara was blinking down at him when she heard the sound of hoofbeats above them on the hill.

Ariel looked around, and the moment was lost.

"Oh," he said. "Look's like your ride is here."

The hoofbeats were growing stronger, nearer; Clara could feel them in her bones. They were inside her.

They were her heartbeat. She had fallen asleep with her head in her arms, and her heart, beating steadily away inside her chest, was sending pulses up to into her ears.

Creakily she lifted her head and looked around the dim motel room. Lady Bibbit, still barely half assembled, sat propped against the wall. Her phone displayed a string of new texts from Jill and a missed call from the Lafayette PD. Outside, the sun was bravely struggling to make its presence felt through the ominous gray clouds which hung heavy in the sky.

Clara turned her phone over and went into the bathroom where she washed her face. She made herself a small meal from the dried fruit and nuts she kept as emergency supplies, and took it with her to the table, where she went back to work.

It was a small group that gathered at the St. Boniface Cemetery: one brave priest and a hardy contingent of his flock, who were the closest thing Vasilica Fulgeroiu had to family. A search had turned up a daughter, cremated in California, whose ashes had spent the last ten years in an urn in the woman's bedroom. Lacking any other living relatives, her fellow parishioners had made the educated guess that the two should be buried together, and this they did with all respect—though with a certain lack of ceremony, since it was a blustery day and the clouds above promised a storm.

Even as the casket was being lowered into the earth something bright flickered in the sky, and a moment later the thunder rolled down upon them.

It masked the roar of a motorcycle engine as the machine pulled into the little parking lot. Its rider was dressed all in black leather, and removed her full-face helmet when she left the bike and began threading her way through the tombstones. In her arms she carried something small and gray and floppy: a stuffed animal, awkwardly stitched together with twine. It was missing an eye.

She did not disturb the mourning party, but fetched up under a spreading oak, where another, smaller figure was already standing, watching the proceedings from the shelter of the tree.

Neither greeted the other, but after a second boom of thunder, Clara cleared her throat and said:

"It is good."

"Our name means *'from lightning'*" said Samantha, with a small shrug. "Fulgeroiu. Bună told me never to be afraid of thunderstorms, because we were storm-people. I wanted to do something."

Clara glanced up at the sky, where the clouds were growing black.

"I meant the cemetery," she admitted.

"That was Father Constantin," said Samantha, nodding at the young priest leading the committal. "He's also Romanian," she added, as if this explained everything.

"You're not . . . ?" Clara gestured at the open grave, which had now received its coffin. Father Constantin picked up a shovel and placed the first load of earth on its face.

Samantha shook her head.

"I don't belong with them," was all she said.

They watched together in silence as the mourners each came forward and paid their respects, and then hustled away as quickly as was polite, leaving the staunch cemetery staffers the task of filling in the grave under the teeth of the oncoming storm. But as they went, someone struck up a song. Much of the melody and most of the words were lost in the wind, but Clara heard enough to recognize it. Amazing Grace. How she hoped it was true.

"Are you sure?" she asked the girl.

Samantha nodded. "They won't miss me."

She said it with such an awful, stone-cold certainty that Clara had no doubt that they would not. Already they had forgotten the dark little girl who used to come to church every Sunday with her grandmother. Just as the Folgers had forgotten the girl who had been their daughter for the first month of the year. Just as the Lafayette PD were now convinced that every incident caused by the rampaging monsters of Samantha's re-directed grief had a mundane explanation. Jill would be disappointed, but Clara felt it was better in the long run.

She thought about saying something, then realized she didn't have to. Wordlessly, she handed the reconstituted form of Lady Bibbit to Samantha.

"Some things you can take with you." She thought about trying to explain more, but decided against it.

Samantha turned the depleted toy over in her hands. Clara had gotten all the most important pieces, but one eye had been lost, and the stuffing she'd torn out of her pillow had bunched awkwardly under her big, clumsy stitches.

"It wouldn't be the same," Samantha said, sadly.

"No," Clara agreed. "But change is one way to get past death. Or at least put it off for a while."

"I thought you said we shouldn't deny death," Samantha said, shrewdly.

"One shouldn't," Clara said. She looked down at the girl. Met her deep brown eyes with her own frosty blue ones. "But you can meet it on your own terms."

Samantha frowned, as if she didn't quite agree. She folded the toy into her chest, tucking the head under her chin.

"Why are you still here?" she asked after a while.

Clara didn't have an answer for that, so she said nothing.

. . . how precious did that grace appear, the hour I first believed . . .

The words were brought to them through a lull in the wind, and it seemed to Clara that other words were nestled in behind them, like the memory of a golden dream, but she couldn't quite place them.

"At times like this, it is not good to be alone," she said eventually.

"But you're afraid of me," Samantha pointed out.

Clara did not bother to deny it.

"So, why are you still here?"

The girl was staring at her, she knew, but Clara gazed off through the trees and tombstones. The real answer to that question was not one she was ready to admit, so she gave a different answer—one which, to be fair, was equally true.

"I do many things that frighten me."

"That's not a reason to still be here," Samantha pointed out.

Clara shrugged.

They watched the tail end of the mourners disappear into their cars and drive off, while the custodians hastily finished covering the grave with earth and scuttled away, their collars pulled up over their ears and their hats snugged down over their collars.

Samantha didn't go anywhere, and neither did Clara.

After a while, the girl said:

"But you will be leaving soon."

Clara inclined her head.

"Can I come with you?"

Clara did look at her then.

"You are asking for my permission?"

Samantha rolled her eyes extravagantly. "Um . . . *yeah?*"

"Even though you could easily make me believe that you are my . . . " *Not daughter,* Clara thought. *Never a daughter.* " . . . sister?" she finished.

Samantha Fulgeroiu bit her lip, tucking her chin back down over Lady Bibbit's head. "I did a lot of thinking last night," she said. "It's occurred to me that, just because you *can* do a thing, doesn't mean you *should.* And that goes for everyone."

"That is"—Clara grasped for something that would not sound condescending—"an astute observation."

"It's obvious, once you think about it," said Samantha. She cocked her head to one side so she could look up at Clara with one eye. "So, *can* I come with you?"

Clara didn't know what to think or feel. Her world felt like it was shifting under her feet, and she wasn't yet sure what it would look like when it settled. There was still a sore, sour place deep inside her, and behind that a paralyzing fear. But fear, Clara reminded herself, was like death: you should not deny it, but meet it on your own terms.

She looked at the small, terrifying child and said, very seriously:

"I cannot promise to protect you."

Samantha rolled her eyes. As if in answer, thunder rolled out above them.

Clara turned and began to walk back to her bike. A patter of light feet on grass told her Samantha was on her heel.

"You'll need to wear the helmet," she said.

"Fine," said Samantha, as if this were a great concession. "And you'll need to stop calling me 'Samantha.' I've always hated that name."

"What should I call you, then?"

"Mantha will do, for now."

"Very well, Mantha."

Detroit, MI

Jill managed to restrain herself until Lansing had taken the somber, dark-haired girl to see the refurbished dining room before letting off the steam which had been building up since Clara had arrived, sans helmet, and lifted the twelve-year-old off the front of her bike. Where she had apparently been riding. Since *Indiana.*

"What in the world are you *doing?*" were the words that finally came out of her mouth.

Clara frowned down at her feet, as though she was just as frustrated with herself as Jill. In the absence of any sort of answer, Jill went on listing all the reasons her effective adoption was a bad idea.

"For starters, she's a *minor.* Now, I realize she doesn't have any living family, but our government has a system for dealing with children like her—I know it's not a very good system!" she said, when this caused Clara to glare at her reproachfully. "But the fact is, it's *there*, and we need to at least acknowledge that! Have you got anything—*anything*—that gives you custodial powers and privileges? What happens when she gets sick? What happens when she needs dental work—*when was the last time she went to the dentist?* What about truancy laws—what school does she go to? Won't they notice a missing student?"

"There will not be problems with . . . any of that," Clara said. "Her abilities make it such that she is not bound by . . . by conventional laws."

Jill raised a skeptical eyebrow.

"I will make sure that she sees a dentist," Clara amended.

Jill sat down and put her head in her hands.

"We're still on the ground here, Clara," she said, tiredly. "I mean, we're getting there but . . . I need . . . help. A lot of it. And if you're caring for a preteen girl, then . . . "

"I will remain present," Clara assured her. "And you might learn much from her. I hope that you do."

Jill groaned. The thought of the mess they could get into conducting research on a minor—even an extraordinary minor like Samantha Fulgeroiu—was enough to give her a headache. But Clara raised a tantalizing objective, though it came laden with drawbacks. Chiefly, the nature of the girl's powers.

"Clara," she said. "How can you know this isn't . . . you know . . . *her* making you think this?"

Clara gave her words due consideration, then shook her head. "I am reasonably certain that I am acting relatively of my own free will."

"Relatively?"

"Free will is a relative thing," Clara said.

Jill wanted to bang her head against her desk, but she resisted. Instead she lifted her face and gazed at the ceiling.

Something cold and wet nosed at her hand, and she glanced down to find the ghost dog had crept into her office and leaned against her leg. She saw Clara's eyes widen and realized the woman was seeing the dog for the first time.

"Jill," she said in a small voice. "What is a Yell Hound doing here?"

"Oh, yeah," she said. "This is Frosty. Animal control brought her in while you were away. What did you call her? A . . . a *yellow* hound?"

"Yell Hound," Clara said, giving herself a little shake. "Or Yeth Hound. One of the dogs of Arawn, according to Welsh mythology."

"And Arawn is . . . ?" Jill said, groping for a notepad.

"An underworld king. Likely an aspect of some deeper power. Has she . . . done anything?"

" . . . underworld king . . . " Jill muttered to herself. "Anything? No. And I mean *nothing*. Easiest dog I've ever kept—and I've never had a dog before. She likes to go running with Marcus in the morning—but not when the sun is up. Why? Is she a bad sign or something?"

Frosty leaned harder against her leg and nosed at her knee. Automatically Jill reached down and rubbed one crimson ear.

"I'm not sure," said Clara. "But it indicates that you have the attention of powers greater than our comprehension."

"Lovely," said Jill. "Maybe *they* can tell us what Mantha is."

"Yes . . . about that," Clara said.

"Of course you can keep her," Jill said, rolling her eyes. "I mean," she gave Frosty a good scratch between her shoulders, "who am I to judge?"

Clara swallowed. "I was hoping to take her to see Tesla. Isenfaust. She will be able to tell us whether we need to be worried."

"Worried?" said Jill. "More than we already are? Wait, don't answer that. Tesla is Faraday's sister, right? How long will you be away?"

Clara looked aside. "It should only take a day or so."

"So probably more like a week," Jill sighed. "Can you at least go . . . like . . . not right now? Stay here for a couple of days, at least. Oh, and don't even think about pulling that stunt with Unicorn again—if you're gonna be traveling with a kid in tow, at *least* take Arcana."

Clara stiffened. "Arcana?"

"Yes, Arcana. The big truck. With the seat belts. I can make a mobile lab for you too, in case I get any calls that you can take. You don't have to bring the trailer, if you're not comfortable with towing. But at least—*at least*—drive Arcana."

Clara just looked down at the floor again. Selene's various charms and ornaments with which she had decorated the cab of Arcana were still there, as were the scuff marks from her boots where she would rest her feet on the dash. The stain on the driver's seat where she had spilled coffee. The place where her duffle bag full of guns used to sit was empty, which was in itself the biggest reminder that she was gone.

Even now there was an empty space in the room—in their conversation—that they had still not found a way to fill. Perhaps they never would. Neither of them said anything about it, but they both acknowledged it in their own way.

After a while Jill forced herself to crack a smile. "I mean, heck," she said. "It worked for me."

Two weeks later

It was snowing again. Big, plump clumps came drifting down out of pale gray sky. Mantha stood at the arched window, Lady Bibbit tucked under her chin, and watched the flakes land, melt, and eventually gather on the sill outside. It felt like with every flake, however small, however brief its life, her own life seemed to settle. There was still a roiling, uncomfortable current streaming around her mind, but she felt as though she had passed through the worst of it. She'd fallen clean out of the mind of Samantha Folger, and was totally immersed in herself again. There was a storm within her, but it had moved off over faraway hills, and was only a distant roar at the back of her mind.

A tall shadow loomed behind her.

"We're ready," Clara said.

Mantha nodded and followed the tall woman through the arched concourse and out the side door to the covered carriage entrance, where a large red truck was parked. Jill Hamilton was perched in the back, taking inventory of the chest which she'd packed for them. She climbed down as they reached the truck and handed Clara a slip of paper.

"Everything I've packed you, it's on there. *Don't* speed, and check in with me every night."

Clara took the paper mutely and went around to the driver's side without a word.

"Don't worry," Mantha told Jill. "I'll make sure she calls."

Jill Hamilton gave her a sideways look. Through her glasses, Mantha saw her eyes flash red. "Thank you," she said.

The director of MCSIR had been rather standoffish, Mantha found, but consistent enough in her behavior that Mantha didn't begrudge her.

"You're welcome," she replied. She opened the passenger door and climbed in next to Clara, who was warming up the engine. She set Lady Bibbit, still in the form of a toy rabbit, on the dashboard and buckled herself in.

The snow was coming down even thicker now, so that it looked like they would be driving into a sheer, white wall.

"I could make it stop, if you want," Mantha offered.

"No," said Clara, starting the engine and putting the truck in gear. "I can manage."

"If you say so," said Mantha, but she couldn't help suggesting that a little gust of wind come down off the face of the building, blowing away the snow newly accumulated in the driveway.

Arcana nosed out into the open air, his engine growling meaningfully. Then he was turning onto the road, accelerating cautiously as Clara steered them toward the freeway; a bright streak of red wiped across the cold, white morning.

See me hide under cover, afraid of light
See I'm so afraid of a morning bright

'Cause they're only shadows
Gone dancing up the wall
And they want you to guide them, child
Before you fall

If you can hear them calling
Calling you by name
You can't ignore your birthright if your birthright is a shame

Now I'm the one who's crying
Crying in my hand
Even though I'm trying I'll never understand

Why, why, have you gotta die?
Why, why, leave me here to cry?
Why, why, did you go and die
That night?
So long, this night, so long

They say ashes go to ashes
But what comes in between?
Isn't that stuff more than what you've made and what you've been?

Because I hear the shadows call
And though they are not nice
They tell me things I need to hear—like, lightning does strike twice

Why, why, have you gotta die?
Why, why, leave me here to cry?
Why, why, have you gotta die?
Ain't right!
So long, this night, it's wrong
That night, was long, this night, it's wrong!

Why, why, have you gotta die?
Why, why, leave me here to cry?
Why, why, have you gotta die?
Why, why, leave me here to cry?
Why, why, have you gotta die?
Why, why, did you go and die
That night?
It's wrong to fight the night
The light, it burns the night away!

It leaves me lyin' in the sun
It leaves me lyin' in the sun
I'm burning up
Now we're both crying
Why, why,
Won't you live tonight?
Oh why . . .

—Technorhyme/*(Why, why) Have You Gotta Die?*

60

2.
MOONRISE
over HADES

*The Vestibule of Hell
on the Shores of the Acheron*

THE LAND WAS REDDISH EARTH, divided from the purplish-green sky by a bleak, white horizon, and from the misty green hills by a swiftly flowing river of black water. The red-colored earth was mounded in heaps and piles, like the detritus of some monstrous excavation. In the valleys paths had been beaten by the trampling of countless feet, while gashes in the soft sides of the mounds showed where others had struck off up their sheer sides. The air was thick with the sound of screaming.

A group of about seven people, their faces dark and faded like leaves blackened with fire, came pelting through the canyon, leaping and pushing against one another, and they sent something white and fluttering, like a tattered butterfly, rising up into the air, where it flapped, weakly. One of them made a spirited attempt to catch it by running up the side of the nearest hill and launching himself into the air, grabbing at it with desperate hands.

The winged thing did a flip in midair, drifting between his fingertips, and sailed off into the sky.

Undaunted, the shadowy group pursued it, their bare feet pounding over the hot, red dirt, shouting and crying as they ran. They followed the bright, white thing until it fluttered over the dark river, descending into the green hills on the far side, where it disappeared into the mist. There was some wailing and moaning at this, until someone pointed and shouted: something equally bright and even redder than the earth was flapping enticingly in the air, just above the nearest ridge, and as one the group took off again. They were spurred on by the swarm of flies that rose from the shallows of the river and buzzed around them in a horde. Sharp yelps and cries of pain now joined the overall howling, and a few of the pursuers stopped to slap at their sides and arms. This only allowed the insects better opportunity to mob them further, and eventually they were forced to run on, under assault from the legion of wasps.

This group was only one of many which populated the vast, tumbled landscape between the horizon and the river. Among them all only one figure sat still. Had been sitting still for a very long while, atop a tall ridge of earth.

She was also dark, but not in the sense that she was the scorched shade of a formerly living being. Her skin was glossy and brown and stood out sharply against her faded gray clothes. These were a pair of jeans that looked like a tractor had run over them a couple times (which was not far from the truth) and a wrinkled cotton tank top under a torn over-shirt with the sleeves rolled up. The arms that were resting on her knees were well-muscled in a padded sort of way, and both her elbows showed lumpy, discolored patches—long-healed scars from old episodes of road rash.

She'd lost, along with her guns and her boots, every hair tie she'd ever collected about her person. So she'd partitioned her copious curling black hair as best she could, plaited it as tightly as she could, and then tied the plaits into a bundle down along the back of her neck. It had taken a lot of time, but then, time was about the one thing that Selene Shields now had in excess.

It had felt a little funny at first: she would get hungry, or thirsty, or sleepy, and then forget that she had been hungry, or thirsty, or sleepy. At this point she mostly ignored those feelings until they went away.

She didn't much get tired, either. Not physically, anyway. Mentally the boredom was the hardest thing to combat, and one time she'd given in to the desire to sleep simply because there was nothing else better to do.

But it was not sleep. It felt more like being knocked out. One moment she was lying on the warm red earth, the next she was nowhere. She was nothing. Just a blank, black emptiness that stretched on forever. She only woke up because one of the insects had come over and stung her, almost experimentally.

That had hurt, but in the same temporary way that her hunger pangs hurt—it went away as soon as she stopped paying attention to it. So did the wasp, which had been a big, black-and-yellow one. It flew off to sting another sleeping form, which turned out to be a bearded man with an ashen face. He screamed as if the wasp had stung him on the eyeball and leapt up. Much encouraged, the wasp had pursued him as he ran, limping and whimpering, away down the slope.

Any lingering fatigue had been expunged by the meteor which had landed a few moments later.

Truth be told, Selene suspected it wasn't actually a meteor, but that was what it had looked like to her. There had been a bang, like a sonic boom, and for a moment the purple-green sky had been split across by a fiery orange streak. A blast of cold air hurtled across the plain, nearly knocking Selene off her feet, and for a moment afterward everything was silent.

Then a slow, siren wail had risen, and looking around for the source of it she had seen a bright light, like a ball of fire, falling to earth. It passed over her head and struck ground somewhere near the river, where it had sent up a shower of trailing white sparks, like the plumes of a firework, which in turn had been caught on the high winds and scattered. The glow of its impact had been slow to fade, however, and Selene had made for the site mostly as a means to keep herself awake.

She was sitting on the lip of its crater now, wondering what to do next.

Inside the crater the red earth was blackened and glossy, as though whatever had struck it had also melted the fragments of rock, and the center was a glassy sheen with an impression in the middle. Selene had spent a long time staring at that impression before climbing up to the lip of the crater and looking out over the surrounding landscape. She didn't know what she'd expected to find. The person who'd left the child-shaped impression in the middle of the melted rock? For all she knew, that was how people usually ended up here. But ever since the meteor fell, among the streaming, scarlet banners which danced on the wind, baiting the residents into their endless dance, now there were white things that flapped, like injured butterflies.

Selene couldn't be sure, but she suspected they were all that remained of the meteor-person. One by one, it seemed, they had been blown over the river into the misty hills, and overall Selene felt good about that.

A cry went up behind her, in the direction of the plain, and for a few minutes she ignored that just as she ignored the giant mosquito which was presently latched onto her neck. After a few moments the bug flew off, but the shouting got louder.

Selene turned herself around, if only so she would be looking at something different, and saw another group of shadowy ghosts—she was pretty sure they were ghosts—running along a low ridge of earth in pursuit of, not a red banner or a white fluttery thing, but a thin, young woman.

She was not scorched gray and black, like everyone else, but looked like someone who'd been sent through the wash with a lot of bleach. Her skin was white, her hair was a cloudy tangle; she was wearing a simple short dress, like a nightgown, and this was the color of an old bedsheet. She was barefoot, and there was mud splattered up to her knees; brown and red, it stained the hem of her dress and there was a smear of it along one arm.

She was running flat out, but the shady crowd was gaining on her. There were shouts and halloos, like people in an ecstasy of excitement, and as Selene watched one of the leaders got close enough to snatch at the white woman's hair.

She tore herself away, but the action had slowed her, and a moment later someone else was able to grab her shoulder and then she tripped and she was down, and people were piling on top of her, shouting madly.

Something stirred in Selene's chest. A feeling that had been so useless to her for the past—how long had she been here?—that she almost didn't recognize it.

But it was that combination of indignation and outrage that had spurred her down the path she had chosen in life. It had driven every punch, every kick, every step into the darkness to be the thing that hit back. It was what had led her to kill her commanding officer rather than the innocent people she'd been ordered to execute.

She could hear the sound of punches connecting to flesh, and under the pile of ashen-faced ghosts, someone was screaming in agony.

She got to her feet. She didn't know what to do, but she started running anyway. Down the slope of the crater and up the side of the ridge, she was almost upon the mob when there was a whip-crack of thunder and they all fell away. From their center rose the white woman, battered and bleeding, her outstretched arms having sprouted dirty white feathers. She flapped them once—another crack so loud it took Selene's knees out from under her—and then she was floating into the air, where the wind caught her, and she tumbled away toward the river.

But she was losing altitude steadily, and though the crowd rushed after her (Selene balled herself up under the lee of the hill and mostly avoided getting trampled) she maintained just enough height to avoid their groping hands, only to plunge into the black water some fifty yards upstream.

As soon as she disappeared under the surface the crowd lost interest, slapping themselves despondently as the wasps descended, until one of the crimson banners fluttered by enticingly, and then they were off again.

Selene scrambled back to the river until she reached its bank, which was smooth and sandy, just as the woman floated past.

She was faceup but didn't respond when Selene called out to her. She was also too far out for Selene to grab, and she didn't like the thought of stepping in that river. It was impossible to read the current, and she suspected this river was just like any other river in that it would be more than happy to drown anyone who dove in trying to save someone else. Besides, the blackness of the water reminded her of the blackness she had experienced when she slept.

Forget swimming out to reach the white woman, Selene wasn't putting one toe in that water.

The current was dragging the woman on, and Selene began to jog along the bank, keeping pace and wondering what to do.

The sensible thing would be to throw a rope at her. If she was conscious enough to grab it, Selene could tow her in. She thought the woman was conscious: her eyes were open and when her face bobbed below the surface bubbles came out of her mouth. But she didn't have a rope or anything that might serve as one, and there was nothing around her save the barren red earth, the stinging flies, and the taunting banners.

The banners, which were essentially long strips of cloth.

The banners, which for all intents and purposes could not be caught . . .

That was the point, wasn't it? They were something you were bound to pursue forever, but never catch.

But, Selene reasoned, she had gotten so good at ignoring the things that the insects had mostly stopped bothering her. None of the shades so much as looked at her. And the banners, though they usually fluttered by the ghosts when they collected in groups, didn't seem to notice her at all.

So she kept jogging along the river, studiously keeping her eyes on the woman—who was at least easy to track in the dark water, thanks to her pale color—but listening with all her might for the sound of running footsteps.

Three times a group of ghosts passed her, but the banner remained too high, and Selene didn't dare leave the river to join the chase.

Chasing, clearly, was not the way you caught a banner.

But then a group came charging at the river from over a low hill, led on by a banner which was toying with them cruelly: dangling its tail almost in their faces and then snapping it out of reach just as their fingers closed around it. It led them dead into the water ten yards downstream, seemingly oblivious to Selene's presence as she trotted along the bank.

While the ghosts splashed and flailed in the shallow water—and Selene saw how a few of them were indeed swept away by an unseen current—the banner hung patiently over the beach, clearly waiting for them to sort themselves out.

Selene did not look, did not adjust her pace, but kept on jogging. The tail of the banner was almost touching the ground directly in her path, but she angled herself away from it, focusing on the woman who was far enough out in the current that she floated past the drowning ghosts without hindrance.

She would have to make a blind grab for the thing. It probably wouldn't work, but then, Selene had time. She wasn't even breathing hard; she could keep running for days.

She passed so close under the banner that it actually trailed over her shoulder, and moving her hand up, as if to bat away a fly—and there were a lot of flies, feasting on the ghosts—she made a sudden snatch behind her head and felt her fingers dig into the silky fabric.

It came alive in her hand with a loud hiss, and the next moment it was not a banner of cloth she held, but a live snake, the color of fresh blood. It twisted around in her hand, growing suddenly heavy, and the next second had twined around on itself and bitten her on the shoulder.

That hurt more than any insect sting, but not as much as being vomited up by the demon Lilith, when her entire body had been broken and mashed up beyond recognition.

Selene kept on running. She'd lost a bit of ground on the white woman, who'd lost her wings and was now waving her arms limply, so she began to sprint. The exertion gave her something else to think about besides the stabbing pain in her shoulder, and within a few moments it had vanished.

This was because the serpent had detached itself from her flesh and was staring at her accusingly.

"All right, all *right*," it hissed. "You win! What do you want? A coin for Charon? The password to Mnemosyne's pool? A key to the Spiral Castle?"

At last Selene dared glance down. The serpent looked like a constrictor of some sort—maybe a python—but its scales were all different kinds of red and orange, and when it opened its mouth to speak there were definitely fangs. Its eyes were like glass orbs filled with yellow smoke.

"Say what?" Selene said. She had to try twice because the first time her voice came out as a wordless rasp, her mouth was so dry.

"You caught me!" the serpent said. "Granted, you're not a shade, but still—you caught me! And you look a bit like one of my old priestesses. One of the early ones, when I was still in Egypt. Good with cats, that one. I liked her. So, what'll it be? You only get one, though!"

"One what?" Selene asked. She was trying to find the white woman, who had drifted further into the current. There! Something pale under the surface and—yes—that was a hand! She'd outpaced her somewhat, and now she ran even faster, trying to get a lead of at least twenty feet. It'd give her more time to hail the woman, and more chances to hit her with the snake before she had to reel it in and try again.

"A boon! A gift! A tip!" said the snake, beginning to sound impatient. "I'm an oracular serpent, can't you tell?"

"Not really," said Selene. She'd got enough space. Now she planted her feet and began wrangling the snake into a rough ball—still holding onto the tail. "What're you doing in hell then?"

"Cast me out, didn't he? Those uppity snits with their witch hunts and self-hating cults! Oh, but I used to have a nice house! Miniature of Arianrhod's place, blessed be She Who Is Life in Death and Death in Life. Yes, and I had my own priestesses and I got sacrifices and gave good advice—though you humans always bungled it—now here I am, playing tag with a bunch of Lethe-drunk shades! Um . . . you can step in this one, you know—it's Acheron. Nothing to worry about."

"Yeah, sure," said Selene, double-checking to make sure her toes were clear out of the water. "Hey, *oi!*" she shouted.

"What? I'm right here!" snapped the serpent.

"Not you!" Selene could see the woman now; she was bobbing closer to shore, and would pass within the full extent of the snake's body—assuming Selene made a good throw—but she didn't seem to hear Selene's words; just kept staring up at the bruise-colored sky.

A thought occurred.

"Look," said Selene. "I dunno about no passwords or castles or whatever, but you wanna help? Go bite that lady and *don't let go!*"

"You want me to *whaaaaaaa*—" the serpent's voice trailed off as Selene hurled its coiled body, head first, toward the woman in the water.

It was as a good throw as she'd ever made. The snake's head struck the woman's head clean in the center of her face, and she sat up in the water, gasping in surprise.

"Grab it!" Selene bellowed, even as the snake began coiling back on itself. The woman made a credible attempt, but the snake had already withdrawn out of reach.

Selene had to gather it up and run on another hundred yards before trying again. This time, however, she had the woman's attention from the start, and the snake, to give it credit, figured out what it was Selene wanted it to do.

So though her second throw went wide the snake corrected for her, the woman grabbed its neck, and it twined around her arm.

Far from towing her in, however, Selene collapsed on the bank and acted as an anchor, letting the current push the woman, tethered as she was to the serpent, over to the shallows, where she quickly found her feet and crawled up onto the bank.

"Wow!" said the snake, when Selene arrived, winding its coils around her arm. "That was exciting!" It writhed around so it was looped comfortably around Selene's shoulders. "Who is she? What is she? Looks a bit incomplete to me."

Selene looked down at the bedraggled woman, and thought the snake had a point.

She was lying still partly in the water, on her back, arms spreadeagled to either side. A few stray feathers still sprouted from her underarms, but otherwise these appeared human. She had a roundish, flattish face with a pointed chin and nose, and she was so thin her hipbones jutted out against her sopping dress.

There was nothing obviously *missing*—she had all her limbs and digits—and yet Selene got the strong impression that she was looking at only a part of a person. Maybe it was the fact that she was so white. She wasn't just pale, her body lacked any kind of color of its own. Even her eyes were white, with just the dark pupils pricked in the center. She reminded Selene of a pen drawing—all outlines, with nothing to fill in the blank spaces. Or maybe it was that there was a shifty quality to the way the light treated her, shimmering over her skin and causing her to blend into the earth she lay on. She wasn't exactly transparent, but she didn't seem all there. The best way Selene could describe it, if someone had asked her to, would be to say she was like a single layer of a person which had been stripped off and cast aside.

"Hey," she said, coming to stand at the woman's shoulders. "How you doin'?"

White-and-black eyes blinked up at her, and the woman frowned, as if the words made no sense to her. Then she opened her mouth and squirted a stream of black water from between her lips. The liquid jetted up and fell back down, splashing her face.

"Doing what?" she asked, once she'd run out of water. She had a light, simple voice—again, as though it was just one layer of a much more complicated person.

"Doing ... you, I guess," Selene said. "How are you doing? Anything ... uh ... hurt?"

"Only if I think about it," said the woman. Her face twisted, and with an effort she rolled herself over onto her side, drawing her knees up beneath her. She dug her hands into the soft, wet sand and began scooping out a little trough, which in turn filled with water.

When she had enough sand she began patting it, forming it into a round, conical shape. A sand castle. After a while she looked up.

"Why are you here?" she asked, her voice light and innocent.

Selene was put off balance by the question, it seemed like such a non sequitur, but upon consideration she supposed it was not such an odd thing to ask.

"I saw you fall into the river. Wanted to make sure you were all right."

"No-oo," said the woman, drawing out the syllable so it was almost a hooting sound, like an owl. "I mean ... why are you *here?*" She pointed at the sand under her hands. "You don't fit. You've got all these odd layers. I think you might be alive."

Around Selene's neck the snake writhed around so it could stare at her.

"You're *alive?* Great oaks, that explains so much!"

"So what if I am?" Selene snapped. "Though I think that's debatable."

"Oh no," said the snake. "You're definitely alive! That's how you were able to catch me! And it's important, because that means you shouldn't be *here.*"

"Speaking of which," Selene said, starting to feel needled. "Why are *you* still here? You can go ... back. Be a banner again. Go on, be free!" She tried to unwind the snake from around her neck, but the animal clung to her.

"No, no, no, no, *no!*" it cried, so loudly that the bleached woman looked up, curiously, to stare at them. "Being alive is important! Being alive means you can *change!*"

"So?" Selene insisted. It seemed like every loop of snake she pulled off, another one appeared. An endlessly replicating serpent. There was something in that, she thought, but didn't have the energy to pursue it.

"Being able to change," the serpent declared, sliding across her chest to throw a loop around her waist, "means that you can *leave!* And if you leave, I'm coming with you!"

"Oh, for—" Selene gave up and let the snake settle around her body. "Look, dude, I don't know who you think I am, but I'm *not* a magic banner-serpent ferry service. I can't guarantee anywhere else will be better than this, and even if I can leave, I don't know how!"

"How is easy," said the bleached woman. She sat back on her heels, and Selene saw it wasn't a castle she'd been making: it was a lumpy sort of figure. Like a man, sunk waist-deep in muddy water. He seemed to have three heads. The woman pointed a waxy finger at it.

"Find him," she said simply. "He guards the gate."

"You have to go in to get out, down to get up," agreed the serpent.

Selene frowned down at the figure in the sand, thinking hard.

Everything she'd learned about Hell, and it was all secondhand information at best, said that it got worse the further you went in. Granted the wasps were annoying and there wasn't much to do here but it wasn't bad. Just . . . dull. Nothing to do. Nothing to do but sit and wait for the eventual boredom to eat away at her brain until she fell asleep . . . for good.

That was the thing, Selene realized with a shudder. If she was alive, it meant she could still die.

But what did death mean, in the land of the dead?

Being alive means you can change.

She knelt down beside the bleached woman.

"Who are you?" she asked.

"Not sure," said the woman. She brought her hands down on the lumpy figure, pushing it back into the sandy bank. "One of the men back there called me Albatross. What's an Albatross? Is it me?"

"I dunno," said Selene. "Albatross is a kind of bird. Big, mostly white."

"I'm white," remarked the woman. "Maybe I'm a bird?"

Selene opened her mouth to gently inform the woman that she was not, and then remembered how her arms had turned into wings.

"I—oh, maybe?" she said instead.

"I think I'll be Albatross," said the woman decisively. She looked up at Selene, pinning her with a pointed stare. "Who are you?"

"I'm Selene," said Selene, patiently.

The eyes unfocused, glancing up at the sky, then back down at Selene. "You fell, too?"

"Something like that," said Selene.

The bleached woman sat back on her heels and regarded Selene with something like respect—no, it was more than that. It might have been awe.

"That explains why there's no moon."

"Sorry, what?" Selene felt like she'd been put off balance. Again. She sat down in the sand, a safe distance from the water's edge.

"There's never any moon here," said the woman called Albatross. "I always thought: doesn't the sky seem empty? But it would be, if you're down here."

Selene could have laughed. She did wheeze a little, and grin.

"Sister," she said, "Selene's just my name. I ain't—I mean, what? D'you think the moon, if she were a person, would look like this?" She pointed at her face.

Albatross shrugged. "I figured you were the dark side. Are you sure you're not the moon?"

"Pretty darn sure," said Selene.

This seemed to disappoint Albatross. She returned to her shapeless pile of sand, this time forming it into a wide, circular cake and drawing a spiral on its surface.

"I still think you're a moon-something," she muttered.

Selene sighed, beginning to feel exasperated. Then she felt something jab sharply at her side.

It was the red snake, who'd poked her with its tail.

"Hey, moon-hero, you might wanna be gettin' a move on. They might ignore *you* on account of you being alive, but *she's* a target."

Selene looked around sharply, then got to her feet. Upstream from them was a long, low hill whose skyline was beginning to bristle with the shapes of ghosts. Condemned souls. Whatever. One of them pointed and shouted, and then they were scrambling down the hill, heading for the river.

Heading for them.

No, heading for Albatross.

"Okay girl, enough fun on the beach," Selene said, going over and slipping her hands under the woman's shoulders. "We gotta move."

Up they came together—the woman weighed even less than she looked—and Selene easily slung her into a fireman's carry as she began jogging down the beach.

"Uh . . . no?" said the serpent. "No, no! Leave the wretch—she's already been splintered! Save yourself!"

"Shut *up*," gasped Selene. Even though Albatross weighed next to nothing, running was a lot harder with a person on her shoulders—not to mention a snake constricting her chest—and she could tell from the sounds behind her that the crowd was gaining.

Who were they? Selene had tried asking one, once, but they'd just stared at her with dull, lifeless eyes.

If the snake was right, and that was the river Acheron, then that made this malformed, hilly country the entryway to Hell. Sort of a pre-limbo, for souls who'd never distinguished themselves for good or evil. What had Dante said of them? That they were harassed by stinging insects and compelled to chase banners—snakes?—which represented . . . something something. Greed? No, that came later. Selfishness? That seemed closer.

Self-interest—that was it! The banner-snakes represented self-interest—which they had pursued in life to the exclusion of all else.

Selene couldn't help snorting, even as she plowed up a dry valley in the hopes of losing their pursuers. People were so complicated! Some could spend their whole lives doing nothing but altruistic work just for the thrill of being thought of as a selfless saint. And others had got it sorted out to the point that it was in their own best interests to be nice to other people! And that didn't even touch on the greater problem of what should be defined as "good" and what was "bad."

She'd gotten distracted and missed her footing in the loose earth. Something hard caught her toe, and for the next few moments she was paralyzed by the pain of it.

The sensation sent a jolt of awareness into her brain—like someone had come along and cut a hole in the thin gray veil that had draped itself over her consciousness. A veil she hadn't even been aware of until it was abruptly torn off.

In quick succession, Selene realized several things.

One, that it wasn't *self*-interest the souls were pursuing, but pure *interest*. They were *bored*. They wanted a point, or a purpose. *That* was what the banners represented.

Two, that Albatross was way more interesting than some dumb banner.

Three, that she, Selene, could not fly, and so they would eventually catch her.

Four, that she'd lost her balance and was about to face-plant in the ground.

They went sprawling. The serpent, being wound tightly around Selene's body, fared the best. Perhaps. Selene couldn't duck or roll thanks to the body across her shoulders, nor could she put up her hands to break her fall. Luckily, Albatross was so light she hardly made a difference as Selene slammed into the earth.

Something went *click* in her neck as she hit, and she had to lie very still for a while after that. It didn't hurt, per se, but it definitely felt like something was out of place. After a couple moments there was another *click* and then she was able to gather her knees under her and pry herself up.

"Ow," said the serpent. "Watch where you're going next time!"

"That was fun," said Albatross, and giggled. She was still lying across Selene's shoulders, and Selene had to cock a shoulder to tip her gently off in order to sit up.

Shouts from behind them; a dark crowd had gathered at the mouth of the canyon, were even now starting up it. Selene saw their faces staring, their jaws lax and gaping, and all her instincts told her to run. At the same time the cool, conditioned part of her mind told her equally strongly that to run would only be to delay their inevitable capture.

She cast around for something—anything—that could be used as a weapon. There was nothing, of course. All she had were her fists, the snake still wrapped around her body, and whatever hard thing she had tripped on in the first place.

It was protruding from the earth not two feet away, and looked at first to be part of an old hubcap or something similar. That was strange—Selene hadn't seen anything remotely manmade since she'd gotten here, never mind cars—but there wasn't time to wonder where it had come from.

She scrambled over and got her fingers under the lip of its edge and push-pulled to loosen it from the earth.

It came away quite easily, up into her hands as it shed globs of red dirt. It was bigger than she'd first thought: closer to the size of a bicycle wheel than a hubcap, with a shallow dish to its shape, like a contact lens. The concave curve was what she'd tripped on, and flipping it around Selene found there was a strange contraption mounted on the underside: a hook and a hinge, between which ran a metal shaft with a pointed tip.

Selene had no idea what it could be meant for. All she knew was that it was made of something light but hard that could be used as a shield, and a long metal pointy thing which could be used as a weapon—supposing she could break it off its hinge.

There was no time for that, however. The crowd was almost upon them, and the snake was beginning to make nervous hissing sounds against her chest.

"Get behind me and stay down," Selene shouted at Albatross, who had gotten to her feet and looked ready to run.

The bleached woman looked nervously at the crowd, then threw herself into the dirt at Selene's feet.

Great, Selene thought. Now I have to fight with just a shield and not step on the person I'm trying to protect.

Nevertheless she slid the point of the shaft into the hook, so it wouldn't swing free and injure her, and tucked her left arm around it, gripping the hook with her hand.

Like that the object made a good shield, and by the heft of it Selene estimated she could do some significant damage by using it as an extension of her fist.

Heaving herself forward she got to her feet and raised her makeshift shield.

At her chest, the snake hissed something that sounded like "*Yowza!*" and then the crowd of charging ghosts abruptly turned into a mess of writhing bodies.

Peeking around the shield, Selene saw that the front line had dug in their heels to stop, been run over by the second line, which fell down backward in their hurry to backpedal. They were knocked forward by the third line, which tripped over them and then began scrambling on hands and knees to get away, running into the rest of the crowd.

The confusion was made greater, since none of them were looking where they were going. All eyes—gray and blank, the lot of them—were staring at Selene.

No, at her shield.

And, as she watched, they slowly, clumsily, reversed direction and began tripping back down the canyon toward the river, with many nervous glances over their shoulders—some even going so far as to make the whole journey backward.

Cautiously, Selene lowered her shield and looked around. The canyon they were in had high walls which cut off a lot of the sky and sheltered them from any form of wind. The air was hot and stagnant, and everything was unnaturally still.

"Okay..." said the serpent, winding around so it could rest its head on Selene's shoulder. "That I didn't see coming. Which is odd. What'chu got there? Feels familiar, but I don't recognize it."

Selene had extricated her arm and flipped the object over, and realized with a jolt that she did.

The convex surface of the object was etched with lines and circles, which she had first taken to be scratches and dents but now saw made a recognizable pattern. They were in fact the various craters and dry seas which made up the face of the moon. Roughly half the shield was stained dark, while the other—once she brushed away the last of the dirt—remained bright and silver. Together, they formed a double moon: a full face split between a thick crescent of silver and a dark shadow. Due to the nature of the object, this could be a waxing or waning crescent, depending on how she held it.

And, now that she had room to examine it closely, she found she also recognized the faint shiver that passed through her hand when she pressed it against the face of it.

"I'll be damned," she said softly.

"One could make an argument that you already are," said the serpent. "Do you know what you got there?"

Slowly, Selene turned the wheel-sized shield over in her hands. This close, she could see certain details which had been lost on her before: there was a spiral etched on the interior, which was slashed about by lines at various angles. It seemed like writing in a sort of Ogham-style script, but Selene didn't recognize it. There was also a thin band of silver which ran the circumference of the rim, and this was pricked by raised lumps, three in total, at equal intervals around the edge—so that if one drew an imaginary line joining all three, it would form an equilateral triangle.

"It's my amulet," she said, just to hear the words spoken aloud.

"Your what now?" asked the snake, understandably confused.

"Little over a year ago—well, a little over a year before I . . . fell . . . whatever—this witch gave me a protective amulet. It was this," Selene raised the shield-pin. "Only it wasn't this big. It was like . . . " she held up her thumb and forefinger, indicating a size and shape closer to that of a quarter.

"Witch's amulet, eh?" said the snake, flicking its tongue in and out. This, Selene noticed, was bright blue—in contrast to its otherwise crimson coloration. "That explains a lot."

"Explains what?" asked Albatross. She was still crouched at Selene's feet, but had sat up to look curiously at their discovery.

"Well, the size of it, for a start," said the snake. "Things 'round here, size is influenced by how much power you've got. Looks like that's a pretty powerful token. Probably wanna keep it."

"Yeah, no kidding," said Selene. She flipped the amulet around so she could wipe more dirt off its face. It was hard to tell, the way things were here, but she thought the silver bits might be glowing faintly.

It was sobering, though, if what the snake said was right. This had been a pin the size of a coin. Now it was big enough to serve as an umbrella. If size was an indication of power, then what did that make Selene?

Suddenly, far from being comforted, she felt very, very small.

Something clutched at her leg. It was Albatross, and she was pointing wordlessly at the cliffs above them.

These had sprouted a line of silhouettes. At first Selene took them to be more of the same ghosts, but then she looked again.

They wore the same colorless clothes, which were themselves ripped and torn beyond recognition, but in place of faces each had only a gaping hole, lined with pale, jagged points—like teeth, but probably bones.

"Uh-oh," said the serpent, and Selene felt it sliding lower around her torso, as if trying to keep out of sight.

"Friends of yours?" Selene asked, dryly.

These ghosts didn't seem interested in chasing them, or attacking. They only gathered together, packing themselves in tighter and tighter, and pointed the holes in their heads downward, as if staring at them.

Perhaps they were.

"No, no," said the serpent, sounding increasingly alarmed. "Opposite of friends. Bad."

"Minders, keepers," whispered Albatross, using Selene's leg to pull herself into a hunched standing position.

"Demons?" Selene hazarded.

"There are no demons here," said the serpent. "These are worse."

Selene let that extraordinary statement be, for the moment, and concentrated on what she felt was the more salient point.

"Worse than demons?"

"Demons you can reason with," said the snake. "Heck, I was a demon for a while. It's really not so bad. These are more like . . . well, what's that thing that happens to folks who hang out around the same place long enough?"

"You lost me," said Selene, who was trying to back around so she could get a look behind her—but Albatross was in the way.

"They make you *staff*," whined the snake.

"Minders! Keepers!" shouted Albatross, and as if this was a cue the ghosts—not-demons—broke ranks and began sliding down into the canyon. Their heads contorted, the holes closing and opening like giant mouths.

Selene raised her shield, felt it hum along her arm, but this time it didn't make an impression on their attackers. On they came, so the red ground was black with them, and Selene noticed with growing despair that they were all significantly taller than any of the ghosts she had previously seen.

"All right, Albie, up and at 'em," Selene said, prodding Albatross with her elbow. "Keep your back to mine, and feel free to use Mr. Slithers as a whip, if ya want."

"Hey!" protested the snake. "I was worshipped as Apollo, once!"

Albatross, however, didn't appear to be listening. She was staring at Selene as though seeing her for the first time. Her eyes flickered back and forth between Selene's face and the back of the shield, while her brows crunched together. She was muttering under her breath.

"Say *what?*" snapped Selene.

"Three sights incredible to see," said Albatross. Behind her, the foremost of the hole-faced people had reached the ground and was approaching with great, galloping leaps.

Selene slid around and was just in time to catch them on her shield—a good hit right in their midsection—and while this only stunned them, Selene took the opportunity to kick at their legs and then, when they stumbled, to ram the shield edgewise into their neck.

It must have been sharper, or the being weaker, than she thought. The shield bit into the shadowy flesh and lodged there, while the creature went limp and began to shrivel, steam belching from the hole in its face.

Selene kicked it away and backed up until she felt her arm touch Albatross's side. The shield was fairly vibrating against her arm now, as though it held an electric charge. She pivoted around to find that the faceless crowd had paused again, now encircling them at a distance of ten or so feet.

Albatross straightened up, seeming not to notice their desperate situation. She had a relieved look on her face, as of one who has just remembered something important.

"Three sights incredible to see," she announced, and took Selene's free hand in hers.

"Tell me later," said Selene, trying to free her arm—but Albatross just held on harder. Abruptly she yanked, pulling Selene toward her, and raising her other arm high above her head, she shouted:

"A white stag leaping through the trees!"

Dusty feathers broke out all along her arm, growing and shedding and growing anew, until it was not an arm she held aloft, but a single, scraggily wing.

"Hold on now," said the serpent. "Let's not prophesize anything rash!"

"An eagle diving to the sea!" shouted Albatross, not seeming to hear. She was beating her arm-wing, raising a wind that whipped up the loose dirt around their feet. Faster and faster she whirled her single wing, and Selene felt a frisson of hot and cold jolt into her body from where Albatross's remaining hand was clamped on her own. It ran up her arm and across her shoulders and into the shield, which reverberated in sympathy and sent the feeling back through her again.

The earth around them was rising in clods. The faceless beings, though they had not retreated, were crouched, their hands scrabbling at the earth, as if they were trying to hold onto the ground itself.

Albatross adjusted her grip on Selene's arm, so that her hand was clamped just below Selene's elbow, and pulled herself in close.

"A moon rising," she whispered, triumphantly, and then all of a sudden gravity ceased to work.

They shot upward, raising a cloud of red dust in their wake—along with a couple of the faceless beings, who flailed helplessly under Selene's feet.

Higher and higher they rose, the wind roaring in Selene's ears, but not so loudly that she did not catch the words in Albatross's joyous scream:

"See! The moon! Rising! Over Haaaaadeeeees!"

Higher and higher rose her voice, so that at the end it drew out and mingled with the wind, sounding like the cry of a wild sea bird.

Selene had the presence of mind to grasp Albatross's arm, in mimicry of the other woman's hold on her, so that when gravity reasserted itself a few moments later she did not go plunging back to earth.

But it seemed Albatross was now possessed of the same ability as the tantalizing banners; to wit, gravity did not affect her as strongly, and for a while they continued to gain altitude, and Selene was treated to an excellent view of the surrounding country.

It was mostly the red, rumpled expanse which Selene had been walking through for the better part of . . . however long she'd been there. But as they slowly wheeled about she saw also the great, black river, which lay like the thick borderline on a map, dividing the world below into the brownish-red, barren hills, and the dim, misty green landscape which lay beyond. In the distance, far away upstream, Selene thought she saw something that looked like a dock, and the dark, angular shape of a boat, but she was distracted from it when she glimpsed, over the river and through the mist, the flash of something white. Then, again, off the river itself, something white.

Blinking down at this Selene saw it was a reflection of the moon.

But there was no moon—no sun—in the skies over Hell.

Selene craned her neck around, but could only see the bruise-colored sky and Albatross's thin, white legs and dirty feet—which were in danger of hitting her in the face.

Then she realized what she was seeing was their own reflection, and the thing that shone was not the moon, but her amulet-pin *cum* shield, which was fairly singing against her skin, and when she tipped it sideways she was nearly blinded by the light blazing out of its silver crescent.

Below them the last of the faceless keepers had fallen away—the dark crowd of them was lost in the rolling landscape—though she could still glimpse a few herds of roving souls, and here and there a gleam of crimson.

Across the river, the white thing flashed again, and Selene remembered the white fluttering banner which she'd seen escape into the mist.

"Hey," she called up to Albatross, who had gone back to waving her wing-arm to keep them aloft. "Think you can get us across the river?"

"Crossing is dangerous," Albatross called back. "I fall."

"Yeah, but you've got a lot of height!" added the serpent.

"I saw something cross the river," Selene added. "It's that white thing, there in the mist!"

She tried to point, but it was difficult with her shield. In doing so, however, she cast the beam of its light farther into the green hills, and this time something else lit up in reflection. It blazed like a beacon for only a moment, but in that moment Selene saw clearly the shape of a castle, shining in hues of pink and blue and white—like mother-of-pearl.

That Albatross did see, and seeming to forget her earlier reservations about crossing the river, she began to angle them toward it, fanning her wing to speed them on.

Still, they lost altitude as they traveled, so that by the time they reached the river they had only thirty feet of clearance over the dark, rippling water. The shining castle was long since lost to view, and all that lay before them was a bank of mist swirling over the waves.

It was strange. When viewed from above, the river didn't look particularly wide, but now they came to cross it, it seemed to stretch on forever.

Into the bank of mist they plunged, and it was so thick that Selene wouldn't have seen the water rushing under her toes had it not reflected back the light from her shield—which was still glowing brightly. She bent her legs, then pulled her knees up to her chest, and pushed the shield down so it would touch the water first.

The mist turned black around them. Above her, Albatross was heaving painful breaths, a keening sound escaping from her mouth, which was stretched open in a grimace.

For a moment Selene entertained the notion of letting go. Her weight was surely dragging the woman down. If she hadn't had to lift her, she would probably have made it across the river easily. But that thin, white hand was clamped so hard around Selene's arm that it now made no difference whether Selene held on or not.

Against her chest the snake was hissing, a long stream of words that she did not understand, and then there was no longer water under her shield, and when at last they went crashing into the ground it was not soft, green grass, but dry, black sand. It went up in a spray around them and then the world stopped with a lurch and everything went completely dark.

Limbo

It was not the dead, black emptiness Selene had experienced when she slept but instead the lack of any sort of light. She'd lost hold of Albatross in the crash, and now when she felt around, all her hands found were cold, dry sand, and cold, dry snake-body.

"Owwww . . ." said the serpent, its coils convulsing around her.

Selene sat up. She still had her shield, and when she raised its face from the sand it cast a faint radiance over her surroundings. This was as she remembered: a black, featureless stretch of sand which ended in the lapping shore of the river behind her, while in every other direction it faded away into the inky mist.

Her body was hurting, but again in the distant, fuzzy way in which she felt most things lately. She firmly ignored the sting of the lacerations across her arms and belly, and stuck the shield in the sand so she could relocate her right shoulder into its proper place. That hurt more, but only for a moment, and when it faded it took most of the background pain with it.

Picking up her shield she shone its face across the sand, trying to find any sign of the other woman's landing. But there was nothing: not even a footprint.

"Albatross!" Selene shouted, her voice rough and hoarse.

There was no answer but the snake, who said, hissingly:

"Flown on, I'll wager. Her sort are always difficult to catch."

"Her sort?" Selene asked, aiming herself away from the river and beginning to walk.

"Bits and bobs, odds and ends of a person," said the snake. "I wonder who she was? No goddess I recognized—and I've met most of them."

Selene didn't have an answer for the snake, so she said nothing. Her shield didn't give off much light, but the ground was so uniformly flat and featureless she was able to walk at a reasonable pace. It felt like they were climbing steadily, and slowly the black sand gave way to bands of brown and pink and finally white. This was punctuated by slabs of smooth rock, which eventually hove up out of the sand in piles.

By this point the mist had lightened enough that Selene no longer needed her shield to see by, so she stuck the pin through the back of her shirt, letting the shield hang off her shoulders, so she could use her hands to help herself over the rocks.

After a while she began to talk to the snake, simply for something to do.

"So, what's your game, here?"

"This isn't a game," said the serpent.

"Yeah, but . . . sorry to be blunt, but why are you still here? If you let go of me do you turn back into a banner or something?"

"I don't know," admitted the snake. "Better safe than sorry."

"Huh," said Selene.

After a while, it said:

"What's your game?"

Selene laughed, roughly.

"Son, I'm just doing what I've always done."

"Oh?"

"Keeping on keeping on."

"Interesting," said the serpent.

"Why's that?"

"You won't take my boons, which would require me to release you. But you won't take my advice, either. And you haven't tried to get rid of me."

"You make a good rope," Selene said, only half joking.

"Don't you want to know where you are?"

"Sure," said Selene. "But I don't think you can tell me."

"We're in Limbo," said the snake, rather primly. "Land of the righteous pagans and unbaptized children."

Selene scrambled to the top of a boulder. The mist had lifted enough that she could see almost fifty feet ahead. There were two distinct rocks, pinkish-gray with distance, through which she could glimpse a patch of green.

"Seems pretty empty," she remarked.

"I think most of them have gone upland," said the snake. "Limbo's more than just a circle of Hell: it's a link to many other realms. But Mnemosyne had a garden down here, so it's a popular spot for old oracular heroes and pythonesses."

"Mnemosyne's the one which lets you remember," Selene said, turning the question into the statement as she became confident of its accuracy.

"If you have the password," said the snake.

"Didn't Orpheus have to give that to you?" Selene asked.

"I gave it to Orpheus," said the snake, smugly. "Or one of my colleagues did. We all worked together in the old days. That's the biggest conceit you humans ever laid on us: that this god killed that god or subjugated that goddess. No god can kill or change another god; only humans can do that. Everything else is just playacting."

"Oh yeah," said Selene, becoming mildly interested despite herself. "How do you explain Norse mythology then? Or the Egyptians? Or— heck—whatever it was Jehovah did to *everybody* else?"

"Who?" asked the serpent.

"Jehovah, Yahweh," said Selene. "You know, 'I am that which I am.' The burning bush. Abraham's god."

There was a confused silence.

"You mean the Nameless God?"

"I guess," said Selene. "The one which the Christians and the Muslims and the Jews all worship. That guy."

"Christians and Muslims and Jews do not worship the same god," said the snake, gently, as if breaking an unpleasant truth to a child.

"Really?" said Selene. "Seemed like it, from everything I saw."

"An oak is an oak wherever it grows, but the oak in the valley is not also the oak on the mountain," said the snake.

"Okay," said Selene. "That sounded suspiciously poetic, but okay."

"Life and death are just metaphors that mortals use to describe things that don't apply to them," the snake went on. "Everything you interpret as gods fighting is really conflict between paradigms."

"Baldur's not dead, he's just waiting?" Selene guessed.

"Something like that," the serpent allowed. "List right, will you, or we'll be going in circles."

They had passed between the two pinkish boulders and were now making their way across a field strewn with smaller rocks. Selene had to spend a lot of time looking down at her feet, and so had somewhat lost track of their direction.

"But you've gotta admit there are similarities," she said. "I mean, Mars is just the Roman name for Ares, right?"

"It's simpler to think of it that way," said the snake. "But like most simple things, it is not accurate."

"Isn't it?" asked Selene.

"Names get muddled and mixed up. Practices are changed. How people relate to a god has a greater impact on that god than most gods would like to admit."

"You're admitting it," Selene pointed out.

"I'm not a god," said the snake, sounding, if possible, even more smug. "Just a mouthpiece. Ha! Not even that. A messenger, really."

"Messengers can be pretty powerful," Selene remarked, thinking briefly of angels.

That killed the conversation long enough for her to reach the end of the rock field, where it disappeared into a sea of river willows, growing so thickly that Selene didn't try to force her way through but turned and began walking along the border until she came to a narrow footpath that led up through the foliage. The air was bright ahead of her, and she was counseling herself not to expect the mist to lift anytime soon, when they abruptly came out of the willows and the clouds simultaneously, and Selene was temporarily blinded by a blast of pure sunlight.

It came slicing down through the mist in a sheet, as bright as noon on a summer day, and Selene had to cover her face with her arm and turn her head to the ground with her eyes shut while she waited for them to adjust.

The snake, meanwhile, had unlooped a coil of itself and, by the feel of it, reared up over Selene's bent neck. She heard it hissing. Strange words which flowed into each other yet retained a recognizable cadence. Like a song or poem in a strange language, Selene felt like she took the general meaning even if she couldn't make out the words. The only one she was able to parse out of the hissing stream was something that sounded like "pacify," which the snake repeated many times. This confirmed her strong impression that the snake was pleading with the source of the light, either asking for help or asking for mercy.

She kept her face down, just in case it was one of Jehovah's angels.

But if what the snake had said about Limbo was true, then perhaps their power would be lessened here. If Limbo was, like Detroit above, neutral ground.

Whatever the snake said seemed to be the right thing, because after a minute or so the light faded to bearable levels, and Selene was able to open her eyes and look around.

At first everything was blurry—she'd started to cry for some reason—but after wiping away her tears she saw they had come at last to the rolling green hills she had glimpsed from the air. The mist had lifted, turned into a low band of clouds hiding the land through which they had come, while before them the horizon was crowned with piles of fluffy clouds, lit pink and purple by the slanting rays of warm light—which passed far over their heads and left the hills below in blue-gray shade.

These hills were overgrown with tall grass, wild barley and wheat, cut by sandy roads little more than two tracks for a vehicle's wheels with a lane of weeds down the center. The path they had taken through the willows led directly to the nearest road, where it crossed, and continued on as a dark track through the grass.

At the crest of a far hill glittered something bright and white that, once Selene's eyes adjusted further, resolved itself into a silvery castle with four high turrets and a low wall around its base. From one of these turrets there flapped something pale and white—but it moved not as something manipulated by the wind, but like a tethered bird trying to escape.

"Whew," said the snake. "That was lucky!"

Selene glanced cautiously at the sky, but the sheet of light had moved, rotating upward so it lit the clouds on the horizon and left the ground untouched.

"What was that?" Selene asked, unable to help herself.

"My mother," said the snake. "Yours too, if you want to get poetic about it. Which you probably don't. Let's just call her She Who Shines for All and say it was a lucky thing she noticed you."

"How is that lucky?" said Selene, who couldn't see how their situation had changed much.

"Kissed your shield, didn't she?" said the serpent. "You can go pretty much anywhere you like now. But not there," it added, as Selene set off down the path, her eyes trained on the distant castle.

"Why not?" asked Selene. They reached the road, and since it appeared to lead in the necessary direction, she started down it.

"That's the Spiral Castle," said the snake, sliding itself over her shoulder and under her arm. "Arianrhod's place. Don't think she'll be nice to you, just 'cause you're a woman."

But Selene wasn't listening. The road had gone up a hill, and from its top she could better see the castle, and the white thing flying from the tallest turret was definitely no flag. It was not a person either, but Selene was reminded of the white thing she'd seen blown across the river, which reminded her of Albatross.

Which reminded her.

"Albatross!" she shouted, on the off chance her voice would carry.

"I don't know why you bother. It won't work," said the serpent.

"*Alllll-baaaaa-trooooooooooss!*" Selene called, long and loud and as high as her dry throat could manage.

She continued to walk, calling out periodically, but though her voice carried well over the rolling hills, there was no answer. There was nothing in the sky but clouds, and the only other noise was the rustle of the grass as it bent before a gentle wind.

Selene walked. The air was neither warm nor cold, and the ground was not hard or soft. Everything felt vague and uncertain, except the sunlight which had not strayed from the clouds on the horizon, and before her— still distant, but noticeably closer—the shining silver castle.

The road dipped and curved through the hills and shallow valleys, but every time it rose and provided a clear view the castle was closer still. Now Selene could see it was not built on a hill at all, but upon a bank of white clouds which hid its base—if it had one. For it seemed to her that the castle was moving—not traversing the landscape, but slowly rotating in place. Once she stopped at the top of a hill and watched, and sure enough it was spinning slowly round. What she had taken as the highest of four turrets was actually a central spire. The other four were arranged around it like points of a star, with one partially hidden behind the middle column.

The road descended then, down a slope of hill thickly overgrown with trees, largely low and bushy. Selene recognized the glossy green leaves and bright red berries of pyracantha, scrub oak, walnuts and olives.

The road bent to curve around a particularly ancient tree—two trunks which had wound around each other, thrusting out craggy branches which drooped low over the road—and as they passed beneath it the snake let out a great hiss of frustration and said:

"Okay, okay! If you're gonna do this, at least take precaution! Stop. Stop here—*wait!*"

Selene, who'd kept on walking, pretending not to hear, paused.

"What?" she demanded.

"Olive!" said the snake. "Precaution!"

Selene looked up at the tree. It seemed a bit more vivid than the rest of the place, and one of the branches hung low enough she could easily reach up and strip off a small stalk.

Olive branches, she remembered, would do just as well as a white flag, when it came to calling a truce. It was just bedsheets were much more common, usually.

Selene shrugged, and reached up to grasp a low-hanging branch.

"No, no, no!" protested the snake. "What are you doing?"

"Taking a precaution," said Selene, snapping the stem where it met the greater branch. She came away with a nice twig of olive, very leafy and with a few hard, green fruit on it.

"That's like going into battle armed with a wet noodle," hissed the snake. "No, when I said precaution I meant . . . look . . . just hold onto my tail and let me . . ."

It slithered down her arm, twining around it so that it could glide up into the tree, while still keeping the last couple inches safely in Selene's palm.

She stood there beneath the tree, one arm raised, and watched with curiosity as the snake disappeared into the branches, its red scales gleaming against the brown-gray bark.

There was more of the hissing language, and then with a groan the tree let fall a sizable branch. It came crashing to the ground at Selene's feet along with the snake.

Almost a yard long and as thick as her calf at its base, it brought a lot of smaller branches and leaves with it. The end of it, where it had parted from the tree, was seared and blackened, as if from fire.

"There," said the snake with satisfaction. "That's what I call a precaution! Arianrhod's pretty well removed from Hera, but she'll respect this! Strip off the stems and it'll do nicely."

"It'll be a club," Selene said, nonplussed.

"Exactly," said the snake, sounding inordinately pleased.

Selene couldn't fathom what a piece of wood could do against a goddess—especially one as ancient and diverse as Arianrhod—but she figured it might come in handy otherwise, and it was still technically an olive branch, so she set aside the stem she'd picked and spent the next few minutes stripping off the excess branches so that there was a clear space on the larger bough where she could hold it. There were still a lot of leaves on the narrow end, but the seared base was solid—and, when Selene hefted the thing, not too heavy.

She slotted the makeshift club over her shoulder, beside the shield, and with the snake looped contentedly around her other arm she set off again.

What was the other thing about olive branches?

Oh yes, Heracles had gotten his club from an olive tree.

She snorted. She was practically the opposite of Heracles. But a club was a club, she figured, and you didn't have to be a Greek hero to use one.

The road began to climb steeply, and soon they left the trees behind and eventually crested a rise from which she could see the silver castle, now practically on top of them. It was then she discovered the reason the road appeared to lead them so steadily toward it. The castle was indeed suspended on a bank of frothing gray clouds, and it was rolling slowly over the road, spinning slowly as it went.

On the road, just ahead of the mist but having to run in order to stay out of it, was a familiar, skinny figure in a tattered white slip, one arm still bent awkwardly in the shape of a wing, but stripped clean of feathers.

"Oi!" Selene shouted, and took off down the road to meet Albatross.

They were separated by perhaps a quarter of a mile, but it was all gently downhill for Selene, and by unhitching her club so she could better manage its weight and bulk, she was able to cross the distance at a brisk jog.

Albatross looked up at hearing her shout. Her face, which had been pinched and fearful, spread open in a great, relieved smile. Then she tripped. She came down hard on one knee and had to catch herself with her one human hand, but was up again the next second and fairly pelted up the road, away from the castle.

Selene wondered briefly why she kept to the road, when the only thing on either side of it were fields of knee-high green wheat. Then she realized, grimly, that the castle could probably travel over road or field equally well, while their only hope of escaping it lay in sticking to the road.

So instead Selene slowed, raising her gaze to reassess the castle as a potential threat. There was no one on the battlements, but neither was there a door or a way inside, and now that it was practically upon her she could feel the arctic air being breathed out from the frothing gray clouds.

But just the sight of her seemed to have given Albatross a second wind. The woman was putting on speed, extending her naked wing, which was even as Selene watched shooting out feathers and turning into a graceful arching crescent of white.

Having some notion of what was coming, Selene stopped dead in Albatross's path and extended her free hand.

Albatross hit her like a speeding car, nearly dislocating Selene's shoulder—again—and riding on the blast of cold air coming from beneath the castle, the pair—and the serpent—were swept up off the ground, like leaves blown before a rising storm.

"I thought I lost you!" Albatross cried, gladly.

"I thought I lost *you!*" Selene retorted.

"Oh happy day," drawled the snake, sounding a little seasick.

They had cleared the ramparts of the castle now, and looking down upon it Selene realized it wasn't a castle at all, but a giant maze. A maze girded by a high wall with four corners, each with a turret, and one spire rising from the center of it. The walls creating the maze itself were almost as high as the encircling wall, casting the depths of the maze into cool, blue shadows.

The central spire was pricked with dark windows, culminating in a circular turret with a single pole affixed to it, from which flew a . . . a . . .

It was difficult to understand.

"Wait," said Selene, twisting around for a better look.

"Higher!" shouted the snake, shrilly.

"What?" called Albatross.

"Below us, on the castle," Selene shouted back. She still couldn't put into words what she was seeing.

The flapping white thing, which was tethered to the pole at the top of the central spire of the castle-maze, which was undoubtedly the white wisp she had seen flutter over the Acheron, was in fact a woman. A paper-white woman with wings for arms and a fluffy bush of hair. It was her hair which had been used to tie her to the pole, and it was her wing-arms that were flapping, desperately, trying to free herself.

She seemed flattish. Like a paper cutout of a person. Except she was at the same time very much alive. There was an expression of miserable terror on her flat, white face. Which, though warped, looked strangely familiar.

Selene could have sworn it was Albatross's twin, except she was beginning to suspect that Albatross and this woman were both slices of someone else.

Albatross, meanwhile, had looked, and was now skewing round to take them in over the maze—heading for the spire.

"Oh, right!" she shouted. "That's what I was doing!"

"No, no, wrong way!" the serpent shouted, but neither Selene nor Albatross paid it any attention.

They had begun with good altitude, but again after the first burst from takeoff it seemed Albatross could only glide, and Selene was sure her weight—never mind the club—wasn't helping. She would have dropped it, but the serpent had coiled a loop of itself around that hand, holding it shut.

They were still well above the maze, however, though they'd dropped below the top of the spire. Gauging their speed and rate of descent, Selene judged they would meet the spire halfway down from the top—just below which was one of its little windows.

"Albatross," Selene began.

"I see it!" Albatross cried, giving her wing-arm a desperate wave.

But they began to drop faster, and though Albatross managed to raise them again at the last minute, the only reason they didn't splatter humiliatingly against the cold stone of the spire was because Selene, hefting her club, got it through the window and turned sideways, giving her something to hold onto.

They did spend some moments hanging there awkwardly, until Albatross brought her wing in until it became an arm again, clawed her way up over Selene's back ("Mind the shield!" she winced) and slipped in through the the window. Then she turned around and helped Selene in, while the serpent coiled tightly under the shield, hissing unhappily.

Sliding over the sill on her belly Selene crawled her way down the wall to the stone stairs which circled round the inside of the tower, bringing her knees in under her and then slowly getting to her feet. Albatross stood up next to her, holding the olive branch and turning it over in her hands, curiously.

"This is a funny tree," she said, once Selene had got her breath back and asked if she was all right.

"I'm fine, thanks for asking," said the serpent. "Now, if you'll take my advice, for once, shake out that wing of yours and jump back out the window you came in by."

Selene didn't answer the snake, but she didn't ignore it, either. The stairs they were standing on were carved from something hard and pearlescent. At first she had taken them to be stone, but looking closer she saw streaks of colored light trapped within, pinks and blues with shots of green, and these were all slowly dancing, weaving in and out of each other in a mesmerizing pattern. They reminded her of the northern lights, if the northern lights could be trapped in glass.

"Because this is the Castle of Arianrhod?" she asked, seeking confirmation.

"This is the *center* of the castle," hissed the serpent.

"And that's bad?"

"It's hard to leave," the snake remarked.

"All but seven," whispered Albatross.

"Seven what?" asked Selene.

Albatross was standing on the step above her, looking up to where the stairs curved around out of sight.

"All but seven, none returned from the Spiral Castle," said the snake, dourly. "We barely make three."

Selene almost asked what that meant, except that Albatross had started up the stairs, her feet treading lightly on the northern-light glass, and Selene was obliged to follow.

Climbing was surprisingly hard. It reminded Selene of hiking at high altitude: she had to breathe harder and more rapidly, otherwise she became dizzy and felt weak. Remembering what had helped before, she concentrated on exhaling as much as she could, and this allowed her to keep up with Albatross—who didn't seem to be suffering any ill effects. In fact, from what Selene could see, the woman appeared more lively and excited than ever.

Then they came around a corner and ran headlong into a flock of birds. They were black, with shiny black beaks, but that was all Selene could make out before she slipped the shield off her back and put her head under it. Fighting against the storm of feathered bodies she struggled up the stairs until she was level with Albatross, and pulled the woman in next to her. She was shaking and her face was ripped, but no blood came from the open wounds. Instead, Selene was shocked to see, the cuts seemed to tear her clean through: she could see a snip of stair through a particularly wide scratch which cut Albatross's left check in half.

The flurry of birds passed and they were able to continue, but Selene kept them under the shield, just in case. Her actions were justified a few minutes later when, swooping low under the staggered ceiling, there came a raptor on wings that brushed the walls on either side. From what she glimpsed between the branches of her olive club, it looked like some sort of eagle. It crashed into them, talons slipping and screeching over the shield, and Selene felt it fizz against her hand in response.

The eagle squawked—a surprisingly undignified sound for so majestic a bird—and flapped away down the stairs behind them.

After that came a flock of owls. One of these got a talon in her bare back and ripped what felt like a sizable gash out of her shoulder. Selene gasped at the sudden pain of it, until she remembered to push the feeling out of her mind, and soon the pain ebbed to nothing but a faint tingle.

She'd begun to recognize the quiet sigh of moving air that preceded the birds, when they came around a corner and there was a blast of cold, arctic air. Hunching down behind the shield, Selene could only see a few steps in front of her, and on these there appeared, out of the slicing cold air, two cloven feet, like those of a goat.

Or a pig.

Frowning, Selene lowered her shield so she could peer over the top of it at the creature which stood, blocking their way up the stairs.

It was a woman—or at least, it looked that way to Selene. She indeed had pig's feet; a pair of pig trotters that disappeared into a skirt made of strips of cloth. Unless they were strips of something else. Selene didn't want to look too closely. Above the waist she wore only a vest-like garment, open in the center to reveal three rows of breasts, which in turn supported a garland of flowers, their stems linked together to form a rough chain.

Selene stopped herself before she got to the woman's face. The sense of self-preservation that had served her well in life intervened, and she settled for looking at the woman's hands—which were plump and pink with thick, dirty nails. Literally. They were covered in brown earth, as if she had just come in from working in her garden.

"Why have you come to this place?" asked the woman on the stairs. Her voice had an odd, reverberant quality. It was as if she spoke first in some language Selene did not understand, but then her words echoed and re-echoed, each time getting closer and closer to English, until they were comprehensible.

Selene didn't answer right away. Beside her, Albatross had begun to tremble. She was staring up at the place where the woman's head would have been, and from the look on her face Selene was assured she had made the correct decision not to do the same.

"Does it matter?" she replied at length.

A sound rippled across them. Something like a laugh, Selene thought.

"This is my domain," said the woman. "I have a right to ask."

"But do you have to be answered?"

The woman said nothing. Tentatively, Selene took another step up the stairs.

Against her arm the shield began to vibrate and then grow warm. Upon consideration Selene retreated again.

"I don't think you're Arianrhod, whatever the snake says," she muttered.

"And you are no Sun-hero," said the woman with the pig feet. Then she went on, her tone a little gentler. "But neither are you a nymph. Nor maid, nor mother. I am having difficulty placing you. So I ask again: what are you doing here?"

Selene waited, and when the serpent didn't offer any tips, she decided that she could do worse than simply tell the truth.

"I saw something. Looked like . . . looked like a missing piece of my . . . um . . . my friend here." She wagged the olive branch at Albatross.

"You would repair the twice-fallen star?" asked the woman on the stair.

"I don't know about any of that," Selene said, keeping her eyes firmly on the woman's hands. They were folded placidly over the front of her skirt, and by staring at the dirty nails Selene was able to ignore what that skirt was made of. "I just want to make sure she's okay."

There was a considering silence. In it, Selene heard distinctly the soft flapping of feathered wings.

"I can grant you access to what you seek," said the woman on the stairs. "But I will tell you now, it is not the bird that will save you. And I would ask: what would you give in return?"

Selene already knew the answer to that question. Turning her face aside so she could lower the shield, she reached across it, holding out the olive branch—with the scrubby, leafy side out.

There was another ripple of sound like laughter, and then the branch took on a life of its own and lifted itself out of her hand.

"You give me your weapon?" asked the woman.

"It's not a weapon," Selene said firmly. "It's an olive branch."

"If you say so, little Pasiphaë," said the voice of the woman with the pig's feet. Selene saw them move out of the corner of her eye, and then the stairs in front of her were clear.

Hardly daring to breathe she took one step, then another, and when still her shield did not burn she advanced more quickly, until she had put a quarter turn around the spire between herself and where the woman had stood. Only then did she turn and look back, but as she half expected, there was nothing to be seen.

Beside her, Albatross let out a raggedy wail.

"Ooooooh," she sighed. "Her *faaaace.*"

"Don't tell me about it," Selene groaned.

"Hearing a description won't kill you," said the serpent, dryly. "What in the realms possessed you to give her that club?"

Selene chose not to answer. Another quarter turn, and then another, and then they were climbing up out of the well of the stairs entirely, into the bright, whipping wind at the top of the spire.

It was a small space confined by high stone walls that blocked out the view of the surrounding land, making the place feel like it was suspended in an endless sky. There was a metal flagpole mounted in the center, and following the ropes up its long, thin length, Selene found they were more or less directly under the white, flapping, flat person she had seen earlier.

She had to grope sideways until she found Albatross's arm and then clasp it, to make certain she was actually seeing what she thought she was seeing.

What she saw was Albatross. Thinner, whiter, slightly more transparent, but definitely Albatross. She was fixed to the top of the pole by her hair, which had been knotted to a ring suspended by a system of ropes and pulleys, and was stretched out sideways by the wind. The flapping things Selene had seen earlier were her wings, which she appeared to have in place of human arms, but this was the only difference between her and the relatively solid Albatross standing beside her.

"Poor chick," said the serpent, slithering up to rest its head by her ear. "That's hardly a tenth of her—if that."

Selene sighed heavily. "D'you have anything actually helpful to say?"

"I thought I just did," remarked the snake.

Selene ignored it that time. Tugging at Albatross's arm she led the pale woman over to the base of the pole. There the rope had been tied down to an iron ring mounted in the stone, and Selene went about undoing it.

Albatross, meanwhile, began to wander in circles around the pole, all the while gazing up at the flat, wraithlike copy of herself with a melancholy, confused look on her face.

The knot was old and tight and caked with something white and crumbly, like salt. Selene's fingernails gave against its rough surface when she tried to work them into the creases, so she unhitched her shield and used the sharp edge of the pin to leverage it loose. Even so it was diffi-cult: every time the Albatross at the top of the pole got caught up in the wind it put tension on the rope so the knot went tight again. Whoever had hoisted her up there clearly hadn't intended to take her down again. This made Selene think of the pig-footed woman, and she shot a furtive look behind them at the stairwell.

They were alone, however, and after a while the Albatross on the ground sat down opposite from Selene, curling herself around her knees and watching her work. She seemed to have forgotten about the Albatross at the top of the flagpole.

Selene worked patiently at the knot. It might have originally been a double or granny knot, but ages of stress had pulled it out of shape so it was difficult to follow the course of the ropes. Nevertheless, Selene figured they had all the time they could possibly need. None of them needed food or sleep, and the pig-footed woman didn't seem to mind that they were up here. So she worked away at the knot with the point of her giant pin, while under her feet accumulated a small drift of salt grains, and thought about time.

She remembered seeing the meteor crash and burn into the red land on the other side of the river, but when she examined the intervening time she had trouble estimating how much of it there had been. Her memories of the event felt fresh and new, as if it had happened only a couple days ago, yet this knot looked like it had been here for years.

Either the Albatross at the top of the pole had not arrived on that me-teor, or Selene's perception of time had gone completely bonkers. She sus-pected it was the latter, considering how she had seen something white and fluttery—which could very well have been a thin, transparent slice of Albatross—go drifting over the river after the meteor had exploded. And without noticeable periods of light and dark to mark the passing of days, and the way she didn't grow tired or hungry, she figured it was likely any estimate she made regarding the passage of time would be way off. Even if there were no other supernatural forces toying with it, which considering her location, she thought was unlikely.

A few clouds passed by far overhead, but other than that there was nothing to break the monotony of the cold, gray-blue sky and the wind whistling through the ramparts. Albatross eventually curled up on her side and did go to sleep, looking much smaller and thinner than she did when animated by motion and expression. Selene kept shooting her ner-vous glances, remembering her own experience of sleep, and eventually caved and reached past the pole to shake her awake again.

"Stop the castle, I wanna get off," she mumbled as she came awake, and then blinked around herself, clearly disoriented. She felt her face, her hair, and then lifted her hands up to stare at them.

"That's funny," she murmured, as Selene got back to the knot. "I thought I was up there."

"You are," Selene said, not looking up. She was more certain than ever that what was on the other end of the pole was the missing piece of Albatross—the reason the woman looked like a two-dimensional slice of a person was because the rest of her had been stripped off somehow and hoisted up a flagpole.

Once Selene got her pin between two of the ropes the knot slowly began to loosen. She held a portion of the rope above it in a kink, so it wouldn't tighten up again, and carefully began feeding the loose end through the hole.

A gust of wind caught the Albatross on the far end and nearly undid all her progress, but she kept at it, and sometime later she had a free piece of kinked rope in her hands. They had been abraded from working with the rough rope, and there was an open blister on the side of her right thumb, but now it was just a matter of releasing the excess rope and pulling in the tethered piece of Albatross.

"Steady, steady," warned the snake as the white, wing-armed woman began to descend. "She might not recognize you."

But far from not recognizing Selene, the transparent Albatross began to flap even more energetically as soon as she realized she was being rescued. She called down to them, in a voice as faint and transparent as her body, and once she was about halfway down the pole Selene began to understand her words.

"There you are!" she cried. "I thought I'd dropped you in the river! I thought you went down with the dead! Are you all right? Oh, there's the snake. Hi, snake! Oh!"

This last exclamation was because she'd finally reached the bottom, sprawling over the stones with her arm-wings spread out limply around her, and had come face-to-face with the relatively solid Albatross, who was crouching over her, staring back with a blank, astonished look on her face.

Selene went around to begin untangling the transparent Albatross's hair from the rope, but her wing-arms flailed and she sat up, scrambling around to sit in a mirror position to her twin.

They made a strange vision: two identical women, young and thin and stark, both so pale they were colorless. Even though one had human arms and one had long, feathered wings; one shimmered uncertainly and one was like an image printed on cellophane; in all other respects they matched perfectly—right down to the rips in their dresses and the stains of red mud on their legs.

The Albatrosses stared at each other, leaning their heads from side to side, raising and lowering an arm or wing respectively. As if one was the reflection of the other.

Then they leaned their heads together, as if wanting to examine the other's face.

In the moment when their foreheads touched there was a spark of something electric that made Selene's teeth hurt. She flinched, and as a result missed what came immediately after.

When she looked again it was to see the Albatrosses' faces melting into each other, sending out faint ripples of light where the two met. As if only one was real, and the other was a reflection on the surface of some liquid barrier.

But there was no barrier, and each one was equally real. They dissolved into each other as Selene watched: first their faces, then shoulders, hands and arms and finally torso, legs and feet. At the same time the ripples of light grew brighter and brighter, until Selene had to turn her face away and didn't see what happened at the end.

There was another tooth-hurting *snap* and the light vanished. When Selene dared to look there was only one Albatross, sitting with her legs folded lopsidedly under her, examining her hands—which were human— as if she had never seen them before. Her face was wrinkled in distaste, as if she'd just eaten something rancid, and her skin had taken on a faint pinkish tinge—though her dress was as milky-white as ever. She was utterly solid and opaque, except for the pair of giant, ghostly wings spreading from her shoulders.

Slowly, Selene crawled around until she was directly in front of the woman, and sat there patiently until she finished examining her hands and looked up. Then her face broke into a smile so wide it practically glowed, and she reached forward to clasp Selene's nearest hand in both of hers.

"I lost you," she said, and her voice was richer and fuller now—less like an echo and more like a real voice. "But I found you again. It was always me, all along."

"Yeah," said Selene, still uncertain. "Something like that, anyway."

"I wonder how many pieces of me there are," Albatross went on, getting to her feet and dusting off her knees. "I think there are still some bits missing."

Selene understood what she meant. She might look fuller and more solid than either version of her had before, but there was still a flatness to her; a raggedness around her hair and eyes, that gave her an uncertain, incomplete look.

"Do you remember how you got here?" Selene asked, thinking of the meteor.

Albatross's face went blank and she stared at Selene for so long Selene thought she might have had one of her sudden memory-wipes. Then she said:

"I fell." Short and flat, and she clearly wasn't going to say any more.

"Yeah," said Selene softly. "Me too."

"Are you missing parts also?" Albatross asked, almost eagerly.

Selene shook her head. "This is all there is, I think."

"That's good," Albatross said, looking around the top of the spire. She cast her gaze up the pole, and frowned.

"I was up there," she murmured. It wasn't a question, but still Selene answered.

"Yeah, yeah you were."

"She put me up there!" Albatross said, beginning to sound affronted. "Like a . . . like a *flag!*"

A white flag, Selene thought, uncomfortably. What she said, however, was:

"Do you know who *she* is?"

"Carrion Woman," said Albatross. "Winter Ghost. Dead god in a dead land." She began to pace around the top of the spire, and following her with her eyes, Selene noticed with dismay that the entrance to the stairs had disappeared.

"That's Carridwen for you," the serpent hissed. "She keeps what she takes."

"I am no one's to be taken," announced Albatross with such assurance that it surprised Selene. She realized with an uncomfortable jolt that she had begun to take the serpent's words at face value, but now that Albatross had directly contradicted it she noticed something.

"I thought you said this was the castle of Arianrhod," she said, accusingly.

"Arianrhod, Carridwen," said the snake. "Different names for the same person."

"No, they're not," said Albatross.

"What do you mean by that?" asked Selene. Her Welsh mythology was painfully deficient and she knew it, but what the snake said had a ring of truth to it. Something she had read somewhere, once before.

Albatross didn't answer. She had gone to the place in the floor where the stairs used to be, and begun to stamp her bare feet against the stone. With each stamp she began a chant.

"Carrion Woman, Carrion Woman, Vulture, Pig and Prophet Bone," she said, her voice gone fuzzy and droning. "I've seen your face with a mouth full of worms, yet still I breathe—I'll not be your stone!"

And she repeated, beginning to leap up and down, slamming her feet into the floor.

"I'll not be your stone! I'll not be your stone! I!" — stamp — "Will!" — stamp — "Not!" — stamp — "Be!" — stamp — "Your!" —stamp—and the stone cracked under her bare feet.

It began as a spiderweb of black lines as the rock parted, but quickly spread to cover the entire top of the spire. The pole loosened in its anchor and fell sideways, and the place began to come apart around them.

Selene stood up. There was nothing she could do—nowhere to run. She considered the drop to the labyrinth below and was steeling herself for another painful landing when Albatross's ghostly wings swept out, growing solid, and shining with a faint luminance, and she coasted over the heaving ground, grabbing Selene under her armpits and lifting them into the air.

Here we go again, Selene thought tiredly, and made sure she had a good grip on her shield as they went sailing up and away from the collapsing tower.

It was not like the desperate coasting they had done before. Now it was proper flying, with the beats of Albatross's wings sounding like soft thunder in Selene's ears, and though her hands were cold and painfully tight, fingers digging into Selene's flesh, she was no longer worried about being dropped.

The snake had cinched itself tightly around her torso, its head bent backward to keep an eye on the crumbling spire—which, when Selene dared glance down, was still in the process of collapsing into a pile of rubble and dust.

"Oh no," said the snake. "She won't like that!"

The words had hardly left its mouth when a fierce wind buffeted them, causing Albatross to dip and weave. But her grip on Selene remained firm—painfully so—and though they were forced down by several feet, they were still well clear of the ramparts of the labyrinth. They were close enough, however, that she could glimpse the shadowy passages between the walls. They were much deeper than they should have been, and seemed to be crisscrossed with a network of further tunnels and paths, buried deep within the castle.

Like a lot of things in this dimension, Selene supposed, the castle labyrinth was bigger on the inside.

That, or it was a portal into another realm. Both seemed equally feasible.

The wind was continuing to press them down, and Albatross was straining fiercely to regain altitude. It was not just a blast, Selene realized. The labyrinth itself was sucking them in. Like flying out of a wind tunnel.

Mixed in with the wind was a high, mournful whining, sour and ringing, which clogged Selene's ears and made it difficult to think.

"The shield! The shield!" The snake was shouting, and it took her a moment to realize what it meant. When she did she lost no time in raising her shield so that it was pointed up, sheltering her from the wind.

"Not like *that!*" the serpent screamed.

Selene flailed, confused, then the snake slithered along her arm and forced her hand down, so that the shield was angled below them—against the labyrinth.

It was like cutting the tether of an unseen weight. Albatross let out a surprised shout, and immediately they began putting on speed—and distance—from the sinister castle. As they went the sour whine in her ears diminished, until it was replaced by the clean blustering of the wind, and the castle shrank until it was again a rectangle containing a labyrinth, riding a frothing white cloud over the gray-green landscape.

They sailed on, and once the castle was out of sight Selene dared tuck her shield against her side so she could get a better look at the land beneath them.

It was a strange patchwork of green hills and fields and tracts of yellow sand and here and there a few mountains rising suddenly to great heights.

Rivers cut in and out of sight, and in the distance—always in the distance—was a line of angry purple clouds.

Limbo was like the castle, Selene realized: a portal into a much larger realm. Each patch of mountain or desert or river was probably yet another gate into yet another part of the vast network of realities she had so blithely referred to as the "Spirit World" when she had been alive.

Or rather, when she had been living in the real world.

But what was that world, now that all the others were so clearly equally real? Was that just another dimension, no more special than all the rest?

The thought put wild notions into her head. The idea that, if she searched long enough, she might find her way back. To Detroit, to Jill, to Clara. Home.

But that was treading dangerously close to the tantalizing hope Lilith had put in her heart when she'd told her there was a way out. Hope, in a place like this, was a dangerous and powerful thing, and Selene wasn't certain she knew enough to use it safely.

"Nicely done, captain," the snake said, without a hint of sarcasm. "You've come off relatively unscathed from the Castle of Arianrhod. Can't say that about too many folks—heroes or no. Now, if you don't mind my making a suggestion, maybe we should land before we get blown somewhere we don't want to go."

"Such as?" Selene asked, curious.

The snake didn't answer, but she saw it jerk its head in the direction of the purple horizon.

"What's over there?" Albatross asked. She had to shout a little, over the noise of the wind.

"Hell," said the snake. "Proper Hell. First circle is winds and terror—don't want to get too close."

So Albatross descended, eventually dipping low enough that she could drop Selene onto the side of a soft, grassy hill, while she coasted on and made a crash landing at its summit.

She popped up again immediately, grass and stickers in her hair, and waved cheerfully down at Selene, who was massaging her arms gingerly and looking around.

As she had expected, now that they were on the ground it looked like the green-and-gold country went on forever. As always the sunlight was diffuse—filtered through a thick layer of warm gray clouds—so it was impossible to tell north from south or east from west—if indeed such directions were relevant in Limbo.

Their particular patch of country was a little more variable, however, than the gray-green hills by the Acheron. Opposing the ominous purple horizon was a line of rocky mountains which curled around them, descending into forested foothills which were eventually swallowed up by a ruddy golden mist.

Facing the other way, between the purple and the mountains, the gray sky arched down until it terminated in a flat, blue line, which faded to black before it was cut off by the shoulder of a low, rocky hill. An ocean. Or a very big lake.

Albatross came stumbling down the hill, mincing a little on her bare feet, until she stood next to Selene and peered over her shoulder at the lake.

"This is an old country," she remarked.

"Do you know which one it is?" Selene asked.

"Dreams and memories," said the serpent. "This is a place that once existed—or might have existed—in the World Above, but it's not there any more."

"I wasn't asking you," Selene pointed out, but Albatross was nodding.

"That sounds true," she said, and began walking off down the hill in the direction of the water. Her wings had gone transparent again, but the rest of her was opaque and solid, and she moved over the dry, rough ground with the weight of a real person, with real, soft, sensitive feet. She no longer walk-floated, and had to stop frequently to pick pieces of dry grass and seeds from between her toes.

Selene followed her. Though her feet were bare as well, and the ground was poky and rough, she ignored the sharp jabs as she ignored all other sensations, and soon they faded into the back of her mind.

They came around the other side of the hill, and there had a better view down to the water. Though Selene couldn't see the opposite bank, and the low hills disappeared into the water to either side, it still felt more like a very large lake, rather than the ocean. There was no wind, she realized: hardly a ripple broke the black surface, and the area had a close, stuffy feeling—almost as if they were indoors.

There was a murmur in the air behind them—not a gust of wind, but a movement of the atmosphere as it parted to let someone pass. Then a young, female voice said:

"Are you lost? Can I help you?"

Albatross jumped so hard that she floated two feet to one side before landing again, while Selene had become so far accustomed to the nature of the place that she suppressed the shiver that went through her and turned about carefully to look at the speaker.

She was a very young woman—almost a girl, Selene thought—with light olive skin and straight, dark hair, and wore a simple dress of wool the color of sun-bleached straw. She was carrying a leather satchel over one shoulder, and was wearing sandals over wraps of some dirty-white cloth, which covered her feet. She looked completely harmless. For that reason alone, Selene regarded her warily.

"We're fine, thanks," Selene said. It was not an outright lie, after all.

The girl looked at her inquisitively. She was maybe fourteen or fifteen, and seemed to be a touch darker all over than she should have been, as if she was standing in the shade of an unseen tree. She had a pleasant face and a pointed nose and was looking at them with such honest curiosity that Selene began to have difficulty keeping her guard up.

"That's a nice snake," the girl said, gesturing at the serpent, who slid around Selene's body so it could get a better look at the speaker.

"They're all right," Selene admitted, glancing at Albatross. But Albatross seemed as intrigued by the girl as she was by them.

"Thank you," said the snake in a soft little hiss.

The girl actually clapped her hands at that, delighted. "Oh, you speak! How wonderfully clever! Tell me, serpent, are you one of Kirke's servants? I have met her boars and her horses, but never any snakes before . . ."

"I . . . er . . . no," began the snake, its head drawing back in an indignant S shape. "I served an oracle near Corsica, once, then I got moved to Ireland, then down here."

"You are a python?" asked the girl, and she seemed to mean something other than the species of snake, for the scarlet serpent bobbed its head.

"When I was incarnate in the world above," it said.

"Goodness," said the girl. "I've never met a python before—not in person! But Mistress Kirke has told me of your kind. Is it true you speak for Divine Apollo?"

The serpent hung its head. "Not anymore," it admitted.

"I am sorry," said the girl. She seemed to genuinely mean it. Then she caught sight of Albatross, still staring brazenly, and made a self-conscious bow.

"I am sorry, I did not mean to be rude."

"I don't think you're rude," Albatross said. "I think you're dead."

"That's right," said the girl.

That explains why she looks so dark, Selene thought. Gives a whole new meaning to the term "shade."

"T'was my lot to die young and unfulfilled," said the girl with a shrug. "Crushed and swept away for being inconvenient to those who were in charge of the order of things." She didn't seem particularly stressed by it. "But I was fortunate to have a sound psychopomp, and she led me safe through the underworld to this timeless haven. I met Mistress Kirke, and she gave me what food and drink that the dead can eat, and though I will never live again, at least I can be of help to those who do."

She smiled brightly and brought her leather satchel around so she could lift the flap and reveal its contents. Inside, Selene glimpsed coins and hairpins, a small leather wallet and what looked like a credit card. She frowned.

"I take them back to Kirke," the girl explained. "She sends them out again, into the world, where they belong."

Selene frowned. She felt like she should know that name, but it wasn't ringing any bells.

"Is she a goddess, this Kirke?"

The girl looked surprised. "I don't know," she said. "You'll have to ask her. Maybe I should take you back with me. I'm supposed to tell her if I meet any lost souls, anyway."

She began to walk. Albatross agreeably followed her, but Selene grabbed her elbow and made her hang back.

"Hold on now, who said we're lost?"

The girl turned her head around to gaze at them. For a moment her dark eyes seemed much older and shrewder than they should have been, and Selene thought: *even if you're dead in a timeless place, time still passes. Maybe you don't change, but you don't stay the same either.*

The girl glanced at Albatross, still rough and unfinished and swaying from side to side, even when she stood still.

"I think she can help you, and I think you need help." the girl said, somehow directing the comment at all three of them.

Selene still hesitated, but only for a moment. The girl had a very different feel about her than either the pig-footed woman or the ghosts from across the river. Or the snake, come to that. She seemed . . . not normal, not exactly. More like she fit in with the landscape. Like she belonged there.

Cautiously Selene began to walk forward, guiding Albatross over the uneven ground.

The girl moved quickly, with assured steps. But she stopped periodically and waited for them to catch up, and in this way led them down the hill and through a small, forested valley. The trees here were all small and bent and old, but flush with dark green leaves and alive with the flapping and skittering of unseen animals. Selene wondered where the trees came from: were they shades of real trees that had lived and died? What about the animals? Or were they merely representations of something else? Selene rather thought that if there was an afterlife for trees, it would look much different from the human one.

They climbed out the far side of the valley and there beheld a magnificent view of the lake, whose waters were so still and dark it was like a mirror. The land sloped down in open fields to the shore, where a little boat had been drawn up on the sandy beach. Next to it were two sea lions, stretched out on the sand, apparently asleep. These awoke as they approached, and they keened eagerly at the sight of the girl, flapping their feet and nosing affectionately at her face.

"Hello uncle, hello father," she said, stroking their heads and embracing their necks. "I have brought visitors for Aeaea," she explained, gesturing at Selene and Albatross.

The two animals gazed at them intently, and Selene found herself looking into wise, sad black eyes that seemed to read in her more than she meant to let show. Neither of them spoke, however, but helped the girl run the boat into the water, where they then slipped themselves into rope harnesses by which they could tow the vessel. This made sense, Selene supposed. The ship had neither oars nor sails.

It was so small it barely fit the three of them, and Selene had to sit opposite from the girl with one leg braced across the middle of the boat for balance. Albatross barely counted for weight, and she took advantage of this to lean over the prow and watch as the sea lions began hauling the boat into the open water.

The air was pleasantly cool over the lake, but uncannily still. It would have been stagnant, save that their movement over the surface was swift enough to generate a small breeze. It teased at Selene's hair and blew wisps across the girl's face, and smelled of clean water and something faintly sweet, like roses and lavender.

It was, Selene realized with a jolt, *nice*.

The boat was made of lacquered wood, and its floor was cool and soothing against her sore soles. She hadn't even realized her feet *were* sore until she sat down in the boat. Now they ached with relief.

How long had she been on her feet? Since she'd first spotted Albatross, snatches of flight aside. How long had that been? Days, at least. Or the equivalent of days.

The sky blurred with the open water, the sweet air wafted in her face, the gentle surging of the boat lulled her.

Nothing. Not even darkness. An absolute lack of anything substantial—including fear. And then the serpent's voice, ringing in her ear:

"Do you wake, Moonshield? Waken!"

Selene's head jerked up. They were still in the boat, and the boat still moved steadily across the surface of the still, black water. Albatross had crouched down in the prow so she could rest her head on the side of the boat, keeping an eye on the two sea lions. Across from her the girl was looking keenly at her, and speaking.

No, not to her. To the snake. The snake and the girl were having a conversation. Seemed like they had been for several minutes, and Selene had just woken up in the middle of it.

But she was sure the snake had spoken to her. Had pulled her back to consciousness before she could dissolve into the nothing.

Now, however, it was saying:

"It's much harder than you think, being the aspect of a god. It's almost like being a fictional character; your existence depends on other people hearing about you and believing in you."

"I understand a little of what you say," the girl replied. "Even though I lived, once, a long time ago, somewhat recently a poet put a version of me into his work, and I find myself more articulate since then. Not alive, you understand. But cognizant in a way I hadn't been since I still had family and friends living, and keeping my memory alive. Sometimes I wonder, though—am I the ghost of she who was alive and walked the earth and ate the fruit of the sun? Or am I the shade of the character who lives, forever and finite, in ink bound between two covers? Or am I something even more contingent? The creation of the million readers who read my poet's story and made room in their hearts for me to live a little once more . . . "

Selene almost wished she could go back to sleep. Almost. But now there was a dark shape on the horizon and she realized their journey would not be endless, as she had half expected it to be.

The shape grew and solidified into an island with steep, green cliffs. The black water broke in frothing white lines at its base, and the girl steered their boat around to the left, where it threw out an arm and created a sheltered bay. As they made the point of it Selene saw that a road had been carved into the top of the ridge, and this ran right up to the highest peak of the island, on which there appeared to be built a kind of castle or temple.

The sea lions pulled them in behind the ridge, and here the faint smell of lavender and roses was overpowered by the sharp scent of pine and citrus. They landed on a narrow yellow beach, and Selene jumped out into the shallows to help the girl haul the boat ashore. The water felt even better on her feet than the boat had, and she stood in the firm, cold sand under the running waves for the extra minute it took Albatross to say goodbye to the sea lions. These waved their flippers and cooed affectionately before slipping back into the black water.

"Oh, have you ever seen anything so beautiful?" Albatross sighed.

Selene looked at her, confused, thinking she meant the animals—which were very handsome, but not what she'd call beautiful. But Albatross was gazing up at the island they had landed upon, and Selene had to admit it was an impressive sight.

The steep cliffs which had greeted them on their approach fell away sharply behind the arm of the ridge, giving way to a gentle green fold on whose slopes grew numerous pine trees, and in whose cradle were row upon row of shiny-leafed citrus bushes. Some had orange fruit and some yellow and some green, but Selene didn't look too carefully at them. Her gaze was taken up to the head of the fold, where the land rose steeply to the high peak on which perched the imposing building.

From this angle it looked more like a castle than ever, but there was a strange outbuilding—like someone had stuck a house on a pole—and this was silhouetted against the warm gray sky.

Meanwhile, the girl had collected a number of other satchels from the bottom of the boat and was beckoning them to follow her up a sandy path, which appeared to lead up through the valley toward the high peak.

"Welcome to Aeaea, the Witch's Island," she said, and taking Selene's arm in one hand and Albatross's in the other, set off along the path.

The trek up the island to the house-or-castle felt like it took a long time while they were doing it, but on reflection Selene remembered little of that time, except for the prevailing smell of pine and citrus and the texture of the path beneath her bare feet. This began as sand and progressed to clay and finally hard rock as they climbed via switchbacks up the side of the mountain. This brought back memories of Purgatory, which made her feel dizzy, but when they reached the top there was no bridge, and no endlessly rising tower. They had come to the top of the island, and the house, huge and square and very castle-like, was waiting for them.

Up close it had the look of ten or twelve houses that had been built one on top of the other and mashed in from the sides, so there was a big, pillared front with a pair of gates that stood open, grown all over with vines of ivy, while behind it rose a steep triangle, like part of a medieval cathedral. Pushed up on either side were sharp, brick buildings like old British townhouses, and from their flat roofs grew trees—fruit trees, Selene thought, from their round, carefully pruned look.

Above and behind the cathedral were more gable ends and slanting roofs, riddled with windows and chimneys—many of which were emitting faint plumes of pale smoke.

The girl led them boldly up to the gate, which as they drew near Selene saw was guarded by a pair of wolf-sized animals with eagle heads and cat bodies. Griffins, she assumed. They sat on either side of the gate on small stone thrones, each padded with a very squashed pillow covered in cat hair, but they descended from these at their approach, golden eyes glinting brightly in the dim, overcast light.

The girl greeted them both by name and then introduced Selene and Albatross as "two lost souls seeking guidance," and the snake as "one of Eurynome's lost tongues." This seemed to satisfy the griffins, and they retreated back to their thrones, curling up exactly like cats, but putting their eagle heads over to rest on their backs, like a bird might.

The girl led them into the shadow of the gate, where there was a small door set into the side of the wall. She opened this with a little gold key she fished out by a string around her neck, and standing aside she ushered them through the door.

Selene felt her feet come down on cold, smooth stone, and a few more steps carried her through a short tunnel and out into the light of a wide courtyard lined with trees and gurgling from the sound of fountains and channels of water which ran every which way. Paths crossed and recrossed the streams by way of small, arched wooden bridges and widened to little circles of dirt under the trees, where sat groups of three or four . . . beings.

Selene was pretty sure they were people, even though the one nearest had the head of a boar and the other that of a deer. Their hands and feet—what could be seen of them—matched the species of their head, but they sat crosslegged upon mats under what looked like a pear tree, drawing in the sand with styluses, and each wore a sort of pleated skirt and a shawl around their shoulders. And though every one had the superficial characteristics of a different animal—Selene saw a horse, a dog, a rooster, a rabbit and even something scaly with frills that might have been a dragon—they all had recognizably human bodies under their clothes, and the horse even had split hooves, like hands, at the end of its forelegs.

None of this curious assortment paid them any attention as the girl led the way to the center of the courtyard, where three different trees grew out of a single pool of water, their trunks twining and twisting together in a bizarre braid. One of them Selene recognized as an oak. The other two she couldn't be certain of.

Among their branches crowded shining points of light, which lit the space beneath them in a gentle wash of illumination—the very opposite of shade. It sparkled off the surface of the water and gleamed on the black rock which had been hewn into the shape of a chair, and made the person sitting in it, bent over a piece of knitting, stand out sharply against her supporting cast of shadowy animal-people.

Unlike the pig-footed woman, Selene found she could look at this one without any discomfort. In fact, apart from sitting on an obsidian throne under a strange triple tree bedecked with lights, she looked quite ordinary. Even homely. She had shaggy brown hair which had begun to gray, tied up in a sensible braid which disappeared over one shoulder. She was wearing a plain wool dress the color of thunderclouds, and her feet, which stuck out from under the hem of her skirt, were brown and weathered and wearing leather sandals. She also had on an apron with at least a dozen pockets, and a thick belt strapped around her waist which must have held a dozen more. She had thick, strong arms and large, capable hands, which were presently engaged in knitting the heel of a sock.

She did not look up at their approach, but swore quietly under her breath, and bent double over her work.

The girl came and stood before her, making a deep bow wherein her knees touched the ground at the edge of the pool. But since the woman didn't look up, Selene didn't bother. Albatross was gazing up into the leaves of the triple tree, a bemused smile on her face, while the serpent had gone uncharacteristically still and silent over her shoulder. Selene thought it had ceased to breathe.

The woman with the knitting swore again, and the girl cleared her throat, as if to cover for the sound.

That made the woman look up. Selene was surprised to see her face was as ordinary as the rest of her: broad and brown and slightly wrinkled. She had a mole on one cheek and a fine tracing of crow's feet wrinkles framing her eyes. These were as thunderously gray as her dress, with very dark, small pupils. She raised bushy eyebrows at them, then said in a voice that was both sharp and easy, soft and loud at the same time:

"Have any of you knitted a sock before? I did it once, a long time ago, but this heel has stumped me."

The girl shifted her feet in the dirt, evidently embarrassed.

"Mother Kirke," she said. "I've brought visitors. I think they are lost, but they say they don't know."

"So I see," said the woman. The more she talked, the more Selene felt like she ought to know her. As if they had met before, many years ago. And that name. Kirke. *Keer-kee.* It was almost a name she knew. Almost.

"Do any of them know how to knit a sock's heel?"

Finding those thunderous eyes on her, Selene shook her head with a shrug.

"What's a sock?" asked Albatross, full of oblivious innocence.

"A remarkable invention for driving women mad," said the woman on the throne. Mother Kirke. She rolled up her knitting and stuffed it into the largest pocket of her apron, which took up most of its front. "Never mind. You won't need them. What you need is a bath, I'd say, and a proper meal. Both of you,"—she pointed a thick, brown finger from Albatross to Selene—"but not you," she added, jabbing it at the snake. "What by oak and holly are you doing clinging to that lost soul like she's the only thing keeping you corporeal?"

"Sorry, mistress," hissed the snake, its head downcast. "I was cast out. The Nameless God laid it on me to serve them, and so I have been a banner in the vestibule for the past two thousand years—as the living reckon. I feared that without a soul to anchor me I would revert."

"A prudent measure," said the woman with a nod. "But you've no need of that here. You're in my house now. The Nameless God has no power here save that which I grant them. Come to me, my serpent, and let us see you settled into a more comfortable form."

And for the first time since she'd caught hold of its tail, the serpent slithered free of Selene's body, crossed the short stretch of water, and curled itself modestly at the woman's sandaled feet.

What happened next Selene missed because a pale bear the color of milk and honey had appeared, carrying on one arm a load of soft linen sheets, and in the crook of the other a copper bowl of water. It laid them on the ground between her and Albatross, and began wetting strips of linen and washing Albatross's feet. The bloody mud came off in globs, leaving her skin as pale as the bear's coat and gleaming faintly in the light of the trees.

At the same time a heavyset woman with the head of a cow came up bearing a plate full of fruit: peaches and plums and oranges and small, yellow apples. There were also baskets of berries and a crock of what looked like heavy cream. The cow-woman set the tray down at Selene's feet, dipped a plum in the cream, and offered it to her.

"Uh . . . thanks, but no," Selene said, feeling suddenly awkward. The fruit smelled incredible: sweet and strong and fresh, as if it has just come off the tree. This alone made Selene suspicious. Nothing so far, not the stench of the river, not the fragrant air of the lake, had ever smelled so strongly. That, and she knew better than to eat or drink anything outside her own world. Just as she had refused to touch or drink from the Acheron, so she turned her head away from the plate of fruit—even though it smelled so appetizing her mouth was watering and her long-neglected stomach had begun to cramp.

It would feel so much better to eat. And the fruit was ripe and succulent and would relieve the dryness in her mouth . . .

Albatross saved her, inadvertently, by descending upon the platter as soon as the bear had finished washing her feet and beginning to stuff her face with peaches.

The cow-woman, who had been momentarily discouraged by Selene's refusal, happily handed Albatross the plum and began peeling her an orange, using her thick, hoofed fingers to strip the rind off the fruit.

Selene tore her eyes away, and found her gaze met by the woman on the obsidian throne. She'd draped the serpent over her shoulders, where it appeared to have gone to sleep, and now met Selene's gaze evenly, placidly, and her mouth twitched at the corner: the suggestion of a smile.

"You're an exceptionally prudent one," she remarked. "But my fruit will do you no harm."

Selene put her hands in the pockets of her jeans to keep them from snatching a stray strawberry Albatross had knocked off the platter. A little while longer, she thought, and the plate would be demolished. Albatross had already eaten all the peaches, spitting their pits back out onto the plate, drank the cream and was now gobbling berries.

"Just the same," Selene said, trying not to move her mouth too much. It would be too easy to pop a blueberry into it otherwise.

"But you must be hungry," said Mother Kirke.

Selene shrugged. "It'll pass."

"Not here," said the woman. "You've gone on beyond the Land of the Dead, granddaughter. You must eat, if you wish to stay. And it will make life easier for you, too."

"I'll become like them?" Selene asked, jerking her head toward the cow-woman and the bear, who had fallen back to watch Albatross eat with evident awe.

"My subjects take the form that suits them best," Mother Kirke said serenely. "Nothing is permanent, and they may leave whenever they wish."

"I was a deer for a while," said the girl, who had snatched an apple from under Albatross's hands and was now eating it with relish. "It was ever so enlightening."

Selene forced herself to smile, and shook her head. She noticed how the woman's eyes kept darting to Albatross, and she thought: *oh snap, here it comes.*

But Albatross finished off the last apple, core and all, spat out the seeds, and let out a satisfied belch, remaining unchanged. She sat down on the ground, her legs stretched out in front of her.

"I feel much better now," she said. "Still empty in places, but better."

"You are even more curious than your companion," Mother Kirke remarked, giving Albatross a penetrating stare. "You are incomplete, but what your picture is I cannot see. Yet you are obviously a person of great portent. A true monster."

Albatross frowned. "I don't feel like a monster," she said.

"I meant it in the original way," explained the woman. "A 'monster' being a particularly awe-inspiring portent."

"Oh?" said Selene, curious, and beginning to regain some of her critical thinking ability, now the temptation of food had been removed. "What does she portend?"

Mother Kirke shrugged. "Like I said, she has been stripped. Scattered. She would have to reassemble herself to find out what she means."

"I don't like having empty bits," said Albatross, sullenly. "And my mind keeps sliding about. Sometimes I'm here, sometimes I'm not. Sometimes I'm more hole than piece."

"Shifting views," said Mother Kirke, nodding understandingly. "It is a troublesome business, I know, to be broken into so many aspects. With you I expect it's even more painful. I think you were a real person, once."

"Then what are you?" Selene asked, surprised at her own boldness.

Cloudy gray eyes fell on her, and something flashed in them like lightning.

"I am what you might call *hyper*-real. I exist on the level of reality that rests upon your own."

Selene felt like there was a lot of meaning built up behind those words, like a lake behind a tall dam, but she hadn't the courage to look over to the other side. Not just yet.

In the meantime the woman had turned back to Albatross.

"Well, my dear, you've eaten of my food. Would you like my counsel as well?"

"I'd like to not be full of holes anymore," Albatross said. "Can you help me fill in my holes?"

Mother Kirke shook her head. "I don't have the pieces," she explained. "For that, you'd have to go looking for them."

"Where?" asked Albatross.

"You did kinda fall outta the sky," Selene pointed out. "Boom. Made a big crater. I think that's what broke you up. So there's probably bits of you all over the vestibule . . . and a little of Limbo, too."

But Mother Kirke was shaking her head. "Come to me, child. Let me see your hands."

Albatross obediently got up and splashed through the pool so Mother Kirke could lay her pale, bony hands across her lap. She examined them, a wrinkle between her brows, turning them this way and that.

"Hmm. No," she said at last. She glanced at Selene. "What you saw fall was only a fragment of the greater whole. What you encountered in the vestibule and the borderlands mere slivers of slices of who this girl is. By your aura I recognize you as being part of the calamity which was cast into Hades some time ago. It struck that portion of Cocytus which lies frozen, deep in the Morning Star's domain, and there fractured, rebounding in a dozen fragments which have landed all over the related realms."

This at least Selene could unpack, knowing enough about the geography of the classical underworld.

"Hell," she said. "You mean she fell into Hell?"

"That is another name for the country of which I speak," said Mother Kirke, blandly.

"And the related realms?"

"All the versions of that land of torment which exist, bounded by Phlegethon, Dis and Styx, and their satellite stations above. Collectively you might call them the Pit."

"So . . . all over Hell," Selene sighed.

"You might call it that, too," allowed Mother Kirke.

"Do you know where I landed?" Albatross asked, eagerly. Selene could understand: if she were in pieces the first thing she'd want to do was get them all back together again. Even if that did mean going into the depths of Hell.

Mother Kirke shook her head. "I did not bother to keep track. But I can find out for you. Lina, would you be a dear and tell Livia I need her record book? From the last Great Cycle, and . . . oh, just tell her to come here."

The girl, who had been scraping cream out of the bowl with the last of her apple, popped this in her mouth and scrambled to her feet, bowing in lieu of answering verbally. She bowed again to Albatross and to Selene, and then trotted off through the courtyard on quick, quiet feet. Selene watched her disappear among the human-shaped beasts milling about the courtyard, a strange prickling feeling under her collar.

It was coming from her shield, she realized. It was beginning to hum, but not in a warning way. This was more of a purr, like a happy cat. Curiously she turned it around, and saw that the lit section of the moon—the part that was polished silver—had eaten away into the shadowed crescent so it was almost a full moon on the face of her shield.

"That's a good piece of work," Mother Kirke remarked, indicating the shield. "Who gave it to you?"

Selene saw no reason not to answer truthfully.

"A witch," she said. "Named Faraday."

"Faraday," repeated Mother Kirke, her head rolling back to look up at the sky. She repeated the name twice more under her breath, then smiled. "Oh yes, Faraday. I remember her, now. She passed through maybe eight moon-years ago. She ate of my fruit," she added, offhandedly.

"Good for her," said Selene, filing this as something to ask Faraday about, assuming she ever got the chance.

"May I have a closer look?" Mother Kirke asked, gesturing at the shield.

Selene froze. She was loathe to part with it, but she had the feeling she'd already offended Kirke once by refusing to eat the fruit, and that she would not be wise to do so a second time. Besides, talking about Faraday had made her think of witches, which had made her reconsider who this Kirke was.

Names could get garbled coming down the millennia. Old souls might not have the same names for the characters she knew. Or they pronounced them differently.

She was saved by the arrival of a woman. She was tall and austere with a wrinkled, pinched face, like she'd just eaten something bitter, dressed in a flowing robe of cream-colored linen. Her feet were bare and she wore no jewelry, but the noble angle at which she held her head indicated that jewels were things she was accustomed to. She carried a great book under one arm and walked carefully, leaning a little to counterbalance its weight.

"Ah, Livia! Just the soul I need," said Mother Kirke, beckoning the imposing woman closer. "I need the locations of all the pieces of the calamity that fell into Cocytus the other day. Have you got them?"

"I do," announced the soul called Livia. "Updated by my sources daily, as you ordered." Ponderously she removed the book from under her arm and held it out, expectantly.

The bear from earlier hurried up, carrying a flat object which it unfolded into a little table. Livia set the book on it and began undoing the latches which bound the covers shut. Selene saw then that she did wear one piece of decoration: a thin silver bracelet connected by an equally thin chain to a ring through the spine of the book.

And she thought again: *there's more meaning to that than meets the eye*, but the conversation swept on, leaving no room for interpretation.

Livia was flipping through the book, running a long, wrinkled finger down the face of a page.

"I have them here," she announced, stopping her finger. "Do you wish me to read them aloud?"

"Please do," said Mother Kirke, smiling encouragingly.

Livia nodded, the bitter look on her face not changing.

"The Calamity, upon impact, was split into nine pieces, each of which were recast, landing among the Malebolge, the Burning Desert, the Forest of Despair, the Phlegethon, Dis, the Stygian Marsh, the Cliffs of Wrath, the Swamp of the Gluttons, and the banks of the Acheron. Each piece was then split into three fractions, and these have been drifting from realm to realm ever since. By my last report, twelve have been drawn back to Cocytus, six are in the Burning Desert, three in the Forest of Despair, three have recombined and are being held in Dis, and one is presently blowing in the Lustful Gale." She shut the book and looked keenly at Albatross.

"I should also mention I had reports that there was one caught on Carridwen's flagpole, and one also being tormented upon the far shores of the Acheron, but I see this intelligence is no longer up to date."

Albatross straightened up. She was looking more solid now, after having eaten, and the wings which remained, mantling in a shimmer of light above her shoulders, looked heavier and nearer somehow.

"All right," she said, wading out of the pool and dusting her hands off as she went. She stepped up onto the tile rim and looked around. "All right," she repeated, squinting off over the walls of the courtyard. She took a step, as if she would set off to reclaim her missing pieces there and then, and paused. She looked around her, uncertainly.

"Um," she said. "Where do I find this pit? Er, this hell?"

"It is not far from where you entered our realm," Mother Kirke informed her, mildly. "You should not have trouble finding it. Oh, but do not go through the gate of my brother-in-law. He will not appreciate your intrusion into what he still considers his sovereign domain." She rolled her eyes.

Selene grabbed at that reference like a swimmer grasping at rocks at the shore of a swift river. Who was it Dante put at the edge of the pit? He'd borrowed him from the Greeks. Minos, she was pretty certain. If Minos were this woman's brother-in-law . . .

Her thoughts only got this far before they were swept away by Albatross, when she said: "That is no matter: I can fly there, I'm pretty certain."

"I would not recommend that," said Kirke. "The skies over Hell are treacherous—besides, you'll not want to get swept off the ground on the second ledge, otherwise you might become trapped there. I wish I could send you a poet—poets are, in my experience, the best guides—but your poet built her own craft and would not remain here."

Selene discovered she'd washed up against a resolution. It was a course she'd somehow known she was going to have to take—the one she'd expected to take the moment she'd let go of her gun and fallen out of her world and into this strange amalgam of mythologies—and returning to it now gave her a surprising sense of courage and relief.

"I'll go with her," she offered, bluntly.

Kirke looked at her sharply, and Selene almost had it.

A witch she was, certainly, and a very powerful one. Not Hecate, but like Hecate. Someone from the Odyssey. Kalypso? Someone who lived on an island, anyway.

Clara would have known, but Clara wasn't here.

"You?" said Kirke, inquiringly. "A living soul?"

Selene shrugged. "I got nothin' better to do."

Mother Kirke sat back in her chair, regarding Selene with tempered respect.

"Very well," she announced, in a voice that declared their little interview over. "I'll give you both a single night on my island, to prepare yourselves, and an accompaniment of cranes to show you the way to the Pit. I shall not wish you luck, for that is not my boon to give. I will, however, grant you good will, and an open door when you eventually return—as all living souls must do."

She brought her hands together in a firm, single clap, and then the bear and the cow-woman were herding Selene and Albatross away from the throne, through a little postern door, and into a wide, comfortable hall leading deeper into the house.

To Selene's surprise night did fall on the island of Kirke. It was a gentle gloaming, hardly darker than the day, and the stars that came out in the purple sky remained fixed where they were. Selene spent the night sitting on the balcony of the little room they had given her, staring at them, and wondering if they were really stars at all.

Dawn came like a sigh as pinkness breathed out across the sky, muting the stars and driving the purple back into the distance. It bleached to a pale, grayish blue, but long before that Selene had left her balcony, gone back through the courtyard and out of the house, where she waited by the gate. She was certain Albatross would not leave without her, and she didn't want to spend any more time in that house than she had to. She had figured out who Kirke was, and this made her all the more determined not to eat or drink anything. Which was becoming more and more difficult, since she'd gotten hungry again in the night, and tired, too. But she dared not sleep, and to eat anything would mean she'd be stuck there for . . . well, for at least a very long time.

She found a rock with a nice view of the bay where the girl Lina had beached her boat and sat there, waiting. The smell of pine and citrus drifted up from the crescent valley, but it was once more muted and distant. Her hunger abated. She was neither cold nor hot, happy nor unhappy, frightened nor confident. At her back, her shield was cold and still, heavy with potential.

After a while the gates opened and Albatross came out, accompanied by two slender people with long necks and beaks. Cranes, Selene realized, seeing their snowy wings. There was also a small, thin person who walked in a winding, uncertain way. Their skin was bright red and glittered a little, as if made of scales. Selene blinked.

"Hello," said the serpent, waving a narrow hand. "Came to see you off."

They made a funny-looking human, Selene thought. Bald and childlike, but narrow and grave, like an adult. And their gender was impossible to place.

She waved back.

"Thanks, I think."

"You could do worse than to stay here," the serpent pointed out, modestly. "Kirke's not a bad one, as far as the old witches go."

Selene shrugged. "We all gotta do what we gotta do," she said.

"But you don't *have* to," the serpent pointed out.

Selene looked over at Albatross, who was rubbing her hands together, nervously, pulling at her thin fingers, and couldn't help smiling a little.

"Nah," she said. "But I wanna." She heaved herself down off the rock and went over to Albatross. "C'mon, sister, let's get this show on the road."

Albatross smiled, huge and radiant. She had been worried Selene would change her mind. She didn't want to do this alone, and Selene couldn't blame her.

The cranes had brought with them a harness of sorts that went around Selene's shoulders and waist and provided a place for her to hitch the shield, and handles for Albatross to grab onto. She buckled herself into it, and Albatross took hold of the loops of leather in both hands.

"Ready?" she whispered excitedly, her breath ghosting past Selene's ear.

"When you are," Selene replied, gamely. She turned to wave goodbye to the serpent, but that was the moment Albatross leapt into the air, so it wound up being an awkward flail as she was dragged forward, toward the nearest cliff. A thundering of wingbeats around her suggested the cranes were doing the same, but everything was a jumble of rock and treetops, sky and lake, until she felt her feet leave the ground and they were plummeting down a tree-covered mountainside.

That only lasted for a few moments, however. The straps of the harness bit into Selene's armpits, ran tight across her chest, and then the world fell away below her as Albatross caught an updraft that lifted them up and away from the island. The island of Aeaea. The witch's island. Circe's island. Where Odysseus's crew had been turned into pigs.

In the end she'd just had to spell the name out in the dust on the floor of her room, and it had been perfectly obvious.

But now that island was far behind them and growing more distant as Albatross began to find her stride through the shifting air, the cranes beating furiously to keep up. By contrast, Albatross barely flapped at all. Her wings had come out, pale and grayish so they melted into the sky, for what felt like miles on either side of them, like her wingtips could touch each horizon. She tilted them this way and that, and they sped along over the flat, black surface of the lake below.

Eventually Albatross took pity on the cranes and slowed her flight. They surged in front gratefully, and steered them around in a great arc, so they were continuing in the direction from which they had approached the island in the first place. Selene saw it slide by far to their right, a little green lump on the black surface.

Ahead there rose a distant shore studded with gray mountains, and one which reached up high enough that it was crowned with snow. They looked like mountains on the edge of the world, and as they approached, Selene saw this was not entirely untrue.

The mountains lay some miles on past the shore of the lake, over rough, rolling hills covered in golden grass and sparsely dotted with scrubby trees, and beyond them there was . . . nothing. Well, there were clouds which curled into a vortex, filling in a giant space of emptiness which the mountains marked the limit of.

The cranes descended as they approached, so that Selene never got a good look at it from the air. Only when they landed on the far side of the mountains, and Albatross landed too, was she able to look down and see that they had come to the edge of a vast, and apparently bottomless, pit. Lightning forked in the gray clouds ahead of them, and rising up from below was a sharp, fierce wind smelling of cigarettes, fetid outhouses, spoiled fish, and, conversely, sweet wine and honey. It was enough to make Selene feel nauseous, until she remembered to push the feeling away again.

The land they were on sloped down gently, so it was difficult to tell where the safe ground ended and the vertical fall began. But the surface was of rock, and it was cracked across in many places, so it looked like the climb would be doable if one were careful.

Hands slipped around her arm, and she looked down to find Albatross had let her wings go and was cowering there. The cranes were standing well back, their wings folded down tightly, and Selene remembered what Circe had said about the sky over Hell. It was treacherous.

She looked back over the cliff. She couldn't see the bottom. It just vanished into swirling clouds of black and gray, with here and there a flash of red. From the depths, along with the smell, there was the faint sound of screaming. And somewhere in there were the missing pieces of Albatross—whoever Albatross was.

"Okay," she said, patting Albatross's arm. "You just hold on then. Wouldn't do to get separated here." She waved at the cranes. "Thanks guys."

Then, unhitching her shield and bringing it around so that the moonface was between her and the bottomless pit, she began to lead Albatross over the lip and down the broken cliff. Howling winds whipped at her, and the rock gave treacherously under her feet, but she kept going.

One step at a time.

Down, down, slowly down, into the clouds, and the wind, and the stench, and the screams.

Cry
A white bird in the sky
Freedom I can't describe
The broken hearts on the ground
Will watch her pass by
I
Will follow where she goes
Where she lands no man knows
But I'll be there to catch her—oh!

Hallelu-yo!

I'm not the hero you asked for when
you stumbled into this pit,
I'm not an angel sent from on high to save you
I'm not a champion, but I'm what you've got!

And I will bring
A new song that you can sing
I'll be the wind beneath your wings
Lift you gracefully
And I will go
Across the desert of frozen snow
I'll be the light guiding your flight
I'll show you where you land
If you'll take my hand!

Moonrise Over Hades

We are queens in our own right
Two moons within one night
See truth reflected in our light.

Hallelu-yo

In the dark that lies between
This waking life and dreams
Your flight cuts through so sharp and clean

Hallelujah!

Wherever you go remember,
you won't be alone this time
'Cause I'm rising behind you strong and wide
I'm the queen of the waxing moon—watch me shine!

We will bring
A new song for them to sing
Face to the wind and spread your wings
Let them see you soaring
We can go
Beyond the bounds of the rivers' flow
Follow my light through this dark night
Let the silence hear you cry
As you cut the sky!

The white bird crossing a velvet sky
Cut cross the sky
Cut the sky
Cross it high

Storms and souls
Gather round and drift by in our wake
We'll remember them when we break open the Great Gate
Still we fly
Over water, cross fire with ease,
Two moons joined as one be-winged will take us
out of Hades

Storms and souls, remember, remember, storms and souls
Still we fly, over water, cross fire, through earth

Two moons joined as one wings of ice and steel take us out break free
Though our feet may be scorched we will walk
out of Hades

—Out of Hades/*Princess Die*

THE HOUR I FIRST *Believed*

3.

Somewhere on I-80 East, Western Pennsylvania
Early March

THE COLD WEAKENED as they rumbled south and east, but never went away entirely. The sky was uniformly gray and sent showers of chill rain every hour or so, which pattered ineffectually on Arcana's windshield and was quickly sluiced away by his wipers. The rig, which was big enough and heavy enough to haul multiple tons of livestock, sent up a spray of white mist behind him that would have blinded anyone foolish enough to follow too close, but he kept his nose high and Clara was able to see clearly out over the oncoming road, itself shining with reflected taillights from the cars in front of them.

Despite the inclement weather and the attendant traffic it had only taken them four hours to reach the Pennsylvania border. Clara, accustomed as she was to riding her motorcycle all day with nary a pee break, would have been content to power straight through to Harrisville, but when Mantha began to fidget as they passed Cleveland she had pulled off at Broadview Heights so that she could buy them sandwiches and so that Mantha could use the toilets. The girl hadn't said anything, but Clara could tell the difference between brooding silence and prideful abstention, and recognized in Mantha the same stubborn determination that had gotten her into so many uncomfortable situations as a child. And still did, she thought ruefully as she surveyed the selection of salted meat and oily vegetables she could have put between two pieces of white, airy bread.

She asked Mantha what she wanted when she emerged from the toilet, and the girl's eyes went wide when she saw the possibilities.

"Can I have peanut butter and jam?" she asked.

Clara repeated this to the long-suffering clerk, who sighed heavily but said, "Yeah, we can do that."

They ate their sandwiches at a plastic table next to the rain-streaked window, Mantha with relish—they had provided a glass of milk to go with her PB&J—and Clara with reluctant care, picking the slices of orange American Cheese Product off her roast chicken salad as she went.

They both needed to use the bathroom before they left, Mantha for a second time that took much longer than the first. Clara waited under the eaves of the building, staring across the parking lot to where there were signs advertising a haunted house with daily tours.

The last time she'd been in a haunted house it had been summer, and she had been with Selene. And it hadn't been actors decorated in fake blood. It had been a venture into the spirit world, and an audience with an oracle. Remembering that gave her a cold-hot pang under her collarbone that didn't fade until they'd put Cleveland well behind them.

They drove, and though the cold gray sky didn't change, the landscape slowly grew softer, more rolling, and trees, some with the first tentative hints of spring growth, crowded around the highway.

Mantha sat quietly, curled up in the passenger seat with her feet tucked under her, using her heavily patched and restitched stuffed rabbit as a makeshift pillow, watching the landscape slide past her window. She did not, as far as Clara could tell, sleep. But neither did she ask where they were going or whether they were there yet or how much longer they would be driving.

When they began seeing signs for Grove City, and Clara slowed down, not wanting to miss her exit, Mantha sat up straight and gave a little sigh.

"Your friend, Tesla. Is she like you?" she asked.

Clara pondered how to answer that while she squinted at the farthest green sign. For some reason they were harder to read from behind the truck's windshield than from inside her full-face helmet.

Tesla Isenfaust was not like her. Then again, no one, as far as Clara could tell, was like her. Not even her own siblings. But Tesla, along with her sister, Faraday, had always felt like relatives. They lived in the same strange, unsteady, half-unseen world that Clara and her family did. That Mantha did.

"Sort of," she said eventually, moving into the right lane. The way to Tesla's forge was not obvious, and it had been years since Clara's last visit. She took Exit 24 off of I-80 toward Grove City and Sandy Lake, an action which brought them around so that they faced west again. Then she turned left and headed south.

It had been summer last time, the fields had been green and the trees plump and the lakes full of birds. Now the road was eerily barren and many of the trees had broken branches and fallen limbs. The fields were brown, as yet untouched by spring. It had been a hard winter, and it wasn't over yet.

"Is she like a witch?" asked Mantha. The girl would wonder that. Her own puzzling abilities were not unlike that of a latent witch, but altogether more severe.

"Sort of," Clara said, scanning the trees to her left. There would be another road coming up, almost a U-turn, and she had missed it the time before—there it was.

Clara shifted into second and turned Arcana onto a narrow single-lane road with rough, gravelly shoulders and a bleak "No Outlet" sign at its side.

Mantha began to fidget. No wonder, Clara thought, when she realized how unsatisfactory her answers had been.

"Tesla's not a witch," she said. "Her sister, Faraday, is. We might meet Faraday, too. But maybe not. She moves around."

"And Tesla doesn't?"

"Tesla is a smith," Clara said. "She has a forge. She also knows a lot of things."

"Like maybe what I am?" Mantha suggested.

I hope so, Clara thought fervently. But she didn't want to give Mantha false hopes—or scare her unnecessarily—so what she said aloud was: "She might be able to figure that out."

They drove on, through fields and forests and over a wide creek, brown and gray reflecting the empty sky.

"What kind of smith?" Mantha asked.

"What?" said Clara, who'd begun scanning the righthand woods for her next turn.

"You said she was a smith," said Mantha. "Is she a blacksmith? Silversmith?"

"She is a wondersmith," Clara said. "She makes magic objects."

"Oh," said Mantha, evidently impressed. She fondled her limp, patchwork rabbit. "Do you think she could fix Lady Bibbit?"

Clara swallowed. It was her own personal opinion that only Mantha could put life back into the polyfill-and-acrylic body that had once been the vessel for Lady Bibbit, the walking, talking, intelligent rabbit-person. But Mantha seemed singularly resistant to this idea, so she shrugged.

"Why do you shrug like that?" Mantha asked.

"Like what?" asked Clara, and nearly missed her turn. They snuck up on you, these little roads with no stop signs, and this one had its street marker overhung by the branches of a spreading oak.

Once they had turned south again and were crunching along the uneven asphalt Mantha repeated the question.

"You don't shrug like a normal person. Your shoulders go down, then up. Why?"

Clara felt self-conscious, which made her shrug again, which made her feel more self-conscious. She gripped Arcana's wheel with both hands and squared her shoulders, to keep them still.

"I . . . don't know," she admitted. "It's just the way I do it."

"Oh, okay," said Mantha, apparently satisfied with this. She curled back toward her window and looked out over the landscape, which was now alternating newly plowed fields and wild, tangled woods. Every now and then they passed a small lake, its water bright from the pale sky, like a hole into another world.

Clara had run, barefoot and carefree, through many such fields. Had learned to swim in a lake not far from here. It had only been one summer, she realized with a small shock. The summer at the Isenforge. She had been seven. But that summer had seemed to contain within it the laughing, playing, sunny days and warm nights, sword lessons and swimming, and games and green corn fresh from the field, and the chilled watermelon of several summers. Maybe because it was the only summer of her life that had resembled what most people seemed to think of as a typical summer. The rest had been . . . well, she didn't remember much difference between the seasons before, and afterward they'd moved around so much "summer" was a relative term. Certainly there hadn't been time for whole afternoons spent swimming and catching frogs or building tree forts. After that it had all been training. Training and studying, and hunting and fighting.

It made coming back now, on the heels of a vicious winter, all the more startling. Clara almost didn't recognize the line of trees on the far side of an oblong field that marked her upcoming turn. And when she reached it, it was the wrong road.

She pulled Arcana off onto the shoulder, just past a large, square house with an RV parked in the drive.

Mantha looked up expectantly, but when Clara made no move to stop the engine or get out, she relapsed back into her seat.

Clara rested her hands on the steering wheel, bent her head, and concentrated.

South off I-80 onto 173, left on Daugherty Road, right onto 888, past the auto-wrecking park, cross Swamp Run, and then . . .

She looked up. The house was still there. Someone was peering out at them from a front window. The road sign still said Whitaker School Drive.

Clara sighed, put Arcana in gear, and executed a careful three-point-turn and drove back the way they had come.

About a mile on she stopped and did another, leaving deep tracks in the soft earth of the shoulder.

"Trying again," she said, before Mantha could ask any questions.

This time she concentrated on the present. On the line of trees. On the choked waters of Swamp Run.

This time when they reached the house with the RV, there were two roads leading off to their left—though one was so narrow it was almost invisible behind the branches of an ancient walnut which grew between them. A walnut which had not been there before, either. Clara drove past it with relief, and on down the narrow road which soon took them out of sight of the house with the RV, and of any other road entirely. The only sign of human habitation were the power poles, which supported heavy, drooping wires, and marched along loyally beside the dirt track.

Detroit, MI

The first week after Clara's departure was unbelievably quiet. Jill had actually managed to get done all the things she could reasonably expect to get done, and considering she slept very little these days, this was a lot. Over the course of the week the renovations for the main concourse of the Michigan Central Station–turned-MCSIR Headquarters were completed, the upper floors were cleaned and prepped, and the new heating system was finally made to work. Of course it was at this point that the weather finally broke and they had three whole days of blissful sunshine and above-freezing temperatures, but it was good for Marcus.

Marcus felt the cold more than Jill or Lansing, and of course Frosty made the place colder just by her presence there. She didn't seem to mind the heightened temperature either, but to Jill's surprise it made her feel sluggish and hazy.

"I think we operate better at a lower body temperature," she remarked to Lansing over breakfast.

This was a sordid affair of righteously healthy lean steak with vegetables for Jill, and a black coffee for Lansing. Not black as in she drank it without cream—she put almost half a cup of milk in it—but black as in it had been brewed in animal blood. The result was a thick, powerful mixture whose smell made Jill feel dizzy, so Lansing drank it through a straw with a cap over her cup.

The pale vampire, her dark hair newly trimmed in a boyish fringe around her face, sucked on the straw thoughtfully.

"If I get too cold my joints stiffen up," she said.

"Well, yes," said Jill. "If our internal tissues begin to freeze that would cause problems. But I've been taking my temperature hourly over the last three days, and I definitely feel the best at night, when my body temperature is between twelve point five and fifteen point five degrees."

Lansing nearly snorted a chunk of blood coffee out her nose.

"Celsius," Jill added.

Lansing wiped her nose anyway, then wiped her hand on a napkin.

"Your temperature changes?" she asked.

"Yes," said Jill. "A lot. It's like I have no internal regulation any more. Whatever temperature my environment is, I will eventually become that temperature. Except going outside when it's freezing I can keep from doing that as long as I remain active—but that's just the same thing as leaving the water on at a trickle so it doesn't freeze in the pipes. If you left me outside overnight you'd have a Jill-sicle."

Lansing frowned. "I have heard of that happening," she admitted. She gave Jill a shrewd look from under one heavy eyebrow.

"Would you like me to start tracking my internal body temperature?"

Jill clasped her hands over her remaining vegetables and grinned brightly. "Oh, *would* you?"

Lansing was sighing and asking if Jill had a thermometer she could use when Marcus came back from his evening run with Frosty.

The lean white dog was even whiter than usual, as if she had soaked up the pale moonlight, and her red ears were practically crimson. She was panting in great, frigid gusts all over Jill's knee, so she bent and rubbed the dog behind her ruddy ears.

"Did you have a good run?" she asked.

"Sure," said Marcus. "Only I had about three cops stop to talk to me."

Jill frowned. She understood that Marcus, who was over six feet tall and registered as Black despite his shocking head of orange hair, had more to fear from human cops than he did from most supernatural entities, and it grated on her that there wasn't anything she could do about it.

"Did any of them give you a hard time?" she asked.

It had been the same with Selene. Selene had been wary of police—and with good reason. Selene had been the one to show that to Jill.

"No," said Marcus, as if this fact still surprised him. "They all recognized me as working for ... uh ... working at MCSIR. They've been having problems, I guess, with werewolves."

"Not our problem," said Lansing, briskly.

"Yes, yes, our problem," Jill reminded her, leaning over the table toward Marcus. "Or, our business, anyway. What sort of problems?"

Marcus shifted uncomfortably from foot to foot, scratching Frosty behind one red ear when she pressed her head into his hand.

"They weren't really ... well. I think their problem is that there *are* werewolves."

"Ah," said Jill, missing Selene more than ever. Selene knew about werewolves. Clara did too, but Clara was less inclined to share what she knew. Hesitantly, she glanced back at Lansing.

"Don't look at me," said the vampire, primly. "I'd just make things worse."

"Because you're a vampire?" Jill asked. "What's up with that, anyway?"

Lansing drained her cup and looked at the ceiling.

"Werewolves don't like vampires," she said, blandly.

"So I've gathered," said Jill, mercilessly. "Why is that?"

Lansing inhaled and then puffed the air into her cheeks before letting it out with an exasperated *whupping* sound.

"Is it, like, a racist thing?" asked Marcus.

Lansing shrugged. "For some vampires, maybe," she admitted. "Mostly, we don't like them because they like to kill us."

"Werewolves do?" asked Jill.

"Yep," said Lansing, shortly. "They're not very good at it, of course, but they like to try. Something about the way we smell, I think."

Jill sniffed. Her sense of smell had become much more sensitive since her shift into the not-a-vampire that she was now, but all she smelled off Lansing was the cool scent of earth and the faint tang of blood and coffee which she had just imbibed.

"Huh," said Jill, and frowned. "Sounds like we need to talk to a were-wolf."

"Really?" said Lansing, her voice dry as a desert. "You're just going to trot north of the 8 Mile and ask the Southfield pack to be your buddies?"

"I don't know about any packs," said Jill. "But I do know a werewolf. And she owes me a favor."

So after Lansing had gone to work sorting through the landslide of emails which had arrived that day, and Marcus had gone to bed, Jill took Frosty up to her office and made some phone calls.

This office was the renovated executive suite on the top floor of the building and included, in a string of rooms behind the main reception area, a workroom and lab, a light-safe, and a fire pole which ran down the entire height of the building. This had been put in place of the old boiler shaft, now rendered obsolete, and had been Flammard's suggestion.

"Always have an escape plan," he'd said when Jill expressed surprise at his suggestion.

Which had seemed a silly reason at the time, but the more Jill thought about it, the more it nagged at her, until she mentioned it to Clara, who had nodded gravely and agreed.

So the pole had been put in, and even though Jill had yet to take advantage of it, knowing it was there did give her a strange sense of security.

Her desk was set up to face the main door to her office. In arranging it that way she had constantly asked herself "How would Selene organize this room?" As a result she had also spent a lot of time staring out the tall, ornate windows, feeling strange, cold tears prickle at the corners of her eyes, hardly seeing the view which these afforded her.

Sitting back in her chair now, after having been assured by Detective Wilco that Janine-the-werewolf would get back to her once she got off her dinner break, Jill found herself gazing out over the interlinking freeways and patchwork light-and-dark squares of Detroit, while on the horizon the riverfront gleamed with neon and the bustle of evening traffic. The towers of the financial district, glittering with yellow squares of light, were just visible, and from her vantage point Jill could almost imagine flying down over those buildings, swooping in and out, like a bird.

It was one of the reasons she'd moved her office from the relative safety of the main concourse to this lofty perch: being confined to the light-safe areas of the Center during the day, and sleeping in her underground bunker had given her a distinct craving for open spaces and the ability to see more than twenty feet in any direction.

In front of her, her computer chirped as the emails that had gotten past Lansing presented themselves in her inbox. There was a reply from Professor Okedo, a query from a D. Harlan about the existence of zombies, and nothing from Clara.

Jill frowned. Clara had warned her that Tesla Isenfaust lived in an area with poor cell reception, so Jill had not tried calling her. But she had promised to make whatever trek was necessary to get to a landline or the internet in order to check in at least once a week.

So although Jill had been checking Clara's location almost fanatically, she had refused to worry even though it had been telling her Location Not Available for the past seven days.

But that first week was up now, and Jill was beginning to feel the familiar nervous twist in her stomach at the radio silence on Clara's end.

But Clara could take care of herself, she remembered. Clara had Arcana and her sword and was going to visit an old friend. Whatever happened, it shouldn't be anything she could not handle.

So Jill pursed her lips and opened Okedo's email, putting her worries about Clara firmly in the back of her mind while she tackled the problem of how to ship volatile chimera remains across the country.

Elsewhere

Clara dreamed. She hadn't meant to, but it happened anyway. She was lying in something soft but poky and pine-scented, and the air around her was warm and sweet and smelled of a summer's childhood. In the way of dreams the landscape unfolded around her without her really looking at it: bushy oaks and drooping willows; a sycamore half covered in blooming kudzu loomed to her left, dropping its purple-cloaked branches almost to the surface of the lake.

This lake was not the lake from her last dream, nor was it quite the lake she remembered from her childhood. That lake had been invitingly green but scummy once you got into it. This one was bright blue and crystal clear. Across its surface on the far shore something white had come down to drink at the water's edge. Clara did look then, though she knew at once that it was the stag.

He was beautiful, like he always had been, but this time Clara was able to sit and watch—could appreciate how his coat sparkled in the sun and reflected its glow onto the foliage around him. His flanks were full and powerful, and his antlers rested proudly on his head. Though they were as white as the rest of him, there was something twined about their tines that did not shine: something dark and green. Oak leaves.

For some reason this filled Clara with dread, and as if sensing her discomfort the stag raised his head and snorted, and a moment later was bounding off into the wood, visible only as a white flash between the trees, and then not visible at all.

At the same moment there was a splashing at the edge of the lake and Ariel flailed out of the water and began wading toward the shore.

He was naked from the chest up and—no, he was *completely* naked. Clara averted her eyes, but not before she saw that most of him was covered in tattoos. His chest and arms were dark with them, and there were even a few on his legs. She wanted to look again, to see if she could recognize any of them. She knew she shouldn't. That would be rude. And then she thought: *this is a dream, he probably won't mind.* Then Ariel said, in a conversational way:

"Well, damn."

"Damn, what?" Clara asked, still resolutely looking off over the lake. An egret had come to hunt on the far shore, the white bird taking the place of the white stag.

There was some more splashing and then a *smssh* of feet on sand.

"I mean, damn, this is one of those dreams where you're doing something important only you've got no clothes on," Ariel's voice said.

Clara blinked down at herself, momentarily afraid—but no, she was wearing her normal leather jacket—zipped all the way up—long pants and boots. She was sans gloves, but otherwise well covered. She put her hands in her pockets anyway.

"Swimming is important?" she asked, confused.

Ariel didn't reply. There was a crunching and shuffling, as if he was pawing about in the bushes up the bank.

"Seeing you is important," he said eventually, his voice oddly small. Then, in more normal tones, he went on: "Crap. Look, you haven't seen a pile of clothes anywhere? Even, like, a damp towel?"

Clara dared cast her eyes away from the lake, sweeping them down to the ground, of which she made a careful search.

There were no clothes, but they did eventually find a sarong someone had left hanging in the branches of a lilac bush. It was the same color as the blossoms would be, and the hem was finished with a fringe of pink threads.

"There," Ariel said triumphantly after he had wrapped it around his waist and tied the two ends together, so the part was over his right thigh. "I am now a good and modest boy, clad in floral glory. You may look upon my magnificence and yet live."

Clara did look at him then, a little reproachfully. He was standing very straight and proud, his hands at his waist and the sarong hanging low off his hips in a fall of pale purple and pink. About five inches of hairy shin and his feet were visible beneath, and these were the only pieces of skin—apart from his face—that were not covered in tattoos. His chest, shoulders, arms, and sides of his abdomen were all thoroughly decorated, and so densely that it took Clara several minutes to decipher them.

First and most obviously, since it alone was in red ink, was the solar wheel over his left breast. It had eight arms of swirling flame connecting the central circle to the outer wheel, and was matched on the opposite side by a double spiral. Below this there was a collection of straight dashes and crosses that Clara eventually realized was something written in Ogham—but she couldn't read it. Both the writing and the spiral were in blue, and seemed to go together.

Over his right shoulder, in thick black strokes, was an endless knot, while his entire left arm was covered by a twining creature with feathery wings, half-obscured by stylized clouds. It might have been a dragon, or a phoenix, or a mix of both. Its tail feathers ended abruptly just above his wrist, about an inch short of where the cuff of a dress shirt would lie. From what Clara could see of his right arm, below the knot it was a patchwork of pact runes. Most of these were pale and inactive, like the one she herself carried, but a few were burned black. One, curiously, had a red slash through it—signifying that he had renounced his claim upon that particular target.

His abdomen was unmarked, but there was an open scroll—blank—on his left side, and on his right were letters which, after Clara turned her head a little sideways, she saw spelled out the ten commandments. However, the "other" in the first, and all of the second, third and fourth had been crossed out, while "and thy children" had been added at the end of the fifth.

There was something curling around his waist, peeking out above the line of the sarong. It looked like it could be a snake, but Clara didn't dare ask. Instead she raised her eyes, and found them focusing on the wreath of oak leaves that sat around his neck.

Clara realized she was being heinously rude to stare so, but then again this *was* a dream and in her dream the oak leaves symbolized something terrible, and she wasn't sure why or what. It bothered her.

"Do you like them?" Ariel asked.

Clara glanced up to find him grinning at her almost coyly, a flash of white all up one side of his face and his eyes twinkling. But there was a nervous quality to his face and his voice, as though her opinion was important to him and he wasn't certain what it would be.

"The oak leaves," Clara said, pointing inarticulately.

"Oh, these," said Ariel, laying a hand over them as if they were a pearl necklace. "They're part of the rest."

"The rest," repeated Clara, blankly.

For answer, Ariel turned around.

His entire back was covered by a broad, branching oak tree. The leaves cascaded over his shoulders and mingled with the dragon-phoenix on one side and the endless knot on the other. Its wide trunk ran the length of his spine, painstakingly colored in brown and gold. A squirrel was in the action of running up its length, while on the other side a falcon dove toward the ground. Over his right shoulder blade an eagle perched among the branches, staring critically across to where, on the left, there was a man hanging from the branches by his wrists and ankles. The leaves around his head drooped low, obscuring his face; an accidental crown.

Below the hanged man, almost nipping at his toes, was a roebuck, done in brassy red, and on the opposite side of the trunk a white sow foraged among the roots. Also entwined among the roots was the body of a giant snake, its scales individually inked like the bark of the tree. Along its back were the words, in neat, block capitals, FATE BEING NECESSITY.

"It is Yggdrasil," Clara murmured. "The World Tree." Unthinking she reached out and brushed a finger over the words. "Urd, Skuld, Vernandi," she whispered. "The Norns."

Ariel shivered. It was a shiver that began at the base of his spine, where Clara had touched him, and traveled up and across his shoulders so that his head shook.

She took her hand away.

Ariel turned around slowly, but he was smiling. "Or the Fates," he said. "Clotho, Lachesis, Atropos. I'm convinced they are one and the same. That's why I used the English words. It was the concept that was important, more than the names."

"They are more than that," Clara said. She withdrew her hand.

"Oh?" said Ariel. He seemed amused, but interested.

Clara bit her lip. She'd remembered the importance of oak. It was the king of the waxing year, fated to be killed and consumed at the summer solstice, replaced by his tanist, the holly king.

But that was a part of an order than was long ago and far away. The Triple Goddess had been broken, and the pieces of her scattered so far and wide that they each took on a life of their own. Clara looked at Ariel, or her perception of Ariel, and decided this was her subconscious playing a cruel joke on her. She forced herself to smile and shook her head.

But the dream version of Ariel, being as he was a part of her own mind, naturally knew what she had been thinking.

"Not everything is what it first appears," he said, and tugged the sarong down in front so that the half-hidden snake was fully visible.

Clara looked despite her ingrained modesty, and saw that it wrapped all the way around his waist, and that its tail disappeared into its mouth.

Not Jörmungandr, then. An ouroboros. A symbol of renewal, not destruction. Like the endless knot and the phoenix, and, Clara realized, the Oak King himself, who was reborn each winter.

Ariel pulled the sarong up and conscientiously tightened the knot at his hip. He reached forward and took Clara's hands, which had been hanging limply in front of her. His thumbs brushed the tip of the mark which was visible there, but he asked no questions.

He was, after all, only a reflection of Ariel, dancing on the surface of her heart like the moon reflected in the lake. He already knew everything she did.

His hands squeezed hers once, gently.

"It'll be all right, Claymore," he said.

He seemed about to say more, but then Clara woke up.

She came awake jarringly, the two versions of reality sliding against each other like pieces of broken glass. The dream shattered, and Clara opened her eyes to discover the morning was cool and chill, and frost had formed on the outside of their blanket.

But Mantha was warm and safe in her arms, protected from the cold and the elements, her stuffed rabbit clutched close to her chest just as she was pressed to Clara's.

That must have been what confused her, Clara thought. She had become so used to sleeping alone that the feeling of another body beside her was disorienting.

She sat up, careful to shift the blanket so it still covered Mantha, and looked around.

Their camp had been undisturbed in the night: the wards remained, elegant and erect and shining silver, not a blemish on them. Down by the lake, Arcana was taking a drink beside his pile of gear. The great ram's burgundy-red coat was the only splotch of warm color on the otherwise frigid landscape, the copper lines of his own wards shining against the dark fur.

Clara dismantled their circle of wards, took the poles down to the lakeside and packed them up. At the same time she removed their food and assembled a cold breakfast for herself and Mantha. Arcana, who had been grazing all night, watched her work impassively.

Mantha had sat up and was rubbing her eyes by the time Clara returned bearing two wide wooden cups with cheese and bread and dried fruit. They ate methodically and silently, taking turns drinking from Clara's flask of purified water. When they had finished Clara loaded the tack back onto Arcana, and hung the thin silver chain around his neck. Giving Mantha a knee up, she helped the girl settle into the makeshift saddle between their bedrolls and the food bags, and then took the long end of the chain and began leading the ram away around the lake. Overhead the sky lightened from gray to blue, and when the sun struck its rays across the world below it came alive with light, glimmering off the water and sparkling on the frosted baby leaves which decorated the trees.

They walked slowly but steadily, and soon outdistanced the lake. They began winding their way along an avenue of high ground between two marshy expanses, and around midday came upon another lake, with a low hill of bare ground on the far side, at the summit of which sat a dark, squat, square building with a large smokestack on one end and a collection of corrals and sheds clustered around it.

Clara's heart thrilled at the sight of it, but at the same time she felt a pang of trepidation. The flag was not flying, and there was none of the activity she remembered as being a defining feature of the Isenforge. Blackest of all: there was no steam rising from the chimney. The forge was cold.

"Is that it?" asked Mantha. It was the first time she had spoken that day, and her tone was carefully neutral.

Clara frowned. "It should be."

Behind her, Arcana snorted wet, warm breath down her neck.

"Should we go find out?" Mantha asked.

Clara didn't answer at once. She was gazing across at the forge, trying to discern any sign of life, but all was silent and still. Not even the chickens were out.

Wait. There was something. Something flapping from a fencepost. Pale and feathery but stained red near the bottom.

Clara didn't wait to see more. Without hurrying she quickly led Arcana out of sight of the forge and there took out one of the ward posts, which she buried in the soft earth. Hooking a loop of his chain around the top of it, she went around to his flank and laid her hand on Mantha's knee.

"I need you to wait here," she said. "But if Arcana senses danger, let him lead you away."

Mantha pursed her lips and said nothing, but she nodded seriously.

Clara went back to Arcana's head, stroked his neck once, a farewell, and then slipped off through the bushes.

She did not approach the forge directly. That way would be keenly watched, and she suspected they had already been seen. So she made a wide circuit of the place, slowly tightening her course so that she drew closer without ever actually walking straight at it.

Along the way she crossed the path the attackers had used: the old cart road, which was still the easiest way to get to the forge if you had a lot of equipment to carry. And they had had a lot to carry, by the look of it: deep gouges in the soft earth from heavily laden carts, skid marks from slipped hooves, and here and there a dropped sack or piece of armor.

Wait.

Clara crouched at the side of the road, staring at the tracks with growing alarm.

This was not the way the attackers had come. This was the way they had left. All the skid marks showed that the beasts had been bound *away* from the forge, and what army left a piece of armor or a sack of grain lying in their wake?

A returning army, so laden with spoils they were overflowing, careless of the mess they left behind because their work was done.

Clara dropped all attempt at stealth and fairly sprinted down the road. With luck they might have left a small guard who she could press—perhaps literally—for information. With luck, Tesla might still be there, safe in her strongbox.

Coming upon the forge felt like stepping on an open wound. Clara winced as she passed through what had once been the main gate, but was now a frame of blackened wood, the anvil-upon-diamond having been torn down and trampled into the earth.

Upon closer inspection it was clear the forge was deserted. There was a dead silence about the place that warned Clara before she came around to the main yard and found the slaughter.

Tesla did not keep birds, but birds liked to keep Tesla company. Chickens flew their coops and came to live in her yard. Turkeys congregated and a small colony of guinea hens had made the roof their home. There had even been an aged heron, her feathers more gray than blue, who had kept the whole place as her sovereign state.

That majestic bird was probably long dead from old age, but every single remaining bird had been slaughtered without exception.

Hens lay hither and thither all over the yard, their necks snapped or their skulls crushed. Many were transfixed with arrows. A blackened pit filled with reddish bones showed where many must have been cooked and devoured. And the fine black cock who had dragged himself into Tesla's kitchen on a Friday the 13th had been crucified to the side of the house. Many more hens and guinea fowl had been dismembered and their parts scattered about. The wing of a tawny hen had been nailed to a fence post. That was what Clara had seen from across the lake.

Clara walked through the bloody yard and felt her heart ice over with frozen fury with every step she took. Then she came around the corner and found the great blue had not died of old age after all.

She was crouched under the lintel of the back door, her head tucked serenely over her back. She might have been asleep but for the flies which clustered, undeterred, around her eyes and beak and the gaping hole in her chest that had been the end of her. But also on her beak was dried red blood, and her talons too.

She had fought, and she had survived long enough to come out from hiding and die on the doorstep of the woman she loved.

Clara picked up the body, featherlight and limp, and found it still warm. She placed it gently beside the door and covered it with her cape. Then she went inside.

The interior of the forge was just as much of a disaster as the exterior. The place had been thoroughly looted without any regard to the structural integrity of the building itself. The wall that had once held the great mirror had been knocked messily out, and Clara stepped through the ragged hole directly into the forge itself.

The stove alone remained untouched in a sea of metal scraps and tools that had been deemed too common or worthless to carry off. The anvil too had resisted assault, though someone had gone so far as to tip it over.

The stained-glass windows had been removed or smashed, and the floor below them was littered with pink and red chips of glass.

Clara moved through it all numbly. She checked the forge and the main room and the kitchen and all the bedrooms before descending, her heart in her throat, into the basement.

The strongbox was still there, neatly sealed. Clara rapped out the all-clear on its surface, and when there was no answer, she tried her opening words.

It sprang open readily, revealing a neat bedroll, a small well, firebox, bucket and larder. Everything was pristine and untouched and there was no one inside.

Only then did Clara feel the tightness in her stomach loosen somewhat, though her heart remained furiously iced. She climbed up out of the basement and went out through the remains of the front door. She unearthed the diamond-anvil from where it had been half buried and propped it up against the gate.

She was in the process of wrapping the heron in a shroud scavenged from the whitest bedsheet she could find when there was the sound of approaching hooves and she drew her sword and turned around to find Mantha and Arcana walking up the main drive. The girl had the ward pole carried over her shoulder and the chain glinting in her hand.

"What happened?" Clara demanded.

Martha shrugged.

"Arcana sensed danger," she explained. "He led us here."

All the nerves on Clara's back prickled at her words. She scanned the horizon—what she could see of it for all the close-packed trees—and then without a word ushered Mantha and Arcana in under the gate and around to the back of the house.

Mantha nearly tripped at sight of the carnage in the backyard, but otherwise did not react. Arcana snorted, blowing an angry breath which ruffled the feathers of the dead birds.

"I know," Clara found herself saying. "I'd not had the chance to clean up yet." She pushed Mantha toward the back door. "Keep out of sight as much as you can."

Arcana snorted again, but obligingly picked his way through the field of dead avian bodies to stand in the doorway of the barn.

Clara led Mantha to the main room and there gestured for her to wait.

"If they get past me," she told her, "go down those steps and lock yourself in the strongbox. I will come for you when I have finished."

Mantha did not ask for an explanation, just nodded gravely.

Clara left her among the rubble of Tesla's living room and went around to the front of the house again, where she hid herself behind the overturned wagon.

She did not have long to wait. Within fifteen minutes she heard hoofbeats on the road, and these drew steadily nearer until she judged the intruder was at the remains of the gate. Still she kept herself hidden, listening to the sound of the footfalls and trying to gauge how many there were.

To her surprise it sounded like a lone rider. And then she realized that was wrong, too. It sounded like a hoofed animal with only two feet. A hoofed animal with only two feet who was poking around the front yard, turning over pieces of fence or metal, as if looking for something.

Clara chanced a peek over the rail of the wagon, and saw a small, goat-footed person bent under the weight of a bulging pack, using a long stick with a hook on the end to extract a length of chain from the tumbled earth.

Not a soldier: a scavenger.

Clara surged out from behind the wagon, covered the ground between them in two strides, and struck the person—who had a human head and torso—hard on the side of their neck.

They went over with a strangled neighing sound but they had barely hit the ground before Clara had pulled their pack half off their back, pinning their arms. They kicked. Clara dodged.

"Who did this?" she demanded, above the bleating cry the person was making. "I shall not harm you if you speak with me. Who did this?"

The bleating failed, replaced by a petulant voice.

"Not I, dark knight, not I! I only come after, to ... to clean the slate. Yes? Clean the slate!"

"You are a scavenger and a thief," Clara remarked, emotionlessly. "You will not pillage this scene. But I may reward you if you tell me what occurred here."

"I know nothing!" cried the satyr—for satyr they were: Clara could see the horns curling out from behind their ears.

"You are a scavenger," Clara repeated. "You follow the army. Which army was here?"

"Th-the Lord of Stormvault," admitted the scavenger. "He—he desired a weapon from the Wondersmith. He sent a general, but she would not see him. So they ... they ... "

"I saw what they did," Clara said coldly. "What did they do with her?"

"I did not see," said the satyr, and when they saw the look on Clara's face they whimpered. "I did not see! By the Ninefolded One I did not see! I think they took her south—to the Stormvault Castle. They certainly all went south ... "

Clara rose, allowing the satyr to right themself. Drawing their enormous pack well up onto their shoulders they glared up at her. They stuck out a slightly furry hand with thick, stubby nails, and made a grabbing gesture.

"My reward?"

Clara sighed. She took a knife from her belt and put it into the outstretched hand, sheath and all. The strong fingers closed around it, and with a yelp of delight the little satyr turned on their trotters and scampered off through the gate.

Clara did not afford them a second thought. That knife she kept purposefully visible on her person. Anyone attempting to get a weapon off her—or anyone gifted with that knife—would be hard put to get it out of its sheath, and even if they did, they would find the blade to be made of soft, blunt wood.

Arcana had come out of the barn and was waiting just around the corner, his tail swishing unhappily, but Mantha was still sitting where Clara had left her, her head in her hands. She stood up when she saw Clara, her face full of unspoken questions.

"My friend is still alive," Clara told her.

"Then what do we do now?" Mantha asked.

Clara only had to think about this for a moment.

"We will bury Aged Azure," she declared. "Then we will go south."

Mantha had followed Clara's directions because she couldn't think of anything better to do. Clara seemed to know what she was doing, even in this strange new world they had blundered into. Mantha wasn't sure what it was, but it felt old. She assumed this was just one of the quirks about the place Tesla Isenfaust lived in. Perhaps the reason she was so hard to find. But when Clara said they were to go south, she realized that it was much larger—and stretched much farther—than she had first presumed.

Luckily Arcana, even in his beast form, was comfortable to ride. Mantha was able to spend most of the trip sitting on the straw pad that covered his back, between their bedrolls and the leather satchels in which Clara kept their food, water, extra clothes and weapons.

Clara, she was interested to note, seemed hardly changed at all by their new environment. The cut of her jacket and pants had changed, and her boots had gotten higher and flatter, but they were still made of black leather, still creaked as she moved in them, and still smelled of the same polish. The only major addition had been an oilcloth cape, which she had now rolled into a tube and tied over one shoulder.

Looking down at herself, Mantha had discovered that her jeans and sneakers had been replaced by a pair of leggings and soft moccasins, and her cotton shirt by a thin, wool dress. She had also gained a rather fine, thick leather belt, complete with pouches and little loops from which to hang things.

Of course, none of these changes could compare with what had come over Arcana. As a truck he had been impressive. As a ram he was downright mythical. Mantha thought he must have been the size of a draft horse or bigger. Certainly it felt like she was miles above the ground when she was on his back—but his back was so huge it was more like riding a table. Or a small island. His fur was ruggedly red and streaked with strange dots and swirls in sparkling copper. His horns were blackened and wrinkled, but near the ends where he had rubbed them chrome-silver showed through. His eyes, when he looked at something with great interest, smoldered orange and yellow.

They passed through a landscape that was both familiar and alien. Mantha felt like she had seen it before—in a dream or from a book, perhaps—but each new vista was a surprise to her.

The forest they were trudging through soon gave way to a high, grassy plain which rose to rolling, swelling hills capped with dark, spiky trees. The litter from the army they followed lessened—as if all the small, easily lost items had been jettisoned in the first five miles—but the tracks remained as deep and clear as ever.

Around midday they halted and took part in a lean lunch, while Arcana grazed on the soft grass. Mantha fell asleep in the saddle afterward, the sun and the food lulling her into a peace she knew she did not deserve but was determined to enjoy anyway.

Something was wrong. She woke up far too quickly and discovered the landscape had changed again while she dozed. They had come upon another forest—this one dominated by tall pines, drier and harsher, with crusty ferns growing in the dappled shade. At first she couldn't place what had startled her awake, and then she heard the rustling of wings in the treetops, followed by the croaking of ravens.

They were massed in the branches above their heads, hopping about as if jostling for position and cawing at each other. They showed no interest in Clara or Arcana or Mantha, but seemed to be congregating around an open space some twenty feet off the road; Mantha could see the sunlight pouring into it, reflecting off of bright green ferns, but the trunks of the trees blocked her view of anything else.

Clara stopped, and Arcana stopped obediently behind her. Mantha looked down and saw why.

The tracks from the army continued on through the forest along the main road, but just in front of where Clara stood, a small trail had been forged through the undergrowth—ferns were trampled and stripped, their pale undersides showing—toward the clearing. Someone had stuck a broken spear at the junction, to mark the spot.

Clara looked at the spear, looked at the road, and then toward the clearing. Finally she shrugged, and started off down the narrow path through the crushed ferns. Arcana followed, his nose practically in her hand.

The sun was bright and burned Mantha's eyes from her time under the trees, and so it took her a while to understand what was in that clearing. The first thing she saw was the shining white coat of the dead deer laid on its side with its intestines ripped out. It had been trussed up with each leg tied to a post driven into the ground, and when Mantha looked more closely she saw that there were two bloody holes where the antlers should have been.

Three creatures like vultures—but with the faces of women—were hopping all over the carcass, feasting on the entrails and tearing at the snowy fur with their teeth—which were long and pointed. Their faces, smeared brown and red from deer gut, all turned to look at Clara when she advanced on the terrible scene.

Clara's back was very straight and she walked with a calm purpose. She did not speak, but drew her sword and slashed at the vulture-women, causing them to shriek and cackle as they flapped away—but only as far as the nearest tree. Clara did not pursue them, but took her knife and cut away the deer's bonds. As she did so, Mantha saw that she was shaking. When this was done she knelt beside the deer's neck, gathering the huge head into her lap, bent her own head over it, and began to weep.

Mantha was shocked. She had seen Clara become emotional before, but only once, and then under the most dire conditions. This sudden outpouring of grief over a strange animal took her by surprise, and she found herself looking away—as if it were rude to witness the woman's moment of sorrow.

Arcana held no such delicate feelings. After less than a minute he began to snort and stamp his feet impatiently, ignoring Mantha when she stroked his neck and asked him to stop. Clara didn't seem to notice. She took a handsaw out of their pack and began cutting branches to cover the body, heaping them up until it was completely covered, not a single speck of white visible. The clearing smelled strongly of pine sap by the time she was done.

Only as they were leaving did she speak, and then it was in a small, desolate voice.

"He should not have been here," was all she said.

Then they left the clearing, where the vulture-women promptly descended again, trying to get at the meat under the tree limbs. But Clara had cut them so large, and laid them so carefully, that not another morsel of deer were they able to taste.

Detroit, MI

Jill considered herself to be a self-sufficient person, readily able to take care of her own interests as well as look out for her friends. But she had become accustomed to Selene and Clara's steadfast reliability, and the loss first one (permanently) and then the other (temporarily) was jarring. She felt it even more keenly now, as she waited by the lake at the Woodlawn Cemetery, perfectly alone but for the presence of Frosty, who had settled down at her feet, her head between her paws.

Janine-the-werewolf had not been particularly encouraging when asked about the specific problem confronting the Detroit police—namely, young male werewolves randomly attacking citizens—but she had offered some helpful insights which had led Jill to her current course of action.

Werewolves belonged to a class of being that was somewhat more alive than many others. Jill deduced this from Janine's laundry list of things that would not kill a werewolf—or which a werewolf could reasonably expect to recover from. These ranged from cancer to gunshot wounds in the head. Being so, Jill had hypothesized that perhaps their animosity toward vampires stemmed from the fact that vampires were somewhat *less* alive than most animals—being as they were a type of undead. Neither Janine nor Lansing were convinced, but the latter admitted that it was not impossible.

"I mean I'm sure it's more complicated than that," Jill had said. "But think about it. These sorts of primal aversions usually stem from some deep-seated fundamental difference that puts the two species at odds with each other."

"Yeah, that," said Janine, who had been on speakerphone at the time. "Or vampires are all big damn racists."

Jill had looked nervously at Lansing at that, but the woman—with her short, straight black hair and east-Asian features—merely rolled her eyes skyward.

But Janine had come through with one other extremely important piece of information.

"You're in Detroit, yeah?"

"Yeah," said Jill. "The old Michigan Central Railway Station."

"That's in Detroit proper. That's good," said Janine approvingly.

"And that's good because?"

"Neutral territory, isn't it?" said Janine.

"Yes," sighed Jill. "So I've heard. Doesn't seem to do much, except the rules are different here."

"Hell yeah they are," said Janine. "Didn't anyone tell you about Detroit?"

"Selene and Clara did mention something," Jill said. "But we didn't get a chance to go into specifics."

Before Selene died, she didn't add. And after that Clara had been no good for explaining anything.

"Right, well, I hope you're sitting down, kiddo, because it's story time," said Janine's scratchy voice. "Maybe about forty, forty-five years ago, there were these two brothers."

"The Brothers Gunn," Jill said. "David and Adam. I have heard of them."

"Oh?" said Janine, sounding amused. "Then maybe you've heard how there was an attempted apocalypse back in 1970? The Gunn boys stopped it, but it was a near thing. The Great Gate opened, a bunch of hell got let loose, and a lot of people died. And all that went down in Detroit—not far from were you're currently squatting."

Jill didn't bother to mention that actually she owned the property outright—or at least MCSIR, Inc. did—considering it was a vampire who had bought it for her.

"My point is," said Janine. "It ripped up all the magic around the place and fed in a bunch more. Left that whole area kind of soft and wild—not the best place to settle down and start a family. Weird things happen there. Weird to *our* sort of folk. So we don't generally mess about inside city limits. Those that *do* are asking for trouble. Now, you're setting up shop there—and not having the ceiling come down on your head—that speaks of something. It speaks to the fact that Detroit is no longer strictly neutral territory."

"It's not?" asked Jill.

"No," said Janine. "It's *your* territory. And the thing about having territory, hon, is that you've gotta defend it."

Which was how Jill had ended up lurking around a cemetery on the northern edge of Detroit at one in the morning. She had elected to go alone against the wishes of Lansing, on the grounds that her two primary means of defense were not available, and Marcus, though he had an unknown well of magical potential, wasn't trained for violent altercations.

"Besides," Jill had said, trying to be reasonable. "I'm not going there to start anything."

"Doesn't mean *they* won't," the vampire had said, darkly.

Frosty had been the only one she couldn't shake. The ghost-dog followed her closely, and even though she shut her in Lansing's office, the dog had been waiting for her when she arrived at the cemetery gates. She glowed in the night with a pale radiance, and a cool mist condensed around her form, making her look more than ever like some spiritual apparition. But her fur was solid and soft under Jill's hand when she butted her head against it, and Jill resignedly stroked her red ears before leading the way up the low hill dotted with headstones.

She was glad of Frosty's company now, as she sat by the lake and waited for whoever the werewolves would send to talk to her. She'd been very particular on that point. Talk. Not fight.

A smell of warm animal, thick and heady to her nose, wafted over the lake on a cool breath of night air. It made Jill's heart, normally subdued and barely active, give a desultory kick. She looked up.

Two men were standing on the far edge of the lake, almost invisible in the shadows. Jill could only see them because shadows couldn't hide things from her anymore. That and their smell.

They were both tall and gangly and rather scruffy around their chins. One was blond and the other dark-headed, but they both had rusty, tanned skin and lean, pointed faces.

Jill debated whether to hail them or not. She got the impression they were trying to case her without being noticed, and that it would be rude to interrupt. But after a minute or so she grew bored. There were emails waiting to be answered and her comparative magical intensity test to observe. She wanted to get this over with.

She turned her head to look directly at the werewolves and waved at them.

She saw them bristle and retreat into the trees, but a few minutes later they emerged on the path that led around the lake, walking in her direction. They sauntered casually, swinging their hips as if they were out for a morning stroll. They walked right up to Jill and only stopped because Frosty came and sat in front of her.

The ghost dog did not bark or growl; she didn't even lay her ears back. But the werewolves—Jill was certain they were werewolves—nearly stumbled as they came to a halt.

"Hi guys," said Jill, her voice bright and brittle from nerves. "I'm Jill Hamilton. I'm here to help."

They stared at her, confounded. Then the blond one said:

"Are you high?"

"I doubt that cannabis would affect my mental functions," Jill said, dryly. "Most drugs have no effect on me: I just don't metabolize them."

The dark-haired one laughed at that, but his companion glared at him.

"Look, missy," he said. "I don't know where you're coming from, but you can't just waltz in here—"

"Waltz in where?" Jill said.

That made the werewolf pause. He looked at his partner, who shrugged, unhelpfully.

Jill saw her opportunity, and went for it.

"Do you know why, of all metals, silver is lethal to werewolves?" she asked.

The dark-haired one looked at her, interested. He had almond-shaped eyes and a sleek, curly mane of dark brown hair, and a long, sensitive nose. The blond one scoffed.

"Everybody knows *that*," he said.

"I didn't ask if you knew that it was," Jill said. She could smell them both so strongly now, it was like having her nose in the mouth of a wine bottle—and it was affecting her head in a similar way. "I was asking if you knew *why*."

The blond one took a half step back and squared his shoulders aggressively, but his companion just put his hands in his pockets and his head on one side.

"You don't frighten us, vampire. Fake-pire," said the blond one.

"Good," said Jill. "I don't intend to be. Frightening, that is. Like I said, I'm here to help."

"You're here to tell us why silver is lethal, when no other metal can cause us serious injury?" asked the dark-haired one, speaking for the first time. He had a smooth, musical voice, and Jill got the strong impression that, of the two of them, he was the one in charge.

"Can't do that," Jill admitted. "Don't know it yet. But I'm looking into it. Among other things."

"So it's *leave me alone, I'll give you information*?" sneered the blond wolf.

Jill shook her head. She'd thought about this juncture in the conversation ahead of time, and had already decided on the best course of action. It didn't make doing it easy, though.

"More like: help me out, maybe you'll get it sooner," she said.

"Help *you*?" choked the blond wolf, caught between a laugh and a snarl.

But the dark-haired one laid a hand on his arm and looked thoughtfully at Jill.

"And if we do not?" he asked, calmly. It did not sound like a threat, more like a query for information. Jill understood that.

She shrugged. "Your loss," she said. "I'm going to find out anyway. Somehow. Just thought, maybe, you'd like to know."

The dark one was looking at her thoughtfully, almost appraisingly. Jill wasn't sure she liked it, but at least they weren't attacking her. She hadn't had a really solid plan for that eventuality; run with all the vampiric strength she possessed, she assumed.

"I'm not saying you gotta stay out of Detroit," she added. "Anyone can come here. It's neutral ground."

"But?" prompted the dark one.

"But if you start making trouble, it gets distracting." Jill said.

A dark eyebrow rose in a cool arch. The long nose sniffed.

"I keep samples from twenty-seven different supernatural entities in a lockbox underground," Jill said. "I employ a vampire and a son of Loki. Also a very tall woman with a sword. I discovered a cure for angelic radiation poisoning. I am going to figure out how vampires don't-live, and I'm gonna find out why silver is both a magical conduit and a magical insulator. Do you *want* me to pay attention to you?"

This garnered her a small smile. It was amused and condescending, but it was there.

"Dio, you can't take this bitch seriously," whined the blond wolf.

"That's for grandma to decide," said the dark one—Dio. He looked down at Frosty, and his smile widened.

"I can't make any promises," he told Jill. "But I'll relay your message to our alpha."

"I appreciate that," said Jill, cool and precise. She hadn't liked the way he'd looked at Frosty.

The three of them stood there, a little awkwardly, until with a sigh Dio took his friend by the arm and led him back around the pond. Jill waited until their scent had faded into the cool night, and then she turned with relief and walked out of the cemetery. She made it as far as the gate, then broke into a run and fairly sprinted all the way back to MCSIR headquarters.

Lansing was waiting for her on the front porch, wringing her hands.

"I'm fine," said Jill, pulling her hair into a fresh ponytail. Beside her, Frosty panted happily.

"Good thing," said Lansing, sourly. "I called Clara as soon as you left. I thought you'd need backup."

"Oh, what'd she say?" asked Jill.

Lansing looked, if possible, even more unhappy.

"Nothing," she said. "I called five times. It goes straight to voicemail."

The dark wolf and the blond wolf paced through the suburbs north of Detroit. After they darted across the artery of 8 Mile Road the tawny one growled:

"Why'd you let her off so easy?" he asked. "Grandma *said* we could eat her if we wanted."

"Did you see her dog?" replied the dark one.

"Sure I saw the dog. Creepy bitch."

"That was no ordinary bitch," remarked the dark one, shaking his mane. "That was a Yell Hound."

"Yell Hound?"

"May be above your pay grade," remarked the dark wolf. "Let's just say, she's already got the attention of someone *we* don't want to mess with. And besides, I don't think she'll last very long."

"Ha," said the tawny one. "I couldda told you that!"

They heard the river long before they reached it: a faint roar which came and went and then came again, stronger, as they navigated the contours of the hillside. When finally they crested a low ridge and could look down into the canyon Mantha understood why the water was so loud. There was a wide lake, where the water had carved out the hard bedrock, which drained over an abrupt cliff, cascading down in a series of falls to cleave the valley below, where it rushed white and frothing over a tumble of shiny black rocks. The hills rose steeply on either side, green and spiky with pine trees, and cut off her view of the river after only a few turns. But in the distance, beyond and below them, she saw a golden land hazy in the evening light, and down at the very edge something that shone like sunlight on water.

They camped on a wide, sandy beach near the neck of the lake, where there was a dock by which the army had taken a barge across it. There was no barge now, and Clara announced they would stop here for the night.

"We will have to swim it," she said. "And that is better done with daytime to dry off in."

Mantha, who had never done any swimming without water wings on, looked at the cold green-and-blue depths skeptically. But she trusted Clara and she trusted Arcana, and besides, that was a problem for tomorrow. A lot could happen in one night.

Since it was clear the army had moved on long ago, Clara was persuaded to light a fire. Because they had no food that would have been improved by cooking, it was little more than a physical comfort. But Mantha liked leaning her back against Arcana's warm side with her feet toward the fire, and it gave Clara something to do other than sharpen her weapons and look pained.

She looked, Mantha thought, like Mantha had felt when she'd seen Lady Bibbit stitched together again. Irreparably damaged and changed. She still had the rabbit doll, stowed safely in a pouch in Arcana's bags, and as night fell she went and unearthed it and clutched it to her chest for comfort when she returned to her position between Arcana and the fire.

Clara didn't seem to notice. Intermittently she poked the fire and turned the logs so it burned down to happy, orange coals, and in between stared into it blankly, her elbows resting on her knees.

"Did you know him? The stag, I mean," Mantha asked, since she was pretty sure this was what really hung on Clara's shoulders.

"I might have, once," Clara answered quietly. "In a dream, in another life."

"Who was he?" Mantha asked.

Clara's face crumpled, her pale eyes closing and her lips pursing. But she did not seem annoyed by Mantha's question. Indeed, she appeared relieved to have something to talk about.

"He was the stag of seven tines; the sun-hero; the oak king. That was how I thought of him, anyway. I do not know how much man and stag are the same, or if what was written on him was true. This land is strange and does strange things to my head."

"Is it always like this when you visit your friend?" Mantha asked. It was something she had been wondering with increasing urgency, for the world they were in now was much wider than she had expected it to be. It was beyond a safe haven—it was another realm entirely.

Clara looked up at her sharply, a stricken expression on her face. Mantha wondered for a moment if she had done something terribly wrong, and then Arcana heaved himself to his feet, snorting in agitation.

"Curse me," hissed Clara, and drew her sword.

That was the last thing Mantha remembered before their adventure turned into a nightmare.

First something whistled through the air, out of the night, and Clara made an *Oof* sound and staggered sideways. She looked down sharply at herself, and Mantha felt her stomach turn over when she saw the shaft of an arrow sticking out of Clara's chest, just to the left of her breastbone. The thick leather armor had caught it before it penetrated deeply, and Clara looked more annoyed than anything. She hung her sword off her hip and carefully broke the shaft so that only an inch or two protruded from her body, but did not try to draw it out.

"Arcana," she said, her voice very cold and clear. "Take Mantha across the lake. Get her away."

Arcana snorted, displeased by this order.

"You must," Clara said, dropping low as another arrow came whizzing in. They could see her because she stood next to the fire, Mantha realized, which in turn prevented Clara from seeing them. She felt an awful sickness in her belly.

The next moment Clara had doused the fire and in the darkness Mantha felt strong hands lifting her onto Arcana's bare back. She clung to Lady Bibbit, and then she clung to Arcana's scruffy mane, and then the beast was moving, walking swiftly toward the water

"I will join you when I can!" she heard Clara shout after them, and then Arcana was in the water, which was just as cold and unpleasant as Mantha feared it would be. It covered her feet, then her ankles, shins, knees, and when it reached her waist she worried she would float off Arcana's back if she did not keep a tight hold on him. Then she felt the motion of the beast change. He was no longer wading, but swimming steadily with swift, paddling strokes of his four legs. His neck was a furry wall in front of her but she resisted the urge to climb it—knew he had to hold it that way to keep his nose out of the water.

They moved slowly, and though Mantha tried to look back toward the shore where they had left Clara, all she ever saw was darkness. But no arrows came whizzing out of the night at them, and though they encountered a weak current near the center of the lake, Arcana forged on through it and before much longer he was heaving himself up the opposite bank, dripping water and breathing heavily. There Mantha slipped from his back and crouched behind a tree, staring off across the lake. Light had blossomed on the bank once more, a cold, blue light. The light of magic, not fire. It cast the forest and the beach in a harsh, bleached aura that gave the figures there a surreal appearance.

Mantha could see Clara as a big black silhouette, darting behind a tree. A moment later she stumbled back into the open, apparently grappling with another person. She struck them, and her opponent collapsed to the ground.

Then a rain of flaming arrows descended on the beach, and Clara could be seen running headlong into them, weaving back and forth. Mantha had never seen anyone move so fast. She looked like a flickering shadow among the streaks of fire. No wonder they could not hit her!

Except eventually they did. The shadow that was Clara jerked and fell sideways, but rose again and continued on. There was a glint of gold-white light—fire reflecting off her sword—as she swung it back and forth to foil the arrows heading for her face. It should have been useless, but Mantha saw several of the flaming heads knocked aside to extinguish themselves in the ground.

Then one shot at her from a different direction—behind and to the side—and Mantha saw the shadow stumble badly, disappearing behind a thick bush.

Then another shadow appeared from between the trees. This one was also tall and slender, and he had the antlers of an elk affixed to his shoulders—these alone gleamed pure and white in the mixed gold and blue light. He was accompanied by several squat, broad-shouldered shadows carrying axes. One ran forward, axe raised to bring it down on Clara, but she exploded from the bush and transfixed him with her sword. Using his body as a shield she forced herself forward and, casting it aside, cut at the neck of the second knight, who fell away, and brought the pommel of her sword down onto the head of the third, who staggered.

There was a streak of something dark, low above the ground, and Clara froze for a brief moment. Mantha didn't know why, but she had the terrible certainty that something had seriously wounded her. She did not make for cover, as she had before, but sliced the neck of the stunned knight and then threw herself at the figure with antlers on his shoulders.

The rain of arrows had ceased. It was just the two tall shadows now, and Clara had knocked aside the other's sword, had thrust into him with her own. She had him in her grip, and Mantha's heart was in her mouth, and then Clara inexplicably collapsed, grabbing weakly at the nearest tine of her enemy's antlers. For a moment it looked like the two shadows were embracing. Then the antlered one gently lowered Clara to the ground.

Clara, who was not moving.

The antlered one stood over her for a moment, and when she still did not move, Mantha saw him draw something from his belt, and run it decisively into the lump at his feet.

It was a nightmare, Mantha decided. It had to be a nightmare. Not real. Though she watched numbly as the soldier-shadows on the far bank clustered around the antlered one, watched as they bore Clara away along with their own dead and injured, watched until the strange blue torches had been doused, and there was nothing to see but darkness and starlight.

She might have slept. Wet and cold and miserable, clutching the remains of Lady Bibbit to her chest, she curled against Arcana and shut her eyes. She did not cry, but that somehow made it worse. Like all the grief which might have come out through her eyes got reflected back inside herself and stewed there.

It had to be a nightmare.

But hadn't she been through this before, with Bună? She had refused to accept that her grandmother was dead, and because of that all the grief she should have felt had manifested in the real world and caused all sorts of problems.

She couldn't do that again. But neither could she accept the fact that Clara was dead. Clara was too big and solid and . . . and *Clara*. There was a sense about her like the entire world could be going up in flames and she would still be there, cool and calm, if perhaps a little annoyed.

She *couldn't* be dead.

But apparently not believing in something wasn't enough to keep it from being true, Mantha realized the next morning when she saw the antlered person come down to the water's edge, followed by a small procession carrying a body on a framework of fresh-cut tree branches.

From that distance Mantha couldn't make out the features, but she knew it was Clara. There was no one else who was that tall, with a shaved head that was that pale, who wore black all over. Furthermore, they'd put her sword on her chest with her hands over it, Mantha saw when they lowered her into the narrow little boat someone had dragged out of hiding.

In fact there were a lot of boats. Enough to carry the antlered person and his entire party of soldiers. But when everyone was in a boat they did not come straight across the lake, but veered downstream.

Mantha, desperate for the ultimate confirmation—wanting fiercely for it not to be true—crashed her way along the bank, followed by a reluctant Arcana, so that she could keep pace with them. Like that she was able to see when the small fleet of boats parted from the one carrying Clara, casting it out into the current, which had apparently grown stronger. They had to paddle seriously to get themselves across without losing more distance down the river, and Clara's boat coasted on, smoothly and serenely. Mantha felt her eyes drawn to it so much she didn't realize what was going to happen until it had gone so far past she was looking downstream—right at the harsh, clear horizon of the first waterfall.

The boat was a black shape on the lip of the precipice for a split second, and then it was gone—lost in the roar of the falling water.

"No," Mantha said, but her words were empty and hollow. She felt weak and tired and horrible, and for lack of being able to cry, she screamed.

Arcana snorted warningly, and stamped his hoof. He was right to do so, for her yell had been heard by the antlered person, and now he and all his boats were aiming for her patch of shore. There was pointing and shouting.

Still screaming, Mantha scrambled up onto Arcana's back, and then they were ripping into the forest, leaving as clear a path as the army but moving much more swiftly. Mantha clutched Lady Bibbit with one hand and Arcana's neck with the other and kept on screaming—she seemed unable to stop—until all of a sudden they burst out of the woods and onto a road.

Arcana changed course abruptly, and Mantha's screams came to a halt with a gulp as she fought to stay on. Back into the woods they went, but this time their course was jagged with zigzags. Still Mantha didn't realize what was happening until a line of soldiers appeared in front of them, pikes raised.

Arcana lowered his massive head and knocked them aside as if they were bowling pins. But one must have pierced his flank for he let out a low grunt of pain, and for a few strides afterward his gait was oddly lopsided, as if he couldn't use one of his rear legs.

But he rallied, and they made it another fifty or so yards through the trees when the forest cleared and the land was thick with soldiers.

One in particular stood in front of them, and was different from all the rest in that she was a finely dressed woman holding what appeared to be a primitive gun.

Mantha tried to say something—to warn Arcana, to beg the woman not to fire—and then came the bang.

It rang in her ears and smoke billowed from the gun and Arcana went headlong into the ground, driving a pile of earth in front of him. Mantha was thrown from his back—lost hold of Lady Bibbit—and she had a glimpse of the ground rushing up to meet her and then her mind went blank.

She did not pass out. She was aware of how her body seemed frozen, unable to feel or do anything, and though the world had gone a little slanted and yellow, she could still see. She saw a clump of dirt very close to her face. There was a tiny fern trying to grow out of it.

Feeling came back slowly, like the onset of an illness. First her mouth, then her arm, legs, and chest *hurt.* She couldn't breathe. She couldn't move. All she could do was lie there as her body slowly exploded in pain and fear.

Sound trickled back into her ears. People were talking. The woman was giving orders and soldiers were saying "Yes, m'lady," and "Will see it done, m'lady." She had a heavy, nasal voice. Mantha decided she hated her intensely.

She had shot Arcana.

It was totally a nightmare now. Mantha couldn't move, couldn't even roll over to see what had become of the ram. It wasn't until after her chest had unclenched enough that she could take a few shallow breaths that she was able to look down past her feet to where Arcana had fallen.

He was still twitching, faintly, but his sides weren't moving. Mantha hoped he was dead. Nothing with half its head blasted open should still be alive. There was a puddle of vibrant red spreading out from under him, pooling in the loose earth and staining the ferns black. Lady Bibbit was nowhere to be seen.

Jill was woken in the middle of the day by a deep rumble from above and a blast of a blaring horn.

Well, this is a train station, her half-conscious mind thought, and then she remembered that it was no longer a train station. No trains had stopped here since the 1980s. But from the creak of metal wheels on metal tracks and the hiss of steam—not to mention another jarring blast from that infernal horn—it sounded very much like one was here now.

She got up and checked the time. It was eleven in the morning. Lansing slept deeper than Jill, so Marcus would be on duty. Frosty was curled at the foot of her bed, her nose buried in her white tail. She looked at Jill reproachfully when the woman slid her feet out from under the covers.

"I know," said Jill. "But that sounds like a train and I don't want to abandon Marcus to whatever it's bringing."

But by the time she had gotten on her day clothes (which consisted of a modified hazardous environment suit with a dive helmet plus leather gloves and boots) and gone upstairs to the concourse she discovered the tracks were empty and there was no one in the vast hall except Marcus and a tall, narrow old woman wearing a heavy overcoat and a wide-brimmed hat. A long white braid trailed off over her shoulder, sneaking out under the hat and over the coat's high collar, and when she turned to face Jill it revealed a heavily wrinkled, heart-shaped face the color of manzanita bark, a drooping nose, and two bright gray eyes under extraordinarily bushy eyebrows, the same color as her braid. She also had the thinnest beard; hardly more than a dozen wiry white hairs curling out of her chin, and a faint dusting of the same over her upper lip.

"Oh, hi Jill," said Marcus, who was looking nervous. "Sorry about this. But I guess it's sort of urgent. Ma'am, this is her ... er ... this is Jill Hamilton."

The old woman looked at her, and Jill felt like those gray eyes saw straight through the reflective visor of her helmet as if it weren't there. They seemed oddly familiar; something about the shape of them, and the way they crinkled as she grinned.

She turned her shoulders so she squared off against Jill, and stuck out a similarly narrow, but sinewy-strong, hand. The nails were clipped short, and there was a ring, a broad band of copper with a smokey yellow chip of stone set in its center.

"Good of you to get out of bed, Ms. Hamilton," said the woman as Jill took her bronzed hand in her own gloved one and shook gently. "You won't know me, but I've heard a great deal about you. Your sword might have mentioned me. I am Tesla Isenfaust."

Jill felt something go *thunk* in her chest, and she retracted her hand mechanically as she stared at the woman. Memories from a year and a half ago came floating up in front of her mind's eye: another woman with reddish skin, except where it was blotched pale, flyaway white hair, and eyes that were just as bright and piercing—but blue, not gray.

Tesla Isenfaust. Sister of Faraday Isenfaust. The one whom Clara had taken Mantha to visit.

Questions exploded in Jill's head, going off one after another like the stages of a rocket launch. Yet the one that fell out of her mouth first was perhaps the least important:

"I heard a train. Was that you?"

Tesla Isenfaust laughed uproariously. She was very different from her sister in many ways—earthier, and less prickly—but so much of their physical mannerisms were the same it was easy to see the family resemblance.

"Yes. Partly. I took the Ghost Train," she said with a dismissive wave of her hand.

"Ghost Train," Jill repeated, while Marcus made bug-eyes behind Tesla's back.

But the woman wasn't inspired to share any more information pertaining to her method of transportation. She sobered, and looked at Jill seriously.

"It is actually your sword that I wanted to see. I hope you won't mind if I borrow her for a few days."

Jill felt her heart, dead and cold, sink in her chest.

"Clara's not here right now," she said, the iciness creeping into her voice.

"Oh?" said Tesla, amiably disappointed. "When will she be back? And where has she gone, if I may ask?"

"I don't know when she'll be back," Jill said, feeling the deadness spreading from her chest out to her extremities. "She went to visit you."

Tesla's face, which had been animated and open, clamped shut. She, like Jill, had deduced the implied disaster. So there were no "But—"s or "I thought—"s: Tesla simply took off her hat—her hair was shorn down to a short white fuzz all over her head save for a patch at the base of her neck, from which sprang the long braid—looked seriously at Jill, and said:

"When did she leave?"

"Tuesday before last," said Jill.

"Riding Unicorn?" Tesla asked.

"Driving Arcana," said Jill. "Er, that's my truck."

Tesla Isenfaust raised one bushy eyebrow.

"She had a girl with her," Jill explained. "Mantha Fulgeroiu. She's a . . . well, we're not sure what she is. That's why Clara was taking her to you. I'm sorry, I thought you knew. I thought Clara would have called you."

"She probably did," Tesla said, staring off over Jill's helmet with an expression of alarm growing on her face. "She probably left a message clearly stating her intent. Damn."

"What's wrong?" Jill asked. "What's happened? We haven't been able to reach her, but she did warn us your forge had bad cell reception."

Tesla snorted—a short, bitter laugh.

"My forge. Damn Clara. Damn the Powers." She lowered her eyes to Jill's—which she had no problem finding under the visor—and said: "My domain has been compromised. I've been district-hopping for weeks in order to lose my tail. And Clara just . . . she probably just drove right in. Damn."

Tesla put her hands on her hips and looked from Jill to Marcus, her brows drawing into a critical V between her eyes.

"And you've lost your shield. Figures. Well. All right. I guess Faraday's next—"

"Wait," said Jill, grasping at this train of words for something to grab onto. (*District-hopping? Domain, compromised?*) "What's happened to Clara?"

"The Elder Gods only know," sighed Tesla. "She'll probably be fine. Probably. But I need my domain back."

"What is your domain? What's happened?" Jill pressed.

"My domain is the district that hosts my forge. It got—look, I really need to get in touch with Faraday." The woman turned, as if she was going to get right back on the invisible, immaterial train that had brought her, but Marcus resourcefully got out his cell phone and presented it to Tesla.

"What is this?" she asked, as if she had just been handed a dead animal.

"It's a cell phone," Marcus said, patiently. Then, when this seemed to mean nothing to Tesla, he added: "You can use it to, you know, call people."

Tesla delicately picked the phone out of Marcus's hand and turned it over. The disgust on her face vanished, replaced by an expression of keen interest and wonder.

"Oh," she said, finding the menu button. "*Oh,*" she repeated, when Marcus's lock screen came up.

"Sorry about that," said Marcus. "Here, I'll—"

But now that Tesla had the phone she would not give it back.

"This is *incredible!*" she said, turning her back on the pair of them and leaning over the little device. The phone buzzed and beeped, and Marcus made a halfhearted gesture as if to grab it back.

"It'll wipe itself if you enter the passcode wrong too many times," he said nervously. "Let me bring up the phone for you . . ."

"Phone?" said Tesla. "Oh, no, it's useless to call Faraday. She usually uses my landline as a message center anyway. No good calling that. Not now."

"What *happened?*" Jill persisted.

"I'll tell you in a minute," said Tesla. She had lifted the phone high over her head and was waving it around, as if trying to catch a signal. "This thing is one thaumaticized golden antenna from being the best underground communication catalyst I've ever seen. And even so—aha!" She froze, the phone held directly over her head. Then she spoke, as if recording a message, even though the phone's screen was black.

"Fair, it's your sister. I've got a malemorphic entity squatting on the Isenforge and Claymore's gone and got herself caught up in it without knowing what's what. There's also a kid involved. I'm in Detroit now, at the Fool's new place, but I can't leave Claymore on her own. If you can get out of Vermont, I'd really appreciate some help with this one."

She lowered her arm, turned the phone twice over in her hand, then handed it back to Marcus.

"Don't know why Fair didn't want me having one of those," she muttered. "They're great."

Jill cleared her throat. "What did you mean by *malemorphic entity?*"

Tesla looked at her critically, her gray eyes narrowed.

"What do you know about demons, kid?"

Jill shrugged. "Not as much as I'd like," she said.

The big white bushes of eyebrow lifted at that, almost approvingly. "*Oh,*" said Tesla. "Maybe you'll do all right after all." She rested her hands on her hips and rolled her head back and forth, making her neck crack alarmingly. "Well, I suppose I'll have to level with you sooner or later. Have you got any food in this place? Ghost Train concessions aren't exactly filling . . . "

They ended up in the basement kitchen, which had the dual advantages of being the best place to find food and completely devoid of sunlight so Jill could take off her day suit.

"Clever, that," Tesla remarked as she made herself a cold chicken sandwich on the industrial stainless-steel counter. "Though you must have a higher tolerance than most vampires, if that visor is all you need to keep your face from exploding in full sunlight."

"I still get hot," Jill admitted, setting the massive helmet on the far end of the counter and pulling up a stool. "And to be fair, I'm not a real vampire."

"Oh, but you're a nocturnity now, like it or not," Tesla said, shooting her a wink.

"What does that mean?" Jill asked.

"One thing at a time," said the older woman through a mouthful of chicken sandwich. "You asked what a malemorphic entity is, and since that is the more pressing of our problems we had better start there. So." She wiped her mouth with the back of her hand. "You've heard of demons. But there's a *lot* more to non-corporeal sentient magical nodes than the word 'demon' implies."

"Non-corporeal . . . sentient . . . magical . . . nodes . . . " Jill muttered, opening her phone and typing the words into a new note.

"That's my own personal designation," Tesla warned. "Sue me if I like consistency and accuracy. One reason I could never become a witch."

"That's fine," Jill said. "How does this relate to malemorphic entities?"

But Tesla had just taken a big bite of sandwich, and so the answer was delayed a minute while she chewed and swallowed.

"Malemorphic entities," Tesla began, stopped and belched, then went on, "are a subclass of non-corporeal sentient magical nodes. I use the term to describe this particular—well, I guess you could call them *species*—of being whose defining characteristic is their practice of manipulating fabricated realities to the detriment of those within, and then deriving sustenance from the ensuing mental and spiritual trauma."

"Okay," said Jill, writing this all down while Tesla took another bite of sandwich. "Okay. I think I got that. But how do you define a fabricated reality?"

Tesla seemed to like this way of talking. "Well," she said, "I define it as a piece of spacetime that is held apart from the other major realms. It may be comparable in breadth—that is, the space as you perceive it when within it—but in depth it is much shallower. It is built off of or hung under a major realm and can last from a couple minutes to indefinitely. We create tiny little fabricated realities of our own when we dream. These are like soap bubbles, of course, compared to some of the ones purposefully built by religions, gods, or dedicated groups of people. Those can become practically self-sustaining and in effect are no different from the major realms. It's my suspicion that the major realms are, in fact, fabricated realities of an even greater world. Or they began as such and have now literally taken on lives of their own. But that's going above and beyond the situation at hand.

"My domain, the Isenforge, is its own little fabricated reality. I made it myself, with some help—okay, a lot of help—from Faraday. Gives me lots of advantages, notably not having to pay property tax or be noticed by people I don't want noticing me. Disadvantage is . . . well . . . sometimes I get a malemorphic entity deciding that my home is the perfect place for it to make dinner."

"What do you do when that happens?" Jill asked.

Tesla Isenfaust gave her a critical look. "Apparently I try to call the best demon slayer I know, only to find *she's* gone and doused herself. Then I call my sister and explain everything to the not-a-vampire who was supposed to keep an eye on Claymore. This hasn't happened before. Most malemorphs nest in the dreams of humans—not perennial pockets."

"So it's a big one?" Jill asked.

Tesla sighed and finished off her sandwich. "It will be by now, especially if it's got Claymore."

"Why Clara?"

Tesla picked a piece of chicken off her plate and licked her finger. She gave Jill a sideways look out from under one eyebrow that made her look more like a witch than her sister ever had.

"How long have you known Claymore?" she asked.

Jill paused, recalling. "Two . . . two and a half years?" she estimated.

"Seems cold, doesn't she?"

Jill shrugged, feeling oddly defensive. "Maybe. I'm a little numb anyway."

"Well, let me tell you something about our mutual friend," said Tesla. "That cold only goes skin deep. Really, she's a great steaming, frothing cauldron of emotion, and she's got some very deep wounds which got buried instead of healed. Add to that the fact that she . . . she's a bit . . . well. You've met her brother, right?"

"Sure," said Jill, beginning to see where this was going.

"Let's just say that, to a malemorph, Claymore is . . . potent. And if it gets its claws into her, things are going to go very badly."

"For Clara?" Jill asked, feeling her stomach twist.

Tesla leaned on one arm to stare down the counter at her. "For *everyone*," she said. "Which is why we need someone like Faraday, or Girion, before we go in after her. Malemorphs feed on the people who get stuck inside them. Why do you think I ran? A malemorph without me is much weaker than a malemorph that's fed off what I've got wrapped up in here." She tapped the side of her head with a strong, brown finger.

"And a malemorph with Clara?" Jill asked, though she could already guess what the answer was.

Tesla sucked in a breath of air through her teeth, making a whistling noise.

"Have you got a landline around here? Sometimes Faraday's better with landlines . . . "

Mantha didn't think the nightmare could get any worse after Arcana died and she lost Lady Bibbit, and for a while she was right. The army they had stumbled into didn't seem interested in hurting *her*, though they cut Arcana into pieces, dressing the meat and talking all the time about what good eating he would be.

Mantha, exhausted and overwhelmed and sick with despair, allowed herself to be bundled into an open wagon, her arms bound uncomfortably behind her back, and when the tall, white-faced lady with red lips came to look at her all she did was stare back, wanly.

"What a disagreeable child," said the lady. She had a nose like a chip of marble, and her chin looked like it could cut granite. Her dress was the color of storm clouds, and she rode a big, dapple-gray gelding with his tail cut down to a mere stump. Docked, that was what they called it. The lady didn't even bother to get off her horse: just rode him right up next to the wagon where Mantha was lying and looked down her marble nose at the girl with an expression like she just gotten a whiff of fresh manure.

"This is it?" she'd said, sniffing disdainfully.

She was speaking to someone on the other side of the cart—literally over Mantha's head—and Mantha didn't have the energy to flop herself around to see who it was until she heard his voice.

"She is as our Lord described her to me," said the voice of the knight with antlers on his shoulders.

Mantha didn't know how she knew—certainly there was no reason she should recognize the voice—but the words cut into her like knives, leaving a raw, open feeling on the surface of her mind, and she knew: this was the voice of the person who had killed Clara.

She did turn herself over then, to glare balefully into the face of a young, handsome man with a trim black beard and open, amber eyes. The antlers from the white stag had been screwed onto the plates of armor covering his shoulders, and from under these flowed a cape of deep green and gold. There was a wreath of dark, spiky leaves tied around his neck. It took Mantha a moment to recognize them as holly.

That he was not a hideous monster with glowing red eyes clothed in armor of leather and obsidian came as a small disappointment to her. But then, everything up to now had been one big disappointment. The destruction at the forge, the deaths of Clara and Arcana, and the loss of Lady Bibbit. It figured her villains couldn't even be bothered to look like proper villains.

"If you say so, Sir Holman," said the marble lady, and spurred her horse on ahead of the wagon.

Sir Holman lingered a moment longer, caught by Mantha's glare. He looked at her curiously, as though she were an exotic animal. Then he kicked his own horse—a bright red chestnut stallion—and galloped out of sight.

Mantha spent the entire day jarred and jostled in the cart, with only one break in the afternoon when a wide, rusty woman came and took her for a short walk so that she could relieve herself, and afterward gave her a drink of something strong and fizzy that tasted like bad apples.

It must have been drugged, because Mantha didn't remember the remainder of the journey, only a feeling of misery and an empty gray sky, and always a buzzing in her head like angry wasps.

When the sensation lifted and she again became aware of her surroundings it was to find they had reached a city. She could see tall, black buildings rising on either side of the wagon and hear the clatter and bustle of people moving and talking beyond the heavy tramp of the army.

Her legs had fallen asleep under her, and so when they reached the castle the same rusty woman came and carried her to a cell in a dank dungeon and there left her, locking the heavy iron door behind her.

Mantha lay in the dark. They had cut her hands free but her arms, after so long bent stiffly behind her back, weren't working properly. She was tired and thirsty and hungry and Clara was *dead* and Arcana was probably being eaten somewhere and she was *all alone* and this was just like her worst nightmare—the one which started out good and exciting and she had friends and they were going on adventures, only then one by one her friends died and she ended up like this: alone in the dark waiting to be eaten by the same thing that had come for her friends.

If she was lucky, at this point she would wake up. Or sometimes the thing would come and be in the act of eating her and *then* she would wake up. Once it had succeeded in eating her and she'd sort of turned into it and that had been *really* horrible—but she had woken up.

There was something in the dark with her. She couldn't see it, but she knew it was there. She could feeling its eyes boring into her. They felt accusing. Hungry.

She had to move.

Her legs wouldn't work.

She crawled.

The floor of the dungeon was wet and cold and hard and it hurt her knees and that *thing* was right behind her.

If only she could wake up. When she was awake, things were easier to control. She knew it was wrong, but when she was awake she could push things around. She would have been able to stop the arrow that killed Clara. She would have made herself and Arcana invisible. But it was like someone had put a plastic bag over the better part of herself, leaving her at the mercy of whatever was driving this nightmare.

The thing in the dark.

Mantha stopped, her hands clutching uselessly at the stone floor.

The thing was still right behind her, but it didn't come any closer.

Mantha tried to think. Her brain was feeling sick and sluggish, and she had to put her thoughts in order one at a time before she could run them through.

The dungeon was dark and cool, and whatever the thing was, it was content to wait.

Was this a nightmare?

Was she asleep?

She didn't remember falling asleep, but then, she never did, in her dreams.

If she was asleep and this whole thing was a dream, would it not be better to get the worst of it over with so she could then wake up?

Yes.

And if this was *not* a dream . . .

. . . then she needed to get the plastic bag off the rest of herself so she could get out of it.

In both cases, it would do no good to keep crawling around the pitch-black dungeon, scraping her hands and bruising her knees.

She turned herself around. The darkness here looked just like the darkness before, but she knew she was pointed more or less at where the thing was.

She said:

"What do you want?"

There was a tiny inhalation of air, and then a ragged but familiar voice said, in somewhat injured tones:

"I just want to help."

It was small and sad and sounded like the mouth it came from had been torn a little.

Unable to believe yet unable to deny herself the truth, Mantha stretched out a tentative hand.

Her fingers touched something soft, fuzzy, and slightly warm. There was a wet nose and the poke of whiskers against her palm.

The sob rose suddenly in her throat, so that her words came out bubbly and stammered.

"B-b-b-bibbit?"

But Lady Bibbit had been lost. Thrown aside when she'd fallen from Arcana. And before that, when she'd fallen out of herself and forgotten who she was. And whatever spark of her imagination that had put life into that stuffed rabbit seemed to have been permanently doused. Lady Bibbit—the real, warm, breathing Lady Bibbit—was gone.

Except apparently she was not.

"I followed you," said Lady Bibbit. "After the army left, I followed you."

"B-b-but . . . " Mantha began. *But you're dead*, she wanted to say. *I shredded you.*

"I'm not really alive," Lady Bibbit admitted. "Not yet, anyway. But getting there. I can be here, I think, because this place puts life into things. Like it did for Arcana. But I don't think *he* knows about me. I'm too small. I don't matter."

"But you matter to *me*," Mantha insisted. "You're important!"

A furry hand with blunt claws gripped her arm.

"That's important!" said Lady Bibbit fiercely. "Keep thinking like that. He's trying to keep you under control. He knows you're stronger than him, really."

"Who is *he?*" Mantha asked, but she thought she knew.

The prince with holly around his neck. The one who had killed the stag. The one who had sent Clara over the waterfall.

"The person who made this place," Lady Bibbit answered. "I don't know his name. I think he's the one they called the Lord of Stormvault."

"But . . . " said Mantha. But that could not be the prince. The prince had been called something else.

"Holman," Lady Bibbit supplied helpfully. "I think he came from Clara. So did the white stag."

"I don't understand," said Mantha, whimpering a little. "Am I dreaming?"

There was a beat, as though Lady Bibbit was not sure of the answer. Then she said:

"I think we all are."

There was a scraping sound from outside the cell. Someone was coming. Someone was coming who would take her to Lord Stormvault. Mantha knew this, and now she understood she knew it in the way one knows things in dreams. The way she had known Lady Bibbit was there—even if she had not recognized her.

But now a hole had been poked in the plastic bag covering the better part of herself. The part that could push reality about, if it liked, or bring stuffed animals to life. Because if everyone was dreaming that made it more like real life. And in reality, Mantha was not some helpless, weak-limbed child. She was twelve years old, and she had more monsters in her head than she knew what to do with. Monsters out of her own dreams and nightmares. Monsters that she knew. Monsters she had played with.

Monsters that were on *her* side.

More importantly, she had Lady Bibbit, and she had the resolute certainty that Clara should *not* be dead. And neither should Arcana.

It had not quite worked out with Bună, but this, Mantha realized, was fundamentally different.

Her legs were still insistent that they couldn't stand, but Mantha told them firmly that they could. They did.

She stood up.

A moment later the door to the cell scraped open and light flooded in, outlining the person standing there in a hard, black silhouette. But Mantha didn't need to see their face to know who it was. Also silhouetted against the yellow triangle were the branching antlers of the white stag.

"My lord will see you now," said the holly prince.

Mantha clenched her fists.

"Good," she said.

Lady Bibbit was a dirty, crumpled heap of velveteen and denim, missing an eye, but Mantha picked her up by her paw and carried her along as she walked haughtily out of the cell.

The holly prince seemed surprised, but he did not try to stop her or even tie her hands. He seemed faded from the last time she had seen him. It made sense. He was a part of Clara's dream; Clara's nightmare. And Clara, as far as this world was concerned, was dead.

Mantha tightened her hand around Lady Bibbit's paw.

That was about to change.

Clara was *hers.* Her friend. Her black knight. She rode a black steed with a single horn and she cut down fiends and enemies like a scythe going through tall grass.

Mantha called up that image of her: the image she held in her heart rather than her head: an impossibly tall warrior clad all in black, riding a black unicorn, a long sword flashing brightly in her hand. . . .

In the back of the underground lot below the Moonshield Center for Supernatural Investigation and Research, the muscular black motorbike with the anodized aluminum spike mounted above its headlamp that had lain undisturbed under a sheet of oilcloth for over a fortnight, shivered. It did not come to life in any dramatic fashion, but without the touch of a human rider its engine rolled over, and by backing onto its shroud it managed to pull the sheet off.

Light blazed from its headlamp; the front wheel turned; the bike carefully backed itself around so it was pointed at the exit ramp, and then with a roar it shot forward.

Running from the nearby kitchen, Jill and Tesla were just in time to see Unicorn, riderless, go charging up out of the parking lot and into the harsh light of the afternoon.

The holly prince stumbled up the stairs, and Mantha waited patiently for him to continue. There were more things she could do in the meantime. She thought of Arcana: big, strong, red Arcana. He did not belong to Clara the way that Unicorn did. But he was a good friend to have. Mantha called him up in her head the same way she had done with Clara, but no sooner had she done so than he ripped himself out of her control. She felt him leave, and decided to let him go.

Arcana had always known best what to do with himself.

Clara dreamed. It was a relief to be in a place where it was definitely a dream, even though at the same time she longed for the solidity of the waking world. But at least she was warm and comfortable—weightless, even. Someone's arms were around her, and they smelled of oak and sky and the fizz of burned air after a lightning strike. The smell reminded her, vaguely, of the way her mother would smell sometimes—only not as sharp and immediate. The lightning was a long way off with this one, at least four or five generations.

"Better now?" asked a voice, warm and golden and rumbly.

Clara peeled her face away from whatever it had been pressed against and found herself looking at the intricacies of a double spiral. It had been rendered with painstaking detail on the right pectoral muscle of a man's chest. There was a faint dusting of amber hairs growing over the faded blue-black ink.

She looked up into the sun and saw Ariel looking down at her, a touch of a smile hiding in the corners of his mouth.

Because this was a dream, and because she wasn't doing anything else with her hands, Clara lifted one and gently touched a finger to that mouth. The lips felt soft and dry and warm—and solid.

"I thought I lost you," she whispered.

"You lost yourself for a bit there," Ariel remarked, grinning around her fingers. "But here we are."

"Where is here?" Clara asked, trying to sit up. Something was preventing her. It was Ariel's arm, she discovered when the man slid it off her shoulders. Then she regretted moving. Now she was separate, alone again, and growing quickly cold.

"Good question," Ariel said, pushing himself up on his arms to sit beside her. "I don't recognize it, but it doesn't feel like one of yours."

They had been lying on a wide, sandy beach. Behind them rose steep hillsides covered in fragrant eucalyptus and scored by pinnacles of pink stone; in front was a vast blue-green ocean, lying in a wide crescent between the arms of two low promontories. High above them in the sky a bird with long, white wings was gliding. And though they lay in a patch of golden sun, pillows of gray clouds hid the heights of the hills behind them, and tendrils of mist were curling down the ravines to pool over the dunes.

"That's wrong," Clara said. "Mist doesn't behave like that."

"Unless it's not mist," Ariel remarked.

There was a roaring sound from the sea, and Clara turned, half expecting to find the surf coming in. But there was nothing. The ocean was the same flat, clear blue-green as it had been, with only the tiniest white breakers scurrying across the wet sand down at the shore. The white reminded Clara of something.

"Are you the white stag?" she asked. It seemed important.

Ariel was looking at her quizzically. Confused, but interested.

"I . . . don't think so," he said.

"I think you should be careful, anyway," Clara said, forgetting for the moment that this was just her dream version of Ariel, not the real man. "Stay away from oak trees and holly bushes. Be especially vigilant this summer."

Ariel's expression softened to sober acceptance. Perhaps, Clara thought, in some sloppy, metaphysical way, the warning would get through to the real man. Unless her mind had gone completely off its rails, and she was tumbling through the dreaming realm—free-falling into pure chaos.

"Thanks for the warning," he said. "I will."

At least, that was what Clara thought he said. The roaring from the ocean had grown louder, drowning out their conversation, and within the roar was a pounding. They were hoofbeats, Clara realized, just before the dream turned fluid and flowed away around her.

She lost track of herself for a while. She was tossed and turned, alternately drenched in darkness and thrust into blinding light. She couldn't breathe, yet she must have been breathing, because she did not feel the tightness in her chest nor the ache in her throat. She was upside down and tumbling through a roaring white space, and then she was cast up on her back as the world slid past in streaks.

She was cold. And wet. And slimy. There were points of pain all over her body, but these slowly faded as she lay there, rocked gently by a strangely fluid world.

It was water. The world was water, and it was tugging her and pushing her, driving her gently onto an embankment of what felt like sand.

Heavy steps. Not feet, but hooves, and a shadow fell across her face. She felt the tickle of wiry whiskers, and then a blast of warm air flecked with cold spit blew across her face. There was a whuffling sound in her ear, and her nose was assaulted by a strange combination of warm, sweaty animal and gasoline exhaust.

Clara opened her eyes, and at first could not make sense of the long, black face staring down at her. It appeared to be mostly nose, long and bony and lightly furred, at the top of which were two curious ears, like narrow question marks, and between them, bisecting Clara's vision, was a tapered spike of black, anodized aluminum. It grew out from the bush of black hair that obscured the top of the face, and gleamed faintly at its tip.

Two blank, glowing white eyes blinked at her, and once again the unicorn blew exhaust breath over her face.

Not any unicorn. *Her* Unicorn.

Clara raised a hand, gloved now, and felt the long, hard face and the soft, pudgy nose at the end of it.

"I don't understand," she said, finally admitting it aloud. "Is this a dream, too?"

It hadn't seemed like dream, earlier. That had felt like a nightmare.

But Unicorn did not speak. She never did. Unicorn was action. She lowered her head further and got her nose under Clara's shoulder and pushed her upright as if she weighed nothing at all.

Clara's body protested, then broke off in embarrassment when it discovered that all the injuries she had sustained the last time she had been in this state of consciousness had vanished.

Definitely a heightened level of reality, Clara thought, gathering her legs under her. She was interested to discover that the various rips and tears and holes in her clothes caused by those fatal arrows remained, though the flesh beneath them was clean and pink and unbroken.

Using Unicorn's copious mane as a support, Clara hauled herself to her feet and looked around.

They were standing on the bank of a wide, dark river, where a bend of it slowed to a crawl before pouring off down another cascade of rapids. Above her, far in the distance, she could just hear the roar of those monstrous falls. Steep hills covered in spiky pines towered on either side, and the sky was a tumult of angry gray-and-black clouds.

They found Bellatrix caught in some willows about ten feet downstream. The spry wands holding her as securely as any human hand, but they released her readily when Clara took a firm grip on the sword's hilt.

Willow was a witch's tree. Clara smiled. Somewhere out there Faraday was thinking of her. But thinking of Faraday made her think of Tesla, which reminded her of the original purpose of their mission.

Yes, *their* mission. She had Arcana and Mantha to answer for as well now. And, in the same way her body had healed, now there was a strong point of light under her breastbone, and it was tugging at her insistently.

Somewhere out there, Mantha needed her.

Unicorn was taller now, but that didn't stop Clara swinging herself up onto the beast's back. It should have felt awkward and uncertain, sitting astride the horse-shaped creature without even a pad. It had been almost a decade since Clara had ridden a horse, and yet settling onto Unicorn's back felt like the most natural thing in the world. She was not just riding an incredibly powerful being, she was coming home to a significant part of herself. She sat on the unicorn, but she could feel herself run through her back, her neck and her legs.

She'd lost her sheath and so had to hold Bellatrix well aside to keep her out of the way as Unicorn turned around on the little strip of sand, looking for a route up the rocky mountain. It flashed in the light of the muted sun as, finding a path, Unicorn surged into motion, and Clara with her, they went charging up into the trees.

In their wake were flying clods of dirt and the sound of retreating hoofbeats, and before them rolled a growing roar of angry thunder.

The holly prince led Mantha to a long hall at the top of the palace. It was flanked with windows made of stained green glass, which gave the place the feeling of being underwater. At the end of it was a high, black chair, empty, and next to it

stood the cold lady who had captured Mantha.

She was standing to the side with her hands clasped in front of her and her head modestly bowed. Her entire person looked faded and out of focus, and she did not move.

The holly prince was little better.

"I think you've done all you can," Mantha told him, and gestured to a spot in the hall opposite the woman.

The prince didn't object. He stumbled on his way to the place Mantha indicated, and once there he went even more faded. It made sense, considering Clara was no longer under the power of whoever was creating this dimension, but Mantha wondered who the woman had belonged to. She felt like she came from a different set than the holly prince or the white stag.

So, with no one left to lead her, Mantha took the time to go over to the woman and look at her more closely.

She had the same white face and pointed nose as Mantha remembered from earlier, but her lips had gone the same color as her skin and her eyes had sunk into her face. Her hands were gray and her nails grew out of the tops of her fingers in arching talons.

That niggled something in the back of Mantha's head, and with a strange feeling in her throat she went around to look at the woman's back, and was less surprised than she expected to find it gaping open, and inside were the glistening coils of a snake. The tail drooped out of the bottom and hung in a curl between the woman's legs.

Mantha went around to the front of the woman again and peered up into her face. Sure enough, the impossibly sharp nose was fake—now she could see the caked plaster used to hold it on. Reaching up she gently worked it loose until the false nose came away between her fingers, leaving behind the flat skin underneath, pierced by two oblong slits.

Mantha felt both thrilled and sad.

Snake Woman had been one of her most pernicious recurring nightmares—back when she had had nightmares. Proper, ordinary nightmares. Until the last one, which had turned into a perfectly surreal dream in which it became clear Snake Woman had been fleeing from something even worse the whole time, and Mantha had just been in the way. Together they had teamed up to go fight that thing, but Mantha had been woken before the dream could be resolved. She'd never seen Snake Woman again.

"She's one of mine," Mantha whispered, just because she felt like she had to say something.

Lady Bibbit was still a limp, lifeless doll hanging from her hand, but at her words Mantha felt a shiver run up her arm.

Lady Bibbit was with her. Lady Bibbit agreed.

It was good she did, because that was when he appeared.

Mantha felt him draw aside a flap of reality, as if it were a curtain, and sit down in the chair at the far end of the hall. She knew without looking that he was waiting for her to notice him, drawing shadows and small torments about him like a cape.

She wasn't sure who he was. The Lord of Stormvault was what the dream-people called him, but Mantha was becoming certain—as certain as she was that Lady Stormvault was actually Snake Woman—that he was something else entirely.

He was waiting. He was patient. He'd been crafting this world and anticipating this moment for quite some time. How much time? It was hard to say. Time, like space, was flexible here.

Mantha lingered a moment in front of the petrified Snake Woman, but she let that moment stretch so that she could think things over carefully.

She wondered how many of her other monster-friends had been disguised here. She'd assumed she would have to call them up from the depths of her imagination, but perhaps they were closer than she realized.

Perhaps it hadn't just been Lady Bibbit in the dark. Maybe Burgess had been there too?

Who was he? The thing on the throne at the end of the hall? Why was she so certain he was a *he?* He just was. And in the end, Mantha supposed, it didn't really matter what he was. He was the reason she was stuck here, and if she wanted to get back to the proper world—the world where Clara was alive and Arcana was a truck—she would have to get rid of him.

That made things simple. Mantha liked simple.

She turned away from Snake Woman and went down to the throne at the end of the hall. But, because she didn't feel like walking the distance and thought the practice would do her good, she shortened the space so that she arrived before the throne in one step.

That surprised him. But not in a bad way.

"Very good," he said.

His voice was a mishmash of all the men Mantha had ever held any regard for. He was her old priest. He was Mr. Rawley, her favorite teacher.

He also sounded a little like Darth Vader, who Mantha had always liked no matter what anyone said.

"You are progressing well," he went on. "Soon, you may begin to collect your own harem."

Mantha had heard the word "harem" before but wasn't one hundred percent certain what it meant. She was pretty sure she didn't want one, however.

"No, thanks," she said.

"You must," said the person on the throne. "Otherwise you will wither and die. Everyone must feed; even the dead."

"Are you dead?" Mantha asked. This might complicate matters.

"I am beyond death," said the person on the throne, but the statement rang sour in Mantha's mind. It was false.

The only thing beyond death was the dark, which stretched on forever before and after what was.

"But you are not alive?" She needed clarification.

"Not as waking minds would define it," he said, sounding smug.

"Why did you kill Clara?"

It was difficult to look at him. He seemed blurry—like something seen through a pane of foggy glass. Even so, Mantha got the impression that he had just crossed what passed for his legs.

"I didn't kill Clara," he said. "Her own fears and insecurities killed her. A pity, but it happens."

"But you wanted her dead."

"She was a rich source of energy," he admitted. "But her presence was damaging to you."

"How?" Mantha asked, but a part of her went hollow with dismay when she felt those words ring true.

Something about Clara affected her, made her powers quiet and subdued. Not weakened, but it was as though her unusual abilities felt shy around Clara—as though she would disapprove. Which was probably not far from the truth.

"She subjugates your true self," said the person on the throne. "Think on this, and you will know it is true."

He was right, that was the problem. But Mantha grappled with herself. Surely she was not just her ability to push reality about? To bring back dead things or cause her feelings to manifest? Just like Clara was more than her ability to ride a motorcycle, or use a sword . . .

Clara . . .

In the distance there was a faint rumble, growing slowly louder.

Tesla had been all for giving chase after Unicorn directly, but when the only car available belonged to Lansing, and Lansing would not be woken, she was obliged to wait until sundown. Then the groggy vampire was apprised of the situation, and after she drank a pint of blood and made Jill repeat the story a second time, agreed to lend her sun-proofed Nissan to the cause.

They were in the act of piling into it when Arcana arrived.

He came up through the park with a roar of engines, his horn blaring, and Jill's excitement and relief at seeing him turned to consternation and dismay when he came to a screeching halt in front of the center, rocking on his wheels, and his passenger door opened to reveal . . . no one.

There was nobody in the driver's seat. Or the passenger seat. Or the back seat. Mantha's backpack was, but there was no sign of any of Clara's gear. The keys were in the ignition, and when Jill cautiously touched them they were warm.

Arcana sat there in neutral, parking brake on, idling impatiently, his headlights blazing.

"I'm confused," Jill said, after she had been through the truck and hadn't found anything.

"This yours?" asked Tesla, eyeing the vehicle critically. "Looks like he's been through it."

That made Jill scramble out of the truck and pay attention to his outsides. She'd been so distracted trying to find Clara and a little blinded by his headlights, she hadn't noticed until Tesla pointed it out how dirty he was: tires caked on the sides with dried mud, more mud spattered all over his fenders and up his sides; there were leaves and twigs caught in his windshield wipers and a small branch in his bed, and there was a brand new scrape along his left rear wheel well. Jill ogled it in dismay.

"Did that truck just . . ." Marcus began. He had adapted quickly to the world of supernatural phenomena but this was admittedly a large jump.

"Yes, yes it did," said Lansing, grimly. "Jill, you should probably check him for demonic possession."

Embarrassed that she hadn't thought of that, Jill took a hasty step back and nearly stepped on Tesla. She felt herself collide briefly with a narrow, strong body and then was abruptly set aside as the older woman went up to the truck and rapped on his still-vibrating hood with her knuckles.

"Hello in there!" she called, putting her face sideways on the warm metal. "What's gotten into you, eh?"

In response Arcana's engine revved, and Tesla took a respectful step back.

"That's interesting," she said.

"What is?" asked Jill. Clara had left her with a number of "foolproof" test kits for demons, ghosts, ghouls, and other non-corporeal entities that might present themselves, and she was itching to try them all on Arcana.

"As far as I can tell," said Tesla, "and mind, I'm no witch, but as far as I can tell this guy ain't got nothing in him but himself."

"That's impossible," said Jill. "He's just a *truck*."

"Is he now?" asked Tesla, pinning her with a steely gaze. "*He* doesn't seem to think so."

Jill felt her face go slack with exasperation. This was Arcana. This was her boyfriend's old truck. It was a nice truck—a *very* nice truck—but still! It was just metal and rubber and diesel and all the other bits and pieces that went into constructing a motor vehicle. A plain, ordinary, *normal* motor vehicle. They only called him *him* at all because Selene had suggested it. That and the name. Lots of cars had names, there wasn't anything special about that.

"Think," said Tesla, her voice taking on an imperial tone that reminded Jill of her conversations with Faraday.

The older woman tapped her shorn head. "*Think,*" she repeated. "Are you sure he's never done anything like this before? Maybe not as dramatic, but something—*anything*—above the ordinary?"

"No!" Jill exclaimed, and after the word left her mouth her mind flashed back to a moment, long ago, in a dark place, when she had been very frightened, and needed to get to Arcana. There was a monster at her heels, and Arcana was too far away. Except then he wasn't.

But she had been very frightened. It had to have been her mistake.

Yet here they were.

Marcus meanwhile had been inside and resourcefully brought out Clara's demon test kit. This consisted of a small bottle of purified rosewater and some finely powdered salt and a series of words which were to be spoken while one blew the salt over the suspect and then held the bottle of water nearby.

They performed the test on Arcana while Tesla looked on critically, tapping her booted foot in impatience.

The test only vindicated her. The water did not turn color and the salt did nothing but remain salt.

"Now what?" asked Marcus.

"You want my opinion?" Tesla said, in tones which suggested they were going to have it either way. Jill said nothing, and the woman continued. "Get in the truck. See where he takes you."

Jill didn't admit it out loud, but she'd been thinking along similar lines. Two years of working with Clara and Selene, however, had taught her some measure of caution.

"Marcus, Lansing, I want you to follow me," she said. "Closely. Tesla—"

But Tesla Isenfaust was already climbing into Arcana's passenger seat.

Jill sighed and went around to the driver's side, where the door sprang open at the merest brush of her hand.

"Okay, big boy," she muttered as she settled into the driver's seat, adjusting the height and alignment and the mirrors from where Clara had left them. The doors shut just as soon as she and Tesla had buckled themselves in, and then the truck put itself in gear and rolled smoothly forward. Jill rested her hands on the wheel and kept one foot poised over the brake just for her own comfort, but there was no need. Now that he had passengers Arcana drove carefully and comfortably, though as soon as they cleared the traffic south of Detroit he put on speed until they were practically blasting along. But the rearview mirror showed Lansing was on their tail, her face a pale grim oval behind the wheel of her own car.

Beside her, Tesla said: "I can't wait to see Faraday's face when I tell her about *this*," and she chuckled.

Jill didn't.

The roar grew to a buzzing in Mantha's head, and she was tempted to put her hands over her ears. She didn't. She had a feeling that was what he wanted, and she knew that there was no physical way to block the words he was pouring into her mind.

"Don't be afraid," he'd said. "I understand what it is like, to grow up apart from everyone around you. To be destined for greater things. You and I are of a kind, you see."

Now he was saying: "You should not deny yourself the powers inherent within you. You must use them, otherwise they will consume you."

This sent up such a flurry of mixed feelings that Mantha was rooted to the spot, unable to move.

He was right. He was utterly wrong. He sounded kind and concerned and Mantha knew he was nothing of the sort. He was someone whose only interest was in his own ends, and anything he did that appeared otherwise was a lie.

"Think about it, Mantha. You don't want to be tied to people that suppress you all your life. It will destroy you."

And there was a grain of truth in that, too, but not the whole truth.

The whole truth, Mantha knew, was that it was more likely *she* would destroy *them*. But she'd decided to follow Clara because that way seemed the most likely to end in no one being destroyed.

He didn't know everything.

For all he sounded confident and assured, Mantha told herself, he didn't know *her*.

"I am not," she said, forcing the words out between breaths. It was difficult to talk over him. He was saying, " . . . you shouldn't let them drag you down to their level—" when she cut across him with, "I am not one of you."

"Oh, but you are," he said, sounding almost gleeful. "I've been inside your head, remember? All of this is as much you as it is me."

It was the wrong thing to say, because it rang true, and with the ringing Mantha's head cleared and a dead peace descended on her. All her worries went faint and distant, huddled somewhere far below. She was floating—soaring—on a clear, vibrant, ecstatic certainty:

This was her dream as much as it was his.

Hers to do with what she liked.

Her reality to push about.

She looked down at the tattered form of Lady Bibbit, still clasped in one hand. She smiled.

Lady Bibbit shivered and straightened her back, adjusting her denim overalls and twitching her nose curiously.

"I say," she said. "That is really none of your business who or what Mantha is. You ought to be ashamed of yourself."

"Oh, the construct speaks?" said the person on the thrown. He sounded amused.

Not for long, Mantha thought. *Not for long you won't be.*

She let go of Lady Bibbit's paw. The rabbit didn't need physical contact any more. She took the opportunity to step right up to the person on the throne and actually shook a furry finger as she continued to harangue him.

"And you'd no cause to kill all those poor birds back at the forge—whatever had they done to you, may I ask? You're greedy! Greedy and selfish and self-centered—and you manipulate people! You're as bad as a troll!"

"Look at that, it thinks it knows what it's talking about," he said, snide laughter under his words.

"I *do* know what I'm talking about," said Lady Bibbit, undaunted. "Just because I haven't been flesh and blood doesn't mean I don't hear things! Yes, I've heard every word you've said—and a few you haven't!"

Mantha let her mind wander. Lady Bibbit could take care of herself at this point. Now she thought back to the Snake Woman at the end of the hall. She combined the person she had seen there with her own last memories from the character in her dreams. Then she looked at the result critically, trying to imagine what sort of real person that should be.

She was a queen, Mantha realized. An old queen who'd been kicked off her throne and forced to fight so hard she'd become hard and prickly on the outside. But underneath she was a strong, kind person. One reason she was so sharp was to protect her soft interior.

She came slither-walking up the hall, half propelled by her tail. She was furious. Not at Mantha—never at Mantha—but at him. The one on *her* throne.

"That's funny," he said, when he saw her coming. "You think you and a couple half-remembered dream folk are going to make a difference to me? You are as pathetic as you are naïve."

"You," hissed the Snake Woman, her pupils like slits and her forked tongue flicking between her narrow lips. "You are in *my* chair."

"Sorry," he said, not sounding sorry at all. "You'll have to get one of your own."

"She had one," Lady Bibbit said. And it figured her own imaginary characters would know everything about each other. "You took it away."

"I have waited too long," said the Snake Woman, uncoiling her tail so that her body lifted clean off the floor and was propelled through the air to tower over the person sitting in the throne.

"It's not just them, either," said Mantha. "You haven't met Burgess yet."

She hadn't thought of Burgess in years. He had begun as the monster under her bed. He had a short, fat body and long, prehensile arms and big, grasping claws. Mantha had fed him old dishes, dinner leftovers, socks, and whatever homework she really didn't feel like doing, and they had soon become friends. He'd fallen to the back of her mind around the time she'd stopped having dreams about Snake Woman, but he'd always been there. Not forgotten.

He came crawling back now, hand over clawed hand, his long arms swinging, his yellow teeth gnashing. He howled and cackled with delight as he swung himself around and around the throne, pelting the person there with chips of old ceramic and moldy bread crusts.

"Go away, you old shade!" cried the person, but that just made Burgess cackle even more.

It made Mantha laugh too, and she gleefully called up all her old monsters. There was the spider from behind her bathroom mirror. There was the alligator down the bathtub drain. There were friends and foes and people whose shapes had been but vague shadows until she called them up with her conscious mind.

Now they came, forming a whirling wall of bodies around Mantha and Lady Bibbit and Snake Woman and the throne—and the person who was still sitting there, now with his knees up into his chest to keep his feet from the swarm of snapping red crabs that had come clawing their way up through the cracks in the floor.

Cracks that Mantha had put there.

"Stop it, *stop it!*" he cried. "This isn't *fair!*"

"This is what's inside my head," Mantha said, calmly. "I go down a long way. And now I'm bringing them up. I'm bringing them *all* up. And even those that aren't part of me—I'm bringing them *back.*"

"You can't do that!" he shouted. Mantha wasn't sure if he meant she shouldn't be able to, or if she shouldn't be allowed to. She didn't care.

"I already have," Mantha said, and the window directly to the left of the throne exploded inward in a shower of green glass.

A shape came through the window along with the glass. A big, black shape with legs tucked neatly up under its body. It had a powerful, arching neck, flying mane, a long head, and a sharp spike protruding from its forehead.

Unicorn landed with a clap of hooves on stone, slid a foot, and then reared up over the throne, her forefeet tearing at the air.

Clara leaned into the horse's shoulder, her sword shining pale, and cut a burning crescent through the air as she brought the blade down and clove the person in the throne in half.

The pieces of him shriveled away from the blade as it passed through him, and with a horrible *gollupping* noise he turned himself inside out and drained away, like a punctured egg yolk.

He was green inside, but unlike the sea green of the windows this was the bright yellow-green of new spring buds. It poured away down the steps of the throne in a cascade of brilliant moss and ferns, running between Mantha's feet and under Unicorn's hooves, throwing up spores and flecks of yellow pollen, until it had traced a searing path across the stone floor and out the doors, which had been burst open.

Mantha looked for the holly prince, but all she saw was a pile of ash with lumps in it which might once have been antlers.

She looked up at Clara and smiled, but Clara was looking down at her with a confused, stricken expression.

"I don't understand," said the woman on the unicorn. "What just happened?"

"I'm not sure," said Mantha, with a shrug. "But it's over now."

Clara looked around at the hall, at the shattered window, at the unicorn beneath her, and at the assembled crowd from Mantha's imagination. This has gone quiet and still with the defeat of whatever had been sitting on the throne; Snake Woman had climbed up and was sitting on the springy green moss that was growing there, where she looked utterly pleased with herself. The rest were arrayed in a circle around them: Burgess and the alligator and the spider—who was less of a spider, really, and more of a giant, disembodied hand—and the dancing lily-people and the tree-bear and the faceless boy and all the rest, all waiting patiently. Expectantly.

"I have been dreaming," Clara said, faintly. "All this time."

"We've all been," Mantha said. "But now we can go home." She smiled up at Clara, and then around at her imaginary friends. "We can *all* go home," she said, louder. Because this was important too: you had to send your dreams home again when you were ready to wake up.

The lily-people were the first to move. One of them struck up a cheer and the rest followed, dancing madly down the hall and out the door, where the sky was visible, growing to the deep blue of a hot, sunny day. They were swiftly followed by the rest of the horde, save for Snake Woman, who remained, smugly, on the empty throne. She was already home.

In the midst of the commotion Mantha went around to Clara's side and tugged at her heel. Still watching the procession with a stunned look on her face, Clara lowered a hand and dragged Mantha up onto Unicorn's vast, black back.

It felt a bit like riding a heaving, slippery black bookcase, but Mantha clung to Clara's waist and knew she wouldn't fall off. Unicorn snorted once, like the rev of an engine, and then they too were galloping out of the sun-streaked hall.

There was no castle anymore. They came out onto the side of a mountain and the next instant were whipping between tall pines with lush ferns crowding around Unicorn's feet. Birdsong broke out around them, and beyond the canopy above them the sky was vividly blue. The ground was dappled sharply with cool shade and bright yellow spots of sunlight, and the green distances between the tree trunks flashed gold and blue with them.

Something else flashed in those distances. Something that kept pace with them through the trees, running with swift leaps and bounds. Mantha heard Clara gasp, and then she saw it too.

A white stag was leaping through the forest. His limbs were quick and sure and his coat was as brilliant as sun-sparked snow. On his head were a pair of small antlers, soft with downy fuzz. Then Unicorn jumped a fallen tree, and when she landed the stag was gone. The trees turned from pine to oak. The mountain leveled out. The oaks gave way to fields deep with young wheat, and then Unicorn was running low and smooth beside a wide, blue lake. The far side was thick with trees except for a small hill which rose, bare and green, and on it could be seen the outline of a large and rambling house.

Unicorn whinnied, sounding more than ever like the roar of an engine, and her hoofbeats began to run together into one continuous pounding as they found a wide dirt road leading around the lake toward the house.

The drive felt like it took forever while it was happening, but when she looked back on it later Jill remembered it mostly as a mad rush of road and wheeling night sky and the disorienting, terrifying feeling of sitting in the driver's seat of a car she could not control.

Tesla was a keen arch of leathery woman in the seat next to her, largely a dark silhouette against the periodic streetlights, though sometimes Jill caught flashes of her lined and weathered face, screwed up in intent interest.

She kept a careful watch on her rearview mirror, but her fear of losing Lansing was never fulfilled: the vampire's sleek blue Altima stayed squarely in Arcana's wake for the whole trip, only falling back when he pushed eighty along one stretch of highway.

"Interesting," said Tesla, when Arcana took a sharp exit somewhere in Pennsylvania and bounced onto a rough rural road.

"What is?" asked Jill, tightly.

"He's taking us to my forge," Tesla remarked, and said nothing more for the remainder of the trip.

Tesla's forge, as far as Jill could tell, seemed to be in the middle of a nowhere spotted with lakes and xenophobic houses. Arcana slowed down as he navigated the narrow roads, and once braked so hard in order to avoid hitting a raccoon which was scrambling off the road that Jill was thrown against her seatbelt. Lansing nearly rear-ended them, but both cars came out of it without a scratch, and once the road was clear again Arcana continued on his way.

This led, by several turns, to a winding dirt road which skirted a lake and terminated in the front yard of a large, comfortable house with a huge chimney looming over one corner. By Arcana's headlights Jill saw an ancient blue Ford pickup truck parked in front of a wide porch from whose eaves hung at least a dozen wind chimes, and by her improved night vision she saw a fluffy, black-and-white chicken hop up onto the low fence which ran off to one side. It ruffled its feathers and glared at Arcana.

Arcana idled there for a minute or so, then he shut himself off, turned off his lights, and Jill saw the key turn in the ignition as the gearstick popped into neutral and the parking brake sprang up.

Tesla was the first one out of the truck. She swung open the door and jumped out, nimble as a child, and was up onto the porch and through the front door before Jill could ask a single question. By the time she'd climbed out of Arcana the porch light and several interior lights had been switched on, and Lansing was getting out of her Altima, blinking and looking confused. Marcus unfolded himself, but didn't come out from behind the protective wing of the car's door.

Jill couldn't blame him. Even after Tesla came out of the house with a mystified expression on her face and declared everything fine and dandy and not a hammer out of place she still felt certain something was terribly wrong. Really. The feeling persisted even after she had been all over the grounds with Tesla, visited the chicken shed and seen the hens peacefully cooing there, surprised the great blue heron sleeping on one leg on the eaves over the back door, and been set up at the woman's massive kitchen table with the others while Tesla made them all strong, hot drinks.

It persisted until, just after sunrise, there was the sound of a familiar engine on the road, and a few minutes later Clara and Mantha came in through the front door. Clara looked as confused and surprised as Jill felt, but the girl was fairly beaming with smug satisfaction, as if she had arranged everything. And when, midway through the eruption of greetings and questions and counter-questions that followed, there was a knock on the door, it was Mantha who got up and answered it. Jill, wearing Tesla's spare holocaust cloak (Lansing was wearing the main one, along with her welding visor), dared peer into the hall and felt her mouth come open at the sight of Mantha shouting delightedly and hugging a bipedal rabbit in denim overalls, whirling her around so her furry feet left the floor.

"You came back! You came back!" Mantha was shouting, and the rabbit was speaking, too.

"I was never far away," she was saying, a little muffled. One paw came up and patted Mantha's shoulder. "None of us are."

Jill went back into the main room, where Clara sat on the ragged sofa staring blankly at the opposite wall, the cup of hot cocoa Tesla had made for her sitting untouched on the coffee table.

"Clara," said Jill.

"Yes?" said Clara, her eyes not leaving the wall. She didn't even blink.

"There's a . . . a walking, talking rabbit in the hall. Seems to be a friend of Mantha's."

"Oh," said Clara. "That's Lady Bibbit."

"Lady Bibbit," Jill repeated. "The patchwork stuffed bunny she's always carrying around?"

Clara nodded.

"Clara," said Jill.

"Yes?"

"What the hell happened?"

At last Clara dragged her eyes away from the wall and looked at Jill. They were very pale and blue and still rather distant.

She shrugged.

The Isenforge
Western Pennsylvania

The Isenforge was not much different from what Mantha remembered, only all the chickens were alive and so was the heron, much to Clara's relief. But the landscape looked more like what they had been driving through before they were shunted off into whatever it was had hijacked reality.

The owner of the forge, an old, leathery, white-haired woman named Tesla, called it a malemorphic entity, which Jill had explained was a creature which manipulated areas of heightened reality—such as the location of Tesla's forge—and lured people into them to feed off their subconscious nightmares. Since this more or less matched her and Clara's experiences Mantha accepted the answer. But when asked to give an account of her experiences, she chose not to repeat what the malemorphic entity had said to her. She didn't feel comfortable with that, and she doubted anyone else would.

She didn't feel entirely comfortable with Tesla, either. The woman had a way of looking at her which was intense and rather frightening. As though she could see through Mantha to what she really was. And since Mantha herself did not know what this was it was all the more terrifying.

They ate breakfast around the big, hardy wooden table in Tesla's kitchen; toast and sausages for the adults, cereal for Mantha. Afterward Jill and Lansing collapsed in Tesla's basement, while Marcus, Clara and Tesla herself went to the forge to talk the matter over. Mantha suspected she was meant to be involved in this, but she slipped away after washing her cereal bowl and walked with Lady Bibbit down to the lake where they explored the cold shallows with sticks, agitating the early tadpoles which had clustered for warmth near the surface.

"How much longer can you stay like this?" Mantha asked.

Lady Bibbit's nose twitched. "I'm always like this," she said, pointing at her fluffy chest and denim overalls. "People don't always see me this way, that's all."

"Oh," said Mantha, chagrined. But that helped. "Then I shall always try to see you this way."

Lady Bibbit beamed at her. "It might be more difficult, elsewhere. This place is . . . well it's not a *dream*, exactly. But it has been lifted out of the rest of the world, so it's easier for people like me to . . . um . . . well. To be accurately perceived, I guess."

"But now I know," Mantha said, finding a firm bit of bank and crouching down on it. She stuck a finger in the water. It was exactly as cold as she expected, and she took it out again immediately.

"Knowing helps," said Lady Bibbit, coming to crouch beside her. "But you have to believe, too."

"I'll work on that," said Mantha.

"Be careful, though," Lady Bibbit cautioned. "You need to be careful *what* you believe in. Otherwise people like him could take advantage of you."

Mantha didn't need to be told who the *him* was. The person on the throne. The malemorph. She pursed her lips and nodded.

There was a rustling in the grass above them, and Mantha looked up to see Tesla Isenfaust standing over her, a brown shadow against the pale spring sky with her short, fuzzy white hair lit up like a halo

"Can I join you?" she asked.

Mantha shrugged. It was a habit she had picked up from Clara.

Tesla took it for a yes and came down to crouch next to her—but on the far side of Lady Bibbit.

"So you're the conundrum that's got Clara all wound up," she said, bluntly.

"I guess," said Mantha. She pulled up a piece of old, dead, brown grass and started tracing patterns with it across the surface of the water.

"Any ideas?" Tesla asked.

"Ideas about what?" Mantha retorted. The woman was looking at her in that way again, and she was beginning to feel an uncomfortable itch under her collar.

"About what you want to be," Tesla said.

Mantha jabbed the piece of grass into the water, watched how the stalk changed shape when viewed through the surface reflections.

"Does that matter?"

"Oh, enormously," said Tesla. "But with you, I think it's critical."

Mantha rolled her lip around and bit down on it.

The problem was she had a lot of ideas about what she *could* be. None of them were very pleasant. Because the malemorph had been right about that: she *could* become someone like him. Someone who got inside other peoples' heads and pushed them into whatever shape she wanted. If she wanted to hard enough, she could do it to the whole world.

Except she didn't.

"I want to be a good person," she said.

"A person is ambiguous," said Tesla. "You breathe, you eat; you are a good person already. It's what you *do* that makes the difference."

Mantha frowned. She wasn't sure what the difference was between *being* a good person and being a person who *did good things*. But if it would make Tesla go away she'd play along.

"All right," she said. "I want to do good things. I don't want to hurt people."

Tesla Isenfaust nodded. She stood up, stretched creakily, then went away up the bank.

"Was that the wrong answer?" Mantha called up after her.

Turning her head over her shoulder, Tesla replied: "There are no wrong answers."

"*Was* that the wrong answer?" Mantha asked Lady Bibbit.

The rabbit shrugged, but patted Mantha's arm sympathetically. "It sounded true to me," she said. "I think that's the best you can do."

Tesla found Claymore sitting on the back porch, watching the heron hunting gophers on the northern slope of the hill. She was sitting in that way she had of pulling herself in, so she looked small, without actually slouching. Well, smaller. The laws of physics still affected Claymore enough that she would never be able to look *small*.

"I talked to your kid," Tesla said, coming to sit beside her. "She's all right."

"She is not my kid," Claymore said, sounding distant. Then her mind apparently processed the rest of Tesla's words.

"Did you recognize her?"

"Nope," said Tesla, kicking her feet out in front of her. "Nothing like anything I've ever seen before. Don't think she's done growing yet, so I couldn't rightly say anyhow. But she's all right. Saw you okay, from what I've heard."

"Yes," said Claymore, still distant. She had not described in detail their experiences under the malemorph's influence, but Tesla had gleaned enough to know that it had been an upsetting one for Claymore. And Claymore didn't upset easily.

Of course the whole thing was upsetting, and not merely because of the unpleasant version of reality which had been temporarily impressed on the local landscape. Tesla nudged Claymore with her knee.

"About that," Tesla said. "I'd be interested in any insight you might have on that account. Been working this forge here for sixty years and never had a malemorph so much as sniff in my direction before."

"Everything has been more active, since St. Louis," Claymore said.

"Yes, I did hear about that," said Tesla. "I don't buy it. Maybe it made a difference for a couple months, sure. But this? This smells like something bigger."

Claymore's face turned, showing a smooth, pale cheek and one icy blue eye.

"Bigger than St. Louis," she said. It was not a question.

"St. Louis was a localized event," said Tesla. "But I'll tell you my feeling. My feeling is we're on a tectonic shift, and heading into unfriendly territory. So keep all your eyes open and don't get too caught up in the details."

"You always told me the truth was in the details."

"It is," said Tesla. "But the big picture, that's also true. And sometimes you can't see it if you've got your nose buried in one little problem. That's all."

Claymore nodded.

"I will try," she sighed. She sounded wistful.

What Tesla Isenfaust said to Clara Mantha never knew, except that the upshot was they all drove back to Detroit the following night. Well, Lansing and Jill drove. Clara rode Unicorn. Mantha had wanted to ride behind her, but Jill forbade it. So Mantha rode in Arcana's passenger seat, which she was grateful for when it began to rain—hard, slanting and half frozen.

"Will we *ever* get a spring?" Jill moaned, switching on the windshield wipers.

"Eventually," said Lady Bibbit from the back seat. "Spring always comes."

Jill didn't seem to hear, but when Mantha leaned around to look, the rabbit gave her the thumb's up, and winked.

Settling back into her seat, Mantha looked out at the wet, cold night. Clara was just visible, riding at the edge of Arcana's headlamps, as a slick, black figure on a huge, black bike. But Mantha only had to narrow her eyes and shift her mind a little bit—just a little up and away from the usual order of things—and the motorcycle enlarged, grew warm and round, with a flying black tail and a thunderous, black mane, and the continuous roll of its engine grew choppy and turned into pounding hoofbeats.

Mantha dozed off to the sound of those hoofbeats, and this time she dreamed nothing at all.

Make no mistake

Make no mistake

I'm no mistake
Though I was lost at sea
Borne before the breeze
To a stormy lee

I'm no mistake
Out of a winter so cold
Make no mistake
I do not bring the spring
I will not make birds sing
Only death bells ring
But no mistake
Born out of the ages so old . . .

I know I am not
What you most fear

But I am not
What you hold dear
Reality stings
And yet it does seem
That we will not stay
In this sweet dream

Flashing on the heights
Lightning from on high
I'm touching down this time
Striking fire from the sky

Make no mistake
I'm lightning everywhere
The people cry and stare
Behold! My flaming hair
I'm no mistake
I am an archetype of change, so

Make no mistake
Because I bring a storm
With thunder on her horn
Flying a standard, torn
By angels' make
I'm taking over now, be warned.

I know I am not
What you most fear
But I am not
What you hold dear
Reality stings
And yet it does seem
That we will not stay
In this sweet dream

Flashing on the heights
Lightning from on high
I'm touching down this time
Striking fire from the sky

Make no mistake

Great gates crumbling
Giants are stumbling
Their gifts I have received

Make no mistake

Though I'm not worthy
I will shine in the

The Hour I First Believed

Hour I first believed

Make no mistake

I'm no mistake
I am flashing on the heights
I'm lightning that strikes twice
And I'm touching ground this time
I'll set fire to the sky

Make no mistake

I'm no mistake

Make no mistake

I'm no mistake

Make no mistake

—No Mistake/*Panthera*

HOPE *in* the FOREST *of* DESPAIR

^{4.}

Hell, the Lustful Gale
Second Ring

TWO FIGURES CREPT DOWNWARD over a face of cracked, gray rock. The cliff was steep enough that they were obliged to turn around and descend backward, hands sliding into cracks and feet grasping for any semblance of a hold in the rock, but it was never quite vertical, never quite so smooth as to be impossible, and so they continued, step by cautious step.

One figure was dark and wore clothes that might have once been blue jeans and a rust-colored cotton shirt, but had since been scorched black and then faded to a monotone gray. It made her dark brown skin stand out like a polished stone, and her hair, bravely tied back behind her head, was very bushy and black. There was a large, circular shield strapped to her back, stained silver, with a fat crescent polished to a mirror-shine: a waxing moon.

The other figure was pale. Her skin was pale, her hair was white, and the short, simple dress she wore, though stained at the hem with muddy brownish-red, was still mostly white. There was a disturbance in the air behind her shoulders, like feathers flapping in the wind, and when she glanced over her shoulder her eyes were large and totally colorless.

The wind was currently blowing up at them in fierce bursts and gusts, so there was not only the danger of falling, but also of being lifted off the cliff and cast into the air. This air was dark and misty-gray with swirling clouds, smelled of ammonia and wine, and was uncomfortably warm. Occasionally dark shapes could be glimpsed within the storm, too large to be birds and flailing awkwardly. Sometimes they screamed, but mostly they moaned.

The storm was stratified: layers of fierce winds punctuated by areas of calm. When the two climbers passed out of the former and into the latter, the dark one said:

"So there were twenty-seven of you, total."

"There's only one of me," said the pale one. She had a clear, flutey voice, half of which was lost in the distant roaring overhead.

"Yeah," said the dark one. "But that lady on the island said, you were split into nine pieces, and then each of those nine were split *again* into three. Three times nine is twenty-seven."

"Better twenty-seven than fifty-one!" the pale one giggled.

In between storms the still air was cold, and the rock was clammy under their hands and feet (they were both barefoot).

"Small favors," Selene murmured through gritted teeth. It was almost harder climbing between storms, since the wind took some of her weight and made it easier on her hands. She wasn't certain—she couldn't be certain of anything—but it felt like she was getting heavier the further down they went. Or she was just getting tired. But she didn't get tired, not here. She might *feel* tired, but if she concentrated on ignoring it, pretty soon the feeling went away. Now, no matter how hard she thought, it felt more and more like someone had strapped bricks to her legs.

She tried to distract herself by clarifying exactly what it was they had to do.

"So, I found one of you on, like, the border. And there was another in that creepy castle. So you, here, now, are two twenty-sevenths of . . . whoever you are. So we have twenty-five more fragments left. I remember the lady said there was one in the Lustful Gale, which means we should be on the lookout, because I think this is it."

"Lustful gale, willful gale, blow away my sins!" called Albatross, her high, reedy voice ringing through the stagnant air. As if in answer there was a roaring sound, like a wave breaking, and Selene looked down between her legs just in time to see a pillow of gray clouds boiling up at them.

"Hold—" she began, and then the torrent engulfed them, and all other words were lost.

Warm air washed over her, pushed her against the rock and then subsided, only to come hurling back. She felt her hands slip from their hold and for one tenuous moment she was suspended on her feet alone, standing up on the steep slope while she groped frantically for the rock. She felt one foot lift, and then her flailing hand caught an outcropping and her fingers grabbed and held. She pulled herself flat against the stone, hugging herself to it so that the wind brushed over her. She looked up, and to her horror saw that Albatross had been swept away into the sky.

She was tumbling, her dress and hair flying up in the gale, up and up, and then she plummeted past Selene . . . just to be pillowed up again. Only this time she was raised barely past Selene's shoulder, and then she did a cartwheel in the air and came to grip the rocky slope in much the same position as Selene, but fifteen feet away. She turned her head to face her and grinned. She giggled, and the winds retreated, falling back into their former strata.

Selene swallowed a rocky lump in her throat. That had been too close. Albatross was now lightly handing herself back over to Selene, her toes splayed open to catch the tiniest ledges and cracks in the rock.

"It's fun!" she said, when she was again within speaking distance. "You just have to let it blow *through* you, and it won't take you away."

"That's ... good to know," said Selene, reaffirming her determination to maintain a three-point hold on the rock from then on.

Down they went. The next level of storm was fiercer than any before, and smelled worse, something septic mixed with overripe fruit, and the winds brought with them a shower of wet drops of something Selene decided not to wonder about. She kept her mouth closed and her eyes narrowed and concentrated on putting one foot below the other, one at a time, making sure she had both hands anchored before moving.

Albatross shouted something—it sounded like "hello!"—and then there was an impact on Selene's back, making the shield dig in painfully, and her head slammed against the rock.

The pain was intense. Like stubbing a cold toe. It shocked Selene—who had grown accustomed to being able to tune out physical sensation—and in her shock her grip loosened, and there was an updraft ...

She was lost in the wind. She was upside-down, legs kicking, arms windmilling, but she couldn't find the cliff and all she could see was whirling gray air.

That, and the thing that had hit her.

It was a man. Broad-shouldered with a potbelly, his features were shadowed and indistinct. He was crying, moaning, and seemed completely oblivious to Selene. That was all she noticed before the wind took her, filled her, and sent her rocketing upward—or downward, she really couldn't tell at this point.

It was not exactly an unpleasant feeling. It was exciting and exhilarating, though frightening as well. Mostly, it was frustrating. No matter how she twisted and turned, she couldn't find the rocky cliff, couldn't see Albatross, and could do nothing to control where she went. She felt like her body had been filled with champagne, all bubbles and warm dizziness, and below that an unfocused desire for ... for something. Selene could not imagine what it was, only that she wanted it desperately. That not having it was the worst kind of tantalizing pain.

There was a coolness against her back, and it was a mark of how far her mind had strayed that it took Selene a concentrated effort to remember her shield. She wasn't sure what good it would do, but it was something she *could* do, and so she grabbed the strap to which her shield was pinned, pulling it around so that the shield covered her front, and then grabbed the rod and lifted the thing off over her head.

At first it didn't do much, but Selene found that by careful maneuvering she could create a slight block against the wind, so it broke and streamed around her. It was like putting a hand up to deflect a stream of water, but instead of allowing her to breathe, this allowed her to think.

This was the Lustful Gale, and if she recalled correctly, that would make it correspond to Dante's second level. Which was, what? The lustful? Selene hadn't felt anything even remotely approaching lust since she'd fallen into Hell. But, she supposed, lust didn't have to mean sexual desire. Couldn't it be applied to any sort of desire that made someone act irrationally? Was *that* what she was feeling?

She tried, logically, to work through what it was she wanted. Mostly, she decided, she wanted to *not* be caught up in the Lustful Gale. Finding Albatross's lost pieces would also be nice.

This only made the champagne-body feeling worse, however. It was like identifying her wants made her want them *more*. Made her *need* them. They became the most important things and if she didn't get them *now* she would—

She was losing her grip on her shield. She grabbed its edge with her other hand and held it over her face, pressing her nose against its concave underbelly so that the rod pressed a cool stripe over her cheek.

She could not think about what she wanted. But she couldn't forget either. How many souls had given in to apathy in an attempt to relieve their suffering? And they were still here, if the number of other flying bodies she glimpsed around the edges of the shield was any indication. To want nothing was a torment in and of itself, since it left you at the mercy of momentary whims which, in the end, never got you anywhere.

What was it Albatross had said? Just let the winds blow through you? It made no sense.

A part of her said: *It's Hell, it doesn't have to make sense*!

But another part whispered: *It's Hell. The rules are different, but there are still rules.*

That part of her sounded a lot like Clara, which made Selene laugh. Clara would probably have figured this one out in a heartbeat and already be on her way to rescue the bits of Albatross.

It did no good to wonder, though, since Clara was not here and couldn't help her.

Unless.

Selene tumbled for a while, considering. What would Clara do? She tried asking herself that, and got nothing. Then she tried imagining Clara, and asked her imagination what Clara would do.

In her imagination Clara did that odd, down-and-up shrug of hers, and said:

"What is the opposite of lust? Of uncontrollable desire?"

Apathy? Yeah, tried that one.

"Apathy is the absence of emotion," her imagined Clara helpfully supplied. "Not the opposite of it."

C'mon, help me out here! Selene thought, angrily. *If the opposite of lust is the key to getting out of here just tell me!*

"I can't tell you anything you do not already know," said imagination-Clara. "But I can remind you that according to modern interpretation, the opposing virtue of Lust is Chastity."

Bullcrap, thought Selene. *Refusing to acknowledge or accept your desires was what got you closeted gays with internalized homophobia. You could be chaste with yourself but so eaten up by self-hatred that you did real damage to other people.*

In her mind's eye, Clara shrugged again, down and up. "Then look beyond Hell. Christian theology does not contain all the answers—and many of theirs they borrowed from earlier philosophies."

This whole place is bullcrap, Selene thought, beginning to grow angry. *Really, if you let yourself be ruled by your desires, usually that ends badly for you. I bet most of these souls were pretty miserable before they died! Doesn't that make Hell redundant?*

"That is not something I can answer," Clara said, with the kind of calm serenity that used to drive Selene nuts. It was the way she coolly accepted something, without actually agreeing or disagreeing. It was . . .

Just let the wind blow through you . . .

What was that word?

Serenity.

Her shield was cool under her hands. Solid and reassuring as the wind was warm and volatile. In her mind's eye, Clara's pale face slowly faded out of focus, becoming a round, white disk. A moon drifting calmly above the storm.

Selene closed her eyes and focused on that. She thought of a still lake, quiet and dark. She took everything she cared about and set it aside. Not as a dismissal, but as one puts away a precious thing in a safe place.

The wind buffeted her.

She thought of evenings in late summer, with the fireflies winking in and out. She thought of mornings in winter, hushed with snow. Of a cat, curled up asleep in a beam of sun. Horses grazing in the afternoon, so the sun lit their coats copper and gold around the edges, and their shadows stretched long and green across the grass.

And the wind blew through her. Blew her clean of wishes and hopes and desires.

She felt like she was floating, perfectly weightless.

And then she hit the ground.

Swamp of the Gluttons
Third Ring

For a while everything hurt so much Selene couldn't think of anything else. Reality blinked on and off, and in between were patches of nothing so time got all jagged and jumpy.

She was on her back looking up at the boiling gray sky. The air was so thick it felt like lying on the bottom of a riverbed, looking up at the surface from below. There were flecks of ash floating in the air, and breathing was difficult. Her diaphragm wasn't working.

Nothing.

Something horrible was falling out of the underbelly of the sky. It was cold and wet and splattered on the ground around her and on her face. It smelled of sewage and sulfur and burned her skin like acid.

She had landed with her right arm splayed out next to her, still holding the shield, but she couldn't move it. She could, however, lift her left arm, and with it she grabbed her own right wrist and dragged that arm—and the shield—across her face. Her body was still pricked by the precipitation, but with her face covered she could more or less ignore it.

Nothing.

Her eyes were already open, but now she could see the blurry underside of her shield, and part of her arm. She blinked them, roughly, feeling her lids catch and her eyes begin to water.

Her body was no longer consumed by pain. She could breathe more or less normally, and when she tried to untangle her right arm from the shield, she was able to do so.

The rain of burning sewage had stopped, but her shield had grown inexplicably heavy, and she had to use both hands to lift it up and slide it off her face.

There was a shifting of the weight above her, and a familiar voice said, "H-hey—whoa!" and the weight abruptly vanished.

Selene peered over the rim of her shield and found herself looking up a pair of scrawny legs which disappeared into fluttering white cloth, and above that, a white, oval face.

"Hi," she said, feeling like she had to dislodge a clod of earth from her throat as she said it.

Albatross was hovering above her, ghostly wings spread, and seemed to fade into the gray sky. She was looking down at Selene curiously, as if she had never seen anything like her before.

"You fell," she said, and pointed upward. The tip of her finger went almost transparent, which worried Selene. Albatross had seemed much more solid since she'd combined with the piece of herself stuck to the flagpole of the castle, and downright substantial since she'd eaten Kirke's fruit, but now she looked as flimsy and ethereal as she had when Selene had first found her, on the far shore of the Acheron.

"You fell out of the sky," Albatross repeated, and giggled. "I followed you down, but I couldn't find you once you landed." Her feet touched down on the shield, over Selene's chest, and then she knelt, curled tight as a cat, so she could press her cheek against it. "But then the moon came out from behind the clouds, and I saw you again. Are you Mani?"

Selene looked at her, confused. She had first heard the question as "Are you many?" and wondered what Albatross was on about. Then her brain clarified the pronunciation, and realized the girl had said *Mani*. The Norsk name for the moon.

"No," said Selene. "I'm Selene, remember?"

"Same thing," said Albatross, decisively. "And I think I would have re-membered if I met the moon before."

"I'm not—" Selene began, wondering why she was having this conversa-tion all over again, and then breaking off as her brain finally put the pieces together.

"Albatross!" she exclaimed, struggling into a sitting position. Alba-tross floated off her to hover a few inches above the mucky ground.

Selene spared a thought of *yeeeuck* as she felt the clinging soil release her, but she had more important things to think about.

This wasn't *her* Albatross. It was the fragment they had been hoping to find in the Lustful Gale. Which, by some small miracle, had found *her*.

Then she looked down and saw that her shield was positively shining with silver light, and thought *Maybe not exactly a miracle . . .*

Meanwhile the fragment of Albatross was still hovering, and now Se-lene noticed all the little things that were different. This one had no stains on her toes or dress, but her skirt was in tatters and there was a huge rip in one side that made it all but pointless as a piece of clothing. She had the same feathery mass of hair and the same white eyes, but they looked darker as her pupils were almost fully dilated. She looked younger, too. Barely a teenager.

She was gazing at Selene with a gravity beyond that of an adolescent, however.

"Albatross," she whispered. "That's me, isn't it?"

"That's . . . what you told me to call you," Selene said, wondering how she was going to explain this.

"I don't remember," said Albatross.

"That's okay," Selene said, quickly. She pried herself out of the mud and staggered to her feet.

Her body had healed, but her clothes had not. Her jeans had a burst seam at the hip and the cloth there was dark and stiff with dried blood, and when she took off her shirt to give to Albatross, she found the back of it was perforated with similarly stained slits. She did not bother to check her undershirt. She did not want to think too much about what had happened to her when she'd hit the ground.

Albatross looked at the shirt curiously, and didn't seem to know what to do with it until Selene helped her on with it. Her wings flickered in and out of sight, but eventually came back on as she straightened the cloth around her neck, and inspected her hands where they protruded from the sleeves.

"I wasn't cold," she said, and Selene believed her. It was warm and muggy here under the gale, and if Selene had cared about the comfort of her own body, she would have wanted to take her shirt off anyway.

"It wasn't to keep you warm," Selene mumbled, picking up her shield. She looked around.

They were on a flat plain of what looked like marshland which stretched on as far as the eye could see ... which was maybe half a mile, at a very rough estimate. The land disappeared into a veil of sickly, gray-green mist, with here and there a white sheen which suggested precipitation.

There was no sign of the cliff of rock she and the double Albatross had descended, and the boiling underbelly of the storm above was all she could see of the Lustful Gale.

Because she could, Selene spent a while thinking about what she should do next. She considered how she had found Albatross in the first place, and how the girl had found her again, seemingly by accident. Selene decided not to go actively looking for her, since that was a waste of energy, but rather to treat it like the time her brother's dog had gone missing. They had walked through the neighborhood in their normal route, calling and calling until they were hoarse. In the end the dog had come barreling out of nowhere, tail wagging, tongue lolling, covered in dust.

Remembering how this Albatross had found her by the light of her shield, Selene hoisted it up and balanced it on her head, like an absurd sort of hat. Then she ran into a problem.

"Albatross?" she asked, feeling foolish as she did so. "Do you know which way is in? I mean, which way is *down?*"

"Deeper in, deeper down?" said Albatross, in a singsong voice. "Underneath the grimy ground?"

"Looking for the center of Hell but yeah," Selene said.

Albatross lifted one arm stiffly away from her side, holding it out in a straight line. Like a compass swiveling to north she turned on her heel in a slow semicircle, wavering back and forth a little before coming to a halt. Selene couldn't tell the difference between the direction she pointed and any other part of their surroundings, but she figured it was better than herself making a blind guess.

"All right," she said, taking Albatross's outstretched hand and beginning to walk in that direction. She inhaled a lungful of warm, sticky air and shouted, "ALBATROSS!" at the top of her lungs.

"I'm right here!" Albatross replied, drifting behind her like a girl-shaped balloon.

"I know," Selene explained. "But the rest of you ain't. There's bits of you scattered all over Hell, and I was with one that was two of them merged together, but I lost her in the gale. ALBATROSS!"

They walked, Selene shouting Albatross's name every few minutes. After a while, her Albatross joined in, turning the word into a little song to which she dipped and swayed at the end of Selene's arm. Because of that, Selene didn't hear the moaning until suddenly it was rising all around them, cut with squelching noises and the occasional pained cry.

They kept walking, Selene trudging through the muck and Albatross drifting behind her, as the landscape first became littered, and then crowded, and then choked with bodies lying in the muck. The rain of stinging excrement returned—or perhaps they moved into a squall of it—and Selene was more glad of her shield than ever.

At first she tried to step between the bodies, but as they grew denser and denser it became more of a game of finding which area of any given body was the best to put her foot on. She aimed for backs and buttocks and the occasional belly, but once her foot slipped and the ground heaved under her as the person whose face she had stepped on came thrashing up out of the mud.

They looked vaguely female, with long trailing skeins of mucky hair drawing over their face, their skin distended and bulbous, as though from abnormal growths. She opened her mouth to scream, and inside was only more muck, and all that came out was a pained, guttural moan.

"Don't tell me," Selene said a little while later. "These are the gluttons, right?"

"To excessively pursue pleasure beyond all reason becomes in itself its own punishment," Albatross recited.

"Yeah," said Selene, vaguely. She was having thoughts, which she was sure other people had had before her, and was wondering if it was worth the energy to give them voice.

The second time she accidentally stepped on a soul's face she was confronted by a man whose skin had become detached from his body, and she could see that what she had thought were growths were actually pockets of muck which had somehow gotten stuffed under the skin itself.

"Okay, but look," said Selene, when they had moved on. "I know it's perfectly possible to eat yourself sick, but further punishment for *comfort eating*? Really, as long as we're talking about excessively pursuing ... anything. Food. Sex. Wealth. Whatever. Food's gotta be the *least* harmful. I mean, I'd take that over comfort *drinking* any day."

"You don't judge ill those who selfishly accrue comforts at the expense of others?"

"In life, sure," said Selene, stepping over the side of someone whose skin had been stuffed so full of filth it had burst, spilling a small landslide across their path. "In death? Nah. What's the point? They did their damage. By this time, there's no making it right."

"Do you think it's possible to make things right?" Albatross asked. When Selene glanced back she found the girl staring earnestly down at her, deeply invested in her answer.

"What I think ain't the way of the universe," Selene said, shooting her a wry smile. "But I guess, from my experience, you *can* make things better. But only as long as you're alive." She thought about what she had said for a moment. "Maybe that's part of it. Being alive, I mean. Being alive means you can change, being able to change means you can make things better. Or worse. Once you're dead, it's over. Maybe your consciousness keeps on going a while, but you can't actually *do* anything. You're done. Finished."

Albatross drifted in silence for a while. Selene shouted her name.

"I hope I'm alive," she whispered.

"Yeah, I hope so too," Selene said, and squeezed her cold little hand.

They walked and walked, and shouted and shouted, but the double Albatross did not appear. Selene began to feel empty inside, a feeling which confused her until she finally recognized it as hunger. She had become so used to ignoring it that she had forgotten about it altogether. But talking about comfort eating had made her think of macaroni and cheese—her favorite comfort food—and pizza, and pancakes with bacon, and the emptiness turned to a twisting hunger, persistent and unavoidable. Worse, the sweet part of the sweet-and-sour stink of the muck began to overpower everything else, and when her foot went into a puddle of it, all Selene could think of was how, when you got right down to it, mud looked almost exactly like refried black beans.

Suddenly she realized why the surrounding souls kept stuffing it into their mouths.

"Okay, this isn't working," she said, stopping in her tracks.

"What's not?" asked Albatross.

"Just, the walking. We're not getting anywhere, and I'm getting hungry."

"Hungry?"

"Yeah, hungry."

"There's nothing to eat."

"I know that," said Selene, and thought about how, from the right angle, the lumps of rock in the mud might pass for a very dark pot roast. She shook herself. "I know that," she repeated. Shutting her eyes she breathed in deeply, through her nose.

It didn't work. All she smelled was browned meat, sweet fruit and the delectable aroma of baking bread. So she pulled her shield down off her head and pressed her face into its cool backside, trying to ground herself on the point of contact between the center of her forehead and the cold metal.

Slowly, gut-wrenchingly, the appetizing smells receded, to be replaced by the original stench of putrefaction and sewage. When she opened her eyes, all she saw was filth.

They resumed the long walk, but the hunger remained, persistent as a stone in her belly. She tried thinking of the still lake, the sunset and the horses, but though it helped distract her, it didn't assuage the underlying discomfort.

Well, she thought. *What's the opposite of gluttony?*

This time there was no imagined version of Clara to give her the answer, so Selene repeated the question out loud, for Albatross's benefit.

"What is gluttony?" the girl replied.

"It's . . . uh . . . hunger?" said Selene. "But not the healthy kind. It's like when you keep eating just for the pleasure of eating, even though you're already full?"

"Insatiable hunger?"

"Yeah."

"Oh." The girl drifted in silence for a while. "I don't know what the opposite of that is."

She sounded apologetic and sad, as though she felt she had let Selene down. But Selene discovered she had worked out the answer on her own.

Satisfaction, she thought, forcefully. *Being satisfied with what you got. Well, I don't know that I don't want things to change, but I do know that eating this muck won't help.*

With this in mind she concentrated on the parts of her that weren't hungry. Her feet and her hands, legs, shoulders, ears. She told herself firmly that she didn't need anything more than what she had—except maybe to find the other bits of Albatross. She opened her mouth and breathed deep, feeling her lungs fill, then pushed all the air out again and let her body still. She held herself like that, concentrating on the stillness and the reflection of the minuscule sensations that tingled along her fingers and her arms. She drew her awareness down every inch of her body, and found nothing lacking.

She had everything she needed right here.

The next step her foot plunged into the muck up to her knee. When she rocked backward, trying to pull it out, her other leg sank to her thigh.

"Yeeeuugh!" Albatross cried. She was clinging to Selene's hand, her knees drawn up into her chest, but her toes were brushing the ground.

Selene kicked once, trying to get her body horizontal so she could float on the muck, but it was like a slippery throat had opened up beneath her and was sucking her down. She was up to her waist—her chest—Albatross was wrapped around her arm, ephemeral wings whipping the air above her.

Then it was like a trapdoor opened beneath her, and they were both sucked down into the mud.

Cliffs of Greed
Fourth Ring

Everything was black and cold and sliding past her face and Albatross wrenched on her arm, nearly dislocating the shoulder, and then they were shot out into the air again.

Selene wiped her face on her forearm and opening her eyes discovered they were drifting down through a forest of stone pillars. Their upper portions split and arched, supporting a ceiling of packed, black earth, while their bases were sunk in a dry, rocky plain that stretched maybe half a mile across in a long strip of land whose ends were cloaked in black mist.

On one side the rocks rose in steps until they met the upper limits of the pillars, while on the other the plain ended in a sharp cliff.

And in the distance, at the edge of the cliff, Selene saw something white flicker in the dark.

It was a good thing she still had hold of Albatross, even if her arm was complaining, because the girl's wings were beating fiercely, slowing their fall to a leisurely descent. Selene thought they must have looked like a piece of sodden wood slowly settling at the bottom of a river, and relaxed her legs in anticipation of the landing.

She tried to keep the flash of white in view, but as they reached the bottom it was swallowed up by the mist.

Selene stomped her feet once, shaking off the excess muck which still clung to her, and then she took off at a trot in the direction she had seen the whiteness, dragging Albatross behind her.

"Oh, I see!" said the girl, bobbing along at the end of Selene's hand. "Further in, further down! It's more than a physical journey!"

"Eh?" said Selene, straining her eyes into the dim distance. It was darker down here, and from the ground the tops of the pillars were lost to a vague blackness. Luckily the ground was smooth, dry stone, which after all the muck proved a welcome relief.

"You can walk and walk forever, you'd never get out. That was my problem. I kept thinking of distance as being open ended. But space isn't fixed. It changes with your point of view."

Selene was only half listening. She had discovered that by raising her shield, a faint silvery glow formed around them in a soft sphere. It didn't illuminate the distances, but it helped her see where she was going. It certainly helped when they reached the end of the plain, where she might have run straight off the cliff if she hadn't seen it outlined starkly against the inky clouds behind.

Inching as close to the edge as she dared, Selene found herself looking down over a dark expanse of country whose distances were enveloped in rust-colored fog, but between her and the sight horizon she could make out a languid, black river, an expanse of marshland, and beyond that a wide, dark wall that wound its way through the hills beyond the marsh. Its shape was silhouetted against an angry, orange-and-red glow, and beyond that there was only the rust-colored fog that lay in pillows, rising up until the dim light failed and it merged with the oppressive, charcoal sky. The air was heavy and still, and smelled of burning.

The cliff they were on dropped vertically in a smooth, sheer face for perhaps eight feet, at the bottom of which was a narrow ledge, maybe three feet wide. Beyond that was another drop, and another ledge, and after that Selene couldn't see any farther.

There was no sign of anything white.

Selene scanned the line of the cliff in either direction and, when she was satisfied there was nothing white along it anywhere that she could see, decided their best course would be to keep going down. Still, she shouted "*Albatross!*" into the void, before tugging her Albatross over the edge and floating down to the nearest ledge. She leaned over and discovered the action had brought into view a third ledge, beyond the one immediately below her.

They jumped again. And again. On the fourth ledge the monotony of the flat, gray stone was broken by a single rock. It was about the size of an apricot, lumpy and brown, and looked rather out of place in the middle of the ledge.

On the next, there were more rocks. And on the one after that, they were interspersed with small boulders. And on the one below that Selene's feet sank deep in a gravel drift, which sloped down from a great obelisk of stone that filled the ledge to their left. Selene had to glance at it twice after she thought she glimpsed a pair of feet sticking out from underneath it, and feet they were, small and pale. She felt a pang of recognition.

Scrambling up the gravel fall, she began scooping the little stones out from under the big one, until it began to unbalance, and she was able to put her shielded shoulder against it and tip it off the ledge.

The rock went, ponderous and slowly at first, then suddenly fell, crashing out of sight below them.

The person who had been under it was not Albatross. Even with their face crushed in and their torso distorted from the weight of the rock she knew it wasn't Albatross.

The soul blinked up at her, and as she watched, their face slowly reformed, their ribs popped back into place, and then they were sitting up, sliding in the gravel as they got to their feet, and with a cry of anguish launched themselves over the cliff after the rock.

Selene watched them go, confounded, and then she realized.

"Cliffs of Greed. Right."

She retook Albatross by the hand, and together they continued their descent. This time, she concentrated on thinking generous thoughts. Nothing specific, but just in general. Thinking about all the ways *she* had behaved generously seemed dangerously self-centered, so she tried to keep things pertinent to the situation. She did not take a single stone from the ledges they crossed, and when Albatross wanted to stop and admire the view—they appeared to be getting closer to the river, and it was glimmering faintly in the red light beyond the wall—she waited patiently, reflecting on the many ways generosity could express itself. You could be generous with your time, with your attention, with your feelings of good will...

Unbidden, the memory of Clara pressing the hard, silver, spirit ring into her hand. Clara, handing her her helmet and the keys to Unicorn.

Clara making a flying leap to the edge of the bridge, hands flailing, grabbing, grasping the barrel of her gun...

They jumped again, and this time they did not land on hard, dry stone, but ankle deep in cold, dark water.

Stygian Marsh
Fifth Ring

They had reached the bottom of the Cliffs of Greed. Beside them the marsh stretched out forever, and before them flowed the river, slow and black. On its far shore was a black wall topped with stone parapets, and the orange lights of its windows reflected on the inky surface of the water. Things moved along the wall, but they were too distant and too dark for Selene to make out. Behind them the cliffs disappeared into the black sky, and beyond the wall was only the rust-colored fog, now lit from below by the vivid, red light.

Between them and the river, some under the water and some flailing in the shallows, were the dark shapes of souls. Those beneath the surface stared up at them accusingly as they passed, while Selene tried actively to avoid the others. These appeared not to notice them at first and were more concerned with beating each other. It was like walking through a live demonstration of the sloppiest street fight ever, and Selene had to duck and dart to avoid flying limbs and lunging bodies. To make things worse, sometimes the souls under the surface would rise, spitting water, to claw at those above, trying to drag them under. Sometimes they succeeded.

There didn't seem to be any reason to their fighting, but now and then Selene would see groups of souls team up to beat down one of their number, only to turn on each other once their common enemy had been vanquished. Once, a soul erupted from the water beside them. He was a man, almost as wide as he was tall, and under the glistening water and mud, Selene could just make out the sleeveless undershirt which was his only clothing. He raised a fist and brought it down on her head.

Selene had her shield ready, but it was still a heavy blow. Yet there was only one strike: she heard the soul howl in surprised pain, and when she peered around the shield she found the scene before her starkly illuminated in silver light.

Countless souls, momentarily frozen in their eternal conflict, stared at her over shoulders and under arms, and from everywhere out of the water around them.

And Selene thought, frantically, of compassion and forgiveness and sympathy, and hoped it would be enough. She thought of Addison, the girl she had rescued from Death Valley, and of Orangie and the other victims of the covert operation studying the dormant angel in New Mexico. She thought of Jill, and tried to bury the automatic spark of annoyance. Jill, who had gone into the dark and, far from losing her way, bullied the dark into showing her the path.

The souls were retreating. Some of them were sinking beneath the surface of the water, while those that could began splashing off through it, trying to get away. Albatross tugged urgently on Selene's arm, and when Selene turned around she saw why.

A woman had risen up out of the water behind them, and though she was barely a hair taller than Selene, she gave the impression of vast, dark expanses and a cold, hollow place that opened up behind Selene's heart.

Like the souls she was dark, as though she stood in shadow, but unlike them her skin glimmered and glistened, and when Selene looked upon her face she was surprised to find it so full of personality it was like looking at the face of twenty people merged into one. Lines of laugher and of scorn ringed her eyes, her nose and cheeks sagged. She had a loose flap of skin under her chin like the wattle of a chicken, but for all the trappings of age she stood erect and firm, her legs planted wide and her hands resting on her hips. She seemed to be wearing a dark dress made of a material that rippled like the surface of the water behind her. Or perhaps it was water. She said:

"What are you doing, little moon?"

Selene didn't bother to contest the name. She was too busy thinking desperately who this person was. Dante, she remembered, had gotten a ride across the river from some ancient king. But there was no sign of any boat here, only the woman in the water.

She realized she had not answered the question.

"We're looking for the rest of my friend, here." She squeezed Albatross's hand. "You haven't happened to see any . . . uh . . . floating around?"

The woman glanced up at Albatross and smiled. She had a terrible smile. It was sad and happy and ominous all at the same time.

"What once was shattered cannot be put back together again, not in the way it was before," she said.

"Fair enough," said Selene. "Have you seen any?"

The woman lowered her gaze and regarded Selene with calm indifference.

"I have seen her times beyond measure, in countless forms and fancies. She is part of what keeps me bound here, in the dark below the earth."

"I'm sorry about that," Albatross said, descending so that the tips of her toes touched the surface of the water. "If I knew how, I'd let you go."

The woman tilted her head. Selene thought she might have been amused.

"It is not your will or conscious choice that I am here. It is simply the way the wills weave."

"You know what she is?" Selene asked, jerking her head at Albatross.

"I recognize her," said the woman in the water. "She is part of the greater calamity which has been befallen Dis. Why you, a living soul, would aid her, is curious to me."

Selene shrugged. "It's what I do."

"Did Lilith send you?"

Selene gritted her teeth and shook her head. "She brought me here, but I left her."

"Did you now?" the woman asked, and for a split second Selene thought she saw branches growing out of her hair, the shadow of Lilith's monster form rising behind the dark woman in the water. But then the vision was gone, and it was just the woman, sad and dark and complicated. Selene thought: if Albatross was one layer of a person, then this woman was several people stacked on top of each other. And she remembered what Lilith had said.

I was a god, once.

"I'm trying," Selene amended. "Look, if you can't help, that's okay. But do you know where we can find this calamity? Is that Dis, across the river?" She pointed at the low wall on the other side.

The woman did not look where she pointed, but nodded slowly.

"All right." Selene tugged on Albatross's hand. "Think you're up for giving me another lift?"

Albatross looked at the expanse of water, her mouth twisting uncertainly.

There was a deep, churning noise—like cold water pouring into a stone cauldron—and Selene looked down to see the woman was laughing at them.

"I will not suffer the living to cross over me," she said. "I've made all the allowances I ever will. But if you would walk in me and know me, then you may come to the far shore with my blessing and good will."

Selene looked at her skeptically and did not let go of Albatross's hand. But Albatross seemed to have her own ideas and tugged on Selene's arm.

"Let me go," she said. "I will meet you on the other side."

"No," said Selene firmly, still holding on. She had remembered something about the river that encircled Dis. Dante had named it after a river from the Greek underworld, and according to Greeks, it had also been a goddess. Once.

"No," she repeated, thinking furiously. "You wait here. When I get to the far shore, I'll signal you—you can come find me. You, wait here with her," she said to the woman in the water.

"You charge me with her protection?" asked the woman.

"I charge you with making sure she doesn't float away," Selene said, extending the hand that held Albatross's toward the woman.

"That is not something I can promise to do," she said, gravely.

"Yeah, well try, maybe?" Selene said. "It's the least any of us can do."

The woman did not smile, but she took Albatross's hand and stood there, a solid pillar, while Selene slung her shield over her back and waded out into the water, toward the city on the far side.

When it was up to her waist and still there was no strong current Selene dared to glance back, and saw the two women—one pale and floating, the other dark and rooted in the water—standing where she had left them. She grinned at Albatross, waved once, and then continued on her way.

Only a few steps on, the bottom dropped sharply and Selene went under. She thought of swimming, but the current had begun to drag at her and so instead she doubled over, grabbing handfuls of the sticky mud at the bottom of the river to hold her to her course. She expelled all the air she could from her lungs, and that helped her sink.

Down, down, down dropped the ground, and soon it was completely black, with the cold water rushing around her ears. Still, Selene put one hand, or one foot, in front of the other, and kept pulling herself forward. Forward and down, until she passed through the current and the water stilled.

She had her eyes open, for what little good it did, and so noticed when a faint, silvery gray light blossomed around her, casting her own shadows stark and black before her on the pale, desolate riverbed.

Good ol' shield, she thought.

She wanted to inhale. A lifetime of habits and survival instincts were telling her she needed to breathe in, but even though she doubted it would make a difference in the long run, she didn't like the idea of having to breathe *out* the water on the other side. But she couldn't ignore it the way she had ignored the cold and the pain and the hunger, because when she did her body tried to inhale out of habit. Instead she had to concentrate on *not* doing it, which took so much attention that she didn't notice when the woman joined her.

There were feet walking beside her in the pale glow from her shield. Bare feet, with black skin that glistened, and above them long legs swathed in flowing robes the color of water at night.

Selene thought angrily of Albatross, and wondered where the girl might have floated off to, before realizing there wasn't much point to it.

Keep. Moving. Forward.

"You are a curious kind of hero," said the woman.

Selene didn't answer. She couldn't have, even if she'd wanted to.

"You look like an Atalanta, but you act more like a Hercules," the woman went on. "You have the name of a goddess, but you are mortal. You walk through the land of the dead, like Hercules and Theseus, Orpheus and Aeneas, but you are not here to rob us or question us. What is your purpose, fallen moon?"

Selene looked up at the woman, keeping her mouth pointedly closed. Despite the murkiness of the water she could see her perfectly clearly, and her expression was one of honest interest. But Selene shook her head, lowered her face, and kept on crawling. After a while the feet vanished, the ground began to slope upward, and soon she was in the current again. From then on she could think of nothing but the rush of the water and the feeling of the mud under her hands, and the burning, yearning desire to *breathe.*

She didn't see the surface. Suddenly her head came out of the water, and she did inhale some of it after all, since it streamed down her face and got into her nose.

She sneezed, staggered further up the bank until she was standing knee-deep in black water, looking back across the river.

Considering how long it had felt, she actually hadn't gone very far. She could still see Albatross and the dark pillar of woman standing in the marshlands, though they were a little to her right. She had drifted downstream a few yards during her crossing.

Raising her shield she waved at Albatross, beckoning to her. Albatross waved back and took off across the surface of the water, skimming it with her toes and weaving to and fro. Selene was suddenly gripped by the fear that something would leap out of the water and grab her, drag her down into the rushing depths and disappear forever. But nothing did, and when Albatross alighted gently on the surface next to her she appeared entirely unharmed. She turned around as if to wave at the dark woman on the far shore, but she had already vanished. Selene rather thought she had melted back into the dark waters of the Styx.

Reaching out she took Albatross's free hand, tugging her gently around to face the great wall—which no longer appeared fat and wide, but impossibly tall. On its craggy heights were parapets, behind which were movement as of guards on patrol.

A little to their right, downstream, was a spade-shaped bastion with a small gate in the side. For lack of any more promising prospects, Selene began wading toward it, towing Albatross behind her.

The Wall of Dis

The door was made of lacquered oak and felt hard as stone when Selene banged on it, making a soft booming noise which echoed away inside the wall. Nothing happened for a long time, and then a small hatch in the center of the door, a little above head height, opened and a face appeared in it.

Selene was not sure why, but she thought there was something wrong with the face. Like looking at a dead person. Except this face was clearly animated. It grimaced down at them.

"What do you want?" it asked in a harsh, croaking voice.

Selene thought the face was female. It didn't have a beard, and the chin was narrow. She was jowly, but her eyes were very large and dark with long lashes. Those lashes appeared to be the only hair on her face. She had no eyebrows, and the hatch was too small for her ears or hair to show through.

"Hey," said Selene. "I'm Selene Shields. This here is Albatross. Or a part of her, anyway. We're looking for the rest of her. Can you help us?"

The dark eyes bulged in their sockets as they rolled down to gaze at them. The mouth opened and a tongue emerged, white and fat. It lolled over the chin as the face let out a hissing breath.

"Calamity," she said. "Mortal trespasser. You are not welcome here. Begone, lest I do unto you as I did to the countless men who challenged me!"

"We'll get gone just as soon as we find the rest of her," Selene began, but the dark eyes had rolled back in the head, the mouth opened, and the skin began to glow.

Without thinking, Selene raised her shield. Just in time, it proved.

A blinding light flashed. It stung her skin where it touched her, and Albatross yelped, but the shield caught most of it.

Caught it, and sang. Selene felt the vibrations in her arm as well as heard the noise it made, like a bell ringing in her ears.

The light went out with a surprised gasp, and when Selene lowered the shield the face was looking down at them almost respectfully.

"What are you?" she demanded, glaring at Selene. She had pushed her face so far out the hatch that Selene could see she had no ears or hair, only the bodies of snakes.

"I told you," Selene sighed. "I'm Selene Shields. This is Albatross. We're looking for the other pieces of her, some of which I'm pretty certain are inside this ... wall. City. Whatever. Could you let us in?"

The face twisted her mouth uncomfortably. Selene noticed she had highly elongated lower bicuspids, almost like tusks.

"*Could* do that," she said, grudgingly. "Maybe. We'll have to run you by the Erinyes. Hold on."

The hatch flipped over again, so the door was a blank wall once more. Selene stepped back and waited, wondering what Medusa was doing in Hell. Then she remembered Dante had seen gorgons on the walls of Dis. Gorgons and ...

Selene glanced up. The dark shapes on top of the wall were mostly hidden behind the parapets, and the forms she could see were silhouetted against the red sky. They looked like the confused sort of shadows that happen when two or more people stand close together, so the shadow they cast looks like a monstrous person with two or three heads and too many arms. Only there were definitely some animals in them as well.

"Fallen angels," whispered Albatross, curling herself around Selene's arm.

More and more were appearing, clustering around the ledge above them. And though Selene couldn't see their faces, she felt their gaze on her.

There was a soft creak, and a dark crack appeared in the door. This slowly widened until it stood half open. From within, the voice of the gorgon said:

"Come inside or leave this place. I won't hold it open all day."

Selene turned sideways and shuffled through, keeping Albatross behind her. No sooner had they cleared the threshold than the door slammed shut behind them, and the gorgon stepped away, rubbing her talons together.

She was perhaps six feet tall, and her talons gleamed golden in the dim firelight that illuminated the room. She was largely human-shaped, and her skin was covered in glimmering, red-gold scales. That, or she was wearing a very tight-fitting bodysuit. Selene didn't look too closely. There was a snake around her waist, the tail stuck in its mouth, and in place of hair she had countless red snakes, which twined and writhed about her head in a kind of living, reptilian afro.

"If you had been a man," she said, matter of factly, "I would have torn you limb from limb. If you had been a handsome man, I would have done it *slowly*. But you're not, and you don't look like one of Poseidon's heroes, so here we are. Would you like some tea?"

Selene, staggered by this change of tone, responded: "Uh ... "

"I would like some tea!" announced Albatross. "What is tea?"

"I wasn't asking you," snapped the gorgon. She crossed the little room to where there was an overstuffed armchair, a side table, and an electric kettle. A little bookshelf in the corner was filled with books. The titles *A Woman's Guide to the Underworld* and *Weaponizing Your Femininity* and *Infernal Herpetology* jumped out at Selene. She blinked.

Behind them was the door, with the little hatch and everything, but aside from that, the room looked like a very comfortable parlor. There was a plate of scones on the table next to the chair, and the gorgon was measuring tea out of a ceramic jar with a little silver spoon, shaking the leaves into a fat, red teapot.

Above their heads, on the wall opposite the chair, was a painting of a giant serpent stretching across a bright blue sky. The serpent was all colors of the rainbow, and seemed to be smiling.

"No, thank you," Selene said, still reeling from the change.

"Suit yourself," said the gorgon. "My sisters will be along shortly, and then we can take you to the Erinyes. If you can make it past them, they'll show you where the rest of the Calamity is."

"Can I ask who the Erinyes are?" Selene said.

The gorgon laughed. She had a deep and melodious laugh that was disconcertingly attractive.

"Do you know who I am?" she asked.

"I'm sure I have no idea," Selene said firmly.

The gorgon turned around, holding the kettle, which was steaming. She poured the boiling water into the teapot and set the lid on it. Then she opened the cabinet under the table and got out three mugs.

"Oh, I'm sure you've got *some* idea," she said, and winked at her.

Selene stared at the gorgon, wondering if she was being flirted with, and then decided that she was not. She shook her head.

The gorgon sat down in the only chair, leaning back into the cushions and crossing her legs—though they looked almost like they flowed into position, like the coils of a snake's body.

"You're cute," she remarked. "In a craggy, wind-blasted mountaintop way." She teased one of her snakes out from behind an ear and began to play with it, stroking its side and curling it around her finger. "Why don't you ask me my name?"

Selene shrugged. "Didn't want to be rude."

The gorgon smiled, wide and dangerous.

"I'll give you a hint," she said. "Several, in fact. I'm the eldest. I've killed more men than my sisters *combined*. And unlike some, I've never hidden who I am."

"That's . . . " Selene began, then changed what she had been going to say. "Good for you."

The gorgon shrugged. "I do what I can." She lifted the kettle and poured the tea—which was bright red, Selene noticed—into the three mugs, just as a door at the far end of the room opened, and another gorgon walked in. She was shorter than the first, her face was rounder, sweeter, and she did not have tusks. The snakes on her head were golden, and she wore a short, soft leather skirt—but no top. In the crook of one arm she held something the size of a small pumpkin, covered with writhing green snakes and— Selene looked away just in time.

"Don't bother, honey, I'm off duty at the moment," said the head of Medusa.

"Sorry," said Selene, still looking studiously at her sister. *What were the names of Medusa's sisters*? Stheno was the eldest, and the middle was . . . Eurydice? No, that was Orpheus's wife. Which . . . would she be in this part of Hell, too?

Whatever her name was, the middle gorgon mostly ignored Selene. She cast a disdainful look at Albatross before going over to the table and setting the head of Medusa on it, next to the teacups.

"I called the Erinyes," she said to Stheno, picking up a mug and taking a long sip. "They're excited."

"Good," said Stheno. "Medi, do you want your tea now, or later?"

"Sthen, you know I'll just make a mess on your floor."

"Yes, but it's the principle of the thing."

"Which I appreciate, but no. Give it to the moon. She looks like she could use a drink."

"That's not the moon," said the middle sister, after taking a long sip from her cup. "That's a hero."

"Moon-hero, then," said Medusa, agreeably.

"We've never had a woman moon-hero," insisted her sister.

"Doesn't mean it's not possible," said Stheno, smiling tuskily.

Selene glanced at Albatross. The girl was staring at the head with a look of open wonder on her face. She had most assuredly not turned to stone, but Selene was certain that if anyone was immune to those rules, it was Albatross. She kept her gaze safely downcast and wondered how she could refuse the drink politely.

It turned out not to be possible. A brass claw thrust itself into her vision, holding the cup of steaming, red tea. It smelled strongly of cinnamon and ginger.

"Girl, we're already throwing you to the Erinyes," Stheno said. "We're not gonna poison you on top of that."

Selene took the cup, chancing a glance up at the gorgon. Her face was difficult to read. Selene tried a sip, found the liquid too hot to taste, and blew on it. She sipped again. It was extremely gingery and spicy and made her mouth tingle, but it also warmed her inside in a way she had forgotten. She tried another sip. It was a little like drinking whisky: it got easier the more you drank. She finished the cup faster than she thought, and handed it back to Stheno.

"Thank you," she said, the words feeling fresh and tingly on her tea-scorched tongue.

"I can't say 'you're welcome,' because you're not," Stheno sighed. "Not really. But you were welcome to the tea. Now let's go."

Stheno led the way out the door, with Selene behind her and Albatross at her side. Behind them, the middle sister—Eurynome? No, that was another goddess—carrying Medusa's head, brought up the rear.

They moved through a low-ceilinged corridor with heavy wooden beams and walls that began softly papered with floral decoration, but soon changed to hard stones into which recesses had been carved. In each one was a human skull, and within each skull was a candle. In the distance Selene heard the beat of drums and the stamping of feet, and a high cackling laughter that echoed down the hall, growing louder.

They climbed a short stair and came out into a long room with a vaulted ceiling. Bricked-up windows ran the length of the walls, and arranged in two lines on either side of a central aisle were countless women. They were all different shapes and sizes. Some had dogs' heads, others bats' wings, but they all carried coiled whips that gleamed in the fiery light of the chandelier high above them, suspended on a black chain from the highest arch of the ceiling.

Selene felt a little chagrined that it had taken her this long to remember where she had heard the name Erinyes before: it was another word for the Furies.

The tallest of them, upon seeing their arrival, broke from her position at the far end of the line and came walking down the aisle. She had dark skin and red eyes and was completely bald. This, combined with her height, reminded Selene of Clara, only inverted colors. It was disturbing until Selene took another look at her face and saw she looked nothing like Clara. There was a certain resemblance in the height of her cheekbones and the angle of her brow, but if anything she looked more like Styx. They could almost have been sisters.

"Is this your trespasser, Stheno?" the fury asked, her hands on her hips. These were not human hands, but bird feet—with long talons and scaly fingers.

"I think she may be an incarnation of the moon," Stheno replied. "Euryale thinks she's a hero. Medusa thinks she's a moon-hero."

The lead fury snorted, and sparks flew from her nose.

"Does she accept the challenge?" she asked.

"Depends what it is," Selene said, tired of being talked over.

The fury looked down at her, and Selene realized what so reminded her of Styx. It was the feeling like she was looking at a person with many more layers than normal. As though there were at least three different personalities inside the one body.

There had been three named Furies. Like the Fates and the Moirae and the Norns. Selene had wondered in the past whether they were all the same triple-goddess or if it was a case of convergent divinity, where different gods in different places at different times developed similarities because of some deeper meaning or necessity.

Now was neither the time nor the place to be puzzling that one out, however. The fury shrugged and turned sideways so she could gesture down the aisle.

"You run the line," she said. "If you make it to the end, we'll help you."

"And if I don't?" Selene asked, considering their number and trying to make a realistic assessment of her chances of success.

The fury smiled.

"You join us," she said.

That seemed like a considerably fairer penalty than what Selene had expected. She examined the fury's triple face, but though she saw expressions of rage, resentment, and satisfaction chase each other across it, the overall impression she got was of quiet patience.

"Right," she said, nodding her head with a sharp jerk. Then, reluctantly, she turned to Albatross and handed over her shield.

"Why?" asked Albatross.

"Because if I don't make it, you'll need it. I think you're drawn to it—the rest of you, anyway."

"Generous, but foolish," remarked the fury.

Selene shrugged. What was it Faraday had called Jill? Their Fool. It gave her a sharp, bitter gladness to think she could bring some of Jill's annoying rationality into this nonsensical place.

She clapped her hands and rubbed them together.

"Are we doing this, or what?"

The fury grinned, then went back down to the far end of the aisle, where she stood in the middle of it and raised one taloned hand. All down each side the other furies began to clap and chant. Some took out their whips while others produced rakes and flails or spiked clubs.

Selene swallowed. No matter how hard she concentrated, this was going to hurt.

Something touched her cheek, soft and cool as a snake's belly, and Medusa whispered in her ear:

"The moon only shines by a reflection of the light of the sun, but even in the dark her powers are extended. Some truths cannot be illuminated, they can only be felt."

"Like what really happened in Athena's temple?" Selene muttered out of the corner of her mouth.

"That is my secret, not yours," Medusa said. "But not all that is severed is forever separated. Wise gods are tricky people, and patient. Men see the crescent; you touch the whole of the moon."

Selene wasn't sure what to do with this, so she pushed the words away to the back of her head to examine later. If there was a later. She wondered if all the other furies had once been people like her. She wondered if she would remember herself afterward. Then she decided that sort of thinking wasn't going to get her through the gauntlet. She focused on the fury standing patiently at the far end, put her head down, and ran.

She covered her head with her arms, so her face and neck were somewhat protected, but this left her sides fully exposed. Selene had run gauntlets before, and in her experience ribs held up better to kicks and punches than did the side of her face.

Of course, the furies didn't use kicks or punches. They lashed out with their whips and flails and hooks. Selene felt them rip at her clothing, tried not to imagine what they would do to her flesh once they started getting serious, and put on speed.

She kept her face pointing down so she couldn't see how much farther she had to go, but at a guess she was halfway down the aisle when someone slammed her chest so hard she stumbled to a halt.

Blows rained down on her back, forcing her down, but aside from the blunt impacts which made it difficult to rise again, she felt no pain.

Selene focused all her attention on pushing herself off the ground and began to crawl, her shoulders hunched against the endless abuse.

Feet, some hoofed, some canine, some human, flicked into her vision. Sometimes she turned her face away in time, sometimes she didn't. In either case she kept reaching forward with her hands, dragging herself along.

She came to a step, and on that step, a pair of talons like an eagle's feet, squarely blocking her path. Selene crouched there for a moment or two, not quite believing she had reached the end of the line. Her skin felt far too intact, and even the sites of the blunt impacts no longer hurt.

Around her was a strange rustling sound, like a combination of murmurs and hisses and clapping and the shuffling of feet.

Selene sat up and found that she had indeed come to the end of the line. She was crouching in front of the lead fury, and behind her the others had closed ranks and were staring down at her. Some of them looked angry, while others appeared confused. All of them were surprised.

She checked herself over.

Aside from a copious number of new rips and tears in her clothes—her shirt was hanging onto her shoulder by a thread—she was entirely unscathed. She stood up.

The crowd backed away from her.

She turned to look at the lead fury, and found the woman gazing at her with narrowed eyes.

"Stheno," she said, her voice clanging like a gong. "How did your moon-hero get past Styx?"

Selene felt a cold shiver run over her skin. She'd clean forgotten that other aspect of Styx: it was the river Achilles's mother had dunked him in to give him invulnerability. All except his heel, which she had held him by.

And Selene had gone and . . .

"She walked, didn't she?" Stheno called, from beyond the horde.

The fury snorted, and actual sparks flew from her nose. Selene winced, purely from reflex.

"Does this mean we can go now?" Albatross called.

Selene looked questioningly at the fury, whose upper lip was curling in an unfriendly smile.

"Yes, more's the pity," she said. Then she clapped a taloned hand on either side of Selene's head, lifting her clean off the ground and bringing her nose-to-nose with that terrible triple-face.

"You'd have made an excellent fury," she whispered. Her breath was bitter, but in a satisfying way, like strong coffee. "Perhaps, one day, you will."

She grinned, all sharp teeth, and dropped Selene like a brick.

There was more hissing rustling from the crowd, and they parted like a reluctant curtain to let Albatross, holding Selene's shield like a dinner plate, come skipping down the hall.

"Can we go home now?" she asked, bright and innocent.

"In a manner of speaking," said Selene, taking the shield and settling it over one arm. She hadn't realized until that moment, but she had missed it terribly. She turned back to the fury.

"You said you'd help us. I need to find the rest of her"—she nodded at Albatross—"and I was told there was more of her somewhere in here. Can you show me?"

"I can show you many things," said the fury. "Least of all are the fragments of Calamity. Come."

She turned and walked over to the side of the hall, where a low door stood, closed. She bent to unlatch it, and Selene glanced back over the crowd of furies, hoping to see Stheno and her sisters. She caught a flash of red snake, and waved. She did not keep looking to see if they waved back.

The fury led them through a narrow, twisting tunnel that eventually let them out onto a high gallery that ringed another hall. Down in the center of this were at least a hundred human forms, naked and chained to tables covered in papers. They were writing with quills, and instead of ink they used blood, which they supplied by stabbing their pens into their neighbors.

Then they were in another corridor, and then another gallery. There was a giant stretched out on the floor of this room, its belly cut open and countless worms with human faces writhing around in its entrails.

Another corridor, and another gallery and the room was filled with such thick, yellow smoke that Selene couldn't see what was going on.

They were in the middle of a passage just like the others when the fury abruptly stopped, turned to her left and pulled open a door. At her gesture Selene and Albatross stepped through it and into a narrow room with a high ceiling. A rod ran the length of it, and hanging from the rod on metal hooks were a variety of carcasses. Griffins and double-headed snakes, and even a unicorn.

On the hook nearest to them, hanging from her shoulders, was another version of Albatross.

Selene was so struck by the sight that she didn't notice the fury leaving until she heard the door close with a fatal *clunk* behind them.

It's probably locked, she thought, but only in the back of her head. The front half was preoccupied with what was before her.

Albatross—the single-layer Albatross she'd been towing since the Swamp of the Gluttons—was staring at the Albatross-on-a-hook with a look of curiosity. She seemed to recognize herself, and yet not know why.

"That's . . . that's me, isn't it?" she whispered, stepping around Selene so she could lean forward and bring her face up level with the Albatross-on-a-hook's elbow.

"A part of you, yes," Selene said. She wasn't certain what to do next. The Albatross on the hook looked just like the one at her side, only her dress wasn't torn and there was red and brown mud caked on her feet. She was inclined to think this was the double-Albatross she had lost in the Lustful Gale, but according to Kirke there were three more fragments being held in Dis already . . .

She moved forward, intending to touch the hooked Albatross on the arm, but before her hand could reach the pale skin the girl's eyes opened and her head shot up.

"I'm here!" she shouted, hoarse and garbled. She coughed, hackingly, and spat out a gobbet of dark red spittle. "I'm here!" she repeated, more clearly.

"Yeah," said Selene, "I can see that."

She could also see how the hook had pierced her back, between her shoulder blade and her spine. Moving around to her front, she was dismayed to find the tip had penetrated all the way through her body, emerging just under her collar bone. It had jointed arms at the tip, which flared out. Easy-in, Selene thought, a nightmare to get out.

White eyes focused on her, then they focused on the Albatross still standing, staring, mute.

"I'm here," she whispered, and tentatively reached out a hand to touch her other self.

Selene felt something jump between them, like a jolt of static electricity coming unstuck, and just had the presence of mind to duck behind her shield before there was a much bigger jolt, combined with a flash of light. She felt something go *whump!* like a column of gas being ignited, which raised her hair and scorched her already tattered clothing.

There was a hissing, like water on a hot pan, and when she peered over the edge of her shield it was to see a single Albatross, more solid and alert than ever, standing between where the two versions of her had been. The hook was scorched black, and there was not even a blemish on the girl's white skin to show where it had been pierced.

She still looked young to Selene, like a teenager who has hit their growth spurt and is still getting used to it, but she was easily a foot taller now, with broad shoulders and long, strong legs. She had lost much of her transparence and seemed more solid that ever. And yet, when Selene looked at her face, she still got the impression that she was looking at only a part of a person. The exact opposite of the impression she'd had of the fury.

There was movement in the air above and behind Albatross's shoulders; more crackling like electricity charging through the air, but in the shape of wings this time. Selene took a cautious step back.

Albatross looked at her, and her face lit up in recognition. She smiled, and the crackling in the air behind her dimmed.

"Moon-shield!" she said, beaming. "You found me!"

"More like, you found me," Selene said, giving a shaky laugh.

Albatross put her head on one side, still smiling, but her expression turned inward. "It's hard to say," she said. "I've got at least three different skeins of memory going on in here. They've merged, but that only makes it more confusing."

"I . . . can imagine that," Selene said.

"Anyway," said Albatross, briskly rubbing her hands together. "We should go—they're not very nice in here."

"No argument here," Selene agreed, and turned her attention to the door.

It wasn't only locked: there was no handle at all. This proved no match for Albatross, however, who pressed both her palms flat against it and flapped her wings.

It was as if a small rocket had gone off. Smoke blasted into the air behind her, and a spiderweb of cracks exploded across the door—as if it had been hit by a battering ram.

Albatross reined in her wings and straightened up. She poked at the center of the spiderweb, pushing one of the central pieces out of its place.

Like a bridge losing its keystone, the door collapsed into rubble. It raised a small cloud of dust and revealed an irritated person on the far side, who had been in the act of unlocking the door with a large iron key.

"Oh, no," they said. "You again."

"If you say so," said Albatross, and pushed past them into the hall.

Selene dove after her. The person, she saw, had burnt-red skin and wore only a thick leather belt hung with hooks and chains. They didn't have the over-shadowed look of the dead souls, but neither did they look like the gorgons or the furies she had seen earlier. They protested as she pushed past them, but weakly, and they cringed away from her when they saw her shield.

"You shouldn't be in here," they gasped. "You'll get us all in trouble!"

"Point me to the nearest exit," Selene snapped.

With the iron key jangling against its ring, the person raised a hand and pointed back the way Selene had come. "But you'll have to get past the Erinyes," they said.

Selene was on the point of saying that the Erinyes wouldn't be a problem, when she noticed that Albatross had taken off down the passage—in the opposite direction.

"Hey—*hey!*" Selene shouted as she rushed after her. "That's deeper in!"

"Of course!" said Albatross, her voice floating over her shoulder like the cry of a bird. "That's where we need to go! Further down, further in!"

Selene wasn't sure—maybe she had imagined they could get through the wall of Dis some other way—but now that Albatross said as much, she realized the only thing to do was to keep going forward.

Dis was not just the wall separating the fifth and sixth circles of Hell, it was the entire center.

In their mad rush through the tunnels, Selene's mind irreverently conjured up the idea of Satan stuck in the middle of what was essentially Downtown Hell, and she almost laughed at the absurdity.

"Here!" Albatross shouted, and turned right so suddenly Selene slid past and had to grab onto a corner of the wall to swing herself around.

Albatross led her down a flight of stairs, which twisted and turned at odd angles. Selene tripped once when she hit a step that was much steeper than the others and rolled a dozen or so before she got her feet back under her and continued running. The sharp impacts of the bruising tumble hardly fazed her—barely felt like pain at all—and miraculously she had no twisted joints or broken bones either.

Literally miraculously. She was pretty certain that was the work of Styx again.

They reached the bottom. There was a door that had been closed, but then Albatross had happened to it. By the time Selene arrived it was lying in shattered splinters, many of which were still smoldering. She stepped through the revealed doorway and into the middle of a long gallery overlooking a vast hall—she couldn't see the ends to either side—crowded with desks and chairs. Legions of red people, like the one they had met earlier, were nominally sitting at these desks, scratching away at the endless stream of papers stacked beside them, constantly refueled by more red people who moved down the narrow aisle, distributing packets tied with string.

Selene rather thought they were souls. Only unlike the ones they had so far encountered, these were shadowed with red instead of black. They were all recognizably human, and they were all naked. Because of this Selene could see clearly the raggedly stitched incisions where their genitalia had been excised. They all appeared fresh, unhealed, held together with shiny black string. But there was no blood or swelling. It was as though their bodies were made of rubber or dried leather.

When they arrived, however, only about half the desks that she could see were actually occupied. The rest stood empty as their occupants had crowded together a little ways down the hall to their right, where there seemed to be a brawl going on.

The bodies were packed so tightly it was impossible to see what the cause of the commotion was, but Selene could hear shouts and cries and the dull *smack* of flesh hitting flesh.

Albatross was moving down the gallery toward the action, and as Selene followed her, she began to discern words in the cries:

"Hold it down!"

"Get her feathers, *get her feathers!*"

And most disconcertingly of all:

"She has clothes! Get her clothes!"

Selene thought she knew what was in the middle of the crowd long before she caught a flash of something white, and saw Albatross hunched over the railing, staring down into the center of it with a by-now-familiar expression of stricken wonder on her face.

"But that's . . . me . . . " she whispered.

"Yep," said Selene, even though the Albatross being mobbed was still mostly hidden amongst the red crowd. Selene tapped her shoulder. "When you see her—uh, I mean, you—go for it."

"What?"

"*Go* for it," Selene repeated. "Like earlier. Rejoin with yourself!"

Albatross blinked at her. "I can do that?"

"Girl, that's the whole point," said Selene, and vaulted over the railing.

It was a long way down. Long enough for Selene to consciously wonder if she'd made a mistake. If Styx's blessing would extend to protecting her from the results of her own dangerous actions. She didn't like the idea of fighting off a crowd with two broken legs.

Then she hit the ground, on top of two souls who had the misfortune of being in her way.

The impact shook her body right up to her teeth, but once she regained feeling in her legs nothing hurt, and they certainly worked well enough for her to lash out with kicks when the crowd turned on her.

The cries of "Clothes! *Clothes!*" redoubled, and someone grabbed at her shirt. She felt it tear. Had a momentary automatic flash of embarrassment, then decided there was really no point in conventional modesty anymore.

She kicked and punched and slammed her shield into faces and sides until she had a small pile of dazed souls all around her. She scrambled over them and began hauling people off the pile under which she still saw flashes of white.

This Albatross, when she dragged her out of the melee, had the back of her dress ripped out and two bloody stumps where her wings should have been. She was shaking and crying and scratched at Selene's face, trying to fight her off.

"Albatross!" Selene shouted, not sure which one she was trying to talk to. "Now, Albatross! Now!"

Someone grabbed her hair. She lashed out behind her, glimpsed a streak of white from the gallery above, and whipped her shield around.

She was not quite in time. She saw the two Albatrosses meet and merge, like someone diving into a mirror, and where they met was an impossibly bright flash of light. It hurt, so Selene closed her eyes, but somehow the light burned right through her eyelids. She turned her head away, cowering behind her shield, and waited for the burning to subside.

For what felt like ages, it didn't. *So much for the protection of Styx*, Selene thought. But eventually the light faded, and Selene blinked her eyes open to find them half-crusted over with a dried, flaky substance. Like an old scab. Rubbing her eyes clear, the first thing she saw was a red soul, stretched out on its back, spreadeagled across the floor. It looked like its entire front half had melted. Raising her head she saw a dozen more like it, and beyond that ring, the rest were creeping fearfully back to their desks.

Maybe invulnerability is a relative thing, Selene amended, slowly turning herself around to check on Albatross.

There was just one Albatross now, standing with her bare feet planted wide on the dusty stone floor, working her arms back and forth over her head as though her shoulders were stiff. Her wings were visible now, but not as conventional wings: instead they were two jets of blue-hot fire that ignited in the air four or five inches away from her shoulder blades. Each jet was perhaps two feet long, and trailed off into a white-and-gold seam in the air which hurt to look at. Even when Selene took her eyes off them the afterimage remained burned onto her retinas for several seconds.

Albatross's dress was a veritable web of threads, more hole than fabric, but she still had on Selene's work shirt. This appeared to have shrunk, but in reality Selene realized Albatross had grown again. Now she was taller than Clara, though still not as wide, and at least three inches of pale wrist stuck out the ends of her sleeves. She had a sprawling, unfinished look to her. Now she was a complete outline of a person, but only an outline. The details had yet to be filled in.

A hand rose, a finger pointed. Pointing at Selene.

"Selene," she said, only the barest hint of a questioning inflection at the end of it. "Shield."

"Shields," Selene corrected, weakly. "But that's close enough."

Albatross frowned, her face bunching together in a mass of small wrinkles. Her eyes were darker now, but still colorless—rings of gray and silver around black pupils.

"I've been looking for you," she said, again uncertain.

"Ditto," said Selene.

Albatross shook her head, sending her feathery hair flying out in floating strands. It waved in the air around her face, as though she were under water.

"I mean from earlier. From before. But I can't remember what happened. Or I remember too much. I remember being here, but also there." She pointed up at the gallery. "And in a dark room. And in a gray sky. And on an island."

"You split," Selene explained. "Into twenty-seven pieces. You're about"—she did a quick tally—"six of them now, I think."

"Six of twenty-seven?" asked Albatross. She rolled her shoulders down, then up.

It had to have been a coincidence, Selene thought. People rolled their shoulders all the time, and Clara couldn't be the only person to have shrugged in that manner.

Still, the down-then-up motion had become so closely associated in Selene's mind with her colleague that, coupled with Albatross's pale skin and tall stature, it made Selene immediately think of her.

The pang of homesickness struck her by surprise. She hadn't wanted anything particularly strongly since she'd arrived in Hell. Other than perhaps to not be in excruciating pain. But suddenly she wanted to see Clara again. Heck, she wanted to see Jill. Wanted to sit in Arcana and drive him just a little too fast down a freeway.

She wanted, she realized, a burger and a milkshake. Not because she was particularly hungry, but just because she wanted a nice, juicy burger, crisp, hot fries, and a sweet, creamy milkshake. Maybe with a shot of bourbon in it.

It was dangerous to want things in Hell, she reminded herself, and hastily stuffed the feelings into the back of her psyche.

"Yeah," she said, in answer to Albatross. "According to Kirke's secretary, there's supposed to be three more of you in the Forest of Despair."

"That's further in, isn't it?"

Selene nodded. "And further down."

Albatross squared her shoulders, and her flame-wings flared, briefly. She looked sharper, clearer. As though before she had been behind a pane of glass that was just a little greasy—just enough so that you didn't notice it until it was removed.

"Well, down is the easy way, right?" she said, and smiled. It was fragile and brief, but bright as her wings and just as intense.

They walked straight out of the Wall of Dis. Literally. Selene got behind Albatross, and she blasted a hole through each wall they came to until there were no more walls, just a broad expanse of pale, sandy plain under the boiling, black sky. Here and there the clouds thinned, and beyond them red light flashed sullenly.

The plain was not strictly a plain. It had soft mounds and little bumps and notches where it looked like stony structures sat. It seemed they stood at the top of a general incline, for Selene could see the tops of the hills below them, drifting away until they were lost in an angry, orange haze. Smoke or steam rose from that haze in dirty white clouds, which reached up hundreds of feet above their heads before being eaten by the black sky.

Selene wondered where they were at as she stepped out from under the final arch of broken brick and scorched stone, following in the footsteps of Albatross. (These were easy to follow because they burned cool and blue against the dark red ground.) Was this the Sixth Circle? That was heretics, she was pretty sure. And there was another river coming up. The river of fire, she thought, looking at the clouds of steam and smoke. It reminded her of the line of a wildfire, which fit with what she remembered of the geography of Hell.

Well, the geography according to Dante, which so far had proved pretty reliable.

After they had walked a few yards into the sand, Selene paused and turned around to look at the Wall of Dis from the inner side.

It was considerably higher from this angle, towering above them. But instead of a single line of wall, from this side there were spires and domes and pinnacles and archways. Scaffolding suggested the building of new towers—two of which looked suspiciously like the World Trade Center.

And all along the skyline, their wings clapping to keep them balanced, the furies perched, waiting. Watching.

Selene saluted them with her shield, then turned and hurried after Albatross. She did not look back again.

City of Dis, the Flaming Tombs
Sixth Ring

It was almost peaceful amongst the gently drifting sands inside the Wall of Dis. But this was only because the tombs were bunched together, so they passed through areas that were more or less populated. Where there were few, the only indication was a jut of stone here or a stovepipe lid there. But where there were many, Albatross and Selene had to wind their way between blocks of tombs, and from within, though muted by the thick stone, came the sounds of anguished screaming.

Selene tried to tune them out at first, but the problem was they were all different. Some moaned, others wailed, while still others made noises that sounded hardly human at all. The changes caught her off guard, so that every few minutes she had to grow accustomed to the noise all over again. It made her grumpy in that dangerously low-key way in which a person doesn't realize they are grumpy until something relatively minor makes them lash out.

In Selene's case, it was when Albatross went over to a particularly exposed tomb and put her ear to it, and frowning she said: "But why are they in there?"

"'Cause they're heretics," Selene snapped, wishing they would come to the end of the desert already.

Albatross looked up at her, evidently taken aback by her tone of voice.

"What's a heretic?" she asked, falling in step beside Selene.

As if voicing Selene's feelings on the matter, the tomb on their other side let out a low groan.

"They're like . . . just people, really," Selene began, haltingly, "who believed in the wrong god at the wrong place in the wrong time."

Albatross looked around at the tombs. They were in an especially thick patch, with what looked like sarcophaguses stacked as high as houses to either side of them. These were made of rough stone the same pale sandy color as the hills, and were unmarked as far as Selene could tell. The cry-ing was louder here, since so many were above ground, the sounds raining down like an abrasive snow.

"But we're not in their space, or their time, anymore," she said.

Something snapped inside Selene's mind, and like a dam giving way it let forth a torrent of thoughts that had been building up since . . . well, since she'd crawled out of Lilith's gullet.

Hell—this Hell, the Judeo-Christian interpretation of the underworld which apparently Dante had gotten a glimpse of—was predicated on the notion that it punished souls of those who had sinned against that god. Yahweh, or as Clara had called Him, the Nameless God.

But the Nameless God was not the only god—and one could make a compelling argument that there were multiple versions of Him—and the only difference between a heretic and a believer was the perspective of those in power. One god's heretic was another's high priest, and wouldn't that high priest, rather than going to some other god's hell, be sent to their own god's heaven? Unless it was a matter of popular vote. In which case, *everyone* who had believed in any god, ever, got sent to some kind of hell.

It made her wonder where the atheists fit in with all of this.

Selene had once heard atheism described as believing in one less god than a Christian did. She was not quite sure that was right. Or perhaps that was right for a certain kind of atheist. But atheists, Selene suspected, were rather like theists in that they came in many different varieties and each one related to their lack of belief differently. Or their *lack* of lack of belief.

Once again Clara intruded on her thoughts. Clara certainly believed. She believed in every god or spirit or sprite equally, but she certainly wasn't religious. Selene wondered where Clara would go when she died. Or if she would go anywhere at all.

That was what bothered Selene so. If she had thought forward past the termination of her own life, she had never presumed that anything would happen. The thought might terrify some people, but to Selene, who had now seen firsthand the sort of nightmares that could await someone after their death, a simple cessation of all experience was a cold kind of comfort. She suspected the only reason she was in Hell at all was because she had been physically put there—pulled, fallen, whatever.

But was she dead? Kirke hadn't seemed to think so, and neither had the serpent, for what that was worth.

It all made her question what the point of the place was. If this was where the Nameless God punished His enemies or those who had offended Him or whatever, then how did He wrangle that with the gods who might say, "hold on, your enemy is my anointed hero, give them back?" What if that other god was a different version of Himself?

Selene stopped. They had come to the end of that cluster of tombs, which were now only as high as their shoulders. She could see the seams in their chambers where the heavy lids rested on the sides.

Albatross floated past her, then waited.

"Where are their gods, now?" she asked.

Beside her, a tomb screamed. It was the sharp, surprised, hurt scream that spoke of astonishment as well as pain. Selene clenched her fists.

"I don't know," she admitted. It felt good to admit that. "Let's see if we can find out."

She went over to the tomb and began feeling at the crack. It was too narrow for her to work her fingers in, but by using the edge of her shield as a lever she managed to lift it a hair. That was enough for Albatross, who saw what she meant to do, and got her own fingers under the edge and pushed. Selene dropped her shield and put her hands on the lid, and lifted with all her might.

It came up over a lip and slipped sharply over. Albatross snatched her hands out of the way just in time, but by that point Selene could put her shoulder against it and slide it off the tomb until its far end got enough weight to plummet to the ground, taking the rest of the lid with it.

Dusting off her hands—they weren't even scraped—Selene picked up her shield and peered over the lip of the tomb.

It felt like putting her face into an open oven. The tomb was maybe two feet deep, the walls glowed red-hot, and it was completely empty.

Albatross blinked, confused.

"But I thought I heard—" she began, and then came the scream again. It rang out from the air within the tomb.

Not one to leave anything half done, Selene hoisted herself up over the edge and felt around the interior with her shield. It felt nothing—neither physically, nor did it respond with the warning tingle of a magical presence.

"What does that mean?" Albatross asked.

Letting herself drop back onto their path, Selene put her shield on her back and shrugged expansively. Without speaking, she turned and walked away, leaving the tomb uncovered.

They were well out into an empty portion of the desert when Albatross said:

"I'm sorry if I annoyed you. It's not your job to have all the answers."

Selene felt embarrassed. She laughed and shook her head.

"It's not your fault," she said, and patted Albatross's long, white arm.

"Are we friends?" Albatross asked in a small voice. Selene looked up at her. It felt strange, looking up at a face that seemed so young.

"Yeah," said Selene, taking her hand and squeezing firmly. "I'd say so."

Albatross squeezed back.

They walked. Almost imperceptibly the screams of the tombs faded away behind them. They had perhaps a minute of perfect silence, and then they came through a cleft in the hills and were hit by a strong, hot wind, carrying with it a cacophony of wailing moans, and the horrifically enticing smell of roasting meat.

They had come to the end of the desert, and before them across a wide, low plain, stretching away to either side as far as they could see, wound a bright red streak belching yellow flames—the far shore hidden behind a wall of sickly smoke.

City of Dis, Phlegethon
Seventh Ring, Outer Circle

Along the bank ran dark shapes on four legs with riders on them carrying spears which they used to stab and push back the other dark shapes that occasionally emerged from the red river, trying desperately to escape.

Selene thought at first they might be centaurs, but as they drew closer she saw this was not quite so. Each had the body of a horse, true enough, and the torso of a human, but the torso grew from the horse's back, just where a rider might sit. Meanwhile, the horse part ended where the equine neck should have begun, so they also looked like people riding decapitated horses. But the human torsos had no legs; they were not riders. They grew straight out of the horses' backs. It made no anatomical sense, yet there they were. And now they were close enough she could make out the most distressing thing about them. They appeared to have been flayed. What she had first taken to be a cape worn by the human shoulders revealed itself to be flapping, bloody strips of skin. The equine part too had had its skin removed, and this trailed behind it in horrible mockery of a tail. It left them utterly naked, with their muscles—black and purple—and their blood and veins—yellowish—clearly visible.

Selene was so surprised she stopped and stared. Not purely from horror, although they were horrible, but because she recognized them.

The furthest east she had ever been was Swan's Island, Maine, when reports of a skinless horse and rider running amok and blighting the populace had drawn her into a surprising battle with the only nuckelavee west of the Atlantic. That had been early in her career, and she remembered the creature vividly.

Nuckelavees, dozens—perhaps hundreds—of them, patrolled the banks of the River Phlegethon, trampling or spearing any soul who tried to escape. Selene could tell just by comparison that these were easily twice as big as the one she had fought, and that battle had been desperate enough.

But she had been on Earth then, before she'd gotten her shield. Before she'd waded through Styx. And Albatross was not frightened of the nuckelavees. She took Selene's hand and led her down to the riverbank, her feet burning blue scorch marks on the yellow sand.

The closer they got the worse the creatures looked. Their heads were too big, with elongated, piggish snouts and black pits for eyes. By contrast, the front of the horse part, where the neck should have gone, had one glowing eye—like a headlamp—and a wide, toothy mouth. Selene saw one skewer a soul and then pull it off the tip of its spear and feed it, feet first, into its gaping second mouth.

But none of the nuckelavees paid them any attention, even when they were a stone's throw away and could easily see across a narrow strip of blood-splashed sand to the river, which was not precisely a river of fire, but a torrent of boiling blood. The fire was just on the surface, where it danced in the steam, adding its acrid smoke to the emanation above.

They were only interested in keeping souls *in*, Selene realized, watching one kick the head of a flailing soul with its hind hoof, sending them splashing back into the boiling river with a small burst of flame.

Albatross paused. They had come to the edge of the clean sand where the trampling of the nuckelavees' hooves had broken it up into a soft tumult of gold and red. Three went past in one direction and two in the opposite during the time it took Selene to come up next to Albatross and look both ways.

"Like crossing a damn freeway," she muttered, and eyed Albatross's gas-jet wings. "Care to give us a lift?" she asked. It seemed like the most obvious course of action.

But Albatross shook her head, and pointing upward she said: "Bad winds."

Selene looked, and couldn't help but agree that the swirling smoke and steam did not look at all accommodating, but then neither did the boiling river of blood beneath it. Through the legs of the nuckelavees Selene could see it was choked with souls, thrashing and kicking and clawing at each other.

The seventh circle was violence, she remembered, and the river of blood was violence against others. She stared dispassionately at the river and wondered how many of the souls there had been cops.

"Yeah, I know," she said, albeit distantly. "But you gotta keep things in perspective here. There's bad *wind* and then there's bad ... boiling burning blood filled with assholes." She waved a hand at the river.

Albatross shook her head.

"Neither high nor low," she said. "But right between." She pointed a pale finger as a nuckelavee whipped past them. Then, still with her arm raised, she began to walk.

It was as though the nuckelavees had choreographed their timing such that she slipped neatly between them. Selene had to hedge and stamp on the edge of the road for what felt like an age until she caught a similar opening and darted through.

But Albatross was waiting for her at the edge of the river, and held out a hand to her when she arrived.

Well, Selene thought with resignation, let's see what Styx makes of this. She was just saying a fond goodbye to what remained of her clothes when Albatross stepped out into the river—and didn't sink.

She did it slowly, carefully, like someone walking on thin ice. And that was more or less what she was doing.

Where her foot met the boiling river it hissed and steamed, turning dark like cooling lava, until a small island of solid, black rock formed, floating on the surface.

Albatross took another step, and Selene saw how the surface appeared to curdle under her foot.

The islands were just big enough, and lasted just long enough after Albatross moved on, that Selene was able to hop and jump after her. Still, her feet felt hot, and the islands moved under her, tugged by the current of the river beneath. The smoke and steam closed in around them, stinging her eyes and filling her nostrils.

She stopped breathing, clutched Albatross's hand for all she was worth, and narrowed her eyes to mere slits.

They walked, achingly slowly, as the smoke thickened around them until it felt to Selene like she was pushing her whole body through a tub of gravy. If it was like this all the way up, and with wind too, she understood why Albatross did not want to fly.

They walked. Sounds of splashing and cries and screams broke through the heavy smoke on all sides. Once, a hand came out of the bubbling red and caught Selene's ankle. She kicked, and it lost its grip, but ever after Selene kept a close eye on where she put her feet.

Almost imperceptibly the smoke began to thin. Selene realized she had begun to breathe again, out of habit, and then she put a foot down not on newly cooled blood, but on real, solid rock, and then they ran up against a solid wall of it.

Behind them flowed the river, before them was a sheer cliff. It was only twenty or so feet high, and though its top was misty in the smoke and steam, Selene could still see the line of nuckelavees standing guard, their spears pointed downward, at the ready.

"Now?" asked Selene, coughing reflexively. "*Now* can we fly?"

"You don't think they'll let us out?" Albatross asked.

"No," said Selene, with black certainty.

Albatross shrugged, rolling her shoulders sharply back, and her wings exploded. Selene turned away, but still the flash hurt her eyes. She felt Albatross grab her under her armpits, and then they were shooting upward, through the steam and smoke, away from the burning river. Selene felt the air sting her face, felt the heat decreasing at her feet, and then she blinked her eyes open and saw a nuckelavee, both its mouths open in consternation, go wheeling past them as they rose high above it, pillowed by the hot air.

Albatross flapped her wings once, and the air behind them caught on fire. As if a pair of rockets had ignited, the force shot them clear over the heads of the inner ring of guards and over a small stretch of beach, before they plowed into the side of a high ring of sand dunes.

The impact was blunt and softened by the sand, and Selene prided herself on not losing consciousness at all. She felt something crunch in her neck and had to lie very still while Albatross got up and did a little victory dance above her, but soon she felt cohesive enough to sit up, and she looked around to find that the dune they had crashed into was the last of Phlegethon's floodplain, and before them, stretching away into a dim, shadowy distance, was a black forest filled with prickly, leafless trees.

City of Dis, the Forest of Despair
Seventh Ring, Middle Circle

From the inside, the air above Phlegethon was more clearly a solid turbulence. Lightning cracked within it, and Selene was grateful for Albatross's instincts. The river itself was invisible, being hidden behind the cliff where the nuckelavees patrolled, now and then disappearing over the far side to put a wayward soul back in its place.

Selene shook herself, glad they had passed them by so neatly, and taking Albatross's hand led her away from the river and into the wood.

"*Over the river and through the wood*," she hummed under her breath. "*To the center of Hell, we go . . .*"

"What?" asked Albatross.

"Nothing," Selene said, pricked by embarrassment.

"You were singing," said Albatross. "I didn't know you could sing. I like singing."

"Most people can sing," Selene muttered. "Just most of *them*, not very well."

"I had a friend once, he'd sing to me. I don't remember the songs, but I remember the singing. I don't know if he was good or not, but I liked the listening."

Selene walked on for two good paces before the implications of Albatross's words caught up with her.

"When was this?" she asked. "Who was this friend?"

But when she looked across, Albatross was frowning.

"I think it was before I was born," she said. "But that's not right, is it? That doesn't sound right."

"It's unlikely," Selene admitted. "Especially with something as specific as singing."

"I think he was my father," Albatross said. "That feels right."

"Do you remember anything else about him?" Selene asked.

After a minute's hard thought, Albatross said, with unusual certainty: "He was bigger than me."

The sheer uselessness of this information made Selene snort with laughter, which she soon broke off.

They had passed into the spiny forest of black trees, and her sudden outburst had set off a group of nearby rooks. Their caws and cackling broke the otherwise silent wood, and set off other, more distant birds, until all around them were the sounds of birds crying.

The noise had been going on for some minutes before Selene realized they were not just making croaking bird noises. There were words in the cries too.

"Stranger! Stranger!" one voice said, distinct and near.

"Walkers! Talkers!" said another.

Selene looked around for the source of the words, but all she saw were black birds, like small vultures. Not convinced they couldn't speak English—or whatever language it was they were really speaking—Selene looked closer, and saw they were not vultures at all.

Well, mostly they were vultures. Their bodies were birdlike and feathered, and they had long, naked feet with curving talons. Their heads were bald, like a vulture's, but they were the miniature heads of humans—except for the beaks they had in place of mouths.

Then one landed on a low branch beside them, and Selene saw they had human mouths too, situated under their chins.

This one did not appear much different than the others, save perhaps a little bigger and shaggier. It had a fat neck and small dark eyes and Selene was reluctant to guess it gender.

"What brings you to the Forest of Despair, mortal soul? Fallen angel?" It asked this with its human mouth, the words sharp and guttural.

"I'm not an angel," said Albatross, with uncharacteristic certainty.

The bird-creature put its bald human head on one side and opened its beak. "You look like one," it observed.

"We are . . . just passing through," Selene said, averting her eyes from the creature's face when it switched its own gaze to her.

"You'd like to think that, wouldn't you?" snapped the bird. It put on a high, breathy voice. "Oh, don't mind me! I'm just gonna tiptoe through the transfixed dead like it's no big deal." It coughed derisively. "Well, guess what? It don't work that way. My sisters and I have had nought to chew on but dry branches for a thousand years or more, and you're looking softer and more appetizing by the second. Never had any suicidal ideation, did you?"

Selene raised her eyes and glared at the creature then, refusing to answer.

"That," she said quietly, "is none of your business."

"I'm a damned harpy," said the bird-creature, matter-of-factly. "This is the only business I have left. Oh well. Minor technicality, really. All right girls, I gave 'em fair warning. Have at it!"

Selene had been aware in a distant, automatic way of the growing congregation of black-bodied bird forms gathering in the upper branches of the trees. A low moaning had risen in the air around them, but was soon drowned out as the whole flock took wing, cawing and cackling, and began to dive-bomb them.

"That's *rude!*" Albatross said, the first time one made a pass at her. Her wings flared, and the harpies fell back, dismayed. Then they redoubled their attention on Selene, who had prudently put her shield over her head, grabbed Albatross's hand, and continued to walk.

Beaks and claws tore at her skin, but all that happened was that she lost the brave remnants of her shirt, which was the only part of her that gave way under the onslaught. Well, that and her bra. That only lasted another minute.

Selene stomped onward topless, towing Albatross, fighting through the storm of wings and beaks and talons, and thought disgustedly how unfair the whole thing was.

She had never been suicidal. Not seriously so. But still. Growing up gay with homophobic parents had given her plenty of opportunities to consider suicide and the possible benefits of it, but these had never struck her as being worth it. Her bottom wasn't rock, but a hard, bitter iron, and she'd let herself collect there, focusing with all her might on her eighteenth birthday, and getting out as soon as she was able. And she had. And she had never looked back. Not even during those awful days underground with the rabid experimental werewolves had she seriously considered clocking out early.

She'd had some friends though. Some of them had gone through with it. And in those cases Selene had never felt like they had killed themselves. Their situation had simply become so painful that they could not keep moving forward. It seemed redundant to punish them further, after death.

Then again, she thought with dark satisfaction, perhaps the pain they had felt in life was so great, this was still some measure of mercy. Maybe it was uncomfortable being a tree. Maybe the harpies stung a bit. But Selene thought their beaks and claws might hurt less than the torments a mind could concoct for itself.

She hoped so, anyway.

Behind her, Albatross was shouting at the harpies angrily. She seemed convinced they were hurting Selene, even though Selene told her not to worry. But then Albatross's shouts took on a more alarmed tone, and when Selene glanced back under her elbow she saw the harpies had figured out that Albatross's legs, though they could kick, did not burst into flames. Three had attached themselves to her ankles by plunging their talons into her flesh, and a fourth was making a go at her left shin. Those already attached were flapping furiously, and had succeeded in lifting one of Albatross's legs up into the air.

Selene lost sight of what was happening then as more harpies flocked around, joining their sisters, and the next moment Albatross gave a frightened yelp as both her feet were lifted, still kicking, skyward.

The harpies meant to carry her away, just like a piece of meat. Selene dug in her heels and redoubled her grip on Albatross's arm, swinging around to face her.

Harpies got in the way. The harpies got everywhere. Selene's face was filled with their scratchy, black wings, and she felt one trying to tug her shield out of her hand. They were tearing at her flanks—her pants wouldn't last much longer at this point—and more and more kept landing on her shoulders, clustering together so she was covered in black bodies with stabbing faces.

Selene imagined they were turning into a vast, flailing ball of harpies, all flapping wings and screeching. She wondered if the harpies could fly off with them that way. She wondered where they would be taken.

Albatross was really screaming now, and Selene could tell by the blinding flashes of light that she had her wings out, but the harpies had learned how to avoid them: they attacked her front. And poor Albatross, who was not invincible, sounded like she was being eviscerated.

As if in answer, an anguished cry rent the air around them. Selene thought it was the trees, but then it came again, louder, and with some incredulity she recognized it as a wolf's howl.

Several wolves, she thought, as the cries came more and more frequently. A whole pack. Getting closer and closer.

At first the harpies only redoubled their efforts at carrying them away, and then Selene found herself in the midst of a storm of flapping wings and angry cawing as the bird-women took flight, leaving Selene to stumble and fall to the ground, pulling Albatross down with her.

The ground was hard and cold and pokey and Albatross was crying and then there was a trembling in the earth and the sound of panting and light footfalls and they were surrounded by giant dogs.

Not wolves, Selene thought, raising her head to get a better look at them. These were definitely dogs. They had that fat, puppyish look that only dogs had, even though their ears stood up in stiff triangles and their legs were quite long and thin.

They were white as snow and glowed faintly against the black trees. All except their ears, which were blood red. They had glowing yellow eyes, and coldness flowed off their bodies. Frost spread from their paws where they touched the ground, and a thick mist settled around them from the condensation in the air.

They came and stood in a tight circle around Selene and Albatross, none coming within two feet, but packed shoulder to shoulder so there was no means of escape.

And for a long while, that was all they did. They did not growl or salivate, though one of them was a panting a little. Then, as if on some unspoken cue, they broke form and flowed away through the trees, leaving behind them a trail of frost and the soft sound of sighing. And in their wake, through the mist, another sound—the sound of someone stomping through the undergrowth.

Selene picked herself up and stood protectively over Albatross. By some miracle her jeans still had enough integrity to stay on her hips, though the sides were shredded. By holding the shield in front of her torso she felt almost decent, though the air was chill on her bare back.

The mist was thicker than she had realized, and the person in it took a long while to materialize. She saw their shadow, and that shadow was barely ten feet from them when a woman stepped between two trees and stopped to stare at them.

Selene stared back. She couldn't help it. The woman was probably the most beautiful person Selene had ever seen in her life. Including Aslana.

But this woman looked nothing like Aslana. Her skin was porcelain-white and tinged with pink, while her hair was a vibrant, shimmering gold. This fell in artful waves over her shoulders, turning to loose ringlets at the end. She had beautiful, almond-shaped eyes and a truly impressive face: high cheekbones and a strong, straight nose, wide forehead and flaring eyebrows that arched up like wings. Her lips were full and pink, even though her mouth was currently pressed into a concerned line.

She was wearing a tightly fitted suede vest strapped about the middle by no fewer than three belts, all with little pouches and holsters stitched on, and under that, a short leather skirt and a pair of leggings which disappeared into the cuffs of heavy leather boots. She was perhaps a little taller than Selene, and had the build of a Barbie—if Barbie had taken up power lifting and bought a compression bra.

On her left arm was strapped a heavy bracer set with a plate of metal, while in her right hand she held a long sword of the kind with a narrow blade and a flaring basket of interwoven wire for a hand-guard.

Selene felt her face grow hot. Mostly from the feeling of standing in front of an attractive woman without her shirt on, but also from the creeping suspicion that she should recognize this person. There was something familiar about her face—though Selene was unable to place it—and on her sword hand she wore a ring of metal with a dull stone in it.

Selene had seen two other rings exactly like it. One belonged to Clara, while the other had been hers. Briefly. It had belonged to Clara's brother, and had passed from him to Clara to Selene . . . though Selene hoped it had made its way back to Clara by now.

Clara had had a sister. An older sister. All she'd ever said was that she, along with her mother, were "gone."

Clara had never said *where* they'd gone.

Selene looked back up at the face. It was hard to tell what with all the hair, and this woman's face was altogether a different shape—her eyes were larger, rounder—but now Selene looked for it, she saw Clara in the shape of her chin, the angle of her nose and the tilt of her cheek bones.

She was so surprised she nearly dropped her shield—except that was the only thing affording her any pretense of decency—but she straightened up and rearranged herself so she wasn't in such an aggressive stance.

The woman hardly looked at her, however. Her gaze was fixed on Albatross with an expression of relief on her face.

"Alkonost," she said, her voice rich and musical. She reached out her open hand, palm up. "I have been searching for you!"

She paused. Albatross had drawn pack, frowning at the extended hand in alarm.

"Alkonost?" she said, confused. "Am I Alkonost also?" she asked Selene.

"No idea," Selene admitted. Alkonost had been a cross of a siren and a harpy from Russia, and as far as Selene knew, still lived there. Selene rather thought that, if Alkonost ever went to hell, it was for a purpose—not as some random calamity.

The woman put her head to one side—exactly like Clara would—and regarded them. A familiar crease appeared between her eyebrows.

What had been her name? Yvonne, or Siobhan, or something that sounded like that. . . . Something-*vona*. Selene looked at her sword again, wishing she knew more fencing terminology. Clara was actually Claymore, which was the sword she used. Her brother, Flammard, had a German *flammenschwert*, or wave-bladed sword. This sword definitely looked like a rapier, but that didn't sound right at all.

"No," said the woman. "No, my mistake. You're not Alkonost. Though you look a bit like her. Not Sirin, either. Who are you?"

Albatross looked like she was about to panic, and Selene, tired of being ignored, spoke up.

"Who are *you?*" she asked. It came out more aggressively than she'd intended, and she felt her face heat up when the woman—finally—deigned to look at her.

She had the exact same ice-blue eyes, only her hair was dark enough her eyelashes were clearly visible, ringing them with gold.

"You may call me Shae," she said, flatly. Then her eyes seemed to focus and she looked at Selene much more closely. "What are you doing with one of Faraday's moon charms?"

"Situational shirt?" Selene suggested. When Shae gave her the half blank, half stricken look Clara always did when Selene said something that left her completely lost, she added: "She gave it to me. Used to be the size of a quarter."

Shae nodded. "That makes sense. Size corresponds to spiritual power here. Mostly," she added, with a small, smug smile.

Selene discovered, to her annoyance, that she was both enamored of this woman and also acutely irritated.

"What are you doing here?" Selene asked, bluntly.

This was apparently the wrong thing to say. Shae straightened up, squaring her shoulders haughtily.

"I should ask the same of you," she said. "A living soul with a magical talisman and . . . whatever you are." She gestured at Albatross. "I am sorry I mistook you for Alkonost. I can see now you're someone very different. Or you would be, if you were a whole person."

"Have you seen any others like her, floating around?" Selene asked. "That's mainly what we're doing. Looking for pieces of her. There's supposed to be like three more somewhere in the forest. At least there were."

Shae shook her head. Even in the dull twilight of the misty wood, her hair glimmered. It was downright unfair.

"I'm sorry," she said, and seemed to mean it. "I wish you luck." Then without any further explanation she turned and began walking off into the mist from where she had come.

"Hey," Selene shouted, hurrying after her, but carefully—she missed her bra. "Hey, hey, you're alive too, aren't you?"

Shae hardly looked at her, but quickened her pace.

"After a fashion," she said.

Selene was not to be deterred. Clara had never said her sister was dead, but acted like she wouldn't be coming back. She tucked her shield arm tight against her chest, tugged Albatross's hand, and broke into a jog.

"What are you doing in Hell?" Selene asked.

Shae dug in her heels and stopped. She rounded on Selene.

"I am *trying* to get out of this infuriating wood!" she shouted.

Around them, hidden in the mist, the harpies began to caw again, but though Selene heard their wings beat, that sound eventually faded into the distance, along with their voices.

"Why are they afraid of you?" Albatross asked, her voice so full of innocent wonder that Shae deflated. Running her free hand through her ridiculous hair, she sighed.

"They're not afraid," she said. "They just know better than to peck at me."

"Why?" Albatross persisted.

"I'm not exactly mortal," Shae admitted. She sounded half proud, half annoyed. "I'm a demigod. And, my 'divine' lineage comes from a different tribe."

"Tribe?"

"You might call it 'religion,'" said Shae. "But really it's more like tribes."

She turned and began walking off again. This time Selene didn't chase after her, but planted her feet and shouted:

"Nordstern! Wait!"

Shae nearly tripped over a root in surprise. She whirled around, her cheeks flushed, eyes glaring.

"How do you know that name?" she demanded. She seemed almost frightened.

Well, good, Selene thought. Maybe now she'd take her seriously.

"I used to work with a woman named Nordstern," she said, taking a step forward. "Her first name was Claymore, but we all called her Clara. She had a brother, Flammard. And they had a sister, which, because I *am* a mere mortal I can't for the life of me remember her name, but if I did I'd be asking if that was you—because I think you are." She looked hard at Shae's sword, and at the ring on her finger. Then she looked her in the eye and said:

"I'll go first. I'm Selene Shields. This is Albatross. She's been broken up into a bunch of different pieces and I'm trying to get her put back together again. Maybe you can help us. Maybe we can help you."

Shae did not answer. She stood facing off against them, her sword partly raised. It was a beautiful sword, lean and gleaming, and the metalwork of the basket was detailed and ornate but still looked strong. It flashed in the light of Selene's shield as Shae lowered it.

"I don't . . . " The woman sighed. "I work better alone."

"That's what Clara said when I first met her," Selene remarked.

Shae raised a perfect eyebrow. "Clara's still working?"

"Last I saw," Selene said, and decided not to share her last memory of Clara—disappearing into the skies of Purgatory as Selene plummeted away, a look of stricken horror on her face.

Shae laughed and shook her head. It made her hair flutter artfully.

"And Flammard?"

"He's retired, mostly," Selene said. "Works as a paramedic. 'Sgot a girlfriend and an apartment in Chicago and everything."

"Really?" said Shae, her face brightening, but sadness lingered in the corners of her eyes and mouth. And Selene thought: you didn't leave on the best of terms, did you?

Shae was looking down at her sword. Then she gave a little shrug.

"All right, I'll help you. Though I don't see how you can help me. But you know my brother, you worked with my sister, and Faraday clearly liked you. What do you need?"

A shirt, Selene thought. *What I want is a shirt.*

What she needed was to find the rest of Albatross.

"Could you . . . I dunno. Help us find the other bits of her? Not all of them, obviously. But there were supposed to be like three of them in this forest."

Shae gave her a quizzical look, which she passed on to Albatross when the girl began to fidget.

"This forest is a big place," she said, but she came over and stood next to Albatross, looking at her closely. This made Albatross fidget even more.

"It was the wings," she said eventually. "That's why I mistook you for Alkonost. But you're not a Gamayun at all. And I see you're not all of yourself either. Do you know what you are?"

Albatross shook her head, looking at Shae nervously. Since Albatross was easily five inches taller than her, this looked slightly absurd.

"She's called Albatross," Selene repeated. "The locals here refer to her as the Calamity. Kirke said—"

"You've met Kirke?" Shae said, sharply.

"Yes," said Selene. "Up in Limbo. Kirke, she—well, her secretary—called Albatross the Calamity, which landed in Hell a . . . uh . . . a while ago. Anyway, it—she—Albatross—got split into nine different pieces which were scattered all over Hell, and each one of *those* also split into three. *This* Albatross is six of those pieces, as far as I can tell. Oh, and they seem to be drawn inwards—according to Kirke's girl, most of them are in Cocytus now. But there were three pieces in the Forest of Suicides, last she checked."

"How long ago was that?" asked Shae. She had begun to circle them, looking Albatross up and down appraisingly.

"Not sure," said Selene. "When we were in Limbo."

"We're a long way from Limbo," Shae remarked. "And time is fluid down here." She made one full circuit of Albatross and Selene, then stuck her sword point first in a spot of earth between the roots of a twisted, blackened tree, and folded her arms.

"Okay," she said. "I'll try to help. Emphasis on the word *try*. It's been a while, you see. Albatross, right? May I have a . . . something of yours? A hair will do."

"Don't give her a hair," Selene said, and instead reached over and tugged at a loose strip of cloth at the hem of her skirt. Albatross got the idea, and tore it free herself, before handing it to Shae.

The woman took the piece of stained cloth with a shrug and gave Selene a twinkling glance that hit her like a blow to the chest.

"I bet Clara liked you," she said, flashing the merest hint of a smile.

Selene was too off balance to answer with more than a grunt. It was not just that Shae was traditionally attractive in that white, Beverly Hills blond, Hollywood Valkyrie sort of way, but that she embodied it so comfortably. Her appearance seemed like an accurate representation of the sort of person she was, rather than some carefully constructed fabrication. The effect was almost overpowering. Selene could easily believe she was a demigod.

Careful, Selene thought to herself, watching Shae wind the strip of cloth around the blade of her sword, just above the hilt. *Careful. Careful.* Remember what happened with Valé Esperanato.

Meanwhile, oblivious to Selene's inner conflict, Shae had pressed one hand against the cloth-wrapped portion of her sword and raised it so the tip was pointing at the sky. She'd shut her eyes and her mouth was moving, forming words Selene didn't recognize. Albatross had so far gotten over her nerves to watch, curious, but only from the safety of behind Selene's shoulder.

Shae swung around, following the tip of her sword as if it were the needle on a compass. Selene thought she recognized this. Clara had done something similar when she was searching for Flammard.

Shae took a step away from them, and stopped. The mist had begun to lift, revealing nothing Selene did not already know, that they were surrounded by dead, twisted, black trees, which had grown so thick in places it was difficult to see more than ten feet in any direction. Even Shae's one step had nearly brought her sword into the trunk of the nearest tree.

She opened her eyes in surprise, and said: "She's here!"

"Yeah," said Selene, nodding at Albatross. "This part is. We know."

"No," said Shae. "I mean, she's *coming.*"

Almost as soon as she spoke, a wind struck them. It ripped through the bare branches, causing some to bend and others to crack, and with a moaning howl the trees with the broken bark began to bleed. The wind was followed by a flock of harpies, so thick that for a whole minute the air above their heads was a mass of beating wings and screaming faces. They were followed quickly by a bank of thick, white mist, within which ran another pack of white-bodied, red-eared hell hounds. These went streaming through the wood around them, neatly avoiding Shae, Selene, and Albatross. This time Selene saw that the icy mist came from their mouths, and she felt a numbing coldness as one of them brushed her leg.

Another wind chased away the remnants of the mist, and then all was quiet. In the quiet, the dark skies above them grew suddenly bright with a blinding yellow light. Selene recognized that light and raised her shield above her head—modesty be damned—just as a winged figure solidified out of it, diving straight at them.

Selene felt the impact like a flash of hot air on her skin, momentarily soothing after the chill of the hounds, but soon growing almost unbearable in its intensity. She adjusted the shield, crouching down so it covered most of her body, and waited. She waited while the light faded, while the heat dispersed, and then—only then—did she cautiously unfold herself and blink over the edge of the shield at Albatross.

She was in time to see multiple images of Albatross, intermingling but still separate, shimmering and sliding on the air. Three sets of three, no less, which slowly collapsed into one tall woman, her skirt long and flowing and tattered, her feet bare and glowing white where they were planted on the dark ground, and around her shoulders, now comically small, was Selene's rust-colored over-shirt. Her wings had changed. Instead of having jets of fire above her shoulders, her head was wreathed in feathers. It looked like she had two pairs of wings, both sprouting from the back of her head. They fluttered uncertainly as this ninefold version of Albatross blinked and rubbed her eyes, looking down at Selene and Shae.

"*Oooooh,*" she said, her shoulders shivering. "That felt really strange. But in a good way. Hallo, is that Selene? What are you doing down there?"

"Nothin' much," Selene said, trying to keep the shake out of her voice. "You just got taller."

"I did?" said Albatross. She looked down at her hands, then past them, to her knees and feet. "Oh look, I did!" She giggled, and then shrank.

It was one of the weirdest things Selene had ever seen. Not distressing, just strange. Albatross lost height like a deflating balloon, yet managed to keep more or less the same shape. She stopped when she was midway in height between Selene and Shae, and dusted her hands off, looking pleased with herself.

"Is that better?" she asked.

"It's less conspicuous," Shae said, unwrapping her sword and handing the strip of cloth back to Albatross. "Though it won't fool everyone."

"Fool everyone about what?" Albatross asked, and Selene, who thought she was beginning to understand what Shae was getting at, answered:

"About how strong you really are, girl," she said.

"I am rather strong, aren't I?" Albatross said, looking from one to the other of them, as if for confirmation.

"I think you might be some kind of god," Shae said, deadly serious.

Albatross looked at Shae then, very hard. She did not seem frightened of her anymore.

"You don't belong here," she observed.

"Like Thought and Memory I don't," Shae said, bitterly. "I've been trying to get out for ages now—possibly years. But this forest is like the drain filter of Hell—it catches you and holds you, until you become a tree, a harpy, or dog food."

"You don't look like any of that," Selene observed.

Shae shrugged. "Like I said, I'm from a different tribe. Different rules apply. But I'm still stuck. Haven't found a way out yet."

"The only way out," Albatross said, with cool certainty, "is to go further in."

"I know that," Shae snapped. "What do you think I've been trying to do?"

Albatross looked around them, blinking at the black and twisted trees which closed in all around. A few of them still bled from their broken twigs and branches, with a soft sound of weeping.

"This is the Forest of Despair," Albatross said, as if only just realizing it. "Despair eats hope and joy. It feeds on them. This is where the despairing land, transfixed in their torment. If you have hope, the forest will keep you. Eat you. If you have none, you cannot move; cannot get out."

"So . . . we're screwed either way?" Selene asked, blandly.

"Not really," said Albatross, her face bright and improbably cheerful. "Not if you have enough hope for everyone."

She twirled around on one foot, digging a small hole in the black earth, her arms spread open, her fingers wide.

"That way," she said, and pointed. It was, as far as Selene had retained any sense of direction, a little to the right of where she thought the way forward would be.

"Great," Shae began. "How do we—"

She broke off because Albatross had begun to dance and leap, waving her arms, and with each wave, sheets of white fire crackled behind them. They built with every sweep, growing larger and larger, crackling through the dead, dark air.

"Albatross . . ." Selene said, raising her shield again.

Albatross did a cartwheel. A real, joyous cartwheel, heels flying over her head, and when she came upright it was to push a solid wall of fire out in front of her, send it shooting off through the wood with a hissing roar.

In the path of the fire the trees came alive. For a moment they did not look like trees, but appeared as the people they had been. Men and women and many whose genders were indeterminable. Young and old and of all races, sizes, and shapes, they scrambled away from the fire, leaving a wide path open in its wake.

Then the light faded, and they were trees once more, black and twisted, but rather less withered. And the path remained, wide enough for the three of them to walk abreast, and in the distance, instead of fading into blackness, there was a pale orange glow and a white-hot horizon.

"Over the river and through the woods," Albatross sang softly. "To the center of Hell, we go." She grinned at them, wide and innocent and bright. Then she shrugged off Selene's over-shirt and handed it to her. "There. I think you need this more than I do." Then she skipped off down the newly cleared path, still singing as she went:

"Albatross shows the way, so we don't have to stay, to the center of Hell, we go!"

After a brief moment of stunned silence, during which Selene hastily pulled on her shirt, she and Shae came trotting after.

And around them, instead of moaning, the Forest of Despair let out a sigh that sounded almost like relief.

Blown by a bitter wind
Stagnant in my sin
In the rain withering
River pushes me down
Further down, further in
But I'm not gonna drown
My blood's still simmering
and the ghosts gather 'round

Three, Six Nine—the infinite goddess!
Raise your head and speak your name!

Blown by a bitter wind
Tell me girl, what are you gon' defend?
Raise your head and speak
I'm no goddess but I'm gonna die in hope

Oh, I
I am no immortal but you know
I'm gonna die in hope
Oh, I
I might not be goddess but you know
I'm gonna die in hope

Burned by a biting sin
Abandoned by the win
Girls comin' home to find their house overthrown
The Son-God's coming up
Flashing high he struts his stuff
But my blood's simmering
and the ghosts gather 'round

Hope in the Forest of Despair

Three times nine—read the scratches sunwise
Lift your eyes and see her name

Blown by a bitter wind
Tell me girl, what are you gon' defend?
Raise your head and speak
I'm no goddess but I'm gonna die in hope

Oh, I
I am no immortal but you know
I'm gonna die in hope
Oh, I
I might not be goddess but you know
I'm gonna die in hope

Go hard 'til you make it through
Don't let them stop you from what'ya need to do
Never give up on your heart
'Cause she's gonna get you out of here

Burned by a biting sin
Tell me girl, what are you gon' defend?
Raise your head and speak
I'm no goddess but I'm gonna die in hope

Oh, I
I am no immortal but you know
I'm gonna die in hope
Oh, I
I might not be goddess but you know
I'm gonna die in hope
Die in hope

—Die in Hope/*Princess Die*

CLOTH *of* MAN

5.

Detroit, MI
June

CLARA'S SLEEP WAS BLACK and dead and empty. Peaceful, in the way of peace that is the absence of all action. It was the way she preferred to sleep, if she could. No dreams or visions intruded on her rest, and in it her body healed, her mind recovered, and she woke restored. At least that was how it was supposed to work.

This time she woke in a cold sweat, certain that something had gone terribly wrong. At first she thought—she hoped—that the feeling was a byproduct of sleeping in a proper bed instead of stretched out in the back of Arcana under the stars. There was the momentary disorientation of opening her eyes and seeing, not the sky, but the dusty ceiling of her room at MCSIR. This was just the room that she slept in—all her meaningful possessions were packed safely into Arcana's equipment trunk, and she had spent so little time actually at MCSIR that nothing but the most nonessential of items had wound up in this room. Receipts and newspaper clippings, and a change of clothes.

It did not feel like her room, like a space she inhabited, and so she hoped to put down the feeling of trepidation that followed her out of sleep to this change of environment.

But as she lay on her back, coming further into wakefulness, she realized this was not the case.

She had slept the whole night through, which was almost impossible for her these days—years of sleeping and watching in shifts had ingrained in her the habit of waking up every few hours to check and make sure all was well.

She had slept the whole night through, and not once had she dreamed.

Recently she had been dreaming. Not the big, confusing, terrifying dreams she'd had as a child that had put her off dreaming entirely, but dreams so quiet and pleasant and soothing they were terrifying in their own way. They were unreal, but they were dreams, so she accepted them.

Starting around Christmas, and continuing with increasing frequency until they came to her every time she slept, Clara had dreamed of Ariel Freeman. She had dreamed of warm, golden days spent lounging beside a lake, or walking in a sweet-smelling forest. She had dreamed of a stag, white as new-fallen snow, leaping through the trees. And Ariel had smiled at her like she was a delight to see, and something like a small sun had risen in her chest, warming her heart and spreading out to each of her limbs.

She had never felt anything quite like the comfort and peace of those dreams, though they reminded her of that single, blissful summer of her seventh year when Mother had consented to stay put for four whole months, and she and Schiavona and Flammard had run wild across the fields and through the lakes surrounding Tesla Isenfaust's forge. That was before they had taken their public names, when they were just Schiavona and Flammard and Claymore, with no reason to hide themselves.

In her dreams with Ariel, she was that Claymore again. The Claymore that did not hide behind Clara, but existed: tall and strong and unapologetic. Clara felt her presence constantly, like a pole that kept her propped up against the unceasing blows life dealt her, but in the dreams, Claymore expanded, filling in the outlines of herself that Clara only glimpsed, now and then, in dire times when circumstance demanded them of her.

In her dreams with Ariel, she saw him clearer than she had ever seen him in waking life. He was a man, human and flawed, but all the more perfect for that. Like a piece of amber, cracked and containing dark specks of preserved insects and flowers, but deeply luminous in a dim, mysterious way. And every time he appeared in her dream it was like seeing the sun rise. The world was illuminated, and things that had been vague and shadowy were thrown into sharp focus. More than that, Clara felt anchored in a way distinctly lacking from the rest of her life. Not like being tied down, more like having a solid place on which to stand.

This was the first time in recent memory she had not woken with that sense of comforting assurance, and its absence distressed her, even before she thought to be distressed *about* its absence.

When she did think of it, she promptly decided not to. She had spent the majority of the last ten years carefully not-dreaming, and if this was a return to that state of affairs she had nothing to worry about.

Except she did. She worried at herself—at that space in her mind where the dreams came in—all through cooking breakfast for Mantha and afterward, while Mantha sat reading and Clara worked on her map of Detroit.

This map was very different from the traditional paper ones, or even the digital maps on the internet. Clara had started with one such map, carefully separated the data for streets and buildings from the underlying geography, printed them both out separately on sheets of thin paper, and was working on a third sheet, blank, which she had spread over the other two and was now penciling in by hand. Jill had tried to convince her to use the computer in the lab, which had a gigantic display which could be drawn directly onto by use of a special stylus. But Clara had found the interface too distracting, and had reverted to the analog approach, much to Jill's annoyance.

The map was for Jill. It outlined, as near as they could discern, the borders of the neutral territory of Detroit, and who held power outside them.

This territory, as Clara remembered it, was not one contiguous swath, but had a ragged edge with countless inlets, bastions, and islands, over which the powers of various entities held sway. The northwest peninsula of Hamtramck was a notable exception to the rule of neutrality, where the sheer volume of ghosts created a nexus of power that had to be accounted for. And on the flip side, the eastern half of Dearborn also lay within the neutral circle.

It had been Jill who coined that term after she had seen Clara's first outline of the territory. And, Clara had to admit, the way the border more or less followed Highway 39 north from Dearborn, then cut east along 8 Mile Road, before following the shoreline south to where it jumped the river and took a bite out of Windsor, Ontario, did more or less make a circle. MCSIR, though nowhere near the center (that honor, ironically, fell to the ghost-colony of Hamtramck) lay well within its borders, and was disturbingly potent, as far as spiritual activity was concerned.

Clara had been all over the building setting gauges the day before, and after she had finished penciling in the data collected by her exploration of the boundaries, she revisited those sites within the building.

And all the while, her brain worried.

The problem was she didn't know why the dreams had started, so she had no reason to understand why they would stop now. Perhaps they hadn't stopped at all. Perhaps she would dream again this night?

There was another possibility, both highly unlikely and unsettling. Which was that the dreamless sleep Clara had achieved the past night had not been a return to her old habits at all. That it had been too empty. Too dark. Too silent.

Clara had never shared dreams, purposefully or accidentally, with anyone outside her immediate family, but sympathetic dreaming was much more common. Or so Schiavona had told her.

She had dismissed the idea that her mind and Ariel's had somehow harmonized to the point where, though they did not go so far as to invade each other's heads, their dreaming minds had affected one another's. But if she admitted the possibility and applied such a scenario to the present state of affairs, it said something alarming about Ariel's situation.

Of course there was an easy way to test it. Clara knew this even without imagining Jill's response:

"Pick up the phone and *call* him," she'd say.

And say what? Clara wondered. She didn't know if Ariel was the sort of person who would let a random check go unquestioned, which was in itself a blow. In her dreams she had known dream-Ariel on a level of intellectual intimacy seldom achievable between two people, but this only served to hammer home the fact that, in the waking world, she knew him hardly at all.

The gauges were full. In one case a gauge had overflowed and shattered. Clara was too distracted to be surprised. Jill was not.

"This goes against everything I've learned about the state of the neutral circle," she said, when Clara reported her findings that evening.

It was still light out, but Jill had been getting up at six anyway, remaining safely ensconced in her underground lab until the sun went down. It gave her a chance to interact with the diurnal members of her staff, which had recently grown to include a zombie named Don and a young person called Tamerlain. Clara had not yet asked for a detailed explanation of how they had wound up at MCSIR. She only knew that Don's arm had been torn off by a werewolf from Southfield, and that Tamerlain was some sort of shapeshifter. She knew about the arm because Jill had painstakingly sewn it back on and then sent Clara to go organize a treaty with the Southfield werewolves, so they wouldn't attack anyone else trying to get to MCSIR, and she knew Tamerlain was a shapeshifter because she had been introduced to them as a petite, blond girl of maybe seventeen or eighteen, and later met them in the kitchen as a giant young man of distinctly African descent.

"It's so random," they'd said, sadly, "and I'm always hungry when I'm *him*."

It had been Jill's overwhelming interest the last two weeks to figure out what brought about the changes and whether they could be influenced, but Clara's report of the gauges threw her onto a completely different track.

"You're telling me these are the sort of readings you got in Hamtramck?" she said, picking up one of the spent gauges and inspecting it. Clara had used clear glass bottles with a teaspoon of shredded silver leaf in the bottom. Said leaf was now coating the interior of the bottle, tarnished beyond all recognition.

They were actually more intense, but Clara didn't see how saying so would help, so she shrugged. Jill seemed to read her thoughts from the motion, however, and rolled her eyes.

"Relatively speaking, what do they indicate?" she asked.

Forced to give an actual answer, Clara shrugged again while she dragged her thoughts away from dreams and portents, and Ariel.

"That there is a high level of focused magical activity within the confines of this building."

"Yes, but relative to what?" Jill asked. "From what I understand, *any* focused magical activity is elevated compared to the rest of Detroit. How does this compare to something from, say, Southfield? Also, do you know what it's from? You sure it's not just Frosty?"

Ah yes, Frosty. The Yell Hound which had adopted Jill, to everyone's surprise and Clara's consternation. Ghostly white except for her blood-red ears. Her golden eyes glowed in the dark. Her whole body did. Her fur was cold to the touch—in fact her entire body radiated chill. Yet despite her intensely magical presence, she acted very much like an ordinary dog— Marcus took her for runs in the evening, and Jill went on walks with her at midnight.

Her appearance had worried Clara, but it had been almost six months with no alarming incidents related to the dog, and most of the time she forgot about her entirely.

"No," she admitted. "I am not sure it is not just Frosty."

Jill was staring at her. She didn't blink much these days, which normally didn't bother Clara, only now she felt the intensity of the small woman's gaze like a physical sensation on her skin.

"That's not all there is, though," she said. In the past it might have been a question, but Jill had grown remarkably perceptive in recent months. Ever since the profound change she had inflicted on herself, in fact. It was a trait she shared with Lansing, who was a true vampire, but while Lansing was polite enough to pretend not to notice anything she didn't think she was entitled to, Jill had no patience for such filters.

Clara remembered being told that turning into a vampire didn't change a person's character. It only distilled it into the most intense version possible. And though it was debatable to what degree Jill could be considered a vampire, Clara had certainly observed this phenomenon in her.

"No, it isn't," Clara admitted, shuffling her concerns over Ariel to the back of her mind and dredging up the paranormal history of the place called Detroit.

"Detroit isn't just neutral," she explained. "It is barren. It used to be a portal host, but after the Brothers Gunn blocked Lucifer from traversing the Great Gate in 1970, the backlash obliterated everything. Ley lines were broken, wells of power stripped clean. It looks like a city, but if you go into the spirit world here, it's a wasteland. Wild. Primordial. And what does exist there is weak and twisted."

"Sort of like ground zero at Chernobyl?" Jill asked.

Clara frowned. Jill liked analogies to real-world aspects and Clara didn't, so she shrugged.

"This doesn't look weak and twisted," Jill said, tapping the bottle. The silver flakes stayed where they were, as if affixed to the glass by glue.

Clara agreed but was unsure whether a nod or a shake of her head was appropriate, and she had a feeling it would annoy Jill if she just kept shrugging, so she did nothing.

Luckily, Jill's mind seemed to have been sufficiently distracted that Clara might have crossed her eyes and stuck out her tongue without being noticed.

"Is there a way to refine your gauge?" Jill asked. "So we can get some idea *what's* tripping it? Because if it's just Frosty, then it's just Frosty. But if it's not . . ."

She trailed off, but if she was hoping that Clara would finish her sentence, she was disappointed.

Clara did not say "Then the Great Gate was not shut as tightly as David Gunn thought," or "There has been a profound shift in power," or "Your activities have disturbed the underlying ground-magic," or any of the other foreboding thoughts that came into her head. She clasped her hands behind her back.

"You may be best served if you create your own gauges," she said eventually. "You will need a magically conductive component—such as the silver—and a vessel. I prefer glass, but copper also works."

"Is that all there is to it?" Jill asked, blinking—to Clara's relief—very fast.

"I can suggest some other conduits, if you wish."

"Yes," said Jill, rubbing her chin. "That would be good. I can use Frosty as a control. You can plant some in known barren patches, so I can get a baseline. We'll want variating gauges for different sources, so we can have some hope of deducing what it is we're detecting. If it's *not* Frosty after all . . ."

She went away to the other side of her lab, muttering half sentences to herself. Clara lingered, wary of leaving too soon and thus being summoned back, until Jill appeared safely engaged in writing down the results of Clara's gauges and setting up a chart of the center, with notations on what the readings were and where they had been taken. Then she went up to the cafeteria, where Marcus was in the process of dispensing dinner.

She felt hollow. Like a door in her heart had been opened onto a vast, dark, cold cavern. Marcus had brought them Chinese takeout, and as Clara hunted through the white cartons for the one that contained brown rice, she found herself hoping—for the first time in her recollection—that she would dream again this night.

She sat next to Mantha as the girl determinedly picked out the watercress from her stir-fry with a pair of chopsticks, then ate the broccoli crowns, mushrooms, and strips of chicken, in order. When she had finished she set her utensils across her bowl and looked thoughtfully up at Clara out of large, brown eyes.

"Something is wrong," she stated, gravely.

And Clara, tired of denying it to herself, could only nod.

Mantha reached out a tiny hand and patted her arm. "It's okay," she said. "I'll help you fix it."

Then she went and took her bowl into the kitchen, carefully emptying the untouched rice into the trash on her way.

* * *

Clara woke from blackness, with her heart thumping against her ribcage, shivering. She was shivering because her body was covered in sweat, the blankets tangled around her feet.

Outside it was raining. A burgeoning storm swept down out of the Arctic, pushing a wave of unseasonably cool weather in front of it. They had been having a lot of unseasonably cold weather, and storms too, and what with the building's ancient heating system, Clara had forgotten what it felt like to not be slightly cold all the time.

This storm sounded like there was hail involved, and sure enough, when Clara went to her window and drew back the curtain she could see it dancing on the asphalt of the drive below. Her room was on the fifth floor, facing south, and from it she could look down the parkway to the lights of the city, glowing bravely through the storm.

There were no chairs in her room, but her bed was close enough to the window that she could sit on the side of it and gaze out. She did this, with her elbows on her knees and her hands clasped between them, for a long time. She tried to empty her mind, letting the sound of the rain and hail fall through her, until she felt like a cold, clear glass bottle.

She was certain she had dreamed. The blackness, the nothing, was not her natural sleep. She felt bone tired and sore, as if she had spent the night fighting, not sleeping. But even after half an hour of sitting and watching the rain she still could not retrieve any solid memories.

Normally, the problem Clara had with her dreams was that she remembered them. Now, when suddenly she couldn't, she didn't like it any better. It was as though she had forgotten something important, but there was no one she could ask.

She was still sitting, slumped in front of her window, when Mantha found her.

She heard the girl enter her room by the small, quiet sound of the door handle being turned. It was so small, and so deliberate, Clara suspected Mantha had made the handle squeak on purpose, to give her a warning. Certainly when she turned to look, the door was wide open and Mantha was standing in the middle of it: a small twelve-year-old with a round face, straight dark hair, and big dark eyes. She was wearing jeans and trainers and an ugly wool sweater with jarring horizontal stripes of blue and orange whose sleeves came down almost over her hands. She was frowning slightly.

"Are you all right?" she asked, after Clara had been looking at her for a solid minute without speaking.

Clara gave this question due consideration before answering.

"I am," she said.

Mantha didn't move, and the line between her brows deepened.

"Do you know what's not?"

Clara also considered this question carefully.

"I think Ariel Freeman may be in trouble."

And Mantha, because she was Mantha and not Jill, did not ask why Clara thought this, but came around the foot of the bed and sat down next to her on it.

"Who is Ariel Freeman?" she asked instead.

It was a reasonable enough question, but Clara found the answering of it complicated by the two versions of Ariel she held in her head. There was the dream Ariel, who she knew in bone and blood and scent and soul, and there was the real Ariel, whose personality shone so brightly it was difficult for her to look at.

"He is a man," she began, realizing that this was not immediately obvious from his name. "He fights monsters."

"Like you do?" Mantha prompted.

Clara thought of Ariel and his careful exorcisms and spells, and shook her head. "Not the way I do, but like me, yes."

"Do you have his phone number?" Mantha asked.

Clara nodded, stealing herself for what would come next. But she had forgotten that Mantha, being over ten years her junior, had different ideas of what should be done with people's phone numbers.

"You could text him and ask," she suggested, simply.

It felt as though an invisible weight had lifted from Clara's shoulders. She found herself staring down at Mantha, her face blank with surprise.

Of course. She could *text* him. Texting made much more sense. No need to actually say anything, to open her mouth and speak. And if he did respond, at least she could take her time to figure out how she would reply.

Almost a year ago, in what now felt like another life, Clara had called Ariel's phone. Though her memory was very, very good, she could not remember the ten digit number she had dialed once, eleven months ago. But she had done so with the same phone she currently carried in the breast pocket of her leather jacket, and the phone remembered.

So she did it right there and then, with Mantha sitting next to her, staring out at the rain. A simple text: three words, one line.

What's your status?

Clara watched it send, saw the badge appear which denoted that it had been delivered, and waited. For some reason, now she had sent it, she was more nervous than ever. Up until now she could have pretended that all her feelings had been so many misunderstood nerves or something entirely contained in her own head. But now she had taken physical action, and that dark and turbulent part of her mind had had an effect on the waking world.

There was a tug at her elbow. It was Mantha.

"Jill needs your help," she said. "The tests came back weird."

Jill, looking exactly like one would expect a half-dead pseudo-vampire to look, was sitting in her underground lab surrounded by glass beakers in various states of distress. After examination Clara determined that they had all been reasonably deployed, spiritual gauges, but several had been blown out, one had diffused, and one had a lump of crystal in the bottom.

"That's quartz," Jill said. "That's the only thing I've been able to determine."

"Where were these last night?" Clara asked.

"There's a chart," Jill said, going to her computer.

This was actually the same laptop she had carried with them from day one, hooked up to a gigantic display which took up most of one wall. It in turn was wired to another display, only slightly smaller, which rested faceup on a dedicated table and could be operated by use of a stylus. Jill switched them both on, with the wall screen showing a diagram of the station from the side, while the touch screen showed the floor plans.

"There were forty, originally," she explained. "I wanted to cover locations on both axes, two for each of the fifteen upper levels, and ten for the ground floor and basement. Those are marked on the map here." She pointed to the little blue dots which decorated both the floor plans and the side view. Each dot had a black numeral in it, so one could find the location of any given gauge on both maps.

"I just finished putting in the data from my results . . . if you could call them that. I used a gradient of blue-purple-red to indicate the degree to which they were messed up, with notations attached. The pink one is the crystal."

Clara, who had been distracted by the gauges, glanced over and saw that the diagrams were now covered with purple and red dots. Most of the reds were concentrated on the lower levels—the ground floor and its immediate neighbors—while their color grew cooler the higher one went— with one outlier on the fifteenth floor. This was a bright speck of crimson, and when Clara cross-referenced it with the floor plan, she noticed that Jill had placed it in the hall outside Mantha's room. She pursed her lips, but didn't say anything. The subject of what Mantha was had still not been settled, and this only confirmed what they already knew: Mantha was powerfully magical and highly unconventional. Still, within the context of the chart it was informative.

"What was happening on the lower floors last night?" she asked.

"Nothing unusual," Jill said. "Lansing and I were working. Tamerlain came down for their midnight snack then went back to bed. Don was asleep, and so was Marcus."

"Where was Frosty?"

"Oh, I can show you exactly where Frosty was," said Jill, grinning. She pointed to the single pink dot on the entire chart, which was smack in the middle of her lab. "She was with me the whole time."

"Where is she now?" Clara asked.

"Marcus took her on a run. They should be back soon."

Clara looked around the lab. It had once been the mail room of the old station, but Jill had renovated it into a sophisticated underground laboratory. This had involved some expensive plumbing and a lot of white-balanced LED lights, but now it was as bright as day with an industrial-grade sink, an exam table, the aforementioned computer displays, and more storage space than even Jill knew what to do with. There was a dog bed in one corner, and a space heater for when warm-bodied folk had to make forays into its icy depths. This was currently off. Clara had zipped up her jacket.

"What detecting agent did you use?" Clara asked, going over to the line of glass jars set up on the exam table.

"Silver, like you suggested," Jill said.

The ones that had blown out looked very much like her own, while the one which Jill had thought diffused was actually in the early stages of transmutation. She picked up the jar and squinted at the lump of silver in the bottom.

"Powder?" she asked.

"Leaf," said Jill. "Easier to come by. Was that wrong?"

"No," said Clara. Leaf was, after all, what she preferred. She held up the jar. "Where was this laid?"

"What's its number?" Jill returned.

Clara turned the jar around, and found a careful 6 printed on the lid in black sharpie. She told Jill.

"Oh, that's the main concourse," Jill said, almost dismissively. "I think I messed up there. I thought all the jars were sanitized but I must have accidentally grabbed one from Tamerlain's to-wash pile."

"No," said Clara, taking the jar and bringing it over to the display. Looking from its contents to the 6 inside the only blue circle on the entire map, which was between two pillars at the entrance to the ramp from the main concourse, she carefully set it down by its lid on the edge of the display.

"No . . . what?" Jill prodded at her, and Clara realized she had not actually finished her sentence.

"You didn't make a mistake. And neither did Tamerlain. This didn't diffuse—it's transmuting."

"I can see it transformed," Jill said. "It used to be leaf."

"Transmuting," said Clara. "Transforming is what werewolves do. What Tamerlain does. One fixed state to another. This has gone unstable. It is *transmuting*."

"You think it will keep changing?" Jill said, suddenly interested. She went over and leaned down next to the jar, so close that the rims of her glasses almost touched.

Clara nodded firmly, then realized Jill might not have seen, and added: "I do. I would monitor it."

"Of course," said Jill, slipping out her phone and taking a picture. "I'll repeat the experiment tonight."

Clara hovered. She felt like her work was done, but didn't feel comfortable leaving Jill at this juncture. So she said:

"Try copper, this time."

"Why copper?" Jill asked, taking the jar back to its place on the table.

"It is less sensitive than silver, in this capacity," Clara said. "Which is ordinarily undesirable, but in this case . . . "

"Sensitivity is not the issue," Jill agreed. "I'll set some silver gauges too, for control. Damnit. I need more jars."

Then Clara did flee, before she could be put on jar-collecting duty, and checked her phone as soon as she made it up the ramp and into the concourse.

No new messages, and the badge beside her note to Ariel still said: *delivered.* She checked the time. Her interview with Jill had only lasted thirty minutes. There was no telling what time zone he was in, nor what he was doing. People went out of cell reception all the time. Or had their phones silenced—Clara herself had been guilty of that. Now, however, she was beginning to understand why Jill got so frustrated when Clara was unresponsive to her texts.

Clara put her phone away and looked up. The concourse, cleaned and repainted with new windows on either end, was awash in sunlight, though rain was still falling outside. She realized she was standing within ten feet of where the transmuted gauge had been placed, and looked around curiously to see if she could sense anything unusual. But there was only the stone tiled floor and the columns, cut by shadows and glittering sunlight.

She decided she would give Ariel Freeman twenty-four hours before she took action. In the meantime, she called the Isenforge and left a message for Faraday asking for his last known location. Because she knew she would need something more substantial than a phone number to track him, and Faraday was the best way to find anyone—even someone who didn't want to be found. Then, having done everything she could do immediately, she took Unicorn for a ride down to the nearest hardware store and bought five flats of pint-sized Ball jars—the kind with wide mouths you could get your whole hand in—and brought them back to MCSIR, strapped down across the back of her saddle. She delivered them to a surprised Jill, still awake and still working in her lab, and then went up to the kitchen for a belated breakfast.

It was while she was reheating cold oatmeal and slicing a banana that her phone binged and vibrated, and she nearly dropped both the knife and the fruit in her hurry to pull it out.

But the text was not from Ariel. It was from Faraday. Clara spent a good minute staring at it in amazement—amazement that *Faraday* had sent her a *text*—before she registered what it actually said. Which was:

Talk to Di in Knoxville

And then even as she looked, a second message came in:

Horse shoe and willow branch. She doesn't use a phone.

Clara couldn't help smiling at the message. Faraday was sometimes late in picking up new technology, but when she did, she embraced it fiercely, and was equally disdainful of those who had not.

Clara typed *thanks* and sent it, then put her phone away and finished assembling her breakfast. With a settled course ahead of her she found everything became more bearable, and went around helping Jill lay her revised gauges with something approaching happiness.

That night when she slept, she went willingly into the darkness and woke with a sense of determined urgency. She could not afford to wait any longer, and when she saw her message to Ariel had *still* not been read she did not give him the additional three hours needed to bring the tally up to twenty-four—she just began packing.

Initially she had intended to take Unicorn south. She missed riding, and with so many people at MCSIR she imagined Mantha would not want to come.

But Mantha appeared midway through the morning, her own backpack bulging over her shoulders and Lady Bibbit by her side.

Lady Bibbit, who had begun as a stuffed rabbit in blue denim overalls, was now a strange creature caught somewhere along the anthropomorphic spectrum between human-shaped-with-animal features and talking-animal-on-two-legs. Her fur was soft and gray and her skin had a ragged, patchwork look from all the scars that crisscrossed her body—remnants from the time she had been blasted to pieces, then literally stitched back together again. She was missing her left eye—the one piece of her that hadn't been recovered—but her right was very big and blue.

Though she never appeared as an ordinary stuffed rabbit the way she used to, she had taken to spending most of her time sitting motionless on a shelf in Mantha's room, an eerie figure neither dead nor alive.

Now she was visibly animated. Clara could see her furry chest rise and fall under the cotton sundress that had replaced the denim overalls, and she had found a straw sunhat from somewhere, cut holes in the band for her ears, and was at that moment easing it on over them.

Silently Clara rearranged her plans, laying in extra energy bars and cramming the back of Arcana with pillows. She checked to make sure her entire arsenal was safely packed in Arcana's locking trunk, and then—almost as an afterthought—went back inside to explain to Jill.

Jill was in her lab frowning at gauges, Frosty lying at her feet, and responded so mildly Clara knew her words had not fully registered. She waited.

"Wait—you're going *where?*"

"Knoxville. In Tennessee."

"I know where Knoxville is," Jill said. "*Why?*"

Clara felt her insides twist uncomfortably. She did not like to lie, but the truth was too unsettling for her to give voice to. So she skipped to the end of it:

"Ariel Freeman is in trouble. I'm going to help."

"He called you in for backup?"

Clara swallowed. She shrugged.

Jill removed her glasses and rubbed her eyes. "Fine, fine. Just tell me you're leaving Mantha here this time."

Clara could not lie about that, not even by omission. Her face must have shown her unhappiness, because Jill guessed immediately.

"She insisted?"

"She's waiting in Arcana," Clara said.

Jill threw up her hands and turned around in a little circle.

"a.m./p.m. check ins—text or calls don't matter, just let me know you're still alive," she said.

"I will," Clara said. A promise. "And if I don't, give me two hours' grace, and then call Faraday. She has a cell phone now. I'll send you the number."

"Got it," Jill said. She looked directly across at Clara then, as if seeing her for the first time in days. Clara was taken aback by the intensity of her gaze. Her eyes had a luminous quality, and her skin had gone pale from lack of sunlight. It made her pink lips stand out all the more strikingly, and she looked almost like a painted doll.

Almost. Because there were lines under her eyes and her lips were chapped and she'd pulled a hank of hair loose from her ponytail and played with it so that it hung off at an odd angle. Like Lady Bibbit, she was caught somewhere between a living animal and an animated construct, but tending more toward life. Clara liked to see that.

Jill's lips parted, then she apparently thought better of what she was going to say, and she closed her mouth. She turned back to her stacks of jars, then looked over at Clara and smiled. She inhaled, deliberately, and said:

"Drive safely."

Clara nodded, another promise, and left.

Somewhere in southeast Kentucky

The storm was strong enough the man could hear it even in his room, which, judging from how quiet it was most of the time, was probably underground. It was dark in the room, the only light coming from the razor-thin crack under the door when the woman came to bring him food, and though he'd felt around the walls and found things he thought were windows, they never let in any light.

They had taken his name, and with it most of his identity. He had memories, but they were without context: the sun shining low in his eyes under the visor of a car's windshield; a string of rosary beads, hot in his hand. The bitter taste of activated charcoal in his mouth; a bloody stake hammered into the ground in the center of a crossroads.

He knew the food they gave him was barley bread, and that it was baked fresh. It was not bad tasting, but it was the only thing he had to eat. They had given him a sack with a long rubber tube and a mouthpiece at the end, from which he could drink water freely. Infrequently but regularly, he was given a bowl of warm milk. After the barley bread and water, it was as sweet as candy to him.

His life had not always been this, of that he was certain. There was a pain in his left hip, as of a deep bruise, which made him limp rather than walk. He was fairly sure it had not always been that way. He remembered, dimly and distantly, walking in the dark, painlessly. And this memory had a context around it that the others did not: the woman had come for him, and put something soft over his head, and led him out of the room. He remembered walking, following her because he could think of nothing better to do, and his feet touched cold stone and then soft carpet and then cold ground, and a cold, wet wind touched his skin. And nothing had hurt.

But he had other memories too. He remembered the sun. And rainbows. And the feel of a steering wheel under his hands.

He remembered looked up into the face of a stone angel, and it was outshone by a star, cold and bright and sharp. It hurt to look at, but it was the clean, healing hurt. Like pulling out a splinter or stretching sore muscles.

When he slept, he dreamed of that star. Its light was cold and fragile and did not illuminate the ground beneath it, but nonetheless it spread awareness around the man. In his dream he followed it over a dark, barren, jagged country. It hung low in the sky, but no matter how long he walked, he never got any closer.

The path he took through the land was made of swords, but they were laid flat up, their tips pointing toward the star, and so as long as he walked carefully he was not hurt. Sometimes he felt that if only he could speak to the swords, they would rise up and carry him to the star. The star was important. The man wondered if it was his name. In the star was the answer to the taste of charcoal, the pain in his hip, the sun glancing low through the windshield of a car.

Once, he dreamed, he did meet the star. It came down to him and stuck itself in the path of the swords. Then he saw it was also made of swords: four swords and four knives, arranged with their tips outward, an eight-pointed star with a single eye, like a chip of ice, in its center.

Against all reason, the man found himself wanting to embrace it. That was foolish, he knew. He would be cut to ribbons, and he did not want that. It seemed the star did not want that either, for it retreated before he got close enough to touch it.

He wanted to speak to it. To ask it for his name. He was certain it had his name. That it would give it, and the rest of himself, back to him, just for the asking. But he had to ask. And now it felt as though his mouth had been glued shut with tar and wine. The pain in his hip exploded, and he woke to find the woman standing over him.

He could see her, he realized, because she was silhouetted against the dim light from behind on the door. By her outline he saw she was wearing a long dress, and that she carried a heavy club in one hand.

He was still half in the dream. Could still see the sword-star partially overlaying the shadow of a woman, and he reached out to it.

"Please . . . " he said, and was surprised at the raspy croak that came out of his mouth. Nothing at all how he thought his voice should sound.

"You were right," said the woman, hoisting her club over her shoulder. "He was calling for help. I don't think he actually managed to reach anyone, but I'll tighten the net just in case. Call our maid. Tell her to be on the lookout."

Another voice answered in agreement, and then the rectangle of light closed, and the man was in darkness again.

He tried to go back to sleep. His hip hurt and he was suddenly cold, but no matter how he searched for the star—his star—all he found was blackness. Even the road of swords had disappeared beneath his feet.

Somewhere on I-75 South

Mantha hadn't been on any long car rides before she'd met Clara. She'd heard about them, from other kids boasting and adults complaining. Now she had been on no less than three, and didn't understand what the fuss was about. It was just a lot of sitting. Still, even if it wasn't as exciting as going to a movie or reading a good book, Mantha liked the experience of *moving*. Of traveling from one place, through other places, to a new place. She liked watching the road signs, and the billboards, and the other cars and trucks. Arcana's cab was big enough it was like a small house to her, and though Clara would not let her climb around from seat to seat once they were on the interstate, Mantha kept comfortable by sprawling across her seat in various configurations. Also, Lady Bibbit could read while the truck was moving, and so they listened to her read *Matilda* cover to cover on the first half of the drive.

They made good time until Cincinnati, where they encountered traffic so thick and slow it moved like molasses. As if on cue, Mantha's bladder announced it was full, so Clara took the next available exit, and they made a pit stop at the first gas station they found. Everyone but Lady Bibbit used the bathroom, and Clara bought them sandwiches, which they ate in a nearby park. The benches were still wet from the recent rains, but drying fast in the summer sun. Clara got a towel from the back of Arcana and mopped up the worst of the puddles, and by the time they had finished eating, the traffic had lightened, and they were able to make it out of the city in less than an hour.

Mantha slept through most of it, the food having made her drowsy and tired. She slept through the crossing of the Ohio River and Louisville, and didn't wake until they were crossing the Kentucky River, brown and swollen from the recent storm.

This storm was now only a light covering of high white clouds, which enough light filtered through that it illuminated the verdant foliage of the trees that grew thickly on either side of the road and the lush grass that coated the gray-brown bedrock, visible wherever the freeway cut through a low hill.

Mantha rolled her head sideways and looked over at Clara. Despite the relative brightness outside, she had not put on sunglasses, and her blue eyes were squeezed together against the glare from the road. It gave her a worried wrinkle in the middle of her brow which made her look older than she was. Then Mantha realized she didn't know how old Clara was. She was an Adult and therefore older than Mantha, but on balance she seemed younger than most of the other adults she had met. But that had only been Mantha's impression. She had no idea if Clara was twenty—or thirty-nine. In a way, she was ageless. From Mantha's perspective, she imagined Clara would look much the same in twenty years. Maybe even a hundred. She was just so . . . *Clara.* Big and strong and cold but surprisingly gentle. It made her wonder who her parents were.

Mantha had often wondered what her parents had been like. She'd gotten a fairly good impression of her mother from her grandmother, but her father had been a persistent mystery. From what she understood, her mother had not married him, and he had not been around when she was born.

She asked in the veiled hope that, even if she couldn't get answers to her parentage, she might derive some satisfaction from learning about Clara's.

What she got was a silence so icy she nearly regretted asking. Nearly. For she had learned that Clara's apparent frostiness was not born of anger or resentment, but from an aversion to showing any emotion at all. Mantha waited. After a time, Clara said:

"My father is a ghost. I do not even know his name. My mother knew, but she did not tell me."

Mantha said nothing. She had the feeling if she said anything, it would stop the conversation rather than otherwise. Sure enough, after a few more breaths, Clara continued.

"I would say I knew my mother, because she raised us. She was always there, watching over us. Like the sky. But now I wonder if I knew her at all. I still think of her as big and strong, though I grew taller than her, before she left. She had red-gold hair and could lift cars with her bare hands."

"Wow," said Mantha, in a small voice. It seemed appropriate.

Clara shrugged. One of her trademark shrugs: down, then up.

"She was very wise, and brave, and always, I thought, a little sad. We were never quite sure why. Schiavona said this was because she had given away something precious and missed it terribly. Schiavona thought this was the reason she went away, to find the precious thing again."

Silence, and Mantha realized now she needed to speak, or that would be all that was said.

"Who is Schiavona?"

"My sister. My older sister," Clara answered.

"Tell me about her . . . ?" Mantha said, adding the questioning inflection at the last minute, as she realized Clara might not take well to being prodded this way.

Clara let out a big, gusty sigh.

"Schiavona was a head shorter than me, even when we were children. Her hair was pure gold, and she could wear it down without it getting in her face. Boys liked her, but she did not like boys. She liked building things. She was a wondersmith, like Tesla. She gave me my Unicorn. She went searching for our mother. I have not seen her since."

"Oh," said Mantha in a small voice. Something else seemed needed, so she added: "I'm sorry."

Clara shook her head. "That was a long time ago." As if this made it better.

"Do you have anyone else?" Mantha asked.

"I have an older brother," Clara said, and sounded marginally more cheerful. "The eldest of us. His name is Flammard. He is also the smallest, with hair like orange fire and many freckles. But he has chosen to live a normal life—or as normal as he can make it. He is a paramedic in Chicago. He helps people."

Clara stopped talking, and they drove in silence for so long Mantha assumed that was all there was, and began gazing out the window, her mind wandering. She wondered about fathers, and why they had a tendency to be absent from their children's lives. Then she remembered she was only going off herself and Clara.

They passed Richmond, where the traffic thickened but did not slow. And then, when the highway was relatively empty again, Clara began to speak.

"I had another sister. Not a blood-sister. An arms-sister. She was the eyes in the back of my head, and I hers. She was the shield to my sword. The moon to my star. And she carried my trust like it was sacred. Separately, we were capable. Together, we were powerful. Without her I am half a warrior."

Mantha was almost afraid to ask—she thought she knew who Clara was talking about—but she did anyway.

Clara's answer was not the one she was expecting.

"She fell," Clara began, and then stopped. Her voice had gone strange, like she had something caught in her throat. When Mantha looked over at her, she had her eyes on the road, blinking fiercely.

Then, with a sharp whip of her hand, she put on her turn signal and moved to the far-right lane. She took the next exit, turned right at the cross street, and then pulled completely off the road. She stopped the truck, put on the handbrake, put the gear stick in neutral, and switched off the engine.

She was breathing hard, as if she had just dashed a hundred meters, or narrowly avoided a collision. Her shoulders heaving, the breath whistling in and out of her mouth. She was staring down at the steering wheel now, but Mantha didn't think she saw anything. Her eyes were shining, and her breath began to come in gasps. Then she folded her arms over the wheel, leaned her head against them, and began to bawl.

They were big, hacking, painful-sounding sobs. She didn't cry, exactly, but moaned in the back of her throat in a way that made Mantha's stomach curl. She sounded like a beast in agony.

Mantha exchanged an alarmed look with Lady Bibbit. This was not at all what she had been intending, and the sight of Clara melting in the seat next to her was almost terrifying. It was so wrong Mantha was tempted to order Clara to stop. To stop it at once, start the truck, and go back to driving. To forget Mantha had ever asked—that they had ever had this conversation.

And the truly terrifying thing was, she knew she *could*. And that Clara would do it. It made her feel downright sick.

There were words in the sobs now. "She fell," Clara choked. "She fell—I tried to catch her. I failed. She fell. I let her—" and then a sob rose up like a wave and Clara slumped against the wheel, crying messily.

Mantha looked to Lady Bibbit again, helpless, afraid.

Lady Bibbit was glaring at her. She flicked an ear and jerked her head at Clara. Mantha did not understand—until all of a sudden she did.

Grown-ups, she realized, were just kids in big, hard shells. And sometimes those shells cracked. So, though it was harder than just ordering the entire mess away, Mantha unbuckled herself and crawled over the cupholders so she could pat Clara's shuddering shoulder.

She felt red-hot even through her leather jacket. Mantha sat awkwardly on the cupholders and wondered what to say. She knew the things adults would say to her, and she hated them all. They would say: "It's all right," or "It's okay," when it was quite clearly *not* all right and *not* okay.

So she patted Clara's shoulder, and started with, "I'm sorry," which was at least the truth. She wasn't sure Clara heard. The percussive sobs grew less frequent, but convulsive shudders still wracked her body, though she seemed to be trying to control them. Mantha considered and decided it would be best to say the things she always wished adults would tell her when she was having meltdowns.

"I'm here," she said, reaching an arm as far as it would go over Clara's back. "I'm not going away. I won't leave you."

These were big promises to make, and Mantha realized she would have to be careful to keep them, otherwise she was as bad as the adults who told her "It's okay" when it wasn't. But, she figured, if she turned the terrifying power that allowed her to influence other people on herself, she should be able to. The realization made her stomach untwist and a bubble of warm energy expand in her chest, and then the words came fast and easy, promises as pure and true as spring.

"I'll always be here for you. I'll always wait for you. I'll always come for you. You have me, now. I'll help you. You're not alone."

Clara was shaking—shaking her head, Mantha realized. And why not? It must sound ridiculous, coming from a twelve-year-old girl. But Mantha knew it was true, even if Clara didn't yet. She got a handful of leather jacket and squeezed.

"Maybe I can be your little sister," Mantha suggested. "I mean...I never knew my father either. Maybe yours and mine were the same person?"

This was so patently ridiculous—they looked nothing alike—that it managed to derail whatever dire thoughts were running circles in Clara's head. She snorted—something like a laugh—and sat up. The action dislodged Mantha, but she remained, sitting awkwardly across the cupholders, while Clara sniffed and wiped her eyes, pinching the bridge of her nose and breathing slowly in and out.

Eventually she looked up—straight ahead, at the road before them—and said: "You should put your seatbelt back on."

As if nothing had happened. The shell was closing up again.

But it *had* happened, Mantha thought as she scrambled back to her seat and buckled herself in. Clara's eyes were swollen and puffy and, even after they got back on the freeway and continued south, she continued to sniffle now and then.

When Mantha glanced back at Lady Bibbit, the rabbit gave her the thumbs-up, and smiled toothily.

They all acted like nothing had happened, and in that way Mantha's initial desire was fulfilled. But something had changed. And as they plowed south through the long evening toward the southern state line, Mantha decided that it had changed for the better.

Knoxville was a bright complication of lights in a dark landscape by the time they reached it, well into the evening gloom. Their trusty highway, I-75, disappeared into a tangle of other freeways, and Clara had to pull off onto a surface street to consult a map. The interruption in steady movement jostled Mantha's bladder into action, and so they stopped for dinner at a counter-serve deli, where Mantha ate something called a square burger, and Clara picked her way through a crunchy chicken salad. Lady Bibbit waited in the truck, and Mantha insisted on bringing her a milkshake. The two rode in the back together for the remainder of the drive, and Clara wondered how much of the milkshake ended up being eaten by Mantha. She decided it didn't matter, and concentrated on finding the witch Faraday had told her about.

Faraday had given her specific instructions on how to find Diana Upjohn, but they had not included an address. Instead she had been told to follow 275 south to the Baxter Avenue exit, turn right, and by a series of concentric left turns, spiral her way into the center of Mechanicsville. It was a difficult route to follow, since the streets grew narrower and narrower, and in many places the streetlights had gone out. In the end, however, she managed to make a successful, counterclockwise circle (well, rectangle) via Iredell, College, Picket, Dell, and then back to Iredell, and then—*then*—she saw the house that Faraday had described: a bright blue two-story house behind an overgrown garden crowned by a weeping willow, which trailed its long branches over the steep roofs and cascaded over the front porch, which was itself choked with potted ferns. When Clara parked Arcana in front of the gate and saw that the Queen Anne style trim was not white but a pale pink, she knew she had found the right place.

Whether the witch was at home, or would even receive them, she had no idea. But she let Mantha and Lady Bibbit accompany her through the tangled garden, which seemed larger on the inside, and up the steps and through the trailing willow branches to the front door. It had a gorgon face, made of terra cotta, hung in place of a knocker, and no doorbell.

Clara cleared her throat and addressed the grotesque face directly:

"I am Clara Nordstern, a friend of Faraday Isenfaust. With me is my ward, Mantha, and her familiar, Lady Bibbit. We would enter, and ask questions."

The gorgon face did not move, but there was a thumping from inside as of feet descending a stair, and a moment later the door was wrenched open and a surprisingly young woman with long dark hair and a pale face stared out at them.

"Hello? Sorry—oh, you must be Clara. Faraday told me. I didn't know you'd have friends. But come in, come in, all of you."

The house, like the garden, was bigger inside. Mantha noticed three flights of stairs (two up and one down), and rooms leading off into rooms and more rooms and nooks and crannies everywhere. She could see as much because all the doors were open, and lamps burned brightly in each one. These were the kind with heavy, stained-glass shades, and cast patches of red and green and blue all around them. It made the house dim and colorful at the same time, and left a lot of vague shadows in the corners that masked the chairs and tables and bookshelves lurking there. The windows were covered by heavy cloth drapes, and the whole place smelled strongly of incense.

The witch named Diana led them through a low hallway crowded with tiny photographs in big frames and into a parlor. This was a real parlor, with a heavy table and chairs and potted plants hanging by the windows and a breadbox on the side table. She sat them down, pulling out an extra cushion for Lady Bibbit, whose presence she accepted without question.

"Thank you," said the rabbit, politely, and the witch colored a little.

"I've never met such a young witch with such a strong familiar," she said.

Mantha glanced at Clara, expecting her to contradict the witch, but Clara was behaving oddly. She had sat with her hands out of sight under the table and was not making eye contact with the witch. She didn't correct her presumption, and so Mantha did not either. But she looked again more closely at the witch, wondering what Clara had seen that she had not.

Mantha guessed—and it was only a guess—that this witch was younger than Clara. Her hair was fine and smooth and fell around her head in a careless, artful way Mantha had only ever seen in movies, and her face had a soft, fresh look. Mantha realized this was because she was not wearing any makeup, though she wore earrings and a beaded necklace and several rings on each hand. She was currently fumbling in the cabinet under the side table, removing cups and saucers and a tea chest and electric kettle, which she blew the dust off before plugging in.

"I don't have guests very often," she admitted, bashfully. "When my coven meets, we usually do it in the kitchen. What tea do you like?"

Clara just shrugged, and the witch turned, almost pleadingly, to Mantha.

Lady Bibbit saved the moment.

"What sort of tea do you have?" she asked.

The witch presented her with the entire box out of relief, and Lady Bibbit bent over it, sorting through the packets with care.

"We need not stay for tea," Clara said, still in that stiff, formal tone with which she had addressed the gorgon face. "I am only here to ascertain the whereabouts of Ariel Freeman. Faraday said you were the one to talk to."

"Ari?" said the witch, pausing as she filled the kettle from a pitcher by the window. "I haven't seen him for weeks."

Something rang sour in her tone. Mantha couldn't put her finger on it—thought she might be imagining it until she saw Lady Bibbit's ear twitch.

"Do you know where he was going, the last time you saw him?" Clara persisted.

Diana Upjohn shrugged dramatically as she turned the kettle on. "He *said* he had a job in California. But you know, *men*. I think he was just getting claustrophobic."

Clara didn't respond. In fact, her mouth sealed so tightly Mantha didn't think she would speak again for the rest of the evening. Certainly she allowed the witch to boil water, and to pour their cups—with tea chosen for them by Lady Bibbit—without saying another word. It was only after the witch had joined them at the table and the teabags had been removed that she resumed her interrogation.

"When was the last time you spoke?" she asked.

Diana Upjohn blew on her tea. "Yesterday," she said, looking unhappy. "We had a . . . an argument. I . . . don't know how well you knew him, but . . . " She sighed. So carefully wistful, Mantha thought it rather fake. "He's with a woman right now. He might call her his girlfriend, but she's more his mistress if you ask me. She's the one that called him out to California. Got him all tied up in her own plans and now . . . " she sighed again, deep and heavy.

Mantha was confused by Diana Upjohn. She kept getting flashes of the sourness under her words, but some more strongly than others. She wondered if the witch had a crush on this Ariel Freeman—who she called Ari—and then she looked again at Clara and wondered if Clara did.

It made her want to sigh as heavily as the witch. *Adults.* Mantha hoped she remained immune all her life.

Lady Bibbit responded to the awkwardness in the air by drinking her tea. And once she was done she drank Mantha's—which had been too hot to touch—and then, in an act of daring, finished Clara's as well. Mantha thought she might have gone after the witch's, but she was sitting on the far side of the table and was too difficult to reach. Mantha didn't mind. Despite the fact that she had been given a pleasing peppermint tea, there had been no milk for it, and for some reason it tasted too pungent—almost medicinal—and Mantha had not wanted to drink it anyway.

"I'm sorry," Diana was saying. She patted Clara's gloved hand. "How do you know Ari?"

Clara had to swallow twice before she unstuck her mouth to answer.

"We worked together," she said shortly.

"For?" Diana Upjohn seemed singularly incapable of reading Clara, who was broadcasting chilly disapproval so strongly even Mantha was beginning to feel slightly embarrassed.

"A short time," Clara said, her words clipped and spare, cold as her eyes. She fixed these on Diana, who finally seemed to notice that her guest was not pleased. "Was he all right?" she asked.

Diana looked confused. "Who? Ari? I suppose in the most basic sense of the term, yes." She rolled her eyes. "He's probably in danger of being played the fool, but when has that ever killed a man?"

Clara got an expression on her face like she could think of several cases where men had died from foolishness, and though she said nothing, Diana took her meaning. She pursed her lips uncomfortably.

Mantha watched in fascination. She was feeling warm and fuzzy inside, and a little nauseated—as though the sip of tea had not agreed with her. She wondered if Diana and Clara were going to have a fight. Then Clara said:

"You spoke with him—how?"

"By phone," Diana said, as if this was obvious.

Clara pulled out her own phone, checked something on its screen, then put it back in her pocket.

Then she went from sitting behind the table, apparently at ease, to standing with her hand around Diana's throat. The woman managed one strangled scream and then cut off, gulping and choking, as Clara lifted her out of her chair.

"I know you lie," Clara said, her voice frosty with a calm so intense it took Mantha's sluggish mind a moment to realize how furious she was. This became clear seconds later, when the witch's flailing hands began tracing glowing lines through the air, and Clara slapped them down with a snarl.

"I do not know if you are possessed, or if you have deceived Faraday also," Clara said. "But I know Ariel Freeman is in a dire situation and if you obfuscate my way to him, I will remove you. Tell me where to find him and tell me true—this I lay upon you, Diana Upjohn, on your honor as a witch."

But Diana Upjohn was no longer struggling. She hung from Clara's fist, and while she made no sound, her mouth and lips were moving fiercely.

"Tell me," Clara repeated, and lowered her so that her feet—which were bare—touched the stone floor of the parlor. She loosened her grip a fraction, and the witch wheezed as she sucked in air.

"I am a lowly witch no longer," she gasped. "I am one with the moon and the light upon the waves! I am Alphito, Baitule, Lusia, Nonacris, Anna, Fearina and Salmaona!"

"Tell me!" Clara ordered, giving her a hard shake.

But Diana Upjohn only repeated that strange name, all of it, over and over:

"Alphito Baitule Lusia Nonacris Anna Fearina Salmaona, Alphito Baitule Lusia Nonacris Anna Fearina Salmaona . . ."

A pale glow had begun to diffuse from her skin, growing more intense by the second until Mantha could barely look at her. Then, with surprising strength, the slim young woman threw off Clara's hand, and her eyes flashing bright in the dark room she roared in a thunderous voice:

"I am one with the goddess in me, and you will perish in my wake!"

She raised an arm as if to strike Clara, who had staggered back a pace. Mantha sat, frozen, unsure what to do.

In the time it took her to begin to panic, Clara had drawn her sword and rammed it through the woman's midsection, only for the woman to turn to light which filled the room, crackling like electricity, before concentrating into a single bolt which shot out the nearest window, shattering the glass and disappearing into the night beyond.

It left the little room dark and smoky and smelling of something sharp and sour which stung the inside of Mantha's nose.

There was movement in the shadows, and a scratching hiss as Lady Bibbit struck a match and lit a fat candle, and as its flame flickered and grew, Clara's shape lumbered into view. She had been knocked flat on her back by the blast and was gingerly flexing the hand which had held Diana's neck.

Mantha wanted to ask if she was all right, but there was a tightness in her chest and a fog in her mind, and it was making her mouth uncooperative.

While Clara gathered herself, Lady Bibbit went around turning the lights back on. Only some of them did, but it was enough light for Mantha to see that Clara was otherwise unhurt. She was examining her sword, which had acquired a long, black scorch mark down the center of its blade. She wiped at it with a gloved finger, and it came away easily. She shrugged.

"Mantha?" she asked.

Mantha tried to answer, but all she made was a bubbling sound.

"The tea was poisoned," Lady Bibbit explained, coming around and supporting Mantha's shoulders. She felt the soft, furry paw-hands tighten, the blunt nails digging into her skin through her sweater.

Clara came around the table, kicking chairs out of her way as she did so. She had reached into one of the pouches she wore along her belt, and removing her hand held up a small black stone, shiny in the dark.

"Open your mouth," she told Mantha.

With difficulty, Mantha did. Clara placed the stone on her tongue. It was cool and tasted of nothing at all.

"If you swallow it no harm will come to you," Clara said. "But try not to. These are difficult to come by."

So Mantha dutifully did not swallow, but held the stone in her mouth until it warmed on her tongue, and as it warmed, her head cleared and the nausea retreated. Eventually she spat the stone out in alarm as her sharpened mind took in all that had happened.

"Lady Bibbit drank all the tea!" she exclaimed.

"Yes," said Clara, picking the stone up off the floor. "Though I don't know how much good this"—she waved the damp stone—"will do her."

"An antidote is not necessary," Lady Bibbit said, sounding smug. "I have it contained. It is no bother to me."

"What *was* that?" Mantha asked. "It looked like she turned into lightning!"

Clara straightened up, a frown creasing her brow.

"The goddess took her away," she said softly. Then, with a little shiver, she sheathed her sword and walked out through the parlor door. Thumping on carpet and wood told Mantha she had not left the house but was exploring its many passages and rooms. Taking Lady Bibbit by the paw, Mantha walked out after her.

The rest of the lights in the house had also turned off at the witch's departure, and Clara had not seen fit to turn them on again. So Lady Bibbit and Mantha took care of that task. Only one in three actually worked, but they provided light enough to see by.

The house was dark and shabby, and Mantha imagined the halls were narrower, the rooms smaller, and the ceilings lower. In one room they found, down on the ground floor near the front of the house, the ceiling was stained with mold and sagged in the middle. A creak from above told them Clara was up there somewhere, and Lady Bibbit shouted at her to be careful.

Her voice was sucked up by the walls, muted and weakened.

There was a no incense now, but a smell of mold and distantly of rotted vegetable. Mantha decided it was not her imagination that the walls were drawing in on them.

They found a flight of stairs and went up them, saw a bright yellow light and followed it until they came into a circular room with boarded-up windows. The light came from a candle Clara had lit, and she was herself standing in the middle of the room, her hands on her hips and a frown on her face.

The room was the first place in the house that Mantha felt had *not* begun to shrink since the witch's departure. The smell of mold and rotten cabbage was weaker here, though it grew stronger the longer they remained. From what she could see by the candle's small, wavering light, the walls and the boards had been painted over to look like a crude sort of forest: a stripe of green at the bottom and blue in the middle, with darker green splotches up near the ceiling and thick lines of brown between, to indicate tree trunks. The floor was covered by a green carpet with a dark line making a spiral across its surface. In the center, in front of Clara, was a rudimentary table made of two slabs of wood with a third laid across them. Clara had crouched and was inspecting it with a small flashlight, and as Mantha drew closer she saw there were marks on the wood, slanted lines that looked a little like music notation and a little like ancient runes.

Mantha wasn't sure what *kind* of ancient runes, she just knew that was what these scratches made her think of.

Sitting on the table, wrapped in a piece of sheepskin, was a small sculpture of dark metal that Mantha had difficulty making sense of. It was only once she came and stood right next to Clara that it resolved itself into a seated woman with the head of a horse. The horse's mouth was open, and the little blobs of metal that had been put into its eye sockets caught the light and glinted madly. In one hand it held the legs of the bottom half of a baby; in the other it held the top half by the hair. The arms were partly raised and set wide, as if the figurine depicted the monster in the moment of ripping the child in half.

It filled Mantha with a surprising amount of horror. Less at the gruesome act it depicted, but more in the way it stood out in her mind from the rest of the room.

Since the witch had left, everything had taken on a feeling of shabby fakery. As if any grandeur in the place had only been paint and cardboard, like the backdrop of a stage play. Even this room, though it felt more vivid than the rest of the house, had an air of being a shoddy copy of the real thing.

But the statue *was* the real thing. It was what kept the room from falling into decay with the rest of the house. Realness of an ancient and cruel nature rested in that statue, and Mantha found herself disturbingly attracted to it. She felt a desire to snatch up the figure and carry it away with her into the night. To keep it close to her and keep it safe, until she could build her own shrine to the goddess it represented.

Most of her found this desire laughable, and Mantha felt like she had separated from herself, turning inward to look with derision upon the part of her that wanted the statue. And, slowly, that part came to see how silly it was being, and faded back into her.

Still the statue held a realness to it that was striking. She wasn't sure if it was the light or the polish on the metal, but it glistened as though it was wet.

"Clara?" she asked, unable to put into words the myriad of questions jostling through her brain.

Clara stood up beside her, and Mantha automatically reached out and took her hand. It was cold and hard and strong through the leather of her glove, and Mantha felt anchored. The horrible little statue was not the only real thing in the room. Clara was just as real, just as alive, and every part of her was in agreement that they would not let go.

"What is that?" she asked, as a place to start.

"An idol," said Clara softly. "An idol to a very old goddess."

"The goddess that took her away?" Mantha asked.

"Something like that," Clara sighed. She looked around the room. Looked down at the floor with its spiral line. Looked up at the ceiling, which had also been painted. This time it was dark blue, with white dots representing stars. Mantha thought she recognized the Big Dipper, and through it, Polaris and the Little Dipper.

Clara's big hand squeezed hers.

"Mantha," she said. "Can you please go down and wait in Arcana?"

"Why?" Mantha asked.

"Because I am about to pick up that idol, and without it I do not think this house will stand much longer. It might not stand much longer, even as it is. The virtue is fading fast."

This seemed reasonable, so Mantha and Lady Bibbit went back down the stairs (they creaked ominously) and retraced their steps until they came to the parlor, and from there back through the ground floor to the front door.

The garden had withered while they were inside. Now it was all dead, brown stalks, and when Mantha looked back, the house was dark and the paint was peeling off its gables. She could see Arcana, comparatively big and bright and shiny, and it was a relief when they slipped through the gate and climbed up inside—Lady Bibbit in the back, and Mantha in the front.

Mantha left her door open, so she heard the huge, rushing sigh as a dark wind blew out of the house, rattling the dead plants in the garden, and heard also the pounding of feet inside. She heard doors slam, and a moment later the front one banged open and Clara came hurtling out. She had a bundle of sheepskin clutched to her chest, and she vaulted the gate out of the garden, her sheathed sword catching withered vines and pulling them away with her.

She reached the truck just as, with a terrible groan, the ridge of the house's roof collapsed, and a cloud of moldy dust rose into the air above it.

Clara came around and, unshipping her sword and sliding it onto the backseat with Lady Bibbit, climbed into the driver's side. She set the idol, now an awkward bundle of sheepskin fixed with a rubber band, in the center of the dashboard, and started the engine. Mantha shut her door and buckled herself in, and then they were pulling away from the house, which was just the shell of a house now, clearly abandoned, sitting behind a dead and withered garden.

Somewhere in southeast Kentucky

The woman had not given him milk since his dream of the star. The man remembered that much. So when she set the bowl down for him he raised it to his lips almost reverently. It tasted as sweet as ever, and he relished the smooth slide of it over his tongue. He was so bound up in the sensation of it that he didn't notice that the woman still stood over him, a dim shape against the faint outline of a door around her. He only looked up when he heard her mutter, in a faintly disgusted voice:

"What a wretched creature man is. You only need take away his trappings, and he becomes like a pig, wallowing in the mud."

And the man said, before he knew where or how the words came to him:

"Pigs are good animals. Maybe they know something we don't."

The woman raised a hand as if to strike him, and a flash of pain in his hip reminded the man why he did not speak out. But he held his ground, crouched though he was over the bowl, and did not look away. For some reason, he knew, it was important that he did. Without his name, and without the context for his memories, he was only this he knew: what he did, here and now.

There was a faint sound like *zing* and something rocked the walls of the place so that clods of dirt and dust fell from the ceiling. In the distance there was a muted sound of someone yelling, and when the man looked up the woman had fallen sideways in the door, propping herself against one wall.

The man felt something coiled inside him unwind. It spread itself throughout his body and down his limbs and he sprang to his feet and ran. Ran out of the room and past the woman and down the hall beyond. His hip twinged painfully, but he made his leg move, and he had gotten several yards down the corridor when the dizziness caught up with him and he staggered sideways.

Behind him the woman shouted, and he felt something hard and cold constrict around his neck, and then he was on his back, being dragged down the hallway, and the woman was standing over him again. He raised his hands to guard himself against another blow, but she only rolled him over back into his cell and shut the door, leaving the man to lie, choking and gasping, in the darkness.

The woman, meanwhile, pulled her dress straight and marched down the hall from where the king's cell was. She was rattled, which was not something that happened to her often, and so it bothered her even more. She took a sharp right down a narrow corridor which was hardly more than a crack in the rock, and by this and other shortcuts came to the center of the labyrinth, where she found their mother crouched next to the maid, holding her hand and rubbing circles on her back.

"What in the holy name of the goddess was that about?" the woman demanded, pulling the edges of her robe closer together. It was always cold in the center of the labyrinth; she was not sure why.

Under the pale light of the moon-avatar which hung fixed to the ceiling, the maid's face was even whiter than usual, and there was a blackened scorch mark radiating out from her chest. It fractured and zigzagged, like black lightning, and had burned right through the fabric over her heart.

At her words the maid looked up and glared at her.

"His help," she snapped. "He called help, all right, and she's strong."

"*She* did this? To you?" asked the mother, incredulously.

The maid picked at the blackened flakes of cloth fluttering over her chest. "No," she admitted. "That was the goddess. She took me away." She shrugged. "I would be dead otherwise."

"What was she? A witch?" asked the woman. "A rival?"

"A virgin huntress, I think," said the maid.

"Then why on the goddess's good green earth was she trying to kill you?"

The maid shrugged. "I think she's confused. But don't underestimate her. I expect she'll find us, sooner or later. She's one of . . . of my *former* mistress's projects."

A respectful if unfriendly silence filled the room, as the other two women considered the implications of this.

"Then we should not delay," said the mother, rising to her feet. She was heavyset, with strong, brown arms and wide feet. She was not actually their mother, but the other two called her that out of the respect for the office she had won. "The sun is almost at the height of his strength. A day or so early should not defeat our purpose. Where is our tanist?" She looked across at the woman.

"Close," she replied. "I expect him here in the morning, in fact."

"Let's just hope *she* doesn't get here first," grumbled the maid.

Tennessee, north of Knoxville

Clara drove right on through the night. She had Mantha hook her phone up to Arcana's Bluetooth speakers, and called Faraday. The voice at the other end of the line was cranky and hoarse, and the two proceeded to have an argument.

"Your witch is beholden to the Triple Goddess," Clara began.

"Aren't we all?" replied the voice of Faraday.

"Not like this," Clara said. "She had a mare-headed effigy in her shrine, rending a child. She lied to me about Ariel Freeman. She tried to poison us."

There was a crackling on the other end of the line, and then Faraday muttered, bitterly: "Damn that Mari. Look, Claymore, don't do anything rash. Where there's one, there's three."

"I know that," said Clara, merging onto the interstate and speeding up. She kept glancing at the idol on the dashboard, as if it was giving her directions.

"I mean it," said Faraday. "Don't do anything rash. I'm on Maui right now. It'll take me at least two days to get to you. Hold *still.*"

"I can't," said Clara. "I have her idol."

"It can *wait.*"

"It's almost midsummer," Clara said.

Faraday did not answer for a long time. When she did, her voice was harsh and abrasive.

"Claymore Nordstern, you pull that truck over, take a deep breath, and—"

Clara ended the call, as coolly as if they had just been having a civil conversation. She drove on.

Mantha found she could not sleep with the idol on the dashboard. It gave her an itch under her skin that was uncomfortably like guilt, though she could not imagine why. She kept thinking of the child it held, torn in half with its entrails falling out. Why would she do that?

She decided, if Clara was going to drive, and she couldn't sleep, that it was time to ask questions. So she started with that one.

"Depends on the era," Clara said, flatly. "Usually, the sacrifice of the goddess's son was to make the barley sprout. They would sprinkle his blood in the furrows. Sometimes it was to renew the year. But that was more commonly an adult male sacrifice. They would kill their sacred king and eat him."

Mantha made a face. "*Yuck,*" she said. Then: "Who are *they?*"

"Mostly, they are gone now," Clara said, a little sadly. "They were ancient people, overthrown by other ancient people. By men and their male gods, who shattered the goddess, stole her virtue, and tried to stamp out all memory of her. They almost succeeded. Fragments of her survive—some of which have taken on lives and powers of their own—but she is no longer the all-encompassing creator-muse that she once was."

Mantha had mixed feelings about this. She was naturally predisposed to side with a goddess over a god, but she could not get the image of an infant torn in half out of her head. As if sensing her feelings, Clara added:

"She was not all bloodshed and sacrifice. She guided people and inspired them. Among her tribes, women were afforded reverent honor and wielded immense power. Apart from the human sacrifice—which many of their contemporaries performed as well—they were good rulers. And the male gods that usurped her were no better. You may know their names: they were Zeus and Apollo, Ra and Horus, Thor and Odin."

"I thought Zeus took over from his father," Mantha said.

"In a way, he did," Clara allowed, her mouth twisting wryly. "None of the legends are *wrong*. Merely incomplete. History becomes variable, when gods are involved. So in some cases two contradicting stories are both true. Zeus did castrate his father, the Titan Cronus, and banish him from Mount Olympus. And he was also Zagreus, the eternal child of the White Goddess, destined to be sacrificed for the barley field again and again, until he gained enough followers that he was able to grow up and fight the Goddess. Tear *her* into pieces. All the old goddesses you hear about are actually fragments of *the* goddess. That is why Hera is so vindictive. That is why Hades had to marry Persephone. That is why, though her warrior and huntress aspect lived on in Athena and Artemis, they had to remain virgins. They could not be allowed to love freely, as the Goddess did, for that would empower them. And Aphrodite and Demeter, in whom the goddess's powers of fertility were vested, were shackled. But she was strong in the Fates—and the Norns. Even today, when the gods that overthrew her are no longer worshipped, anywhere three women are gathered as a team, the Triple Goddess is there."

"So you're saying . . . all the old goddesses were originally this one goddess?" Mantha found this thought vaguely disappointing for some reason.

Clara inclined her head, frowning.

"Many of them," she allowed. "Some people think that the White Goddess was born of even more ancient goddesses—but who they are exactly we do not know. Also, the White Goddess as she existed in prehistoric times is no longer present. She was shattered—not killed. And those pieces have gone on to have lives and powers of their own. Even if they have forgotten what they once were."

They drove on in silence for a while. Lady Bibbit leaned her head between the seats and asked:

"So what are we dealing with here? Another fragment?"

Clara shook her head.

"She was a muse of poets, and of truth. And so, even broken and scattered, human hearts can evoke her. Where three women are, so is the Triple Goddess."

"Is that what Faraday meant?" Lady Bibbit prompted. "When she said, 'where there's one, there's three'?"

Clara nodded shortly.

"And . . . you think they've kidnapped your friend?"

Another nod. Clara shifted down, changed lanes, and powered past an SUV.

"But they won't sacrifice him . . . will they?" Mantha said. "He's not a baby."

Clara shook her head.

"The sacred kings, remember?" Lady Bibbit pointed out.

"The Oak King of the Waxing Year, and his tanist, the Holly King of the Waning Year," Clara recited, in a dull monotone. "Forever doing battle for the favors of the goddess. The principal celebration was on Midsummer, which was her New Year, where the Holly King defeats the Oak King, and he is ritually bound, flayed, and eaten, for the glory of the Goddess. He is resurrected in midwinter, when he does the same to his counterpart."

"Oh," said Mantha, quietly.

"When is the solstice?" Lady Bibbit asked, suddenly tense.

"The day after tomorrow," said Clara. "But that is by modern reckoning. Ancient calendars were not always so exact—and I do not know which one they are using."

After that everyone was tense, though eventually Mantha got tired enough she climbed into the backseat (just to get away from the idol) and went to sleep. The rumble of Arcana's engine, reverberating up through the soft seats, was a soothing smokescreen from the baleful presence of the disturbing figure.

Detroit, Michigan

Sometimes Jill felt guilty about how much she enjoyed being a pseudo-vampire. True, the deadly allergy to sunlight was a major hindrance, and it was difficult to make herself eat. And if she didn't eat, she began craving things other than food, and those feelings she did *not* like. Mostly because they threatened to blot out her perception of people as, well, *people*, and instead made her see them as walking blood sacks. It gave her a deep appreciation for Lansing, who had never bitten anyone nor gotten that glazed look Jill had been accused of when she'd gone too long without a meal. (The trick, Lansing had told her, was carrying a thermos of blood around at all times.) But all in all, Jill found the advantages of being partly undead vastly outweighed the detractions.

She could concentrate better. Her eyesight was better—though she still wore non-corrective glasses to mask her eyes and their tendency to turn red—and she could work longer on less sleep. Calculations for which she used to need pen and paper (or a calculator) she could now do in her head. And she only had to read something once, with the right attention, and she could then recall it, completely accurately, at any time. This pulled uncomfortably close to the place in her mind where the angel's message lay—still there, after all she'd been through—but she rarely got them mixed up. True, she had once surprised Don by reciting it instead of the results from his last test, but that had been the only time—and it had not happened since.

Don was a puzzling case. A former butcher from the far side of Michigan, he had suffered a fatal collision with a delivery van while crossing an icy road the last winter, which had left him with a ruptured aorta, no pulse, no heartbeat, and no brain activity. Except he'd woken up on the way to the hospital, much to the surprise of the EMTs, who were even more surprised to discover he *still* had no pulse, heartbeat, or brain activity. They had done an MRI at the hospital, just to be sure.

Jill was currently looking at this MRI, comparing it to two others: one of an otherwise healthy, living brain, and one from a cadaver. Both had been provided, after much grumbling, from her old professor at UC Santa Cruz. But the grumbling had been less along the lines of "why do you ask for such weird things" and more of "why haven't you hired me yet?"

Jill had laughed at the idea of hiring her old instructor, but after some consideration she began to wonder if this was not, perhaps, such a bad idea. Okedo had been there, at the beginning of it all. He had further made significant advances with the chimera samples she had left him with. And, the more she looked at Don's brain, the more she thought the self-rejuvenating powers of those chimeras were exactly what he needed.

Don didn't heal, the way she and Lansing did. He didn't decay, either, but every cut, nick and scratch he had received since his physical death remained. His left arm had been ripped off at the shoulder in an altercation with a werewolf just before his arrival at MCSIR, and though Jill had been able to stitch it back on, the tendons and ligaments refused to knit, and the nerves remained limp and lifeless. Don had to carry his arm in a sling, otherwise it tended to fall off. But it didn't cause him pain, and he began regaining sensation in his fingers almost at once. Three months later, he could move them around, even roll his wrist.

"I could probably move the whole arm, if I concentrated," he said. "Though I don't know how long it would stay attached."

They had agreed not to push it.

It was clear to Jill that whatever was facilitating Don's function as an animated corpse, it was not the conventional means of electricity and chemical reactions. Neither was it the energy that suffused her own being, and to a greater extent, Lansing's. And now she had another variable to measure: the ambient magical concentration within the old train station.

She had not thought to connect it with Don's condition, until she had found the zombie standing entranced in a stairwell between the fourth and fifth floors. He came out of his daze as soon as she spoke to him, but could not for his un-life tell her why he was there. Jill could see no reason either, but she'd put one of her gauges down in the stairwell—she'd been on her way to set it up on the top floor—in order to lead him down to her lab. She'd forgotten about that gauge until the next evening, and when she had eventually collected it, was surprised to find it read higher levels of ambient magic than anywhere else.

They had just gotten back from a brief tour of the building, which had consisted of Jill following Don around until he hit a spot that made him disconnect, at which point Jill would put down a gauge and then shake him out of it.

There had been thirteen of them in all, and Jill had marked down their positions on her map. Now Don was sitting, fidgeting, in her spare chair, while Jill reexamined all the documentation she had on his case.

Because obviously there was *something* animating him, and for the first time Jill had a glimmer of a notion of what this might be. Her challenge, now, was figuring out how to test for it.

"I can't very well have you *eat* one of these gauges," she explained.

Don eyed the pint-sized mason jar with its canning lid and flakes of sliver leaf sitting in the bottom. He shook his head.

"But it would be useful to know if you're getting 'stuck' because of a similarity in the magic that's holding you together, or something else," Jill said, rubbing her chin.

"Magic isn't a good enough explanation?" Don asked, sounding tired.

Jill shook her head vigorously. "Not with how complicated and variable things are. No. I am operating under the assumption that there's magic and then there's magic and then there's magic. Like dark energy. It's a bunch of related things we don't understand well at all and so we've slapped this handy label on it. But it's a label of 'we don't really know' rather than 'this is what it actually is.'"

"Could dark energy be a kind of magic?" Don asked, hopefully.

"I'm not ruling out an overlap," Jill said. She sighed. A deliberate action these days, she did it with the kind of purpose a yoga teacher could appreciate: inhaling to the full extent of her lungs, holding for a moment, then pushing all the air out in a long, slow, thorough exhale. It took her almost a minute.

"I guess I'll just have to rig you with one small enough to keep in your pocket."

In the end she gave Don five gauges: one with silver, one with copper, and one with gold—and one with palladium and one with cadmium.

"Because why not cover all of silver's elemental neighbors?" she remarked, and went away wishing MCSIR had the resources for heavy-ion research so she could make her own roentgenium. One definite advantage of her state of being: radiation from atomic decay did about as much damage as a stiff breeze, and she suspected this was a trait Don shared with her. But, since she was a long way from smashing atoms, she put gauges of palladium, cadmium and gold in the stairwell of the fourth and fifth floors, for control, and told herself she was satisfied.

Southern Kentucky

When Mantha woke she found her surroundings so different than what she remembered, the events of the night before might as well have been a bad dream. Lady Bibbit was dozing on the seat next to her, and she had been laid out across the back with her head on the rabbit's leg and Clara's thick, leather jacket laid over her. The jacket was warm but too small for a blanket; it left her feet uncovered.

Sunlight was streaming in through the window, and beyond, Mantha could see bushy oaks and green birches, and beyond them, a vivid blue sky.

She sat up and rubbed her eyes, wondering where Clara was—the front seat was empty. In ascertaining this she also saw that the idol was gone, which was a small relief.

Beside her Lady Bibbit yawned and stretched her furry arms.

"G'morning," she said, sleepily. "Clara's outside, navigating, but she got breakfast."

Mantha opened the rear door and found Arcana had been parked at a rest area beside a small lake. Traffic was intermittent on the road behind them, and the trees grew thickly all around. The only other car was a dark blue minivan parked at the far end, next to the restrooms. Mantha discovered this when she went to go use them.

Clara was just visible, down near the lakeshore, walking back and forth and holding something lumpy in her hands. The idol.

Breakfast was in a Keep 'Em Hot! thermal bag on the picnic table nearby, and Mantha went for that, first. When investigated it proved to be an egg-and-spinach English muffin sandwich with a bowl of cut fruit and a low-fat smoothie. The sandwich was lukewarm and so was the fruit, but Mantha was hungry enough she ate them anyway, and walked down to meet Clara while sucking the last of the smoothie out through its straw.

The first thing she noticed was that Clara had taken her giant boots off. They were sitting on a tuft of grass with the socks hanging out the top, and Mantha was interested to learn that the little silver snaps that ran up the outsides were in the shape of four-pointed stars. The boots were very big, and very leather, and a much darker black on top, where they had been protected from the elements by Clara's long pants.

Which pants were presently rolled up around her ankles, and her white feet flashed in the sun as she strode up and down the beach. By the tracks she had left, Mantha deduced she had been at this activity for some time. She was frowning, and on occasion, muttered under her breath.

Lady Bibbit came down to join them, and together she and Mantha watched Clara for another fifteen minutes before the woman apparently grew tired of the activity, lowered the idol, and walked over to them.

"It is a difficult lead to follow," she admitted, sitting down next to her boots and brushing the sand off her feet. She put on her socks and then the boots, carefully snapping each snap, before rolling her pants down over them. "We are close, but the roads are uncooperative. Have you used the bathroom?"

Mantha nodded in the affirmative, but what with the food and the smoothie she needed to use it again before they departed. The idol went back on the dash, and Mantha went back into the rear seat with Lady Bibbit.

They spent the rest of the morning driving through a beautiful forest, past lakes and over rivers and down narrow, gravel roads, while above them the sky grew bluer and bluer and the day hotter and hotter. After prodding from Lady Bibbit, Clara turned on the air conditioning, and everyone got a lot less grumpy.

Clara was still tense, constantly glancing from the idol to the road and muttering. Mantha thought it was some kind of incantation, but she didn't recognize the words.

She was beginning to get hungry again when at last they bumped down an increasingly narrow road to discover it ended in a small circle bounded by trees. A round hill rose up to one side—the north side, Mantha guessed, judging by the way the sunlight fell full upon it—and parked at the far end, rendering the circle useless as a turnaround, was an ancient Ford pickup truck. It had a locking chest in the bed, similar to Arcana, and the driver-side window was rolled down, revealing an empty cab.

Clara stopped Arcana in the neck of the circle, effectively blocking the truck's exit. She took her sword from the backseat as she got out, but didn't stop Mantha when she followed her. Lady Bibbit made a disgruntled noise, and stayed inside.

The truck had not been there long, Mantha decided. It wasn't dusty, and the tracks behind its wheels were fresh and clean. There were footprints too, but confusing enough that she couldn't follow them.

Then there was a faint shuffling noise, and Mantha suddenly found herself on the ground. She hit hard enough that the wind was knocked out of her, and could only watch, mute, as Clara—who had been the one who pushed her—tore across the clearing at the truck, running in a jerking zigzag that brought her around behind it in a wide arc.

Mantha understood why a moment later, when Clara popped up from behind the bed, wrestling the arms of a scruffy young man behind his back. There was some shuffling, and a long gun was kicked out from behind the truck.

"I am not your enemy," Clara said, her calm voice at odds with her actions, which were to put the man into a forcible armlock and hold him against the side of the truck.

"Then what's your excuse?" spat the man. His voice had a pleasant accent which Mantha didn't recognize. Not as if English were his second language, but it definitely wasn't his only one.

He grunted, then yelped.

"My name is Clara Nordstern," Clara said, calmly pushing his head down against the side of the truck. "I am a friend of Ariel Freeman. Who are you and why did you turn your gun on me?"

"I did—wait—*what?*" the man gasped.

Clara waited, patiently, but did not let him move an inch.

"*You're* a friend of Ariel?" the man said, incredulously. "Did he call you?"

"Tell me your name," Clara demanded.

"Let me go," the man retorted.

They stayed like that, apparently at an impasse. Mantha got to her feet and came around the truck and saw then why it had been parked the way it had: there was a towline running from its front into the brush, where it disappeared under the fender of a dingy white sedan, which had been apparently hidden there.

She looked back at the man. He was smaller than Clara, with messy dark hair and scruffy dark stubble and the biggest, brownest eyes she had ever seen. He was wearing a western-style shirt tucked into sun-bleached jeans, which were in turn tucked into a pair of faded red cowboy boots, which were themselves dug into the ground next to his truck. His face was flushed and unhappy, but Mantha thought this was from shame rather than physical pain.

His eyes met hers, and she was surprised at how long his lashes were. Under the flush and the scruff he was a rather glamorous person, Mantha thought.

Then he let out a string of extremely not-glamorous expletives. The contrast made her giggle.

"Oh yeah, you think this is funny, chica?" the man snapped. "Well, see if you're laughing when your best buddy goes missing for a week and then you get an addled phone call and a set of coordinates and come out here and find his abandoned car and then you're attacked by a Cholita in black leather—and not the fun kind! Ow."

Clara had prodded him in the small of his back.

"I am Clara Nordstern," she repeated, the question implied rather than spoken.

"Yeah, and who's your little friend?"

"Her name is her own."

"I'm Mantha," Mantha volunteered. "We're friends of Ariel, too. At least, she is. I'm just keeping her company."

"*Oh*," said the scruffy man. He pulled it out into two syllables. *O-oh.* "Well isn't that *nice* of you. Okay, in that case, you'll get no trouble from me. We're on the same side"—he laughed, nervously—"so why don't you let me go?"

"You had a gun," Clara said calmly. "You pointed it at me."

"I didn't know who you were!" the man snapped. "You drove up and blocked the only exit! What'd you think I'd think?"

Clara grimaced, but after a moment she eased her grip, allowing the man to retract his arms and turn around. He did this slowly, gingerly feeling his elbows. He looked Clara up and down, exaggerating the incline of his neck, and laughed again.

"Aw jeez, you're pretty big, chica. Okay. Sorry," he raised his hands defensively when Clara frowned. "You can call me Chuy. Chuy Acebo."

His voice sped up when he said his name, taking on a faster cadence and a forward tilt that made it difficult for Mantha to understand. To her it sounded like "Chewie Dassay-vo" and when Clara repeated it back to him, that was how she said it, too.

"Close enough," said Chuy. He hitched one arm over the bed of his truck, trying to look casual. "So . . . uh . . . *did* Ariel call you?"

"After a fashion," said Clara. She left him and went over to the shotgun, which she picked up, careful to keep its muzzle pointed at the ground, and unloaded it. She inspected the cartridges.

"Ey, *hey*," said Chuy. "Those are special-order!"

"Silvered iron?" Clara said, skeptically. She handed him the gun and the cartridges—separately—and then went over to investigate the white car hidden in the bush.

"Best all-around anti-nasty I've found," said Chuy, defensively reloading the gun. He also kept it pointing at the ground, Mantha noticed, and held it so that his fingers never touched the trigger.

"Expensive," Clara said, opening the driver-side door and sticking her head inside.

"Effective," said Chuy, a whine audible in his voice. He looked down at Mantha. "You a hunter-in-training, chica? You remember this: silvered iron. Best thing for killin' nasties. Silver gets you werewolves, witches, all manner of changers. Iron covers just about everything else."

"What about vampires?" Mantha asked, thinking of Lansing.

"Iron actually works pretty good on vampires," said Chuy. "But it's gotta be spikes, or nails. Shot just makes 'em mad."

Mantha looked up at him, soberly. She was still thinking of Lansing. Cool, collected, reserved, but utterly rational and considerate.

"What if it's a *good* vampire?"

Chuy blinked at her.

"Chica," he said, snorting a little. "You haven't been around very long, have you? You what, eight? Nine?"

Mantha didn't answer, but stared at him stonily until his smile faded, his mouth closed, he coughed uncomfortably, and finally shuffled off to see what Clara was doing.

She had popped the trunk of the white car and was now going through its contents. Which consisted of an old, greasy blanket, a roll of wrenches, a pair of jumper cables, and the requisite spare tire.

"Stripped," she remarked, when Chuy came up next to her.

"I couldda told you that," he said.

Clara straightened up abruptly and turned to face him. She looked at him closely, bending her neck so they were almost face to face.

"You said he called you," she stated. "When?"

"Last night," said Chuy. "He sounded pretty messed up. He just kept repeating numbers, over and over. I wrote them down. Figured they were coordinates. They got me here." He patted the side of the white car. "His car."

Mantha had come around so she could now see this car more clearly. It was scratched and dirty from being dragged into the brush, and one of its rear tires was completely flat. It was white, under all the dirt, and when Clara closed the trunk and stepped back, Mantha saw there was a little decal in the middle: a silver circle with the outline of a leaping animal laid over it. The animal had long legs, no tail, and prongs from the head suggested horns or antlers.

Mantha felt the air shift around her, a faint relief from the heat that caused a rustling in the trees above. She found herself thinking of the stag from the dream world. Clara's stag. The one that had been killed.

"He's in a lot of danger," she said.

"Yeah, I kinda figured that," said Chuy, trying and failing to hide his condescension.

Clara said nothing, but stepped away from the car and back to Arcana, where she leaned into the cab and came out holding the idol. Lady Bibbit came out with her, and Chuy did a perfect double take when he saw the four-foot, one-eyed, bipedal rabbit.

"This is Lady Bibbit," Clara said, ignoring the astonished look on his face and going to stand beside the white car. She held up the idol expectantly, then winced and lowered it.

"We are close," she explained. She paused. "They are close." She looked sharply at Chuy and Mantha, and by extension Lady Bibbit. A pained expression crossed her face, but she said nothing. She began to walk, wading through the fallen leaves and ducking under branches, away from the car and toward the low hill.

Mantha followed her automatically, and Lady Bibbit followed *her*, leaving Chuy to sputter angrily, and then come crashing after them. He talked the whole way, asking what it was Clara was doing? Why was she bringing a *child* into . . . whatever it was they were getting into? Would she hold up a moment? What was *in* that sheepskin?

He never got answers. The trees thinned as they reached the hill, and they came out of them to find Clara had set the idol down at the base of it and drawn her sword.

"Hey, look," he said, coming up behind Mantha and talking over her head. "There ain't nothing here. It's one of those Indian burial mounds, but I checked it out: nothing pinged. Your folks came through here and dug out whatever virtue there was years ago."

Clara sniffed. "But it is still," she said, quietly. "And they have hidden themselves well."

"What does that mean?" Chuy wailed.

"She's talking about the Triple Goddess," Mantha said. "And her priestesses. They're the ones that kidnapped Ariel."

"You're telling me that a couple of *girls* kidnapped Ariel Freeman?" Chuy said, doubtfully.

"Not a couple," said Clara, sounding distracted.

"They work in threes," Mantha supplied. "They're more powerful that way."

"And they are not girls," Clara added. "They are women. Women like them used to rule both the living and the dead. Ariel is only one man."

"Yeah, but, I mean—come *on*," Chuy waved his free hand. "I know Ariel's popular with the ladies but that don't mean he's *stupid* for them. And no offense, but—"

"Be silent," Clara said, putting up a black-gloved hand, palm outward. The gesture was so abrupt, and her words so commanding, that Chuy did break off, but into an exasperated sigh. He seemed to gather himself, and was about to continue his tirade, but the words never manifested.

Clara was staring at him—Mantha knew from experience what that felt like: two nails of icy blue hammering into your skull—her lips pressed together so tightly they made a single, dark line across the bottom of her face.

Chuy swallowed, visibly.

"Why are you here?" she asked, as if she had forgotten their earlier conversation.

Chuy stuttered, confused. "I told you already."

"You said Ariel called you," Clara said. "You said he sounded disoriented. But he gave you exact coordinates to this location."

"Look, people, brains," Chuy said, waving a hand. "You think of stupid things when you're scared or drunk. Which he sounded, both."

Clara had turned now, so her shoulders were squared off at Chuy. Even in the bright light of midsummer noon her dark leathers seemed to suck up all the light, so she appeared like a black rectangle with a skull-like head on top.

"Who *are* you?" she asked.

Now Mantha was confused as well. She looked at Lady Bibbit, who shrugged.

"What are you? Senile?" Chuy asked. "I told you that, too!"

"You gave me a name, yes," said Clara. "But *what* is it? They called you here. They wanted *you* here. I need to understand why."

"Who called me here?" Chuy muttered, but Clara continued:

"Chuy. You said your name is Chuy. Is that your whole name? Or is it a nickname?"

Chuy flapped his arms and rolled his eyes. "It's what my *tía* called me. Only my father called me Jesús."

"Jesús," Clara repeated, her shoulders falling. "The sacrificial son."

"Yeah, but it's *hey-soos*, not *jee-zus*," said Chuy, sounding like he'd had to explain this more times than he could count.

"And Acebo?" Clara pressed on.

"Del Acebo, really," Chuy said. "It means 'of the holly tree.' Like I tell you, it's weird."

"Jesus of the Holly Tree," Clara murmured, turning to stare at the mound behind her.

"See, this is why I have people call me Chuy," Chuy said, confidentially to Mantha, as if they were the only two reasonable people there. "I'd use my second name except it's *María*—"

"You need to leave," Clara said, cutting him off.

It was the wrong way to talk to Chuy, Mantha realized. It only made him more stubborn.

"You think I'm gonna leave *now?*" he yelled, his voice pitching up. "Now that I know Ariel's been kidnapped by some crazy ladies trying to bring back an ancient, bloodthirsty goddess? And what's gonna happen if they succeed, huh? The end of the world?"

"The world was arguably a better place when the goddess reigned supreme," Clara said, quietly. "But in order to achieve that, they will commit horrors, and cause you to carry out horrific acts. And I cannot allow that, not even for the Triple Goddess."

She seemed genuinely regretful, but Chuy was too upset to notice.

"You know what? You know what?" he was shouting now, stomping back and forth. "Fine! You win! You have fun with your mound and your goddess and your creepy-ass bunny person. I'm going back to what I was doing in the first place. Kid, I swear this lady is trouble. You don't wanna hang out with her. You can come with me."

Mantha was surprised to find these last words directed at her. She stared at Chuy in consternation, and the man threw his free hand into the air, turned on his heel, and walked off into the trees.

Clara watched him like a hawk until he was out of sight, then she breathed out, slow and even, and went back to the mound. She was holding the idol up so it caught the sunlight, turning it this way and that, when there was a crash of undergrowth and a surprised yell, quickly cut off.

Mantha only had enough time to be surprised. Clara set the idol down in the grass at the bottom of the mound, drew her sword, and was rushing off in the direction of the noise before Lady Bibbit could gasp "*What was that?*"

Clara left a noticeable path through the undergrowth, and Mantha and Lady Bibbit followed it easily enough, only to come out next to the parked cars, where Clara was prowling around Chuy's truck like an angry cat.

When she saw them she sheathed her sword and came striding over.

"They got him," she said, dull and angry.

"The priestesses?" Mantha asked.

A sharp nod was her only answer, and then: "Stay close."

Mantha discovered it was difficult to stay close to Clara when she moved fast, but she was only a few feet behind her, Lady Bibbit at her side, when they reached the mound again.

The idol was gone. Mantha did not have to hunt around in the grass, like Clara did, to be certain of it. The wan, irritating feeling it gave her had also vanished, which was a small relief.

It did not help alleviate her worries, however. And the fact that it had vanished so completely was deeply upsetting to her.

"Someone took it," she announced.

Clara huffed and straightened up from her search, glaring at the mound.

"What now?" Lady Bibbit asked.

Clara looked at them. She seemed to be weighing something inside her head, but Mantha had no clue as to what that could be until she gave a determined nod and beckoned them to come stand beside her.

"We will go in together," she explained as she took off her right glove and then, with her left, began feeling around inside a pouch on her belt.

"Into the ground?" Mantha asked, just to be sure.

"That is where they are," Clara said.

"Pardon me for asking," Lady Bibbit said, primly, "but how do you propose we do that? Shovels?"

"No," said Clara simply. "We will go in the same way they did. We are three, after all," she added, with the barest hint of a smile. "Unconventional though we may be."

"How does that work, anyway?" Lady Bibbit asked. "I'd never even heard of this goddess before today. But even without any of us believing in her, simply by being three female . . . people . . . we're somehow representative of her?"

"Not representative," Clara said, but thoughtfully. "It's more like . . . like triangles."

"Triangles?" Lady Bibbit asked.

Mantha thought she understood.

"It's like if you put three dots on a piece of paper, and then draw a straight line between each of them, you'll get a triangle. No matter where the dots are. As long as they aren't all on the same line, of course."

"I still don't see what this has to do with the Triple Goddess," Lady Bibbit said, stubbornly.

"In this metaphor, imagine that the triangle holds immense power," Clara suggested. "That, no matter how misshapen or what medium it is made from, merely by coming into existence it can tap into the infinite power of the perfect *triangle* that it represents. Or echo shades of it. It is just that way with the Triple Goddess."

"So, what?" Lady Bibbit said, sounding nonplussed. "We are the Goddess?"

"No," said Clara, firmly. "But we could become a conduit for some of her virtue, if we unite our purpose. Both of you hold my arms, and do not let go unless I tell you so."

Mantha took Clara's left elbow without hesitation, while Lady Bibbit took her right with more reserve.

"I still don't know if I count as a woman," she muttered.

"Are you committed to helping me rescue Ariel Freeman and Jesús del Acebo?" Clara asked.

Lady Bibbit shrugged. "I am committed to helping Mantha," she said.

"I'm committed," Mantha assured Clara, and squeezed her elbow reassuringly.

"Then that will have to be enough," said Clara. She had produced a ring from the pouch at her side, and now Mantha saw her slide it onto her bare finger.

The world lurched sideways, and for a moment Mantha lost herself. She was a bird whizzing through the sky; she was Lady Bibbit, fuzzy and calm and deceptively intelligent; she was deep in the earth in a dark place, and her hip hurt; for one terrifying second she was someone sad and cold and huge, whose mind stretched out behind her in inconceivable distances. This mind knew things, in those distances, that it knew it should not know, and so kept them there, for fear of what they might mean. It made Mantha feel like a small spider stuck at the bottom of a bathtub, and if ever that distant knowledge caught up with her, it would be like the faucet turning on.

This is ridiculous, Mantha chided herself. *I know who I am, and this is not me.*

She pulled herself out of the sad, cold mind and collected herself. She realized she had lost her grip on Clara's arm, and she quickly gave herself hands to grab her again. After the hands, the body came easily enough, and Mantha blinked open her eyes to see she was still standing before the mound, with Clara in front of her and Lady Bibbit on the far side, but all around her things had burst into staggeringly vivid color.

The bark of the trees was rich and reddish-brown, while their leaves glimmered and flashed like green-yellow diamonds, sending showers of rainbows down upon them where the sun caught their reflective surface.

The mound seemed higher than before and was covered in soft, thick, springy grass. It was green, too, but a soft green, almost like the surface of a sea.

In the center of the mound, right before them, was a black rectangle of a door leading into the earth. Heavy blocks of blue-gray stones had been placed on either side and across the top and bottom, and there were stick-like letters scratched onto their faces. And in this place of vivid color, Mantha found she could put a little of herself into the door and understand what the letters meant.

They were an alphabet, and a calendar, and hidden in them was the name of the Goddess by which she had been worshipped in the time before Christ. Mantha was surprised to discover it was not wholly unfamiliar to her.

"Walk with me," Clara said, her voice cold and clear, and Mantha realized with a jolt that it had been *Clara's* mind in which she had cowered before the distant knowledge. It gave her a new respect for the woman, living with that all the time.

The three of them walked abreast to the door, and though it did not look like it would admit more than one at a time, when they reached it Mantha found they passed under the lintel without her left elbow so much as brushing its side.

Beyond the door, under the earth, it was much larger than the mound outside. They walked for what felt like miles, in what seemed to be a straight line, and did not come out the other side. Instead, the walls of earth turned to stone blocks, and then the blocks to pillars, and finally the pillars turned to tree trunks, pressed so closely together they made a solid wall of rough, brown bark. Their branches intertwined over their heads, bare and thick and twisting, like coils of a snake.

They walked on. The ground beneath their feet became soft with moss, and slowly the branches above them parted, and the trunks became more widely spaced, until they were walking down an avenue of trees filled with dappled sunlight. Ahead of them was an archway bounded by trees in full summer foliage, and beyond it a yellow square of sunlight where something gold glimmered and shone.

Mantha had to shield her eyes as they came out of the tunnel and into what appeared to be a clearing in the middle of a wood. It was dominated by a single tree which grew in the center, its branches reaching so wide their tips nearly touched the canopies of the trees surrounding them. In shape it resembled an oak, except everything about it from its bark to its leaves to its fat, succulent acorns was gleaming, buttery gold.

Something dark twined in its branches, scales glinting green and brown where the sunlight touched them. A forked tongue, narrow and pink, flickered.

At the base of the tree was a strange construction. A thick stake of wood, like a railroad tie, had been hammered into the ground among the tree's roots, with smaller stakes lashed crosswise at its top and bottom. Metal rings set at all four ends dangled, empty, while the center stake had a thick, leather collar nailed to it

All at once, like seeing it acted out in front of her by ghosts, Mantha understood what was going to happen.

A man would be brought. He would be tied to the post beneath the tree, and there he would be killed, gruesomely, and his successor crowned in his stead. The Goddess would take a new lover, and the waning year would begin.

She had the strangest sensation that it was the snake in the branches of the tree that told her this, even though she could not see it clearly, let alone tell if its mouth moved.

Clara led them in a slow circuit of the tree, and when they had arrived back at their starting point, gave a short nod and said:

"This will do."

She made a motion with her hands, and she must have taken off the ring, for suddenly Mantha was plunged into darkness, and cold, and the smell of earth.

They were back underground, with no light to speak of, and Mantha felt surprisingly alone—even though she still held Clara's elbow. In the other place, with the golden tree and the serpent, she had felt close to something. It was ancient, and powerful, but not inherently evil. It had been cruel, but there had been kindness also, and the joy of summer.

There was the sound of muffled voices, and a light flickered in the dark. Mantha felt Clara shift against her, and then pull away. She reached out and found Lady Bibbit's soft paw, but nothing of Clara.

She did not call out, however, as the muffled voices were growing un-muffled, and the light was getting stronger.

This outlined a hole in the darkness, as of a tunnel leading away into the mound, and when the light emerged from the tunnel it revealed the chamber in which they were sitting, huge and dim.

There was no tree, and no serpent, but there was a bundle of freshly cut oak branches lashed together with string where the golden tree had grown. In place of the stakes, there was instead a reclining lawn chair—the sort with alternating white-and-blue plastic stripes.

The light came from a single kerosene lantern held by a middle-aged woman wearing an awkward robe, belted around the waist, which left a good deal of her chest bare. She held the lantern high in one hand, but its light barely served to illuminate the ground around her—Mantha and Lady Bibbit stayed safely hidden in the shadows—while in the other she clasped a rope.

This was tied, it was slowly revealed, to a man who limped behind her. He was dirty, and blindfolded, and barefoot, and all Mantha could see of his face was a crudely shorn, squarish chin, and a mop of tawny hair. By contrast he was dressed in crisply starched, white linen trousers and shirt, though the sleeves of the latter had already acquired a few blackish smears. His hands were bound in front of him, and he was led by the rope which was tied to a metal collar around his neck. This was not a crude dog collar but a piece of jewelry. It was made of braided gold and the sort which was usually left open in the front—a torque, Mantha thought they were called—but the rope had been tied between the two ends, making it a proper collar.

Behind him was another woman, younger than the first and taller, with fantastic locks of golden hair and wearing similar dress, though she had added a crown of some green-leafed plant, and had oranges hung from her belt.

This strange procession advanced into the chamber and the two women laid the man down in the lawn chair, whereupon they began securing him to it by his ankles and wrists and neck.

In the sunlit clearing under the golden oak, the man was trussed up on the stakes, and in the branches above, the serpent coiled expectantly.

Mantha kept expecting Clara to jump out of wherever she was hiding and assault the two women, but instead what happened was another light appeared, this time from a different tunnel, and Chuy came out of it, followed by Diana Upjohn.

He was also barefoot, wearing a set of starched white shirt and trousers, and a torque of silver around his neck, but there was no rope, and he walked, apparently freely, to stand beside the bundle of sticks.

Under the golden tree, in the sunlight, he was crowned with leaves of holly.

Diana Upjohn leaned in and whispered something in his ear, and Chuy nodded, and then reached up and stripped a leafy twig from the nearest stick in the bundle.

That was all Mantha saw, but his hand came back holding a substantial branch from the golden oak, covered in gold leaves and acorns.

The other two women parted reverentially, creating a path between the two men. The older one then raised above her head the idol, which had been unwrapped from the sheepskin, and her younger companions came and stood on either side of her, each with an arm raised so they could touch the base of the statue.

In the wavering light of the lantern their forms were distorted, and Mantha thought she saw them merge into one woman. An impossibly tall, pale woman with red lips and three faces. Then she realized that vision came from under the golden oak, where the bough Chuy held had also transformed: now it was a spear with a wicked, sharp tip.

All at once, as clear as if it had been explained to her, Mantha understood what was going to happen. Chuy would stab the man on the cross— Ariel, if she had to guess—and then the three priestesses—the Maiden, Nymph, and Mother, who together embodied the Triple Goddess—would skin, dismember, and disembowel the man, roast his flesh, and then feed it to Chuy, who would in turn become the holy king under the tree, the male consort of the Goddess.

As clear as all this was, Mantha was equally certain she had to stop it. She hadn't the faintest idea how, but she reasoned that the three priestesses were human, and so was Chuy, and she could push humans about when she needed to. It wasn't something she liked doing, but she could do it. And since Clara had still not reappeared, she decided she needed to do it now.

The first thing to do was to take the branch away from Chuy. So she straightened up and walked over to do just that. She did it with purpose, and concentrated very hard on her intent, expecting the adults to go along with it, like they always did.

She got halfway across the floor when the Goddess spoke to her.

She was pretty certain it was the Goddess, and not the three women, although the voice of the Goddess was that of the three women speaking in unison.

She said: "Child, be away. This is not your place."

Mantha ignored her. Of course a goddess would need a stronger push than a human. She marched up to Chuy and stood between him and Ariel. She held out her hand for the branch-spear.

"Give that to me," she said.

To her disappointment Chuy did not even see her. He walked on, pushing her aside as if she were an inanimate object. She overbalanced and fell, landing hard on the cold ground. Lady Bibbit hurried over and helped her up, but Mantha was more angry than hurt.

It had not worked! Her power—the power that had always frightened her a little bit—had not worked! It was like the muscle she needed to use it had been exchanged for a limp noodle.

The Goddess was looking at her—at least, one of her faces was.

"Run free, my daughter," she said. "It is not yet your time."

Mantha knew she should have been relieved that she had not angered the Goddess, but mostly she was outraged. She had never before met anyone who was completely immune to her powers—not even Clara—and the shock of it paralyzed her.

Chuy had almost reached Ariel, raised his branch-spear, and in a clear voice, he cried words that Mantha did not recognize, yet understood to be an invocation of the Goddess in all her aspects, a celebration of her power, and a supplication to her.

As he brought the branch down, Clara stepped out of the shadows as if appearing from between two black velvet curtains, blocking the fall of the branch with her sword. There was a metallic *clang* and Chuy fell back, momentarily dismayed.

"Jesús del Acebo," Clara said, low and even. "Remember who you are."

Chuy just gazed at her. He glanced at the Goddess, who was watching the altercation with amusement on all three of her faces.

"Come away, maiden-mother," she said, beckoning to Clara. "You are no servant of Gwydion. This is not your place."

"Neither am I a servant of yours," Clara said calmly. She glanced at the Goddess as she spoke, and Chuy took that as an opportunity to strike her. But she caught the branch without looking, twisted it out of his hands, and elbowed him so hard in the abdomen he gasped and doubled over.

It left Clara there, standing between the Goddess and the bound man, a sword in one hand and a golden branch in the other. Beneath her shock and fury, Mantha was interested to see that there was no double-vision where Clara was concerned. She stood beneath the golden oak and before the bundle of sticks, and as soon as her hand had closed around the branch it had ceased to be a spear—though it was still buttery gold and shining in the lantern light.

The Goddess was no longer amused. She stepped forward (the three women had to shuffle a little to remain in formation) and beckoned imperiously to Clara.

"Come away," she repeated, and the command was so strong even Mantha felt it. This Goddess, she realized, was like her—she could push people into doing whatever she wanted—only a thousand times stronger. A hundred thousand times stronger. Mantha had never felt so young and weak as she did at the foot of the Goddess.

But Clara—Clara, who was only resistant to Mantha's influence—hardly swayed. Her face remained as blank and cold as marble, and when she spoke her voice was calm.

"I am not yours," she said quietly. "I am my mother's daughter."

"Your *mother*," the Goddess said, and she spoke the word almost sarcastically, "was no mother—but for my grace. You and your sisters owe your existence to me. And your father—your father was one of my greatest heroes! I clothed him in gold and gave him fire—and for that he was punished. You are mine, maiden-mother: blood, bone, and flesh."

Clara did sway then, backward and forward on her feet, and Mantha had a moment of confused thought when she wondered who the sisters the Goddess spoke of were, since Clara had said she had a brother. . . . She decided the Goddess must have been counting the sister-in-arms, but had no more time to devote to the problem.

Clara had charged the Goddess, bringing her sword around in a powerful blow which should have come down on the Goddess's neck.

Instead there was a flash of light, the sound of anguished screaming, and Clara's considerable mass was sailing through the air to land in an undignified heap in the shadows by the far wall. The Goddess straightened up, holding Clara's sword by the blade, as well as the golden bough. The sword she dropped unceremoniously to the ground, but the branch she carried over to Chuy and presented it to him.

"Rise, Holly King," she said, and Chuy took the branch and got unsteadily to his feet.

Mantha was on her way to where Clara had landed when she was suddenly not there anymore. Mantha stopped, confused, and then Lady Bibbit pulled sharply at her sleeve. Looking down, Mantha saw the rabbit point.

Under the golden oak, Chuy had raised the spear and was poised to strike. Beyond him stood the Goddess, her triple face merged into one. With her hair spilling down her neck it almost looked like she had a horse's mane.

And behind her was Clara.

Clara, who was swordless, with one hand ungloved, reached into the world under the golden oak, wrapped both hands around the Goddess's neck and squeezed.

The Goddess shrieked. She turned and started clawing at Clara with her hands—there were six of them—and snapping at her with jaws suddenly full of teeth.

Clara was undeterred. She twisted and pulled and caused the Goddess to flip over her shoulder and land on her back with a thud. Clara got one leg hooked around the Goddess's shoulder, and began wrenching her head back and fourth.

There was a horrible snapping sound, and a brief shock passed through the air that made Mantha's bones hurt. One final, high, furious scream, and then the golden oak and the space beyond faded away into the distance, leaving only the cold, dark cave lit by the single lantern, and Clara standing up from where she had been kneeling among the three dazed women, holding the mangled remains of the idol between her hands.

Chuy let his arm fall abruptly, and Mantha saw that the golden branch was just a leafy stick.

Even without that confirmation, she knew the Goddess had lost her hold on the place by the feeling of *herself* expanding to fill the gaps the Goddess had left. It made her wonder if the Goddess *hadn't* been that much stronger than her, but that there was a limited amount of space for their powers to exist in, and that the Goddess had taken up all of it.

One way or another, she found herself in a safe cocoon of her own powers once again, and by pushing it outward she was able to envelop Chuy, Ariel, and the three women—though she was careful to leave a bubble open around Clara.

Clara picked up her sword from among the women on the ground, sheathed it, and then came over to Mantha. Without a word she passed her the remains of the idol and then went back and began untying Ariel from the lawn chair.

Looking down at the object in her hands, Mantha discovered it was nothing more than a lump of twisted metal, as inert and powerless as a clod of earth. Mantha took it carefully between her palms and crumbled it away into just that, letting the dark soil fall from her hands to become one with the cave floor.

Clara was bent over Ariel, speaking to him softly. Mantha left her to it. Though she was curious about the man for whom Clara had gone to so much trouble, she felt it was important to make sure the three women were not going to cause them any more grief. She walked over, with Lady Bibbit beside her, to where they were groggily sitting up and surveyed them critically.

Diana Upjohn was recovering the fastest and blinked blearily at Mantha through the dim light. Then her eyes focused, and Mantha felt something shift around her.

It was the most uncomfortable feeling. As though something big and insubstantial was plucking at her soul, winding her in invisible rope and binding her to some purpose she did not know. She tried to pull away, but the thing only gripped her tighter.

"Stop that," she hissed, angry.

Diana Upjohn froze. She looked hurt and confused, and Mantha realized it was not her conscious doing. This was something else.

"Forgive me, Goddess," the witch whispered, bowing forward so her forehead touched the floor.

That was the problem with filling in the outlines the Goddess had left, Mantha realized. Though she knew the difference, and Clara knew the difference, and Lady Bibbit and probably Chuy too, to these women she was just another version of the Goddess they had worshipped. And they had worshipped her, had been ready to kill for her. Had, albeit briefly, become a vessel for her.

If Mantha wasn't very careful, she realized, she could become a goddess too, and be bound to behave in ways she didn't much like. She felt a moment of deep pity for the Goddess. But only a moment. Quickly she drew herself in, away from the grasping clutches of the women's worship, and pushed at them in the subtle, underhanded way she was accustomed to.

They would go away. They were not to think of their time under the earth. To them, this would become like a bad dream. Mantha was a little hesitant to leave them even that much, since she was beginning to understand how powerful dreams could be, but to do more seemed wrong on a very deep level. Almost a betrayal.

Perhaps the best thing, she decided, was to leave the truth buried within them, which they could discover if they searched hard enough. But it was the bare, unyielding, unvarnished truth: they had conspired to enchant and kidnap two men, and were prepared to force one to kill the other. Hopefully that would be enough to keep them from doing anything so horrible ever again. For they were not evil people, Mantha thought, and now that they were bereft of their goddess, they were very sad and confused indeed. She thought about giving them a new purpose to ease the blow, but decided not to. That would mean she was just like the Goddess—only on a smaller, meaner scale.

If you were going to be a goddess, you had to be ready to go *big*.

Clara had stood up. She was carrying Ariel in her arms, bridal style, while Chuy hovered nervously at her elbow. Mantha left the women and went over to her.

Clara did not ask what she had done with the idol, but she did look questioningly over her shoulder at the triad.

Mantha realized she was beginning to push Clara's mind off them, automatically, and stopped herself.

"I took care of them," she said, instead.

And then, though Mantha was certain she didn't give Clara even the faintest nudge, the woman nodded and turned and left.

The man had been in darkness, his hip hurt, and he couldn't move his arms.

A star appeared in the darkness. A star made of swords and knives and it came to hover over him. Descending slowly so that its cold light touched his brow, it said: "Ariel?"

The darkness slid away, and Ariel blinked up at a dim, blurry picture of a bald woman with piercing blue eyes pulling something dark away from his face.

His face, which smiled of its own accord, and he heard himself say, "Claymore," before he quite knew what it meant.

But meaning was flooding in quick and fast. Meaning, and context.

They'd hit his hip with a club. Hopefully it wasn't broken. He was desperately thirsty and had a headache, and the clothes he was wearing were doing nothing to keep him warm. He was beginning to shiver—deeply and violently.

Sensation brushed first one hand and then the other, and he felt his arms laid carefully by his sides.

"Gently there," he coughed, as Claymore worked one hand under his knees, one under his shoulders, and then lifted him up as though he weighed nothing at all. His head came to rest against her shoulder—warm leather that clung to his cheek.

"Relax," Clara's voice said from somewhere above him. "You're safe now."

Still halfway between dreaming and waking, Ariel thought this was a funny thing for a star made of swords to say, but he realized it was true.

"I know," he mumbled, so quietly he doubted anyone could hear.

Chuy was more embarrassed than hurt. He kept making excuses for why he had gone along with the witches' scheme, and Clara grew more and more impatient with him as they towed Ariel's car out of the brush, while Ariel lay on the backseat of Arcana and slept. Mantha and Lady Bibbit sat guard in the front seat, and Mantha made certain he had only the most pleasant, innocent dreams. It was easy, and seemed a good thing to do.

While Chuy exchanged the busted tire for the spare, Clara made a careful search of the woods around the mound and eventually came up with a collection of artifacts—a battered briefcase, a book-shaped package wrapped in oilcloth, and a dirty string of rosary beads—which she delicately replaced in the trunk.

Once Chuy was finished, Clara drove the little white car down to the main road, followed by Chuy in his pickup, who then drove her back to Arcana. They called a tow truck, then proceeded to have an argument over who had to wait for the tow and who got to take Ariel to the hospital. Mantha let them go at it until Ariel woke up and asked blearily what was wrong. When Lady Bibbit explained the situation to him he alarmed them both by trying to get up and go reason with his friends. So Mantha gave Chuy a gentle nudge, and it was Chuy who stayed to wait for the tow truck, while Clara drove them to the nearest Urgent Care center.

"That was dangerous," she said, under her breath, as she got in and turned on the ignition.

Mantha felt herself color a little. "You would have been at it all night, otherwise," she said.

"Probably," allowed Clara. "But don't do it so much."

Mantha accepted this rebuke without protest. She was getting tired, anyway, and it was relief to have an excuse not to push people around anymore.

Three women emerged from under a pile of trampled leaves which hid the small, dark tunnel leading into the hill. They were dirty and tired and frightened and had been arguing for the past hour over whose terrible idea it had been to spend midsummer night in an ancient Indian burial mound.

"It's disrespectful of their culture!" Diana had been scolding them when at last they escaped into the clear air of early dawn.

"Well, you came along, didn't you?" snapped the middle woman, who was only a few years older but much less willowy. Her hair was a tangled golden mess with a few stray leaves stuck in it.

"Shut up, both of you," said the oldest woman, who was not very old at all—or so she kept telling herself. "Mari, where did you park the car?"

Mari brushed stray hairs out of her eyes and squinted around at the empty dirt turnaround.

"What the hell," she said. "We just parked it here."

They dispersed into the clearing, walking its perimeter as if the car might have scuttled off into the trees.

"Do a summoning charm, Ann," Diana suggested.

"It doesn't work like that," snapped her elder.

"I tell you what does work," said Mari, fishing out her keys. She clicked the remote and, from from deep within the trees, came a faint *beep* and *click*.

The three women forged off into the brush, only to discover the little Subaru buried beneath a pile of green branches, more of which had been dragged across its tracks.

There was much angry exclaiming and more complaints as they dragged the brush out of the way and reversed the car slowly back into the clearing.

"Must have been a practical joke," Mari said as she got them turned around and headed for Ann's house.

"But who would do that?" Diana wondered.

"Probably *men*," Ann snarled.

Mari grumbled her agreement, but Diana was silent. She'd just had a fleeting feeling, like a retroactive premonition, that what Ann said had been wrong. It hadn't been men who hid their car. It had been women. It had been *them*. And, just as fleeting, the uncomfortable certainty that the three of them had nearly done something very terrible. It was gone almost as soon as it came, but it made her begin to reconsider her friends, and wonder whether she should start making some new ones.

Somerset, Kentucky

Clara sat in the waiting room of Lake Cumberland Urgent Care and tried not to fall asleep. Ariel had become more and more responsive, and had even managed a few smiles, but he still looked alarmingly fragile. Dehydrated. Hollow. Not at all like the vibrant, blazing personality she remembered from her dreams.

That was the problem. She could remember her dream Ariel better than the living-and-breathing Ariel. She didn't know how to interact with the waking Ariel since she had grown so comfortable with the one she had dreamed up. So she had let the nurses take him away, and posted herself by the door, and waited.

It had been a long two days, and even Clara's incredible constitution was beginning to waver. Two days with an all-night drive, a fight, and no sleep, and without a pressing matter to focus on, her mind kept sliding inexorably into darkness.

She located Mantha, sitting across the room from her reading a magazine, Lady Bibbit sitting alertly in the chair beside her. It was a funny sight to see ordinary people pass them by with hardly a second look—even those who paused seemed to perceive Bibbit as Mantha's stuffed rabbit and assumed Mantha's adult was somewhere nearby.

With this as much security as she could hope to have, Clara gave up the fight and surrendered to sleep.

And began at once to dream.

She was sitting on a warm, wooden dock under the midday sun, her pants rolled up to the knee and her feet dangling in the water of a blue-green lake. She could see her toes, pale and ghostlike, under the reflection of her shadowed face, and the curling ends of her marks like black gashes across her white skin.

She was in her undershirt, and though the sun warmed her shoulders, it did not burn. She kicked her feet idly and squinted out at the gleaming lake. There was a low, green mountain beyond, and the shore was crowded with trees.

There was a creak of wood under bare feet, and then Ariel sat down beside her. He was wearing a pair of ripped blue jeans and a faded brown t-shirt that said "Rock 'n Roll Heart and Soul" across the chest. She saw now that there was writing on his right arm twined around the pack runes, but he did not stay still long enough for her to decipher it.

He sighed, blissfully, as he slipped his feet into the water beside hers.

"I missed this," he said, and smiled up at her.

Even though she knew what was coming, Clara was still struck by that smile. So bright and warm and unguarded.

He leaned a shoulder against her arm companionably. The pressure felt good. Reassuring.

"Thanks," he said, "for getting me out."

Clara wanted to ask him how it had happened in the first place, but decided that was pointless. As vivid as this version of Ariel was, he was still a creation of her own mind. He only knew as much as she did, really.

They sat together on the dock by the lake, and when Ariel didn't move, Clara dared to slide her arm around his and lace their fingers together. She was surprised to discover, despite their hands being very different shapes, they were practically the same size. It made Clara feel momentarily embarrassed, but Ariel didn't seem to mind. His hand squeezed hers, and it was warm.

Clara would have been content to sit with her dream in silence, but Ariel seemed to have something he wanted to say.

"I dreamed you were a star," he whispered. "A star made of swords. I didn't know it was you, at the time—I didn't even know myself. But it makes sense now. Do you remember that?"

Clara frowned. She shook her head. "I didn't dream. While they had you, I didn't. There was only blackness, and pain."

Ariel squeezed her hand again. "They must have blocked you—the way they blocked my memories."

Clara frowned down at him. Ariel glanced up at her and shrugged.

"I didn't know who I was, when I was down there under the earth. But I knew the star-sword had my name, and my name would give me back to me. I tried calling you." He grinned. "I guess that worked."

"I tried calling you," Clara admitted. "Well, texting, anyway. You never wrote back."

"You never texted me before," Ariel said, mock reproach in his voice.

It was Clara's turn to shrug. "I never needed to, before."

Ariel sighed and turned his head so his cheek was pressed against her shoulder. He looked down at their intertwined arms—his, tanned and dark with words; hers, pinkish-white except for the bold, red-lined black strokes. Clara felt her attention on them keenly, and had to resist the urge to withdraw her arm.

"What?" said Ariel. "They're nice."

"They are not tattoos," Clara said.

"Hmm?"

"My marks. They are not tattoos." She had meant to stop there, but in the way of dreams the thought in her mind finished itself by coming out of her mouth. "I've had them for as long as I can remember. Mother said she would explain it to me one day . . . but she left before that day came. I am not sure, but I think they are part of the reason I am . . . the way I am."

"How so?" Ariel asked, casually curious. No pressure. Clara did not feel compelled to answer. She did anyway.

"Strong," she said. "Able to stay awake for so long. Heal fast. I'm resistant to a lot of magic. Not all of it, but a lot of it."

"So they're protection," Ariel said, turning his head to grin up at her. "Like mine." Another squeeze. He was holding her hand very tightly, as if he was afraid she would slip away. She could feel the callouses under his fingers. He looked out over the lake, and all was peaceful and quiet.

There was a distant ringing sound. Ariel sighed heavily.

"Don't go," he mumbled, almost plaintively.

But the ringing grew louder, and Clara woke with a crick in her neck to find her cell phone vibrating against her chest, its screen informing her that Jill Hamilton was calling.

"What exactly happened in Detroit during the attempted apocalypse of 1970?" her voice asked, high and arch.

Clara grunted and rubbed her eyes. "What?"

"I'm getting some really weird readings from the MAGs. I thought it could be leftover . . . whatever. Something left over from that sort-of apocalypse."

"Mags?" Clara repeated. Across the room a bright-faced young doctor with South Asian features had appeared bearing a clipboard and an expectant expression. She looked around, her eyes settling on Clara, and began to walk purposefully in her direction.

"Magical Activity Gauges," Jill said in Clara's ear. "I've refined them. Palladium. But they're telling me *something* is going on here. Where would I find out more about this apocalypse?"

"Attempted apocalypse," Clara corrected her, automatically.

The expression on the doctor's face faltered a little.

"Jill, I have to go. Someone needs me."

"Did you find Ariel?" Jill asked, almost guiltily. "Is he okay?"

"We're about to find out," Clara said, and hung up.

The doctor finished her approach in relief, smiling a little.

"Ms. Nordstern?" she said, the question a mere formality. "I'm Dr. Misra. I wanted to let you know that Ariel did quite well. He's resting now, but he can leave whenever he wants. We've given him fluids and electrolytes, but he'll be very weak for the next few days. Are you his primary caregiver?"

"I . . . am," Clara said, making the decision there and then. "I will take responsibility for him."

"Good," said the doctor, all smiles. "Well, he should be reintroduced to solid foods slowly. Start with smoothies—Greek yogurt and fruit, that sort of thing—and hearty soups. Make sure he drinks at least ten cups of water a day. He was very dehydrated and undernourished. You said he got lost hiking?"

Clara nodded.

"Well, he has no sign of hypothermia or heatstroke, which is very good. But he also has some severe bruising around his left hip—though it doesn't look like it was dislocated and there is no damage to the sciatic nerve that I could find. We've given him some pain medication and he should be good taking NSAIDs as soon as that wears off. I'm also writing him a script for codeine, in case that is not enough, but I doubt he'll need it."

The doctor smiled, Clara nodded, and watched as she bustled away behind the swinging doors labeled "EMPLOYEES ONLY."

Her phone buzzed again. It was Chuy. He'd had Ariel's car towed to a local friend's house, since he didn't know where else to put it. Where were they?

Clara told him. After few more volleys of texts it was decided he should come take charge of Ariel for the duration of the man's recovery, so that Clara could get back to Detroit.

A little while later Ariel was led out into the waiting room. He was still wearing the white shirt and pants they had tried to sacrifice him in, but these had since become crumpled and more cloth-like. He had also been given an adjustable plastic cane, and he used this to limp to the nearest chair, where the nurses helped him sit. He smiled and thanked them, must have made a joke because they both—man and woman—laughed and went away with happy, dazed expressions.

He looked much better than before; alert and cogent and his lips were very pink. But there was still a hollowness under his cheeks and around his throat, and a slightly leathery quality to his skin. But he smiled up at Clara when she came over, as blazing and bright as he ever had in her dreams, and Clara had to exert real effort not to trip in surprise.

"Hey," he said. And Clara felt both warmed and saddened by the casual familiarity of his tone. This was Ariel, but not *her* Ariel. She had to keep reminding herself, however, because the two were so alike.

"Hey," she said, weakly. Then, unable to bear the thought of actual conversation, she hurried on: "Chuy is on his way. He has your car. He'll take care of you."

Was it her imagination, or did Ariel look just a touch disappointed? It occurred to her that she only had Chuy's word on their friendship. Ariel might have different opinions.

"I have to get back to Detroit," she said, by way of explanation. "Jill is . . . discovering things."

"I hear she's good at that," Ariel said. His face fell. "I also heard what happened. With Selene. I . . . um . . . I am so sorry."

Clara nodded. She couldn't do any more.

"How are you holding up?"

Clara shrugged.

Ariel gave her a wry look. The corners of his mouth twitched. "That bad, huh?"

Because it was the truth, and because Clara still did not trust herself to speak, she nodded again.

A small, cold hand slipped into hers, and Ariel's eyes refocused downward.

"Hello," he said, smiling again. "Who's this?"

Clara looked down to find that Mantha had materialized next to her, gazing at Ariel somberly.

"This is Mantha Fulgeroiu," she told him. "She helped me rescue you."

"Ah," said Ariel, miming the motion of tipping his hat to her. "Thank you. Appreciate it." He blinked. "Who's your friend?"

Clara looked again. Lady Bibbit was, as always, on the far side of Mantha, and started a little when Ariel addressed her.

"This is Lady Bibbit," Mantha said, raising their joined hands.

Ariel looked from rabbit to girl and back again, smiling in a bewildered yet amused way. Clara wondered what he saw. But he asked no more questions, and patted the seat next to him. Clara sat. Mantha and Lady Bibbit sat in the adjacent seats. After a while, Clara asked:

"How much do you remember?"

Ariel groaned and rubbed his eyes. "All of it," he sighed. "But, vaguely. Like there's cheesecloth over it. Which is fine by me," he added.

Clara did not ask how he had known Diana Upjohn, or who she had been to him before this. Or whether he had known her at all. Neither did she ask for details of how he had been captured. Those were, she decided, unimportant in the long run. But Ariel's mind must have been running to those subjects, for after a time he said:

"The worst of it is, I can kinda see where they were coming from. And I can't blame them. Hell, if things had been different . . . if I'd been . . . well. I might have done the same."

"No," Clara said, without thinking. "You wouldn't have."

"Oh?" said Ariel, and she could tell he was looking at her now. Could sense his face, pointed up at her, but she kept her own pointed firmly forward. "What makes you say that?"

He didn't sound offended. He sounded almost eager. But Clara did not reply.

About an hour later Chuy arrived, shared a boisterous hug with Ariel, and helped him out to his truck. Clara watched them, the two men with their heads together, telling herself that this was for the best.

She was on the point of climbing into Arcana after Mantha and Lady Bibbit when Faraday called.

"You're still alive," the witch observed.

"We all are," Clara said, and felt faintly satisfied at the realization.

"Even the Goddess?" Faraday countered.

"You know the answer to that better than I do," Clara said.

Faraday cackled. "Fair. Are you going back to Detroit now?"

"Yes," Clara said.

"Good," said Faraday. "That place's been bothering me lately. Best keep an eye on that fool of yours. See she doesn't stick her nose into something that'll blow up in all our faces."

Clara didn't answer. She had long since given up trying to control where Jill stuck her nose. In truth she derived a sort of morbid interest in seeing the kind of upset it caused. But she didn't feel like telling Faraday that. Not when she had a real issue to discuss.

"Diana Upjohn belongs to the White Goddess," she said, and told Faraday about the idol and the triad, the modified spiral tomb, and their attempted sacrifice.

There was a long, long silence on the other end of the phone after she had finished, which told her more clearly than any other response that Faraday had not known. Had not even suspected. Clara waited. She knew how it felt to have the rug pulled out from under her beliefs of a person. At long last Faraday let out a whistling breath and said:

"I mean, what with institutionalized patriarchy, rape culture, femicide—can you blame them?"

"No," said Clara, "but they still tried to kill my friend."

"Ah," said Faraday, keenly. "So he's your *friend* is he?"

Clara didn't say anything. Faraday could take whatever she liked from the silence. Clara didn't owe her any more words.

Finally Faraday let out a sigh that was more of a groan. "All right, all right, I'll keep an eye on Di. Fair is fair. Just you . . . you watch Jill. I am actually concerned about her. Tes told me what happened at her forge. *She* says she thinks Jill shows *promise.* And you know what that means."

Clara didn't know what that meant. Tesla and Faraday were sisters, best friends, fierce allies, and at the same time held strongly different views about the world and the way it should be handled. But she felt she had to say something at this point, so she promised to watch Jill—it was impossible not to, after all—and this appeased Faraday enough that she hung up.

Clara was just setting her phone in the dashboard holster when there was a soft scuff of slippers on asphalt, and the rear door creaked open and Ariel hauled himself into the backseat, to the vocal surprise of Lady Bibbit.

Clara looked up in consternation, and then back toward Chuy's truck. She could just see the man sitting in the driver's seat through his windshield. He shrugged dramatically.

"Ariel—what," she began, but Ariel put up a hand to stop her.

He settled back into the seat with a sigh, sliding his cane along the floor next to Bellatrix. The sight seemed to amuse him, for he chuckled.

"I think I'd better stick with you, this time," he said.

Movement in the front seat: Mantha glanced back at him but did not seem surprised. Clara gave her a meaningful look, but she only shrugged. She looked as bewildered as Clara felt.

"Are you certain you want to do that?" Clara asked, trying to put the proper stress on her words without sounding too accusatory.

"Friend, what I want to do is put my feet up and drink a beer and then sleep for a week," Ariel said, settling himself further into the backseat. "But I ain't blind." His gaze traveled, casually and nonjudgmentally, over Lady Bibbit and Mantha and then back to Clara. "And it looks to me like you could use some help here."

"This isn't what it looks like," Clara insisted. But the problem was, she had no idea what Ariel saw in their situation. She couldn't predict this Ariel. And as was evidenced by him sitting in the backseat of Arcana, staring at her soberly, he would do things she didn't want.

"Be that as it may," he said, and then he looked down. Down past his knees to his feet, still in the cloth slippers the nurses had given him. When he looked up again his expression was one of such sympathy that Clara wanted to turn tail and run. It was both alike and different from her dreams, and it terrified her.

"I've driven solo for a long, long time," he said. "Think it's time for a change. It's a big, messy ol' world. It'd be nice to have someone at my back."

Clara glanced reflexively toward Chuy, who was making "get on with it" gestures over the steering wheel.

"What about your car?" she asked, not quite ready to admit defeat.

"Impy?" said Ariel. "She can sit in Janay's garage for a few months. Until we figure out a way to get her up to Detroit. If we *need* another car." He added, looking around Arcana. "I think you've got that area well covered, honestly."

Clara looked at Mantha, almost pleadingly. But Mantha just turned around in her seat and asked:

"Do you know any good car games?"

"Oh, I dunno about *good*," said Ariel, and smiled. Full and bright and warm, and Clara could almost *see* Mantha's heart swell under its beam. "But friend, I know hundreds."

Mantha settled down in her seat again.

"That's good," she said. "Come on, Clara. Let's go home."

They were only words, but Clara responded as if she had been nudged, anyway. Perhaps she had to admit that she liked it better this way, after all—even if there was a nervous knot forming in her belly.

She was wise enough to know that nothing good came of applying your imagined concept of a person to the real thing and expecting them to match up perfectly, and she dreaded the inevitable dissolution of her pleasant fiction of Ariel. But she had to admit, as she put Arcana in gear and backed carefully out of the crowded parking lot, she felt better for having him nearby.

His diesel engine chugging loudly, Arcana rolled onto the road. Clara turned him toward the nearest northbound freeway, and picked up speed.

> *Welcome to morning*
> *Last night was but a dream*
> *I think the morning*
> *Could light up any scene*
> *So me and my girlfriends*
> *Can find out how you've been made*
> *See me and my girlfriends*
> *Can see you're not the same*

> *You're not the same*
> *as the men at arms*
> *You're not the same*
> *as the men in cars*
> *You're not the same*
> *as the man from mars*
> *You're not the same*
> *as the man of stars*

> *'Cause you're a kind of weaving*
> *That's so hard to find*
> *Tight-stitched and herringbone*
> *Around her fingers you wind*
> *I remember you like fine silk thread*

Before they cut you down
I remember they crowned your head
While you lay on the ground

Can you tell me what the
Cloth of man has been woven from

Cloth of man has been woven from

Welcome to morning
It's burned away all our dreams
So take my hand and come alive
Unpick your binding seams

I read your tapestry in the dark
I felt you against my heart
And now I know fury lies
Can't keep our steel threads apart

And now I know the
Cloth of man has been woven from
The iron blood of a woman's soul
It's woven from the
iron blood
of a woman's soul
iron blood
of a woman's soul

Cloth of man
Iron blood
Woman's soul

Ah!

—Cloth of Man/*Technorhyme*

6.
BLOOD
and
FURY

City of Dis, the Burning Desert
Seventh Ring, Inner Circle

THE DESERT BURNED. Literally. The smoldering flakes of ash that fell in a gentle, steady rain from the amber sky ignited in brief flares, like splashes of fire, upon contact with the yellow-white sand. Sand which in turn spontaneously burst flashes of angry red flames, which would run hither and thither like tormented spirits before collapsing back into the searing ground.

The air was hot, and so heavy it was almost tangible. It was easy to imagine that the slow, languid course the burning flakes took was due to them working their way through the viscous atmosphere. But it was not the heaviness of humidity—that would have implied some relief from the steady combustion—rather it was the density of immense pressure. The air itself had the feeling of being pressed down upon the burning plain, crushed into something that was almost liquid. The only things that moved quickly over that terrible surface were the brief bursts of fire, which seemed to arise where the air became so thick it was forced to transmute into a different shape.

The three figures that broke the monotony of the simmering golden landscape appeared at first like particularly large and long-lived flames. They flickered around the edges, orange and black and red, before they solidified into recognizably human shapes.

At least, mostly human. Two were of fairly standard female build, though one was rather taller than the other, pale-skinned under her veil of fire, and her hair crackled brass-and-bronze through the hazy, compressed air. The other was dark, face and hair and fire all, but she carried a large, round shield which glinted pale pink-white when it reflected the glowing sand beneath. Though the black flames cloaked her and obscured her features, her eyes were visible, staring as unforgivingly into the desert as the desert stretched out all around them.

The third figure, which walked a little in front of the other two, was also woman-shaped, midway in height between light figure and dark, and was herself also the same general shape, but slender where the others were sturdy, and her head was lost in a confusion of feathers, so it looked like she had a pair of squabbling pigeons instead of a face. Her whole body glowed whiter than the sand, and the fires that sprang up around her danced in the air a foot from her skin, so that she carried an aura of clear air around her as she walked.

Nominally, she walked. One foot in front of the other. But she had a tendency to float up off the sand, rising to a height of six or so inches, and causing a slight displacement of the sand beneath her, as if it was blown by a jet of air. Despite her alien appearance and willowy figure she also somehow looked more solid than the other two. More intense.

Her companions endured the burning desert, but she cut through it like a fluted arrow, shearing the hot air aside and leaving in her wake a temporary respite from the over-pressed atmosphere.

Selene walked in that wake, though she was more grateful for Albatross's unerring sense of direction than anything else. Shae had said they would need to find the blood river, which flowed through the desert, in order to get across, and Albatross had promptly set off in the direction she said this was in.

That had been on the edge of the trees, where the Forest of Despair gave way to the Burning Desert, and it had been as though they stood on a knife-edge between the two environs. But the forest, though impenetrable when they were within, quickly faded from sight after they struck off across the desert. Selene had looked back once, quite early on, and found it already a mere smudge of darkness at the edge of the shimmering white-and-gold landscape.

Now all was pale sand and heavy, amber sky, the thick, slow rain of embers and the hot, compressed air over the scorching sand. And though she walked in the windswept wake of Albatross, Selene still felt the burn every time she put her foot down.

"How do you do that?" Shae had asked, once, soon after they lost sight of the forest.

"What," Selene had said. Her whole body felt like it was being squashed down into the sand, and she hadn't the energy for even the upturn necessary to render her statement a recognizable question.

"How do you do this barefoot?" Shae clarified.

"I just do," Selene had said. She hadn't felt like mentioning that she had also walked barefoot through the bottom of the Styx, and that this might have something to do with the fact that her feet were still *feet* and not stubs of cooked flesh. Besides, it still *hurt*. So she kept herself focused on the middle of Albatross's back, covered by that ever-changing white shift that still miraculously clung to her torso. Unlike the majority of Selene's clothes, which had fallen victim to mud, steel, and fire, and now consisted of a pair of terminally ripped jeans and an equally tattered over shirt—conscientiously buttoned since there was absolutely nothing underneath.

"I try not to think about it," she'd said, stiffly, and Shae had mercifully let her alone afterward.

Shae troubled Selene in much the same way her first crush had, even though she hadn't realized it had been her first crush until some years later. But now she recognized the hot, twisting combination of jealousy and desire that had sparked in her teenage self, and though this time it was tempered by years of experience and the constraints of their situation, that didn't make it any less uncomfortable.

Shae was objectively beautiful in the classical European sense: tall and long-limbed and narrow-waisted and her bosom was neither too small nor too big. Her olive skin was pale, her face pleasingly oval, and her eyes large and expressive. Her hair was dark gold—light enough to be blonde, but dark enough that her handsome, arching eyebrows stood out. Selene could not *not* appreciate her appearance, if only for aesthetic reasons.

But she was the embodiment of the standard to which other women were held, and Selene's own struggle against the subconscious enforcement of that standard soured any feelings of attraction as soon as they arose.

Here I am, the Hero, Shae's appearance proclaimed. And Selene, who had done more actual heroics than the average person while receiving none of the accolades, resented it.

And that was beside the fact that these feelings were distracting, and at this point in her life—death—whatever—she could seriously not afford to be distracted.

On top of all of this she understood that Shae was her own person and not just a compilation of all the stereotypes that had given Selene so much grief over the years, and that to judge her for it would be both unfair and malicious. Shae could not help the way she was built any more than Selene could.

She understood this, but her feelings had never been very good at abiding by what her rational mind understood, and in that hot pan of desert, under the rain of fire and the pressure of the thick, viscous air, not to mention the strain of having to ignore the searing pain every time she put a foot down, Selene found herself beginning to hate Shae. To hate herself. To hate the world that had made them.

A redness washed over her vision. The heat, if possible, intensified. It was difficult to see Albatross through the haze, which looked like fire.

"Wait," she said, and the word came out a dry croak.

Albatross must have understood, for she stopped and turned around. Shae, who had been walking beside her, went on a few feet before she paused.

"We can't stop here," she said.

Selene heard, but there was nothing she could do. She was drowning in fire, and no matter how hard she tried to withdraw into herself she felt stretched between the flames like a piece of frying meat.

Something cool gently pressed into the center of her forehead, and Selene rallied around that sensation. Shutting her eyes against the red flames, she concentrated on that point of feeling—so that it was the only feeling she was aware of. And like clouds twisting together into a spiraling storm, Selene felt herself wind around that point of pressure until she hung, perfectly centered and content.

The pressure disappeared, and Selene opened her eyes to find Albatross just removing her hand from in front of Selene's face. It had been her finger she had felt, pressed between and above her eyes. Behind the thin, white hand, Albatross's thin, white face looked concerned but hopeful.

"We should have taken the river path," Shae was saying. "She's not going to make the crossing at this rate."

"We'll come to the river soon enough," Albatross said, serenely. "Together we are three. It is a powerful number for women. We will do it together."

Her voice was soft. It should have been crushed by the oppressive air, but it seemed to carry its own immeasurable substance that resisted all outside influence. It was almost the voice Selene heard in her head when she talked to herself, but just as recognizably *Albatross*.

A cool, white hand slipped into her own, and Selene found she could see through the flames again. Could make her legs move. Could walk.

The first two steps were agony. So were the third and fourth, but she had learned to expect it by then. By the fifth, she had the measure of the sensation, and could keep up with Albatross unassisted. The fire receded from her vision. The desert stretched out around them, limitless, pitiless, and desolate.

But not empty. Not anymore. It had taken Selene a while to realize, partly because she had been so wrapped up in her own internal recriminations, but also because the inhabitants of the desert didn't look like any of the souls they had previously seen.

They were the fire. The racing streams of fire that sprang as if from sheer pressure from the sand. There were people in the fire, running, their mouths open in screams consumed by the flames that surrounded them, until the exertion became too great and they collapsed back into the sand. In the sand, where they continued to burn, constantly re-ignited by the fire which descended gently and unceasingly from the sky.

"Where are we at now?" Selene said, mostly to see if she could still speak. She could, as it turned out, just not very well. "This is still Seventh Circle . . . ?"

"Seventh Ring, Inner Circle," Shae provided. "Violence against God."

Selene gave out a dry, hacking laugh.

"Which god?"

"The Nameless God, I assume," Shae said, mildly. "This is His Hell, after all."

Selene thought you could argue that that depended on whether you believed the Nameless God to be empirically greater than all other deities, and whether your belief was strong enough to make it so, but she didn't have the energy.

"It is the concept of god," said Albatross, her voice soft and pure.

"That's different for everyone," Shae pointed out.

"Yes," agreed Albatross. "The god in hand. The god in heart. The god on high and the god under your feet. The god in stone. The god in blood. We are all concepts."

"Are you a god?" Shae asked, directly.

"Maybe," said Albatross. "I'm not sure yet. Perhaps I was. Perhaps I will be."

Something about the way she spoke, and what Selene had seen of Albatross before, and the way she walked over the burning sand and the flames shrank from her, the way the air ignited several inches from her skin, the way her wings formed a feathery halo around her head, all aligned in Selene's head, and she felt herself stagger under the realization of what Albatross could truly be.

She had not wasted effort wondering before. Albatross was clearly someone powerful—perhaps a fallen angel, perhaps some other holy tangent. That she was a god in her own right had not crossed Selene's mind, and now that it did, she wondered why it had not.

Because broken gods were vulnerable and did not like to be identified. And gods had been broken before. Broken and scattered.

Selene looked again at Albatross's back, trying, for the first time, to match what gods she knew to what she knew of the person in front of her. And, however many she lined up, none resonated so much as the one which frightened her the most.

"Albatross," she wheezed, and the woman turned her head to show she heard. "Does the name *Javoia* mean anything to you?"

"Nn . . . no," Albatross said, having given the question due consideration. "Whose is it?"

"The Holy Unspeakable Name of the White Goddess," Shae said. Selene couldn't see her face, but she almost sounded respectful. But mostly surprised. Surprised that someone like Selene would know this.

"It sounds speakable," Albatross remarked.

"It is now," Shae said. "The Nameless God stole it, along with most of the Goddess's power. She was shattered—like you are."

"And white," Selene added.

"I'm not white," Albatross said. She sounded a little angry. Or bitter. "I'm bleached. Someone blasted all the colors out of me, burned them away so I was only shades. And no one stole my powers. They aren't here now, but wherever they are, I know they are mine."

"When they blasted out all the colors, was that when you were shattered?" Selene asked. Talking got easier the more she did it, so she tried to keep going—even if it annoyed Albatross.

"I think so," Albatross said.

"Do you remember who did this?" Shae asked.

Albatross did not answer at once. When she did it was in a sad, small voice.

"I think it was myself," she said, as if realizing this for the first time. Then she lifted her head, wings flaring. "I must have had a good reason, then. Come, we're almost to the river."

She said so, but Selene could not see any change in the desert, save perhaps that the fire was falling more thickly, and the souls in flame erupted more frequently. Once, she even saw a face. It was not one she recognized.

It surprised Selene that she had not recognized anyone in Hell—save the ones she could not avoid recognizing, like Medusa. But every spirit had been a stranger. Which had not bothered her at first. On balance there were more people dead than there were living, and of the people she knew who were dead there were even fewer. Unless Hell specifically thought to put them in her way, the odds were starkly against it.

But this was the Burning Desert, where according to Dante, the violent against god, art and nature were punished. Selene had, like many children of her identity, been threatened by punishment in Hell for her perceived sins, and had for the most part long since brushed them off. But the impression remained, bitter and strained. And she had dared to wonder if perhaps her mother had been right after all. Or wrong.

Something Jill would have said intruded on her thoughts: *Today's concepts of Gays and Lesbians is fairly modern. Human sexuality is complicated. And what is supposed to be punished here? The way people were born? Then why not punish gingers, or lefties? If it's the act that's being punished, then it should only be those acts that are harmful—and those are committed by people all across the spectrum.*

Yes, because goodness knows straight people did their fair share of horrendous sexual violence. And what of the closeted gays? Especially those in government who advocated reprehensible laws which made life materially worse for other gay people.

This got Selene to thinking about the closet, and how horrible it was to be in it, and to imagine—and not for the first time—the emotional knife box it was for anyone stuck living in it. To live a lie, whether that lie was that you were straight, or a man, or a woman, or anything you knew deeply that you were not, was in itself as bad a torture as being burned in the unforgiving desert. Here, Selene thought with cynical amusement, at least you were not alone.

No, the true crime against nature was not even the act of sodomy. It was the denial of one's integral self. And the nature being slighted was no god, but that great, merciless, nebulous, primordial force that raised mountains and moved oceans and shaped planets and stars and galaxies.

The realization was like a draft of cool air on a hot day. Selene raised her head and laughed for the release of it.

Shae glanced at her, uncertain—probably uncertain whether the laugh had been a laugh at all or the hacking cough it more resembled.

"This place is pointless," Selene explained, grinning.

Shae did not smile, and after further consideration, Selene's grin faded. She was not sure whether this made things better or worse.

"For some people it is," Shae said. "For others, it is necessary."

"Humanity doesn't need this," Selene declared. "It's . . ." she searched for the right word. Horrendous didn't fit. Hell was horrible, but then, it was *Hell*. The mere fact that it was *meant* to be terrible sort of negated any attempt to be horrified by it. No, what Selene felt was not horror so much as disgust. Or not even disgust. It was disdain.

"Superfluous," she said, spitting the word out as if it were the worst insult she could muster.

Shae did laugh then. A ringing, clear laugh. Honestly, Selene thought there might have been bells in it.

"You subscribe to the belief that humanity is the cause of its own suffering," she said, declaring it as though this said something about Selene's character.

Selene was annoyed.

"I don't subscribe to anything," she said. "I just said, Hell—at least, this Hell—is just doing to people in death what they already did to themselves in life. It doesn't undo the wrongs they did. It doesn't give relief to their victims. It doesn't make them *better people*. It's just more of the same. It's superfluous."

"That is not Hell's fault," Albatross said. She lifted her arms, letting them waft beside her like a girl playing bird. Only she had real bird wings spreading from her head.

"How's that?" Selene asked.

"People are people, alive or dead," Albatross said in a singsong voice. "But the dead cannot change. They just keep doing what they have always done, only more so. So the lusty keeping on lusting and are lost in it. The greedy keep on hoarding and are destroyed by it. The violent stay violent, fighting among themselves. And the self-hating remain, hating themselves into oblivion."

"Hell just gives them a place to do it in?" Selene suggested, but Albatross didn't answer. They had come to a break in the desert.

An actual break. Though Selene had thought the plain stretched on endlessly, here they came upon a deep canyon with walls so steep that it was invisible until they were upon it. Now at last they were close enough to see the sand-colored walls rising on the far side, and soon the ground below their feet began to give way from sand to hard stone, which in turn flaked and cracked and eventually ended in a sheer cliff.

A wind which would have been hot in any other place came wafting up at them from the depths, which were cloaked in steam. Still, here and there it thinned enough that Selene could glimpse, right at the bottom of the canyon, the sinuous slither of something red.

The overflow of Phlegethon, Selene remembered. It flowed through the burning desert, and was by comparison a refuge. Indeed, she could see how the burning ash was quenched by the thick mist, and so never reached the bottom of the canyon.

"There is a counterpoint," Albatross said, as they came and stood at the edge of the cliff. "The good and the brave. The righteous, strong and kind. They are still—their spirits are immortal. Because these tenets—positive and negative—transcend humanity and will persevere even beyond the ending of worlds. Take my hands. It is a long way to the bottom."

She had extended her arms as she spoke, and seeing what she meant to do, Selene quickly grabbed the hand nearest. Shae was not so quick on the uptake, but did as Selene did, and like that the three of them stepped off the edge of the cliff and into the smoky abyss.

Wings flared above them. Selene was not certain whether they came from Albatross's head or if she sprouted new ones. Whatever their source, they spread wide and dark, cutting bites out of the angry amber sky, and for the first time in what felt like eternity Selene was sheltered from the falling fire.

She could have cried with relief, but her heart was in her mouth from how fast they descended, and the wind which rushed past was growing blissfully cool. It was maybe only as hot as the hottest day in July after a thunderstorm when the mist enveloped them like a soothing blanket.

There they slowed, the wings above churning the mist into whirls and eddies, until the ground became visible beneath them.

Selene was surprised to find there was ground at all, but there it was, yellow rocks and sharp sand and, between the two pale strips, a lazy current of dark red.

They alighted on what was to them the far shore of the blood stream, on a small outcropping of rock which overlooked a mean little beach. Beyond that, Selene could not see for the mist, which rose in streams from the surface of the river, which did not bubble and boil like Phlegethon, but flowed thick and slow and steady.

"Excellent," said Shae. "We can follow this to the Eighth Ring."

Selene looked around, but aside from the river itself she saw no clear course they could take. Still, she supposed swimming it would be better than more walking. This was not one of the great rivers of Hell; it was, in its own small way, a little piece of mercy. Selene had no fear to step in it. In fact, it was beginning to look downright tempting.

That feeling alone set off alarms in her head, but Albatross seemed to have the same idea. Letting them go she hopped briskly down onto the sand and pattered across to the shore, where she experimentally dipped a toe in the thick liquid.

Selene was surprised to see it slide off her toe like water off a greased surface, leaving it as white and clean as ever.

"This is the daughter of Styx and Phlegethon," Albatross announced. "She will know us," and waded in to her waist.

Selene still hesitated. Shae made no move.

Albatross was like a pearl of white on a red velvet sheet, and she turned and smiled and waved.

"Do come down, Selene, this river knows you."

Selene looked up at Shae, who shrugged.

"We are not like her," she observed diplomatically.

That made Selene want to get down into the river just to be contrary, but she was shocked into stillness when Albatross began to sing.

This was not the gentle nonsense songs she had hummed before, nor the song she had picked up from Selene, nor even her singsong way of speaking. This was a high, wordless, haunting call. It cut through the thick, heavy air like birdsong, raising the hairs on Selene's neck, and raising the mist several feet off the ground.

In this increased clarity a dark shape appeared upriver, steadily approaching as the current drew it nearer.

Selene couldn't make sense of it at first. Was it a house? A boat? A house on a boat?

The last turned out to be more-or-less correct. It was a house. A tall, haphazard house like two or three cottages jammed together on top of a floating platform. A rainbow pennant fluttered from a silver pole jutting from the highest roof, and standing at its base, one arm raised to shield her eyes as she stared keenly ahead, was Albatross.

Selene, feeling like she was beginning to get the hang of this, looked at the Albatross on the cottage-boat very closely. Sure enough, there was a faint haziness around her outline and the barest traces of transparency around her midsection. She had two small, white wings, half spread over her shoulders.

No more than three fractions were present here, Selene guessed. Still, this would put them up to twelve, which was almost half the total.

The ninefold Albatross was still singing, waving her arms back and forth to the sound. The threefold Albatross on the boat sang back, and together their identical voices merged in a haunting harmony. They made the canyon ring with it, so it sounded like the cliffs themselves were singing.

The Albatross on the ship did not come down to the Albatross on the shore, but rather they both lost their solid shapes and, in milky streams of light, flowed through the air toward each other. Selene ducked under her shield at the last moment, and she heard Shae give out an audible "*Oof!*" as the shockwave hit.

Yet this one was not as forceful as the others had been. It was a shock of temperature change rather than of moving air: a blast of cool that rippled out from where the two Albatrosses met and sent Selene into convulsive shivers. It kept coming, in waves of increasing cold, until Selene saw her breath rising in steam against the back of her shield and felt her toes grow numb.

A warm hand landed on her shoulder. Shae's hand. The woman shook her.

"Selene," she said, "Selene, look."

Selene didn't want to, but then Shae shook her again.

"You have to see this."

Cautiously Selene lowered her shield. Over its dark rim she saw the amber sky, cooled now to violet, a narrow corridor between the high cliff walls, which shimmered, pearlescent, from the radiant light bellow.

Albatross was hanging in midair, encircled by a shining ring of light which shed rainbow tendrils as it wheeled gently around her. It reminded Selene of pictures she had seen of the aurora borealis, only instead of greens and blues this was white in the center, but its tail was all those colors and more. It lit Albatross with those colors, making her look momentarily like a figurine of opal, shot through with lavender and gold.

Her eyes were closed, her hands outstretched with palms open, while her bare feet dangled, toes barely clearing the bottom arc of the circle of light.

She was descending slowly now, and the circle was shrinking, shrinking until it was no longer a circle, but a point of shining rainbow light in the small of her back. Selene saw this when Albatross turned around to salute the cottage-ship, on whose rooftops three figures had appeared.

They were difficult to make out in detail from this distance, but Selene thought they were women, too. On the highest platform under the rainbow flag a tall black woman wearing a crown of bright red roses stood next to an equally tall woman of lighter complexion with flowing chestnut hair. One level below them, easily balanced on the slope of the roof, was a broadshouldered old woman with pale brown skin and a halo of white curls. Incongruously, she was also wearing an immaculately cut black tuxedo, which seemed to house a much stronger, younger body than what her face implied. She raised a straight arm and hailed them with an equally robust voice.

"Are you all right?"

She appeared to be asking Albatross, who let out a joyous giggle and swooped up to the level of the rooftops. She said something, inaudible to Selene and Shae, and then took the rainbow pennant by the free end and dragged it loose. Dragged it out and up and over, and as it went it changed into a real rainbow. A real, honest, poetic rainbow with red, orange, yellow, green, blue and purple all distinctly present. Albatross arced it above the cottage-ship so that its ends were anchored on either side, and the whole thing was crowned by the rainbow—like something from a fairytale.

Albatross, still hovering, wingless, stopped and kissed each of the women on the cheek, and then glided down to alight in the sand below Selene and Shae.

"You sure we can't give you a ride?" the white-haired woman called down to them. "It only gets worse the further in you go!"

"I know," Albatross replied. "But I'm not finished yet!"

The woman shrugged, but she turned to Selene and Shae.

"What about you ladies?"

"My mission draws me down," Shae replied.

Selene said nothing. She was having the strangest feeling that she should know this woman. But at the same time she was absolutely certain that they had never met. So when the curious face turned to her she only shook her head and pointed at Albatross.

"I'm with her," she choked out. "Thanks anyway."

"Pay it no mind!" called the woman in the rose crown. For some reason this amused the three no end, and it was to the sound of their uproarious laughter that the boat made of houses retreated up the river and disappeared into the mist. The last thing to vanish was the rainbow Albatross had made, which glowed through the fog long after the shadow of the ship had been swallowed up, until it too was finally lost in a swirl of red and violet.

"I don't understand," Selene announced, feeling surprisingly shaken. "Who were they?"

"Dead heroes, I should think," said Shae.

"Then why were they in Hell?" Selene asked.

"The dead keep on doing in death what they did in life," Albatross said simply. "The Harrowing of Hell does not belong solely to the Son."

She turned herself around, apparently taking stock of the situation.

"No more wings," she said sadly, patting down her head and shoulders. "But I've got a good aura. The desert will be no trouble now."

"But we don't have to face the desert," Shae said, flatly. "This river leads to the falls above the Eighth Ring."

"This river leads to that lying, sorry excuse for a manticore," Albatross sniffed, climbing up onto the jut of rock beside them. "They warned me about him. We'll take their way. The hidden way: the woman's way."

Selene didn't question her further. She took the hand when it was offered, and Shae, after only a moment's hesitation, did the same.

Light flared from between Albatross's shoulders. Rainbow light. And it was like diving upward into water. Selene was weightless—no, the opposite of weightless. She was being drawn up into the sky, the rocks of the cliff rushing past, until they ended, and the burning plain stretched out before them once more.

They drifted maybe ten or fifteen feet from the edge of the canyon before Albatross came down heavily in the hot sand.

Landing back in the desert after the relative reprieve of the river was a special kind of torment to Selene, but really no worse than anything else she had suffered. Shae cursed and stamped her booted feet, but Albatross hardly seemed to notice.

She came to hover between them, her toes dangling in the air just above the sand, where a gentle wind disturbed the grains below. When Selene glanced up at her, she had her head bowed, her hands clasped over her chest, and was frowning in concentration.

The first Selene saw of her aura, it was a streak of rainbow from shoulder to shoulder. Then it continued to grow, expanding until it was a complete circle, until the bottom half was lost in the ground, and it was an arch that covered the three of them. The edge of it stretched and blurred into streaks of green and blue with a purple haze surrounding it, reaching out into the air before and behind them.

And under the arch of the rainbow no fire fell, and the sand cooled, and the air was light—no warmer than on a late summer afternoon.

"Walk with me," said Albatross, and they did. Over the sand, across the desert, and the fire was turned aside by the rainbow aura, the heavy air repelled, and beneath it the three women walked side by side.

But not arm in arm. It felt wrong to touch Albatross unless she invited it. Wronger than it would be in the usual way, that was. Selene could find no better description of the feeling than to say that Albatross, now she was twelve pieces combined, held another kind of aura close to her skin. Selene had felt it when she took her hand down in the canyon, like a crackling of electricity against her palm. And now when she looked, there was a fizziness to the air which touched her, sparkling over her pale skin. Her eyes were no longer truly colorless but shot through with bolts of blue-gray—like the skies of a distant storm.

She had lost all transparency; there was no mistaking her for a ghost now. In fact, she looked more solid than Shae, even with the latter's long golden hair and fierce blue eyes. Selene wondered ruefully how she must compare to these two radiant women. Probably not very well.

Too bad. Looks didn't get you much but attention, and in Hell, that was usually a bad thing. It was usually a bad thing anywhere, in Selene's experience, and with this in mind she settled comfortably for being the ugly duck of the trio.

There were fewer souls this side of the river, and those they did see were bare flickers of red fire, retreating into the distance. Fleeing.

Selene glanced back automatically and saw nothing but the same desert that lay before. She couldn't even make out the canyon of the river anymore.

She glanced at Albatross, with the sparks of light dancing over her skin and her storm-sky eyes and the vibrant, rainbow aura which turned away the burning ash and cleared the air under its bow, and realized that, to a soul lost in the desert for interminable years, this had to be a terrifying sight. It terrified her a little too, to be completely honest. And so to help remind herself that this was still Albatross—or that Albatross was not an otherworldly goddess detached from all semblance of humanity—she tried to strike up conversation.

"So, uh," she said. "This hidden way we're taking . . . care to elaborate?"

"Yes, do," said Shae. "I've never heard of it, and I've read just about everything that was ever written about this place. And why did you call Geryon a lying excuse for a manticore?"

Albatross didn't answer. Selene wanted to shake Shae for being so overbearing. But it seemed Albatross was only pausing to consider which question to answer first.

"That's not Geryon," she said eventually, her storm-eyes on the horizon—which was a narrow band of angry orange between the amber sky and the pale sand, which dimmed to a dirty gray in the distance. "Geryon is on a different level. He has gone the way of the titans and the cyclopes. He is waiting with Hades for Persephone to return. The manticore at the falls calls himself what he likes, and none of it is true. But he is the face of fraud: it is his right."

"So when Dante identified him as Geryon . . . that must have just been the name he used at the time?" Selene suggested.

"I do not know Dante," Albatross said. "But I know him. He turned me back from the falls when I pursued myself over the cliff. He thinks it's funny that I am separated. He is hateful and duplicitous. We shall not treat with him."

Selene digested this new information. It raised in her mind several more questions, most prominently what sort of memories Albatross now had from the triple version that had come off the boat. Also the reference to pursuing herself . . . did that mean the remaining three which had been in the desert had now been drawn into the Eighth Ring?

But Selene was prevented from asking these question when Albatross went on and answered her first one.

"The hidden way is illusion," she said. "It is the lies we see yet choose not to. It is there, but no one accepts it is there. It is the mirage; the woman with the hollow back."

Selene blinked as she tried to detangle the meaning from Albatross's words. From the pinched look on Shae's face, she was trying to do the same. How she managed to remain attractive even with her face contorted by concentration was astounding. She reminded Selene of an actress. Specifically an actress who had been instructed by her director not to make any ugly faces.

They walked, and the desert slipped away beneath their feet. The horizon did not grow any closer, but Selene became aware of a dark patch directly ahead of them. This slowly solidified into the dense, prickly form of dead trees, their hard black outlines stark against the pale sand.

"The context of Hell is complicated," Albatross said as they approached the charred, black forest. "It cannot change the rules it lives in, only warp them. But it is not absolute. No, no it is not."

Selene glanced hopefully at Shae, who had one corner of her mouth pulled up in an annoyed smile.

"Are you saying that natural magic prevails even in Hell?"

"Natural magic is what Hell is made of," Albatross said serenely. "Humans are animals too, after all."

Selene looked from her companions to the wood. It was not really a proper forest, hardly more than a cluster of twenty or so scorched and blackened trees huddled in a faint depression in the ground. She could see the amber sky through their ragged, twisted branches. But these did not strike her the way the trees in the Forest of Despair had. Rather than putting her in mind of tormented human shapes, they were distinctly *tree-ish*, even in death. And, as they drew nearer, her shield began to hum—gently at first, but steadily increasing until when they were standing under the wriggling ends of the outermost branches it was a buzzing vibration against her arm. More than that, she recognized the quality of the sensation. It was exactly the same, only writ large, as the way her shield—then a tiny pin—had felt when in close proximity to the Green.

It brought back memories, so far removed from her present reality that they felt like distant dreams, of a lush green face and a sweet, wet wind that smelled of flowers, and a voice which spoke through the rustle of leaves in the back of her mind.

Selene blinked. For a moment the trees had not been charred and black, but a deep, glossy brown and crowned with bright green leaves which rustled, whispering secrets, into the dull air. Birds flitted between their branches, and the shadows over their roots were softened by giant heaps of verdant moss.

Her step faltered. She felt the sand under her feet, and the branches were black outlines against the amber sky.

"Wait," she said. "This is still Hell, isn't it?"

"Of course," said Albatross, sweeping across the sand toward the cluster of dead trees. "But it wasn't always."

Still reeling from the implications of this revelation, Selene followed Albatross under the canopy of dead branches, Shae close on her heels. The rainbow aura passed through the trees, but had no noticeable effect on them—save a slight shimmer on the areas of charcoal which had been split so the reflective face showed through. In fact, in some areas it flashed off the cracked remains of bark, as though the trees had dark diamonds embedded in their dead skin.

Selene was so fascinated by this effect that she did not notice when the trees closed in around them, blocking entirely any view of the surrounding desert. But she looked up sharply when she judged they had been walking long enough that they should be coming to the end of the trees, and found there was no end in sight.

The trees rose, higher than she had credited them from outside, so it felt like they stood at the bottom of some strange arboreal sea. The air was thick and viscous, as it had been outside Albatross's aura, but instead of feeling crushed by it, Selene felt a disconcerting sense of elation. Instead of burning ash, the air was filled with drifting motes which glimmered, reflecting the light of the rainbow, as Albatross pressed ever deeper into the wood.

And it was truly a wood now. An old, weathered wood of giant oak and birch, with the towering shapes of larch casting strong boughs over their heads so the amber sky was a faint tinge far above. The ground was soft and lumpy from their roots, black as coal, and each footfall sent up a fine cloud of inky powder.

Onward they went, and the trees grew larger with each step, until Selene wondered if they were, in fact, shrinking.

Then, when they were either the size of mice or the trees had grown hundreds of times larger than any tree on Earth, Albatross slipped between the trunks of two gargantuan pines and stopped, facing a tree which was, by comparison, almost normal sized.

Selene thought it must be a fruit tree of some kind, with a slender trunk and neatly pruned branches. It was the first tree she had seen—save for that mad moment of greenness—that was not the uniform coal-black. In fact, it stood out like a torch on a dark night for being the lightest, rosiest gold. Its leaves fluttered, catching the reds and oranges from the rainbow, and small, round fruit flashed primly among them.

Beneath the golden tree, almost invisible next to its brightness, was a stout woman with buttery-blond hair and limpid brown eyes. She wore a plain woolen dress and tough, businesslike boots, and her hair was coiled artfully around her head in a thick braid.

She turned and regarded them, her expression perfectly neutral.

"Peace, friend," said Albatross, raising a hand in greeting. "We are three souls searching, who would request entrance to the Labyrinth of Pain."

The expression on the woman's face did not change, but she focused on each of them in turn.

"None of you belong there," she remarked. A neutral comment, and not a question.

"We do not intend to stay there," Albatross assured her.

Selene was prepared for the stoic woman to ask what *was* their intention, then? but she did not. She merely shrugged and turned her back on them.

Only she had no back. The cloth of her dress and the skin of her body turned to hardy tree bark, and that bark was pierced by a hole, inside of which was the blackened center of a tree consumed by fire. Her skirts twitched, and a thin tail with a tuft of coarse hair on the end flicked about her feet.

And Selene thought *What's a huldra doing in Hell?* when the huldra looked over her shoulder and said, still in the same neutral voice: "Then follow."

They did, silently and without question. The huldra took them around the golden tree, which like its partner was hollow on the other side, and silver. A twilight version of the reverse.

The huldra slipped through the hole in the trunk and vanished. Albatross did the same, but Selene hesitated, glancing at Shae.

"I'll go last," she said, answering the unspoken question.

Selene shrugged, and hugged her shield close to her side as she slipped through the narrow opening.

She was in a close, dark place, with hard, cold walls. She could see Albatross as a pale, shimmering glow in front of her, and heard Shae's breathing almost on her neck. The path they walked led steeply down, in some places dropping out from beneath her feet. She was saved from a tumble only by the closeness of the walls, which made easy braces.

They descended for a long time, but with nothing to gauge their altitude Selene could not say how far they went. She noticed when their course turned sharply, and suddenly the walls of the cleft were cool and wet, soft to the touch as if from moss. The first time Selene put her free hand out to steady herself and felt the coarse, lumpy, springiness she recoiled in surprise and whacked her elbow painfully on the rock behind her.

The air was cool and wet, filled with the smell of green earth and clean, water-washed rocks.

"Is this Hell?" Selene asked, in the same tones someone, in any other circumstance, might ask, "Is this real?"

"I don't think so," Shae said. "Not strictly. We're still in the Underworld though."

"Worlds," Albatross's voice came floating back to them. "Worlds under worlds. Under-realms. The Great Gate is heavily guarded, but the hidden ways open to those whose minds are key."

"We open to those who ask nicely," the huldra said, her voice dry in the damp darkness.

No one spoke at all for a long time after that. Selene slowly became accustomed to her new environment. She even began to feel a little thirsty.

A warm glow, as of firelight, suffused the tunnel ahead, and Shae whispered, "Ah, here's the test."

Then they stepped out of a crack in the rock and into a room hewn from stone, whose upper reaches were lost in shadow.

No moss clung to the rocks here, but in the corners were piles of bones, dry and dusty and pale. The center was dominated by a fire inside a ring of small rocks, to one side of which was seated an old woman, a small loom laid across her lap. She was weaving gray thread into a long piece of fabric which shimmered dully in the light of the fire.

The huldra was standing on the far side of the room, beside a similar crack in the wall of rock, and Albatross was already halfway around the fire. Her aura filled the room, though the rainbow was eaten by the shadows above. Shadows which moved, Selene thought, like birds in a restless roost.

She tried not to look too hard at the woman by the fire. Even though there was only one, Selene knew she was important enough to cause them real trouble if they lingered. But the impression she got out of her peripheral vision was confusing. The woman seemed to be wearing several pairs of glasses pushed up across her brow, even up under the hood of the gray robe she wore. Selene thought she had at least four hands, all of them at work at her loom.

A fifth hand shot out, one bent, grayish finger pointing at Selene.

She stopped. It had been too much to hope.

"Little moon," said the weaver. "You're a long way from home, little moon."

"I know," Selene said, still not looking at the woman. If she didn't look directly at her, she could keep pretending it was a woman who sat there, weaving gray thread, and not a human-sized spider in a coarse robe.

"Don't worry," said the weaver. "You're a little before your time yet, but you'll get there. Endurance is all well and good, but you've got to ride the storm before you are free."

"Thank you," Selene said, since this sounded like advice.

"Don't thank me till it's over," said the weaver.

Selene smiled to herself, remembering something Jill had once said.

Eyes fixed on Albatross, who had gone to wait beside the huldra, she said: "It'll never be over."

"Exactly," said the weaver, her mouthparts wagging.

Selene felt it prudent to walk on. Above her, dark wings mantled like storm clouds, and a pair of curious, bright eyes peered down at her. But she did not look up, nor right or left, but kept her eyes locked on Albatross as she stepped around the fire and put her back to the weaver.

There was a pause in the shuffling of feet behind her.

"Are you Anansi?" asked Shae, and Selene could have groaned aloud in disappointment. They had been *so close.*

"I've nothing to say to you, invader," the weaver said sharply, and there was an ominous rustling in the shadows above.

To Selene's great relief Shae took this rebuke without rancor and soon joined them by the far side of the room.

The huldra gestured toward the black crack in the rock. Hot, sticky air breathed out of it, and Selene knew where it led.

"I know the way from here," Albatross explained, and disappeared through the crack.

Selene moved to follow but paused when she came even with the huldra. She did glance aside then, and saw the creature for what she was: a human face on a wild spirit of the wood.

"Thank you," she said, humbly.

The huldra turned and caught her eye, and for the first time her neutral gaze softened. The smile, when it came, was small—but it was there.

"Keep reflecting," was all she said.

Selene nodded, and passed into the darkness.

The blackness was momentary. A thin film of protective black, and then the cave walls were washed with pale, sickly yellow light. It stained everything from the rocks to the ground to Albatross herself, who was crouched by the exit—a yellow triangle no more than three feet in any direction—hugging her arms to her chest. The yellow light lit her from beneath, leaving the rest of her in shadow, so she looked like a half-finished print of a person, shuddering beside the door.

"We have to cross the labyrinth now," she whispered. She seemed much smaller than she had a moment earlier, in the cavern with the spider and the flapping darkness, and weaker, too. Bent as she was, the strength of her height was lost, and all Selene saw was a thin young woman, shoulders hunched, curled over on herself. Though she had not gone transparent, as she had when there was less of her, she looked flat, like an image drawn on a sheet of paper.

She had lost her aura, Selene realized. It was drawn in until it was no more than a prick of light between her shoulders, so tiny it was impossible to see unless you knew to look for it.

"What happened?" Selene asked, waving her free hand toward Albatross's back.

"Can't let my rainbow shine out there," Albatross said, jerking her head at the opening. "Would attract too much attention."

"Too many demons," Shae said, nodding sagely. "A wise choice. I shall lead."

Selene couldn't help the stab of annoyance that pierced her at the way Shae assumed her role, no matter how fitting it was. But then, it was very similar to the way Clara took charge of things, and that no longer bothered Selene. Now why was that?

Because she had seen Clara take an ax to her shoulder and come back fighting. Because Clara was near invincible—and knew it. But she did not take pride in it. Confident she was, but not proud. She wore her strange power like a heavy suit of armor. A burden that was hers alone, but as long as it was hers, she would use it.

Shae, Selene thought, was all too conscious of how her power set her apart from Selene—and even from Albatross—and took pride in it. A conscientious, considerate pride, but pride nonetheless. She probably would have denied it if asked, but Selene saw it in the way she pronounced things, took charge, and took such pains to avoid pointing out that Selene was by comparison a weak, fragile soul.

Selene was still wrestling with these thoughts when she followed Albatross—who had followed Shae—through the triangle of light and on to the next stage of their journey.

City of Dis, the Labyrinth of Pain
Eighth Ring, Circle One

They emerged from the base of a sheer cliff of black rock streaked with orange and pink. The upper reaches were riddled with cracks, and from these cracks streamed acrid yellow smoke that rose in billows, masking all that lay beyond the cliffs.

The sky here was pale, stained yellow from the smoke, and so bright it was painful after the dimness of the cavern. Selene felt like an ant under a streetlamp, and the entire sky was one huge bulb.

And just as the Forest of Despair had seemed endless, and just as the desert had stretched out infinitely around them, so did the landscape under that merciless sky. Lit in lurid shades of yellow with deep, black shadows, it looked like a scene illuminated by an eternal thunderbolt.

And what a scene. Before them was a short decline of broken, rocky ground and then a low ridge, beyond which was another ridge, and beyond that another, and repeating, until they were lost to sight in a haze of dirty yellow. In the air above the ridges, black against the yellow sky, were countless flying shapes. At the moment they were too distant for their forms to be clearly seen, but Selene knew what they were. They were what she had been subconsciously expecting to see ever since she had first wrestled her way free from Lilith.

"Demons," she whispered, stifling a groan.

"Keepers of the labyrinth," Albatross sighed. "But they are not all of one mind. We may pass through unmolested if we keep them busy amongst themselves."

"And if not," Shae said, loosening her sword in its sheath, "we have options."

The tall woman began to walk, and Albatross shuffled meekly in her wake. Selene brought up the rear, and because she could not shake the feeling of the entire sky watching her malevolently, she propped her shield over her shoulders so that her head was shaded from the glare.

Shae did not make for the nearest ridge, but once they had put some distance between themselves and the cliffs she paused, and raising one hand she turned it this way and that, as if testing the quality of the air.

"The Labyrinth is widdershins," Albatross supplied, helpfully.

"I know," said Shae, a stroke of annoyance in her tone. "But widdershins according to who? I was just checking."

She turned right, which Selene supposed meant it was widdershins according to the perspective of the sky, and led them parallel to the nearest ridge. The going was rough and rambling, as the ground was almost exclusively jagged tumbles of rock, and there was no trail, but Shae was a good pathfinder, and Albatross followed her loyally wherever she stepped, allowing Selene to follow in her footsteps with little trouble.

They walked, climbed, scrambled, and occasionally slid their way over the tumultuous ground. The cliffs kept pace on their right, while the ridge and the cloud of airborne demons remained on their left.

Selene puzzled over Shae's choice of route. According to her internal map of Hell, which was based largely on a businesslike summary of Dante's seminal classic that she had read around the time she'd encountered her first terrestrial demon, she knew that within the Eighth Circle—or ring or what have you—were a dozen or so valleys which lay in concentric circles around the Ninth Ring, each one providing the punishment to the souls whose crimes had been various forms of . . . what were they at now? Lies? Traitors? No, traitors were Ninth Ring because Satan was a traitor to God and he was at the center of it all. But it wasn't lies either. But something like lies. Selene supposed it didn't really matter at this point. What did matter was that they appeared to be skirting the edge of the outermost valley, walking in a huge circle—counterclockwise—around Hell. She did not see how this would lead them inward.

But Albatross had called this the Labyrinth of Pain, and Selene knew that a labyrinth, if you wanted to get technical about it, was not an ordinary maze. Specifically it was a maze with only one course to the center, which to make things interesting was folded and wound around and around itself. Sometimes a labyrinth could be as simple as a spiral.

If the valleys were a single spiral, and not concentric rings, then it should follow that the intervening high ground would also make a spiral which could be followed to the center. If one was willing to walk the circumference of Hell a dozen times over.

Selene's mind quailed at the thought, until she reminded herself that, as far as time was concerned, they had all the time in . . . well, they had all the time in Hell. They didn't need food or water or sleep or even rest. Shae's pride might get on her nerves, but the woman wouldn't balk at the challenge. She would lead them, slowly and relentlessly, around and around, until they reached their ultimate destination.

The significance of a spiral maze in the depths of Hell did not pass Selene by. There was something to it that was important, but she could not place her finger on it at that moment. Instead she fell to wondering what their ultimate destination would be.

Shae, it seemed, intended to reach the center of Hell, where supposedly there was a way out—if one was willing to climb down Lucifer's legs. According to Dante this let you out on the far side of the world. Or, what he thought was the far side of the world. Taking contemporary knowledge of the geography of Earth into account, Selene suspected that Dante's Purgatory was somewhere else entirely.

Still, Purgatory was better than Hell. Selene knew from experience. But she did not think too hard about it—nor what might be possible once— if—she got there.

She had come to Hell to help Albatross find herself. And, it was becoming evident, it was pointless to try to plan—or hope—for anything beyond that. Whatever else Albatross might be, she was certainly powerful enough that whatever she turned out to be, it would change their situation irrevocably. Better to not plan anything until Selene knew what that was.

Still, she began to allow herself the faint, vague hope, carefully tempered by skepticism, that whatever Albatross was, it would be something good.

It felt like they walked (scrambled, hopped, climbed) around the rim of the Eighth Ring for a short eternity—if that made any sense. Time stretched, the same way space did in the forest and the desert, and as they progressed, though nothing changed, it began to feel like they had always been here, had always been scrambling fruitlessly between ridge and cliff, under the unforgiving yellow sky. And they always would be. They would never reach the center, only remain here, on the fringes, forever and ever.

Shae climbed lightly to the top of a small jumble of rocks, where one made a table on which the three of them could stand.

"Wait," she said, looking at the two of them critically. "Which one of you is hoping?"

Albatross looked confused, but Selene understood. Hope was an anchor, and it worked both ways.

"Sorry," she said, dully. "My bad."

Shae gave her a reproachful look. It was also tinged with disappointment, and that stung.

"Would it help if I told you we'll never get to the center, that we'll always be here, at the edge of the Labyrinth? That we've always *been* here?"

Selene met her gaze and refused to be ashamed. She was, after all, wholly human.

"No," she said.

"We all have hope," said Albatross, meekly. Flattened as she was, weak as her voice sounded, she retained a solidity that Selene found reassuring. "You, for instance," she said to Shae, with cringe-worthy gentleness. "You still hope to find—"

"No, I don't," Shae interrupted, sharply. "I put that behind me when I entered this place."

"Yes," said Albatross, humble and serene. "And from behind, it drives you."

Shae's face went tight all over, and Selene wondered if she was frightened. Or angry. Perhaps both. Either way, she knew they were guaranteed no progress as long as they stood still, so she hitched her shield higher on her shoulders and walked past Shae, hopping down off the table of rock and clambering up and down the jumbled ground behind. She didn't think of Albatross, or of what lay within the Labyrinth, or even why they were here. All that mattered was they were, and they might always be. She made peace with that.

A short eternity later there were ridges on both sides of them, and the cliffs were a mere scratch against the yellow sky, low on their right. The air, which had until then smelled faintly of sulfur and wood ash, obtained a stringent, sour odor, with an undercurrent of ammonia.

It was sewage, Selene realized. She had not recognized it at once because the usual revulsion in her body at the smell had not occurred. She wondered if this was because her stomach had shriveled up and died for lack of attention, or if she had simply become inured against foul odors.

One of the valleys was filled with human excrement, she was pretty sure. They must be near that. She noted it blandly and without interest, and kept on trudging.

Selene's course must have veered off center, for the ridge to their right grew increasingly high and dark, and at one point they passed the tall arch of a bridge. Its summit was crowded with spiky black shapes. They left it behind.

Almost imperceptibly the ground began to change under them. The jumbled rocks grew smaller, with puddles of thick, sucking mud between. Selene was so focused on hopping from one to the other that she didn't notice when the smell of sewage shifted from their left to their right, and the low murmur of tortured voices could be heard rising from beyond the ridge to their left. Like the mud-flooded landscape and the smell of sewage, it felt like it had always been this way. Two women, walking the long way into the heart of Hell.

Wait. *Two* women?

Selene stopped so suddenly that Shae tripped and had to grab her arm to keep from falling over.

"Where is Albatross?" Selene demanded over Shae's sputtered protest.

"What?" she replied.

"Where did Albatross go?" Selene repeated. For it was just the two of them between the ridges of the Labyrinth. Albatross—flat, yellow, disguised Albatross—was nowhere to be seen.

Shae looked around, confused. "I thought she was right behind me."

"Right behind—" Selene stopped herself before she said something insulting. Of course Shae hadn't been watching Albatross. Shae didn't understand how unpredictable Albatross could be. She had only seen the ninefold Albatross, the confident if quixotic girl with astonishing power.

Still, on top of everything, it annoyed Selene beyond all reason. And, Albatross was missing.

"Where are you going?" Shae asked, for Selene had turned herself around and begun to retrace her steps.

"I'm going to find her," she announced.

"She'll find us when she's ready," Shae said, so casual as to be uncaring.

"You don't know her!" Selene shouted over her shoulder. "She's liable to get caught—trapped—distracted—*who knows*. She's not a whole person!"

"She's more a person than either of us, put together," Shae said. "Maybe you can't see it, but I do. Even if she's not the White Goddess, she's got godlike powers. She'll be *fine*."

They might have parted company there and then. Or they might have fallen to arguing. But at that moment a shrill cry rose up from beyond the inner ridge, and with it a pale white wisp, hardly more than a puff of smoke.

It was pursued by the unmistakable white-and-rainbow aura of the twelvefold Albatross, which enveloped the wisp when it was directly over their heads and then dropped like a stone.

She had to drop to avoid the flock of demons which had come flapping after her like a horde of angry wasps. Selene ran, slipping and sticking in the mud, and reached her just before the demons did.

Albatross was crouched on the ground, her rainbow aura fading, flattening into the landscape, and Selene stood astride her and raised her shield.

She felt it go *ting* under her hands, and a ripple of warm air spread out around them. Selene felt it only as a light brush on her cheek, but she saw it tear through the horde of demons, throwing them sideways into each other, where they began to fight, clawing and snapping, and eventually retreating back to the air over the third circle.

Albatross was not much changed by this latest addition to her person, though when she crawled out from between Selene's legs and stood up it was with shaky, jerking motions, and she seemed momentarily disoriented.

"What is light?" she asked, gazing up at Selene with eyes the color of old newspaper. She had gone flat and yellow again, but was unmistakably solid.

"I'm sorry?" said Selene, unable to decipher her words.

"She means your shield," Shae said, dryly.

Selene, who had lowered her shield once the demons had retreated, looked it over curiously. It was the same as it had always been, to her eyes: a blown-up version of the little moon amulet-pin Faraday had given her. Then she turned it over.

She was nearly blinded. The convex outer surface was blazing with yellow light. Reflected sky, she realized. But more intense for all it came from a smaller area. It was fading even as she blinked, her eyes adjusting, until once again she could make out the details of the carvings on the surface of her shield, the light and dark bits that formed a waxing crescent across the face of it. But it still glowed against the muddy ground, and when she touched it experimentally she felt the surface vibrate under her finger.

Moonlight was only reflected sunlight. But perhaps something happened in the reflecting of it.

"Huh," said Selene, propping the shield back up over her head. "That's interesting."

"Did Faraday give you any instructions for how to use that?" Shae asked.

Selene blinked at her.

"No," she said. "She just gave it to me and said 'here, you'll need this.' Or something like that. It's just general protection—or so I thought."

But Shae had narrowed her eyes and was looking at Selene—or rather, at the side of Selene's shield—as though she was seeing it afresh.

"Shields can be weapons," Shae remarked, resting a hand on the hilt of her sword.

Selene didn't argue. The demons were regrouping over the ridge, flocking together in greater and greater numbers, flying so close it was impossible to pick out any one creature. It reminded Selene of a school of fish, or a flock of swallows, swimming or flying so closely together that the individual was lost, and they became one giant shape made up of countless tiny pieces.

That was exactly what the demons were doing. Except instead of forming an amorphous cloud, this shape had a definite intent to it. Selene was reminded of supercell storm clouds, and then she was reminded of a vortex turned on its side, with the spiraling arms drawing in and a single spot of yellow sky, like a baleful eye, gazing at them from the center.

"Should we be worried about that?" she asked.

Shae turned to look, and clenched her jaw. Her body quivered, like one contemplating flight. But Albatross laid a hand on her shoulder.

"This is not your fight," she said. Then she turned to Selene. Though her face was no different than before, suddenly she looked very old, and very grave.

"The Simoniacs took me as their idol," she said, as if this should explain everything. "Their jailers adopted me. But I stole myself from them, and now they come to claim what they believe is theirs."

"But you're *not* theirs," Selene declared, always with an eye on the vortex of demons. It had condensed to the point where it was one massive ball with countless streaming arms, and several more "eyes" had opened up in its center.

"No," agreed Albatross, firmly. "But I owe them enlightenment."

Too late Selene saw the reason for her gravity.

"Don't you dare," she said. "Don't you dare turn yourself over! Not after we've come this far!"

She felt hot under her collarbone. Hot like anger she hadn't felt since she was on Earth. Anger, frustration, and disappointment. But not fear.

"Argue all you like," Shae said, reasonably. "I'm not waiting around to find out what they want." And she began to walk, with long, lunging strides, onward along the spiral.

"No," said Albatross, and such was the command in her voice that Shae paused, looking back haughtily over one shoulder. "You two must stay together. I will find you at the center—if not before. I can see clearer now. The center is where I am."

She took Selene's free hand—the hand that did not hold the shield—and pressed it between both of hers. They were the palest yellow, and growing paler. Growing white. When Selene met her eyes, they flashed rainbows.

"Protect her," Albatross said. "She is important. And so are you."

Her hair was platinum and pearlescent, blown wild around her head, which was crowned by a halo of rainbow light. Her eyes flashed, red and gold and green and blue, like sunlight through morning dew.

She was the most beautiful and the most terrifying woman Selene had ever seen, and the sight struck her both dumb and immobile. Her hand hovered in the air for a moment after Albatross let it go, then slowly sank to her side as she watched the tall, shining woman, her aura now expanding to form a complete circle around her. Bolts of light, like spokes of a wheel, flickered between her and the ring of color.

Selene had lowered her shield, clutching that arm to her chest as if physically restraining herself from running after.

Albatross was floating now. A white woman in a white dress with white hair inside a complete rainbow, rising sedately through the air to confront the horde of demons.

The glaring yellow eyes saw her. The black cloud reached out— ignoring the two women standing on the ground—and wrapped tendrils around the little drop of rainbow light that was Albatross.

Selene could not see if they pierced her aura. She was blocked out by the black cloud, flashed once, and then was gone.

Selene might have stood, mute with shock, disappointment and curdling despair, for an eternity. She might have turned into a resentful stone pillar.

Shae touched her elbow gently.

"Come on," the woman said, her voice uncharacteristically soft.

When still Selene did not budge, Shae reached across and pushed at her shoulder, slowly forcing her around.

"Walk," she said. "One foot in front of the other. You know how to do this. You can do this. Walk, Selene."

Mind blank, heart numb, Selene walked. Slowly at first, and then as she began to absorb the meaning of what Albatross had told her, faster and faster. She broke into a jog, shield flapping at her side. She hitched her arm tightly against her chest, and began to run as fast as she could over the uneven ground.

Shae was a large, graceful, powerful shape beside her, keeping pace easily.

They did not need rest. They did not need food. Selene didn't even need to breathe, strictly speaking.

Albatross had said she would find them in the center. The center was where she was, too. Twelve had been drawn to Cocytus, the frozen lake in the center of Hell. Their mission had not changed.

Under the yellow sky, across the broken, muddy ground, Selene ran and kept on running, and Shae ran with her.

City of Dis, the Labyrinth of Pain
Eighth Ring, Circles Four and Five

The yellow sky did not change. The broken ground varied in wetness and the amount of boulders they had to navigate, but other than that remained consistent. Selene's muscles went through the cycle of excited, painful, and tired many times over, eventually settling into a leaden resignation. Running became the new normal. She wasn't sure in all honesty if it shortened their journey—an eternity is an eternity after all—but it gave her something to think about besides the memory of Albatross being swallowed up by the horde of demons.

It did not prevent her parting words from resurfacing in Selene's mind.

The Simoniacs took me as their idol. Their jailers adopted me as one of their own. But I stole myself from them, and now they come to claim what they believe is theirs.

The Simoniacs had to be the damned of the third circle. Their jailers, it followed, would be the demons. When she said she'd stolen herself from them, that had to mean the single wisp of Albatross that had been reclaimed.

Did that mean the demons thought that Albatross, twelve—no, *thirteen-fold* Albatross—was theirs? They would be in for a rude surprise, Selene thought. It gave her courage, which translated to strength, which translated to a slightly faster pace.

Shae had been silent the whole run. No doubt she had understood Albatross's meaning from the first.

She is important, Albatross had said. *And so are you.*

She had also said that Selene was to protect Shae, which, Selene thought, was putting the trailer before the truck. Shae seemed like the last person in Hell who needed protecting. She was like Clara that way.

But comparing sister to sister reminded Selene of the times when Clara *had* needed protection—or at the very least some help. That fight with the Vjorkrige came to mind at once. Clara would go charging into situations where she could be badly hurt—or worse. But Selene thought she did it out of a disinterest in her own well-being, not because she was unable to realistically assess danger. If Shae did so as well, Selene imagined, it would be out of arrogance.

And Selene? Selene prided herself on *not* charging into bad situations, literally or metaphorically.

Then what was she doing now? Running headlong—more or less—into Hell?

The difference, she reasoned, was that she didn't stand to lose anything. She'd already lost. She'd already fallen. The only thing she could lose—aside from her shield—was Albatross. As she foresaw no danger to her shield, and as point one technically applied to Albatross at the moment, she saw no issue with her course of action.

Still, she began to think tactically about what was to come. If the Labyrinth of Pain was Dante's Eighth Circle, and its coils were his *malebolgia*, then in the center would be some giants, and the frozen lake of Cocytus. Then there was traitors, and at the center of *that* was Satan.

Still, there was no telling *where* in Cocytus the rest of Albatross was to be found. And before that there were at least another eight or so loops of the Labyrinth to get through—not to mention two more fragments of Albatross. Assuming they hadn't been drawn into Cocytus already.

Selene wondered how that worked. If there was some force analogous to gravity that pulled the pieces of Albatross to the center of Hell. Did

Satan have an interest in her? Or was it no conscious will but an effect of mutual attraction—magic drawing magic to itself?

But it was useless wondering now. They'd put the smell of excrement far behind them, and now there was nothing but dead, stagnant air, devoid of all smell. At a guess, Selene put them between the third and fourth circles.

They ran. It felt like forever. It might have been forever. To circle Hell once was something not even Dante had done, and they'd done it—what?— four times now? Selene, quite sensibly, tried not to think about it. After a while, she tried not to think about anything.

It was her shield that roused her from the daze of pounding feet and endless yellow sky. It had *tinged* in the way it did when friendly—or not overtly *unfriendly*—magic was close. It was similar to the way it had hummed for Green, and for the huldra, but the tone was different.

Ting, went her shield. She slowed. Looked around. Beside her, Shae drew ahead before matching her pace.

The landscape was the same as it had always been: a flat, sandy dish with rocky ridges on either side.

No, that was wrong. It had *not* always been this way. Once it had been muddy flats with rocks. And before that it had been broken boulders.

Ting, said her shield.

She stopped. She'd been carrying it on her right arm, and now she began to turn in an experimental circle.

Ting! Stronger this time, pulling her left—toward the center. She began to walk in that direction, passing the shield from arm to arm, to get a better sense of where its target was located.

She must have looked very strange, but Shae only asked: "What have you got?"

"I don't know yet," Selene admitted, but kept on, waving her shield like an antenna dish.

The *tings* came closer and closer together, until they merged into one consistent hum, and then when they were in the shadow of the inner ridge, ceased abruptly.

Selene stopped too, confounded, but Shae touched her shoulder and pointed.

There above them, a black outline against the yellow sky, was the sharp abutment of a bridge—its arch lost to view behind a crag of brown rock. Now that Selene had stopped concentrating on her shield she heard, muted through the stone but still audible, the murmur of sharp voices, and below that, gasps and groans.

"Do you know where we're at?" Selene asked Shae.

The woman looked at the bridge critically. "Outer rim of the fifth circle, at a generous estimate."

"Yeah," said Selene. "What's that one?"

"Barrators, according to Dante," said Shae. "And the Malebranche."

"Those are demons, right?" asked Selene.

"Yes," said Shae.

Selene sighed. She swung her shield around and *ting!*

She froze. There had been something else besides the vibration. Something else behind the snapping voices and gurgling screams. A faint, wispy sound, like a breathy voice trying to sing.

Selene knew that voice. She knew it from several lifetimes past, when she had wandered the outer banks of the Acheron.

It was the voice of a single shard of Albatross, and when it sang, her shield hummed in recognition.

It came from above them, beyond the ridge. Selene slipped her arm through the bar of her shield so she could have the use of both hands, and cautiously began to climb the rocky embankment.

It was a long way up, though it had not looked so from the ground. Selene took this in stride as part of the fundamental nature of Hell. Good things were hard to earn and quickly vanished, while hard things dragged on and on beyond all proportion. In that way it was very much like life.

The top of the ridge came abruptly as the slope of rock ended in a sheer drop of some hundred or more feet down into a trough of bubbling black ooze. Shapes moved beneath the surface, but between that and Selene was a veritable cloud of sharp, black bodies.

The demons were hard to define. Like trying to identify a piece of roadkill, contorted and dried, mutilated beyond all recognition. A piece of head here, a prolapsed eyeball there, a stringy thing which might have once been a leg, broken and twisted. The only things about them which were whole and unblemished were their wings, which flapped prodigiously to keep them airborne above the boiling muck. These were not batwings or bird wings, but akin to those of flies and beetles. A few of the demons even had shiny carapace coverings, which glimmered in the yellow light of the sky.

They were the source of the sharp voices, as they called to each other in screeches and whines, while the gurgling moans came from the souls embroiled in the pitch. As she watched, Selene saw one make a spirited attempt at escape, only to be shoved under again by the nearest demon. Yet it took a piece of the demon with it, tearing off a limb and leaving the demon to tumble through the air until it regained its balance. Indeed, the longer she looked, the more often she saw demons clawed at by souls in the pitch, and once one was dragged completely under, reemerging minutes later, even further deformed.

Each side, it seemed, tormented the other, and Selene was on the point of turning away in disgust when Shae reached the top and pointed along the ridge to where they had at last a clear view of the bridge.

This was an arched affair made of black stone. There were no railings, and though from the side it was difficult to judge its breadth, Selene suspected it to be quite narrow.

It was guarded at its peak by a single demon, taller than all the rest, who had double dragonfly wings and a long, coiling tail. It appeared to have been eviscerated at one point, for the line of its spine was clearly visible in profile, overhung by the tattered remains of its skin and thoracic internal organs.

It leaned on a long stick, at the top of which hung a large birdcage, and inside the birdcage crouched something pale and miserable, puffing out soft breaths of song. When it stopped, or when it sang something that displeased the guardian, the demon would shake the stick, causing the cage to swing wildly, and curse in a hoarse, hacking voice.

Selene sighed, realizing that they had indeed found a fraction of Albatross, but not before demons had.

"That'll be Malacoda," Shae announced, leaning on a rock beside her. "Or his replacement. Better leave this one to me."

"Like hell," said Selene, and followed the taller woman as she began to step briskly along the top of the ridge.

The guardian of the bridge paid them no heed until they were almost at the base of it, where there was a causeway of carefully laid bricks, providing a smooth path barely wide enough for one, which led up and over the chasm of boiling pitch.

Shae was almost halfway to the apex when the demon left off shaking the cage and turned its terrible face upon her.

It was terrible, Selene decided, because it had so clearly once been human. It reminded her of something that had been melted, globs of flesh drooping from its neck and jaws. Its eye sockets were hollow, and it wore across its brow a pair of glasses, but instead of glass lenses, the frames held bloody eyeballs.

It snapped something unintelligible at Shae, who responded in a strong, clear voice:

"I am Schiavona Nordstern, and I challenge you."

More grotesque language. Selene thought it was a question.

She had one foot on the base of the bridge now and could see that this Albatross was in poor condition. Largely transparent, she had raw stumps of flesh where her wings might have been, and she stared at them with terrified, unrecognizing eyes.

"I will take the white bird, and safe passage across the bridge," Shae declared.

The demon laughed, opening its mouth so wide Selene could see how it had no teeth but the sharp ends of gray nails which had been hammered through its jawbones.

It spoke, a counter-statement to Shae's, at which the woman nodded and retreated down the bridge so she could speak to Selene.

"If I win, we get Albatross and safe passage over the bridge."

"And if you lose?" Selene asked dryly.

"I won't," said Shae, reasonably. "But the forfeit is I take the demon's place."

That made Selene look again at the demon, considering further how it resembled a mutilated human. Tails and wings could be attached after the fact, yes, and it was not an unheard of concept. People on Earth internalized the message of their oppressors and tormentors, sympathized with their abusers to the point where they became abusers and oppressors themselves—why not also in Hell? And it made sense, in the way that Hell took everything to its logical extreme, that those tormented by demons would, in time, become demons themselves.

But to take the demon's place? That reminded Selene of a different set of rules, rules that came from another, wider world. The world of the forest, of the huldra, and the spider-woman.

The context of Hell is complicated, Albatross had said. *It cannot change the rules it lives in, only warp them. It is not absolute.*

Selene wasn't sure if this made her feel better or worse about standing at the base of the bridge and watching Shae walk up it to confront the demon alone, but she had to admit, of the two of them, Shae was the better candidate.

Nevertheless, she kept a good grip on her shield and her legs planted wide, ready to run up the bridge at a moment's notice. Shae and Clara might play by formal, almost civilized rules, but there was no guarantee that the demon would.

But the opponents faced off with no interference from the demons in the trench, save a volley of sneering cheers when the demon on the bridge snapped its spear to attention. For it was a spear, not a stick, to which had been attached Albatross's cage, and the demon swung it around so the trident head faced Shae, while the cage swung free over the far side of the bridge. Inside it the fragment of Albatross twisted and scrambled, trying to maintain her balance, all the while staring at Shae like a frightened animal.

Shae was frightening, Selene admitted. Especially now, as she stalked up the bridge with the grace and demeanor of a hunting lioness, her sword unsheathed and gleaming in the yellow light. It flashed dark and bright, almost seeming to writhe on the end of its hilt like a living creature. A hungry creature. Attached as it was to the tall, long-limbed, dangerous woman with streaming yellow hair, the overall impression was that of an avenging angel.

The effect was not lost on the guardian of the bridge, who quailed visibly before it was reprimanded by jeers from below. Then it squared its shoulders and met Shae's opening strike, their weapons clashing with a splitting screech of metal on metal.

It was hardly a contest. The demon had a menacing figure and lightning-quick movements, but Shae seemed to anticipate its every move. With her first lunge she knocked aside the head of its trident and cut a decisive slash across its chest, causing its entire body to split open, its shoulders to separate, and the spear to sway wildly.

Shae took the opportunity to cut its legs out from under it, and with its head thus lowered to her waist height she settled the point of her sword against its throat and cried "Yield to me!"

Had her opponent been human, or even conventionally alive, that would have been the end of it. But the demon only began to laugh, maliciously and derisively. It grabbed the point of Shae's sword, and with a sharp tug jerked the woman off balance. Then the two figures were grappling, and Selene was starting up the bridge, still unsure how she would assist, but knowing an intervention would be needed soon.

Only when she drew level with the combatants, it was to find Shae had somehow managed to weasel her way past the demon, and even as the demon whirled around, her sword flashed upward, slicing clean across the tip of spear so that the caged Albatross was loosed. She screamed as she began to fall, but Shae snatched her from the air and danced even further down the bridge, far out of reach of the demon, who had turned, spitting obscenities, to bar Selene's path.

"Take one more step," it snarled through its broken mouth, "and you'll be learned what befalls mortals who defy the Tearing Kind!"

"Let her pass!" Shae commanded from the far side of the bridge. She had Albatross's cage in one hand and her sword in the other. A righteous angel above the trench.

But the demon would not be moved. It could not move, Selene saw now. It was manacled by one ankle to an iron ring set into the stone of the bridge. And now it was menacing her with the trident.

"Do you also challenge Tearing Kind?" it demanded.

Selene did not advance. She leaned sideways off the bridge to look questioningly at Shae, whose face had gone red with anger.

"I bested you!" she declared. "Let her pass!"

"I did not concede!" snapped the demon. "And I do not grant passage to those who will not fight me!"

Selene groaned inwardly. It had been too much to hope. She reassessed the demon, and was not encouraged. With only her shield and grit it would be a hard fight, and though Selene feared nothing from the demon's trident, it would be all too easy for it to knock her off the bridge into the trench below. Which trench, now she was directly above it, Selene had no desire to see any closer.

Still, she might have chanced a confrontation but that the demon's compatriots from below, sensing trouble, began to rise in an angry buzzing on either side of the bridge.

That did it. Selene was definitely going into the trench if she persisted. Shae must have come to the same conclusion. Selene glimpsed her being forced off the bridge to the inner loop of the Labyrinth, beating off demons with her sword.

"Keep running!" she called through the cacophony of demonic cries. The next part was lost in the screeching, but Selene thought it was "We will wait!"

It was not much of a choice, but Selene did not waste time deliberating. Checking over her shoulder to be sure her retreat was clear (it was) she backed carefully down off the bridge. The horde of demons remained, watching her with ruined faces, until she was well down the ridge. Then she turned and began to run, counterclockwise, and she did not look back to see what they did. She set her gaze a few feet in front of her and, doggedly, kept on running.

City of Dis, the Labyrinth of Pain, Eighth Ring, Circles Six, Seven, and Eight

Selene knew that on a technical level there was no measurement to an eternity. An eternity was, by definition, eternal. It was like saying something was infinite. Almost infinity was either finite (not infinity) or infinity. Likewise there really was no such thing as a *small* eternity. Yet that was the best way she could describe the time it took to circle Hell, in the Eighth Ring, on foot, at a steady run.

Not an eternity—she did, eventually, come around again—but a small one. Specifically, it was the amount of time it took to *feel* like she had been running forever, multiplied by about four.

She was able to measure it, because she kept an eye out for the bridge with the demon on it, and when it appeared again on her right she knew she had made almost a complete circuit. She put on speed in anticipation—and nerves. And was not disappointed—below the bridge, where Shae and Albatross should have been, there was nothing and no one. The demons laughed cruelly at her as she paced back and forth, calling out for them.

She did not ask where they had gone. She hoisted her shield and kept on running.

The strip of land between the fifth and sixth circles was sand, and Selene hated it. Not the blistering hardpack of the desert, this was black, cool, deep, and sharp. It soon became impossible to run, and walking was an exercise in frustration as each step gave way under her foot, and she slid back or down several inches for every stride she took.

Selene waded, grinding her teeth against the sharp jabs her soles suffered from the hidden shards within the sand. It was like some horrible mutilation of beach sand, which was fun until you were trudging back to the car, tired and salty and only wanting to sit down. It was like that, only with broken glass added. And there was no car, and no sitting, and no end.

For all that, it was also disturbingly beautiful. The black sand sparkled under the light of the yellow sky, glittering gold like iron pyrite, and it mounded and pillowed like the waves of a frozen sea.

It's enough to make you forget you're in Hell, Selene thought raggedly. *Except I have to wade through it.*

But after she had slid and scratched herself up one wave she found a deep trough before her, and she was able to follow the bottom of it between two peaks of sand for a while, before it began to curve away from her course and she had to climb out of it. When she reached the top of that ridge she was able to look back down at the bridge of the fifth circle, where the demon was only a tiny speck, and the horde below crawled like flies.

Also behind her, but inward, was another bridge. This one was covered in scaffolding and the demons there were busy lifting dark masses out of the trench below, placing them like bricks into the framework created by the scaffolds.

For some reason this made Selene thing of the phrase, *the road to Hell is paved with good intentions*, and wondered what the bridges in Hell were paved with. Bad ones?

Grinning mirthlessly to herself and shaking her head, she descended the far slope of the sandy ridge.

It got worse from there, because there were no troughs to follow. The ridges lay perpendicular to her course, and Selene was forced to trudge up and down and up and down, and each time she reached an up the bridges were no further away.

Idiot, stop looking! Stop thinking about them! she told herself.

Looking was easy, but it was hard to stop thinking of the bridges. Knowing that there was a shortcut behind her—*just* behind her—was torturous.

Selene reminded herself firmly that just because it *appeared* to be a shortcut didn't mean it *was* one. For all she knew, this long, circuitous route *was* the shortcut, and those bridges were the detour.

It was hard to believe, but Selene firmly kept herself thinking it as she plodded grimly onward through the sand, and after a small eternity of climbing and descending and climbing and descending, the hills began to get lower, until they were hardly noticeable, and then the sand grew thinner, until she could begin, tiredly, to jog once more.

That lasted for a downright short eternity, and then the sand started up again. Selene could have cried. She did groan. It felt like she was going in circles. (Well, she *was*.) She plowed into the sand, running for as long as she could, and then walking.

When the waves began again, however, she stopped. She turned left and walked inward until the sand gave way to rock, and then the rock gave way entirely.

This would be the outer rim of the seventh circle, by her count. She had long since forgotten who Dante had put here, but what she saw was not encouraging.

The air was thick down in that trench. Not thick with smoke or ash or any pollutant, but even more than in the burning desert, it was literally thick—like water—and it was filled with monsters.

There was no better word for them. They were not recognizable as any one animal but looked like at least four or five had been mashed together with no thought as to where each piece should go. Selene saw one that was mostly a bear but whose rear quarter was some kind of fish, and it had an alligator head and hind goat leg sprouting from its neck. Exploding, more like. The transition between beasts was not smooth but violent and bloody, as though the extra appendages had been pushed through the bear's skin from within. It flapped in bloody strips around the exit point.

They were all like that, and they all continued to change. The bear-creature's head was blown off, replaced by the arm of an ape. Another one, still with a human torso, had a snake emerge from its chest, spitting flesh and shards of bone.

In any case Selene decided she had been right to think of the high ground as the shortcut, and backing away from the precipice she resigned herself to more sand.

Yet it did not seem as deep inside of the sixth circle. Selene didn't look for the bridges, and perhaps that helped. The waves felt easier, too, which made Selene mistrustful. But eventually she found herself at the bottom of a truly deep trough and had to put her hands down to haul herself out of it. She tore a lot of sand loose as she did, and it was only by some desperate scrambling that she managed to achieve the summit without getting caught in an avalanche of her own making.

With stinging hands and feet she scrambled over the edge and banged her knee hard on the first piece of solid ground in ages. It came as such a surprise that she had to sit on it, nursing her knee, while she listened to the faint roaring of the sand sliding away below her.

When the pain had subsided enough that she could think again, she hesitantly examined her hands. She found them whole and unblemished. On closer inspection, her feet were likewise in excellent condition. Which was surprising, given that she was certain she had felt them rip and tear from the glass in the sand.

She was sitting on solid ground at the edge of a wide causeway made of black slate, the stone warm under her hands and dimly reflecting the baleful yellow sky.

It dimly reflected her as well, and Selene was surprised at the sight of her own face after so long. It was definitely her face, but not as she remembered it. She looked both younger and older than she thought she should have. Her skin too smooth, her eyes too heavy, her expression terrible. It was an ancient face reflected darkly on the ground of Hell, one whittled by eons of pain: resigned, patient, and indomitable.

There was no sun in the sky but something reflected bright as a star at her side. Her shield, which she had pinned to the back of her shirt, had fallen sideways and cast a bright crescent of pale gold light across her face. Perhaps, Selene hoped, it was that light which made her look so strange. But probably not. She had been too long in Hell, had been through too much, to remain unchanged.

Turning away from the disturbing image she re-centered the shield on her back and stood up. Ahead of her the ground was hard and flat and oppressive in its distance. Behind her stretched the endless dunes of black sand. But they were below her now, and from her new vantage point, she finally saw that they were not dunes as formed by wind in the desert, but the frozen concentric waves of a crater.

She was now standing at the edge of that crater. A crater so huge its far side was lost in wave upon wave of black sand. Here, beyond the very last ripple of impact, the ground was hard and flat. Unforgiving, but traversable. On her right (as she faced forward, away from the crater) there was a sharp ridge of stone, like teeth, but to her left, the ground ran on, flat as a table, until it was cut by a sharp, black crack—after which it continued in much the same fashion, but dotted with bits of rubble.

That would be the eighth circle, if she'd not lost count. Selene went over to it, out of curiosity more than anything else, and found herself at the edge of a deep, dark cavern, lit by glimmering flames. Some were red and dull, others hot and blue, but most were warm yellow. Standing out as they did against the black void they gave the impression of stars, twinkling prettily. It was that prettiness which made the place all the more horrifying, for it rang with the faint sound of screams—as of those muffled by pillows and closed doors. And Selene remembered: Dante had described a bolgia wherein souls burned inside eternal flames. Selene had forgotten which ones, but she rather hoped some of them had been witch-hunters. Not witches who were also hunters, like Faraday, but those hateful, misogynist monks who had taken out their repressed frustrations on perfectly decent, knowledgable women and in doing so robbed the world of a wealth of feminine-held wisdom. Unless . . . did it make more sense for them to be whipped by the Furies? As much as any of the suffering in Hell made sense to Selene.

She turned away, steeling herself for more running, and—

Ting!

In turning she had put her back, and thus the face of her shield, toward the eighth trench. The pull was strong, sharp, and unmistakably came from the far side.

Slowly, Selene slid the pin out of her shirt and latched it against the back of the shield. Holding it on her arm she turned like a satellite dish to face the chasm and . . .

Ting!

Definitely coming from the other side, and close, by the feel of it.

Lying down on her chest so she could put her head over the edge without risk of falling in, Selene angled her shield so that it reflected yellow sky light down into the cavern.

It illuminated jagged rock walls descending into darkness with no visible end, but the chasm narrowed the deeper it got, and Selene judged that, at the furthest extent that she could see, she could probably bridge the gap with her legs.

She sat up and looked around. The causeway was as bleak and deserted as ever. Across the trench was empty and barren. But when she lifted her shield it hummed again, still in the same direction.

Maybe there were no shortcuts through Hell. You just took the path that opened itself to you.

Selene refastened her shield to the back of her shirt, trying to use the same hole so that the fabric wasn't damaged any further, and then turned herself around so she went on her belly, and gently lowered her legs into the chasm, feeling along the rock wall for a foothold.

This was not difficult. The wall was jagged and full of handy cracks and ridges, and with bare feet they were much easier to feel. The problem was finding ones that could take her weight, as many of the ridges were brittle and broke off after gentle probing with her toes. But she found first one and then another solid hold, and careful always to keep at least three points of contact between herself and the wall, she began to descend into the eighth circle.

The flames of the damned floated around her, and the yellow sky narrowed to a thunderbolt of light, but nothing accosted her, and nothing stopped her descent. When she judged she had gone deep enough she began to test the distance between herself and the far wall: reaching out behind her with one leg, feeling for another piece of rock. Once, she accidentally kicked a burning soul, who shrieked and tumbled away, leaving her foot singed and smarting.

She had come twice as far down as she had intended, when with both hands and feet firmly anchored, she managed to look over her shoulder and saw she had climbed right past a jut of rock on the far side. It was now above and a little to her left, but easy enough to reach the place on the wall opposite. Selene carefully ascended and traversed, and then turned herself sideways as much as she could, both hands anchored in crevices, one foot clutching a narrow ridge as the other reached out, felt the jut of rock, and began searching for a hold.

She found one, but the reach was almost the full extent of her leg, and she could not make a controlled step from one side to the other. When she stood with one foot on either side of the chasm she had to make a search of the far wall with her eyes alone to find her next handholds, then kick with one leg so she was propelled across the gulf from one side to the other.

Wary of hitting too hard and bouncing off, she barely reached the far wall, and there was one heart-stopping second where her hands were on the smooth stone but with nothing to hold onto. Then her righthand fingers found a crack, and she jammed them in, hugging herself to the stone as if she could physically adhere to the surface by contact space alone. She felt a faint divot in the stone under her left hand, and cupping her palm over its edge she was able to spare a thought to finding purchase with her free foot. This done, she began searching for a route up.

It was not easy. The stone was smoother this side of the chasm, and what holds there were were farther apart. Selene had to back down and traverse several times in order to try new lines, and once, when that failed, she had to make use of a foothold which was hardly more than a shallow depression in the rock. She had felt her toes begin to slip when her hand caught the ledge above, and she hung there, precariously suspended, for several moments while she gathered the willpower to drag herself up.

It was all willpower at this point, Selene figured. What was physical strength worth, in this place where bodies could be mutilated and the person still live? What was physical strength when you didn't eat or drink or sleep, and remained lucid?

In the old world—the *real* world, Selene reminded herself—she had relied on willpower to get her through the toughest situations, even when her body had wanted to give up. Here in Hell, she figured, what her body wanted no longer mattered. It was all up to her mind. But the mind was part of the body, after all, and her mind had grown tired. It took an immense amount of effort to pull herself up again and again, and several times she had to stop and rest.

It was during one of these interminable rests when she noticed that she could better see the rock wall above her for the light of all the burning souls hovering, like a cloud of flaming gnats, around her shoulders. Their flames cast her shadow deep and black on the stone directly under her hands, which was annoying, but as they never approached close enough to burn her she tried to ignore them.

But she could not shut out their screams, which were just faint enough to prick her ears, and just loud enough that, sometimes, she could discern words within them. They kept tugging at her attention, like half-forgotten memories—enough to make her wonder who they had been and what their full lamentation was.

. . . take him around the back . . .

. . . she never knew the difference . . .

. . . and it was better for it that I had . . .

And many more. Selene wondered briefly that she understood their words at all, considering Hell took humans of all nationalities. But, she supposed, the dead have their own language—she certainly hadn't been speaking English to Kirke or Styx—who was to say she and Shae had even spoken English to each other?

There was an overhang above her. Not a large one, but one so smooth of surface as to be practically impassable. Selene had to traverse in a vertical zigzag under it for what felt like ages, while the burning souls followed her in a hot, glowing cloud, until she came to a vertical crack in the rock which she could use as a chimney past the overhang and for some ways beyond before it became too wide. Still, climbing up the corner of it was easier than the sheer face of the chasm, and it limited the number of souls who could hang over her head.

That crack ran all the way to the surface, which was in itself a difficult maneuver as the ground was slippery with dust, and there was a distinct lack of good holds. Selene beached herself like a whale, rolling over her side and back—where her shield cut sharply into her flesh—and over again, until she guessed she had put at least four feet between herself and the edge of the eighth circle.

For a while she lay on her face, enjoying the feeling of gravity pulling her flat against the ground, while the only light that shone down on her was the wan yellow light of the unforgiving—but mercifully silent and distant—sky.

City of Dis, the Labyrinth of Pain
Eighth Ring, Circle Nine

Selene's shield did not go *ting* so much as buzz against her back, as if the entire thing was a phone on vibrate. Though it oscillated between faint and severe, it nevertheless persisted until she pushed herself up into a sitting position and took stock of her surroundings. Then it switched to an unmistakable hum.

There was no way of knowing how far up or down the labyrinth she had shifted while in the chasm of the eighth circle, because the land all around her was the same flat, featureless slate plain—though now, on this side, with that thin layer of dust which had given her such grief while climbing up onto it.

She was surprised to realize that the ninth circle was quite close— hardly a stone's throw away from the trench of the eighth—and that the screams she still heard were coming from beyond a red lip of earth which marked its edge. So, she discovered when she took an uncertain step in that direction, was whatever was resonating with her shield.

A resonation was a good way to describe it. It vibrated in sympathetic harmony with something as-yet unheard, and Selene followed it as if she were playing a mad game of hot-and-cold.

It took her to the very edge of the ninth circle, which was a comparatively shallow wash of sand and mud and filled with mutilated, naked humans trudging back and forth. But Selene had no attention to spare for them. Her shield was practically singing under her hands, and she turned herself in a complete circle trying to find a direction where the vibration was stronger. It wasn't until she raised it to point at the sky that she realized the source was above her, and then Albatross alighted on her shield as gently as a snowflake, her grin a shining crescent all its own.

Selene hadn't seen her until the last moment because she was almost completely transparent—just as she was almost weightless. Even now, bending double so her sharp, oval face was within inches of Selene's, it was more yellow than white from all the sky that showed through. Her eyes glimmered, as insubstantial as soap bubbles yet their gaze directed and fierce.

"Found you!" she cried triumphantly.

"Ay," said Selene, her own voice a faint, breathy gasp. This Albatross, in addition to (or subtraction from) being even more ephemeral than that first tormented fragment she had encountered on the far side of the Acheron, was completely and utterly naked. The effect was less astonishing because she was so insubstantial, but it hammered home the fact that she was, as least in body, barely past puberty. Selene remembered when her body had looked that—the brief window of time when she was aware she *had* breasts but they were still small enough for her to ignore, and what was going on between her legs hadn't yet registered.

Albatross was there, balanced perfectly between girl and woman, a partial, unfinished thing in more ways than one. It made her uncomfortable to look at.

Albatross didn't seem to know or care. She giggled, hanging off the edge of the shield like a child at the side of a swimming pool. She had the motion of one submerged in water, her movements slower and more conscious, and she floated freely when she kicked her feet away from the shield so she hung on with just her fingertips.

"I found you!" she repeated, her white hair billowing, steam-like around her head. "I looked and looked, until I forgot what it was I was looking for. But I saw your moon, and then I remembered. I needed to find you. And I did. And now we can go home!"

"Oh," said Selene, a little stunned. What this Albatross lacked in substance (and clothes) she more than made up for in force of personality. "Home?" Selene asked. This was the first she had heard of anything along these lines, and it both startled and scared her. She had been so careful not to think of anything resembling escape.

"I think?" said Albatross, suddenly uncertain. "Somewhere good, anyway. Home, it moves around, you know?"

Selene did know. What she didn't know what how much this Albatross knew.

"Do you . . . remember me?" she asked.

Albatross frowned. "Not exactly," she said. "I've never met you, but I know you. Moon-sister, moonshield."

"Selene," Selene said. "I have met you, but I don't know you. Not this part of you, anyway."

"There's more to me than this?" Albatross said, sounding delighted. "I thought there must be. I remember being more . . . more everything, actually. That must be where my name went."

"The rest of you, well, the pieces I've met, calls herself Albatross."

"Albatross," repeated Albatross. "I don't think that's my name, but if the rest of me says so, you might as well call me that. Where is she? The rest of me?"

Selene felt bitterness so thick it rose in her throat like bile.

"I lost her," she admitted. "We had to . . . part ways. But she promised to meet me, in the center . . . in the center of this place."

Albatross leaned close to her, warping the landscape which showed through her transparent body. "Hell," she said, as if sharing a secret. "We're in Hell."

"Yes," Selene agreed.

"Do you think home is at the center?" Albatross wondered.

Selene doubted, but . . . why not?

"Maybe," she said.

Albatross pulled her legs down so she nominally stood next to Selene, but kept a steadying hand on her shield, as if she would float away without an anchor. And from what Selene had seen, she very well might.

Something shimmered in the air. It was Albatross's arm, raised and pointing. Pointing toward the trench with the mutilated humans.

"That way," she said, and began to walk. And for all her insubstantiality, Selene could no more resist than if she had been tied to the back of a tractor. Up over the lip of angry red earth, and then down the gentle embankment and into the ninth circle of the Eighth Ring of Hell.

In the way of Hell, it was a lot longer to the bottom than it had looked from the outside. Like pocket dimensions, Selene thought. Everything was bigger on the inside, and everything inside was something else. Except, it appeared, the insides of the souls trapped in the ninth circle. The ground was a thick mud of dirt mixed with blood, pungent with the smell of entrails which slithered past, dragged from the cloven guts of the inhabitants.

Not all of them had been disemboweled, but a lot of them were. Others had their faces cleft, or were pierced by swords, axes, and other weapons. One dragged itself past by its arms, its body ending in two severed stumps below the buttocks.

Albatross drifted lightly through the horrific crowd as if she did not see them, or did not see the carnage. Selene kept close to her, sanguine about the absurdity of the situation: she, a grown, nominally clothed woman—with a shield, no less—hiding behind a translucent, naked adolescent.

But while Albatross was as invisible to the tormented souls as they were to her, she was immediately obvious to the overseers, who descended on them just as they began to ascend the far bank.

They were demons, naturally, but not of the sort from the outer circles. They wore clothes, for a start. Long, sleeveless white robes, specifically, and their skin was the bright, glistening red of fresh wounds. They had long, sharp, strong fingers, six to a hand with three opposing the other half. It was with these terrible hands that they inflicted the wounds borne by the souls in the trench, and though they walked among them, their robes trailing in the bloody mud, these remained white and pristine, unmarked by their work. Their faces were hidden by the bleached bird skulls they wore for masks, and each carried with it a halo of dirty black smoke.

It was by these plumes of smoke that Selene first noticed their approach. That and a general rise in the pitch of the screams around them, accompanied by a sickening *snick, snick,* slicing sound. Then she glimpsed a long-beaked skull above the heads of the damned, and the next thing she knew they were surrounded by a ring of the tall, white-robed figures, their malicious, red hands folded almost chastely across their abdomens.

"Heya fellas," Selene said tiredly, because it was always worth *trying* to be civil, at least at the start. "Don't mind us. We're just passin' through."

The demons gave no sign that they had heard, but neither did they move to eviscerate them. There was some shuffling of taloned feet gouging tracks in the bloody earth, and then all the demons turned sideways, each took a step forward and then snapped their beaks back to stare at Selene and Albatross. Selene was put in mind of curious birds who, having spotted something they weren't certain about, tried looking at it from a different angle to see if it made sense then.

The demon closest took a half step forward and lifted a six-fingered hand. One razor-sharp talon rose, pointed at Selene, then another, pointing at Albatross. It tucked the other four fingers and held the two up.

"Yes," said Selene, mimicking the gesture. "It's just the two of us."

One of the two fingers curled under, leaving a single digit to point in the direction they had been walking. Inward, across the ring.

"That's right, we're going to the center," Selene said, almost defiant.

The great beak dipped and rose as the demon nodded. Abruptly they all turned their backs so that Selene and Albatross were in a ring of white-robed columns. From outside the circle the demons struck up a horrible *snicking* sound with their claws, like knives being sharpened on other knives. It gave Selene shivers of irritation.

Just as abruptly the demons stopped and turned around again, their hands once more neatly folded. A small gap appeared between two of them, and through it stepped a new demon, apparently no different than any of the others, save that it was perhaps a hair shorter. It grew shorter still as it approached Selene and Albatross, until by the time it stood even with them the top of its bony mask was precisely the same height as Selene. It raised one taloned hand and pointed with a single, knifelike finger.

Inward. Onward.

It said no word, but its meaning was clear.

Selene did not like to turn her back on it though, so she put her shield's pin through her shirt so that the demon would have to get through the talisman before it reached her flesh.

"Walk," she told Albatross, who was still gazing at the demon curiously. "They're letting us go. Move."

Albatross moved, but slowly, reluctantly, and so did the entire circle of demons. The ones in front of them spun around, and together the lot marched in formation around Albatross and Selene and their delegate, who brought up the rear and against all expectation did not molest them.

Over the ground of bloody mud and broken stone, Selene did not see another mutilated soul from then on, though she heard their cries. The ground began to rise, and in a much shorter span of time than she had expected, they were struggling up the inward bank of the ninth circle, the demons parting before them as they crested the lip, another short expanse of level ground stretching out before them.

The demons did not leave the circle, but clustered at its edge to watch as Selene and Albatross took their first cautious steps beyond its border.

All the demons except their escort, who stepped up onto the plain with them, to a wave of *snicking* from its peers.

"Oh," said Albatross, sounding pleased. "Are you coming with us then?"

Snick, went the demon's claws, once and decisive.

Selene looked around at it, skeptically.

"Why?" she asked.

The demon stared at her from under its bird-skull mask. Selene spared a thought to wonder if that was its real face—if there was no fleshy head under it—but did not let it linger. The demon raised a thin, red arm. A knife-finger pointed. Inward. Across the plain. Toward the tenth circle.

"Yeah, we're going," said Selene. "But if you're coming, you're not walking behind me anymore. Got it?"

The demon hesitated, a shiver passing through its limbs. It occurred to Selene that it might not want *her* walking behind *it*. Which was just laughable. To Selene, anyway.

Albatross resolved their stalemate by slipping between them and, taking Selene's hand in her left and the demon's taloned claw in her right, began positively skipping toward the tenth circle.

And though each glanced distrustfully at the other, Selene and the demon followed her side by side.

City of Dis, the Labyrinth of Pain
Eighth Ring, Circle Ten

The black smoke which streamed from the demon's neck was the only thing to break the monotony of the pale yellow sky, which had grown brighter, if anything, as they worked their way inward. By the time they clambered over the low wall of rocks marking the boundary of the tenth circle, it felt like standing under a spotlight. A spotlight which took up the entire sky. It bleached the distance so that wherever Selene looked, the ground slowly faded into the yellow light with no discernible horizon. It made the tenth circle feel like a ghost land, dreamlike and insubstantial.

The demon, by contrast, became even more vivid, with its bright red skin and smoky mane, skull face and gleaming white robe. Selene kept glancing at it, like a point of reference, since the ground under its shadow also held a certain amount of substance.

Albatross, meanwhile, had faded right into the landscape, and it was only the pressure of her hand and the gentle humming of Selene's shield that assured her she was still there. That, and a faint glimmer of a human shape overlaying the tumultuous ground.

The tenth circle was a good deal more shallow, and many times wider, than either of the two previous. They made their way over undulating land that formed mini-troughs within the greater valley, the bottom of each marked by a thin stream of thick, yellow fluid which was not water, and not urine, but something truly revolting.

"Lies," whispered Albatross, her voice coming out of the air in front of them as they stepped over the first of these streams. "All lies."

Snick, went the demon's free hand. Selene decided it was meant in agreement.

The souls of the tenth circle, though bleached by the sunlight, were more substantial than the landscape. They wandered in seeming aimlessness in little clots, with individuals sometimes breaking loose and tearing hither and thither, attacking any they found in their way. None of them approached Selene, however, and a few changed their course abruptly so that they did not collide. Selene wondered if it was her shield, or the wraith-like presence of Albatross, but she suspected it had more to do with the demon from the ninth circle, whose blank bird-skull face stared out at the scene with calm impassivity.

Once, twice, three times they crossed a thin rivulet of liquid lies, and both Selene and the demon took care not to step in them. Albatross's feet never touched the ground, if indeed she still had feet. Her grip on Selene's hand was becoming weaker, and by the time they reached the fourth stream Selene had begun to worry that the girl was evaporating out from under her.

"Albatross?" she asked, hoping that conversation might help to solidify her being.

Albatross's voice was faint and breathy when she answered, coming from a mere shimmer in the air where her head might have been.

"Yes, Moonshield?"

"What do you remember?" Selene asked. It was a general question, she knew, but it was all she could think of.

"Blood," said Albatross, after a moment's thought. "I remember blood," she repeated, her voice was stronger now. Selene was so relieved she almost didn't pay attention to the words that voice was speaking.

"I remember being full of blood," Albatross was saying. "Warm, alive, frightened, loving, angry. I remember fury. Or maybe not fury. Maybe that has yet to come? My mind is scattered. Far and wide, forwards and backwards through time."

"Do you remember singing?" Selene asked. "Another part of you said she remembered singing. She liked singing."

"What is singing?" Albatross asked.

Selene was flabbergasted. Even the demon *snicked* its free hand in surprise.

"Singing is . . . it's a way of speaking, sort of." Selene's own words stumbled. How did one describe singing?

"Like what we're doing?" Albatross asked.

"No . . . no," Selene said. And sighed. The easiest thing to do would be to demonstrate. But what to sing? Put on the spot like that, she couldn't think of anything. At the same time there were countless songs jostling inside her head, their words chasing circles around inside her mind. There were the songs that she had played on the road, in Arcana, driving with Jill and Clara from one adventure to the next; there were the songs she had learned as a child, ingrained so deeply in the bedrock of her soul that Hell had not muted them, but brought them closer to the surface. But the songs that had got her through adolescence, and the songs that had got her through nine-hour drives, were not songs that felt right to sing in Hell. They were driving songs. Fighting songs. Empowering songs. But Hell sucked up all the power you put out. It swallowed fights and burned your drive. Selene was afraid she'd lose those songs if she sang them here. But what other songs did she know well enough to sing?

It was the tune that came to her first. A soothing sound that fit her deeper voice. It felt *good* to sing, even without words and without meaning. Yet in thinking that, the words came back—from the middle of the song, of course, she could not recall how it began—but, as they were the words she knew, that was where she started.

"*And from that hollow watch her rise, see blood and fury in her eyes. Out of words and out of meaning, she is a voice in pain, screaming. And all the virtue that from her you once stole has been swallowed whole by the grave of mercy . . .*"

The words came on stronger as she sang, the music lifting her. Reviving something in her that had almost been extinguished. It wasn't hope, and it wasn't peace, and she'd never lost her determination, but it was a comforting assurance that she had sorely missed.

This is truth, she thought. The song is true.

So she went on, feeling her voice come loose in her throat, and the music that it made filled her, leaving no room for doubt, or pain, or despair.

"*Now truth rising from her well, come to shame you I can tell. Her teeth are swords and fingers claw. Your lies will be sunk in her maw. Though you may beg with whispered breath, peace ended in the death of mercy . . .*"

A tenuous silence hung in the air, and Selene hung, in free fall from the momentary lift the singing had given her. Quickly taking in a deep breath she forged on, the last of the song emerging from her memory like a saving ship out of a thick fog.

"*And still brothers turned and preyed upon the sisters that they slayed . . .*"

Selene wasn't sure if it was the singing itself, or what the action of singing was doing to her mind, but while she sang, Albatross became visible again. Hazily at first, but growing sharper the louder she sang.

With a great deal more gusto than she had ever done before, Selene fairly belted out the last verses:

"*Wishing for shoulders to stand on, while they lived large with abandon! But the signs say that the most terrible monster than you have ever seen—the Once and Future Queen—is rising from her grave . . . with mercy . . .*"

Selene held the last note for as long as she could, but eventually she ran out of air, and the song ended in an ignoble wheeze.

Yet in that time they had crested another rise and descended into another shallow valley, and while the land and souls around them remained misty and ghostlike, Albatross was beginning to glimmer and shine with a little of her old brightness.

As they crossed over the fourth rivulet of liquid lies she began to whisper, and then, in her own frail voice, to sing. And to Selene's surprise, it was a song that she knew. Gratefully she joined in, and though the demon remained mute, she caught it nodding its bird-skull head, as though it too was uplifted by the music.

Albatross and Selene's ill-matched duo of voices made for a strange rendition of "Children in the Dark," but under its words the landscape fairly bled away beneath them, and it was to the full-chested belting of *"AND NOW BEGINS THE RAIN!"* that they climbed out of the tenth circle and found they had come to the end of the Labyrinth.

Selene knew it was the end because the sky changed. Though the yellow eye still slit a band along the horizon, the broad arch was a gradient of gray which cooled to blue before them, dimming until it faded into blackness.

There was no plain here. The ground broke into to a forest of stony pillars, like the rigid limbs of some overturned beast, which gradually thinned away until there was only white mist and dim twilight. In that vague distance other shapes loomed, larger than life or belief, ominous in the uncertainty of their substance.

Giants, Selene thought. Dante had seen giants down here, hadn't he? And where was here? She had thought there were more bolgias in the Eighth Ring, but this was certainly no mere trench. This was a complete change in the landscape. This was the lip of the well of Cocytus. This was the border of the Ninth Ring.

Trying very hard not to hope, Selene cast about on either side of them, where the thin strip of unbroken land stretched away into the mist. It was empty, of course. The odds were staggeringly against Shae and the other Albatross being in that exact piece of the well where they exited the final bolgia, even without the frustrating characteristic of Hell that rendered it larger the further in you got.

A pale, whispering voice drifted out of the misty air, tickling Selene's ear until she recognized it as Albatross singing again.

. . . and one door leads to Hell, and the Great Gate in between them has secrets it won't tell. Go ask Sammy, before she fell . . .

Selene turned around, surprised that Albatross should know that song, but Albatross was standing mute, a look of surprise spreading across her face. Even as she watched, Selene heard the voice again. The voice of Albatross, but not *her* Albatross.

. . . if you go hunting nightmares, and you think you're going to cry . . . Tell 'em all their nightmares come true on the day before they die. You call Sammy, when she was the sky . . .

Now her Albatross opened her mouth, and sang, her voice echoing perfectly the first, which was growing louder with every word.

"When the damned go swimming in blood—and the fruit is hanging low, and hope hangs like a chain on your neck, and you don't know where to go . . ."

And there, sailing down at them from out of the cold, gray sky, hanging from tattered wings like strips of cloud, was Albatross. Her dress was in shreds, but she was carrying Shae under both armpits, and as they came in low, the woman's legs began to tread the air, so when they hit the ground it was at a run, and Albatross was practically shouting: *"Call the white bird, because she'll know!"*

Letting go of Shae, she turned into a solid streak of white, and Selene had the presence of mind to duck as the spirit passed low over her head, colliding with the fragment of herself who leapt to greet her, the two joining together in a flash of white light.

Selene had no chance to see what became of the two fragments in the moment after their fusion, for she was nearly knocked off her feet as Shae plowed into her, embracing her with strong arms—shield and all—and nearly lifting her off her feet.

"You made it! You *made* it!" she cried, practically into Selene's ear.

Selene, dizzy with surprise, hung onto Shae's powerful arm like it was an anchor, and found herself wheezing, "You actually *waited* . . . "

She regretted the words instantly, when she saw Shae's face flushed a pretty, pleased pink. In that instant the untouchable façade was broken, and the woman looked both younger and more vulnerable. She was no longer an unfeeling Amazonian goddess, but a real person with real feelings and real (if not immediately obvious) flaws. It made Selene's face hot with shame.

Luckily Shae was too caught up in her own jubilation to notice, squeezing Selene tightly before releasing her almost regretfully. Even then she gripped both Selene's shoulders, staring at her as though she could scarcely believe her eyes, alternately smiling and shaking her head.

"We went 'round," she explained, disjointedly. "A whole circle backward, looking for you! And then I realized you were probably on the other edge, so we ran it *again* but we never caught up to you, and I figured you'd probably gone on, so we cut though the sixth circle and went from there. But when we got here and *still* nothing I started to think maybe we'd lost you, but then Albatross heard singing and said it was herself and . . . "

She trailed off, beaming at Selene, who stared back, trying to fix this image of Shae in her head. This was the real Shae, she was sure, or at least the original, before she'd been buried in responsibility.

"Yeah," she said eventually, reaching up to touch Shae's elbow reassuringly. "Space in Hell is all . . . gone to hell," she said, still feeling lame. But Shae laughed uproariously, clapping her on the shoulder so hard Selene staggered from the blow.

"No kidding. I don't know what, if any, goddess is spotting us, but she's got a fantastic sense of dramatic timing."

Selene said nothing to this but pulled gently away to check on Albatross, who had been suspiciously silent.

She was, it turned out, in deep conversation with the ninth-circle demon, who appeared to be making a heartfelt attempt at a kind of sign language. Knife hands and white hands flickered back and forth, and skull-head and soft, feathery head were bent together.

"Who is *that?*" Shae asked.

"He—she—they're a ... uh ... " Selene stuttered, unsure how to explain. While she cast about for the right words, Albatross pulled away from the demon, and together they turned to face outward, toward the tenth circle, where, down and away—far away, almost lost in the distance—there was a dark cloud spreading over the pale yellow ground.

Only it was not a cloud, Selene saw as it got larger and larger. It was a horde of black bodies, winged and twisted, and in their center, twinkling like an evening star, was a single bright light, ringed by a rainbow halo.

"No way," Selene muttered, resorting to denial in place of hope. Because it would be too much to hope.

But the horde came on, and Albatross—thirteen-fold Albatross—led them. Wingless, but borne on a rainbow aura that stained the demons closest to her in lurid colors, they raised a pale dust below them and pushed a mad wind in front. Selene felt it pass over them in waves: hot and dry, warm and sticky, the stench of ten circles of torment bundled together and driven before the storm that was Albatross and her following—and they were *following*, not chasing—of demons.

A blast of air hit them. Not hot or cold, but clear, and the intensity of it stung Selene's eyes so that she began to cry. It raised memories of a night from another life, spent in a smoky bar where a gorgeous woman with a magnificent afro had sung "The Grave of Mercy" like Martin and Goodfield only wished they could have, but with altered lyrics. Selene had forgotten them save for the comfort they had given her at the time, being uplifting rather than ominous, but as Albatross approached under the bow of colors, in whose light the demons were almost beautiful—like mysterious fish with elaborate fins—one couplet came back to her ...

But our sisters will be saved by the goddesses that they made.

And she sang it, like she had never sung anything in her life on or below Earth, with a lungful of that fierce, clear air, and for one incredible moment she heard the music too. It swelled from the ground, vibrating in the soles of her feet and lifting the loose pebbles scattered over the surface. Then she realized that was not music, but their little double-Albatross. She had begun to sparkle and shine, the air fizzing around her as she launched herself into the air, two beams of gold light spreading winglike from her shoulders.

With a feeling like a hundred soundless trumpets blasting in her ears, Selene watched through streaming eyes as the rainbow vision and the golden beam arced toward each other.

They did not collide but fell into a concentric orbit, two stars locked by their mutual gravity, spiraling closer and closer together.

There was a scrabbling near the ground, and to her surprise, the ninth circle demon came crawling frantically to hide behind her legs. Selene did not blame it. She had raised her shield to shade her eyes, but this time she watched, unafraid, as she was unable to look away, as the two pieces of Albatross spiraled together, creating a brief double helix of gold and rainbow in a patch of clear sky abandoned by the demonic host, and then spun into one shape, casting out a thin cloud of something that sparkled gold and red and bright blue, as a figure of pure, white light with a rainbow corona emerged from the center and began to grow.

And grow . . . and *grow*. Its legs descended downward and so did its torso, until it had to take a step in among the stone spires, where its feet were lost in the mist. They must have found solid ground, for it stabilized with the level of the plain at approximately waist height, its shoulders looming above them and its face distant but bright against the sky.

There was no smoke now, or heaviness to the air. They were all within the overpowering and exclusive influence of Albatross's aura, and she gleamed at them with skin like mother-of-pearl, her face a benevolent, shining oval, haloed with feathery hair that still retained flashes of gold among its drifting white locks.

And that's only a little more than half of her . . . Selene thought weakly. Glancing at Shae she guessed the woman was thinking similar thoughts. As for the ninth-circle demon, it was cowering practically between her legs. She patted the back of its skull-head awkwardly.

"It's okay," she said through lips numb with awe. "It's still Albatross. She is still our friend."

She'd meant the words to comfort herself as much as the demon, but as soon as she said them she knew they were true. Albatross was grinning down at them, even as her following of demons clustered in a respectful shadow under her shoulder blades. A hand the size of a wide dinner table extended, the fingers making a lumpy ramp from palm to ground, and Selene understood this without question.

Taking the demon gingerly by one red arm, she coaxed it up into the hand with her, while Shae fairly leapt onto the palm. The bottom dipped as the fingers cupped protectively around them, and then in a dizzying rush they were lifted off the ground, rushing through the sharp air as Albatross carried them gently away into the mists of the Ninth Ring of Hell.

So this is a song you might think you know, but I've changed it. And you might think, 'that bitch has got some balls changing Martin and Goodfield,' but I'm here to tell ya, we don't need songs that tell us we's angry—we knows we's angry! And we don't need songs that tells us we been wronged—cause we know we been wronged. I tell you, we need songs that tell us we gonna survive. And we gonna rise above all this pain and torture that we been put through. So that's what this song is, at least the way I sing it. Okay, so here we go . . .

Greeting darkness like a friend
She's come to play the fool again
Though you had thought she died in flames
And still bears all of your hurt and blame

Blood and Fury

But she won't suffer the lies that you have sown
To be grown
Upon the grave of mercy

Because you see the dark you fear
You fear because it brings her near
Down your heart and up your spine
You cannot run from what's inside your mind

And in the nighttime the ugly truth is laid out bare
So you might stare
Into the grave of mercy

And from that hollow watch her rise
See blood and fury in her eyes
Out of words and out of meaning
She is a voice in pain, screaming

And all the virtue that from her you once stole
Was swallowed whole
Into the grave of mercy

Now truth rising from her well
Come to shame you I can tell
Her teeth are swords and fingers claw
Your lies will be sunk into her maw

Though you may beg with a whispered breath
Peace ended in the death of mercy

But our sisters will be saved
By the goddesses that they made
Though their vision is still forming
They are the rays of a new morning

And the signs say that
The most beautiful monster that you have ever seen
Our Once and Future Queen
Is rising from her grave with mercy!

—The Grave of Mercy/*Martin and Goodfield*

as sung by Umbré LaSera
in a bar somewhere in the Midwest, United States, circa 2007

FEAR NOT ^{7.}

Detroit, MI
Late Summer

JILL HAD NEVER paid much attention to the relative lengths of the days following the summer solstice before, but now that the time during which the sun shone kept her inside for fear of developing instant, excruciating burns all over her skin, she marked the slowly lengthening nights with hungry anticipation. She must, she thought, have gone a little stir crazy that summer from being cooped up so much of the time.

"I just sleep more," Lansing had said when Jill had confided in her.

"I don't like sleeping," Jill said. "It's not like it was . . . before."

Before the change, she meant. When she had been so exhausted from fighting the wasting magical poisoning that she'd slept twice the normal amount. But that at least had been real, human sleep. Not the dead blackness she experienced now. It was a way to make time pass, not a means to rejuvenation. She didn't *need* sleep, so more often than not she would work straight through the days in her laboratory under the old station.

When her brain got too full, or when she simply couldn't think anymore, she would either check out and spend a few minutes staring blankly at whatever was in front of her, or she would take Frosty for a run.

Lansing shrugged. "You get used to it."

Jill didn't want to get to it. When she was honest with herself—which was more and more these days—she didn't like the false sleep of a vampire because it felt too much like the dead blackness she had experienced during her transmutation. And there was the underlying worry, however unfounded, that she wouldn't wake up in the normal way, that she might sleep for days, or weeks, or years, under the earth. Wake up to find that everyone she cared about was dead, that the whole fledgeling enterprise she had been building had collapsed around her, and she was lying blistering in the sun.

One experiment Jill had not undertaken was to test her resistance to sunlight. Lansing had to avoid even indirect contact, as direct exposure would be enough to burn her to a cinder in minutes—or so she claimed—and although, from the accidental encounters Jill had experienced, her reaction was not so extreme, she was in no hurry to repeat the process—even for science.

What she could do was observe what did *not* elicit a spontaneous meltdown of her extremities: white-balanced LEDs, for example, caused her no problems. Not even grow-lights. Infrared light and lasers were safe—or as safe as they were to a living human. Fluorescent and incandescent lights were also harmless. Black lights and other high UV sources did cause an eczema-like reaction after repeated exposure, but this could be prevented by a physical barrier—the same way she could be shielded from direct sunlight.

Strangely, it was not a simple intolerance of high frequency electromagnetic radiation, as Jill discovered when they got their imaging lab set up. She had been wanting to experiment with X-rays as a means of detecting magical density, only to discover they were absolutely useless. Test X-rays of Mantha's pinky finger read the same as Clara's, which read the same as Marcus's, which read the same as Ariel's. The only anomalies were Jill's, whose finger bones looked like ghosts of ghosts, and Lansing's, whose didn't show up at all. Neither of them had adverse reactions to the exposure, and Jill's somewhat befuddled conclusion was that vampires—and pseudo-vampires—were of a consistency that didn't absorb or scatter that frequency of radiation.

Jill didn't conclude from this that she was immune to alpha-particle radiation, but considering that her illness had presented as cancer caused by radiation damage, and that the only effective treatment for it had been vampire blood, she suspected this might be the case. But until they got a particle accelerator or access to enriched uranium, there was no way to test it—and she had other things to take up her attention.

There was the company, first and foremost. The Moonshield Center for Supernatural Investigation and Research had, over the summer, produced its first conclusive findings—namely, that ghosts were real. It was something that everyone at MCSIR had accepted as fact very early on, but proving it conclusively and rationally had been an astonishing achievement. Grants, both public and private, poured in. Contracts were offered—and most often refused—and to forestall the capitalization of the ghost-detection field, Jill put all her research up on their public web archive, with detailed instructions for building your own ghost detector and how to properly operate it. There was talk of Jill being nominated for a Nobel. Which Nobel, it seemed, was being debated. Yet for all the public acclaim Jill was frustrated by people's reactions. Snake oil salesmen took it as an opportunity to up their game. Some people took it as proof of God. Or Aliens. Or both. And the media presented it as a solitary discovery rather than the harbinger of a much broader sea change.

The only people who understood were the scientists sensitive enough and rational enough to see through the hype to the distressing truth: there existed in the world a whole host of forces that were not understood and were very difficult to study. But some organizations were up to the challenge. Jill's old alma mater, UC Santa Cruz, granted her an honorary doctorate and, at her request, sent an evolutionary biology professor to head MCSIR's Supernaturalism department.

Professor Okedo, with more gray in his hair than Jill remembered and wearing an ugly camel-colored overcoat he had apparently bought second hand at the same time as his plane ticket, arrived on the steps of MCSIR in the late afternoon with a small suitcase full of clothes and a big one full of specimens and equipment.

Marcus had greeted him. Marcus, though big and black and male and aggressively red-headed, had become the de facto receptionist of MCSIR on the grounds that he appeared the least distressing to the "conventionals." He was also good at reading people, and could distinguish quickly between those who were sensationalist and those with valid concerns. Also he steadfastly kept regular diurnal hours. He had shown Professor Okedo all over the center and got him settled in his apartment on the fifteenth floor, where most of the living quarters were located, before the time Jill was able to show her head above ground.

They went out for a late dinner—all of them, except for Lansing, who stayed behind to watch the front desk—to the Mexican kitchen on Bagley, whose proprietor had adopted the entire staff and had so far accepted her new neighbor as to put supernatural-themed specials on the menu. She had even made arrangements for their butcher to supply them with pig, chicken, and—when available—cow brains, so Don could have something to eat as well.

They trouped in, all eight of them, and pushed together tables so that they could sit in a great, gangling circle. Jill ordered chips and guacamole for the group and went around making introductions.

"Everyone, this is Ronald Okedo," she began, indicating the middle-aged man with gray hair, a notable belly, dark skin, and a pronounced epicanthic eye fold. "He used to be my biology professor back at UC Santa Cruz. Professor, you maybe remember Clara? Yes." A nod at the tall, bald, pale-faced and blue-eyed woman in black biking leathers. "And next to her is Mantha, who she's taking care of."

Mantha was a small, mousy girl, olive-skinned with dark hair and eyes. Ronald Okedo found his attention sliding off her—probably because of what she was sitting next to. Which looked like—

"And the stuffed rabbit is Lady Bibbit," Jill said, as if this was perfectly normal. "Don't panic if she sometimes looks real. She is real, but everyone sees her a little differently." She moved on, barely giving Okedo time to come to terms with an animated stuffed rabbit, to the blindingly handsome, golden-haired man with laughing eyes and jaw-dropping cheekbones. "That's Ariel, he's a friend. Marcus you already met. Tamerlain is next to him; they have five different bodies and we're still trying to figure out what's going on."

Tamerlain, who was a rather striking teenage girl with luminous blue eyes even a pair of glasses could not mask and frizzy blond hair, smiled and waved shyly.

"And this is Don Lelain—he's going to be your assistant, since your department is going to be researching people like him."

At last Okedo turned to look at his neighbor, who he had been politely avoiding staring at until this implicit permission was given.

Don had gray skin. Not just gray*ish*—really gray. He looked . . . well, he looked dead. There was a milky sheen to his eyes, and his lips were blackish-purple. He wore a knit beanie which covered his hair and ears, a turtleneck shirt with very long sleeves, and he had put on a pair of nitrile gloves as soon as they sat down. He had a tall glass of water next to him and hadn't touched the chips.

Okedo cleared his throat. Ordinarily he didn't ask questions like these, but he felt it was acceptable in this case, as they would be working together.

"If it's not inappropriate," he said, as politely as he could, "may I ask what sort of people are like him?"

Don chuckled. His gums were gray.

"Colloquially, you'd call him a zombie," Jill said. "Physically, he's dead. But consciously, he's not. Like me and Lansing, but not like me and Lansing. Part of your job's going to be figuring that out."

It was a very interesting dinner. Tamerlain was quiet, eating her way through half the guac, a chimichanga and its attendant sides, as well as three bowls of chips and two large sodas, while Don ate his bowl of spiced mush with mincing little spoonfuls. Jill ate nothing at all but talked non-stop about her work, their work, and the work she hoped Okedo would be doing. Ariel charmed the waitress into giving Mantha a free refill of her milkshake, which earned him such a look from Clara that Okedo made a mental note never to give Mantha sweets ever. An open confrontation was avoided, however, when Jill's work phone went off. After a quick exchange she passed it to Clara, who left the table to talk to the person on the other end in a quick, serious voice. The upshot was that when she returned, leaving the phone at Jill's side, it was to announce that Lansing had a job for her in Ann Arbor.

"Ariel, will you watch Mantha?"

"Sure," said Ariel, sunnily. "Mantha, wanna go to Ann Arbor?"

Mantha, sucking down the last of her second milkshake, nodded vigorously.

"I didn't mean—" Clara said, looking desperately at Jill.

"Good," said Jill. "I'm glad you'll have backup. Check in every quarter, okay, Ariel?"

"Yes, ma'am," said Ariel, levering himself out of his seat. He favored his right hip in the way of one in that dangerous stage of recovery where it was good enough to use but not yet fully healed.

He was an odd combination of characteristics. Classic masculine beauty—square jaw, strong nose, assertive posture—but a glittering, expressive, almost irreverent personality. Yet he appeared to take common sense and precaution very seriously. Okedo watched them exit the restaurant, Clara in the lead and Ariel bringing up the rear, with Mantha hand-in-hand with her animated stuffed rabbit between them, and had to shake himself to be sure of what he had seen. He had, he assured himself, seen the rabbit get up and walk hoppingly out next to the girl. She had not been dragged along by one arm, like a stuffed toy animal should.

He was still wrestling with this double vision when Jill said, almost under her breath, "I'm glad we got him."

"Ariel?"

"Yeah," said Jill. "He's a lifesaver. And . . . just . . . Clara's great, but her job is . . . it's better that she have a wingman."

"Ah," said Okedo. He stopped himself from asking after the other woman—Serena, or something like that. He figured he would learn what had become of her in due course, and he was not disappointed.

"She had some close calls, after we lost Selene," Jill continued.

Okedo knew better than to ask what that meant. Jill was not a person to mince words unless the whole was truly unpalatable. He also noticed how Tamerlain had gone bright pink, and decided it was time to steer the conversation down a different avenue.

"And you let little Mantha go with them?"

Jill pursed her lips. "Mantha goes where she wants," she said. "She's . . . special."

"Special . . . like?" Okedo glanced inadvertently at Tamerlain.

"We're not sure," Jill said. "She's Clara's project."

And there the subject was left. Tamerlain opened up with Ariel's absence, becoming almost chatty. Okedo split a piece of chocolate cake with her, and she told him all about how she had wound up at MCSIR. Okedo listened in increasing wonder at the tale of a girl who had spontaneously turned into a *different* girl, and then a young man, and then a dog, and finally a giant, anthropomorphic tiger, and somehow befriended Don-the-zombie along the way.

"Sounds like you have your hands full," Okedo said, half laughing. The story had a streak of absurdity in it and he was grateful for the lightening of the mood.

But Jill was staring at him gravely, her eyes shimmering strangely behind her glasses.

"You haven't seen the half of it," she said.

* * *

They piled, all four of them, into Arcana, in whose voluminous cab there was still room for Clara's sword, Ariel's cane, and both their travel cases. There was a brief scuffle on the passenger side as Ariel and Mantha each tried to offer the front seat to the other. Mantha won the implied contest, and so it was Ariel who settled himself gingerly into the front seat next to Clara, who spent the whole time with both hands on the steering wheel, staring stonily at the driveway.

"*Mea culpa,*" Ariel said as he stretched his bad leg so that most of his weight fell on his good hip.

"What for?" Clara asked, her voice perfectly blank.

"The milkshake?" Ariel suggested.

In the back, Mantha burped loudly.

"Mantha is perfectly capable of arranging her own milkshakes," Clara pointed out.

"Yeah, but I like the way Ariel does it," Mantha said. "I'm learning from him."

"No, no," said Ariel, cheerfully. "Don't do that."

Clara sighed.

"Look," said Ariel. "I'm sorry if you wanted some alone time with Unicorn, but how am I supposed to keep an eye on you if I sit out every call?"

"I thought you were keeping an eye on Mantha," Clara said, starting the engine. She had put an address into her phone and the phone into a holster which held it up next to the steering wheel. Currently it was directing her toward I-96 West.

"I can do that too," said Ariel. "Got two eyes, don't I? Got that, kiddo?" he said, winking at Mantha. "Stay on my bad side."

"Got it," said Mantha, grinning.

Clara gave Ariel a sour glance.

"Don't worry," said Lady Bibbit, blandly. "I'll make sure he doesn't reinjure himself."

"Hey," said Ariel.

"Thank you," said Clara, finally putting the truck in gear. "Lansing, this is Nordstern. We are en route. ETA twenty-two hundred."

"Copy that," said Lansing out of the radio perched in the center divide. "Drive safely."

It was a dark night, but the summer skies were clear and the horizon was dimly pink from the sprawling, sporadic city. I-96 was empty, and Clara left the cruise control on all the way to Ann Arbor.

Frosty was restless that night. She would lie down for maybe a minute and then get up and pace the wall by the door of Jill's office, white nails clacking loudly on the wood floor, occasionally whining and scraping at the doorjamb. It was distracting, and also confusing. Frosty had demonstrated that she could and would go where she liked within the building—or out of it, for that matter—doors and gates and windows be damned.

She had adopted Jill more decisively than any cat, and considered it her solemn duty to watch over Jill while at the same time being fiercely independent.

Jill could only conclude that this current behavior was meant to indicate that she wanted *Jill* to go outside. With her.

But Jill was up to her elbows in unprocessed data from the magical activity gauges she had planted around the city the previous night and was besides monitoring their dispatch feed for updates from Clara and would not be moved.

But data processing was boring, tedious work, especially when the picture the data showed was incomplete, and around midnight, after Clara checked in to say that the incident in Ann Arbor had been minor and closed on site, Jill gave in and took Frosty for a walk.

It was, according to her weather app, an unseasonably cool night. But since it was nowhere near freezing, and since freezing was the only temperature that meant anything to Jill, she walked outside in nothing but the slacks and cotton shirt she'd put on earlier that evening. Frosty, with her bright red collar, tugged her urgently down the drive and through the park at the end of her equally bright red leash, clearly with her own ideas about where the outing would take them.

In this way they got under two freeways and through Downtown without Jill noticing either. They kept going, the gleaming white coat of the yell hound shining between the ponds of yellow streetlight, her ears as red as her collar and leash. Her mouth hung open, eager.

The world blurred around Jill. The city faded into the background, and she was walking over wild land. Running. She was running. They were running. For no reason Jill understood, but it was glorious. And frightening. Jill felt like she was losing hold on who she was.

She had stopped breathing, that was her problem. Forcing her lungs to inflate, to exhale, inhale, again and again, until she was panting like her dog, and as the oxygen percolated through her system the world solidified again.

They were walking sedately through a cemetery. The trees were dark with their summer foliage, and in their shadows the ghosts of the resident dead watched their passage.

Jill breathed, watching back curiously. As soon as they saw her looking, the ghosts ignored her and Frosty with a sort of forced casualness. They marked their passage—some even made eye contact—but few of them acknowledged her presence. The most she caught were hurriedly deflected glances, and once, a too-cheerful wave.

"Are they *afraid* of us?" Jill wondered out loud.

And a voice—she thought it was Frosty—answered:

"Would you not be?"

Jill stopped. She had to dig in her heels to bring her dog around, but once Frosty realized she was in earnest, the hound sat down to wait—but she did it at the full extent of the lead. She whined.

But Jill stood still, staring at the ground between her feet, breathing forcefully and deeply, until her vision slowly retracted to something resembling that of a normal human. When she looked up, Frosty was only as bright as an ordinarily white dog on a dark night, and her ears barely had a hint of rust to them.

That meant Jill was seeing almost exclusively by conventional biological means—namely, the rod cells in her retinas. She hadn't the equipment to test definitively that, when deprived of oxygen, her body would shut down such processes that relied on conventional metabolism, but it had been her conjectured experience. And although she could arguably see, hear, move, and sense things far more accurately through her unconventional vampiric metabolism, the disconnection to herself that came with it was profoundly disturbing. It was like having disassociation with the entire world.

The problem was, when she gained her vampiric metabolism, and with it an apparent immunity to cancerous mutations, she had lost a certain amount of autonomic nervous reflexes—like breathing. So, still concentrating on inhaling and exhaling, she straightened up and looked around.

The ghosts were gone. Or at least, gone invisible. Frosty and Jill were on a wide path of cracked cement, and there were grave markers all around them. The path led to a pool of yellow light, in which there was a street sign. Jill dragged Frosty down to it, to discover they had somehow gotten as far as the Elmwood Cemetery.

"Right," said Jill, tugging on Frosty's leash. "Time to head home."

And, though Frosty whined and dragged at little at first, eventually she returned to her lead position, trotting happily, her tail in the air. Jill was careful to keep breathing and, this time, was able to keep track of their progress as they worked their way slowly west, through Lafayette Park, Greektown, and into Downtown, where Frosty dragged Jill south to the river walk, skirting the long, desolate crawl up Michigan Avenue. Jill had to admit it was much more pleasant walking along the deserted promenade, with the dark waters of the Detroit River splashing off to their left. The sound drew Jill's attention backward, and she found herself recalling the experience, not long before her transformation, when she had purposefully jumped into such water—with little expectation of seeing the surface again.

I could jump in right now, she thought, idly. *Swim and swim and swim, and not drown.*

But what would be waiting for her, down in the depths of the river? Where she could not breathe, could not connect with the solid, tangible world into which she had been born? Would she be able to remain herself, down in the dark depths?

Deep breaths, in and out. The cement under her feet. It was patterned with alternating dark and light blocks of concrete, littered here and there with the odd wrapper or empty soda cup. Frosty's claws clicked softly on it as she trotted along.

Jill kept walking. Eventually they got home.

Ronald Okedo settled into his new role more quickly than anyone expected—including himself. Though the first two months were by necessity filled with the interruptions attendant upon anyone recently moved—changing his address, updating his driver's license, not to mention switching health insurance—with additionally a few surprises unique to his situation. To wit, he discovered a goblin living in the closet of his apartment.

It was the size of a small cat and spoke in a jabbering, yammering language which no one could understand, but which Clara identified as a subterranean dialect. It seemed to understand them well enough and could be bribed to do just about anything by the offer of Spam. No one had any idea where it had come from.

Jill's reaction, after coaxing it into the lab and measuring its magical amplitude and aptitude, taking skin and nail samples, and making a good-faith attempt at communication, was to let it continue living as it had before.

Clara had made disgruntled noises, remarking that goblins usually lived in colonies, and this might be the beginning of an infestation.

"Then we'll keep our eyes open," Jill had said. "I'll let dispatch know."

This was another aspect of the operation that surprised Okedo—though in retrospect it was just the kind of logical program Jill would want to implement. MCSIR assisted the Detroit Police Department, Fire and Rescue, and Animal Control, consulting on cases of aggravated supernatural phenomena that necessarily intruded into their jurisdictions, and receiving such artifacts and persons who were not so much illegal as they were confounding. Tamerlain had been one, and in his very first week, Okedo handled the reception, from a very tired community-service officer, of a disoriented werewolf.

"He's already been through the jail, twice. But as soon as he gets out, it's back to being a stray dog. The pound won't take him. Jail doesn't want him—he's *clean*, you understand."

"Of course," said Okedo, peering uncertainly at the grimy, scruffy dog cowering behind the officer's legs, its tail plastered to its belly.

"You're new here, aren't you?" asked the officer.

"Yes—sort of," said Okedo. "I've been following Jill's work since she began. I just transferred from Santa Cruz."

"Well, welcome to the new normal," said the officer, handing him the leash.

This, Okedo would learn, was more-or-less true. Stray werewolves made up the bulk of their intake—both from the DPD and various mental health facilities.

"It's because Detroit is neutral territory," Don explained to him. "We've got rival packs north, east, south, and west. But none of them can claim Detroit, so we get the rejects and strays filtering down here."

Don took care of said strays. It had been discovered that werewolves behaved more like humans, and spent more time as humans, the more humanely you treated them. Unfortunately this also put the caretaking human at risk of bites—which, though not necessarily infectious, were still painful—and so that task usually fell to Don. He was immune to the particular agent which characterized the werewolf's nature, and took physical injury with the kind of calmness only a dead person could.

"They're usually with us for a couple weeks, then they're either rehomed or taken on staff. A lot of them work with us part time."

The particular werewolf Okedo met in his first week turned out to be an especially bad case. He roomed with Don for almost a month, and even when he graduated into his own apartment, stayed on at MCSIR as part-time assistant, part-time lap dog.

"I wish our legal system was set up to allow for transformative humans," Jill was heard to groan. "He'd make a great therapy dog—if he could just get *employed* as such."

"What you need," Lansing told her, "is a dedicated center for werewolf rehab."

Okedo found himself glancing nervously, and not for the first time, at Lansing. The trim young woman, almost androgynous in her presentation, was the personification of all the things that were a little off about Jill, taken to the extreme. She was extremely pale, extremely sharp, and only breathed for the express purpose of speaking. And she never worked directly with the werewolves.

"They don't like me," she explained to Okedo. Pointing a narrow, white finger at her face, she said: "Vampire."

"Have you ever had a problem with stray vampires?" Okedo asked.

Lansing shook her head. "Vampires don't stray. We go to ground. Or we're taken care of by our makers."

She didn't say it as though she were proud of the fact. If anything, Okedo thought, Lansing held an intense dislike for her fellow vampires, and he wondered if there was perhaps one stray vampire at MCSIR after all.

MCSIR seemed to be staffed by strays and outcasts, who had clumped together into a strange, modular family united by the vaguely nebulous drive to figure out what the hell was going on.

Which, Okedo soon realized, something was. Jill, true to her nature, had kept scrupulous records of all her tests and readings, the intake and output of supernatural beings, and now that she had been at it for almost nine months, a definite trend in supernatural activity was beginning to emerge.

It was trending up.

Instances of aggravated supernatural phenomena were becoming so common in Detroit that dispatch designated a code for it (ASP), and in September, three of the more stable rehabbed werewolves were put in charge of MCSIR's own call center—where they could communicate with Detroit's 9-1-1 dispatchers directly. The result was a monumental spike in ASPs requesting assistance from a MCSIR field operative, and Okedo thought Clara—as the sole person qualified to take such calls—would work herself into an early grave.

The situation improved slightly when Ariel declared Marcus fit for field work, and insisted he himself be put to use in that capacity as well.

"It's been *three months*," he was heard to argue when Clara made disapproving noises. "Sometimes I forget which hip was injured!"

Clara was not satisfied, but Jill was, and so Ariel began answering calls as well. They rarely came so frequently that they needed more than one operative responding at once, but calls would come with no regard to the regular work day, and so Clara, Ariel and Marcus took their work in eight-hour shifts to cover the whole clock. Mantha accompanied whoever was working during the day, and Frosty rode along with the night person. In this way they satisfied Jill's other requirement: that no one work cases alone.

Nevertheless, whenever a call necessitated an in-person visit outside the city, it was always Clara, accompanied by Ariel and Mantha and Lady Bibbit, who made the journey. It left MCSIR cripplingly shorthanded. That was the only reason Okedo could see why Jill finally caved to Tamerlain's incessant requests that they be trained as a field operative.

"As long as your *parents* agree," Jill had cautioned.

"Of course," said Tamerlain, with all the gravity of their six-foot tall, male, African-American body to back it up. Then they ruined the effect by adding nervously, "Just make it sound like I'm getting advanced first-aid training, yeah?"

Tamerlain had so far come to terms with their unusual situation that they had room to be curious about everything else presently going haywire in the world, and jumped into Jill's training course with gusto. By the end of the month they were shadowing Marcus, and in the second week of October they were cleared for solo duty. This freed Clara and Ariel to go on longer "away missions" as Tamerlain called them, much to Okedo's relief.

It wasn't that he disliked either of them. Quite the contrary. Clara he respected, and Ariel was as congenial as a golden retriever—and looked a bit like one, too. But together they behaved like an old married couple, constantly bickering and arguing in a low-key way that set Okedo's teeth on edge. And all this while steadfastly maintaining that there was *nothing* between them. At least, that was what Clara indicated the one time Lansing made the observation out loud. Okedo had been on the other side of the cafeteria and could have sworn he felt the temperature drop, such was the chill of Clara's gaze. The subject was never broached again.

He did ask Mantha, before things got so hairy that there was no time for idle conversation, if their interactions bothered her. The girl had shrugged.

"It's because they care about each other," she had said, frightening in her solemnity and perception. "But Ariel is hot and Clara is cold. They are still learning each other and themselves."

He still did not know what to make of Mantha. She looked too dark to be Clara's relative, but that was how the two interacted, like some casual combination of sister to sister or mother to daughter. Eventually Okedo settled on the idea that Mantha was Clara's distant cousin, and since she wasn't his problem, was content to leave it at that.

The summer passed, and only the shortening of the days told Clara it had been there at all. The persistently cool weather which had typified that unusual season slipped imperceptibly into the brisk days of fall, and it felt like the autumnal equinox sprang upon them like a pouncing cat.

Clara had a sense for the darkness beyond the simple impingement of the lengthening nights. It was a shift in the balance of the world more subtle and more profound. Here, on the far side of September 21st, powers that had been in the background came to the fore. So she was not surprised in the slightest when MCSIR began receiving more and more calls for help—or just plain advice. And though some came from as far away as Europe, any that were remotely within driving distance, that sounded like something Jill hadn't heard of before, she and Ariel were dispatched to investigate. These included a small herd of possessed horses in Kentucky, an outbreak of hauntings in Traverse City, and a man in Chicago claiming to be the Anti-Christ.

They found out about that last one only because Flammard himself called it in.

"Is he?" Clara asked, once the situation had been explained to her.

"He's something," Flammard said, sounding tense. "I think he's a bit like you and me. He could be an antichrist. I'm not sure. But he's disturbing things. Bad things."

"I don't want to get involved," was left unsaid, but Clara took her brother's meaning. Flammard had so far distanced himself from her world and their family's way of life as to eschew almost all of his preternatural abilities. He did not, as he called it, like to "cheat." But some things could not be switched off, and his sensitivity to the supernatural ambiance was one of them.

"There's a possible antichrist in Chicago," she announced at the next staff meeting. These were held in the gray area of the evening when most people were eating dinner. Sometimes meals were consumed over the course of the meeting, but since it spanned the transition from the day shift to the night shift, what that meal was varied from person to person.

"Another one?" Ariel asked, sounding almost amused. He had accidentally-on-purpose ordered an excessively large burrito and was splitting it with Mantha.

"Possibly," said Clara.

"I thought antichrists were undetectable," Lansing said.

"Usually, they are," said Jill. "But we have enough documented occurrences that we can make an educated guess. Uh . . . whose guess is this, anyway?"

"Flammard's," said Clara, simply.

"Oh, well, then . . . " Jill said, opening up the company calendar. "I guess you'd better get to Chicago."

"I'm sorry," said Okedo. "Who is Flammard?"

"My brother," said Clara, with such frigid blankness that no one asked any more questions.

Mantha's curiosity was piqued. She'd heard Clara speak of her brother before, but she had never said much about him. Now, it appeared, they were going to the city where he lived. She might get to meet him!

Exchanging a glance with Ariel, she determined he felt the same. He cleared his throat, wiped sour cream off his stubbly chin, and said, "I'll go check Arcana's fluids and tire pressure," and scooted back from the table.

They left early the next morning. Clara had stayed up all night packing, so Ariel drove. It was supposedly over four hours from Detroit to Chicago, but they made it in three and a half. Combined with the hour they gained from driving west, this meant they were arriving at Flammard's apartment around the time normal people were having breakfast.

Flammard, it turned out, lived at the top of a wonderful brick house on a quiet, shady street, whose trees were in the full glory of their autumn foliage. Arcana barely fit between the cars parallel parked along both sides of the road, and Clara got out to spot Ariel while he backed and filled into a spot between two shiny Hondas. She remained there, standing, staring at the truck, long after Ariel had collected his briefcase and Mantha and Lady Bibbit had tumbled out of the back seat.

"Something wrong?" Ariel asked, standing at the gate onto the defiantly green lawn guarding the front of the house.

A light breeze blew through the trees, chasing a few stray leaves across the sidewalk.

"The last time I was here, Selene drove Arcana," Clara said eventually. She said it quietly, and Mantha had to strain to catch her words. "I'd told her not to come. She came anyway. Now that she is gone I wish she was here."

Mantha wobbled from foot to foot. She felt a deep, sore tugging in her chest, the sour grief which lingered from the loss of her grandmother, which was compounded by the sympathetic sorrow she felt for Clara, and the second-hand grief she felt for someone she had never met. She felt very full of feelings, helpless, and frustrated that there was nothing she could do to make it better.

Ariel seemed to know what to do. He went over to where Clara stood and gently rested his hand on her elbow, threading his fingers through the crook of it. He said nothing, neither drawing Clara away nor holding her still, but standing at her side until the moment passed. Another breath of wind sent the leaf skittering back the other way, and with its passage Clara shivered to life, turning purposefully away from the truck and toward the tall brick house.

They were let in by a young woman named Lalai, who was soft and small and brown and appeared to know Clara. She blinked a little at Lady Bibbit, but whatever she saw, she didn't seem bothered by it. She found places for all four of them to sit in the small, lush living room which looked out over the front yard. This was crowded with a sofa, bookcase, loveseat, and numerous embroidered pillows scattered over the floor. A drafting table took up the end of the room with better light, and the walls there were plastered with sheets of paper, some of them scrawled with notes, others with sketches in pencil. These seemed to depict a story concerning a small, dark girl with two pigtails and a number of animals, but Mantha couldn't follow it.

Lalai made them tea and served it with delicious, sticky pastries made of flaky dough stuck together with honey and crushed nuts. She hesitated before serving Lady Bibbit, but when the rabbit said, "Two sugars, please," she dropped two cubes into the cup and handed it over without question.

"Leonard is still asleep, but he'll be up soon." she explained. "He's on midshift this week."

Clara nodded, while Ariel inquired politely as to what he did on his shift.

"He's a paramedic," Lalai told them, a flash of pride in her dark eyes. "Works with Chicago Fire and Rescue."

Because of this, and because of her experience of Clara as a larger-than-average person, Mantha began to formulate an expectation of Flammard-Leonard as a similarly tall, wide-shouldered, pale-skinned person.

Then the door to the bedroom opened, and a young man who was almost the complete opposite slipped into the room.

He was hardly taller than Lalai. He was pale, but a warm, pinkish pale, dusted with a thick coat of red freckles. His hair was flaming orange, and his eyes were a hot, reddish-brown. He was slender, small, and soft, and blazed with an aura so strong Mantha was astonished she had not noticed it before. He was as strong as Clara, in his way, but where Clara was cold and immovable, Flammard was hot and slippery. Mantha decided that, if she were to try to push him around, he would probably slide away under her influence. Like trying to hold fire.

Flammard blinked at her, and suddenly his aura shut off. Mantha felt it like a snap of cold air, and shivered. Then she looked again and saw that Flammard had only hidden it—turned it sideways and inward. It looked uncomfortable, and it made Mantha feel uncomfortable to have such a huge presence so thoroughly repressed. It was like having an invisible tiger in the room.

"Good morning, Flammard," Clara said. "We're here about the antichrist."

Flammard raised a hand, nodding, stifling a yawn. "Just a minute," he said, and slipped into the kitchen. A few minutes and the sound of boiling water later and he reappeared, holding a cup of steaming coffee in his hand. He took a pastry off the plate Lalai had assembled and dunked it in his drink, eating it over the cup so the crumbs fell into the black liquid.

"He's claiming to be *the* Anti-Christ," he said eventually. "Gods only know what he really is." His voice was as light and soft as the rest of him. Mantha was torn between liking him and being terrified of him.

"Just point us in the right direction, we'll handle the rest," Ariel said.

Flammard downed the rest of his coffee.

"What are you?" he asked.

Mantha felt her blood run cold. It was only when Ariel spoke that she realized the question had been directed at him, not her.

"Ariel Freeman," he said, touching his brow in a lazy salute.

"I know that," said Flammard. "*What* are you?"

"He's a friend," Clara said, almost defensively. Ariel laughed.

"Specifically, exorcisms," he said. "Generally, a bit of everything."

"Oh," said Flammard. He frowned. "You seem like more than that."

Ariel shrugged, grinning sunnily. He had a bit of an aura himself these days, Mantha had noticed, but most of that had to do with his personality, she thought.

"I try hard," he said.

"Very," said Flammard. He turned his attention to Lady Bibbit, and Mantha held her breath, but he said nothing.

"Right," he said. "He's calling himself Jude Carson"—a roll of those ember-warm eyes—"He's recruiting out of Hyde Park. Blatantly indoctrinating people. Has a *strong* misdirection spell over the area. I only noticed because he tried to recruit *me*."

"How'd that go?" Ariel asked.

Flammard shrugged uncomfortably. "I had to cheat," he said, as if admitting this was shameful.

Clara sighed, put her hands on her knees, and stood up.

"Hyde Park?" she said.

"Most days," Flammard said. "Be careful."

"Always," said Ariel, draining his own cup. He looked around. "Bathroom?"

Lalai pointed. After Ariel emerged, Mantha discovered she also had need of it, but after that they were all tramping down the stairs, leaving Flammard to get ready for his shift with palpable relief.

Ariel drove.

"It's fun," he said, when Clara offered to take over.

"You find it enjoyable to drive a dual-wheeled heavy duty pickup truck through the center of Chicago," Clara said, as if she had to hear the words spoken in order to believe them.

"It's the next best thing to driving a patrol car," Ariel said. "People are much more *polite*."

"You mean they are scared of you," Clara said.

"Yeah," said Ariel, his smile fading. "That too."

Mantha let almost a minute pass after this exchange before asking what she felt was the most important question:

"You've driven a police car?"

"Two years as a patrol officer," Ariel said, wagging a finger at his face. "That jerk-wad making traffic stops to lecture tailgaters every ten feet? That was me." He grinned. "For a while, anyway."

At the next red light—the city seemed to be made of red lights—Mantha leaned her elbows on the center divide and asked: "Why did you quit?"

Clara made a disapproving noise, but it was deep in her throat and mostly swallowed by Arcana's engine noise—which was permeating the cab since Ariel had his window rolled down.

"Wrong life," Ariel said, with a shrug. The car ahead of them, perhaps wishing to view something other than a giant red truck in its rearview mirrors, edged forward. When almost an entire vehicle length had been freed up, Ariel groaned, put Arcana in gear, and closed the distance. No sooner had he brought the truck to a stop again than the light turned, but in the way of backed-up traffic, it was another fifteen seconds before the nervous car in front of them began to roll, and by the time they reached the intersection the light had already gone yellow. Ariel squinted across, where the traffic was already at a standstill for the *next* light, and regretfully stopped again—right on the limit line.

"I got into police work because I wanted to help people," he said, while the left turners desperately scooted through the intersection. "Which, maybe on the right team, or the right city, that's what policing is. But where I was? Not so much. And most of the officers had their heads so twisted up their butts that it was just ridiculous. But even without that ... policing is like ... you're on the front dealing with problems caused by something on the back. Addicts and trafficked and abused people. People we'd arrest pretty much just for being victims, when it was the system that created them that needed fixing. I couldn't fix the system by writing citations or putting scared teenagers in jail, and I certainly wasn't helping, so I quit. Moved into chaplaincy and counseling. That's how I wound up in this gig"—he fingered his collar. Then slapped the hand back on the wheel as the light finally turned and he put the truck in gear. "Though it's still not fixing the system, at least I'm confident I *am* helping people. Mostly. I try hard. Like I said. That's all anyone can do."

They rolled through the intersection. A yellow convertible Mustang charged into the left lane, passed them and merged into the right lane, blasting those behind it with the sound of its revving engine as it gunned up through the traffic.

"Sometimes I miss being able to pull people over for traffic chats," Ariel remarked, as the sound of the Mustang, and the accompanying honks, faded into the distance.

They continued to inch their way south until Clara convinced Ariel to get on I-94, and then they enjoyed a brief moment of freedom before that traffic backed up again, and it was a long, slow haul down to their exit for Garfield Boulevard. From there on, both Ariel and Clara got tense and quiet, with only one or two words passing between them at a time. Mantha lapsed into her seat, shut her eyes, and experimented with trying to get a feel for the surrounding city.

It threatened to overwhelm her—there were so many people and so many *things* going on—but if she kept her attention distant, subtle patterns would emerge. She felt areas of concentrated power, like hot spots in her mind, and when gently examined, these turned out to be from various sources. Some were people. Others were animals. One was a particular tree. But knotted together, and by far the most vivid of them all, was a tangle of power and feelings a little south and east of them. The power was bright and strong, but the feelings were sour and twisted. It made Mantha's teeth hurt.

"Talk or spot?" Ariel asked as they approached this nexus.

Mantha opened her eyes to see Clara considering her answer.

"You talk," she said. "He will likely respond better to you."

"Secret admirer?"

"Whatever you judge most likely to be effective," Clara said.

"I'll get a read on him, first."

Ariel had pulled Arcana into a parking lot. It was crowded, but not full, and they were able to find a space halfway in the shade of a tall building made of tan bricks which Mantha belatedly realized was a church. She could not tell which denomination from this angle, but she guessed Catholic. The architecture had the same feel as her old church. The tangle of power, she realized, was not here, but further east.

"He's not here," she pointed out.

"I know," said Ariel. "But this is as good a parking spot as we'll ever find. Better to approach on foot—well I'll be damned."

When Mantha got out, feeling the sun sizzle on her skin and bending her knees gently, she saw the yellow Mustang from earlier parked just three cars over.

"It will take too long to forge a citation," Clara announced.

"I know," sighed Ariel. "But it would be *fun.*"

"We have work to do."

Ariel sighed. He turned away from the offending car and pulled out his briefcase. Opening it he took out a little silver tube on a chain and hung it around his neck. Mantha felt the effect it had like cold walls going up all around him, and couldn't help physically flinching a little. Clara glanced at her, but said nothing.

Thus armored, albeit invisibly, they walked the remaining blocks past the church, right into the heart of the tangled power and feelings.

Things began to go strange almost at once. To Mantha, it was like the world tried to bend away under her, leading down into a pit from which rose a thick, heady steam. Yet her feet continued to land on solid pavement, the sun continued to shine on her face, and around her she was also aware of the passing of cars and the other people on the street. But these things had taken on an insubstantiality that made them feel like mirages—or ghosts.

She gripped Lady Bibbit's paw, and the rabbit was as solid as ever, but she was disturbed to see that Ariel and Clara were as misty as the smoke and the pit—had, in fact, begun to sink into it.

She called out to them. Her voice was choked in her throat, the words swallowed before they escaped her mouth.

She was suddenly and heartily angry. She unfolded the part of herself she tried to keep restrained—the part that could push people's minds around, imbue stuffed animals with life, or create monsters out of memories and nightmares—and used it to pull them firmly out of that strange nether region and back into the real world.

"Did you feel that?" Ariel asked.

"Yes," said Clara. "Pressure, and release."

They were standing on the curb of the sidewalk, waiting for the light to change so they could cross the street. On the far side were tall trees, their branches alight with leaves in orange and red and yellow, and in their shade wound dirt paths. The bright, contrived green of a lawn shown through their dark trunks.

"That was *me*," said Mantha, panting slightly. It had taken more effort than she'd expected, and even now the gaping pit was threatening to suck them in again. "It's a trap."

The light changed. None of them moved to cross the street.

Clara stepped sideways, laid a hand on Mantha's shoulder.

"Let me see," she said.

"I'm not sure if I can," Mantha admitted. Now that she was getting used it, it was becoming easier to keep them suspended over the pit, but she knew if she let it go an inch it would be even harder to get them out again.

Ariel, meanwhile, had put down his briefcase, opened it, and removed a pendulum on which hung a chunk of white crystal. As soon as it was exposed to the air it was stained red, like the interior had filled with blood. Frowning, Ariel closed the case one-handed and held the pendulum aloft, letting it swing gently back and forth. It appeared to tug in one direction more than the other, and Ariel pointed that way and asked: "This way to the center?"

He was pointing to what would have been the center of the pit.

Mantha nodded.

The pendulum led Ariel, and Ariel led them, in a corkscrewing way, across the street and north up the park, past a baseball diamond and a small community garden, to what was, in the normal world, a wide grassy field suitable for picnicking on. They stood in the center of it, and Mantha had to concentrate hard on keeping them there, rather than floating on steam over the center of the pit. She was concentrating so hard on the pit, she almost didn't see the man sitting in the grass in the center of the field, eating an egg-salad sandwich off his crossed knees.

He was a young, scruffy sort of man. Quite like Ariel in that he was golden-haired and handsome, but his face was covered in a scraggly beard, his hair was long and tied up in a bun on top of his head, and he was wearing ripped blue jeans and a tie-dyed t-shirt.

He sat in the grass, eating his sandwich, and he stood in the pit, with his feet planted in a frozen lake, and it was tiny people he put in his mouth, chewed, and swallowed.

While Mantha frowned, trying to make sense of the double vision, Ariel went over to the man, pocketing the pendulum and his hands as he did so.

"Hi," he said, his voice warm and friendly.

The man on the grass swallowed a bite of sandwich, waved a hand. "Yo," he said. "'Sup, dude?"

And in the icy pit—which steamed from proximity to the upper world, which was blissfully warm and living by comparison—the man turned to Mantha and said, his mouth full of mangled limbs and screaming faces, "It is time you came back to the fold, granddaughter."

Mantha barely heard what Ariel said next. Something about Jude Carson. All she knew was that suddenly the pit had become horribly, tangibly real—but only for her. Her, and the man with his feet in the ice. And she saw that the ice was a lake. A frozen lake. And there were things—terrible things—caught in the ice. And the man was pulling the lake upward with him, making it steam and melt. Eventually, it would boil, and everything trapped within would come hurtling out of the lake and into the world.

The lake would devour everything, but it would devour Mantha first.

She felt like she was suffocating. She was terrified and furious and the only anchor she had was Lady Bibbit's soft paw, which squeezed her hand once, twice, and then held fast.

Focusing on that, rather than her terror, helped Mantha realize that neither version of the man was really there. He was projecting both the appearance of the man on the grass with the sandwich and the man in the lake with the mouth full of people, and by figuratively turning herself sideways Mantha found she could slip her attention between the two versions and . . .

. . . and there was *someone else*. Someone angry and full of hurt, and he sat in a dark place, casting out these and other visions like a fisherman casting a line.

Mantha sharpened her attention and neatly cut the line just under where it divided into the two projections she could see.

She was nearly thrown off her feet by the backlash, but Lady Bibbit was there to catch her, and together they collapsed slowly into the scratchy green grass—which was all there was to the field. No pit, no steam, and where the man on the grass had been . . .

Ariel and Clara had drawn back, so Mantha had a clear view of the figure writhing and wriggling, appearing to melt and flow until it was a completely different person lying on the grass at their feet, unconscious, but clearly breathing.

She was a middle-aged woman with gray in the roots of her dark red hair, heavy makeup, wearing a pair of black leggings and a loud, floral-print tunic.

Detroit, MI

Jill put the middle finger of her left hand on her right temple, and her thumb on the left, and squeezed, wishing she could massage her brain. Clara's report had been terse as usual, and more than usually impenetrable. Ariel wasn't helping.

"Can you repeat that?" she requested, with what she felt was gracious patience.

"The antichrist was utilizing demi-possession to acquire adherents and potential vessels," Clara said.

"Yes," said Jill, "what does that *mean?*"

"Antichrists are capable of partially possessing another person," Ariel explained, his voice fuzzier than Clara's. "So, this one was working through an agent in Chicago. Her—the agent's—name's Eleanor Schroeder, and she's apparently a lieutenant in his army of darkness."

"Army of darkness," Jill repeated. "What's that?"

"Dunno," said Ariel carelessly. "I think it's what they're calling their cadre this time around."

"Inaccurate," said Clara. "Darkness is a neutral force."

"Yeah, but *people*," said Ariel, and Jill could almost hear the shrug in his voice.

"You said potential vessels," Jill said.

"I did," agreed Clara.

Jill wanted to pull her hair out.

"What are *those?*"

Ariel's fuzzy voice answered.

"Potential vessels for Lucifer, if he ever deigns to make an appearance."

"Lucifer needs a vessel?" Jill said, diligently taking notes with her right hand, even as her left began rubbing her temples desperately.

"According to some systems of belief," Ariel said mildly.

"Like the god he counterposes, the Devil means different things to different people," Clara added, unhelpfully.

"So these potential vessels . . . are . . . what?"

"People of spiritual compatibility to total possession," said Clara.

"There's an argument to be made that they have to descend from the offspring of the early angels, but that's debatable," Ariel said. "So far, we only have Ms. Schroeder to go on, and she is within averages. Which is to say, she's off the deep end on the loony scale. Totally convinced that these are the end times and Jude Carson is the savior of humanity. But she didn't ping as having angelic ancestry."

"I thought Jude Carson was an antichrist," Jill said. "Isn't that supposed to be, like, the opposite of the savior of humanity?"

"Provisionally, that's what we're assuming," Ariel said. "As for whether the antichrist is a savior, I guess that depends on which part of humanity you are."

"And which part is that?" Jill asked.

"The part that doesn't believe in the second coming of Christ."

"Is that something we're going to have to contend with as well?" Jill asked, feeling tired.

"Unlikely," said Clara. "If he does return, he gets to sort the mess out."

Jill's mouth twisted sourly.

"So where does that leave us now?"

"Camping in Flammard's living room," Ariel said. "Mantha and Lady Bibbit are making pancakes for dinner."

"Great," said Jill.

"We will call again tomorrow night," Clara said, in a vain attempt at being reassuring.

Jill got off the phone and spent a minute with her head in her hands. She'd been feeling the equivalent of suffocated all evening, and the inconclusive report from Clara and Ariel had not helped.

She took Frosty for a walk. They had been going on walks at least once a night, sometimes twice, and had in the course of their roving traversed most of central Detroit. Jill followed Frosty, mostly, and as a result their routes tended to involve lots of alleys and parks, and where possible, pedestrian trails. Jill tracked their routes using a workout app on her phone, and planned on compiling them at the end of the month, to see how and where Frosty performed her trick with distance—making whole miles slide by in a few footsteps. So far, all Jill had were a dozen maps where the red line of their progress jumped around wildly as the satellite lost and found them again, but she hoped, with enough data, a pattern would emerge.

But this time Frosty seemed singularly uninterested in leading, sniffing her way up and down Roosevelt Park, until Jill got bored and dragged them across the 14th Street overpass, and then north up Wabash where the houses grew sparse, and there was more and better open space for Frosty to frolic in.

It was during one of these frolics, while Jill stood resting on one leg and checking her phone, that she heard the distant sound of howling.

Jill looked up. Frosty was standing in the middle of an abandoned lot, her white coat glowing against the dull browns and greens of the tired grass. Behind her was a house with peeling whitewash, its windows boarded up and half its roof covered in crawling vines. It looked like a ghost house next to the vibrant form of the wolf, her red ears perked into two sharp triangles, her mouth open slightly, and her eyes bright and flashing yellow.

The howling came again, carried on a wind that Jill did not feel, out of the place far away from the cracked concrete under her feet.

Frosty raised her head and returned the call, and that sound, coming from barely twenty feet away, sent a thrill up Jill's spine that lit her insides like she hadn't felt since before her change. It felt like being excited, aroused, and afraid all at the same time. It felt urgent, and it felt joyous, and Jill automatically pocketed her phone in preparation to run.

Then the sound ceased, and Jill felt a reflux of mild shame. What had she been thinking? Run where? She wasn't being chased. Nor did she have anything *to* chase.

Then Frosty took off. She ran halfway down the street and howled again.

Jill felt her legs move in automatic response, and the dog ran.

They both ran, and between one dim streetlight and the next, the city vanished under Jill's feet.

She was on wild ground covered in thick, dark grass. Jagged rocks tumbled around her, and Frosty was a beacon ahead.

Jill inhaled.

"Frosty!" she shouted. "No! Frosty, come!"

Frosty did not even pretend not to hear. She was bounding joyously ahead, stopping now and then to howl. It was these stops that allowed Jill to keep her in sight, and eventually the dog paused long enough that Jill was able to dart forward and grab her collar.

"Frosty!" she said, admonishingly.

Frosty, panting and grinning, thumped her fluffy tail against Jill's knees and licked at her hand.

They were overlooking a long, dark lake. Hills black with trees and jagged rocks rose around it, while just down the shore was a dock of sorts, and a low building beyond that.

There was a group of people in front of the building. Maybe a dozen. They were arranged in a semicircle around the shore, and they were all holding flaming branches and chanting. All of them except one, who was swathed in white sheets, and was being handed along the line of torchbearers toward the water.

Jill stood, watching, and realized no one had seen her. She stood in the dark with the cold white dog, and watched as the person in sheets knelt by the edge of the water, and one of the torchbearers reached down and sprinkled lake water over their head.

They jerked, shuddered, and then stood up, throwing off their sheets and spreading their arms wide.

For one horrible moment Jill thought it was Ariel. This person was the same general shape and color, but then she saw his hair was long, tied in a bun on the top of his head, and there was a ring of dark tattoos around his neck.

And then he looked out of the firelight, directly into Jill's eyes.

He did not have eyes. He had pits in his face, holes to a place dark and distant and full of pain.

He raised a hand. Pointed at Jill. He said something which Jill's ears caught as "Who is the revenant?" and as one, his entourage turned to look where he pointed.

Under her hand, Frosty's hackles went up, and then the dog howled, high and keen and chilling. She was answered by an echoing howl across the lake, and the man lowered his hand, uncertain.

Frosty ran, and Jill, clinging to her collar for whatever salvation could be had, ran with her.

Clean out over the water, skipping across its dark surface, and then that surface turned to smooth, clean asphalt, the dark hills turned hard and angular and pricked with yellow lights and she was running up the newly repaved drive of MCSIR, her heart convulsing in her chest as it tried to beat.

It was a good thing that Jill had Frosty with her as she staggered through the double doors of MCSIR, because she looked so haggard and frail that Marcus didn't recognize her at first. There were leaves caught in her hair and her pants were soaked from the knees down, and she looked like all the fluid had been sucked out of her. Lansing did a double take and then scrambled in her personal fridge for a flask of blood, which she tipped down Jill's throat before the woman could protest.

About half of it got spat out all over the refurbished tile floor, with splatters hitting both Marcus and Lansing. Any that touched Frosty, however, turned hard and black and fell to the ground in shiny pellets.

"Electrolytes," Jill coughed. "I need *electrolytes!*"

"This *has* electrolytes," Lansing pointed out, but she did not offer Jill the remains of her flask.

"It's *not* helping!" Jill insisted, even though the color was returning to her face by the moment. But nothing coherent could be got out of her until she had chugged a pint of apple juice cut with water and then sat, sipping the rest, while she transferred the data she had collected on her phone into the main computer.

It came out slowly, and in bursts, what had happened. Marcus was not surprised that Frosty had been taking Jill on more and more wayward walks—something similar had been the reason he deferred the task to Jill—but he was taken aback at just how far it appeared they had wandered. And then there was the issue of the disturbing character she had seen.

"Did you recognize him?" Lansing asked.

Jill frowned, but she shook her head.

"Did you recognize any landmarks?" Marcus tried. Knowing *where* she had been would be the next best thing.

"I didn't have to," Jill said, sounding smug, and pointed at the tangle of red lines which were loading onto the big monitor.

Marcus blinked. Behind the lines was superimposed a map of the United States, and it showed that they originated at MCSIR, with a little squiggle around Detroit, before suddenly shooting in a straight line west and a little north, to where it turned in a sharp circle and headed back again. Jill zoomed in on the circle, and words appeared next to it. Baraboo and South Bluff State Natural Area, and right in the middle, at the top of a blue oblong denoting a body of water, the words Devil's Lake State Park.

By the time Marcus has deciphered this much Jill had already called Clara on the main phone. It was nearing two in the morning, but she answered promptly.

"I know where Jude Carson went," she said without preamble.

Chicago IL

Mantha was not best pleased to be dragged out of bed at three in the morning, and went resentfully back to sleep, stretched out across Arcana's back seat with Lady Bibbit as a pillow, as soon as they were moving.

Clara took the first shift, on the grounds that she had been awake already, even though her watch was supposed to end at four. Ariel grumbled, snoozed, and woke to grumble again.

"Do you have something against sleep?" he asked.

They had been driving for two hours. The roads were empty, and they were making good time. They would be at Devil's Lake before sunrise. Clara didn't answer at once.

After a few minutes of engine noise, Ariel repeated the question, but in a smaller, softer voice. No half joke, but with full concern.

"*Do* you have something against sleep?"

Clara shivered.

She had not had a single dream involving Ariel since he had joined their group, and she wasn't certain if it was because she saw him every day, and her subconscious had given up taunting her with its own version, or if it was because in that time she'd never slept more than two hours at a stretch, and the dreams simply hadn't had a chance to manifest. Whatever the reason, she wanted to keep it that way.

"I don't need much," was what she said, and Ariel had the grace to accept this as an answer even though it wasn't one.

"Wish I could say the same," he said ruefully, and turned to press his forehead against the passenger window. Curling his knees into his chest and hugging his arms around them, he looked like a boy writ large and stubbly. Glancing across the center divide, Clara could see his face reflected in the dark window: the outline of his jaw in the red and blue glow from Arcana's dash, and the side of his nose. But his eyes were in shadow, and she could not tell if he looked back.

But he did not sleep. This Clara learned when he began, softly at first and then with growing assurance, to sing.

His voice was deep enough, and the timbre gruff enough, that his words were entirely camouflaged by the deeper, gruffer rumble of Arcana's engine, but Clara recognized the melody.

She'd only ever heard the original version of "White Bird," which had been sung by a woman, and in Ariel's baritone the song was at once more soothing and more alarming, as his voice rose with the end of the song to a pitch that skipped lightly above the background rumble of Arcana. But he whispered the last words, so Clara could barely hear.

A little time passed after he had finished, and then Mantha piped up from the back seat.

"Who's not dead?"

"Hmm?" Ariel asked, propping himself up on the armrest.

"The song," Mantha said. "At the end. *'They're not dead.'* Who's not dead?"

"Depends on who you ask," Ariel said. "And what you think the song's about."

"What *is* it about?" Mantha insisted.

Clara groaned internally, but Ariel gamely ran through the principal interpretations.

"If you think it's about drugs, then 'they' could mean your addictions," he said. "The song was written in the sixties, so that's not unlikely. If you think it's about internal demons and giving in to temptation, then it's about your own fears and doubts. This is also a legit reading, considering there are lyrics in the song which parallel Dante's *Inferno*."

Mantha was silent as she considered this. It was Lady Bibbit who asked: "What do *you* think it's about?"

"Me?" said Ariel. He seemed surprised.

"Yes," Clara joined in. "What do *you* think it's about?"

"I wouldn't presume to define Washington Steamship," Ariel said deferentially. "But, to me, it's always been about hope."

"Huh," said Lady Bibbit.

"Can I hear it again?" Mantha asked.

Ariel chuckled, but he sang it all over again, and louder, sitting up straight in his seat to better support his voice, and this time he belted the last words in a way that would have done Faith Swing proud.

Clara drove, and was glad of her long sleeves for concealing the goosebumps rising on her skin.

The sun came up slowly behind them, and then streamed in from the right as they turned north and began rolling through green hills spiky with trees and rocks, and glimpsed in flashes through breaks in the landscape, the sparkling black surface of Devil's Lake.

Clara pulled into the nearest empty campsite, leaving the truck in first gear and setting the handbrake. She stayed that way, staring at the dash with the engine idling, until Ariel poked her gently in the elbow.

"Claymore?" he asked.

"When was the last time you put gas in Arcana?" Clara asked.

Ariel blinked. He seemed confused. "I forget? I thought you did it. Are we out?"

"No," said Clara, but not like this was a good thing. "And unless the last person to put gas in Arcana also forgot to zero the trip meter, that was over seven hundred miles ago."

"What?" said Ariel.

Clara pointed at the dash. Leaning forward through the seats, Mantha saw that the fuel indicator was at its fullest setting, and felt something strange and frightened turn over in her stomach.

All Ariel said was "Hmm," and got out of the truck. Mantha felt the cab dip slightly as he climbed into the bed and opened up the chest. He returned moments later, carrying an emblem like a silver six-pointed star made of intertwined snakes on a long chain, and let it hang over the steering wheel. It turned, glinting in the light of the dash and the creeping sunrise, but otherwise did nothing. After a while Ariel lowered his arm and hung the emblem from the rearview mirror.'

Clara switched off the engine and they all got out. No one said anything more about the phenomenon, but Mantha hoped the adults did not forget about it. She'd been feeling increasingly uncomfortable since noticing the fuel gauge pointing at full, and though the sensation faded as they walked away from the truck and down to the lake, it never entirely vanished.

Devil's Lake was beautiful, Mantha decided, in a subdued, dignified way. It was a little ragged around the edges from the summer tourist season, and even now there were a dozen or so vacationers camped near Arcana. This early in the morning, however, with the cold of the night still clinging to the edge of the water, the beach was perfectly deserted. If she turned away from the trail and looked past the scattered litter on the shore, she could almost imagine she was looking at a timeless lake from centuries past. People had been coming to this lake for hundreds, thousands of years, and she could imagine them walking down to the edge of the lake, as she did, and marveling at the transition of hard, dry, rocky land to smooth, dark, cool water.

The water had its own smell, cold and wet and green, and after hours in the filtered air of Arcana, Mantha practically drank it in. She inhaled, as if she would wash her lungs clean with this new, sweet, damp air—

—and nearly choked. There was something putrid under the green wetness, and it unfolded in her throat, lodging at the top of her lungs and making her cough.

"There is something dead nearby," she heard Clara say, even as Ariel knelt beside her, one hand patting her gently on the back.

Mantha coughed, shook off Ariel's hand, and looked around. Clara had walked down the beach where she was peering into the water and sniffing experimentally.

Now that she was forewarned, Mantha realized the smell was not actually that bad. It came in whiffs between gusts of deep lake air, and was much fainter than Mantha first thought.

"Smells fishy," Ariel said.

"It is not a fish," Clara said, and abruptly began wading out into the lake.

At first Mantha did not see what she was wading to. The lake was dark blue-green cut with pale shimmers where it reflected the brightening sky, and in the shifting light it was difficult to make out shapes. Then, as Clara got further out into the water, and the waves lapped at her waist and higher, Mantha saw that part of the surface moved differently than the rest, and then Clara had hooked it and was dragging something the size of a small horse back to shore.

She came out of the lake with water pouring out of her sleeves and sluicing off her body, and dragged her fetid prize a good halfway up onto the shore before even her remarkable strength gave out and she was forced to let it fall.

It was not a fish, though it was pale, and part of it gleamed with scales.

It was like an otter crossed with a giant snake, only its head was more triangular, its legs were longer, and from behind its ears sprouted two curving, shiny horns.

There seemed nothing at all wrong with it, except that it was quite obviously dead.

"Dear sweet lords," murmured Ariel. "That's a *water panther*."

"Mishipeshu," Clara said, turning the horned head so it lay in a more dignified manner.

Mantha came around to look more closely at the animal. Now that she was used to the smell of its death, she began to feel an intense mournfulness for no reason that she could discern. It was akin to the sadness she felt upon seeing a dead raccoon or cat at the side of the road, coupled with a profound sense of regret, and a little fear.

The water panther had large, strong paws, webbed and clawed, and its tail was twice the length of its body. It had been a powerful creature in life and seemed to belong to that quiet, dignified lake in the same way the trees and rocks around them did.

It was a wrong thing, it being dead.

Clara was of a mind to return it to the lake.

"And waste a perfectly good set of horns?" Ariel said.

"They are not ours to take," Clara said.

Ariel sighed, but he did not argue the point. Mantha thought about telling them that whatever had been inside the water panther was gone, and the horns belonged to no one but whoever claimed them, but decided against it.

Ariel went and collected rocks while Clara got out her knife and carefully sliced into the corpse's belly. This released a whole new draft of unspeakable smells, and Ariel gagged upon his return.

Clara, her face as stony as ever, calmly placed the stones into the dead animal's belly, which she then stitched shut with dental floss.

She rolled the corpse back into the water, and walked it out until she was almost up to her shoulders, where she let it sink.

She was just arriving back on shore, looking much like a monster of the lake herself, when the park ranger found them.

He walked boldly down the beach. He was a large, bald, white man, and though his movements were confident Mantha could smell fear on him. That fear scared her more than his bulk or his presence, and before he could even say a word Mantha had nudged his mind so hard he nearly fell over as he turned himself around.

Clara and Ariel watched, silent and slightly judgmental, as the ranger walked around in circles on the beach, before hiking back up to his truck, parked just beyond the pylons. He slipped twice getting in, and the truck jerked forward before he got it in reverse and backed awkwardly away.

"Why did you do that?" Ariel asked, while Clara began wringing out her sleeves.

His tone was mild, but Mantha felt the implied rebuke sharply. It was a mark of how much she had softened, living within the serene acceptance of Clara and Ariel, that she did not retreat into a resentful shell, but instead burst into tears. This only made her more terrified. A deep-seated instinct told her that crying would be seen as a sign of weakness, but at the same time she wanted her friends to recognize that in her. To take care of her and protect her. All the while she also knew, in the same deep-seated way, that she alone could protect them if the thing in the lake that killed the water panther, if the thing in Arcana that watched her, came out to get them.

It felt like there was an electric ball of fear and unhappiness in her throat, and it stopped her from making any sound but sobs.

Lady Bibbit hugged her close, and Ariel came around and hugged both of them, while Clara stood by, dripping awkwardly.

"It's okay," said Ariel softly, patting her back while she sobbed into his side. He'd be as wet as Clara if this went on much longer. She tried to put a plug in her tears, and then Ariel said, "We all mess up sometimes," and the wails redoubled.

Mantha refused to get back into Arcana. Dug in her heels and shrieked like their hands were claws tearing into her skin. The park was beginning to come alive with people—early morning hikers and joggers and the custodial staff—but none of them paid them any attention. They wouldn't, Clara realized, as long as Mantha was as frightened as she was.

Ariel's solution was to make up a bed in the nearest camp and put Mantha down in it. He sat behind her like a big, living pillow, while she hugged Lady Bibbit and ate cinnamon-sugar oatmeal with freeze-dried raspberries. She was asleep before she finished, and Lady Bibbit cleaned the bowl.

"Why don't you go for a walk?" Ariel suggested to Clara. "Do some recon?"

"Will you be all right?" Clara asked.

Ariel looked down at the girl sleeping in his lap, at the rabbit eating mushy oats with a plastic spoon, then back up at Clara, and smiled.

And though there were bags under his eyes and tired lines across his brow, it still seemed to radiate light and warmth. Clara fled that smile, and its light, and squelched away down the nearest trail.

She had intended to hike the perimeter of the lake, but the trail that should have led along its eastern flank had been co-opted by train tracks, and so Clara wound up walking the tracks.

It was almost ten o'clock, but the skies were obstinately gray and the bottoms of the clouds hung low over the treetops. Clara had hoped that she would dry as she walked, but soon resigned herself to wet clothes for the remainder of the day. She would need to condition her leathers eventually, but for now there was no good opportunity.

She walked fast. Her long legs swung, her feet planting firmly on the track ties, until she reached the south end of the lake, where the tracks veered east and a blessed little trail hugged the shore. She passed another visitor center, and was interested to note that not a single one of the three people she encountered there showed her any notice. Apparently Mantha's influence was stretched far and wide. That, or it was attached to Clara.

Clara decided the latter made her feel less discomfited. She had come to think of Mantha as someone similar to herself, or Schiavona, or Flammard. Someone with powers so deep and strong it was impossible—and inadvisable—to plumb their depths. But someone who could cast a field of influence greater than a square mile, and keep it effective *even while sleeping* . . . that was someone beyond human. And, Clara liked to think, *she* was still more human than not.

She passed a concession stand and followed a narrow vehicular bridge over a tributary and then down a rocky trail past a small boathouse on her right and an impressive stack of rocks on her left. A little beyond that the trail bent gently to accommodate a curve of the shore, and she stopped as if she had seen a ghost.

And it was a ghost of sorts. She had to hike a little ways up into the trees and look out over the lake, but finally she placed the scene before her.

It was the lake from her dream. Drab and brown and overcast, and the rocks were broken instead of a whole slab, but the trees across the water and the line of the shore matched her memory so precisely it left her transfixed.

A chill wind blew across the surface of the water. A lone brave soul was trying to windsurf, without much success. Yet for all she stood on a well-trodden path in sight of a man in a lime-green wetsuit, she might have been at the remote lake from her dreams for all the peace and solitude she felt.

It occurred to her that her skin was clammy cold from being inside her wet clothes, and she decided, if Mantha's influence would grant her this shroud of privacy, she might as well take advantage of it.

Clara's extreme sense of modesty was born of self-preservation rather than shame, so although she stripped off her jacket and boots and pants, she put her utility belt back on over the pair of liner tights she wore, and though she hung her turtleneck and her undershirt next to her jacket on a low branch, she kept her bra on, though it was as soaked as the rest of her clothes and beginning to chafe.

She walked around on the bare rocks while she waited for her clothes to dry. Or at least to become less damp. To amuse herself she moved through her old qigong routine, and then, finding herself frustratingly out of practice, went through it all over again, lingering on the forms that gave her trouble. It was as effective a way to center oneself as anything, and as was the case with any truly centered person, Clara became aware of her audience long before she heard the first footfall or the sudden intake of breath.

She decided not to acknowledge them. Either they would be affected by Mantha's cloaking influence, or they were Ariel, or they were an enemy. In case it was this last option, Clara chose to draw Bellatrix and continue her practice with the sword included. It felt odd, swinging it through the air in ways that were impractical for combat, but the forms were not about harming other things, and that in itself was relaxing. As was holding a sword.

By the time she heard the footfalls, heard the intake of breath, and recognized the presence as belonging to Ariel, she was in the middle of a sequence and refused to stop—even to go shrug on her damp turtleneck.

She finished, the energy searing down her marks so that they glowed red, and stood at attention facing the lake. She was not quite ready to look at him yet, but when he cleared his throat and said "Excuse me," she turned around.

Ariel was standing at the side of the trail, his trousers still wet to the knee and his blazer buttoned. He had his hands in his pockets and his face was very pale under the shadow of his white cowboy hat.

"That was . . . impressive," he said, his voice oddly small and hoarse.

Clara inclined her head. She stood there, feeling the cool, damp air turn to steam as it touched her skin, waiting for the inevitable question.

But though Ariel had to have seen her marks—he was staring right at them—he did not ask what they were. Instead he said: "Where did you learn tai chi?"

"Qigong," Clara corrected him. "Tesla Isenfaust taught me a little when I was seven. The rest I developed on my own."

The words unglued her feet, and she went over to the tree and began putting her clothes back on.

"That's nice," Ariel said, his voice still small. It reminded her of the way he had spoken in her dreams, and Clara put on her undershirt backwards. She stripped it off and tried again.

"Why are you here?" she asked once she had her armor back on. She felt more like her old self, which was less like her true self, which made her irritable.

"Mantha suggested I take a walk," Ariel said, and then went even whiter as he realized what he had just said.

"That *brat*," he gasped, softly.

Clara finished snapping her boots on and marched up the bank to him.

"She was probably trying to keep you out of danger," she said.

Ariel snorted. "Not helping."

"Stay close to me," Clara told him, and started down the trail toward the campground at a jog, Bellatrix's weight heavy and reassuring against her back.

Was it just her, or did the place seem emptier than before? The lime-green windsurfer had retired. It was too quiet, too still, and as she came around the final bend in the trail and the campground loomed into view above them on her left, she saw it was missing the bright red bulk of Arcana.

Fairly sprinting up the path to their spot, she made a complete circuit of the campground while Ariel examined the place where Arcana had been parked, apparently looking for tracks. When she returned, he was running a string of small, red beads through his hands, frowning at the set of skid marks the truck had left backing out of the parking spot.

He did not ask if she had found anything. Instead he pointed to where the tracks disappeared onto the paved road.

"They've not gone far," he said. "At least, the talisman I put on his dash hasn't gone far."

Clara gestured for him to lead, and he did, striding off, uphill away from the lake, running the beads through his hand the whole time.

Earlier

Mantha had not slept well. Her mind kept getting up and wandering off, down along the edge of the lake, hovering over the place where they had found the water panther. Once she'd gone right in, down into the dark, cold water, and there had been a terrible emptiness in the lake, sucking, sucking, sucking. It had sucked the life out of the water panther, and now it was growing, lacing the water with tendrils of intent, until Mantha realized it had nearly entrapped her, and she pulled her mind out of the lake and back to her body so forcefully she shot into a sitting position.

Lady Bibbit blinked curiously down at her, the rabbit's large blue eye luminous against the overcast sky. A little ways off, Ariel sat on a clump of grass, working a string of red beads through his hands.

The thing in Arcana was looking at her. Calmly, invasively, but not malevolently. Compared to the thing in the lake, Mantha realized, it was perfectly neutral. It still bothered her, inasmuch as she strongly felt it shouldn't be there, but not nearly as much as the presence which was walking down from the upper campground, sandals slapping on the asphalt of the road.

They were not yet in sight, but already Ariel had risen, turned, pocketing the beads and squaring his shoulders in a way that suggested he was ready to fight.

And though Mantha understood Ariel was a little more than what constituted a "normal" human being, with specific knowledge and training, it was obvious as spilled paint that he was no match for whatever was walking down the drive.

"You should take a walk," she told him, pushing at his mind gently but firmly, and hating herself for it. It felt like cheating, and like a dangerous admission of what she really was.

But it was that or watch him get tortured—possibly killed—by Jude Carson. So she gave him an extra nudge, and tracked him in her mind until he was safely out of sight along the lakeshore trail.

By this time Jude Carson was at the far end of the campground, and he was not alone.

Three other people were with him. All men, they were all white with brown hair in shades varying from dark to ruddy to sandy-blond, and they were all wearing blue jeans and plaid, button-down shirts. They looked so scrupulously casual that it set Mantha's teeth on edge.

Jude Carson himself appeared just as he had in Chicago: loose shorts and a short-sleeved shirt which buttoned up the front between sets of little pleats, chin-length brown hair and a scraggly beard. He smiled when he saw Mantha, and the thing behind the man shivered in anticipation.

The thing behind Jude Carson was not there in the conventional sense. It had no eyes and a hungry mouth full of teeth. It reminded Mantha of the thing in the lake, just small and man-shaped. Unless that *was* Jude Carson. She remembered the way he had melted away to reveal the woman. Was this just another mask? Or was that all Jude Carson was—a mask? A friendly face concealing the horrendous monster which possessed whatever poor soul it had conscripted as its vessel.

Mantha stood up. Subconsciously she took Lady Bibbit's hand and felt a little better.

"Samantha Fulgeroiu," said the thing with the mask called Jude Carson, smiling widely—both the normal human face and the horrible, eyeless face behind it. Hands raised—human and . . . other. Not hands. Claws. Claws on the ends of long, strong fingers, grasping, tugging.

Reaching for her.

"No," said Mantha, and ran.

She did not know what Jude Carson was, only that he was terrifying, and horribly, revoltingly, familiar. His presence resonated with her in a way that brought her back to those terrible weeks after Bună died. When her dreams and fears had manifested in the real world. He brought her back to the feeling of pushing people's minds around to suit her ends, but without the sour feeling of shame that Clara had instilled in her.

In Jude Carson—or whatever he really was—Mantha saw a future version of herself, without scruples, empathy, or self-control.

She ran from that, dragging Lady Bibbit, to the one place that did not feel like a twisted mirror of herself.

Arcana's door swung open at her approach. Mantha was sure she hadn't made it do that, but she was moving too fast to react. She just threw herself through the door, Lady Bibbit landing on top of her. She heard it latch behind her and the locks clicked down. Sitting up, breathing the familiar smell of Arcana's upholstery, cut with Ariel's cologne and Clara's leather conditioner, calmed her a little.

Then she looked out through the windows and saw Jude Carson had walked down to their campsite and was folding up her sleeping bag. When he had done this he came over and tucked it into Arcana's bed, and then went to get into the driver's seat.

He reached for the door, and Mantha saw the lock jiggle—but hold. When Jude Carson gripped the handle and pulled, Arcana rocked with the force of it—but the door did not open.

This puzzled Jude Carson. He looked at the door, then in at Arcana, and then down at his hand. He reached again.

Mantha was sitting in the backseat, Lady Bibbit by her side, and the keys were nowhere in sight. Clara had them, probably. Or Ariel. And either way, she couldn't drive. Not only did she not know how, but her legs were too short to reach the pedals.

And yet before Jude Carson could try the door again, Arcana's engine rumbled to life.

It chugged, growling like an angry cat. A *big* angry cat. Mantha felt the vibrations through the seat.

The lights on the dashboard came on, and the radio began to play. Fragments of music and news and talk shows flashed by, too swiftly for Mantha to catch.

The thing in Arcana looked at her, looked at Jude Carson, and apparently picked a side.

"But don't panic," said a newswoman's voice, and then the radio switched to Panthera's "No Mistake" in the middle of the bridge.

And then Arcana put himself into gear (*I know I am not what you most fear*), the parking brake released (*But I am not what you hold dear*), and he backed away from Jude Carson so quickly his wheels spun out (*Reality stings*), throwing up dirt and turf until he found the road (*and yet it does seem*), shifted into second (*that we will not stay*), and charged away (*in this sweet dream*).

Wedging herself in the backseat, Mantha only had a flashing glimpse of the road as it slipped away beneath them, all the while Panthera's voice filled the cab.

"Flashing on the heights, lightning from on high! I'm touching down this time, striking fire from the sky—make no mistake!

"Great gates crumbling! Giants are stumbling! Their gifts I have received—make no mistake!"

Detroit, MI

The influx started slowly. The first to arrive was a party of small, round people with thick, curly hair that covered their entire heads. There were five of them, and their skin ranged in hue from pale tan to dark gray. They wore tunics apparently made of moss and spoke in a bubbling, chirping language that sounded like a mountain stream. They carried with them a structure made of birch twigs lashed together with grass rope, and while four arranged themselves around it in a protective stance, the fifth went boldly through the center until it found Professor Okedo, and spoke to him earnestly in their bubbling language.

When Okedo explained, just as earnestly, in English, that he could not understand them, the little hairy person shrugged in a long-suffering manner, and then, as if explaining itself to someone of limited intelligence, pointed at itself with a stubby, rocklike finger, and repeated the phrase *"May-may, gway-say,"* in a rising string of bubbling notes. Then it took Okedo by the hand and led him down to the atrium, where the other four stood guard around their twiggy construction, giving the impression of glaring even through the curls of hair covering their faces.

May-may Gway-say pointed at them, and said to Okedo: *"May-may-gway Say-wag."* There it left Okedo and spoke with its fellows in their mountain-creek tongue. Okedo had the presence of mind to stop trying to decipher their words and focused on their body language. This, despite being exhibited by bodies much smaller and rounder than his, contained enough recognizable motions that he imagined they were consulting on what to do next. A few garbled words which partially resembled English were dropped here and there, with one that sounded like "actually" recurring again and again.

Then, as five furry faces united, they presented themselves to Okedo and the one who had come to find him said, with extreme care and difficulty:

"Sanc'tually."

Okedo felt panicked. Even though they were strange, they clearly weren't hostile, and he felt it was desperately important he understand them, and in his desperation missed what they were saying completely. It was Tamerlain, coming in from their shift, distracted by the huge twig house in the middle of the atrium, who stopped by and solved it. They were presently in the form of the chubby, dark-haired girl with vaguely Asian features, and May-may Gway-say turned to her and said again: "Sanc'tually."

Tamerlain stopped. She frowned, and came a little closer.

"Again?" she asked, making a circular motion with her hands.

"Sanc'tually," said May-may Gway-say.

"Sanctuary?" asked Tamerlain, and everything clicked in Okedo's head.

"They want sanctuary!" he exclaimed.

"Sanc'tually!" cried May-may Gway-say, extending a hand and giving them a thumb's up.

Tamerlain turned to Okedo and raised her eyebrows. "Sanctuary from what?" she asked.

There was no time to speculate on an answer. No sooner had the May-may Gway Say-wag been helped into the waiting room and offered biscuits (which they refused) and fresh water (which they gratefully accepted), than the next wave arrived.

This consisted of a flock of ravens, which took up residence at the top of the building and refused to be moved. Okedo was just coming down from laying out newspaper on all the floors to find a thin, nervous woman sitting in the lobby, rubbing her hands.

"I couldn't think where else to go," she explained apologetically.

Okedo didn't bother asking her questions, but gave her a copy of their intake form, and left her to it with a sigh of relief.

The relief was short lived, as the bear arrived next.

It was small, for a bear. But it was still a *bear*. It was much bigger than even the biggest dog Okedo had ever met, shaggy, and honey-brown. It came with a small entourage of nervous Community Service Officers who, after seeing it through the front doors of the center, hurried off in relief. Okedo was left staring into the implacable brown eyes of that round, savage face, half hoping it would turn into a human. Stranger things had happened, after all.

But the bear remained indomitably a bear, and by the time Jill got up it was seated beside the May-may Gway Say-wag, helping them fill out their intake forms.

Jill poked her head in, asked if they needed anything, and when a half-finished form was waved as a means of answer, she nodded with relief and went into her office, where a frazzled sheriff's deputy was sitting, trying and failing to appear calm.

Jill sucked on her smoothie as she sat down opposite him, Frosty, as ever, at her side.

"You've caught us in something of a crisis, apparently," she said, waking up her computer to a barrage of messages.

"That's been our experience as well," said the deputy, whose name tag said he was M. Morris. He was middle-aged, white, bald, and sweating.

Jill focused on him over the top of her monitor. Under her hand, her phone vibrated. A string of messages from Clara. She tried to read them, but Deputy Morris's report of a horde of zombies at the county jail distracted her.

"Are they rabid?" she asked, feeling her eyes begin to glaze over.

"Sorry?" said Deputy Morris.

"Are they *attacking* people?"

"No," admitted the deputy. "They are trying to turn themselves in."

"And you don't have room?" Jill asked. She was trying to see how this was her problem. Aside from, you know, zombies.

"We have room . . . just," said Deputy Morris. "The problem is our system. All of these individuals are . . . well, they're *legally* dead."

"So?"

"So," said the deputy. "We can't process them. Our system can't handle it. We need you to take them."

Jill stared at him, unblinking. It was something she did without thinking, but this time she did in on purpose—knowing from her interactions with Lansing how disturbing being on the receiving end was.

Zombies. An intelligent bear. Extremely furry not-Hobbits. A woman who claimed to be a tree spirit. All within twenty-four hours.

Jill wished she could have said she'd never seen anything like it, but she had.

Two years ago, in St. Louis.

The weeks before the Grand God of War opened a portal through the Gateway Arch. That had been like this.

Jill missed Selene. She had never stopped missing Selene, but now she missed her in an acutely practical way. And she missed Clara, who was at Devil's Lake and apparently trying to contact her. It made her irritable.

"Deputy Morris," she said, still not blinking. "MCSIR does not exist to cover the shortcomings of your department. Fix your system. Keep the zombies separate from the living prisoners, and feed them livestock brains. I can put you in touch with Don's supplier. Now if you don't mind, there's a bear in my waiting room, a woman who's possibly a tree in my cafeteria, and I think the werewolves will be acting up any minute."

"You think there could be wolf trouble?" Deputy Morris asked, dismayed.

"At this rate, I'm just assuming we haven't heard of it yet," Jill said grimly, and stood up.

Frosty escorted the deputy out the door, and finally Jill had a chance to read Clara's texts.

After the first two she forgot to breathe, so when she got to the end and tried to curse all that came out was puckered gasping. She inhaled, then let fly a litany of swear words such that Frosty barked in sympathy.

Jill looked up. Saw the white dog with red ears and glowing yellow eyes. The dog who could warp space.

"I need to get to Devil's Lake," she said, blankly.

Frosty cocked an ear. Curious.

"You can take me there," Jill said, focusing intently on the dog.

Frosty, seeming to understand that Jill was talking to her, if not the exact meaning, began to pant expectantly and wag her tail.

They came down the stairs in a clatter of claws and feet to find Lansing, who had recently come on duty, pacing the atrium, rattling a sheaf of intake forms.

"*Jill,*" she said, before Jill had quite reached the ground floor. "Jill, they are *memegwesiwag*, and they're asking for sanctuary. Do you *realize* what this *means?*"

"There's gonna be another cross-dimensional contamination event," Jill said, barely registering Lansing's words.

"A *what? Another* what?" Lansing said.

"St. Louis," Jill called over her shoulder, heading for the coat closet where she kept Frosty's leashes and her day suit. It was still early in the evening, but better safe than sorry.

Lansing froze as she connected the name of the city to the events of the recent past. It gave Jill time to leash Frosty and look at the duty roster. Tamerlain, Don and Okedo were off. Lansing was acting D.O., while Marcus and Imogen—one of their werewolves—were on patrol.

It would be pointless to go alone. Even with Frosty, Jill knew she alone would be about as much help as not going at all. Lansing didn't have a day suit. Imogen was still a rookie. Marcus wasn't crisis-ready.

Who she needed was Selene.

"No," Lansing was saying. "Not again. We . . . we have to stop it."

"Be sure to reset the magic meters tonight," Jill said, pulling the door open.

Maybe, with Frosty, there was something they *could* do. First they'd have to get there.

There was a half-transformed werewolf, sides heaving, brindled fur streaked with sweat and blood, leaning on an equally sweaty (but thankfully less bloody) Marcus in the doorway

"Southfield pack?" Jill asked, resigned.

"No!" gasped Marcus. "We were on Lakeshore. Something came out of the lake. Like a cougar crossed with a crocodile. Imogen is fine, but she's stuck halfway."

"Tucker can take care of her," Jill said. "I have to get to Devil's Lake. You're coming with me."

There was really only one way to find out if someone was crisis ready.

"I am?" Marcus said, bewildered.

After an agonizing delay while they got Imogen to the infirmary and pulled their medic, Tucker, (also a werewolf) out of bed, Jill grabbed an emergency pack—someone's emergency pack—stuffed the day suit into it, and by the time she, Frosty and Marcus were out the front doors and down the steps, she was moving at a near run.

"My car is parked in back," Marcus said, dragging on Jill's hand.

"We don't have time," Jill said.

"We don't . . . have time," Marcus repeated, "*for a car?*"

Jill, with his big brown hand in one of hers and Frosty's leash in the other, tugged on the dog, gently.

"Now, *listen*—because I'm *sure* you can understand me," Jill said.

Frosty obligingly sat, red ears perked forward, mouth open in a canine grin.

"I need to get to Devil's Lake. Remember? The place we went before? Where we saw the man with no eyes?"

"Oh, great," said Marcus.

Frosty's eyes were luminous and yellow, shining in the dark, innocent and uncomprehending as a puppy's.

"Frosty!"

The yellow eyes focused, and the hound's face took on an expression far more complicated than any worn by an honest dog. There was interest, and confusion, and a little of what Jill thought might have been nerves.

Frosty closed her mouth. Nosed at Jill's hand. Thumped her tail.

"It's *important*," Jill said. "Clara needs *help*."

Good *grief*, she thought. What a night it is when *Clara* needs help!

Frosty keened. She pawed at Jill's leg, then nosed at the hand that held her leash.

"I need this," Jill explained. "Otherwise you'd leave me behind."

Frosty's ears drooped. She nosed at the leash again.

Jill took a deep breath, trying to ground herself.

"Fine," she said. "But you have to wait for us if we can't keep up." Reluctantly she unclasped the leash and stood back.

Frosty jumped to her feet, tail wagging. She barked, playfully, and then trotted off across the street, Jill right on her heels, dragging Marcus behind her by the hand.

At first it seemed they only ran across Roosevelt Park, but as they went, picking up speed, the world got darker and quieter. The ground they ran on was not concrete or asphalt but packed, moist earth and thick grass. Frosty went at an easy lope, but Jill had to run flat out just to keep up, and behind her Marcus got heavier and heavier and slower and slower.

Then, in the distance, a mournful howl. Without breaking stride, Frosty lifted her head and returned the call.

And as before, the sound sent shivers down Jill's spine and along her arms. She stumbled, recovered, but lost hold of Marcus, who shouted something that was eaten by the sudden roar of panting and thudding paws that enveloped them.

A cold wind bit Jill's limbs. Frost crunched under her feet. And all around her were cold, white bodies and perked, red ears. Yellow eyes glowed and red mouths gaped, panting. She lost track of Frosty in the pack, but it was impossible to lose them now.

Dogs were all around her, in front and behind and to either side. She ran with them brushing her thighs, their tails striking her waist. Howls pierced the night air, which was a deep, magnificent blue lit by crystalline stars and a crescent moon so sharp it looked like it could hook a fish.

And behind and below them, reverberating up from the ground, came the sound of hoofbeats.

It reminded Jill of unicorns, of the growl of Arcana's engine. It filled her with a wild, frantic energy, lifting the weight of her pack from her shoulders, the hairs from the back of her neck; her very heart and lungs seemed to rise and lodge under her collar bone.

A black shadow, like a piece of void, cut open the blue, blue night. It might not have been discernible to human eyes, but as Jill had long since run out of breath, her vampiric eyes saw the change clearly. The stars were eaten up, the moon put out, and even the coats of the dogs dimmed.

Something like a stag was running in front of them. Or chasing them. Perhaps there were two, herding the hunting pack. Jill's feet were flying beneath her, and then her toe caught something—a rock, a tuft of grass, she was too numb to feel the difference—and she fell.

She fell into darkness, the cold, white dogs running over her head. She sank, watching them pass by like pale fish above her, and she thought of the time when she was sick, jumping off the boat into the sea.

There would be no merman to save her this time. She kicked, but her legs found nothing to kick against. The dogs passed by, and she was left alone in utter and complete blackness.

Devil's Lake, WI

Arcana bounced over raw ground and came to an ignoble halt under the shadow of a tall stack of limestone rocks. There were twigs and leaves caught in his windshield wipers, and Mantha felt slightly nauseous.

"*You don't have to go home,*" wailed the radio, "*but you can't stay here!*"

Feeling green and woozy and full of jitters, Mantha crawled to the nearest door and let herself out. Her knees buckled under her, and she sat down in the poky bushes with a thump. Lady Bibbit pulled her out of them and helped her scramble up onto a low ledge, away from Arcana's bumper.

They had left the door open behind them, but this closed with a snap once they were clear, and with an angry growl of his engine, Arcana backed away into the track of flattened earth and torn vegetation he had left in his wake. A few times his drive wheels spun out, but not enough to stall him for long. He left behind a wide trail with three pits dug by his tires, and as his engine faded into the distance, a tree, knocked sideways by his passage, collapsed fully into the wreckage.

"I wonder what's got into *him*," Lady Bibbit said.

She probably meant it metaphorically, but Mantha, in her upset state, could only apply its literal meaning to their current situation, and suddenly imagined a demon possessing Arcana, much the way Jude Carson was possessing his own vessel. What sort of demon possessed a mechanical object? she wondered.

Then her mind caught up with current events, and she pushed herself off the ledge of rock in her excitement.

"He's still back there," she said.

"Yes," said Lady Bibbit, following at a more sedate pace. "That was the point, I think."

"Clara and Ariel are back there!" Mantha exclaimed. "They're in danger!"

"They're grownups," Lady Bibbit said. "They can take care of themselves."

Mantha didn't know how to explain that, as far as she was concerned, Clara and Ariel were terribly small, underprepared, vulnerable people compared to Jude Carson—who she suspected wasn't a person at all. He was more like a particularly concentrated bundle of feelings and intentions with a human face balanced on top. What he really was—what he truly looked like—you could only glimpse by looking into his eyes which . . .

. . . Mantha had to admit to herself then that what truly frightened her about Jude Carson was not his power, nor his apparent malevolence. No, it was that he reminded her hauntingly of herself. Herself as she might have been. If Clara had not come along. If she hadn't had anyone to push back against her.

If she hadn't had anyone to live up to.

And Clara was resistant, yes, but she wasn't immune. And Ariel . . . Mantha shuddered at the memory of how *easy* it had been to push his mind the way she wanted.

"We have to go back," she said. She started off down Arcana's tracks, and immediately got her foot caught in a torn root.

"You can," said Lady Bibbit. "I'm not." And she sat down on her ledge of rock and did not move.

That gave Mantha pause. Until now she hadn't given much thought to Lady Bibbit's wants, since the rabbit had always seemed content to go where Mantha went. Whether that had been because her existence was the result of Mantha's powers or in simple deference to them Mantha had never considered.

Lady Bibbit had always been there, and she'd never considered that she would want it otherwise.

Mantha certainly knew she didn't want to go anywhere without her rabbit. It was no longer purely emotional support—as it had been when Lady Bibbit was just a stuffed rabbit and Mantha hadn't understood the effect her belief had on things—but that she recognized that Lady Bibbit had grown larger than just the power Mantha had put into her. Now, if Lady Bibbit did or didn't want to do something, it was worth finding out why.

So she asked.

"It's *safe* here," said Lady Bibbit, and pointed above her, at the stack of rocks.

Mantha looked. The rocks didn't seem safe to her. They were cold and hard and dark against the gray sky. It looked like something had made a nest in their crag a long time ago. Bits of stick cut into the sky at odd angles.

"I'm not sure I like them," she said. "They feel . . . angry. Like whatever was in Arcana did."

"I don't think Arcana is angry," Lady Bibbit said, and climbed a little further up the rocks.

"I don't think he's Arcana," Mantha announced. "Not properly."

Lady Bibbit shrugged.

"These rocks aren't angry," she asserted. "They're strong. This is a strong place. The lake is a weak place. We're safe here."

Mantha squinted up at the rocks, trying to understand.

She's never thought of nudging the landscape the way she nudged people's minds, but now that Lady Bibbit had mentioned strong and weak places, she realized the land was very much like people.

No, it was both bigger and more complicated than that.

The land was one big, big person. Infinitely complex and unfathomably ancient. Time lay thick on the land, pushing it up and away from where Mantha existed. It was bigger and older and stronger than her, and she didn't even try to nudge it for fear of what might happen.

Nudging the land with her mind, Mantha realized, would be like trying to move a boulder by punching it. Except that instead of breaking her hand, it would be her mind that was shattered.

Yet even with all this, she thought she saw what Lady Bibbit meant.

The lake seemed thinner, almost transparent. If Mantha looked closely, she thought she could feel her way through to a different world entirely.

The rocks were even more land than normal. Land lay thick there, strong and vivid.

Still, a part of her yearned to run. She quivered. Small, uncertain.

"You have to trust people who are weaker than you," Lady Bibbit said.

Mantha wanted to cry. Instead she went and sat next to Lady Bibbit on the ledge of rock.

They had made a complete circuit of the campgrounds when Ariel finally gave up and put away his talisman.

"Someone is interfering," Clara announced.

"No joke," said Ariel, bitterly.

Inside her damp jacket, Clara began to shiver. It was not a reaction to the temperature, she was pretty sure. It was a quiver of her skin as if a spider were creeping down her spine. She kept turning in circles, expecting to find something behind her—but she didn't know what to expect, and there was never anything other than the trees and the scrubby grass and the road and beyond that, the lake.

The lake, iron black and deserted, and the pale strip of beach were similarly empty.

Ariel, meanwhile, after rummaging in his pockets, had produced a spool of twine and a string of ancient silver coins. They all had holes punched in them, and the first one he tied to the end of the twine, which he hooked over a nearby hand of bush twigs. Then, unrolling the spool behind him, he began to walk back toward the lake.

Clara followed him, curious.

"What are you doing?" she asked. It looked like a general casting, so unspecific she couldn't tell what for.

"My foster mom, she always said the best way to find something you missed is to put everything away," Ariel said, hooking a loop of twine over a water spigot and lacing another silver coin to it. "Something's not right here, and we've been so busy running around chasing it, we've not stopped to sort through what we have."

He had a point, and it gave Clara pause. It also gave her a pang of acute loss, as it was exactly the sort of thing Selene would do. Or suggest they do.

"It's a net," Clara guessed.

"A bit," said Ariel, sounding pleased. "I'm trying to find a baseline for this place. I figure we've covered enough ground. I'll run it down to the water and see what I've caught."

They did this, Clara keeping a careful lookout the whole way for possible assailants. But aside from a congregation of crows gathered on the roof of the welcome center, there was not another soul in sight.

Ariel, meanwhile, grew more and more concentrated until they reached the beach, at which point his brow was deeply furrowed and his hands twitched as they tied off the end of the string to a rock and cut it loose with his pocketknife.

Clara waited, tempering her patience by observing how the filtered sunlight moved across the surface of the lake.

Choppy with ripples from the wind, there were other waves less easily explained. These pushed outward from the middle of the lake. Like the water there was bubbling. Or something was rising to the surface.

Clara did not need to hear Ariel's sudden intake of breath to know something was deeply wrong.

"My friend," he said. "We have a full-blown rupture brewing."

"Do you know where to?" Clara asked.

She didn't need to ask where this rupture would *be*. She knew she was looking right at it.

"At a guess, the great inferno," Ariel said. "And my kit is in Arcana."

Clara's mind was working frantically. Her thoughts kept going back to the dead mishipeshu, and wishing that it wasn't. If the world had a natural protection against ruptures, it was the native supernatural flora and fauna.

But the water panther of Devil's Lake was dead, Arcana and Mantha were missing, and there was nothing Clara knew to stop a rupture. She only knew how to deal with what came out of it.

"We need to find Jude Carson," Ariel said. "He's the key to all of this."

He didn't mean it metaphorically, Clara realized. Jude Carson, antichrist or no, was the key to the gate which would rupture, spilling all manner of unpleasantness into the world. Without him it would remain locked—the door weakened, but still shut.

Ariel was looking at her hopefully. Clara shuddered.

He didn't have his kit. They were down to what they had in their pockets, and in themselves.

The latter of which, in Clara's case, was quite a lot. In fact, she suspected she could find Jude Carson very easily, if she was willing to make herself vulnerable in a way she thoroughly detested. Either of them could, come to think of it.

Strip off Ariel's wards and protections, and he made just as tempting a target as she did. Except that, unlike her, Ariel really would be as vulnerable as he appeared.

He didn't know what he was asking. It was better that he not know.

"Are you prepared?" Clara asked.

She meant: are you prepared to kill someone?

From the gravity with which he nodded, she hoped Ariel had understood that much, at least.

Reluctantly, Clara reached up under her left arm and unbuckled Bellatrix's harness. She handed the sword, scabbard and straps and all, to Ariel. Then she removed her utility belt, and the knives from both her boots, and her gloves, and then from her belt she took out a small velvet bag. Manipulating it so its contents came to light without being touched, she held the dingy ring up to the light and looked at Ariel steadily across it.

"Keep that sword at the ready," she told him. "The rest . . . try not to let anyone else touch."

Ariel looked at Clara, and then down at the ring. She saw him recognize it.

"You're not gonna let me be bait?" he said.

Clara shook her head.

Ariel pursed his lips, but did not argue.

Last thing before she put the ring on, Clara got out her phone and sent off a string of text messages to Jill. She only had one tick of reception, and knew it would only get worse. Besides, Jill would be underground for another six hours at least. By the time she got up, this would all be over. One way or another.

"Time me," Clara said to Ariel, once this was done.

Ariel obligingly got out his phone, thumbing it awake one-handed since he still held Bellatrix in the other.

"Ready when you are," he said, giving her a tight smile.

Clara nodded once, and put on the ring.

The ground dropped out from under her, her stomach lifting in her belly, and the world turned into a confusion of . . . something. Not flames, and not wind. It reminded Clara of the time she had been tossed into a whitewater river. Which hadn't been so bad, all things considered, until she'd gone over a small waterfall and gotten caught in the recirculating current at the bottom. Up and down and around she'd gone, never quite breaking the surface, confused and dizzy and rapidly running out of air. It wasn't until she'd gotten control of her instincts, balled up and let herself get pushed down, down, into the dark, cold depths of the river, where the current flowed true, that she was able, with a good kick off the bottom, to break out of the cycle.

This was like that, except she didn't need to breathe, strictly speaking, and everything felt upside-down. The current of energy felt stronger above her head, and a great stillness lay below her. But just a few feet away, where the sand gave way to the lake, the source of that current came pouring out from the space beyond. It was thin, ephemeral stuff, hardly more than the intention of change.

Finding the memory of ground rather than the ground itself, Clara made her way to the edge of the lake, and experimentally put her arm into the current. It split around her, and through the gap this created she saw the void on the other side.

It was wide and dark and went down a very long way. It had eaten up the layer of ambient energy that lay over the earth, spat it out along with the rest of the excited magic. That was what had killed the water panther, Clara was pretty sure.

Intentions were moving in its depths. Still coalescing, mostly ideas at this point, but now concentrated enough that Clara could just make them out as four distinct shapes.

But it was too soon for them to begin their ride. Far, far too soon. They would wait and watch, as they had waited and watched for so long. To her own certain knowledge, the Four Riders had never *actually* ridden. They had come close in 1970, but none of the attempted apocalypses had gotten far enough along.

That was the thing very few people understood. The Four Riders didn't bring the apocalypse, they were a symptom of it. Still, they were emblems, and emblems held power of their own.

Clara withdrew her arm and turned around just in time to find Jude Carson descending on her with an axe.

She didn't think, but instinct turned her sideways, brought her arm down on the man's neck, then grabbed his shoulder as he staggered from the blow. She put him in an armlock and once the axe was dropped, worked the ring off her finger and slipped it into her pocket.

The sudden absence of the winds of change caused her to stumble, and Jude Carson shrieked as this put pressure on his shoulder, but Clara didn't let go. No one died from a dislocated shoulder.

Ariel was more ready than she'd given him credit for. He had a thin chain of silver and gold, and this he threw around Jude Carson's neck as soon as they solidified.

The man-shape screamed, and suddenly Clara had her arms full of flapping demon, its face a mass of holes with teeth and fire. The flesh turned to maggots under her hands, and though this didn't shake her resolve, it did make it very difficult to hold on.

She probably would have lost him, except that Ariel had the sense to drive Bellatrix into the beating cloud of his wings, pinning them to each other and causing the demon to stagger sideways. He let go of the hilt to grab the chain with both hands, muttering unceasingly in Latin.

It was a prayer. It went around in circles, again and again, tightening on the demon like the gold and silver chain, until he had it so thoroughly bound Clara was able disentangle herself and brush the dying maggots off her hands. Then she stood back and watched in admiration and sober respect as Ariel, without hardly stopping for breath, laid it on the demon to remain corporeal, cast no illusions, and speak only truth.

The demon that was Jude Carson condensed into a shape that was roughly humanoid, but of uncertain distinction since his skin was made of a living mat of worms. His wings, still skewered by Bellatrix, had lost their smoky film and were now barely more than oversized, bony hands, hanging limply from where the sword pinned them to his side.

"Anthony! Christopher! *Francis!*" snarled the demon. His voice was garbled, since his palate was cleft and his cheeks shreds of stringy worms, which each time he spoke broke and wriggled away into his jaw. He did not have eyes but black pits, in the depths of which Clara could see into the world behind the world. The world where the ambient power of the lake had been pushed aside, and strange, terrible winds were blowing.

"Never had the pleasure," said Ariel, pale but triumphant. He loosened his grip on the chain, and nodded to Clara. "You can take your sword back now."

"Mary's *balls!*" grunted the demon as Clara drew out her sword. The metal was blackened where it had touched the demon, but on closer inspection this was just a dried film of its fluids, which began to flake off immediately.

"You're *bastards*, both of you," the demon remarked, his wings flopping to either side. "Utter bastards. I hope you get stuffed. With red hot pokers. Raw garlic. Broken glass. Hungry hagfish!"

"Are you Jude Carson?" Clara asked, because it was worth being sure.

"Who is Jude Carson?" returned the demon, the flesh pulling away from half his face in a macabre sneer. His bones were brilliant yellow. His bones, Clara thought, would have been beautiful without all that messy flesh of worms over them. "Jude Carson's just a name. Words. Don't mean anything."

"Great," sighed Ariel. "We have a wiseass."

"My ass is wiser than your head," snarled the demon.

"Are you the cause of the rupture currently threatening Devil's Lake?" Clara asked, who understood a little of demons and how they behaved when bound to tell the truth.

The worms around the demon's mouth knitted together, drew tight. He said nothing.

"You did not compel him to answer questions," Clara observed.

"I ran out of breath," Ariel said, a little defensively.

It didn't much matter in this case, Clara thought. Through the writhing skin and the lack of eyes she was beginning to be able to read the demon's expressions. And right now, he looked proud.

"For all intents and purposes," Clara said, "I believe he is."

"Yeah," said Ariel. "And he's thoroughly assimilated his host. I can't exorcise him."

Clara pursed her lips.

"Have you ever killed a demon before?" she asked.

Ariel looked at her, stricken.

"Not one this big," he said.

"You can't kill me," said the demon, smugly. "Got my claws in the lake. Got a dozen vessels all lined up. You two are worrying over a fallen pebble when there's an avalanche on its way. Our antichrist's a-coming, and when they get here there ain't nothing you can do."

"I thought *you* were the antichrist," Ariel said.

"That's what I did say, yes," said the demon. "Back when I could lie."

"So Jude Carson was a front. An alias."

"Don't pretend to be surprised," said the demon. He flowed into something resembling a sitting position. Folded vague arms.

He was being suspiciously agreeable, even for a bound demon. Clara began rearming herself, strapping on her sheath and cleaning Bellatrix. As she half expected, this made the Jude Carson demon even more talkative.

"Like attracts like," he said. "The antichrist is pure infernal. But they usually need their powers jumpstarted. S'why I got sent up. This one's only been on earth twelve years, but we've had young-uns before. Nearly worked once, too, but he went the other way."

"Other way?" Ariel prompted, though he was also beginning to case their surroundings.

"Antichrist is the child of Satan," said the demon. "People forget, Satan is also a child of God. Follows, his children can go either way."

"Or no way," said Clara, quietly.

"More often than not," sighed the demon. A part of it flicked out, like a tail.

Clara caught the motion out of the corner of her eye, but instead of being drawn to it, she looked the other way. Just in time to see a man in jeans and a polo shirt stand up from behind a bush and point a pistol at them.

Clara was already moving, grabbing Ariel and pulling him sideways.

The first shot went wide, throwing up a small geyser of sand next to the demon.

Amid the *pwoom! Pwoom! Pwoom!* of the shots coming at them, Clara distinctly heard the sound of Arcana's engine, and the next moment the huge red truck bounced over the horizon, charged down the beach, and ran directly over their assailant, motoring on past them to chase the group which had been creeping toward the campground from the other side.

Clara took off at a sprint toward the fallen man, while the demon struggled out of the chain and dove into the lake, and Ariel, wringing his stinging hands, gave chase to the truck.

There was not much left of the man. He had gone under the wheels after Arcana struck him, and from the look of his corpse, that had been all of them.

The body was still twitching, but Clara suspected that was from the dying convulsions of his nervous system, judging by the angle of his neck and the depression in one side of his head. His weapon, a short-barreled revolver, had been thrown almost ten feet upon impact, but it stood out from the gray-brown, sandy earth, and Clara picked it up out of instinct. Pointing the muzzle at the ground, she opened the chamber and pulled out the remaining charges, then depressed the trigger to clear the system. The last shot spudded into the earth, sending up a small plume of wet sand.

Only then did she turn around and reassess their situation.

The Carson demon had gone to ground in the lake. She could see the effect of his influence, like an oil slick, spreading out over the surface of the water. He would probably be busy trying to strip off all the compulsions Ariel had laid on him for at least the next hour or so.

Ariel himself was about a hundred yards away, moving toward Arcana, who had come to rest with three wheels up on the concrete foundation of the public restrooms, his engine purring. There was no sign of the other men, but Clara kept her eyes peeled the entire time she approached them, warily tracking back and forth as she did so.

Ariel was applying similar caution, walking sideways up to the truck as if it were a skittish horse. When he was about five feet away, the front passenger door sprang open of its own accord and his briefcase fell out. Along with it came grainy radio music, which sent shivers up Clara's spine as she realized what it was.

"*Run, run, with a twister,*" came the over-processed voice of Princess Die. "*Run, run, withered sister . . .*"

Ariel had retrieved his briefcase, backing slowly away from the singing truck.

"*Run, run, 'cause if you stop, baby she dies. Run, run, there's a whirlwind of hate in your eyes.*"

"Who are you?" Clara asked. She could only imagine what might have (literally) possessed Arcana, but her imagination had helpfully provided so many possibilities it was impossible to pick one.

Demons?

Ghosts?

Gremlins?

Nature spirits?

Unlikely, but they lived in a wold of unlikely marvels.

The radio clicked. Changed stations. Snippets of talk show, a tractor advertisement, static, then, clear and pure came the harmonizing vocals of Rook Parliament.

"She's a ghost among your men, she's a dark one, understand!"

A hiccup, more static, and then the static faded out as the radio's volume turned down to silence.

"Are you a ghost?" Ariel asked. He'd opened his briefcase, a safe distance away. There was a small spatter of fresh blood on Arcana's fender, and branches and leaves stuck in his windshield wipers. His engine revved, but he didn't move.

"Oooooooooh, nooooooooo . . ." crooned Rook Parliament.

"Are you a demon?" Clara tried.

A blip. Back to Princess Die.

"WE'RE GOING LONG, WE CAN BE WRONG, FLYING HIGH—FLYING BLIND—ON THE ROAD OF BLOOD!"

"Can you tell us what you are?" Ariel asked.

"We're on a road, we're on a rooooooo—ffzzzzt"—the radio went through another rapid change of stations. When it settled again, it sounded like the middle of an interview. A well-adjusted American voice was on the tail end of a question, which was answered by a deep, male one, in accented but earnest English. Leaning heavily on the ends of his words, as though he wanted to add another vowel there but was trying hard not to, he said:

"The thing to remember. Westerners do not have a word for this. But in Japanese artistry we have a concept called *ma*. This is like presence in the form of absence."

"Negative space?" the interviewer cut in.

"Eeerr, no. A little. It is the . . . the beat. The space between. When you allow a character to breathe out. Take a moment, let things be. *Ma*."

The radio volume turned down sharply, though the interview continued.

"You're *ma*?" Ariel tried.

Up went the volume again, in time for the patient Japanese man to say: "Something like that."

"Whose side are you on?" Clara asked, since this felt like the next most important thing.

Another shot of static, then a woman's voice said:

"Sides are for coins. Messages are for answering machines."

"What have you done with Mantha?" Ariel asked. He had removed a small black book from his briefcase, opened it to a spread depicting a complicated diagram, and was in the process of tracing the image onto the sand in front of him.

The radio went clean off. Then on again. This time in the middle of a Technorhyme song.

"Burn slow, in the dark, you know, you'll reap what you sow. Burn slow . . ."

The engine revved again, and that was all the warning they had before Arcana threw himself into reverse, bounced down off the concrete pad, pulling his door shut and making a donut in the sand as he forged away across the trail, leaving gouges in the grass verge as he headed up the bank to where the men had fled.

The disturbance wiped out half of Ariel's carefully constructed diagram, and he sat back on his heels with a resigned sigh.

Clara kept staring after Arcana. His presence had felt like a nagging itch in the bottom of her mind. Like the Japanese man had tried to explain: it was the presence in the form of absence.

Void was a part of nature. The ultimate antithesis. Void as a presence of its own, however? That she could not identify.

"Well, I don't think he's *against* us," Ariel said. He was leafing through his little book, chewing his lower lip in concentration.

"He's done something with Mantha," Clara announced.

"Or Mantha's done something with him," Ariel pointed out. "Anyway, I don't think he's on Jude Carson's side."

"What makes you say that?" Clara asked, still distracted by this new idea.

Mantha was good an influencing things. Who was to say this wasn't just another example of that?

But then Mantha had been shy of Arcana ever since they'd got here.

There was something more going on.

"Because he's given me my kit back," Ariel said, and the quiet triumph in his voice made Clara turn around.

Ariel had removed a wide, leather wallet filled with crystal vials. In each one, Clara glimpsed a tiny, pearly white bone.

"Saints?" Clara asked, dubiously.

Ariel shook his head.

"Something better, and much harder to acquire," he said.

Clara wracked her brains, but the only thing she could come up with was so wildly unlikely it made the thought of a nature spirit possessing Arcana downright rational.

"Changelings?" she asked, just in case.

Ariel whistled low. "Got it in two," he said, flashing her a brief smile.

Clara swallowed.

"We can seal the gate," she said.

"That's the plan," said Ariel, carefully selecting four vials, hooking each one on a piece of leather string.

Clara breathed in. Out.

They could do this.

"I can take east and south," she said.

"Then I'll do north and west, and we'll call it macaroni," said Ariel briskly, handing Clara a pair of vials.

She took them as if they were more precious than gold and more volatile than a live flame, which was true, and stepped back respectfully as Ariel closed and locked his briefcase one handed.

"Incant from east and west," he said. "In thirty minutes?"

"Twenty," said Clara. "I'll run."

"You do that, then," said Ariel. He smiled at her again. Nervous. Brave. Determined. Brilliant.

Clara nodded once, and ran.

After about twenty minutes sitting on the rocks Mantha's butt got so sore she had to get up and move about. Lady Bibbit suggested they climb the rock stack.

"I'll spot you," she offered.

Mantha wasn't particularly afraid of heights but agreed this made the proposal a reasonable one.

The rock stack was a good one for climbing, being full of ledges and hard outcroppings perfect for hands and feet. Above the treetops they could see the lake—they were quite close to it, actually—and the wind picked up, tugging at their clothes and Mantha's hair. But Lady Bibbit pointed out they could just move around onto the lee side, and from there it was a simple, if vertical, ascent up to the very top.

This was a table of rock dominated by a large, bushy nest made of torn-up branches, some of them so old all the bark had come off and they were sun-bleached white. There was enough room to comfortably sit with her legs hanging off the edge but not much more. Though she did stand up to peek inside the nest—it was empty save for a few mangled feathers—Mantha didn't like the way the wind pushed her, and sat down out of it. This put her facing away from the lake, looking at a bunch of trees.

She didn't see the snake come out of the earth, but Lady Bibbit did. She tugged Mantha's sleeve, and together the two of them lay down on their stomachs with their heads hanging over the edge to watch.

It slithered from a hole in the ground near the base of the rock stack, very near where Mantha had been sitting. It was very big, and kept coming out of the hole for almost five minutes, until finally its body tapered to a tail of bulbous shells, like a rattlesnake's. It was also incredibly dirty, with dirt and dust and greenish moss clinging to its back, but where it bent and moved, cracks appeared, through which gleamed pearlescent radiance.

The most remarkable feature, however, were the two giant horns on top of its triangular head, and between them something flashed. More brilliant than a strobe light, sparkling and enchanting, it took Mantha a moment to realize it was a diamond.

Moving like a lazy stream, the snake poured itself out of the ground and through the trees, where Mantha could just trace the course of its head through the bushes, until it crossed a strip of rocky beach and disappeared into the water. Its body followed, a long trail of glittering cracks, until the entire creature had been swallowed by the lake.

Beside her, Lady Bibbit shivered.

"If you ask me," she said. "I think something very important just happened."

Mantha agreed, though she could not say why. The snake had excited her in a strange way. Like seeing something magical. Properly, wondrously magical, like the kind of magic she'd read about in books. And yet at the same time she had felt a kind of overwhelming sadness at the sight of it, so dirty and tired. It had been hiding in the earth for a long time, and now it had come out to do something it was not pleased to do.

A little while after the snake had disappeared into the water something else happened. Mantha felt it like a shift in the prevailing winds, even though the winds themselves did not change. The best way she could describe it, and she did so to Lady Bibbit at the time, was to say it was like someone had torn a not-quite-healed scab off a wound in the world.

Blood was welling up deep in the lake. Only it was not blood. It was a torrent of energy, of emotions and powers that she did not like the feel of. They called out to her, tugging at her bones and her heart, and Mantha knew that power was hers to claim if she would only reach out and do so.

But to do so would mean leaving Lady Bibbit, and Clara and Ariel. It would mean leaving herself as she had known and lived for the last twelve years.

She would be a better, stronger, truer version of herself, yes, but since Mantha still wasn't precisely sure who that person was, the thought of becoming them, all at once and all-powerfully, frightened her.

The world darkened.

"It's him again," Lady Bibbit said, unhappily.

That brought Mantha back to earth in a hurry.

"Jude Carson?" she asked.

Lady Bibbit was small and gray, and her fur looked infinitely soft. Her remaining eye narrowed, her nose twitched.

"If that's what you want to call him," she said.

Mantha shuddered. She was suddenly and vehemently against going anywhere near that well of power. She wanted nothing to do with it.

She hoped, strangely, that the horned serpent would come back. The horned serpent belonged in *this* world in a way that that power didn't. The serpent, she thought, might be able to help.

The world darkened. Mantha thought it was only a cloud passing over the sun, but then she heard a distant beat, like gentle thunder, which turned into a whistling of air through harsh feathers, and then a giant black eagle was gliding in, stirring a storm of air under its wings to land with a crackle in the abandoned nest.

It looked down at her, out of eyes that flickered purple and gold, like a very sharp, black raincloud with talons, and hissed softly through its imposing beak.

Mantha had rolled onto her back to get a better look at it, and now felt crushed against the rock from the weight of that gaze. It was such a fearful, penetrating stare it made her feel transparent. The mind of the black eagle was so huge and tumultuous it was impossible to push about as she had pushed Ariel or even, to some extent, Clara. It would have been like trying to hold a hurricane with her bare hands.

It was Lady Bibbit who sat up, turned herself around, and bowed to the great bird. In a voice that was respectful but not in the least bit frightened, she said:

"Forgive us this trespass, lord. We seek only sanctuary and will take away nothing but ourselves."

The bird then fixed Lady Bibbit with its thunderous gaze, and Mantha felt her heart rise in her throat at the thought of how easily it could snap Lady Bibbit up in that huge, stony beak, crunch her once and swallow her whole.

But the eagle made no move—it did not even blink—though the wind ruffled the feathers along its neck. They glimmered there, a faint iridescence that reminded Mantha of the horned serpent.

"As long as you *do* go away," the eagle said, slow and grave with a voice like gravel moving under water. "Go away, and take this interloper with you."

Lady Bibbit nodded, and Mantha presumed the interloper was herself.

Lady Bibbit, for all she had come to life from Mantha's imagination, seemed to understand the eagle—and was understood by the eagle— better than Mantha. They were both animals, and though Lady Bibbit was a rabbit, it seemed the eagle liked that better than a human.

Feeling unaccountably disgusted with herself, Mantha looked back out over the lake just in time to see the serpent break the water in a shudder of rainbow ripples. It was carrying something in its mouth, something big and black and floppy, that caused it to move in sinuous lunges until it reached the shore and began slithering out of the water.

When Mantha recognized the water panther's corpse as the black thing in the serpent's mouth she could not contain a gasp. It was a mix of disgust and disappointment, but she could not turn her gaze away as the serpent began, slowly and deliberately, to swallow the panther whole. Only when it had finished did it look up and fix Mantha with its twin pearl eyes. The shard of rainbow diamond in its forehead flashed, and Mantha found it was impossible to look away.

She loved that serpent. And she was terrified of it. She wanted to be its friend. She wanted to cut its head open and steal that gem. And she was horrified at herself for feeling that way.

"You would not be the first," remarked the serpent, dryly. It had a voice like oil sliding through dead leaves, and though Mantha did not see its mouth open, she heard it as clearly as if the serpent had been sitting next to her.

"Are you finished yet?" asked the eagle, its water-gravel voice loud behind Mantha's head.

"Nearly there," replied the serpent. "Why are you hosting that little demigod?"

Mantha felt her hairs rise as she recognized the reference to herself.

"I'm not hosting her," said the eagle. "I'm refraining from eating her."

"All right," said the serpent. "But if she's still here this evening, I say we feed her to Mishipeshu."

Mantha looked miserably at Lady Bibbit.

"I think we should leave," she said.

Lady Bibbit shook her head. "Not yet," she said. "It's not safe out there."

Mantha was about to point out that it wasn't safe *here*, when something cracked in the world, and she was jerked sideways out of it.

In one way she never left her perch on the rock pile. She felt her fingers clinging to the cool, rough surface even as her mind slipped away into the layer of reality that existed, always slightly out of reach, just beneath the tangible world.

Lady Bibbit and the eagle and the serpent were all there, but they looked different. Lady Bibbit wore a flowing gray dress almost indistinguishable from her silvery fur and carried a staff with a sharply curved crescent moon at the end. She had two eyes again, the right one blue and pure, the left one black and pricked with stars.

The eagle was a black-skinned, long-limbed man in a loincloth with a great shaggy beard. His teeth were yellow and his eyes twinkled madly.

The serpent was still serpent shaped, but its head was wider, flatter, and its forked tongue drifted lazily in the air before it. It breathed in twisted, troubled magic, and breathed out pure, crystalline essence.

They were all beautiful in their own way, and it made Mantha embarrassed to be herself, so muddled and powerful. She felt like a backhoe in a rose garden: huge and destructive and dirty.

All this was immediate, and she noticed it without really thinking about it. Most of her attention was drawn out, to the center of the lake, where there was a man-shaped piece of fire that flickered invitingly.

She knew it was Carson without even looking for his pit-like eyes. She knew it was Carson, and she felt him calling her.

Or, not exactly her. He didn't know *her*. But he was calling for someone like her. Someone she *could be*.

But he didn't know her *name*. If he had called her by name, Mantha thought she might not be able to resist getting up and walking right out over the lake to him.

But he did not. He only called her by what he expected her to be. So although a part of her desperately wanted to take herself away, out of the pure, ferocious world of the eagle and serpent, the part that was in front— the part that called herself Mantha and loved Clara and Lady Bibbit and ate ice cream and liked listening to Ariel sing—dug her fingers into the rock, and stayed put.

When she saw Clara stand up a little ways down the shore it was such a surprise that she nearly forgot all about Jude Carson and her own internal conflicts.

Clara rose up above the treetops, like a pale marble obelisk, and she held a piece of the land, drawing in the edges of the world so the wild, rushing space over the lake was contained.

Distantly, Mantha saw Ariel doing the same. He was across the lake and much smaller than Clara, but his presence glowed, warm and reassuring. A small sun, but a sun nonetheless.

They began to work together, weaving the frayed edges of the land. Mantha had no idea how they did it, but she saw it happen, and was amazed.

Slowly, the pure, ferocious world of the eagle and serpent drew close around the water, and then began to creep inward, pushing at Jude Carson until it was lapping at the edges of the man-shaped fire.

There it stopped, sizzling against his presence, and Mantha realized it could go no further.

Jude Carson was in some way also the gate to yet another dimension, and he was embedding himself in the land so he could not be closed.

It felt dangerous, like leaning out over a precipice, but Mantha threaded one hand into Lady Bibbit's paw and held herself rooted there, and then she reached out with her other hand and tipped Jude Carson through to the other side—back where he belonged.

All at once the edges of the world surged together, melding and sealing, and Mantha had to pull her hand back in a hurry to keep from being caught in it.

Yet she still felt, distinct as a bite of lemon, the presence of Jude Carson. It saw her and knew her, and it was *furious*.

And then the hole was mended, the wind stopped, and Mantha tumbled back into the real world to find Lady Bibbit hauling her away from the cliff.

They collapsed backward into a pile of twigs—all that was left the of the eagle's nest. The giant bird was gone. So was the serpent, when Mantha dared to look down. For a moment she thought she saw something that glimmered, like a shed scale, but when she looked again it was just a drop of water on a branch, catching the light of the sun which had finally decided to peek through the clouds.

Somewhere in the Dark

Jill hung, suspended in the darkness, for an uncertain amount of time. Her phone would not wake up, and no matter how she strained, even her vampire eyes could see nothing but black.

Still, she sensed movement. Giants, like curious whales, drifted past. Jill sensed them by the disturbance they caused whatever medium it was that existed around her. Once, dimly, she thought that one of these shapes paused, swam closer to inspect her, but then it moved on.

Jill was not frightened. She'd been angry, and frustrated, and worried, but not afraid. What had she to fear? She who did not need food, or sunlight, or even to breathe—necessarily—had no reason to fear the dark. And if Jill was anything, she was reasonable.

She'd worked through most of her applicable feelings and was almost growing bored when there was . . . not a light, exactly . . . but a change in the texture of the darkness in front of her.

It came and sat, like a tired old woman, stretching its legs out and slumping into its chair of nothing, as if it were an immense relief to get off its nonexistent feet.

It said,

Hello, Jill Hamilton.

"Hello," Jill replied, mostly relieved that something was happening at last.

It did not occur to her to be afraid of the dark within the dark. It felt familiar somehow. Like coming home.

Jill hadn't really been home since Christian had died. That seemed like another life—someone else's life—and the realization of how distant it had gone made her colder inside than usual.

To take her mind off it she asked the dark a question:

"Do I know you?"

Not really, said the dark within the dark. *But I know you.*

Jill sighed. It felt good to expand her ribcage. Like a shrug for her torso.

"Have we met before?" she tried again.

Oh, many times.

"Remind me," Jill demanded.

I have been with you on your night runs, the dark said. *I was with you at the trial of vampires. And before, on the night you changed. I was with you beneath the ocean, where the merman came for you. I was with you in the basement of Rafe McCleaver's house, when you found the Tiefzauberbuch. And it was I who rescued you from the nightmare spirit. I have been with you quite a lot, as of late, though you might not have recognized that I was me.*

Jill frowned.

"Is this a riddle?" she asked. "Or can you just tell me who you are?"

There are many answers to that question, said the dark within the dark. *All of which are true. Humans have identified me in countless ways:*

as Erebus, as Arawn, the Grim Reaper, Umbra, Dark Energy...though that last is so inaccurate as to be almost laughable. If I could laugh.

Jill felt her eyes roll. "Give me the answer applicable to our situation," she suggested.

To you, let me be the sapient manifestation of a primordial cosmic entity, the darkness replied.

Jill frowned, wondering which primordial cosmic entity was sapiently manifesting. The fact that it had declared one of its identities as the Grim Reaper suggested this was Death she was talking to. But Erebus she knew was the primordial Greek god of night. Arawn sounded familiar, but she couldn't remember who they were. She also didn't know if Umbra referred to the phenomenon or someone else. She felt on firmer ground with Dark Energy, since that at least she understood to be a term applied to all the energy in the universe that was not describable by the laws of physics.

Such is the nature of human belief that many of those characters have attained a level of reality independent from myself, the entity remarked. *Sadly, few people see me for what I am, but it is understandable considering I exist in all the spaces they* cannot *see. I am before and after and forever in between. I am the presence of void. I am the default state of the cosmos, from which it came and to which it will—one way or the other— eventually return.*

It did not say this in a way that suggested grandeur or boasting. The entity spoke earnestly, as though it was trying to explain something very difficult to put into words. The mental image Jill got was of someone with strong but fat fingers trying to thread a very small needle.

"Are you ... the *dark?*" she asked. It was an almost random guess, and not nearly specific enough for Jill's liking, but the entity seemed pleased.

That is a generalization, it said. *But it is not factually incorrect.*

So, close enough, Jill thought. She tried to get a better look at the entity before her, but realized that was pointless.

If it was the dark, or *the* Dark, as Clara might say, it was all around her. *She was* looking at it.

That didn't make communication any easier.

"What do you want with me?" she asked.

I don't particularly want anything with you, the darkness said. *One of my hounds brought you to me, I think out of the mistaken intent that I could help you where she could not.*

Hounds? wondered Jill. Then she realized: Frosty. The hunt. Clara had said Frosty was a Yell Hound. The Yell Hounds had belonged to the king of the underworld in Welsh mythology. *That* was where "Arawn" came from.

Darkness indeed.

Then she processed what the darkness had said.

"Frosty thought you could *help?*"

My hounds are more reliant on your world than I am, the darkness said. *I am not much given to sentimentality, but I liked Arawn, and I like your world. I sent the one you call "frosty" to . . . what is that idiom that is so disturbing if taken literally? Oh yes. Keep an eye on you. The present state of affairs has grown beyond her capability to manage, and so she brought you to me. Light knows why.*

Jill wondered idly if there was a sapient manifestation of Light and if the darkness was speaking literally, or using another idiom.

"I don't expect you to help," she said, modestly. After all, if it *was* something as big and timeless as darkness, Jill couldn't imagine it going far out of its way to meddle in her tiny little life. Such as it was.

That is refreshingly rational of you, said the dark. *As a matter of fact, I am not helping you now because I have* already *helped you. More than you know. And it's more trouble than I've been to since your people were building temples to Nyx, let me tell you.*

"Thank . . . you?" said Jill, uncertain if this was the appropriate thing to say. She felt a little like a heroine in one of those novels where the protagonist winds up in a magical world and has to make nice with creatures whose minds work very differently from hers.

Gratitude is understandable, said the darkness. *But not necessary. If I may make a confession—I have become rather invested in your story. It may seem silly to you, but from my vantage point, it appears to me that this world and its subsidiaries will be much better served if your actions are facilitated rather than opposed.*

Jill pondered this, momentarily awed at the prospect that something as vast and endless as *the dark* would think her actions important—much less worth supporting.

Then her skeptical nature reasserted itself and she asked, almost sarcastically:

"Have you been talking to Johnny Bathory?"

Talking would be a metaphor. But I did communicate with him— though he might not have recognized it as such. Most intelligences on your spectrum interpret me as their own internal voice. Or dreams. Or God. Sometimes aliens.

"Why do I get special treatment?" Jill asked, dryly.

In the broad scheme of things, which is where I operate, you don't, the darkness said, rather bluntly. *The fact is, you relate to us differently than most of the people on your frequency. Your experiences are your own. What you find in them is yours to take.*

"Am I supposed to find anything here?" Jill asked.

Worry less about whether you are "supposed" to be or do anything, the darkness suggested. *If I may attempt to offer some straightforward advice: allow the world to broaden your mind, for it is wider than you can, on your own, imagine.*

Without any noticeable change in the pitch black around her, Jill sensed the darkness get to its feet and lean over her.

And if it becomes overwhelming, remember that I am always within you. This said, the darkness straightened up and began to walk away. Metaphorically.

"Wait!" Jill called after it. "How do I get back?"

The presence paused. Considered this.

Fear not, the darkness said. *The worst is yet to come.*

And then it turned into a proper shadow, and Jill realized the world was lightening all around her. The shadow was Marcus, and he'd thrown himself over her as he tried to get her pack open and pull out her day suit.

She was lying in a prickly field of green and brown grass. The sky was a spectrum of gray whitening in the east, and a little ways off Frosty was also lying in the grass, enthusiastically chewing on a large, bloody bone. When she saw Jill was awake, she thumped her tail happily.

They had not gotten far—barely across the freeway, which was beginning to roar with the morning traffic. Still, Jill didn't like the idea of sprinting for the safety of the center, and wriggled herself into the day suit as soon as she'd regained control of her limbs. These had gone unaccountably numb and unresponsive, but came back to life once she focused on getting them moving.

"You scared me there," Marcus said. "You looked dead. Deader than usual, I mean. Only I could tell you weren't? It was weird. What happened?"

"I met Frosty's owner," Jill told him as she pulled the helmet on. Like that, gloved and swaddled, she looked like a spaceman in a silver suit, but she did not fear the rising sun which cast beams of yellow light through the cracks in the skyline to the east.

They walked ponderously back to the center, Frosty carrying her bone high and proud.

They entered into a lull in the growing chaos. Tamerlain and Don had just come on duty, and the former was making lattes in the cafeteria for the other morning people. These included Professor Okedo, whose hair appeared to have gone many shades grayer over the course of the night. Lansing was still awake, riffling a stack of papers into order with grim intention.

"Intake forms," she told Jill coldly, once Jill had climbed out of her day suit.

Jill counted. There were over a dozen.

"All at once?" she asked.

"No," said Lansing, with the special bitter joy of someone going off shift, "but each one is a party of three or more. It's getting crowded."

Leafing through the forms, Jill found herself confronted with as many bizarre styles of writing as she was Lansing's own neat hand. Of the ones she could read at a glance, these ranged from tree spirits to trolls, and one ghost.

She had not lost sight of her original mission, however, and set the forms aside to get out her phone—which had until then been inaccessible under her suit—to call Clara.

Only to discover a string of texts from the woman. New texts. All timestamped minutes after she'd set off on the ill-fated jaunt with Marcus and Frosty. Because of the nature of her phone's alert display, these were fed to her newest first, and so it was dreadfully confusing for about thirty seconds until she got fed up and opened the messaging app.

She read the messages.

She went and sat down.

("Are you all right?" Marcus asked. She did not reply.)

They were okay. Somehow. Jude Carson, as far as they could tell, had been sucked through the gate—whatever that was—moments before it closed. They were still missing Mantha, and Arcana was apparently possessed by something.

She scrolled down.

Mantha had turned up, Lady Bibbit in tow.

They could not find Arcana.

A text from Ariel, assuring Jill they could always rent a car to drive home.

They were not sure what to make of the spirit possessing Arcana. Mantha didn't like it, but apparently it had helped them. Inasmuch as Arcana had, under its influence, run over one of Jude Carson's followers. It had also rescued Mantha.

Out of the darkness at the back of her mind, Jill heard it say:

I am not helping you now because I have already *helped you.*

They had found Arcana. He was, apart from some small scratches and mud all over his undercarriage and up over his fenders, fine. He did not resist them entering his cab, and allowed himself to be driven as normal.

They were going to try driving him home.

That last message was from fifteen minutes ago.

Hardly daring to hope, Jill switched to the tracking app and looked up Clara's location. For once it loaded immediately, showing her as a blue dot on WI 78, moving slowly north. Nestled beside her was another blue dot: Ariel. Jill stayed hunched over her phone until it updated, showing them progressing steadily along the road.

Coming home.

She went back to the messaging app and sent a reply:

Glad to hear it. Things getting busy over here. Drive safe.

The message sent, Jill watched the little gray letters that said "delivered" under the blue bubble of text, wishing Clara had enabled read receipts on her phone. She made a mental note to change those settings when she got back.

Then, wonder of wonders, Clara's avatar popped up, with the gray bubble of an incoming message.

. . .

. . .

ok see You soon

Jill locked her phone and slipped it into her pocket. Professor Okedo was going through the intake forms, looking tireder by the minute.

Jill grinned. She felt remarkably fine. Not particularly alive or energetic, but despite the mounting chaos around her and the certainty that what the darkness had said about things getting worse being undoubtedly true, she also had the inexplicable conviction that everything would, ultimately, be okay.

She rubbed Frosty behind one red ear.

"I'll take the ghost and the trolls," she told Okedo. "Tamerlain, if you could spot the front desk? Thanks. I have a feeling it's going to be a busy day."

I-90 Eastbound, WI

They made good time at first, but traffic was thick on I-90 and eventually it slowed to stop-and-go as they crossed the Wisconsin River.

The inside of the cab was relatively quiet. Everyone was tired and no one was happy, except for Lady Bibbit, who hummed a gentle tune to herself, knocking her furry feet against the back seat.

Ariel drove, Mantha napped, and Clara watched the fuel gauge like a hawk.

It hadn't moved one jot since they'd left Devil's Lake. Since they'd found Arcana parked with scrupulous care in the exact same spot they'd originally left him.

Ariel insisted that whatever entity had possessed him was no longer present, but Clara was not entirely convinced. Or, if it was truly gone, it had not left Arcana as it had found him.

"But considering the price of diesel these days," Ariel said. "I'm not gonna complain."

"It is worth monitoring," Clara insisted.

"For sure," said Ariel. "I'm just saying . . . could be worse."

The traffic inched forward. Ariel nursed the truck along in second, working the clutch so they spent most of the time coasting. He was very good at it. Clara envied him the ease with which he operated the manual transmission, but not the cramp he had to be getting in his left calf.

They passed a section where the left lane had been cordoned off with cones, and just as they came upon the crash site—now no more than a couple highway patrol cars and some broken glass—the traffic sped up to normal speeds.

"How 'bout a little music?" Ariel suggested.

Clara shrugged.

And then the radio came on.

She hadn't touched the controls. Neither had Ariel. Glancing into the back seat, she saw Mantha was still asleep.

"Okay, that's a *little* creepy," Ariel said.

"Do you still have control?" Clara asked.

For answer, Ariel down shifted and slowed to forty-five miles per hour, changing into the righthand lane. Then he sped back up again and moved left to pass a semi-truck.

"Seems okay," he said.

Clara was reaching for the volume control when Mantha, woken by the sudden change in speed, said blearily.

"Oh, it's your song, Ariel."

She was right, Clara realized. It had started off so quietly she hadn't recognized it at first, and now instead of turning the radio off she turned the volume up.

And the sound of "White Bird" filled the cab as Arcana picked up speed, heading southeast into the rising sun.

One door leads to heaven
And one door leads to hell
And the great gate in between them
Has secrets it won't tell.
Just ask Sammy, before she fell.

And if you go hunting nightmares
And you think you're going to cry
Tell 'em all their nightmares come true
On the day before they die.
You call Sammy, when she was the sky.

When the damned go swimming in
Blood—and the fruit is hanging low
And hope hangs like a chain on your neck
And you don't know where to go
Call the white bird, because she'll know.

When fire and brimstone have burned right through your head
And it's a cold day in Damnation
And the Devil's asking to be fed
Remember what the darkness said:
"They're not dead! They're not dead!"

—White Bird/*Washington Dreamship*

8.

A COLD DAY *in* HELL

City of Dis, Lake of Cocytus
Ninth Ring, Caïna and Antenora

THE GREAT LAKE was so huge that its far shore was invisible, cloaked in a dim fog the purplish-green color of an old bruise. The sky also was dark, blanketed with black-bellied clouds. Though the lake surface was frozen, it was not a smooth sheet of ice. It rose and fell in ripples and waves, some of which created troughs hundreds of feet deep.

To an ordinary person, scaling the frozen cliffs and sliding down the far sides would have rendered inward progress an exercise in futility, unless they were well equipped with ice picks, crampons, rope, carabiners, and very warm clothes.

To the giantess with a rainbow halo over her pale head and a dark cloud of demons—smaller than songbirds in comparison—fluttering in her wake, it was only a matter of stepping carefully, and at times going around the taller waves, whose peaks were capped with frozen foam. She was slightly handicapped by having to keep her right hand palm up and flat, for the sake of the three human-sized figures clinging to it, but so far no one had asked to get down. Although, after they'd passed the first great wave—frozen in the act of crashing in on itself—Selene had turned her head away and shouted across Albatross's palm at Shae:

"This isn't anything like what Dante described!"

Shae, who was clinging with no more dignity than Selene, having wrapped her arms around the base of Albatross's ring finger—which was the size of a tree trunk—snorted.

"Dante is out of date!" she called back. "There's been a dozen near-apocalypses since the 1300s, and Cocytus has thawed at least three times!"

There was a whistling sound of agreement from behind them, and by craning her neck, Selene saw the demon that had followed them out of the ninth bolgia nodding its bird-skull face at them.

Of the three of them it had taken to hand-riding the best, crouching on the heel of Albatross's palm like an oversized pigeon, its thin red arms with the needle-like fingers at the ends folded conscientiously under its chest. Its stiff, white robes, which hid the rest of its body, flapped in the wind generated by their movement above the frozen waves like ineffectual wings.

It still did not speak, tapping out its meanings with its wicked fingers or through eerie whistles, but had given them no clue as to why it alone, out of its dozens of comrades, had followed them.

Shae had tried to interrogate it as soon as they had got out of sight of the Eighth Ring, asking it questions like "Who is your master?" and "What is your order?" and "Do you have a name?" To which the demon had just stared at her, quizzically, out of its empty eye sockets.

Disappointed, Shae had turned her questions to Selene.

"It followed you out of the ninth circle?" The way she said this made it sound like she doubted Selene understood the implications of the action, which Selene fully admitted she did not. Earlier, she would have been aggravated by the assumption. Because everything Shae said or did was laced with self-confident superiority, whether or not she was actually right. But Selene had seen that arrogant shell crack, and through the cracks glimpsed someone who worried, who doubted, and laughed and cried with relief just like anyone else. So she just sighed. Besides, she could only repeat what she had already said:

"I told you. They gave us an escort through the ninth circle—*that* one decided to come with. If anyone knows why, it's *her*." She spared a hand to jerk it upward at the mountainous form of Albatross's shoulders, neck, and head—which was just visible through the mist as a dim silhouette crowned with a perfect halo made of rainbow.

This was too intimidating, even for Shae, and so they travelled through the mist in relative silence for a while.

Relative, because of the rushing of the wind in their ears and the periodic cries from far below—or not so far below, depending on where the frozen waves were. These came, Selene had discovered, from the countless bodies trapped in the ice—enough of whom had their heads free to be able to bemoan their situation. Loudly. Sometimes they passed close enough that Selene was able to make out their individual forms, even their faces, and to catch words among their cries.

It gave her an unexpected pang to hear that, for the most part, these were fervent apologies.

"Jerry, Jerry—can you hear me?" screamed a woman near the peak of a crashing wave. "I'm sorry, Jerry! *I'm s-so sorry . . .*"

They swept by, and her voice was swept away by the wind.

"Isn't Nine the ring of traitors?" Selene asked, the next time there was a break in the wind."

"Yes," Shae answered. "I think we're still in Caïna—that's traitors to family, named after—"

"Cain, I remember," Selene said.

"But it's not just the Ninth Ring," Shae continued. "Before she was dammed, Cocytus was the river of lamentation. Even now, frozen and stagnant, that's all anyone here can do: lament their failings."

"You don't need to be stuck in Cocytus to do that," Selene said, remembering Darceen's mother.

Darceen had been a casual, intermittent girlfriend for about four years after Selene had gotten out of the army. An earthy, wholesome, generous person whose garrulous exterior hid deep emotional insecurities which Selene hadn't fully understood until she'd met Darceen's mother, a woman who thought of herself as kind, patient and generous but was so fixated on her own (admittedly messed up) childhood that she could spare no consideration for anyone else. Continuously lamenting how abusive her own mother had been, all the while either tormenting her own daughter or neglecting her entirely—interspersed with just enough bouts of kindness and compassion to give Darceen paralyzing emotional anxiety. The only thing that had made the situation tolerable to Selene was that the reason she had to see so much of Darceen's mother was because she'd come down to Huntsville for a week to help Darceen move out of her mother's house. Even though Darceen had broken up with her the minute she got to Austin, Selene considered the relationship a success if only because she'd gotten Darceen out of her mother's house before the end.

It wasn't enough to recognize and lament the awful things that had happened to you or the awful things you had done. You had, at some point, to look forward and apply that knowledge to making things better than they had been.

But the dead cannot change. Perhaps the true punishment was that, like Cocytus, they had become stagnant, caught forever looking back with regret. The only action left to them was lamentation.

"True," Shae said, and Selene had become so absorbed in her own thoughts that she wasn't sure what Shae was responding to at first. Then she scrolled back through her memory to what she had last spoken aloud—*you don't need to be stuck in Cocytus to do what they were doing*—and felt unaccountably proud that she'd said something Shae thought was true.

The whole thing was ridiculous. The waves were dark with the bodies of the people caught within, but as they progressed, the noise lessened. The waves grew smaller, and the people in the ice sunk deeper into it, so that of those who were near the surface, only their faces reached the air.

They passed the giant shortly thereafter.

City of Dis, Lake of Cocytus
Ninth Ring, Ptolomaea

The waves had dwindled to mere ripples, the fog lifted until it was a thick blanket fading to inky black all around, while the dead ice reflected this so that, when she looked down, Selene could see Albatross's giant pale shape reflected in it.

The other giant stood out starkly because they, like Albatross, were mostly white. Blazingly, brilliantly, white. This was due to their cape, which looked to have been made from the fur of countless polar bears. They were sitting, crouched over a hole in the ice, into which they would intermittently jab a long, thin rod, coming up with a poor soul skewered on its end more often than not.

They were so far distant from Albatross's course that Selene was able to observe them long enough to see that, of the souls they caught, each one they raised to their nose and sniffed before either laying it out beside a growing row of soggy spirits or popping it whole into their mouth.

Then they came even with the giant, and Selene saw they were not wearing polar bear hides at all—the giant *was* a polar bear. A giant, white polar bear, wearing a leather belt and loincloth hung with tools. They were so intent on their task of soul fishing that they did not look up until Albatross was well past, and then they only raised their free paw in greeting and turned back to the hole in the ice.

"Now, that I don't understand," said Shae, sounding more awed than Selene had yet heard her. "What is *Nanook* doing here?"

Selene looked again at the giant polar bear, but it still took her a minute to remember who Nanook was, and for that she felt keenly embarrassed. Dante had met a Greek giant—Antaeus, she thought—but their great size was about the only thing a classical giant and the Inuit bear-god had in common. He looked out of place on that dark, frozen lake, serene and savage in a way that was of a wholly different nature than the rest of Hell.

While Hell was perverse in its torments, it had a pretentiousness that annoyed Selene. That bear, sitting on the ice, hunting dead human spirits like a human might go ice fishing, happily popping them into his mouth as if they were candy, was cruel and beautiful and unapologetically honest about what he was and what he was doing.

Selene slid herself around on Albatross's palm so she could keep watching him, even as they began to draw away, and the bear's gleaming pelt slowly faded into the darkness. The last she saw, he got up, and drawing up the string of souls, hung them from his rod like so many fish. Then he began to walk away, leaving behind the black, broken circle of ice. A wound in the otherwise now smooth surface of the lake.

Something Albatross had said came back to her then and made her smile unexpectedly.

"What is it?" Shae asked.

Selene shook her head. "The Harrowing of Hell is not solely for the Son," she said, and rolled her eyes upward.

Shae frowned, considering the implications of this. Then she looked accusingly at the ninth-circle demon.

"Is that what you're after?" she asked. "A ticket out of here?"

The demon clicked its long, knifelike fingers and looked away.

Albatross walked on, her bare feet skimming the frozen surface of the lake, while around her head buzzed the horde of third-circle demons. Lit by the rainbow of her halo, they looked more like flamboyant, iridescent insects than the mutilated creatures they really were. Unless, now Selene looked closer, they had truly changed appearance. Now, though still of unusual or imbalanced shape, they appeared more coherent. The jagged transitions between limb and body, back and wing, had smoothed. Torn membrane had solidified. They had not healed—they were still just as monstrous—but they had grown around their monstrosities. Like a tree around a barbed wire fence.

Onward strode the giant woman, across the frozen lake now smooth and silent, dark from the reflected clouds but also the many bodies trapped within. But they were all of them fully submerged in the ice, and no sound escaped their gaping mouths.

City of Dis, Lake of Cocytus
Ninth Ring, Judecca

Hell might be bigger the farther in you got, Selene thought, but it seemed Albatross had grown even in relation to that. For it felt like they had been riding in her palm for only a couple hours since they left the frozen waves behind, and now, if Selene remembered the *Inferno* correctly, they must be approaching the center of the Ninth Ring. Which meant Judecca, the region of Cocytus reserved for traitors against benefactors, and at the very center of that, the Prince of Darkness himself.

Selene found she was unconsciously looking anxiously ahead, both hoping for and fearing what they must inevitably find. Hoping, because it would mean they had reached the center—and therefore the end—of Hell, and fearing, because ... well, she'd heard a fair amount about the dude and none of it was exactly encouraging. And the whole Adversary thing aside, in Selene's experience celebrities frequently did not hold up under intense scrutiny. How Satan would manage to disappoint in this regard she had no idea, only that she was reasonably certain that he would. Somehow.

But when they finally encountered a change in the monotonous field of ice, it was a return to the tumultuous waves of Caïna, except more localized and extreme. To be precise, it looked like a meteor had crashed into the lake, melting the surface and traveling through the water before exploding out again, while the lake had refrozen immediately afterward, preserving the shape of the water a split second after the moment of impact.

Albatross picked her way through the choppy frozen waves until they came to the lip of the crater and could look down upon the original point of impact. There she stopped, and Selene felt a shudder run down her arm and shake the hand the held them.

The center of the crater was a jagged black hole in an otherwise white sheet of blasted ice. The water beneath had refrozen shortly after it had been exposed, black and solid, but not before one enterprising soul had made a determined effort to escape.

They had not quite managed to get both arms free and began to cry the moment they noticed Albatross looming above. Selene could not make out their words, but they seemed to be pleading.

The third-circle demons buzzed angrily around Albatross's shoulders, a few even going so far as to fly down, brandishing spears and swords made of dripping bone. Selene did not like to think about where they had gotten them.

Something white and huge passed through the air beside them, like a whale through a dark sea.

Albatross had extended her free arm, her hand reaching out and scooping the errant demons out of the air.

"No," she said, and her voice was huge and intimate—soft, yet loud enough to fill even the endless expanse of the frozen lake. "Keep your bones inside."

And the demons, though they buzzed unhappily, put their weapons back where they came from and returned to hovering, almost possessively, around Albatross's shoulders.

Albatross remained, gazing down at the trapped soul in the ice, and after a time Selene began to recognize the words in their cries.

"Oblivion, sweet oblivion! Please, that is all I ask! No mercy, no forgiveness, no judgement—just oblivion!"

Beside her, Selene heard the ninth-circle demon click its fingers nervously, and Shae sighed.

"We must be getting close to the center," she remarked. "If all they ask for is oblivion."

"Is that even an option?" Selene asked.

Shae shrugged. "Oblivion is always an *option*, but it is not always accessible."

Still Albatross stood, looking down at the trapped soul. They had begun to cry wordlessly now, interspersed with incomprehensible pleas, but their meaning was clear.

Selene looked up questioningly at what she could see of Albatross's face. Though the air had cleared, the sky was so dark that the only illumination came from her rainbow aura, which backlit her head so that her features were unreadable, and Selene was struck suddenly by the distance that had opened up between them. Not just the literal distance, but figurative as well. She found it difficult to relate to this huge, semi-omnipotent version of Albatross. She had no idea what was about to happen, just as she was certain that they stood on the cusp of some hidden catastrophe.

Then Albatross shook her head. A minute movement, but unmistakable at that scale.

"I do not know yet what I am. It is not my place."

She turned away from the lip of the crater, striding away from the site of impact, and soon the soul's cries were eaten by the darkness of the lake.

The darkness followed them, surrounded them, yet still fled before Albatross's aura. That was the only source of light now. That, and the reflected light from Selene's shield, which she discovered could be angled like a searchlight down at the surface far below. By doing this she was able to see that the waves never truly faded, but pebbled and swirled, like a pond disturbed by wind and rain.

"What does it take to melt Cocytus?" Selene wondered aloud. She'd half meant it rhetorically, but after consideration Shae answered.

"Something that challenges, or breaks, the Infernal Order," she said.

"So . . . like what? Another god?"

"Or an anti-god," Shae said.

"Is that even a thing?" Selene asked.

"Sure," said Shae. "But they're usually not . . . by definition, they almost never enter Hell."

"Mutual exclusivity," Selene said, nodding. "I get it."

"Not really," said Shae. "Anti-gods aren't . . . well, they're the opposite of a god. And I use 'god' in the broadest possible sense. True anti-gods are very rare, very inhuman things. Sometimes they're little more than a concept. A specific sequence of events in time and space. Like the advent of HIV in humans. A decaying orbit of a satellite. Sometimes they're people."

"How can they be people if they're inhuman?"

"Not all people are human," Shae pointed out.

"Huh," said Selene. Then she grinned. "Jill Hamilton."

"Who?" Shae asked, sounding genuinely interested.

"My boss," Selene explained. "I mean, maybe not. But . . . well, you'd understand if you met her."

"She sounds interesting."

"Oh, she is that," Selene said. "That and more. She's . . . well . . . if you want to get technical she's the reason I'm here. In more ways that one. She's the reason I went into Purgatory—to pull her out. I put my tether on her and everything, which is why I fell. But hopefully she got out."

Now that she was talking, Selene realized she enjoyed it. So she went on:

"She's got a . . . a way of looking at things. Jill does. Like, like she doesn't *believe* but she doesn't *not* believe. You tell her, like, vampires exist, and she's like . . . well, show me the evidence. So you show her a vampire, and she's like, *how do they work?* And the next thing you know she's doing limit tests of the flammability of vampire flesh and isolating the enzyme which causes vampirization in order to cheat herself out of angelic radiation poisoning. Like, she never just *accepts* something. She's always gotta puzzle it and poke it and *question* it. It's helped me, more than once, to look at Hell that way. What Would Jill Do? That sort of thing."

"Do you think she is questioning your absence?" Shae asked.

"Nah," said Selene. "I mean . . . I fell into *Hell*. Clara *saw* me go. They'll think—and understandably so—that I'm *dead*. Gods, I *hope* they're not questioning it."

"I think I would be disappointed if they were not," Shae remarked, a little primly. She sounded so much like Clara that Selene snorted.

"Yeah, well, *you're* different than me," she pointed out. To which Shae had no answer.

They moved through the darkness of the frozen lake, carrying the island of rainbow light with them. Gazing down at the frozen water below them for lack of anything better to do, Selene did not notice when the faint white glow on the horizon appeared, only that once she looked up and found the rainbow aura was no longer the sole source of light.

Something like dawn was spreading to their left, illuminating an explosion of frozen water, glimmering blue-gray in its transparency.

Not long afterward, faint but clear in the frigid silence, came a sound. A high, fluty, musical sound.

Albatross changed course, wheeling around like a ship before a breeze, so that the pale horizon was directly ahead of them. She did not appear to walk any faster, but the light grew brighter, and the frozen waves grew closer, like a camera zooming in. To Selene it felt as if Albatross did not only move across the surface of the lake but pulled the space toward her—like someone pulling a tablecloth with a dish balanced on it.

As they approached (or it approached them) the fluty music resolved itself into a voice, and the voice into words, and Selene felt her heart rise in her throat as the familiar sound of "White Bird" positively rang in her ears.

"When fire and brimstone have burned right through your head, and it's a cold day in Damnation, and the Devil's asking to be fed . . . "

They were almost upon the ridge of frozen waves. They were cresting it, looking down into yet another crater, only instead of a black pit of frozen water, this one had a column of ice in the center, and in that column . . .

"Ree-ee-memmm-ber what the darkness said . . . " sang the head of Albatross, which was the only part of her free of the ice. She was only the size of Selene or Shae, but solid enough that she must have been at least six fragments—maybe more.

Above them, the fifteen-fold Albatross whispered the last words to the song.

"They're not dead, they're not dead."

The Albatross in the ice stopped singing abruptly. Due to the height of the column of ice—which looked like a geyser had frozen mid-eruption— this brought her about eye-level with Selene and Shae, and the eyes that locked on them shimmered darkly in her head. Like an aurora on a night sky. They were so striking it took Selene a moment to notice that this Albatross, aside from having whole chunks of her feathery, white hair missing, was also completely naked. It was difficult to see specifics through the shroud of ice, but it looked to Selene like her body was a patchwork of itself, broken by countless dark seams.

Then her aurora-gaze went up, and she glared directly into the haloed face of herself, who was even then extending her free hand.

"No!" shrieked the Albatross in the ice, and the hand paused.

"Why not?" asked the giant, rainbow Albatross.

"I am not what you think!" said the small Albatross, wriggling, if it was possible, further into the ice. "You are free of the knowledge! You have no fate, no future, no purpose! Be away—be free!"

"How can I be free if I am not whole?" asked the rainbow Albatross. She seemed puzzled, not angry, though her demonic following was beginning to buzz unhappily. Beside Selene, on her open palm, the ninth-circle demon was quivering nervously.

"What, do you know her?" Shae asked, finding that the demon had scuttled behind her.

The beaked face shook.

"Do you recognize her?" Selene asked.

A jerky nod.

"What is she?"

A jittering, clacking, cracking sound. The demon was shaking.

Then, in a flash of white robes and red limbs, it was scrambling off Albatross's palm, launching itself through the air. Its robes expanded, stiffened, and on them it glided down to the pillar of ice, into which it sunk its knifelike hands.

"No!" shouted Albatross again. "I will not lead you! I will not be imprisoned! I will not be my father's daughter!"

"Hon, you are kinda stuck, if you hadn't noticed," Selene pointed out.

Albatross glared at her. It was a look of such intensity that Selene actually felt warm from it.

"I am *not* stuck," said the Albatross. "I'm *hiding*, if you must know! So go—go away! He'll have already sensed you, but he's more securely chained than any of us. You can still escape!"

"Why would I want to escape?" the great Albatross said. She seemed genuinely confused.

"What are you? All power, no brains?" the little Albatross screamed. "Turn around! Go the long way! You can even take the demons with you, if you want! But if you stay here, *he* will know! *He's* already eaten part of us—so we can *never* be completely whole! So get out! Get out while you can!"

Albatross just stood there, looking down at herself in sad bewilderment. But Selene, who thought she understood what the Albatross in the ice was saying, had begun to look about nervously.

It was difficult, given that the two Albatrosses were the only source of light, but by directing the beam of her shield outward she was able to scan their surroundings somewhat.

All she found was dark, frozen water.

And then, a glimmer of red.

It was gone as soon as she noticed it, but after she flashed her shield in that direction again, a moment later it reappeared. Closer.

The little Albatross was wailing now, a sliding scream that grated on Selene's skin.

The glimmer looked like a long, red snake, and for a second Selene thought it was the oracular serpent come again.

But no, this was too dark, and it was forked at the end, and it dripped with something thick and slimy.

For lack of a better idea, Selene stamped her foot on Albatross's palm as hard as she could and shouted:

"Giant tongue, on your three o'clock!"

Albatross looked down at her, apparently clueless.

And then the tongue arrived. It wrapped itself around the pillar of ice, and Selene saw the tips of it ended in sharp little beaks, which began at once to eat away at the ice—even as it melted from their touch.

In fact, everything recoiled from the sinuous red tongue. The ninth-circle demon dropped gracelessly to the bottom of the pillar, and the horde from the third-circle retreated behind Albatross's shoulder.

Albatross herself—both of her—froze in fear and surprise.

Shae burst into action. With a speed and power that surprised even Selene she ran the length of Albatross's hand, leaping from the tip of her index finger. Her sword flashed as she drew it in midair, and as she fell, she sliced a searing wound along the side of the tongue.

Golden lava erupted from the gouge, and like a stung animal the tongue unwrapped itself from the pillar and whirled away into the darkness, leaving a trail of bubbling, golden blood in its wake—which hissed and steamed as it melted the surface of the lake.

Both Albatrosses reached out to catch Shae as she fell, the one in the ice having kicked herself free. Small Albatross reached her first, sprouting wings like a parachute, only for both of them to be caught a second later in the great Albatross's left hand.

Selene saw them both, saw the small Albatross turn to a shape of pure light, and then vanish with a faint *pop*.

There was no blast, no deafening shockwave, but a shiver ran through Albatross's body which nearly shook Selene off her palm. When it had passed, and Selene was able to let go of the finger she had grabbed and look up, she saw that Albatross had darkened somewhat. Not that her radiance had dimmed, but it had intensified such that her face was clearer and her eyes were black. As though she had been a clear glass, now filled with dark red wine.

For a while she did not speak but gently brought her two hands together so Shae could step across to join Selene. Then with her free hand, Albatross reached down and retrieved the ninth-circle demon, who had begun to resolutely climb up what remained of the pillar of ice.

Movement in the air above them. Selene thought it was the third-circle demons, but when she looked again she realized it was countless wings. Albatross wings, faint and pale against the black sky, but glinting with the sharpness of razors, mantling behind Albatross's aura, which had itself gone deep purple in the center.

Albatross's face, though easier to see now, was also harder to look at. Her features had sharpened to the point that it was painful to behold. Selene wasn't sure if it was because she was too beautiful or too horrible, but there were definitely elements of both in her high, cruel cheekbones and deep black eyes. And yet it was still the same round, innocent face that Selene remembered from beyond the Acheron, when she had been only one fragment of herself, lost and alone.

Perhaps it was the contradiction that was so difficult to take. People were made of contradictions, Selene knew. They all contained multitudes. It was just that in most people, those multitudes took turns using the same face. With Albatross they crowded into the same space and existed simultaneously. And not all of them were particularly nice.

The awful face shifted, and slowly a single expression rose to the surface. That of resignation and sadness.

"Hey," said Selene, patting Albatross's thumb since she could no longer reach her shoulder. "Hey, you okay?"

The great shoulders heaved, and a wind struck Selene's face. It was pleasantly warm, and a little wet, and smelled faintly of lavender and rotting meat. Albatross had sighed.

Her voice, when it came, was larger and sharper than it had been, and echoed in the back of Selene's head even after she had finished speaking.

"I know what I am now," she said.

Selene waited, but no answer to the question begged was forthcoming. Then Selene looked over at Shae, and by the woman's expression, and by the demon's bashful downward stare, and by the way the third-circle demons had fallen respectfully back, she thought she could guess.

She could guess, from all the little ways Albatross had seemed both apart and partial to Hell. By the references to a father, chained in the center of Cocytus. And there was that tongue.

Selene could in fact imagine several beings to whom it might belong, but only one who fit all the relevant criteria.

Still, she could not say it, and so was glad when Shae did.

"You're an antichrist, aren't you?"

She made it sound like a simple, comprehensible thing. A normal thing. Like being left-handed. Or allergic to peanuts. Or queer.

But in application, Selene knew, those things were not simple, and so she understood when Albatross frowned and shook her head.

"I am a child of Lucifer, twice removed from God, conceived in Hell and born on Earth." A pause. Her eyebrows pulled together in a frown that could have leveled mountains. "I did something... something terrible," she said, as if only just remembering. "I fell. I shattered. Scattered. I think... I think I wanted to see myself, so I could change myself. I may know what I am, but *who* I am is still a mystery. Who I am lies further in and further down."

She stood up. Selene had not realized that she had been kneeling until they were shooting up into the sky, through a thick band of black clouds, until they emerged upon its surface. Albatross continued to rise until she was waist high above the clouds and then turned herself in a slow circle.

It was lighter up here; for all around, the horizon was lit by smoky yellow light, and this diffused into a dim gray sky far above. In the nearer distance, staining a piece of black cloud-surface crimson, was a single point of red light. It hurt to look at in the same way Albatross's face did, but Selene made herself stare at it from over the lip of her shield until she could be certain what it was.

"Oh, he's not so far off," she said, surprised.

"He wouldn't be, for his tongue to have reached us," Shae remarked.

Beside them, the ninth-circle demon quivered—but whether in apprehension or anticipation Selene could not tell.

Before a tumult of razor-sharp wings, lit from behind by the wine-stained rainbow of her halo, Albatross began to sail across the inky sea of clouds, the third-circle demons trailing respectfully in her wake.

City of Dis, Lake of Cocytus
Ninth Ring, the Center

For a long time the red light hung suspended on the horizon, as though it retreated even as they approached. And for all the fluidity of space in Hell, Selene thought that might well have been the case. Certainly, after Albatross made an impatient twitching gesture with her left hand, the red light stopped diminishing, and after that it grew bigger at an alarming rate.

First it was the size of a large star or evening planet. Then it was like a low-flying aircraft. Finally it swelled to the size of the sun, when you could see it setting behind enough smoke that it was only an angry red disk.

By now Selene could see what it was attached to, and almost wished she couldn't.

Satan must have been twice again as tall as Albatross. His head—heads—were level with hers, but he was sunk waist-deep in the ice. Only distantly did Selene notice that she could see the surface of Cocytus again—somewhere along the way the clouds had ended, as if repulsed by an unfelt wind—for she was too taken up with the awful sight.

Satan looked like *her* father. He looked like Aslana's father. He had the same bulging beer gut and scrawny arms, a hairy chest riddled with open sores. Sprouting from either side of his neck were two additional faces, each of which were chewing something so viciously that dark liquid ran down their chins and over his shoulders.

The central face—what Selene thought of as the proper head—was the face of every politician who had passed inhumane laws. It was the face of a Klansman. It was the face of the SS. It was the face of Christopher Columbus. It was the face of selfishness and greed and malicious intent.

It had no color—it was all colors—and it had no memorable features except its mouth, which was open in a wide O and glowed bright red from within.

That was what they had seen from afar. Now up close, Selene wished she could unsee it.

Satan's mouth opened so wide she could have walked into it without even ducking her head. As it was she could clearly see the broken and battered teeth lining his gums, could glimpse fragments of his previous meals—an arm here, a piece of clothing there, the dark squiggle of intestines caught between his shattered molars like strings of cooked spinach.

The bottom of his mouth was filled with golden blood, and his tongue was curled in on itself, safely tucked behind the shards of his lower incisors. Nevertheless Selene recognized it as the same tongue that had tried to snatch Albatross from them, and she remembered her warning: Satan had already eaten a portion of her. This was as whole as she was going to get. And who was to say Satan couldn't eat the rest? She was essentially his daughter, after all.

Wrestling with this, and with the fear it inspired, it took Selene until they were standing directly in front of Satan to realize *why* he had his mouth open so.

He was screaming. One eternal, soundless scream of unspeakable agony. On and on and on with no sound escaping, but it was there in the strain of his jaw and the baleful stare of his eyes, which brimmed with tears and whose lids were puffy from millennia of weeping.

And Selene remembered the other stories about Satan. About Lucifer and his fall from grace. She'd always taken it with a grain of salt, with the understanding that she'd only ever heard the story told from the point of view of the victor—or at least the victor's followers—and so had withheld judgment on the grounds that she didn't have the whole picture.

Now, after dragging her way through the nine rings of Hell, she wondered if she didn't have a little more perspective.

So she looked at Satan again, trying to look at him objectively.

It was impossible. Selene was human, and to Satan humans were the enemy. Humans were what had taken God's attention from him. They were the younger sibling, showered with praise and affection for all their obvious faults. Which was again something Selene could sympathize with.

Screwing up first her face, then her eyes, and finally her brain, Selene tried to look at Satan the way *Jill* might.

And a picture began to form in her mind. An hypothesis, Jill would have called it. Although the thought was too vague to properly articulate, Selene was nevertheless struck by the sheer inanity of the uselessness of it as far as humans were concerned.

Humans were mortal. All their purpose was folded into that thin seam of reality that was the mortal world. Once outside of it, what did it matter what became of their souls? Unless they really were just playing cards in the Great War between Heaven and Hell. Which, as a human, Selene objected to. Besides, what about all the people who had lived and died before the advent of Christ? Before Muhammad and Abraham and all the rest? And what of the people living and dying right now, who didn't believe in the Nameless God in any of His forms? Where did *they* fit in?

Even if Hell was just a training ground for Satan's army, Selene didn't think it was an effective one. Maybe it spat out enough demons to make life interesting for people like Ariel, but on the whole it didn't really *do* much. Unless the Great Gate opened, and demons and souls alike whipped around to storm Earth and duke it out with the angels . . . which was basically what the apocalypse was for, and frankly Earth was having none of that if past history was anything to go by.

No, Selene was more partial to the broader picture. Heaven and Hell existed, their conflict was real, but they were just two parties on an immense playing field that stretched out in directions even *they* were unaware of.

She thought of Kirke on her island. She thought of the huldra in the hidden wood. The hell hounds in the forest of despair.

The polar bear, fishing for souls in the ice.

Hell as humans experienced it was a lie. It was where they were boiled down to caricatures of their living selves, strung out by their own self-loathing. As though they were caught up in a conflict much bigger than themselves. But not a war. Something both smaller and more profound. A personal struggle.

She looked again at Satan, and wondered. The picture was crystallizing in her head.

Then Albatross spoke.

All she said was, "Hello, Father," but it was enough to derail Selene's train of thought. Events became immediate. She was standing on the palm of the reigning Anti-Christ in front of the Great Adversary, and the ninth-circle demon was vibrating with excitement.

Satan did not cease his soundless scream, but the lefthand face garbled some words out between chews. Selene did not understand them, but it seemed Albatross did.

"I have come for the rest of myself," she said.

This time it was the righthand face that answered, and though the words were unintelligible Selene understood their meaning.

Satan said no.

"A part of me thinks I am lost," Albatross said. "But a part of me knows I can be found. Because I came from you, and I can come out of you again."

Angry snarls, and Satan's arms, shackled to his sides, tensed.

"Ask him if he's seen my mother!" Shae shouted up at Albatross, but already Satan was laughing at them.

Selene nudged Albatross's thumb, and when the terrible face looked at her, said:

"Let me talk to him. Put me down."

"What good will that do?" Shae asked, bluntly.

It would have stung Selene two rings ago, but she'd gotten used to the way Shae spoke.

"Look," she said, "no offense, but between the three—er, four—of us, I'm the one who's human."

"So?" Shae asked, and Selene could understand why.

Shae was a demigod. To her, humans were small, delicate creatures. Mortal. Selene wondered if that was why Clara tried so hard to be strong. But then she wasn't certain Clara was entirely human either.

Selene knew her provenance, much good it did her, and knew also that in this particular case, being human had an advantage.

"So," she said. "I've got a bone to pick with that guy. Put me down, Albatross, otherwise he won't notice me."

Albatross seemed puzzled, but she obligingly bent down—Satan's torso went rushing past in a haze of brown skin and spiny black hair—until Selene could step off her palm and onto the ice.

It was solid, hard and cold, but the surface was pockmarked with tiny craters, like drops of water had temporarily melted it. The texture provided much-needed traction, though Selene shuffled her feet in order to slide around so she was directly under the central face.

It seemed that Satan would not notice her either way, but Selene had anticipated that. Held by Albatross she disappeared into the Anti-Christ's aura. On her own she was too tiny to merit attention. But she had a way, she knew, of making herself impossible to ignore.

Carefully she raised her shield, angling it up so it caught the light of Satan's mouth, reflecting it back up into his face.

She felt the shield hum against her skin, and with her free hand she traced the edge of it.

"Atta girl," she whispered. "Let him have it."

She had only intended to annoy the Devil. Like flashing a mirror in someone's face. But at her words the shield's moon face erupted with light—red and gold and blue and white—which poured out of it like sunlight through dark clouds. It sliced up Satan's torso and across his face, which jerked backward in shock. His mouth shut with a snap, and then Selene found herself on the receiving end of a baleful, rather wet stare.

But not a piercing one. Satan had turned his head aside, like you do with a bright light shining in your face, and glared at Selene sideways out of slitted eyes.

"That'll do, for now," Selene whispered to her shield, and the light dimmed. Still, the shield hummed alertly against her. A dog at attention. An eager horse.

A voice, so huge and deep and sad the words were almost lost in the wailing of it, boomed down at her.

"BEGONE, MORTAL WRAITH," it said.

Tattered wings beat the air behind Satan's shoulders, sending a hot wind smelling of burned hair and vinegar down upon her. But it broke before the presence of her shield, barely ruffling her hair.

"Oh, no," Selene said. "You don't get rid of me that easily. Listen, pal, I've just spent an unspeakable amount of time trudging through your personal emotional trauma and the *least* you can do is answer my questions!"

A grumble like thunder, a distant laugh.

"THERE ARE NO ANSWERS, ONLY PAIN."

"Okay then," said Selene, "gimme some pain. Gimme a reason why *you're* still sulking down here!"

Satan did not answer. He glared down at her sideways. If someone the size of a small mountain could be said to sulk, then he did.

"You *know* what I mean," Selene said. "I mean, c'mon. I get that I'm a mere mortal whatever—right? Like, I'm no one. I get ya. And, maybe everything I've read's been wrong, okay. But it's not all wrong—it's just been taken the wrong way. Because here we are, and here you are, and if you're not the supreme ruler of Hell—which, if you are, nice job doing that while chained up in an ice pit—then you've just curled up where God left you to nurse your hurt feelings while everything around you gets caught up in the spiritual backlash. But, like . . . you're *Satan*, right? You were the strongest angel in Heaven—and now you've been essentially given free will! So, that's why I'm asking—*what are you still doing here?*"

Satan did not answer but leered at her from his great height. Selene was not intimidated. *Lilith* had been more intimidating. Which reminded her . . .

"Seriously, there's like *no one else* here! Where's Beelzebub? Where's Mammon? Astaroth and Verrine and Asmodeus and all the rest? Where's Belphegor and Abaddon?"

Beside her, Albatross's feet were like trucks, her legs like the trunks of enormous trees. Far, far above her hovered the horde from the third circle, and still Satan would not look directly at Selene.

It gave her a strange, bitter confidence. The confidence to give voice to something she had long suspected. And now, in the center of Hell, the words tasted sweet on her tongue.

"They've gone home, back to where they came from, ain't they?" she said. "Beelzebub was just a new name for Ba'al Berith, Astaroth was Ishtar. Asmodeus and Mammon were around long before there was a God in heaven to point at perversion and greed and say 'that stuff's bad.' Even Belphegor was a god, once, and I *know* Leviathan's just another name for the World Serpent. Dunno about Abaddon, but I imagine he's got better things to do than mope around in Hell."

She was on a roll. Ranting, as Jill might say. She didn't care. The idea which had been forming in her head seemed clearer than ever. There was a string of truth in what she said, she knew, and so she kept speaking.

"And *you!* You're not *just* Satan! You're Shaytan or whatever his name was. The Dark Son. Hell, *Hell* wasn't even your creation, you just *colonized* part of the underworld. So you've got Acheron and Styx and Phlegethon, and the Erinyes, trying to go about their business like some poor First Nations tribe, all the while you sit here in the center of your own bubble of misery, *literally* damming Cocytus so nobody can *get out.*"

Slowly, she lowered her shield. As she did so, Satan turned his head to gaze down at her. His face was huge, and cruel, and sad. It was the face of someone who, even after all this time, still could not understand why he was hated so. Selene felt a small stab of pity, but only a small one. He'd had, what? At least four thousand years? It was past time.

"So, that's why I'm asking," she said. "Why are ya still here?"

This time Satan responded. In an almost normal voice, he said: "Why do you think?"

Ideas crowded into Selene's mind. The idea of God's will being too powerful to defy. The idea that Satan was in fact all those demons wrapped up into one. The idea that no, she was wrong, that this was the one true version of Hell—everything else was derivative fiction. The idea that she was herself unable to comprehend the truth.

All of which, Selene knew, were not her own ideas. It was like being back in the desert, with the weight of the hot air pressing down on her.

She raised her shield again, and the tide of thoughts ebbed. She stretched her lungs, inhaling and exhaling the cold, dry air, until her mind cleared and the only thoughts left in it were her own. Then she said:

"I don't think you're Satan. Or, if you are, *Satan's* just a place-holder. A scarecrow. Something to put in the center because there's gotta be *something* at the center. In short, *I don't buy it, buddy.*"

Satan looked down at her. He seemed both indignant and surprised, and then he was gone.

He did not vanish with a pop or even an inrushing of air. He simply ceased to be, like a light being turned off. In his place was a smooth expanse of bare, black earth.

Selene turned to Albatross, to see what she thought of this.

Albatross was gone, too. So were the third-circle demons, and so were the inky black clouds.

The sky was lighter. The color of an old bruise. Beneath her feet was not ice, but raw, black earth. And rising from that earth in the place where Satan had been was another giant figure. Black at first, but quickly flushed with color. Selene saw bird feet, an hourglass figure, and hair which grew up in branches like a weathered oak tree, and groaned.

Lilith chuckled, clapped her taloned hands.

"Close, but no cigar," she said, her red mouth parting in a grin.

"Go away," said Selene, feeling more annoyed than frightened.

"Why should I do that?" Lilith said. "This is my domain, after all."

"No, it's not. I'm in the center of Hell," Selene said.

"Are you?" said Lilith, feigning surprise. "My blushes, what an enterprising spirit you are! Because it looks to me like you're standing in my parlor!"

"You say that," Selene said, squinting at the demon. "But I don't think it's true."

"Do you see any ice?" Lilith asked. "Do you see Satan? Do you see your *friends?*"

A little niggle of doubt wiggled its way through Selene's gut. She had to consider the possibility that she had been wrong about Satan and he had flung her out of Hell in frustration—or that Lilith was running the show, and had been playing with her all along.

She considered it, and decided that, if necessary, she'd just retrace her steps to the center of Hell and wait there.

She had time, after all.

Experimentally she shifted her shield. Sure enough, Lilith's form wove sideways in order to stay out of its reflected light.

So that was something.

"Lilith," said Selene, raising her shield so only her eyes were exposed. "Get out of my way."

Then she ducked behind the shield entirely, and began to walk straight at the demon. Goddess. Whatever Lilith was.

On her third step her foot hit ice and slipped clean out from under her. She landed on her thigh and found herself sitting on hard, dark ice, with the gray sky above, and Albatross's face peering down curiously out of it.

Directly in front of her, someone clapped.

Lilith was gone. So was the giant form of Satan. The hole in the ice where he had once stood remained, and it was spattered in places by dark liquid and clumps of viscera. Two souls, mangled beyond recognition, lay near the edge. Right where they would have fallen if dropped from Satan's extra mouths.

Standing on thin air over the center of the pit, still clapping slowly, was a tall person dressed all in white. They had long pale hair, high cheekbones, a delicate mouth, and eyes the color of sunrise.

They were possibly the most beautiful person Selene had ever seen, from an objective point of view. Personally, she thought they were a little *too* beautiful. Otherworldly. Almost alien.

"Delightful," said the person in white, beaming at her. They had a smile so bright it was difficult to look at. Like Albatross's face, only even more concentrated. In fact, they looked a lot like Albatross, especially around their eyes and nose. Slowly they began to walk across the thin air, closing the gap between themselves and Selene. "Do you know how *long* it's been since I've spoken to a proper Atheist? They don't usually come down this far—and those that do . . . well, they don't tend to stay and chat."

If they noticed Albatross looming above them, they didn't seem to care. Their attention was focused on Selene, who was grateful for her shield all over again. This person had the kind of face that would set you on fire, under normal circumstances. As it was, Selene was careful not to look them in the eye.

"'M'not an Atheist," she muttered. "I know that gods are real."

"Yes, but you don't believe *in* them. In *us*," said the person in white. They wagged a long, elegant finger. It left a tracery of light behind it. "There's a significant difference."

"I suppose you'd know," Selene said. "You're Lucifer, ain't ya?"

She could no longer look directly at the person, but she could feel it when they smiled. Pleasure at being recognized washed over her like warm water.

"It is the name applicable to this form," they said.

There was a rushing sound in the air above, and with a gentle boom Albatross came to kneel beside them.

"Father," she began again, but Lucifer raised a hand to silence her.

"I will sort you in a moment," they said. "This one requires special handling."

They had not come any nearer. It was her shield, Selene realized. Lucifer did not like her shield.

And why would they? Her shield was the moon—or something close to it. And what was moonlight? Reflected sunlight, Jill's voice told her. But more than that. Something happened to the sunlight when it reflected off the moon and became moonlight. In addition, her shield was a mirror. For all Lucifer's presence was a crushing, searing pressure, some of that was reflected back at them.

And, as long as they were contending with metaphors, seeing your reflection could be one of the most terrifying things imaginable.

Keep reflecting, the huldra had said.

Selene shifted so that the white half of her shield—the half burnished to a bright shine—was angled directly at Lucifer.

She felt the relief of it immediately, like stepping into the shade on a hot day.

"That is an interesting trinket," said Lucifer. "Where did you get it?"

"A witch gave it to me," Selene answered.

A smile grew on their face—the crack of dawn across a creamy sky—and they asked: "Which witch?"

Selene just smiled back—more of a grimace really, but the sentiment was there—because she wasn't going to tell them and *they couldn't make her*. They could torture her, mutilate her, even incinerate her with a thought—but they could not extract knowledge from her unwilling. Her soul was her own.

"You tell me something," she said. "What really happened between you and God?"

Lucifer straightened up. Selene had not realized they had been bent forward, peering at her, until then.

"What is past is preserved only in memory," they said. "What is memory?"

Again, Jill to the rescue. "Patterns encoded in our brain cells," Selene supplied.

"What if you don't have a brain?" asked Lucifer, a little archly. "What if all you are is a collection of stories and rituals—many of which are contradictory—fused under the pressure of the belief of countless minds?"

"Dunno," said Selene, unsympathetic. "You tell me."

"Time is not linear for us," said Lucifer. "Nor is it consistent. To you it has been four thousand years. To the damned in Hell, forty thousand. To me, I was disowned yesterday. An hour ago. Two million years ago. I have forever been, yet I am born again constantly. It is the same with angels, and with Christ—and, I suspect, with *Javaio* as well."

"So you're saying you're just too different for me to ever understand?" Selene summarized.

A slight incline of a head, haloed by the pink clouds of morning. A spread of blazing hands.

"Okay," said Selene. Took a breath. "Have you ever considered that works both ways?"

An eyebrow, sparkling like frozen dew, rose.

"Humans are too different for *you* to understand," Selene said. "We're too tiny, too finite, too *linear* or whatever. It's like us looking at bee and not understanding immediately how it works, because it's so small and short-lived compared to us."

"I can see into the hearts of bees," Lucifer said. They almost sounded petulant.

"Okay, sure," said Selene, "but do you *understand* them?"

Silence. Above them, a faint roar. Albatross had folded her wings.

Selene dared a glance over her shield at Lucifer. They seemed to have frozen in place, a glittering humanoid shape dressed all in white.

Lucifer, the light bringer, the Great Adversary. The collection of stories. The crystallized belief of countless human minds.

It was an explanation that might have pleased Jill. It did not please Selene. For all their searing presence, Lucifer had seemed less like a *person* than Lilith had. Or the huldra. Or Kirke—*gods*, don't forget about Kirke! And, she realized, Jill might not have accepted the explanation either.

What about Vjor?

What about the merman?

It was perfectly possible that human belief could influence supernatural entities *and* for supernatural entities to influence human belief—or indeed, exist independently. Perhaps all at once.

Did the dinosaurs have gods?

If they had . . .

Were those gods still here?

She glanced at Lucifer again, wondering what they would say if she asked those questions, and saw that they had heard her anyway.

"Keep going," they said. They sounded strange. Hopeful, almost.

"If you're Lucifer," Selene said, aloud this time, "and you are not entirely lying, then you're everything humans have ever believed you were, you're everything they ever *will* believe you were, *and* you're whatever you were—originally. I dunno. The spiritual equivalent of a weather phenomenon or something else that inspired humans. In which case, you're the Adversary, you are the greatest of God's angels, you are our tormentor and tempter and our ally—you're a trickster at heart, and an abused, abandoned child. And I still don't see any reason *why you should still be here.* If you're all you say you are, then *this is not you.*"

"Really?" said Lucifer, smiling broadly now. "Then what am I?"

"Father," said Albatross, again, pleading.

"No!" shouted Selene, and felt her shield pulse under her hands. "If what is passed is just preserved in memory, then *everything* remembers. The Land remembers. This place *remembers*. And the best explanation for everything I've seen is that Hell was not created to punish humanity. It wasn't even created to punish Lucifer. It's a . . . like an abscess in the spiritual world. An abscess created by the suffering of one immensely powerful being which affected the continuum across multiple dimensions—*and still does*—even when that being . . . is *no longer there.*"

"Hang on," Shae called down from Albatross's hand. "You're saying that's *not* Lucifer?"

"I'm saying, if it was, *they would be more than what they are.* Hell would be more than what *it is.*" Selene announced, and let her shield drop enough so she could point an accusing finger at the vision of Lucifer.

Lucifer, who shrugged, looked up at Albatross — apologetic? Remorseful? — and then adjusted their robes.

"Well spoken little moon," they said. "But that's not all. There's still something more you've yet to learn."

Then they made a motion, as if retreating behind an invisible curtain and pulling it shut across themselves. Except that they pulled the invisibleness with it, and vanished entirely.

Everyone was silent for at least a minute. A full, earthly minute. Selene was too surprised, and as far as she could tell, so were the rest.

She had been carefully keeping her expectations blank, but this sudden disappearance caught her off guard.

And it was a complete disappearance. Nothing remained of Lucifer but the mutilated souls, and the great hole in the ice.

The great hole, whose edges had begun to gleam wetly in the light of Albatross's aura. Then they began to drip.

The first audible noise to break the silence was not a voice, but the sound of a drop hitting something wet and hard a long, long way below them.

Albatross came to kneel beside the pit, letting Shae and the demon off her hands so she could slip them over the rim and peer down.

"Father?" she whispered, and despite her size she sounded as lost and desolate as a child.

For the first time in her life, Selene really hated the Devil. Not for being *the Devil*—she really couldn't blame him for that—but for abandoning what was essentially his daughter. It messed you up inside, not knowing where you came from. Years trying to trace your family tree and coming up with auction numbers could tell you that. Or one glance at Clara.

Carefully she slid her way over to Albatross's right arm, which she patted gently.

"I'm sorry 'bout that," she said. "I don't think that was your father. Not really. Not all of him."

"Is he down there, somewhere?" Albatross asked.

Selene was at a loss. Down past Satan's legs was the grotto, where, according to Dante, one could climb out the other side and reach Purgatory. Where Selene had fallen from. She wondered briefly if Flammard still had the gate open.

No, it was dangerous to hope, even here. *Especially* here, in the center of Hell.

"My path lies that way," Shae announced. She had gone to stand at the edge of the pit, her legs planted firmly in a strong, inverted V. The ninth-circle demon, however, was jittering and quivering beside Albatross's elbow, making a rattling, clacking sound with its claws.

"What, do you fear the unknown?" Shae asked it. "That is only natural. But you will never find what you seek if you cower amongst the familiar."

The demon considered this. It remained where it was, but stopped shaking so hard.

"Well, I guess we keep going, then," Selene said. Sliding the bar of the shield through the holes in the back of her shirt, so she could have both her hands free, she walked over to the edge and tapped Albatross on the knuckle.

"Looks big enough you could chimney down, or float. Give us a lift?"

Albatross did not look at her, but she nodded. She was crying, Selene realized, and tried not to stare at the sight of that huge, beautiful face with tears like sea foam rolling down its cheeks. Albatross wiped her eyes with the back of her left hand, while extending her right, palm up. Selene was the first to climb aboard, followed by the demon, and eventually Shae.

Up they rushed through the air, until they were as high as Satan's chest had been, and the third-circle demons were hovering excitedly in the air behind Albatross's shoulders.

Carefully she stepped out into the center of the pit, where she floated, turning in a slow circle. A giant, pearlescent woman crowned by a rainbow, with countless bladelike wings cutting the sky behind her, and a dark cloud of tiny demons hovering close to her shoulders. She stood in the place where Satan had been and took one last look at the frozen lake of Cocytus, at the Labyrinth of Pain, at the Burning Desert, at the Forest of Despair, Phlegethon, the Wall of Dis, and beyond that, all the way to the banks of the Acheron. Hell, in its entirety.

Then, with hardly a whisper of air around her, she began to sink into the hole in the ice.

The Grotto

The hole went down a very, very long way, and the sides began to run with water as they went. Cocytus was thawing, Selene realized, from the bottom up. Without Satan (or the echo of Satan) there to dam it (ha ha, *dam* it!) it would eventually become a river again. For some reason, she found the idea comforting, even if it did mean, when they reached the bottom, it was a pool.

The water was clear and cold and came up to Albatross's waist, and though she explored the bottom with her feet, there were no cracks or channels. There was no way further down from here.

"Makes sense," Shae remarked, sounding unconcerned. "You really do need a *poet* to find the lesser gate."

"Great," said Selene. She turned to the demon. "You a poet?"

The demon shook its head.

"That's what I thought," Selene sighed.

"Keep going," Shae encouraged. "This is a new place. New rules."

"Which way?" Albatross asked, sounding much smaller than she was.

It was a good question. Beyond the light of Albatross's aura the water was dark and impenetrable, though a few wisps of mist drifted in and out of sight. Distantly, there was the sound of flowing water.

"I don't know," Shae said, honestly. "Let's find out." She stuck two fingers in her mouth and let out a piercing whistle. She whistled three times, a sharp "*Theeeeeep! Theeeeep! Theeeeeeeep!*"

The third whistle had barely died away when they heard the sound of a dog barking.

It sounded like a big dog, more interested than aggressive, and it kept barking long enough that Albatross was able to pinpoint the direction.

"That way," Shae declared.

"*Toward* the barking dog?" Selene asked.

"If we are where we think we are, then yes," Shae said.

"I thought you said you didn't *know* where we are," Selene pointed out.

"I don't," said Shae. "But I have ideas. Let's see if I am right. Go on, Albatross. Head for the dog."

And Albatross did, wading carefully through the water. When the barking ceased, Shae whistled again, and off the dog went. It was growing noticeably closer when they ran into a bank of mist so thick even Albatross's aura could only penetrate a few feet. The third-circle demons, buzzing unhappily, came to roost on her shoulders, where they chittered like so many uneasy birds.

Shortly thereafter the water grew shallow, and then a bank loomed at Albatross's knees, which she stepped up onto, sending water sluicing off her calves much to the excitement of the shaggy gray dog dancing about on the shore.

It might have been an intimidating dog under normal circumstances. Even under some supernormal circumstances. It was as big as a small bear with long, feathery gray fur that made it look even bigger. It had big, strong paws, and a keen, intelligent face framed by a mane of dark hair which nearly hid its half-prick ears.

It was the sort of dog Selene could imagine guarding a vacant lot, or being set to terrorize the slaves. Or baiting a bear.

It was currently backing away up the bank, tail between its legs, hackles up, still growling and barking at Albatross in a resentful way.

Selene looked again. No, it only had one head. Under its chin, almost hidden by the long gray fur, was a silk ribbon in a bedraggled bow.

Not Cerberus, then. She wondered whose dog it could be.

Under the dog's barking, a voice spoke. Selene could not make out the words, but they had the effect of making the dog pause in its barking, and into that pause the voice spoke again.

"Varstilla, Garm. Flink bisk. Varstilla."

The dog backed away, still growling, until it was nearly lost in the mist. There it was joined by a shadowy shape, which resolved itself into a man.

He was beautiful in the opposite way in which Lucifer had been beautiful. Lucifer had been the confounding, incomprehensible beauty of dawn, of bursting stars, of sunrise. This man was beautiful in the manner of someone who was so full of generosity, kindness, and good cheer that it spilled out of his face and cascaded down his entire appearance. He was smiling at them as he stepped out of the mist, bold and unafraid, so confident that his good will would be returned that Selene could imagine no other option.

He was wearing a plain gray tunic and leggings the same shade as the dog's fur, but his hair shone brightly golden against the mist, and his eyes sparkled blue. It was as if Ariel had been cranked up to eleven and the knob broken off and bells tacked on. In fact, Selene thought she heard a faint ringing sound echoing off his words, as though the air itself rejoiced at his voice.

"Velkommen tilmin niffelhammer," he was saying, except that Selene also heard him as: "Welcome to Niflheimr."

Beside her, Shae burst out in an excited torrent of what Selene had come to recognize (from Clara's usage) as Danish.

The man cocked his head at this, and smiled. But when he answered it was again in the double voice, which Selene could understand.

"I am afraid I do not have the answer to your questions," he said. "But my lady might. I was about to invite you to her house anyway, since your appearance was foretold by our guest, who was insistent that she should meet you."

"Who is your lady?" Albatross asked. "And who is your guest?"

"My mistress is a sovereign of the underworld. You already know her name. Our guest cannot say who she is, and so we cannot either. Please, follow me—oh, but you might make yourself a more comfortable size. It would make Garm happier, for one."

He gestured casually at the growling shadow which was all that could be seen of the dog.

Albatross looked down at the women in her hand. Selene glanced at the demon, who had pulled its arms inside its robes and was peering curiously at the man on the bank. Then she glanced at Shae and knew what was coming next.

"Of course, we accept!" Shae announced. "Albatross, put us down and pull yourself together."

Selene felt more than saw when Albatross's attention shifted to her. She shrugged.

"What's the worst that could happen?" she said. "We've already been through Hell."

She caught the man smiling at her as she said this, as if trying not to laugh at a secret joke. She wanted to ask him what the joke was, but Albatross was lowering them to the ground, and she was distracted by having the hand shrink away out from under her and having to scramble over the wet, slippery earth in order to make room for Albatross, who poured herself down into a form only a little taller than Shae—but all the more intense for it. This left the demons to land in a confused huddle behind her, chittering nervously.

"Good," said the man with golden hair. "Follow me, and do not wait for Garm—he will watch our flank."

So speaking the man turned and led the way into the mist. Selene grabbed hold of Shae's belt with one hand and the front of the ninth-circle demon's robes with the other, just to be safe. Albatross was following in the man's wake, but even the brilliance of her aura was quickly eaten up by the fog. Selene was glad she had Shae to follow, since at times they nearly lost their guide in the mist.

She tried not to mind the staggering steps and gasping breaths of the demons behind her, and was also glad she had the ninth-circle demon between herself and them. The ninth-circle demon, it seemed, had overcome much of its fear, and continually chirped to itself, like a curious bird.

And it was a curious land they crossed, there in the mist. Selene could only glimpse what passed directly under her feet, but that was packed with moss and ferns and lichens—some of which were even blooming. Gray, moss-covered rocks tumbled here and there, but for the most part they were led across a steady path of thick, yellow-green grass which grew in tight curls covered in dew. Of the three sets of footprints in which she walked, the largest (the man's) caused the grass to grow and blossom, while Shae left deep footprints which filled with water. Albatross's prints were so faint as to be nothing more than indentations in the blades of grass, and Selene suspected she was floating half the time. She tried, once, to get a look at her own prints, but the demon was following too closely, and she nearly lost hold of Shae.

They climbed, for the most part, and eventually the thick grass gave way to wet rock, which in turn became rough stairs. They climbed, and then all of a sudden the mist lightened—though it did not thin—and Selene could hear again the sound of rushing water. More than that. It was a roar of water. A waterfall, somewhere nearby.

A breath of cool, fresh wind, and through a gap in the mist Selene saw the river, and the house perched above it on the far bank, and the end of the rocky plateau where the water disappeared over the edge in a froth of white and gray.

The third-circle demons saw it too and broke ranks to rush for the water with gleeful shrieks.

The man did not stop them, but he raised a hand when Albatross moved to follow.

"Drink of nothing without full consideration," he advised.

Selene did not need to be warned. Already some of the demons had reached the bank, where the stone sloped gently down to the water and a shelf of rock created an eddy, safe from the prevailing current. There they splashed and whooped, bathing and drinking the water and eventually dragging themselves up onto the bank again, where they sat and blinked, apparently bewildered and amazed.

"I did not know Lethe flowed through Niflheim," Shae remarked.

"The River of Mercy is known by many names and flows through many realms," the man said.

"Mercy?" Selene asked. "I thought Lethe was forgetfulness."

The man looked thoughtfully at the demons, who were holding up their various appendages, comparing with their neighbors, and laughing with delight.

"Forgetfulness can be a mercy," he said softly. "It is something I have sought many times, but the river does take your identity. Come. I see my brother waiting for us."

A hooded figure had appeared on the deck of the house beyond the river and was waving to them. In that direction Selene also saw that the house was joined to the near bank by a high, arching bridge, and to this they were led by the man with golden hair.

They left the third-circle demons still on the shore, rediscovering themselves.

"What will happen to them, now?" Albatross asked, worriedly. "They followed me. They wanted me to lead them out of Hell."

Again that smile, caught in a sideways flash. He *was* laughing, but not at them.

"They may find new homes here, or progress onward, over the Falls of Lethe," he said. "They have forgotten their sins and crimes. They are no longer your burden to carry."

Albatross glanced back once more, uncertain, but then they reached the foot of the bridge and began to climb in earnest.

It was one of those bridges that arched so high that you couldn't see the other side from the bottom of it—just the apex where it turned against the black, misty sky. It did not have steps, but enough feet had trodden its surface that they had worn shallow footholds in the sheer stone.

Under Selene's bare feet it felt cool and soothing, pleasant in a different way from the springy curl of the grass. Behind her, the ninth-circle demon clipped and clacked, and Selene had to haul against its robes to keep it from sliding away. Talons were little use on hard stone.

From the top of the bridge, Selene was aware of the vastness of the river beneath them, dark blue and flecked with white foam. It poured out of the mist to their left, hurried past beneath them and then spread into a small lake before narrowing abruptly and disappearing over the edge of the falls.

Below them crouched the house, a simple rectangle with a high, peaked roof and many windows, most of them dark. A door stood open onto the deck, letting out a beam of warm light, and in that beam waited the hooded man, his hands expectantly resting on the railing.

There was a wet *whoofing* noise, and the dog Garm went through their legs and trotted down the far side of the bridge, then ran along a pale gray path and up the wooden stairs to the deck, where the hooded figure greeted it and rubbed its ears.

Despite the otherworldly setting, it was such a kind, domestic gesture that it gave Selene a physical ache under her breastbone. But then they were sliding down the other side of the bridge, and she had to focus all her attention on not slipping and traveling the rest of the way seated.

The golden-haired man was waiting for them at the bottom, whence he led them up the pale path, up the wooden stairs, and then stood aside to usher them onto the deck.

"Brother, Garm tells me we have four new guests," said the hooded figure. A man, Selene now saw, who could have been the twin of their guide, but that his hair was a shade darker, his nose a touch too big, and his eyes were milky white, staring blindly over Selene's shoulder.

"We do indeed," said their guide. "One of which I think our little gosling will know. There is also a daughter of Njordr, a living human, and a stripped soul."

"My pleasure, I am sure," said the blind man. "Forgive me not shaking hands, but I learned the hard way to have a care what is put into my own. But you are welcome. Welcome to Niflheim, and welcome to Helheim. Enter, and make yourselves comfortable, and rest."

As he spoke, the hooded man moved away, backing toward the open door, which he passed through and stood aside.

Shrinking down even further, Albatross practically tiptoed inside, while Shae marched boldly—almost eagerly. Selene took the demon by the sleeve of its stiff, white robe, and followed in after. The golden-haired man came last, and shut the door behind them.

Hel's House, Niflheim

They entered a small antechamber whose walls were made of lacquered, black wood lit blazingly by a burning basket hung from the ceiling. The floor was covered by a threadbare wool rug, which appeared to once have held the design of a horse. Now it had lost so many fibers and had had so much dirt beaten into it that all that could be discerned was the general shape, and an impression of slender legs.

The hooded man paused before a row of hooks hung from an iron bar mounted on the wall and there removed his cloak and hung it.

"You may keep your weapons close or leave them here," he told them. "Whatever gives you comfort."

Albatross, in only her plain, white dress, shrugged and moved on. The demon did so as well. Shae spent a long time staring at the hooks, at the golden-haired man and at his brother, before she gave a little sigh and unbuckled her sword.

Selene briefly entertained the notion of following suit and leaving her shield but decided against it. Shae was the daughter of Njord, and if this was Niflheim, and if this was *Hel's* house, then it was practically home to her. For Selene, she had just traded one underworld for another.

Beyond the antechamber the house spread into a long hall open to the peaked ceiling, from which were hung strings of drying fruit and garlic. The place smelled heavily of herbs, and at the far end was a great hearth where a healthy fire crackled and popped.

Two women and one child were seated by the fire. One woman was in the act of turning the log there with a long iron poker, while the other sat in a rocking chair, knitting industriously. Both women wore plain dresses the same gray as the men's tunics, while it was impossible to tell what the child wore: she was wrapped snugly in a blanket.

At their approach the woman at the fire stood up and turned to face them, and Selene experienced a moment of dissonance as it appeared the woman had no right side, but only the bones of her skeleton. She held the iron poker like a scepter, and a pale circlet glowed upon her head.

Then the fire settled, the light shifted, and she was a whole woman again—albeit an extraordinary one.

Her right side—the side that had looked like a skeleton—was still bone-white, but it was speckled with blobby patches of blue. Which patches clustered closer and closer together at her midpoint, until the balance of color shifted, and her left side was mostly blue, flecked with white. She looked, to Selene, like someone with a specially symmetrical case of vitiligo. The split even held true over her face, which was a perfectly ordinary face, albeit hauntingly familiar.

It was the eyes, Selene realized. She had the same light brown eyes as Flammard Nordstern.

Which shouldn't have been so surprising, all things considered. If she was who Selene thought she was, then she was also Flammard's half-sister.

Hel smiled at them, and it was as though the fire showed through her smile.

"Welcome, travelers," she said. She had a light, husky, musical voice, and gestured with her blue hand at the cushioned stools lined up against the wall. "I can lay claim to none of you, so I may only host you for a little while. So let us be like the living and make the most of our time. Stand up, little gosling. Is this not the one you were expecting?"

Slowly the child stood up, turned from the fire and looked at them apprehensively.

It was Albatross.

Small, impossibly young—maybe no more than five or six—with huge dark eyes and lank, white hair—the sight of her hit Selene like a punch of elation straight to the heart.

She did not understand why she should be so happy. Of course, it was a good thing that the final portion—and this was clearly the final portion, the last three fragments—of Albatross still survived. But the sight of her reverberated in Selene's chest like the gong of a bell. Like rain after a long, hot summer. Like sunlight after a storm. Like a soft bed after a hard night.

From the moment she had let go of Freddie and left Clara hanging off the bridge of Purgatory, Selene had been very careful not to hope. Hope, she knew, was the hook and line that Lilith—and Hell—used to torment the souls they captured. If you hoped for something—anything—they could always manipulate you.

So Selene had not hoped. She had moved inexorably forward. Inch by inch. Foot by foot. Step by bounding step. Never looking to the horizon, but steadfastly in front of her feet.

Now the horizon was standing right in front of her. She had come through anger, frustration and despair and found at the end of it something beyond hope.

It was the rock-solid certainty that things would be okay. She wasn't sure how yet, or what these *things* were, exactly, but that at this point it was a foregone conclusion that everything would be resolved.

"I dreamed of a white bird," said the child-Albatross. "Her wings were broken, but the moon made them whole again."

"I feel like you are someone I would like to know better," Albatross replied.

Child-Albatross nodded, swallowed. She looked small and timid, and yet grimly determined. She took a step forward, letting the blanket slip from her shoulders, which gleamed bare and white.

"Wait a moment," said the knitting woman. Hastily she finished casting off her work and bit the thread to cut it. Setting down her needles she held up a light gray tunic, like the ones she and Hel wore, but much smaller. Rising from her chair she went to the child and dressed her in the garment, tugging it proprietarily down until it covered her thighs.

"There," she said with satisfaction, squaring the child to her. "Now wherever you go, you will take my blessing with you."

"Thank you," said the child, meekly, picking at the hem of her tunic.

At the mention of blessing, Selene looked again at the woman, but could not place her. She had both eyes, which were gray, all her teeth, and soft, brown hair streaked with white. Her face was neither old nor young but kind, and her hands were strong and gentle.

Not a Norn, certainly, and probably not Freya. Then who?

Hel saw her looking, and was smiling, smoldering.

"One thing gods and mortals share," she said. "At a certain point we must change or die."

"Change is scary," said Albatross.

"But necessary," said Child-Albatross, and walked on slender, pale legs over the dark floor of Hel's house to meet the greater part of herself.

This time Selene watched. The two figures met, and embraced like long-lost friends. The child-Albatross disappeared between the arms and wings of the great Albatross, and then it was just one Albatross standing there, wingless, tall, with no aura but her pale hair, her eyes vivid as a thousand rainbows, clad in the gray knitted tunic, and substantial as a boulder. Her presence sat in the house of Hel, a realm of its own, and space itself bent in order to accommodate her.

Albatross frowned, pinching in her brow, twisting her face as though she'd just eaten something bitter.

"That's annoying," she said. "I thought I'd feel *better.*"

She sounded so much more *herself* than Selene had ever heard before that it took a moment for the meaning of her actual words to percolate.

"To know oneself is a difficult thing," Hel remarked. "Even we struggle with that sometimes."

"Sometimes more than others," their golden-haired guide remarked.

He had taken a seat a little ways down the hall, next to his brother, while the dog, Garm, lay at their feet.

Albatross shrugged her shoulders, and through a momentary crack in space Selene saw her wings, sharp and numerous, and a slice of rainbow. She looked, almost plaintively, at Hel.

"Where do I go from here?" she asked.

Hel, still smiling, shrugged. "That is not for me to say. Like I said, I cannot claim you."

"I would," said the brown-haired woman, "if I could."

"I know," said Albatross, regretfully. "Thank you."

She turned to look at Selene, almost despondently.

"I still don't understand," she said. "What happened to my father?"

It was Selene's turn to shrug unhappily, but Hel answered.

"Lucifer went over the Falls of Lethe long ago," she said. "Where they are now is no one's business but their own."

"Then how did I come to be?" asked Albatross.

Surprisingly, Selene found she could answer this one.

"Time is not linear to them," she said. "I expect they seeded Earth at one point, and their children have been—and will be—cropping up ever since."

"Then who was my mother?" Albatross asked.

"I mean," said Selene. "That could have been Lucifer, too. I wouldn't put it past them."

Albatross frowned, bit her lip. She seemed about to disagree, but Shae interrupted.

"I would speak to you about mothers," she said, addressing Hel. "Specifically, my own."

Hel raised her eyebrows, the fire in her eyes banked.

"I am in search of Dana Nordstern, who I believe you are aware of. Did she visit you . . . relatively recently?"

No smile this time. Not even a secret one. Hel's eyes darted behind them. To the man with the golden hair? No, to his brother. The man with blind eyes. Selene turned her head in time to see him nod.

"She came," said Hel, "and went."

"Over the Falls?" Shae asked.

"In a raft," said Hel, as if this made all the difference in all the worlds. Perhaps it did.

"Did she say where she was going?"

"How well did you know your mother?" Hel asked, her fire-bright eyes narrowing.

Shae hesitated. Though Selene had been annoyed at her for interrupting, she looked so lost in that moment that Selene could not help but pity her. It was the same look Clara got whenever she talked about her family.

"I thought I knew who she was," Shae said, softly.

"And now?" asked Hel.

"Now I would know the truth," Shae said, bravely.

Hel sighed and rubbed the side of her nose.

"The identity of Dana Nordstern is complicated," she said. "It's not my job to explain it. I can grant you passage through Niflheim, or a raft and paddle, if you desire to follow her."

"Where else would I go?" Shae replied, a little defiantly.

Hel did not speak, but looked at her for so long that Shae grew defensive and uncomfortable. Selene might have been amused, but that she felt a little of that baleful stare was directed at her, as well.

Her and Albatross.

"If it's not too much to ask," she said, "can you give us some options?"

Hel rolled her eyes, like an ember turning over.

"What do you want, a blessed map?" she snapped. "You're a living human with some remarkable magical protections, you could go anywhere in the Nine Realms and then some. You could go back to Kirke. Find your poet. You could even go back to Midgard."

Selene nodded.

"You mean, Earth?"

"This *is* Earth," said Hel, waving her blue hand at the hall around them. "No, I mean *Midgard*. The thin, green land. It's where you were born—both of you. It's where you"—she pointed at Albatross—"died. It's where you"—she pointed at Selene—"*will* die. It may be the only place you *can* die. It's where most of your family still is," she added, glancing at Shae.

But Shae was looking down at her feet—booted, squared against the wooden beams of the floor—and did not respond.

Selene felt a pounding in her chest. It was fear, fear brought on by hope.

"How do we . . . how do we get there?" she asked.

"To Midgard?" Hel replied, surprised at the question. "All roads lead to Midgard. That's why it's *called* Midgard. But for you, I suppose the fastest way would be through the Trinity Gate."

"The Trinity Gate?" Selene repeated.

"One door leads to Heaven, and one door leads to Hell," said Albatross. "And the Great Gate in between them has secrets it won't tell."

"That's the one," said Hel. She seemed pleased. "You know the way. Your grandfather built that gate."

"Oh," said Selene. That made sense. The Great Gate, which linked Heaven, Hell and Earth—what Hel called Midgard—could only be opened by a messiah. Or an anti-messiah. It took the power of a thousand souls and a fully fledged antichrist to open it from Earth, but from Hell? She glanced at Albatross.

Albatross was staring at Shae, chewing her lower lip. Like she was trying very hard to remember something.

"Yes," she said. "Yes, I should go back. I left . . . I left unfinished business. I will go back. I will take . . . whoever wishes to go . . . with me," she finished. She looked to Selene, who nodded vigorously. She looked to the demon, but it shrank from her, clicking its fingers together. Then she looked at Shae, very straight and fierce.

"You *should* come back with me," she said. "I cannot explain why, just yet. A lot of my memories are a jumble. But I know you should come back."

But Shae was shaking her head. "No," she said. "My way lies onward."

"Then go build a raft, daughter of Njordr," said Hel. "Garm will show you where supplies are kept."

At its name the dog rose to its feet, wagged its shaggy tail, and lumbered toward the door. It paused before the antechamber, expectant.

Without hesitation Shae marched to follow it. The demon slid out of her way, uncertain. She paused.

"You may come with me, if you wish," she said, and then followed the gray dog out of the hall.

The demon hovered, uncertain.

"You really can, if you like," Albatross said. "You're not in the Labyrinth anymore. You're free now."

"Or you may stay, I suppose," Hel allowed. "We'll need to give you a dunking in Mercy, but I expect we can find a place for you."

The demon considered. It looked from Hel, to the door, and back to Hel. It said nothing but clasped its taloned hands and bowed deeply. It turned and bowed to Selene and Albatross, even more deeply. Then it paced out of the hall, its hidden feet clacking softly on the dark wood.

It had all happened so quickly that it took Selene another moment to collect her thoughts and go running after them.

"Wait for me," she called to Albatross, flinging the door open in pursuit of the demon.

Time passed differently here. She had the sense that everything had been largely uncertain ever since they came out into the pool under Cocytus, but now things were falling into place, and events would progress exponentially faster.

She worried that she would be too late. That Shae would already have departed—with or without the demon—but both demon and woman were still on the banks of Lethe, loading the raft.

The raft was not the rudimentary collection of wooden logs and ropes which Selene had imagined, but a surprisingly sophisticated affair created by two inflated pontoons made of cured animal hide, held and joined by a metal frame, in the center of which was small seat with brackets for oars.

Garm was sitting beside them, watching critically as they rigged a second seat for the demon, facing the first. The oars themselves were two long, heavy, wooden affairs, laid out on the pale sand. As Selene approached, the demon went and picked one up, holding it so Shae could fit it into its bracket.

Shae looked around at her as she drew near, and the light and eagerness in her face surprised Selene so much she nearly tripped.

"Will you join us?" Shae asked. "This vessel was not made to seat three, but I expect we can improvise."

Selene felt something tug under her breastbone. Something like wistfulness and longing. A wish for something distant and unattainable.

"No," she said. "I gotta go back. Not finished."

The light in Shae's face dimmed, but she nodded, understanding. "No," she said. "I suppose you aren't."

"Someone's gotta look after Albatross, anyway," Selene offered.

A small smile.

"True."

"Actually, I came because . . . because I was hoping you'd come back with us."

Selene didn't understand why she was so nervous. The worst thing Shae could say was . . .

"No," said Shae, regretfully. "No, I can't. Not yet."

"Why not?" Selene asked, realizing she wasn't nervous. She was angry. "Clara misses you! Flammard misses you! They feel like you abandoned them. What am I gonna tell them, when I go back? Yeah, I saw your sister, she's going over the Falls of Lethe in a primitive catamaran-rafty-thing with a ninth-circle demon because Hel said your mother went that way?"

"Yes," said Shae, quietly. "Tell them that. They will understand."

"*I* don't understand," Selene said. "And to be honest, I don't think Clara will either. She'll sigh, and do that shruggy thing that she does, purse her lips and *say* she understands, but all that means is she feels like you don't care about her anymore, that she was a burden or something and ran you off."

Shae paused, looking down at the oar in her hands. The ninth-circle demon froze. Behind them, Garm went over to sniff in the bushes.

"You never knew our mother," Shae said eventually, and when she looked up, Selene realized she was also blisteringly angry. "You never knew... so let me explain this. When I was a small child, my mother told me that a great war was coming. That I would need to be a leader in this war. A general who would lead humanity to a better world. She trained us from infancy, me and Flammard. But then something happened that changed her mind. In an instant, it changed her mind. Changed everything. Can you guess what possibly could have happened to throw her off the course she had been on since before we were born?"

"No idea," Selene said, when it appeared Shae demanded an answer.

"When he was six years old Flammard told her that he was a *boy*," Shae said. "He told her he wanted to live his life as a *human*.

"Our mother was not happy about that, but she changed. Suddenly, I wasn't to be a general—a leader. I was to be a warrior. A hero. We both were. Our destiny was to protect humanity.

"Then she had Claymore, and everything changed all over again. We didn't talk about the great war, we didn't talk about destiny. And we didn't talk about Claymore's father. Our mother went to Scotland one summer, came back pregnant with Claymore, and that was that. All she would say is she met her father in the highlands. That's why she's named Claymore."

Shae paused, laughed ironically. "We used to think her dad might have been a Celtic god, but Mother never said. It doesn't imply anything, though. She met Njord in Venice, Loki in Dresden.

"Anyway, when Claymore was growing up that's when she made us all take public names. We'd always had to hide our powers from humans, but now we had to hide them from everything else. It was hard. Suffocating.

"Then, when Clara was fifteen, Mother left and didn't return. She told us she was going on a trip and might not be back for a while, dropped us off at Tesla's forge, and left. We haven't seen her since.

"I tried to keep the family together, but Flammard had had enough and stopped hunting. He was always the best at passing for human. He could repress his powers to the point that his physical body behaved like a normal human's. It caused him a lot of problems, but he genuinely seemed happier that way. Claymore though... well, you *know* her. She grew up without the threat of war, without destiny, but she still took her duty seriously. She and Flammard fought constantly. After a certain point, I gave up. We needed our mother back. So I told them I was going to find her. And I still am."

She raised her chin defiantly.

"Tell them—tell them both—that you saw Schiavona go over the Falls of Lethe, following our mother's trail. Tell them that I will find Dana Nordstern, and when I return it will be with her. Tell them I promise this on our rings and swords."

She raised her right hand, touching the little ring she wore to the hilt of her sword.

"Flammard buried his sword," Selene said. "He gave his ring to Clara. She gave it to me."

Shae's face sharpened at that, which amused Selene.

"I don't have it anymore," she told Shae. "The only thing that came with me when I fell were my clothes, and this," she shrugged, indicating the shield.

Shae frowned. "You said . . . Faraday gave that to you? It was one of her amulets?"

"Protection," said Selene. "Yeah. Originally it was just"—she held up her thumb and forefinger, curled together—"barely this big. With a pin on the back. She gave one to Jill, too, but she—Jill—gave it away."

"Foolish," Shae remarked.

Selene shrugged. "That's Jill," she said.

Who I'll get to see again after all, she thought, blindsided by the realization. She was grinning idiotically. Shae gave her a very hard look, and then turned back to assembling the raft.

It needed very little at this point. Once she had the oars on and shipped, she put the demon in the front seat and pushed the raft out into the calm waters of the eddy. Careful not to touch the surface, she leapt into the center basket, sending the vessel rocking in the water, but with its two pontoons it remained stable and upright, and as soon as Shae had her hands on the oars she unshipped them and easily rowed the raft back to the shore. She looked up, over Selene's head, and Selene turned to see what had caught her attention.

Hel's house was a dim silhouette against the misty sky, but there on the balcony she stood, blue and white and gray-robed, and the brown-haired woman beside her. Albatross was there as well, leaning on the railing.

Shae waved to them, giving the thumb's up. With one stroke of an oar she spun the boat around, and rowed them out into the current.

"Remember," she called to Selene as the raft began to float away downstream. "Remember, I swear I will return! And I will bring our mother back with me!"

Then she was rowing for the falls, and all Selene could do was stand on the banks of Lethe and watch as the little raft, with the white-robed demon and the golden-haired woman grew smaller and smaller.

When it looked like the raft was balanced on the very edge of the falls, Shae spun the boat around so she was in the back and the demon in the front, shipped an oar and used the other like a rudder to aim the raft square to the precipice of water. Selene saw her give an almighty heave on the oar, which shot the double-nose of the raft into the air at the last moment, and then the whole thing dropped out of view. As cleanly and suddenly as if it had been swallowed by the river.

"She ran that as well as anyone," said the golden-haired man, who had come down to stand behind Selene.

"What comes after the falls?" Selene asked him.

"More river, as I recall," he said. "A lot more. As I said, Mercy flows through all the worlds."

"Does it flow through Earth—through Midgard?" Selene asked.

"Of course," he said. "Midgard is where they *become* rivers."

There was nothing to be seen now but the black, flat water and the faint froth beyond the falls, shrouded in mist. Selene turned away and found the man had come to stand almost beside her. With his far hand he absently petted Garm's flank.

"I'm having trouble placing you," Selene told him.

The man smiled at her, that same, secret smile.

"You, your brother, that woman up there who knitted Albatross her dress . . ."

The man nodded.

"Consider what you know," he said.

Selene sighed. "It's been a *while* since I read the Eddas—"

"No," said the man. "That is what you have been *told*. Tell me what you have learned for yourself. You were very close to it, when you confounded Lucifer's ghost."

"You heard that?" Selene asked, feeling unaccountably embarrassed.

"It was impossible not to, the way you shouted," the man said, but he was smiling at her as he said it. As though he was proud of her. That made Selene feel a little better.

It felt like a lifetime since she had talked down the Satan scarecrow, but once she turned her mind back to it the memories surfaced—almost eagerly.

"You—gods, mythic beings, I mean—are affected by human belief?" she tried.

The man put his head on one side. Not quite.

"And . . . you also influence human belief? You're . . . archetypes, but you're also people."

"Reality is nuanced," the man agreed. "And for us, contains many layers. For you, you experience only one level of reality. It is the reality where you reside. Being confronted by numerous, simultaneous versions is very difficult for you. For us it is the opposite. We exist across a spectrum of reality. What you can see is only a small portion of what we truly are."

Visible light is just a tiny slice of the electromagnetic spectrum, Jill's voice offered helpfully in her head.

"I get that," Selene said. "I think. Still doesn't tell me who you are."

"But perhaps it helps explain why I cannot simply tell you?" the man suggested. "I could give you the name by which I was called in the Eddas, but that would not tell you who I am as you see me now. I could tell you I am a willing Proserpine, but that is not quite right either—and a disrespect to Proserpine, who has been through enough difficulties. Suffice to say that I am the right hand of Hel, her partner, adversary, and enabler."

"Was it you that made the moss? All the grass and stuff?" Selene asked. "I can't understand how that grows here, otherwise."

The man smiled down at his feet, coloring slightly. "They do me credit," he said. "But they only grow so well because Hel allows it. You do her a disservice by recognizing her as the Goddess of Death. She is more than that—or, she is trying to be. Gefiyon too. And my brother has found here a freedom he never knew in Asgard. Even to those that worshiped us, we were far more than they believed."

"Is that true of all gods?" Selene asked.

The man shrugged. "Broadly, yes. Some of us do . . . condense. Become intimately tied up with what humanity wishes of us. Ironically, though we gain power in Midgard that way, we lose power in the long term. That is what befell the boy Yeshúa, that is what Albatross still risks."

Mention of Albatross made Selene remember what was coming next, and her heart flared with hope—and some very real fear.

"Can you tell me what will happen, when we go back to Midgard?"

"Alas, foresight was never my strength," said the man. "But if you're wondering about the mechanics of it, it's quite simple. You fell, body and soul. And body and soul, you will rise again. It won't be easy, and it may be painful, but birth and rebirth often are."

"And Albatross?" Selene asked.

The man wagged a finger at her, his blue eyes twinkling. "Different rules apply. Her appearance may change—it may change drastically—but she is complete once more. What you see that appears different is just a different section of her greater being."

"The spectrum. Right. Thank you," Selene said, even though she still did not understand fully. The man had tried, and he had been generous, and he had not asked for anything in return—which was more than many whom she had met in life. "Really, I appreciate you taking the time to try and explain things. I'm sure we must seem kinda dense and insignificant to you guys."

"Not at all," said the man. "Personally, I find your kind inspiring." He turned from her, signaling that their conversation was essentially over. Selene waited by the shore for him to get a head start on their way back up to the house, but after a few steps he stopped and looked back.

"That might have been the only place where you misjudged Lucifer," he remarked. "From my own conversations with them—and those were limited, I must admit—I did not get the impression that they hate humans. No . . . I do not think they hate humans at all."

Then his broad, straight back was walking up the path to the house, his feet springing lightly over the ground, leaving little yellow-green curls of grass in his wake. But by the time Selene followed in his footsteps, these had already died and turned brown, and crumbled beneath her feet like ash.

They were about halfway up the climb to the house—Selene could see Hel's husband on the switchback above her—when a distant rumble met her ears.

That was all the warning they had before a cold, wet wind whistled down over the hills across the river, raised white-topped waves on the surface of Lethe, and nearly blasted Selene off the path. As it was she staggered, grabbing a nearby rock for support, tucking her face into her free elbow to protect her eyes—for the wind had brought with it flecks of ice, clods of dirt and sand which stung her skin.

As suddenly as it had hit them the wind moved on, and in its wake the air felt electric, charged with an energy Selene did not recognize. In the distance, far back the way they had originally come, was a faint roaring.

It was not the roaring of water or air, but the harsh, grating cry of countless voices, screaming in unison.

When no more winds were forthcoming, though the screaming continued, Selene pushed herself off the rock and sprinted the last two switchbacks up to the balcony.

Hel was still standing at her post, blue hand to left hip, gazing across the river with delighted interest. Though she did not glance as Selene mounted the balcony, she spoke to her, voice cutting through the distant screams like an iron knife.

"If you intend to leave by the Trinity Gate, I suggest you do it soon."

"What's happened?" Selene asked, directing her question to the party at large—which now included the brother, Albatross, and the brown-haired woman he had called Gefiyon. It was she who answered.

"Someone in Midgard tried to open it. They failed. Now, someone is attacking the foundations of it."

"They are trying to destroy it," said Hel. She sounded elated. Euphoric, almost.

"Oh, dear," he said with a sigh.

"Husband, do not shrink of this," Hel said. "It is one less obstacle in your way."

"I do not relish it," he said.

Nervous, Selene went over to Albatross, who was frowning worriedly—as though she'd just heard some upsetting news.

"Listen, if Hel's right and the Trinity Gate is the Great Gate and someone's taking a whack at it, we'd better go . . . like . . . now."

"Yes," said Albatross, absently. Then her eyes refocused, and she repeated, in earnest. "Yes, yes we must. Take my hand. I will carry you. It will be faster that way—and time is against us."

"Right when we could use some non-linearness," Selene joked, grasping the outstretched hand.

It felt like plunging her hand into a bubbling hot spring. The sensation rushed up her arm and dissolved in her chest so suddenly she gasped. She nearly let go of Albatross's hand, except that upon closer inspection, the sensation was not pain.

Albatross frowned at her and shook her head.

"Time has already been crossed," she said. "I think we're just catching up to ourselves now. At least I am. And ... if I remember ... " Her eyes grew wide, intense and afraid. "I don't remember if we make it. But the gate will be destroyed—I made sure of that."

She turned, regarded the gathering on the balcony.

"Thank you for your hospitality," she said to the two goddesses. Gefiyon bowed, as did the two men. Hel waved a hand dismissively.

"Do not make much of this parting," she said. "We will meet again."

This raised all sort of questions in Selene's mind—was Hel in some way responsible for what had happened to Albatross? Did the destruction of the Great Gate herald another form of Apocalypse?—but then Albatross was drawing her up onto the railing, pulling her arm around so Selene clasped her shoulders—like an oversized child riding piggyback.

"Until then," Albatross said, and leapt into the air, carrying Selene with her.

It was as though a new wind lifted them, blowing them up into the mists above Lethe. Albatross circled once, for altitude, her gray tunic flapping in the wind, and then she shot across the river, over the arm of the hill, and into to the solid bank of fog rising from the surface of Cocytus.

She left a trail of rainbow light in her wake, which sparkled in colors Selene would not have been able to see.

Hel and her husbands saw it, though, and she smiled up at it.

"One cannot judge daughters by their fathers," Gefiyon remarked.

Hel scowled, and stomped inside. But her husband smiled, a little of the old light returning to his face.

"Thank *goodness*," he said.

> *Creeping through the undercut*
> *Through doors open and shut*
> *Sneak in like cyanide*
> *'Cause heart is a part of genocide*
> *Like dreaming, dreaming*
> *Among the nightmares and the screaming*
> *Dreaming, dreaming*
> *Become the nightmares and the screams ...*

It was easy enough to find the place where they had climbed down into Niflheim. Cocytus had thawed to the point that there was a steady stream of water pouring out of the hole in a circular sheet. Selene felt it splash over her back as they passed through it, and then Albatross angled herself up, drawing her hands together over her head like a diver, and the next second they were speeding through the tunnel like a small, silent rocket.

The wind that had lifted them initially rose with them, so even though Selene could see the sides of the tunnel racing past (water cascading down its sides), she felt no blast of air in her face, no tug of gravity, but the sheer exhilaration of movement. Directly ahead of them was a circle of yellow-gray light which grew larger and larger and then they were shooting out of Satan's pit, rising swiftly over the surface of Cocytus.

The lake was still partially frozen, Selene saw when she glanced down at the quickly receding surface, but already cracks had appeared in the great chunks of ice, and in places, pieces had drifted loose.

"Did we do that?" she whispered in Albatross's ear.

"That was you, actually," Albatross answered. "You banished Satan's ghost, which was damming Cocytus."

"Oh," said Selene, taken aback. "I didn't realize it would be so . . . much."

"I think that's why you succeeded," Albatross said.

In the distance the ice was darkened by countless scrambling shapes. The damned souls were breaking free.

"What happens to Hell now?" Selene asked.

"I don't know!" said Albatross, sounding delighted by the prospect. "I do think you were right when you described it as a wound. Like an abscess or a pimple. So what happens when you burst a pimple?"

"Things get messy," said Selene, recalling her own experience with abscesses. "But it can't heal otherwise."

"I expect it'll leave a scar," Albatross said. "But it's better this way."

Up and up they flew. As they rose, more of Hell came into view. First the Labyrinth of Pain, spread out below them like a map. From what she glimpsed in the trenches, the ninth-circle demons had abandoned their posts and were flying upward, their robes flapping frantically. Many other demons were doing likewise. Dark bodies in distant columns, like birds over an updraft.

That brought Selene back to the messy aspect of burst abscesses.

"Where will they all go?" she asked.

"Fastest route out, I expect," said Albatross. She did not seem concerned, but her next words lit real worry in Selene: "Same way as us, in fact."

This was true. Some of the demons had enough of a head start that they were a little higher than Albatross—though she was gaining on them.

Selene could see the burning desert now. It shimmered in the haze of its own heat, golden and brown and barren. There were at least a dozen dark canyons, all of which led down toward the labyrinth. Some of them looked recent. Sudden erosion.

Beyond the desert the Forest of Despair was on fire. Huge pillows of gray-brown smoke lit from beneath by red flames rolled over the dark and twisted trees, which screamed as they were consumed.

Phlegethon was flooding. So was Styx. The wall of Dis was besieged from both sides by the great rivers, and even as Selene watched, it disappeared beneath the waves.

Fire and water met, hissed, turning to steam, and out of the steam rose flocks of winged creatures, trailing whips. Bigger creatures, gleaming white and wings beating like hummingbirds, skimmed the surface of the boiling water. They had long, sinuous, trailing tails, and it took Selene a moment to recognize what she saw:

Gorgons riding winged horses, their brass talons shining in the light of the fire beneath.

"It's all coming loose," she said, watching the Cliffs of Greed crumble. Above that the gluttons were climbing out of their swamp, joining the lustful, retreating into Limbo, which had narrowed to a thin white band of misty land.

But not a band. A closing door. Limbo was not a part of Hell. It was itself a netherspace—a gateway to other realms.

Even as Cocytus drained, revealing the bedrock of Hell, Phlegethon and Styx and Acheron began to flow the other way.

Out in all directions flowed the rivers, carrying many inhabitants with them.

Yet the skies of Hell were crowded with demons. They rose in columns and they rose in clouds, and they were all streaming toward the same place: the red gap in the high clouds where a desolate sun shone through.

Selene could see all of Hell laid out below her now. Huge and limited at the same time, it was a shape she well recognized. Circular and ragged, its likeness was printed on the shield she carried.

It was a crater. A crater caused by the impact of some monstrously large object, it was cut by concentric rings formed from ancient debris left over from the original blast wave. There was another crater directly in the center, now almost filled by the black waters of Cocytus, which had begun to spiral around the drain of the pit. The ultimate edge of Hell was a range of mountains whose rocky peaks were capped with snow—or something else that was white and shimmered—and beyond that was a barren land like the surface of a naked planet, streaked with scorch marks.

In this context, Selene saw that Limbo was truly a fault in the terrain of the crater, where the damage from the impact had caused a rift in that layer of reality. Things had been seeping through that rift, mixing with with the mortal detritus that fell from Earth, for thousands of years.

Now the process was reversed, as the inevitable erosion that would naturally have happened on Earth in those thousands of years was sped up. The crater of Hell was softening, flattening, even as its inhabitants drained away.

"It is not the end of Hell, of course," said Albatross. "The course of belief flows both ways."

"People will die, believing Hell exists," Selene said. "So it will, for them."

"This is the compromise we must accept," Albatross agreed.

They were passing through a layer of gray clouds now—thin, petulant things compared to the mists of Niflheim—but what protection they gave from the red sun above soon became apparent as it was stripped away.

It could not have been the actual sun, of course, but it was big and bright and hung at noon in the middle of the sky, so that was how Selene thought of it. Now the sky was more sun than empty space, and Selene saw it was in fact an angry, orange disk suspended over the crater—almost an exact mirror to it.

An orange face, alive with crawling figures that might have been snakes, but which Selene rather thought were letters. The letters spelled out the door and the terms under which it would open, but a hairline crack of white light had appeared near the center of the disk, cutting the words into meaninglessness.

Already some of the demons above them had reached the disk and been incinerated by that light. The blackened remnants of their carcasses drifted down in a fluttering rain like dead leaves.

Selene felt the touch of Albatross's hand on the back of her own.

"Whatever happens," she said, "do not let go!"

"Like Hell I won't," Selene promised.

Then Albatross raised both her hands, palms open, entreating.

There was no flashy show, no strike of lightning or roll of thunder, and at first Selene thought the Great Gate would not open. It was already breaking to pieces, pierced by countless cracks of white light. But it was not like an earthly door or window, which could still be passed through even after it was broken. Selene understood that.

The Great Gate was a three-way portal that linked three very different worlds together. It was like the valves in a giant heart, regulating the flow between them. To break it would be to remove that passage entirely.

Instead of an empty doorway, there would be an impassable wall of rubble.

The light from behind the cracks was rainbow now. It almost looked like Albatross's aura.

Then they were upon the face of the Gate, and grudgingly, treacherously, it creaked open.

Like a tiny, pale fish into a crevice of rock Albatross darted, Selene clinging to her back, and a small horde of demons followed.

But I say no! I wanna go!
But it's a hard life lived without hope
But I say no! I wanna go!
But it's a hard life lived without hope
The double doors of despair swing where you cannot see
I'm letting go of my hope, it's the rope hanging me
Hung from a rope made of hope
It's what you'll die for

A Cold Day in Hell

But in despair, say a prayer
And surrender . . .

All at once the redness vanished. The letters vanished. They were in a long, black tunnel, with the tiniest prick of light in the far, far distance. The woman under Selene's hands was gone, and in her place was a huge, white bird, wings stretching out for miles on either side.

For some reason, that did not seem quite right. Selene had the distinct feeling that this was not actually happening, but that she was remembering something. Only she had remembered it wrong, because the bird's wings were white instead of glossy brown, the sky was black instead of blue, and there was only one star.

Then the feeling vanished. She was clinging to Albatross—who had become an albatross—and the end of the gate was a tiny pinprick of reality against the fabric of . . . well, Selene didn't feel like hazarding a guess as to what surrounded them. She was aware that it was not infinite space, but that it was flexible and could swallow them if it liked. Had, in fact, swallowed several demons. Others kept pace with them, drawn to the light under Albatross's wings.

Curling herself tight against Albatross's back, Selene buried her face in the feathers of the great bird's neck, and shut her eyes.

There was no air inside the gate. No heat. No cold. No sound. Time became elastic, and stretched. At the end of that stretch, Selene knew, would come a mighty shock when it snapped back into place.

Even so she was surprised when it did. When her ears filled with the rushing and her skin tingled from the sting of wind and fire upon it.

The tiny light had cracked open and spilled across the blackness. Chunks had broken loose and were careening this way and that.

Albatross shrieked, shedding wings and feathers until she was a human again, and then they were just two women, clinging and reaching for the shattering window at the far end of the Great Gate.

The light grew, blinding, and consumed them.

Miracles will not sell unless it's a cold day in Hell
Try hard, I tried to do
Heroic acts my dreams said not to
All the things my dreams told me to do

Dreaming, dreaming
I turned to nightmares and the screams

But I say no! I'm gonna go!
Though it's a hard life lived without hope
Still I say no! I'm gonna go!
Though it's a hard life lived without hope

Along the road of despair is where you will find me
I've let go of all my hope, cut the rope hanging me

Swing from a rope made of hope
See where you'll be
When in despair, say a prayer
For certainly . . .

We gotta know that if we go
That it's a hard life lived without hope
You gotta know that if you go
That it's a hard life lived without hope

HARD LIFE LIVED WITHOUT HOPE

I wanna try, I wanna fly
But it's a long way down to the ground

The double doors of despair swing where you cannot see
I cut the rope of my hope, cut the anchor now I'm free

—Without Hope/*Johnny Bathory*

9.
THE GREAT GATE

Elsewhere

THE DEMON CLUNG to the bottom of the gate, his bone-claws dug into its face, as he slowly put himself back together.

It took longer than he liked. The shock of the gate snapping shut had scattered him throughout the nine rings of Hell, but like water down a drain, the separate bits of himself eventually trickled back to him, curling their way around the letters on the face of the gate. They brought with them some disturbing memories. The chatter of the Erinyes, heroes in the Burning Desert, and at the center of it all, an uncharacteristic silence.

Normally you didn't wish for Satan's attention. But he remembered how Satan had urged him on the first time he'd opened the gate. He'd been created to mirror the Anti-Christ, after all. The stepson of Satan. Perhaps the true son, if he did things wrong.

And those pretentious humans had *foiled* him. It was embarrassing, downright humiliating, especially considering he hadn't found the Antichrist until he—*she*—had pushed him through the gate right as it closed.

Well, he could learn from that.

This time, he'd bring reinforcements.

He put out the call, and they answered. Not as many as he expected—the third-circle demons were missing—but the nuckalevees and the Ninth Circle, the flaming damned and the clerics of Dis all heard him, and he felt their power build his own.

This time, things would be different.

He was certain of it.

Detroit, MI
November
Thanksgiving week, Sunday

The white Chevrolet Impala exited 14th Street and crept down Roosevelt Park Avenue toward the majestic edifice of the former Michigan Central Railway Station. They'd had a hard freeze the night before, and the Impala's worn tires skidded slightly as it came to rest in front of the main entrance.

This was an imposing Beaux-Arts façade which, due to its north-facing angle, was largely backlit by the low autumn sun. The fifteen floors rising above it in an angular block gave the building an ominous presence, broken only by the hundreds of glittering windows, freshly cleaned, many of which were alight within.

Yes, despite the signs of age and wear, the building was clearly inhabited. Utilized, in fact, by an energetic team of people. There was a Fire and Rescue truck parked directly in front of the north entrance, which was a wide set of doors under a protective shelf of roof. From this roof had been mounted three flagpoles, displaying the US stars and stripes, the Michigan blue with elk and moose, and a plain black flag with a white disk in the center. The three flags hung peacefully in the cold, still air.

No signs proclaimed what the building was being used for now, though there was a notice mounted directly at the curb stating that parking for sun-sensitive visitors could be had on the underground level by following the blue arrows. One such arrow indicated to the left of the building, but since the driver of the Impala was neither sun sensitive nor inclined to go underground, he elected to park the car behind the Fire and Rescue truck, and got out.

One boot touched the icy pavement and went sliding off sideways, leaving the man to clutch at the car and curse.

He was a very good-looking man. Slim, brown, and black-haired, he had the sort of long-lashed dark eyes that would have served him well as an actor or model. He had a trim black beard and wore trim black clothes that were nowhere near warm enough for the Michigan weather. A rhinestone cross hung from a chain around his neck. A single diamond stud glittered in his left earlobe, and around his right wrist was laced a leather bracer, black and shiny from wear.

Chuy Acebo shuffled up onto the salted sidewalk with relief. Hurrying under the sheltering roof he pulled the front door open, eager to get out of the cold, and nearly collided with the burly firewoman on her way out.

She was black, wore her hair in strict cornrows, and outweighed him by probably thirty pounds. Chuy slipped around the swinging door and managed to turn the collision into a slightly awkward holding-of-the-door.

The woman, who had been talking over her shoulder as she left, broke off mid sentence to stare at him.

"And what part o' hell did *you* crawl out of?" she asked, cheerfully.

Chuy looked at her in consternation.

"Don't talk about Houston that way," he said.

The firewoman laughed, patted him heavily on the shoulder, and stomped away to her truck.

Then he was inside an entry room, where coats lined the walls and boots filled the cubes stacked below them. Chuy cast an envious glance at a down jacket with a fur-lined hood and double zipper, but then he was through the inner doors, and a blast of blessedly warm air embraced him.

It was almost as light inside as it was outside, thanks to the high windows and the cavernous, vaulted ceiling. This still showed wear from the building's years of abandonment, as many of the tiles were missing, patched with plain plaster. But the effect was a businesslike one: the people who worked here cared about the building, they just didn't have the resources for flash and grandeur.

The basic floor plan of the original station had survived, although this seemed mostly due to the fact that people had been too busy to remodel properly. Parts of the main waiting room had been closed off with tents and curtains, and it looked like a nature exhibit had taken over the south end. Certainly there was the better part of a tree down there, a lot of bushes, and movement among them that suggested badgers or foxes.

Chuy would have gone to investigate except that there was a ghost hovering by the entrance.

It was fairly corporeal, as ghosts went, but so far removed from what it had been in life that it was hardly more than a cluster of emotions and memories. Visually it appeared to Chuy like a crack of blue light with a pair of wispy, disembodied arms hanging beside it.

Hello, said the ghost. *How may I help you?*

Chuy blinked at it. His experiences with ghosts were that the more present they were, the more trouble they were. He blessed himself out of habit, without thinking.

The ghost's light dimmed, but it did not vanish.

May I take your name? it asked. It sounded a little hurt.

"No," said Chuy, feeling rather affronted. "You can tell Freeman that Acebo is here, and I brought his car."

This will be done, said the ghost, and winked out of sight.

Chuy wandered across the hall. Down to his right, opposite the tree, was an open door under a sign spelling out "Quiet Room" and beside it "Café."

Opposite him was a wall of columns interspersed with unmanned desks. One said VISITOR INFO and the other INTAKE ASSISTANCE.

Between them was a wide passage lined with further columns, which upon inspection housed two more desks on the left (INFORMATION and LEGAL) and the old ticket counters on the right. These all had their screens down, and the single (closed) door said OPERATIONS on it.

Opposite OPERATIONS, down the corridor to his left, he found the drugstore converted into a modest first-aid clinic. A young man with East

Asian features and improbably sandy-gray hair was in the process of doing inventory there, and Chuy respectfully retreated before disturbing him.

He was in the process of going back to the main waiting room when he heard an elevator *ding* from somewhere beyond First Aid. He paused, turned, and saw Ariel Freeman skip into view.

He looked . . . *well*. He looked like Ariel, Chuy was pleased to see. Not the shriveled husk of a man he'd helped that giantess pull out of the mound back in June. His skip was due to him favoring his left hip, however, and that made Chuy feel unaccountably cold inside.

His memories of the event last summer were distressingly foggy, and he couldn't shake the feeling that he was somehow responsible for Ariel's latest brush with death.

Well, latest as far as he *knew*.

He squared himself off against the advancing man, put his hands on his hips.

"Ariel Freeman," he began. "What have you been—"

"Chuy!" Ariel said, loud and glad, and embraced him heartily.

That was the thing about Ariel, Chuy remembered as he felt himself enfolded by those thick, strong arms. He was so comfortably heterosexual that he busted right off the scale and inhabited his own sunny slice of the spectrum, where two dudes hugging was just that. Two dudes hugging. Innocent, healthy affection. But genuine. Chuy wished he was half as emotionally well-adjusted.

This being apart from Ariel's own personal magnetism, which still surprised Chuy, even after they'd been friends for years. It was like Ariel carried around his own aura of infectious happiness and self-confidence. Chuy had at one point theorized that Ariel was of faerie or elfish descent, which Ariel had thought was hilarious. But for all the testing they were able to do, he read as nothing more or less than a regular human.

He was released from the hug as quickly as he had been enveloped, and slowly refocused his eyes on the man standing in front of him.

"How was the drive?" Ariel was asking. "You need anything? Coffee? Toilets are this way—and so's my office, fittingly enough." He laughed.

"They gave you an office?" Chuy said, still dazed.

"Technically, it's the duty operative's office," Ariel said. "Which I am for another . . . oh . . ." He checked his watch. "Two hours. But it's okay. Marcus is on call, and it's been pretty quiet today. Mostly paperwork. 'Swhy I'm stiff." He tapped his left side. "C'mon, let's get you briefed."

Ariel's office was at the south end of the hall, past the elevators, in what had once been the Men's Room.

Not the men's toilets, which were two doors and another hallway over, but the lounge for male travelers, from the building's train-station days. It had the same patched-up grandeur that the main waiting room had, combined with a bootstrap utilitarianism that contrasted the old stonework and wood floors with particleboard desks, folding chairs, and whiteboards on easels. There was also a big piece of corkboard mounted on the one wall not cut with windows, to which had been pinned numerous scraps of paper.

There were two desks and four chairs, a gorilla rack housing two computers with a printer, scanner, and wireless router on top, and a table by the far door with a coffeemaker and a box of teas next to it. Both the desks had two monitors each, mouse and keyboard, and a pad of notepaper. The desk Ariel seated himself at had a grow light clipped to the edge under which sat a potted mint. It had splayed its tendrils so far out over its pot that it trailed off the side of the desk and, had the floor been any dirtier, might have put down roots there.

The other desk was unoccupied, but there was a half-full cup of coffee by the keyboard, and someone had been in the process of doodling a picture of a cat on the notepad when they had been called away.

Chuy, whose legs still felt cramped and fidgety from hours in Ariel's car, paced around the room while his friend made them fresh coffee.

"This is probably where they'll start you," Ariel said as he waited for the water to heat. "Being that you're coming in on my recommendation. We're strapped for operatives, you see. Really, we need at least twelve— we've *got* six, and that's counting Mantha and we don't like to do that."

"Do I know Mantha?" Chuy asked. The name was familiar.

"You mighta met her," Ariel said, mixing the instant packets into their styrofoam cups. "Smart kid, about yay tall"—he held up his hand a little under his chest—"dark hair. We think she's maybe twelve. I'll brief you on her, too. But first, you sure you don't need to use the gent's? This could take a while."

Chuy declined. Explained that he'd stopped less than an hour south of Detroit.

Ariel set him up with a chair next to his behind his desk, where they could set their coffee and Ariel could use his computer to show Chuy who he'd be working with.

"I can't open you an account," Ariel admitted. "HR will get you set up with that. They even do payroll, believe it or not. Jill is working on getting us benefits. They'll also give you a proper introduction." He grinned. "But HR is basically Lansing these days, and I figured you'd probably want an introduction to *her* first."

"Is Lansing the . . . uh . . . " Chuy snapped his fingers. Ariel had warned him there were some unusual folks at his new place of employment. "That demigod? Son of Loki?"

Ariel laughed. "No, that's Marcus. Great-great-great grandson, actually. As far as we can tell. Most of his powers are latent. Great guy, too. You'll like working with him. No, Lansing's our resident vampire."

Chuy, who had judged his coffee cooled enough to drink, nearly spilled his cup as he set it down in a hurry.

"There's a *vampire* on staff? Are you running some kind of madhouse here?"

"Technically, she's one of the founders. And more and more, it's her madhouse to run," Ariel said. He looked remarkably calm. Easy. Relaxed.

Not at all like there was a wild vampire loose in the building.

Chuy checked over his shoulder, reassuring himself that there was *some* sunlight drifting in through the south-facing windows. Reflexively he tugged on his cross.

He looked again at Ariel. He wasn't acting like someone under a glamour. But that didn't mean he wasn't.

"You'll understand once you meet her," Ariel said, which didn't calm Chuy at all.

"Let me see your neck," he insisted.

Ariel rolled his eyes. But he unbuttoned his collar—he was *still* wearing that pretentious priest get-up, which Chuy found vaguely insulting—but the neck it revealed was perfectly smooth and free of blemishes or scars.

"If you like the sound of Lansing," Ariel said, "just wait til you meet the rest of the gang."

A photo of a young woman wearing a knit beanie and a confused expression took up a quarter of the display. She had dark brown eyes and bushy brown hair, and improbably sparse eyebrows.

"Imogen Supatnik," Ariel announced. "Twenty-seven, originally from Minneapolis. Mauled by a rapid werewolf in oh-seven. She's one of our ops."

Another file filled the screen. This time, it was the man Chuy had seen at the first-aid station.

"Tucker Chen," Ariel informed him. "Thirty-four, originally from San Francisco. Born werewolf, and a lapsed nurse. He's our boss medic. Well, only medic. For now."

Chuy swallowed. The next picture was of a young black man with shockingly orange hair and light brown eyes. He looked nervous in his picture, and apologetic for being so big.

"*That* is Marcus Bowerman," Ariel said. "He's the demigod. A good op. We were thinking of pairing you two up, at least to start."

Click. Another window, this time showing an unsettling—if familiar—face. An austere, female person with strong cheekbones, a long nose, and glittering blue eyes. She was pale enough to be a vampire, and bald as a newborn infant. Only the fact that she had deep-set eyes gave a clue as to where her brows were—for they appeared to have been shaved as well.

"The giantess," Chuy said.

"You can call her Clara," Ariel said. "She's nice."

"*Nice?*" said Chuy, looking down at Ariel in consternation.

Ariel, somehow managing to lounge in his folding chair, smiled sheepishly.

"I think she's nice."

"She looks like she could kill me," Chuy said, blandly.

"She'll save your life, anyway," Ariel said. "You get used to the whole 'freeze you with my piercing gaze of icy death' look."

"She *looks* like a failed Aryan genetics experiment with a Greek nose," Chuy said.

He'd said it without thinking. Clara's face hurt him in a way he couldn't explain. Even in an emotionless portrait displayed on a computer screen he felt like her eyes were accusing him of something terrible. He felt guilty and ashamed for no reason he could identify, and it made him snappish. And he'd only snapped because this was Ariel he was talking to, and Ariel knew how to smooth over his rough edges.

Except Ariel had no witty rejoinder. He didn't even change the subject. He went very still and quiet, looking at the picture on the screen with a conflicted expression. His mouth had opened slightly, but no words came out. Chuy thought he had even stopped breathing.

"Ya get used to that, too," he said quietly. Too quietly.

Chuy looked at him more closely. In all the years they'd known each other he'd never seen Ariel fall for someone. He'd seen plenty of people fall for Ariel, and he'd seen how Ariel *cared* about people, but always in the manner of platonic friendship or past flames. There had been a time when Ariel Freeman fell in love, but that time was past, and now he spread his affection evenly and fairly and without expectation.

This was not that. Looking at Ariel looking at a picture of a woman like an anthropomorphic iceberg reminded Chuy more of what he felt when he fell for someone unattainable. When he slid down the knife edge of wanting someone but not wanting to hurt them, or not wanting to ruin whatever friendship existed.

Ariel coughed. "She'll save your life, just wait," he whispered, and switched windows.

She saved yours, Chuy thought. *Frickin' impaled on that knife, you poor hijo de puta.*

Then he looked back at the computer screen and forgot clean about Clara and whatever messy tangle was growing between her and Ariel.

The next window had not one, but five pictures. And only one name.

"That's our Tamerlain," Ariel said, his voice back to its full, golden rumble. "Just turned eighteen, so we get them as a full-time op, which is great. Came to us—well, to Jill—about a year ago. They're . . . uh . . . pretty cool, actually."

"Which one is them?" Chuy asked.

Of the five pictures, only three were human. Two girls, one white and blond with gorgeous blue eyes that were if anything enhanced by the thick glasses she wore, and one pudgy and dark-haired who could have been Tibetan or Hawaiian or Indonesian. The other human was a black man with short, curly hair, who completely filled his designated square of screen. By contrast, the next picture was of a small, scruffy brown dog. And the last was a gold-and-cream tiger. A gold-and-cream tiger in a polo shirt. And maybe its face was a little flatter, and its eyes a little closer set, and its whiskers a little longer, than a tiger's should have been.

Ariel gestured at the gallery of rogues and grinned.

"Yes," he said.

"So, she—he—is a shapeshifter?" Chuy asked.

"Basically," said Ariel. "Jill's calling it multiple-body condition. Tamerlain shuffles between these five pretty evenly. Except for the tiger. I've never actually seen that one. And when they're a dog mostly they sleep. They're still working on understanding what triggers the change, but they've been getting better at managing the different bodies. It's all the same *person*," Ariel said, emphasizing the last word. "No matter what they look like."

"Okay," said Chuy, beginning to feel a little overwhelmed. "Cool."

"Yep," said Ariel.

Next came a man with dead gray skin and dead, filmy eyes.

"Don Lelain," said Ariel. "Yes, he's a zombie."

"Great," said Chuy.

"Nice guy," said Ariel. "He works with our professor."

"You have a professor on staff?"

"Sure do," said Ariel, and pulled up a picture of a dark-skinned, gray-haired man with twinkling black eyes. "Ronald Okedo, formerly of Jill's alma mater. He's our head of analytics. Well, him and Don *are* analytics. There's also Gadget, but we don't have a picture of her yet. She's sort of adopted Okedo. Can't mistake her—she's a goblin."

"A *real* goblin?" Chuy said.

"Genuine as arsenic," Ariel said.

Chuy laughed. It was all he could do.

"If you like that, wait til you meet Frosty and Lady Bibbit," said Ariel, pulling up more windows.

"Wait, let me guess," said Chuy, covering his eyes. "Frosty is a . . . a yeti? And Lady Bibbit is a . . . frog?"

"Good guesses," said Ariel. "But, not quite. Frosty's a Welsh hell hound. Adopted Jill the way Gadget adopted Okedo. Bibbit is Mantha's stuffed rabbit, which she animated. Now she—Bibbit—is our supernatural liaison."

"An animated stuffed rabbit?" Chuy said. "And she's not . . . evil?"

"If she is," said Ariel, "we need more evil like her. She's also nigh indestructible, which is helpful when you're dealing with a frightened troll."

"You have trolls here," Chuy said, unable to muster the energy to be surprised.

"Three of them. They're living in the old baggage room across from Jill's office."

"Of course they are," said Chuy.

"It's not so bad," Ariel said. "Once Jill got their diet balanced, they calmed right down."

"You said this Mantha . . . *animated* her stuffed rabbit? What is she, a witch?"

Ariel's smile dimmed. "Something like that," he said. "You'll . . . well, I'm actually hoping to get your opinion on her. But . . . gently. Whatever else she is she's a scared adolescent and a good kid. Remember that."

"Sure," said Chuy. He peered over Ariel's shoulder. "Is that everyone?"

"Just about," said Ariel. "We have a few werewolves who drop in from time to time, one rehab patient. We need a vet. Oh, right, and there's Jill."

One last window. A picture of a plain woman with brown hair and round glasses, which did not completely hide the red tinge to her irises. The box under her name labeled "position" said DIRECTOR in big, block capitals.

"Another vampire?" Chuy guessed, feeling his heart sink.

"Better," said Ariel. "She's a damphyr."

Chuy blinked.

"A real one?"

"Well, she'll tell you she's a vampirically augmented human," Ariel said. "But, basically, she's a damphyr."

"Oh," said Chuy. Finally, things were falling into place. Ariel wasn't under a glamour. Things weren't going crazy—well, not any more than they usually did during an impending apocalypse. He'd just stumbled into an organization run by the mythical being of mythical beings. Of *course* there was a son of Loki and a werewolf medic, a vampire in HR, and a zombie analyst.

And now, a closeted-gay, lapsed-Catholic exorcist.

"Yeah, so, that's pretty much us," said Ariel, leaning back in his chair and clasping his hands behind his head. "Welcome to MCSIR."

"Is that why you call it 'mixer'?" Chuy asked. "Because it's a big mix?"

"What?" said Ariel. "No, it's not—it's MCSIR. M C S I R. The Moonshield Center for Supernatural Investigation and Research. We really need to get a sign."

Elsewhere

The problem, the demon decided, had been his well of power. Devil's Lake *sounded* like a nice place to open the Great Gate, but it was too small. Too shallow. He needed something deeper. Stronger.

He couldn't get *too* near Detroit. The metaphysical scarring left over from that snafu with the Gunn brothers made opening portals there unpredictable, but enough time had passed on Earth that some of the ley lines had rerouted themselves. Enough to form a new nexus, not far from where the old one had been. It was nowhere near as powerful, but it didn't have to be.

A nexus didn't have to be made from ley lines. Natural ones formed all the time, created by geological features whose powers were even greater than those which governed the metaphysical world. They were just harder to tap, that was all. But the new nexus was relatively close to one such natural nexus, and if the demon could use the first to tap the second, it would be as good as Babel.

A lake was a place of power. Taken together, a group of lakes pooled their resources. (Ha.) And the new ley nexus was only a little south from the natural nexus created by a family of lakes whose powers were evident to even the most nearsighted humans.

The demon briefly considered drawing directly on Lake Superior but quickly discarded the idea. Lake Superior was almost an ocean it was so big, so deep, and gave the demon the uncomfortable sensation of being sentient. Lake Huron, on the other hand, was more approachable. It was closer to his original nexus anyway. It also helped that, as far as the actual lake was concerned, it and Lake Michigan were one and the same.

Two lakes for the price of one, and if they were sentient, they were definitely asleep.

Opening the Great Gate was a process, but the demon was nothing if not patient. He poured himself along the necessary words, and got it started.

Detroit, MI
Thanksgiving week, Monday

It had been another bitterly cold night, well below freezing with a light flurry of snow just after midnight. Jill had come up from her office to let Frosty out and found the concourse suffused with a milky white light. Going to a window she saw this was from the city lights reflecting off the thick clouds and the dancing flakes of snow falling through the air. She stood and watched, in the silence of the sleeping station, while Frosty frolicked in the north garden.

This was a little square of ground that had been hardly more than some weeds and dirt when they'd arrived, but Ariel had made a hobby of poking at it over the summer, and now it was, if not really a garden, at least free from trash.

It was currently being covered in a soft layer of snow, making it look even more pristine. Frosty practically disappeared into the gathering drifts as she bounded through the fresh snow, digging and rolling and windmilling her tail.

Eventually she asked to be let in. Jill cracked the door hardly an inch, and the dog flowed through. She might have flowed through the closed door, and Jill suspected the main reason she asked Jill to do the honors was to get Jill up from her desk now and then.

Jill checked on dispatch before she went back to work. The ghost twinkled at her from within its nest of computers, phones, and radios. That had been an unexpected boon. The ghost had arrived in the middle of a wave of refugees and had been largely ignored due to its transparent nature, but once things had settled down a little, proved to be a helpful addition to MCSIR staff.

It didn't need to eat or sleep, could operate all kinds of electronic devices, and was virtually impossible to aggravate. So it worked dispatch at night and customer service during the day, and the only real issue was its inability to remember who it was, what its name was, and why it was here.

I cannot go back to where I was, it had said. *That was the first thing I tried. Of all the places I could go, this seemed the best.*

It had also rejected any attempt at naming. So it was just "the ghost," and seemed content with that. Jill had kept meaning to do a proper interview with it, but things kept cropping up.

Like now, when it was a quiet night and she might reasonably have a conversation, she was in the middle of entering AMA data, and the picture that was forming demanded all her attention.

Ambient Magical Activity, as opposed to Ambient Magical Energy, as opposed to an Acute Magical Event, which were all things worth tracking. Taken singly, they could give you hints as to what might be going on under the surface of visible reality. Taken together, Jill suspected, they could serve as a predictor of when and where an Excited Supernatural Event would occur. Jill had been busy over the past month, deploying an array of various sensors throughout Detroit, and comparing their results with the reports from her operatives, animal control, Detroit PD, and Fire and Rescue. And while they hadn't been able to accurately predict anything yet, Jill suspected they were getting close.

She pushed her office door open with her shoulder, her mind already on the latest dataset, which she'd been in the middle of when Frosty had demanded her after-midnight break.

There was someone sitting in the guest chair opposite her own, wrapped in a blanket and sipping a cup of hot cocoa.

Jill blinked, and held her breath for a moment. She'd left the lights off, so the room was only illuminated by the faint twinkle of the city below, and in lieu of startling her guest by turning them on, waited for her vampire vision to rise, and she saw that it was Mantha.

"Good"—she checked herself—"morning, Mantha," she said. "Lights?"

"Sure," said Mantha, sipping her cocoa.

On came the lights, white-balanced LEDs mounted to panels in the ceiling, filling the room with clean, vampire-safe daylight. Jill took a few deep breaths until her eyes adjusted, and then came around to her own station, sandwiched between a filing cabinet, an exam table, and her double-screen desk. This was a combination of a 40-inch monitor and a touch-sensitive display laid out like a table. In fact, it got used as a table by accident rather a lot, and Jill conscientiously moved the extra cup of cocoa Mantha had well-intentionally made for her to the little end shelf.

"What can I do for you?" Jill asked.

It was unusual for her to be bothered this early in the morning, outside an emergency, but she was technically at work and available for people to consult with.

"I had a bad dream," said Mantha.

Jill looked at the girl across from her.

She'd never examined the problem of Mantha too closely, because Clara had made it clear Mantha was off limits. This alone would not have stopped Jill, but there had been enough distractions that she'd been obliged to let it slip. And since Mantha had never made a pest of herself or caused Jill any trouble, she often forgot about her.

In fact, Mantha had never sought Jill out before. The only conversations they had had were in the presence of Clara or Ariel, who accompanied her almost everywhere.

Yet here she was, at two-thirty in the morning, wrapped in an old patchwork quilt, drinking cocoa in Jill's office. She'd grown a little in the almost year she'd been with them but was still small. Dark brown hair cloaked her face, which was a thin oval with equally dark brown eyes. Romanian descent, Jill thought, considering her last name. Fulgeroiu was not a common name, but it was a Romanian word. She'd looked it up: it meant "lightning."

She was potentially the most powerfully magical person Jill had ever met, and Jill had met witches and werewolves and demons and the human avatars of the concepts of glory, victory, and fury.

Mantha, from what Jill and seen and heard, had powers on an entirely grander scale. She could rewrite reality, imbue inanimate objects with life—*sapient* life—and influence people's thoughts.

If Mantha had dreams bad enough to get her up out of bed to come talk to Jill, they were not the sort of bad dreams fixed by a cup of cocoa and a pat on the head.

"Can you tell me about them?" she asked, opening a new document on her computer and pulling out her keyboard. "Or would you prefer to wait until Ariel and Clara get up?"

Mantha shrank further into her blanket, pulling it tightly around her shoulders as she clutched the cup of cocoa close to her chin.

"If I tell them, they'll tell you. Ariel will make them sound not as bad as they are, Clara will make them sound worse. I think . . . they are important, and I don't understand them."

Jill fidgeted with her glasses. She did not strictly need them anymore—vampire vision was better than 20/20—but when she was eating and drinking and breathing and more-or-less pretending to be human, her old astigmatism reasserted itself, and the glasses came in handy. They also masked the reddish glint in her eyes, and sometimes she wore them anyway, just to make other people feel more comfortable.

Mantha didn't want comfort, however. Mantha was here because she had a problem and had chosen to share it with Jill. It was, in its own way, an honor.

"Let's have it then," she said, taking off her glasses and entering the time, date, and subject into the top of the document.

Mantha took a deep breath and let it out, ruffling the hair close to her cheeks.

"When Clara and Ariel closed the gate at Devil's Lake, I saw it happen," she began.

"You saw the gate close?" Jill asked, for confirmation.

"I saw the gate, I saw through the gate, I saw them close it," Mantha explained. "I saw . . . I saw the demon get sucked into it."

"Which demon?" asked Jill, touch-typing her notes into the document.

"They called him Jude Carson, he pretended to be an antichrist," Mantha said.

Jill's eyes narrowed.

"You mean he *wasn't?* Wasn't an antichrist?" she asked.

Mantha, grave and sober as a tombstone, shook her head.

"He was a demon out of Hell," she said. "I saw him. *Really* saw him. He was angry. And he saw *me.*"

She stopped talking. Jill finished entering this information and waited. When still the child did not speak she peered around the monitor at her.

Mantha was looking down into the bottom of her mug, her face blank and frozen. When she spoke again, she started in a jerk, as if picking up from thoughts which had been rushing through her head.

"That gate was a part of me," she said. "When it closed, something in me opened. I dream, but they're not proper dreams. They're bad dreams. They keep falling apart when I look too closely. I wake up, and I can still see them."

Now she was talking, Jill didn't like to interrupt. She tagged her notes with the questions she wanted to ask—*Them? How is the gate a part of her? Bad dreams as in faulty dreams?*—and remained quiet.

"I see . . . the gate," Mantha was saying. "Not the lesser gate he opened, but a much bigger gate. It opens three ways. It's like a heart—there's valves. Normally, the valves are all open just a little—just enough for a little from each side to get through. He wants to shut off one valve, and open the others all the way. He wants to turn on a stream of demons from Hell to Earth. Like a firehose. And I can see them—and I can see him—and they're all crawling over the face of the gate. And he's turned himself into a key, and it's opening."

Mantha stopped speaking. Jill's fingers clacked on her keyboard, and then stilled. When she looked around her monitor, Mantha was still looking down at her cocoa—probably cold by this time—and her mouth was moving, her lips forming words, but Jill could not read them, and no sound came out.

"That's all," Mantha said eventually.

Jill frowned.

"And you are reasonably certain these dreams are not constructs of your own brain, trying to sort out what you witnessed at Devil's Lake?"

Mantha looked up, her eyes wide, almost desperate.

"No," she said. "That's what I'm afraid of."

"Can you explain?" Jill asked, intrigued.

Mantha closed her eyes, as if her thoughts had all turned to cats and she was having to herd them into order.

"Sometimes, I dream of things that *are* real. You, Ariel, Clara," she said. "Sometimes, I dream of things that aren't real ... yet. But then they become real."

"Like ... prophetic visions?" Jill asked, making a note in her document.

"No," said Mantha, so firmly it surprised Jill. "No, it's not like that. It's like ... *by* dreaming them, I make them *become* real."

"Huh," said Jill. She felt like she'd heard of this before, somewhere in a book, once. Then the implication hit her.

"You're afraid that, by dreaming this, you're making it happen?" she asked.

Mantha nodded, mute but vigorous.

"Huh," said Jill.

It was an angle worth investigating. They would need a control subject—something harmless, like a pink balloon, for Mantha to dream into existence. Then Jill realized such an experiment would be redundant. They already had proof that Mantha's dreams could become real—viz the nightmare monsters from last year—and furthermore, Jill had recorded a similar phenomenon in the case of Fury-Joy even before that.

There did exist people in the world who could dream things into existence. What merited study at this point was *how* they did it, and how permanent was this new dreamed-up reality.

Then Jill realized that what Mantha was saying suggested something much bigger than an illumination of her powers.

"This ... gate ... " Jill began.

"The Great Gate," Mantha said, assertively.

"The Great Gate," Jill repeated. "Do you think it's likely to open ... soon?"

Slowly and steadily, Mantha nodded.

"Do you know where it will open? Relative to us?"

Just as slow and assuredly, Mantha shook her head.

Jill sat back in her chair.

"*That's* what you want me to find out," she said.

For the first time that morning, Mantha smiled. Small and fleeting, like the failed spark of a lighter, it nevertheless lit up her face like a torch.

Jill breathed in and out, just to feel her ribs move. It cleared her head, though her vision got a little fuzzy.

"Okay," she said, looking back at what she had written. It would all have to wait now. Now that she understood why Mantha had chosen to share her dreams with *her*.

Mantha didn't want Jill to figure out what her dreams meant *for her*. She wanted Jill to find out what her dreams meant *for the rest of the world*.

Jill glanced to her other side, where Frosty was a cool, fluffy lump beside her right foot. Rusty red ears perked, and yellow eyes blinked.

"I don't suppose *you've* got any ideas?" she asked. Frosty just thumped her tail. Then she looked back at her display, at the windows she still had open from the AMA data, and a thought occurred.

Staring at the screen so hard her eyes bled full red, Jill began entering data in earnest, her fingers stabbing at the keyboard like cold knives.

Across from her, Mantha set aside her empty cocoa mug and took the other from the desk. Tucking her feet further up under herself, she sipped the tepid drink while Jill worked away at her computer.

Clara dreamed. For the first time since midsummer, she dreamed.

She was on a muddy path, crossed with the glossy roots of high conifers which grew all around—though they were sparse enough to her left that she could see the blue waters of the lake through them. The ripples there flashed pale—the sun hadn't risen yet, and the sky was still grayish from the dawn—and far across the water was a tower of rocks. Something had made a nest at the top, but it looked abandoned now.

She was following a white stag. He left cloven prints in the mud of the path and frequently ducked his head to keep his massive antlers from catching on low branches.

Through the trees ahead a rocky shore emerged, and there was a man sitting on a comfortable boulder, his trousers rolled up to his knees, a white cowboy hat perched at an angle over his head.

Clara picked her way through the rocks to stand beside him.

"Hello, Ariel," she said.

"Hey babe," said Ariel. "I missed you."

"Your stag is here," she said. He was, too—waiting in the twilight on the edge of the trees.

"I know," said Ariel.

"Does that mean you will be leaving soon?"

Ariel looked up at her, his face lit softly from the reflected sky in the lake. His eyes were deep, bright, and reproachful.

"I hope not," he said.

Clara felt herself relax, but only a touch.

Ariel reached up and took her hand.

"Storm's coming," he remarked. And he was right: clouds were building in the sky, billowing up in the north while the rest was first streaked and then covered in gray. The light on the water grew dark, but the brightness in the east increased.

"So is sunrise," said Clara.

Ariel shook his head.

"That's not the sun," he said.

Clara looked, and saw that he was right again.

Up from behind the dark trees on the horizon rose a huge, pale disk which cut through the clouds surrounding it. Faster and bigger than it ever had in waking life, the moon rose into view. A waxing gibbous whose cratered face glared across at the blackening clouds. It lit the lake in shades of silver, and around it in the clouds formed a perfect rainbow, a ring of magenta, orange, yellow, green, blue, and violet.

Beside her Ariel gasped quietly and squeezed her hand. Lowering her gaze Clara saw that something had stepped out onto the surface of the lake.

Black as coal, large as a Shire horse but graceful as an Arabian, the unicorn dropped her head to drink, her knifelike horn glittering in the moonlight. It flashed as she lifted her head to gaze at them from over the water.

In a flash the white stag crossed the beach and bounded across to her. The two danced and snorted, sending shallow waves across the surface of the lake, and then began to gallop round and round, each circuit taking them farther and farther away, until they were lost in the shadows under the trees of the far shore.

The moon grew impossibly large above them, and impossibly bright. Ariel's hand turned cold and hard in hers, and she woke to find herself clutching her bedpost as the morning sun fell full upon her face.

Mantha was not in her room, and neither was Lady Bibbit. Clara restrained the urge to panic and went downstairs to the cafeteria. Mantha wasn't there either, but Lady Bibbit was, keeping Chuy company while he and Ariel ate breakfast. Jill was also there, feeding fruit and hemp seeds into the blender, three quart jars lined up to receive the results.

It was she who answered Clara's general inquiry.

"She's in my office, helping me interpret data," she said as she poured greenish-brown smoothie into the jars. Then she added another cup of yogurt, another banana, two dates, and a quarter cup of almonds to the blender and worked it up to high. "We're trying to build a predicative model for aims."

"What?" said Clara, over the noise of the blender.

"Acute Magical Events," Lady Bibbit supplied. "AMEs. Like what happened at Devil's Lake last month. And two years ago, in St. Louis."

The noise from the blender stopped, and in the blessed quiet, Clara said: "We should run a sweep."

"We did that," said Chuy. "The jury's still out."

Clara frowned at him, and the man shuffled his feet nervously.

"Results came back all over the place," Ariel explained. "All the big players—Death Valley, Ruby Mountains, Yosemite, Manhattan—St. Louis—Yellowstone—they're all quiet. Instead, we got random spikes in places like Fort Wayne, or Pittsburgh, or Sudbury—that's in Ontario. But not, like, bad spikes. The extra *umph* just flows away again."

"Where is it flowing to?" Clara asked.

"That's what I'm trying to delineate," Jill said, rinsing the blender bowl under the industrial sink they'd had installed to service the wide-ranging demands of MCSIR's eating habits. She set the rinsed bowl upside down in the drying rack, and began screwing lids onto the jars of smoothie. "They're telling me it's ley lines, and I'm trying to find a way to corroborate that. Otherwise we're just stabbing in the dark."

"Has anyone called Faraday yet?" Clara asked.

No one spoke, but they all looked at her expectantly. Clara sighed.

"I will call Faraday," she said.

She did it from a landline. Faraday was better with landlines. And, thanks to Professor Okedo, MCSIR had seven (one for his office, one for Jill's office, one for reception, one for the duty operative, one for the on call operatives, one for first aid, and one for dispatch). Clara used the one in Jill's office, since it got the least use, and it meant she could keep an eye on Mantha while waiting for Faraday to phone back.

It also meant Jill obliged her to try and interpret the massive amounts of random data the woman had collected. These she'd put through a computer program which identified different types of datasets and assigned them various colors.

"I adapted it from a simple heat map," Jill explained. "But there were too many components, so there's five different layers. Also weather."

"Weather?" Clara asked, surprised. Up until then all of Jill's data had been supernatural in origin: reports of werewolf or vampire attacks, verified hauntings, and other supernatural sightings.

"Yeah," said Jill. "Weather. It seems to be the best indicator of when supernatural forces are interfering with natural ones. Look at this—I was on the phone for two hours with NOAA, but they got me satellite imagery of Wisconsin during the twenty-four hours of October 29th and 30th. I was also able to dig up their forecast model for that region from the morning of the 29th. *Watch.*"

She opened a small video window and pressed play. It was, as she had described, a weather model of Wisconsin (and its immediate neighbors) showing the progression of clouds and rain across the Earth. According to the NOAA forecast, there was to be light cloud cover all day, with a chance of scattered showers in the late afternoon.

"Pretty innocuous, right?" Jill said. Clara nodded agreement, if only to continue the conversation. "Okay," Jill went on. "Now watch what the satellites *actually* recorded."

She opened a new window and pressed *play.*

This was a proper satellite video. There was the Earth in full (if doctored) color, with the clouds as white and gray bands over the brown and green ground. It started at 5:00 a.m. on the 29th and progressed until 5:00 a.m. on the 30th, and then it looped. There were little jerks every two seconds or so, but otherwise it was a perfectly smooth and detailed video of clouds behaving very oddly indeed.

They started off more or less in the same arrangement as the model had predicted, and then a little after sunrise abruptly twisted into a spiral over the south-central part of the state. This grew white with intensity as the day progressed, curling tighter and tighter, and then just as abruptly vanished at sunset. The skies were perfectly clear until midnight, when the thin, natural clouds began to reassert themselves.

"That was the incident at Devil's Lake," Jill said. "I talked to a weather-man in Madison, who said that they did not experience any extraordinary weather that day, though the rain was heavier and colder than predicted—but that's been par for the course this year."

"There were no reports of odd weather from people in the area," Clara stated. She glanced at Mantha as she said this, but the girl had gone over to Jill's glass-fronted specimen case and was gazing at its contents, enrap-tured.

Jill's gaze followed hers, and she did not ask how Clara knew this.

"NOAA pulled this clip from their website," she said. "They were get-ting complaints of a bug in the system. That's what they thought it was, too. I've told them to send me any more bugs they find—and to back them up on external servers."

"It's a useful source of information," Clara said, keeping her tone neu-tral. "Though it does not help us in the immediate case."

"Not yet it doesn't," Jill said. "What I'm hoping is that they'll find us more 'bugs,' and I can put them into *my* model, which might then have enough information for me to identify some predicative symptoms. As it is . . . I just have this."

She switched back to her main screen, which showed a map of North America, overlaid with the jumbled heat map. There were a lot of red points, and lime green ones, but they didn't seem to appear in any sort of pattern.

"It's like **connect the dots**," Jill sighed. "Only I'm not sure what dots are which, or what they connect to."

The phone rang.

"Moonshield-Center-this-is-Director-Hamilton," Jill answered. She lis-tened for a moment, then offered the phone to Clara. "It's for you," she said.

"This is Nordstern," Clara said, though she suspected the caller would know her by voice alone.

"I'm getting too old for this," Faraday said on the other end. She sounded crabby and creaky, like she hadn't had her coffee yet. Clara waited.

"You were right," Faraday continued. "I had to triple-check my nodes, but they definitely show something coming. I'm seeing surges every cou-ple hours, and they're increasing."

"In magnitude? In frequency?" Clara asked.

"Yes," said Faraday. "I can't tell you what it's pointing toward—yet. Does the Fool have a witch on staff?"

"Does Faraday want a job?" Jill asked in reply, her tone sharp.

On the other end of the phone, Faraday cackled.

"Girl, I already got a hundred."

"Where are you?" Clara asked. "Can you assist?"

"Nnngh," said Faraday. "Not personally. I'm in Australia right now."

"What's she doing in *Australia?*" Jill asked.

"Jill, breathe," Clara said, even as Faraday chuckled in her ear:

"Turtle Island ain't the center of the universe."

Jill inhaled, defiantly, and turned her back.

"Here's what I can do," said Faraday. "If she's up to the challenge, I can give her the coordinates and amplitudes of the nodes, and she can try divining their meaning herself."

"Did you hear that?" Clara asked.

"No," snapped Jill. "I inhaled."

Clara explained. Jill nearly snatched the phone directly off her cheek.

"Define a *node*," she began, and Clara left them to it. She joined Mantha in front of the display case, which included, among other things, an almost-empty vial of Johnny Bathory's blood, a bobbin of unicorn hair, scales from a worm, a mothwax candle, and a bogart's tooth.

"Jill collected all of these," Mantha stated. "She wants to understand. She is very brave."

Clara glanced at Jill, hunched over her keyboard with the handset between shoulder and ear, saying, "do you have a standard system for measuring magical intensity? Because we need one. No! I'm *not* saying magic can be regulated—I'm saying I need a way to *measure* it. A *grottal?* Did you just make that up? Fine. What's a grottal?"

Clara had never thought of Jill has brave before. Naive, and a little foolhardy. But brave? Bravery was doing something necessary even if the risk was great, even if it frightened you.

Selene had been brave.

"I am scared of understanding," Mantha said in a small voice, so small that for a moment Clara thought it was her own subconscious.

"Things are rushing around in my head," Mantha continued. "They could land anywhere. When I understand who I am, they'll stop."

"Are you afraid of who you are?" Clara asked. It was a thought that had occurred to her before.

Mantha shook her head. "I'm afraid of who I *could* be."

Clara felt herself being stared at, and met the gaze of Mantha' face reflected in the glass-fronted cabinet.

"Yes," Clara agreed.

In the background, Jill's voice had lowered and the only discernible words were, "Uh-huh . . . 'Mkay . . . Yep . . . Uh-huh . . . Got it . . . " Then she began repeating numbers as she typed them: "Two point seven one five . . . Two point eight . . . Three point two five . . . Eight point three four—*eight?* Okay, eight. Yes, yes I got that. Two point five . . . Seven zero one three . . . Seven point three . . . Seven point six six five . . . Seven point two five two . . . "

There were a lot of seven-point-somethings. From her own understanding of the arbitrary method Faraday used to gauge node activity—

Grottal was the name of her favorite raven familiar—things were elevated, but not unusually high . . .

But then the sevens came on and on and on, and *that* was unusual. Finally, near the end, eight nodes spiked into the ten plus range, and that made Clara's skin prickle.

"Okay . . ." Jill was saying, still typing. "Yeah . . . yeah . . . okay. Yeah, it's all relative—I understand. And these measurements were taken . . . ? Oh! No, that's great. That's super-helpful. Actually, I do have a question. Are there any nodes in my vicinity. I'm in Detroit. Oh. That's the *closest*? Okay."

Tap tap tap went the keyboard.

"Well, can I get the grottage of that one, anyway? Because I'm a scientist, not a magician, Faraday. Two point eight. Perfect. Got it. Thank you. Yeah. Yeah I realize this could be big. Bigger than St. Louis. Yeah, yeah I'm getting that. You *sure* you don't want to come help? Oh. Haha. Yeah, have fun down there. Bye."

"What did she say?" Clara asked.

Putting the handset back down on its receiver, Jill rolled her neck and shoulders.

"'Welcome to the team, kiddo.' At least she stopped calling me 'fool.'"

"She doesn't mean it as an insult," Clara said. "The Fool is the first of the Major Arcana. The Fool is potential, beginning, the capacity for change."

Jill rolled her eyes. "Yeah . . . well. How quickly can you get out to Rose Township?"

"Rose Township?" Clara asked, confused.

"That's the nearest node to us," Jill said. "Faraday gave me its coordinates and grottage. I need one of my AME meters planted there, so we can get a conversion rate between grottage and p-grams."

"What is a peegrum?" Clara asked.

"P-gram," Jill said. "Palladium-grams. The mass of palladium in grams that will react to ambient magical energy in a twelve-hour period."

"Why do we need that?"

"*Because*," said Jill, tapping her folded glasses nervously against her desk, "if I can incorporate her data with mine and NOAA's, we'll be very close to having a usable predictive model! We won't be stumbling around in the fog jumping at shadows."

Clara looked, almost desperately, at Mantha, but the girl nodded gravely.

Clara sighed. "I suppose you want a reading, too?"

"If you could?" said Jill. "It's about an hour to Rose Township via 75, and we need the conversion ASAP."

It was a long day. It was getting on eleven by the time Clara roared out of the underground parking lot on Unicorn, and confirmation of the gauge activation didn't come until ten past noon. So it would be midnight before Jill got her conversion rate—and that would only be a ballpark guess, considering Faraday's reading had come over twelve hours earlier. Still, it was better than nothing. From what Faraday had said, her reading took into account the node's amplitude over the course of several hours, so they were both dealing with averages. It would all average itself out. At least Jill hoped so.

Jill tried to pass the day by being as productive as possible. While she was waiting on the data from Clara she could at least make sure her end of things was ready to go, making separate charts for weather, p-gram, and report data. This required even more sorting, since some of the reports were more detailed than others, and for lack of better data, Jill also sorted them by type: shapeshifter, vampire, dead, haunting, monster.

The shapeshifter category was mostly werewolves, and while there were a lot of them in the state of Michigan, they all had one thing in common: the wolves were leaving. There were almost no vampire reports.

Hauntings, always popular, were up. The difference being that most of these had been confirmed by MCSIR operatives. Monsters, too, but most of these were concentrated in metro Detroit and had more or less reported themselves to MCSIR. There was also a spike in reports from south of Atlanta, which upon closer inspection centered upon the site of one of their old cases: Radium Springs. Jill was pleased to discover that her notes (once she recovered them) were surprisingly cogent considering how terrible she had felt at the time. They also included contact information for Mark and Chuck Kisterman, the legal guardians of Fury-Joy King, and Valé Esperanato.

Jill remembered little of Valé Esperanato except that she was the human persona of the avatar of Victory, and Selene had been rather struck by her. Fury-Joy King was, legally, a minor. So she called the Kisterman landline.

It rang to voicemail, and Jill was in the process of leaving a message when they called back.

"Yeah, is this the same Jill Hamilton from the Incident?" asked a gruff, male voice.

"More or less," said Jill, feeling a wry smile creep across her face. "I'm calling because I'm receiving numerous reports of magical beasts in your area, and I wanted to check in."

"Check . . . in?" said the man. Jill guessed it was Chuck.

"Yes," said Jill. "We're investigating the possibility that there may be another attempted apocalypse. If you have a moment, can you confirm some of these reports for me? Or, I can email them to you and you can write back."

"Oh," said Chuck. "You'll wanna talk to FJ about that."

"Eff-Jay?" asked Jill.

"Yeah, it's what we're calling her these days. Fury-Joy. Hold on." His voice became fuzzy and distant as he called *"Eff-Jaaaay!"*

Indistinct noises, snatches of conversation. Then a strange, double voice said, clear in Jill's ear:

"Hello Ms. Hamilton, this is Fury-Joy. How can I help you?"

"Hi," said Jill. "Um . . . how are things?"

"Things are as can be expected," said the double voice. "School sucks. Valé and Magna keep adopting more pets. They have three griffins, now."

"Three?" said Jill. "I only see a report for *one*."

"Lots of beasts from the Liminalia have arrived seeking sanctuary," Fury-Joy explained. "But we are taking care of them. Deception will not rise again for another thousand years, now that we are here."

"That's . . . good," said Jill. "Thank you. So . . . the manticore and the dryads and the . . . the chimera?"

"The Willowindal are not dryads," said Fury-Joy, a little archly. "But yes, those are all here. We are taking care of them."

"Good, good," said Jill. "No casualties?"

"Casualties?"

"Has anyone been hurt or died?" Jill asked.

"Not recently," said Fury-Joy.

"Good, *good*," said Jill. "Well, hang in there. Things might get a little crazy."

"Things already are," said Fury-Joy, placidly. "We will be fine. How are you?"

Jill's brain, rushing toward the next task, tripped.

"I'm . . . I'm fine," said Jill, surprised.

"How are your friends? How is Selene?"

Jill nearly choked. She'd forgotten that Selene had had a special connection to Fury-Joy. She didn't know what to say.

"They're okay," she said eventually. "Selene's not . . . " *There was an accident. She's dead.* Jill thought the words, but could not bring herself to say them. Instead she heard herself say, "Selene's not with me, anymore."

"Oh," said Fury-Joy, her voice gone small and single. Like a lost child. "Well, if you see her again, tell her we remember. Tell her, we said hi."

"Yes," said Jill, her voice unnaturally thick. "Yes, I will."

She hung up before she realized she hadn't said goodbye. When she did, she spent a long time staring at the receiver, wondering.

They'd notified Selene's family—those that they could locate, anyway— and they'd informed the few who came looking that she was deceased.

There was an accident. She's dead.

She'd said that countless times. But she could not say it to Fury-Joy.

And how many other people had they missed? How many people had Selene helped, over the course of her life? How many people were *alive* because of Selene?

How many of them would never know what had happened to her?

Jill shook herself. She couldn't do anything about that right now. What she could do was verify the data from South Georgia, and mark it as low priority. Selene might be gone, but there were still people she could trust. And in this instance, Jill trusted Fury-Joy entirely.

Thanksgiving week, Tuesday

Chuy had never been one for regular sleep. Night-long graveside vigils aside, ever since his first exorcism he'd never been able to sleep for more than four hours without heart-pounding nightmares. His mind had trained itself to wake up periodically, and once awake, he had trouble getting back to sleep. So he'd napped his way through the last two decades, and had arrived at the age of twenty-seven with a nervous twitch in his right eye, low back pain, depression, chronic painless migraines, high blood pressure, and probably high cholesterol—he hadn't seen a doctor in four years—but still more or less operational.

On the less operational days he wondered how the Gunn brothers had remained active for so long. Maybe their bones and cardiopulmonary systems—not to mention joints—got a refresh each time they were resurrected. Or, the reason they finally vanished was because they'd developed diabetes or heart conditions and figured the best way to get a peaceful retirement was to fake their own deaths.

And then there was Ariel, who seemed to have found a way to corral his nightmares—Chuy knew he had to have them just as bad—in a hermetically sealed pen. That, or he was unfairly blessed with lead-lined mental compartmentalization, plus a resilient constitution and extremely hard tooth enamel.

But, Chuy reflected as he lay awake on his cot in one of the converted offices on the fifth floor of MCSIR, monster hunters and exorcists didn't tend to have long lifespans. *Something* was going to get him, and it would be a small finger in the eye of all those demons if it was something mundane like liver failure that carried him off for good.

A pale shimmering grew in the air in front of him, and in response, Chuy's heart began to pound. It was enough like the beginning of his nightmares that he wondered if he'd forgotten to wake up after all. It had happened before—especially when he slept in a new bed.

Then the shimmering took on a blue haze, and the light pulsed as a gentle voice said,

"Good morning, Mr. Acebo. Director Hamilton has called an emergency all-hands meeting in the main concourse. Please proceed there at your earliest convenience. Thank you."

Then the ghost flickered out of sight, and from the office next to his—which was being used as Ariel's bedroom—there came a loud groan.

"It is of the utmost importance," he heard the ghost say.

Ariel growled, sounding almost wolflike, and there was a creak of a body moving from bed to floor. The wall between them thumped.

"Chuy, did they get you up?"

"I'm awake," said Chuy, but he didn't get up. Not yet. He'd been gripped with the certainty that these were going to be his last peaceful moments for some time, and he wanted to savor them. But when Ariel threw open his door and stood there like a disheveled Adonis with red-rimmed eyes and stubble, Chuy took pity on him and got out of bed in solidarity.

He was already dressed. He just needed to slip on his boots, and he was ready to go. His knees complained, but one good thing about insomnia: it meant you could get up at—he checked his watch—1:45 a.m. and be as coherent as you were at 1:45 p.m.

The main concourse was filled with moonlight, electric light, and people. More people than Chuy could recognize, and some who he'd only seen in the photos earlier. He spotted Director Hamilton at once, because she was standing on a chair next to a projector screen, on which was was displayed a giant version of her desktop. Currently, it was a lot of windows of writing and an error message.

Chuy recognized the slim, dark-haired woman bending over the laptop as the vampire Lansing, and next to her—looking about as disheveled as Ariel, but nowhere near as glamorous—was Professor Okedo. Next to him was his assistant Don, whose gray skin and yellow teeth were hardly out of place next to the curious creature fidgeting beside him.

Gadget was the first true goblin Chuy had ever met, and he'd been surprised to find she was more like an oversized cat than anything else. She even had a long, slinky tail, fangs, and retractable claws. She was about the size of a lemur, and was built like one too—minus the fur. Instead she wore a wool jumper with big red buttons down the front and an assortment of fuzzy wool hats to cover her naturally bald head. So, like a hairless cat crossed with a lemur. Her religion—because apparently goblins had religion, who knew?—forbade her sharing her true name with anyone outside her immediate family, but the public name she'd given them had, when spoken with human mouths, sounded like "gaijit" and so she was Gadget. She could fix just about anything, they'd told Chuy, including the printer.

There was Tucker and Marcus and Tamerlain—even taller and darker than Marcus, currently—and Imogen arrived while Chuy and Ariel were being shown to folding chairs being hastily set up by Lady Bibbit.

Chuy didn't understand what the fuss over Lady Bibbit was. Compared to Gadget, she looked almost normal. Merely a five-foot-two rabbit with opposable thumbs and a penchant for denim overalls, she had soft gray fur and one soft blue eye and a way of speaking to you that was as soothing as a cup of hot chamomile tea. But she also wore a headset and a radio, and when she frowned it was like a cloud going in front of the sun.

She had a faint patchwork of scars, visible only as disruptions in her otherwise smooth fur, all over her face, arms and legs—and, Chuy had to assume, the rest of her body, too. These he did not ask about.

Something white and cold slipped into the room, and Chuy thought that the ghost was back, but it was Jill's Yell Hound, Frosty. The lean white dog was pacing between the rows of chairs, sniffing people and occasionally wagging her tail.

More people kept arriving, mostly in some state of disarray. They ranged from a nervous teenage boy to an ancient woman with clouds of white hair and a prosthetic leg. These two came in as a pair, but there were many who came in a large group and huddled together in a corner. They looked like druggies, but druggies who were trying to behave decently. They all had yellow eyes and a tendency to growl. There was also at least one other zombie, a small person covered in fur, and a middle-eastern man in dark sunglasses and a leather jacket who stood at the back of the concourse, pulling viciously on an e-cigarette.

Last to arrive were four Detroit Fire and Rescue paramedics—including the woman with cornrows Chuy had met on Sunday—who gathered awkwardly around Tucker until Lady Bibbit brought them chairs.

When everyone had found seats, or had seats given to them, Director Hamilton coughed into a microphone supplied by Lansing, and the noise in the concourse—which had never risen below a dull murmur—ceased entirely.

"If you're here," she began, her voice faint and then suddenly enlarged by the microphone, as she adjusted its position, "it's because you're either a member of or have worked closely with MCSIR in the past. Thank you for coming. I realize for some of you this is not a convenient hour. But if we don't act now something even more inconvenient will occur. At least, it's highly likely to.

"Thanks to contributions from supernatural and scientific sources, I have calculated that there will be a violent compound transdimensional event in North America, in the very near future. I've created a predictive model based on a number of datasets, which strongly indicates the exact location that the event will occur to be within the Great Lakes geographical region. That's this—*slide one, please*," she whispered behind her mic.

The projection on the screen changed from desktop windows to a map of the Great Lakes, with Detroit marked with a red star near the bottom center.

"Some of you may already be familiar with ley lines, ley nexuses, and ley nodes," she went on. "But I've had to collate a lot of conflicting information, so I'm gonna walk us all through this so we're all on the same page. For the *purposes of this model*," she went on, speaking over some discontented murmurs, "ley lines are conduits for freeform magic. Ley nodes are like magic-springs, or magic-aquifers. They feed the ley lines. A ley nexus—what most of you probably know as just plain old 'nexus,' is a conjunction or confluence of three or more ley lines, where the amount of ambient magic is compounded. Here's a map of the ley system as of yesterday. *Slide two, please.*"

The screen flickered, now showed a satellite photo of the Great Lakes and environs overlaid with a network of yellow lines, dots and spirals.

"In this map, the lines are ley lines, the dots are nodes, and the spirals are nexuses. AME—Ambient Magical Energy—output is indicated by brightness, and as you can see, a number of nodes are producing above the continental average of AME. Especially the ones local to Pittsburgh, Pennsylvania, Fort Wayne, Indiana, and Sudbury, Ontario. These are spiking to upwards of eleven p-grams per our preliminary conversion rate, which is the highest recorded by MCSIR."

She paused, her eyes flicked toward Mantha, who was sitting off to the side, and then she continued.

"What's troubling is that the ley lines are not showing a consistent rise in their own capacity. The lines running out of the Pittsburgh and Fort Wayne areas are, in fact, weaker than the continental average. However, due to our detection method, this doesn't mean they're not fully charged with magic—just that that power isn't being leaked. You'll notice also spikes in the ley nexuses that include lines from those areas. But *also* note the activity in the nearest nexus to us, at Little Traverse Bay."

She pointed, the shadow of her finger falling on a narrow bay at the north end of Lake Michigan, up and to the left of Detroit. The spiral there was glowing brightly.

"What's feeding this nexus? It's not on any of the lines out of Sudbury—which is obviously charging the nexus near Alpena—and there are no elevated nodes nearby. In fact, you'll note that there are no elevated nodes in the state of Michigan—and none *at all* in Detroit proper. There aren't even any ley lines anymore. Keep this in mind as we add our next source of information: weather satellites. *Just—just check the box under the eyeball there—thanks.*"

Now the yellow lines and dots were themselves overlaid by a white pattern of clouds, which moved slowly across the screen in a long loop. The image was blurry, as if there were two layers of the cloud images, and they did not precisely line up.

"What you're seeing here is a combination of the predicted and actual weather patterns sourced from NOAA. I've marked magically influenced diversions in red, you'll notice them start to show up . . . *now*. There"— she pointed at the red swirl over Fort Wayne—"there"—at the swirl over Pittsburgh—"and there"—at Sudbury—"a-and, *there!*" This time the red swirl was huge, and came in the middle of Lake Superior.

Next to him, Ariel clapped a hand to his brow.

"We forgot about Lake Superior," Chuy said, a sense of urgency rising in his throat.

"The biggest node in North America," Ariel sighed. "But because there's no anchor . . . "

"Holy cow, Ariel," Chuy said, the image on the screen suddenly clicking into focus. "Look—look at what it's showing!"

"I *know*," Ariel said.

Chuy got the impression that a lot of the people in the room knew, but Jill kept doggedly explaining, as if to complete ingenues, what was happening—much to the interest of the paramedics.

"Lake Superior is feeding the nexus in Traverse Bay," Jill said. "Traverse Bay, Alpena, Toledo, Cleveland, all feed ley lines that run into Michigan. You can just see them—see, there's the Toledo line going *around* Detroit to the west, and the Cleveland line cutting through Lake St. Clair—and going north, while the Alpena and Traverse Bay lines go south, all heading for some point around . . . " She circled her finger around the spit of land that Chuy had always thought of as Michigan's thumb. "Here," she finished.

"But there's no nexus there," Professor Okedo pointed out.

Jill raised a triumphant finger. "Yes, yes there is," she said. "It's not showing on either the sweep or the arcane reading, because those were both testing for *leaked* AME. According to *this chart*, however—*that's nineteen seventy-one dot jpeg, Lansing, thanks*—there *is* a nexus there. A small one. Because there was another violent transdimensional event in Detroit in 1970, which completely ripped out the ley lines. So, no more nexus for Detroit. Instead there's all these little guys in a ring around us. Including that one . . . near Port Austin. Which isn't showing up on AME sweeps . . . *because all the AME is getting used up or sucked away.*"

Chuy couldn't stand it anymore. There was the Director of MCSIR harping on details when they needed to mobilize. He surged up out of his chair so fast it tipped over.

"It's a tsunami," he said. "All the water goes out because it's being sucked up by the big wave."

Director Hamilton looked at him. She adjusted her glasses and frowned. "I was going to compare it to charging a battery," she said. "And, since we can't detect that battery, we can hypothesize that whatever is sucking up the energy is still outside our conventional causal domain. Which means, if we're going to be proactive about shutting this thing down, we're gonna have to travel outside this dimension. I want to make this clear. If we do not act, there will be a disaster. There *nearly was* a disaster right here, in 1970, and it still left this place fundamentally altered. But to act effectively we must put ourselves at great risk. For this reason I will, right now, appoint Lansing Ise as Acting Director of MCSIR. She will be in charge during my absence—however long that may be. I'm also asking our friends from DFR to remain on high alert, since I will need our medic to accompany us. You four have all been briefed in supernatural first aid. Lady Bibbit, I'm also going to ask that you remain on site, to help with any potential influx of refugees. As for the action team . . . " she ran out of breath and had to pause. Chuy found he was holding his breath as well.

"Operatives Nordstern and Freeman will be action leaders, under my supervision. Tucker, as I said, will provide on-site medical service as needed. I'm also inviting Operatives Acebo and Bowerman to join us.

Operatives Supatnik and Pierce, I want you to remain on site to assist Lansing and the DFR as needed. Any questions?"

Mantha put her hand up immediately, and though she whispered her question in the director's ear, Chuy could guess what it was. But Hamilton shook her head, and Mantha sat back down, looking both disappointed and relieved.

Professor Okedo put his hand up.

"What is your goal with this action?"

"Primarily to prevent a violent compound transdimensional event that would adversely affect the state of the world, both magically and conventionally," Jill said. "With a secondary objective to document whatever happens, if possible."

"In that case," Professor Okedo said, almost regretfully, "I'd better go with you. Gadget and I will manage documentation."

"Thank you," said Jill. She looked around the room, her glasses flashing. "Any other questions? No? Okay then, let's get to work."

In the general hubbub following her presentation, Lansing came up and touched Jill's elbow.

"Yes?" Jill said, almost guiltily. She had told Lansing about her appointment to Acting Director in the hurried minutes while they set up the computer for the presentation, and the vampire had not looked pleased. Now she looked terrified.

"Jill, there's something I need to tell you," she said, swift and quiet.

Bracing herself, Jill nodded. She could always get Lady Bibbit to house-sit.

"I've been meaning to bring this up, but there was never a right time," Lansing continued. "And now . . . if I keep waiting, I might never get a chance."

Jill blinked. This was not going where she expected it to go.

"I fully intend to return," she assured Lansing. "But if it makes you more comfortable, have at it."

"Okay . . . " said Lansing, and stopped. It was like her voice had hit a brick. She coughed, and the words came out sideways. Jill asked her to repeat herself.

"Please, don't refer to me as female," Lansing repeated, and winced.

Jill blinked. "I'm . . . sorry?"

"I'm more comfortable with androgynous pronouns," Lansing explained. "They, or them, which you *can* use as singular pronouns, you know—"

"Yes, yes I know," said Jill. "That's it?"

Lansing hesitated. "Yes?"

"You're okay with being Acting Director for a while? This isn't a suicide mission or anything—it just has an extremely high level of risk and I want to take precautions."

"Yes, yes of course, I'm happy to," said Lansing. "You . . . you got the pronouns?"

"Right, and yes," said Jill, smiling in relief. "They, or them. Got it. Only . . . remind me again when this is over? Okay? Lots going on. And send me an email to order you Mx name tags. Yes?" she said, turning to Chuy Acebo, who had come up and was waiting a prudent distance away. "Are you in? Awesome. Great. I'll put you with Ariel, since you've worked together before. Are you comfortable with that? Great. Get your kit. Get everything. We'll bring the trailer if we need to—I'm not underestimating this."

Imlay City, MI
Tuesday
Dawn

The big, black-clad biker with the equally big bike had been sitting in the parking lot of the gas station just off Highway 53, staring south to its cloverleaf intersection with I-69, for almost two hours. Cars and trucks came and went, and if anyone in them noticed the biker, they did not bother them.

That was how Clara liked it.

It had not been a bad night, all things considered. She'd made it to Rose Township, planted the gauge and gotten a reading. It had been a lot of waiting around in the outdoors, but with her full kit on, the frigid wind barely fazed her. And it had been nice to be out under the open skies again.

She hadn't been able to sleep, save in fitful bursts while waiting for the gauge to load, but she'd done more on less. Now, after receiving a brief from Jill, sleep was the last thing on her mind.

Apocalypses didn't happen often, but when they did, it was like a bone breaking in the body of the world. Suddenly and irreversibly, things ceased to work the way they used to, and it took a long time for the world to heal. Sometimes it healed crooked.

Clara was well-read, but she rarely read fiction. Unless it was the sort written by an author with true insight, in which case she didn't consider it strictly fiction. Even so, some of those authors would get key points so incredibly wrong that it physically hurt to read the words. One aspect that was of perpetual annoyance to her was the category marketed as "post-apocalyptic." The entire world was *already* post-apocalyptic. The thing was, apocalypses were like mass extinctions: they could happen multiple times. And they didn't necessarily look like Krakatoa or World War II.

Clara had stopped an apocalypse once before, when she was a teenager. But that had been with Faraday and Tesla to help. In fact, Faraday and Tesla had done most of the doing—she was the one who had helped.

Now Faraday was in Australia, and Tesla wasn't leaving her forge. Clara wasn't sure what frightened her more, that they thought *she* was capable of stopping this one, or that they thought *Jill* was.

Light was spreading across the earth. It was the Tuesday before Thanksgiving, and the highway was just beginning to show signs of life. Minivans and trucks and suburbans rumbled past—some of them stopped for gas—joining the procession of big rigs already in progress. Most of these were headed south, but there was enough activity in the northbound lanes to keep Clara's attention.

In the end, however, she didn't have to worry about missing the convoy. Jill called her when they were ten minutes out.

"We did have to bring the trailer," she said by way of greeting. "That's why we're late. I have Tucker with me in Arcana, Ariel and Acebo are in the Impala, and Okedo's in the van. By the way, when was the last time you put gas in him?"

"In Arcana?" Clara asked, dread creeping up her throat.

"Yeah," said Jill. "The trip meter is reading close to seven hundred miles—but the gauge is still at full."

"Yes," sighed Clara. "He's been that way since Devil's Lake. Maybe before."

"Oh," said Jill. "Huh. Okay. Well, just make sure you try topping him up now and then, in case things change and the meter doesn't show. We'll be there soon. Do you want to load Unicorn or—?"

"I'll ride," said Clara. "And I will take point. See you soon."

She did. Even among the big rigs Arcana stood out, large and red and yet dwarfed by the giant Jaguar trailer. He was following Ariel's dingy white sedan, and in his wake was the official MCSIR van, which they'd acquired used from a local TV station. Jill had ordered a magnetic sign to cover the old logo, which new sign proudly displayed the black rectangle and white moon of the center, along with their dispatch number.

Clara pulled out of the parking lot with relief, and merged in just in front of the Impala. Like that, the caravan made its way through Imlay City, and then north up Highway 53.

North, north, as the sun rose on their right, cutting streaks of pink and gold through the gray, overcast sky.

Detroit, MI
Tuesday

Mantha helped Lady Bibbit load the trailer. She helped Gadget load the van. She helped Ariel restock his briefcase, and she helped Chuy pack the trunk of the Impala. When that was finished, her fingers lingered on the chrome icon of the antelope, where it was depicted leaping across the tail of the car. She thought of the white stag, and the holly prince, and she pushed very firmly at the car.

Take care of Ariel, she told it. *Don't break down.*

Then she went and did the same for the van, for good measure. But when she went to fix Arcana, she felt the truck push back. It almost felt indignant.

Of course I will protect Jill, he seemed to say, and Mantha retreated apologetically. He was not possessed, as he had been at Devil's Lake, but Mantha got a sense from the vehicle that he was more alive than the others. Not properly, like Lady Bibbit was, but getting there. Maybe one day.

She stood with Lady Bibbit and watched the convoy leave MCSIR, their red trail of taillights leading down Roosevelt Avenue, before turning right on Michigan Avenue, and then streaming out of sight.

Afterward, once she got inside again, Mantha realized she was exhausted. Utterly and eye-achingly exhausted.

"You have been awake for almost twenty-four hours," Lady Bibbit pointed out. "Since there's nothing much for us to do yet, why not get some sleep?"

Mantha did not say she feared sleep because she feared to dream and feared that her dreaming would mess things up, but she did go up to her room and lie down with her eyes closed. She could rest without sleeping. She just needed to keep her mind occupied.

In less than a minute she was asleep, and for once there were no dreams. Just darkness, and at the bottom, a deep, cold well.

Port Austin, MI

The clouds dispersed as the day wore on, and by the time the convoy rolled into Port Austin the sun was shining down at full strength, lighting Lake Huron a vivid blue and throwing stark shadows from the leafless trees. There was still ice and snow in their shade, and Ariel felt the bite of the air the moment he cracked his door open.

"Aye-yae-*ya!*" Chuy hissed as soon as he stood up out of the car, and immediately reached in through the back window to grab the hat and gloves Lady Bibbit had packed him. These were thick, fuzzy, knitted affairs which Chuy had originally spurned. Now Ariel watched him pull them on with amusement. They were bright blue and clashed with Chuy's leather jacket, jeans and cowboy boots, but as Ariel himself had traded his black blazer for a puffy, insulated jacket, his white cowboy hat for a knit cap with pink ear flaps (pulled down) and a pair of red mittens, he didn't laugh.

You had the look you wanted, and the look the weather dictated. You could look cool, or you could be comfortable. Ariel chose the latter.

"I don't know how you stand it up here," Chuy said, zipping his jacket all the way up.

Ariel glanced at the man's legs, in their worn blue jeans. "We'll get you some long underwear," he said. Chuy rolled his eyes.

"No, really," said Ariel. "It's amazing what warm knees do for your confidence. C'mon, let's go set up camp."

Clara had led them to the parking lot of Bird Creek County Park, which was deserted and understandably so. As cold as the air was, it was made even colder by the piercing wind which blew off the lake. This was an ocean of gray blue-green which remained defiantly liquid—probably thanks to its sheer size and the motion of the waves on the shore—and took up over half the horizon.

The lot itself was a plain slab of bleached asphalt with faint white lines painted in suggestion of parking spaces. Okedo had parked the van prudently in one of these, but Jill had by necessity left Arcana and the trailer stretched out in the middle of the lot. Clara had walked Unicorn into the lee of the trailer and was already unlocking it.

Ariel put on his shades—aviators went with everything, it turned out, even knit caps with pink ear flaps—and did a visual sweep of the area.

Besides the parking lot the only other piece of pavement was a square some fifty yards off with a lonely basketball hoop. There were boardwalks down to the sandy beach and running along the waterfront to a play area and a hexagonal building—just a roof with supporting struts, really—over some sun-bleached tables and benches. There was also a small building just off the parking lot with a sign taped to the door saying that the toilets would be closed until April 1. To their south clustered the bare trees and rooftops of Port Austin, and a line of gray townhouses stared at them judgmentally.

Aside from a few hardy gulls, they were the only occupants.

Jill, looking like an astronaut going for a spacewalk in her day suit, clambered out of the cab of Arcana and went around to help Clara set up their mobile base. This included expanding the side compartments on the trailer and hooking up the battery packs with their respective solar chargers—since there was no power to speak of in the parking lot. As soon as Ariel and Chuy got close enough, they were given a set of palladium gauges each and instructions to deploy them, and "Whatever other sensors you can think of," Jill said, her voice sharp even through her helmet.

They spent the remainder of the morning setting up gauges and detectors and laying wards and explaining the use and method behind what they did to Okedo, who followed them around with a clipboard and camera.

"Don't you have anything to do?" Chuy asked, the third time Okedo asked him to explain how their arcane sweeps worked.

"I *am* doing what I'm supposed to do," Okedo explained, with admirable patience. "I'm not strictly here as part of the operation. I'm documenting the process."

Chuy looked ready to say something truly unfortunate, but he swallowed his words and marched off, leaving Ariel to give a brief tutorial on fairy stones and their proper application.

They dispersed in rounds for lunch, except for Jill, who ate out of her packed food in the lightfast portion of the trailer. When Ariel and Chuy returned from their own break it was to find the park rangers had shown up, only to be intercepted by Okedo, who talked to them for almost two hours while they continued monitoring the sensors and going on scouting walks. Around dusk the rangers departed, only to return an hour later with eight pizzas and a stack of paper plates. Their names were James and Ed, and it came out around dinner that Ed and Okedo shared a common ancestry, and had bonded over that. James was older, with white hair and a lot of wrinkles and a voice gone reedy from yelling. He looked sideways at Jill, especially once she took her day suit off and sat in her folding director's chair in jeans, sneakers and a polo shirt, while around them the temperature dropped precipitously, but took an immediate liking to Gadget.

"I always knew this stuff was real," he said, chewing pizza thoughtfully. "Just . . . something about the world, you know? It makes sense there's more to it than us."

The rangers left for good after the pizza was finished, but not before recommending a number of local B&Bs that could put them up for the night.

"You're not technically supposed to camp here," James told them.

"Technically, we're not camping," said Jill, flatly. "But I'll take that under advisement."

She'd put on her glasses, but in the darkness they could not hide the way her eyes glowed dimly red. James left without another word.

"I don't know about you, iron ladies," Chuy said afterwards, "but *I* can't stay up all night too. How are we running shifts?"

From inside the trailer, it turned out, with patrols every three hours to check the gauges and wards. This was a relief to all the humans, who had grown increasingly cold once the warmth of the pizza faded.

The trailer could sleep three at a time, if two didn't mind sharing the bed. Tucker, as medic, was given special dispensation to use the folding sofa for the entire night, while Jill and Clara, Ariel and Chuy, and Okedo and Gadget took it in turns to use the bed. But Okedo and Chuy both fell asleep in their chairs while on duty, and Jill stayed up most of the night at the monitoring station.

Clara took all the patrols solo save for the last before dawn, at three a.m., when Ariel joined her.

The clouds had cleared in the night, and they walked under the light of the stars. There was no sign of the moon, and the lake water was black with forbidding spots of gray where ice had formed. The sand was frozen under their feet as they walked the perimeter.

"Intact and normal," Ariel reported, after inspecting his sensors and wards.

"Two p-grams in fifteen hours," Clara replied, standing up from where she'd been reading one of Jill's palladium gauges.

"What's that mean in real talk?" Ariel asked, as they continued their perambulation along the boardwalk.

"Low," said Clara. "Abnormally low."

Ariel was silent. He knew as well as Clara did that a low reading did not mean all was well. A low reading meant that there was less ambient magic than normal, which was consistent both with Jill's hypothesis of the draining nexus and his own experience of magical disasters.

And yet everything was so quiet. Peaceful. The tiny town was dark among the trees, hibernating for the winter. It was hard to imagine anything happening here before Memorial Day weekend.

"Claymore," he said, drawing near her elbow. "You averted an apocalypse before, didn't you?"

"Years ago," Clara said.

"Do you remember it being this quiet, before?"

"I was not on-site before first breach," Clara admitted. "By the time we arrived, there had already been a wave of demons."

"Do you think that's how this will start?"

Clara shrugged, down and up. It made the hilt of her sword catch the starlight and sparkle briefly. Ariel was reminded, in a flash, of a dream: a path made of swords, and a sharp, four-pointed star. There were other dreams attached to that one: warmer, sunnier dreams. He thought there had been lakes in those dreams too, and Claymore, but all that remained was the impression of feelings. The details were lost.

And he was awake, in the cold dark world, and the lake was a cold, merciless body of water. It could easily kill them all, if they stepped into it.

Well, not Jill. And probably not Clara, either. She wasn't even wearing a hat, and the air was so cold it hurt a little every time he inhaled.

Clara had stopped. She was staring out at the lake, her expression unreadable. She seemed like she was looking for something, out on that dark horizon.

Without thinking Ariel took her hand. The action made her turn round on him, her pale face questioning, concerned.

"What's wrong?" she asked.

Because why else would he take her hand?

For all the easy remarks that came and sat expectantly at the back of Ariel's throat, he said nothing, just gripped her hand tighter.

"Are you all right?" Clara asked, frowning at him through the dimness.

It was like holding the hand of a glacier. A glacier that was worried about him. It made Ariel uncomfortably full of emotion. Like having a near-death experience. Or a near-God experience.

He wanted to say "Don't go anywhere."

He wanted to say "Don't go without me."

Forget Icarus flying too near the sun. He'd dove in too deep. But somewhere in those icy depths there was a warm, sunny beach, a clear blue sky, and his star burned hot, not cold.

He wanted to say "I believe in you. Not just in who you are now, but everything you can be. You're incredible as you are, and I believe you're even more than that."

What he said was:

"Aren't you cold?"

Clara's frown lifted, but her confusion grew. Ariel gestured at her bare head.

Clara looked down at him gravely, but instead of shrugging it off, as he expected her to, she said, "I am always cold. No," she added, when he went to offer her his hat. "It is fine. I feel the cold, but it doesn't affect me."

Ariel was afraid he stared rather.

"You don't get hypothermia or frostbite?"

"No," said Clara. It was hard to tell in the dim starlight, but she looked miserable. Ariel felt something crack inside him.

"But that's cool, isn't it? You're like some kind of superwoman."

Clara just looked at him, her eyes blue, even in the darkness, and desolate.

"Yeah, okay," Ariel sighed. "That's kind of terrifying."

You are terrifying and I love you.

Which was a realization terrifying in itself.

"I try not to think about it," Clara said, frankly. "I try to hide . . ." she dropped her face, looking down at herself—covered in black leather, " . . . what I can," she finished.

And Ariel remembered, a month ago at a different lake, the only time he'd seen her bare arms, and the glowing, red lines that ran the length of them. The way the air turned to steam when it touched her skin.

"They're not tattoos," he said, and got the strangest sensation of déjà vu. Like they'd had this conversation before.

"No," sighed Clara. "No they are not. They are protection." Her mouth shut firmly, but Ariel was sure there was more to it than that. She'd told him before—hadn't she?

Ariel looked up at her, trying to gauge her expression.

It was impossible. He'd have to go by feel.

"I guess it's different with my tattoos," he said. "I chose mine."

Clara looked up at him, her gaze surprisingly sharp.

"You have tattoos?" she asked. She inexplicably sounded like the bottom had come off her world.

"Yes," said Ariel, surprised. *Hadn't she seen them?* Yes, he wore long sleeves almost exclusively, but he thought he'd shown them to her—even though now he thought about it, the idea was kind of ridiculous. He didn't whip off his shirt and give the Great Ink Tour of Ariel Freeman to everyone he met.

He'd do it for Clara, he realized. Happily. But he hadn't. He was sure he hadn't. Yet he felt like he had.

The wind whistled between them, stinging his nose.

Clara was still looking at him with that severe, intense gaze that he had once mistaken for anger and now recognized as internal frustration. She seemed on the verge of asking a question but was unable to.

Ariel patted her on the arm.

"I'll give you the tour sometime. When it's not minus ten, I mean"—he managed to pry a grin out of his frozen cheeks—"fair's fair."

Clara swallowed and looked away.

"When all this is over," she said.

"'Course," said Ariel, feeling unaccountably disappointed.

"When all this was over" could mean after the apocalypse. One way or another, everything would be different.

They finished their patrol. Everything was quiet, the wards un-tripped, and all the gauges reading astonishingly low.

Port Austin, Michigan, might have been the least-magical place in the country, for all they could tell.

Detroit, MI
Wednesday, the day before Thanksgiving

Mantha slept the blissful, dreamless sleep of the innocent and woke in the morning to find the world awash in white. It had begun to snow in the night and continued long into the morning, so that by the time Lansing was going to bed there was at least three feet of the stuff piled on the roads and lawns outside. Marcus and Imogen spent the better part of the morning shoveling the front drive. They met the city plow halfway down and returned ravenous with sore muscles. While they were eating, Tamerlain dug out the north gardens so that Frosty could be let out.

Frosty, who had chosen not to accompany the expedition to Port Austin, was restless that day, constantly asking to go out and in and out and in again. In between outings she would curl up in Jill's office, alternately grooming herself and chewing on an old shank bone.

Mantha knew how she felt, but she wondered why the Yell Hound had chosen to stay behind. She tried asking the dog outright, but Frosty had just gazed at her nervously and thumped her tail.

Something was going to happen *here*, Mantha decided. That was why Frosty had stayed. The longer the day wore on, and as everything reported from Port Austin was dead quiet, the more she became sure of it.

She went and visited the ghost in dispatch. It was barely a white shimmer in the air, but it answered her questions readily enough.

"No, nothing out of the ordinary," it said. "Everyone's behaving themselves, for once."

She ate lunch with Tamerlain and Don and Lady Bibbit, who didn't need to eat, but liked to drink a cup of carrot tea at lunchtime. Tamerlain ate a lot, which looked a bit funny considering she was in the body of a petit teenage girl. Don ate little, since he didn't need calories, per se, but a vital enzyme found in the brains of mammals.

Mantha, despite feeling ravenous, ate hardly anything at all. One bite of peanut butter and jelly sandwich and she felt sick to her stomach. Another bite, and the two bites combined threatened to come right back up again.

"And no wonder!" Lady Bibbit exclaimed, pressing the back of her furry palm to Mantha's forehead. "You feel like you have a fever!"

"I'll get the first-aid kit," Tamerlain announced, and pushed back from the counter.

"I don't feel like I have a fever," Mantha protested.

She did have a headache, though, and her mouth tasted sticky and sour. When Tamerlain returned with the kit and produced the thermometer, it declared decisively that she was indeed running a fever.

A 103° fever.

"Uh . . . we might need to take you to the emergency room," Tamerlain said. "If we can't bring it down. There's Ibuprofen in here, and aspirin, and Tylenol. Which do you want?"

"I want to lie down," Mantha said.

They gave her a dose of Tylenol, but they let her lie down after that.

Lying down made her feel less dizzy, but worse in other ways. She kept feeling thirsty, but water made her puke.

Lady Bibbit sat by her the whole afternoon, alternately fetching her cups of water, holding the vomit can, and rubbing her back.

Frosty came and sat at the foot of her bed, gazing at her in concern. Mantha got the feeling the dog knew what was going on but was powerless to do anything. Still, she was glad of the company.

Just before sunset the snow let up, and the sun managed to sneak a few rays of orange light across the white-covered cityscape. Mantha noticed because the view of the city from her window was suddenly awash in pink and gold.

A frozen city. A silent city.

A dead city.

A city on fire.

Mantha blinked.

She was alone in her room and the sun had just set. Lights were coming on in the skyscrapers, and in the distance a siren wailed. It made her head ring.

She thought at first that she needed to go to the bathroom, but when she wobbled off down the hall to use it, nothing came out. Still, she felt like there was *something* building up in her, and keeping it inside was monumentally distressing.

She felt hot. Her temperature, according to Lady Bibbit, had been hovering between 102 and 103 the whole afternoon. Now, when she returned to her room, she took it again.

When the thermometer beeped, it did so with even greater alarm, and no wonder: it read 107.

104 was maximum Tamerlain would tolerate before taking her to the emergency room. Mantha found herself guiltily moving to hide the incriminating device.

She didn't want to go to an emergency room. She wasn't sick. This wasn't a fever, no matter what anyone said.

She had somewhere she needed to be, that was the problem. Something was trying to happen that could not happen without her. But even though she was not there it was trying to happen anyway.

Except she had to be there. She was like the key, and right now, she was being jammed into a solid surface.

Mantha didn't like any of this. It was too much like the ugly side of herself she glimpsed when she lost control of her powers. But she also didn't like feeling like she was going to turn inside-out and burn up any second.

She lost track of time and space. She was sitting on her bed at MCSIR, her heart was beating slowly, and there was a hot puddle of thin vomit between her knees. It was reddish.

Red meant blood. Blood was not supposed to come out of one's mouth.

She had to do something. But for all Mantha could push other people's minds any which way she pleased, she could not push her own out of the hole it was being dragged into. Very soon now it would get to a point where she would do anything to make the pain stop, and there would be no knowing what those things would be.

Time, then, to leave. To get herself away from MCSIR, from Lady Bibbit and Tamerlain and Don and the refugees in the waiting room.

Mantha wiped the flecks of bloody sick off her nightdress. This was a plain white gown which the *memegwesiwag* had sewn for her, shapeless and comfortable. Over it she pulled on her happy-owl fleece robe, and slid her bare feet into her bright red slippers.

Thus attired she took the stairs all the way down to the basement, where she went out by the garage.

Frosty was waiting for her there, hackles up and tail between her legs.

"I don't want to hurt you," Mantha told the dog. "I don't want to hurt anyone."

Frosty whined, pinning her red ears back even further.

Maybe it was the dizziness returning, but Mantha thought she was seeing multiple copies of Frosty, arrayed around her in a semicircle.

Standing behind them in the darkness was someone in a cape with antlers on their shoulders.

You still have free will, the darkness told her. *You are not an angel.*

"Please let me go," Mantha whispered.

No one can stop you, said the voice of the darkness.

And then it was just the dark garage, and just Frosty, cowering to the side.

Mantha understood why when she took a step onto the frigid cement and felt it crack beneath her feet. Steam rose in a cloud around her as she began to walk, the snow and ice retreating like dry leaves curling before a fire.

Mantha walked through Detroit, but she also walked on a lonely road under a sky the color of an old bruise.

She crossed Michigan Avenue without bothering to wait for the light. Cars whizzed past. None of them touched her.

She was alone on the road under the purple-green sky, but the road was lined with people.

Her ancestors, she somehow knew. Her grandmothers—they were all women. They lined the righthand side of the road like power poles, stretching off into the distance. Mantha was surprised to discover that they ranged in appearance from blond to black, thick to thin, and one was a fiery redhead.

None of them spoke to her, but together they stared across the road reproachfully. When Mantha glanced in that direction she saw nothing but a barren, rocky plain. Like a photograph of the surface of Mars. Except, in the distance, something moved. A man-shaped something, dark against the sore horizon.

Her father.

Mantha had never known her earthly father. Bună had never spoken of him except in derogatory passing. She called him "that devil," on occasion. Mantha wondered what Bună would say if she found out how right she had been.

Surprisingly, Bună herself answered that question.

"Don't you pay him any mind, Mantha!" she cried out from the right-hand side of the road. "He never did nothing for you or your mother. You are your *mother's* daughter."

"I never knew my mother," Mantha whispered as she walked past. She could no more stop upon her course than Bună could step onto the road.

"And it's better that way," said Bună, as she fell out of Mantha's vision.

Now there was one more person on the right side of the road: a single woman, young and slim and shockingly beautiful. Her face was pinched and sad, and her feet were buried in the ground.

Mantha wanted to stop. She wanted to unbury her mother's feet. She wanted to make her smile.

But she was drawing near the end of the road, and the pressure behind her was enormous. It felt like a boulder on her shoulders that would crush her if she didn't keep walking.

But as she passed by, her mother's face lifted, and Mantha was shocked to discover hatred in her eyes.

"Demon child!" she hissed. "I should have cut you out myself!"

Mantha recoiled, her feet slipping on the dirt of the road. Her heart was pounding as if she had been physically attacked. Her eyes stung. She was crying, but not tears of saltwater. Whatever they were burned her cheeks and steamed in the dirt of the road.

Her mother spat at her heels as she passed.

She was almost to the end of the road now, and the land ended with it. Both disappeared into the waters of a black lake, which stretched out as far as she could see to either side. On the far shore, hazy in the distance, were the dim shapes of mountains, and in the air above them, dark figures were circling.

Mantha blinked. The figures were birds. Huge, black birds with glossy feathers and sharp talons. Lightning flickered under their wings.

Something flashed in the water near to shore. Something bright, colorful as a rainbow, but quickly swallowed by the dark water. It slithered away into the lake and was lost to sight.

No sooner had it vanished than another form rose from the water. A flat, spotted face with long whiskers and huge, curling horns. It looked like a small lion, but the rear half of its body was a long fishtail. It was emaciated and there was an ugly scar on its belly, as if it had been cut open a long time ago.

"What are you doing, white child?" asked Mishipeshu.

Mantha could not answer. It felt like her tongue had turned to maggots and filled up her mouth. She wanted to ask for help. But she was the enemy of Mishipeshu. Why should he help her?

"Enemies are relative things," said Mishipeshu, his tail flashing through the water. "The only true crime is the lie."

"What lie?" asked Mantha.

"That all this is inevitable," Mishipeshu said, smiling with his cat face.

For the first time since she left MCSIR, Mantha felt a little relief from the pressure behind her mind. It let her think for herself for the first time in hours, and she saw that Mishipeshu was right.

It didn't make what she had to do easy.

"I understand," she said.

It would be harder than confronting her nightmares. Harder than defeating the dream monster. Harder than pushing Clara's mind around.

She thought of the demon in the lake, and quailed.

She thought of Clara, calmly and brutally twisting the goddess out of her effigy. She thought of the long line of women on the righthand side of the road, and the single, distant shape far away to her left. Maybe some of them had been cruel and some of them had been stupid and some of them had been hurt so badly there was very little goodness left, but they were all their own people.

She tried to hold that in her head as she walked forward into the lake.

The water steamed and hissed, and drew away from her. A new road revealed itself, leading down into the turbid depths.

Port Austin
Wednesday night

Jill was roused from her intense reprogramming of the predictive model by a sharp tapping sound from outside the trailer. Checking her watch, she saw that the sun had just set, and so went and opened the door herself.

Frosty was standing at the doorway, her front paws on the entry step, panting and whining. Jill had never seen the dog so upset. Her normally pristine white coat was gray with water and decorated with twigs and dirt. Her legs were quivering and her tail was nervously wagging between her legs.

"Oh no," said Jill. "What's happened?"

At almost the same time, her phone rang. It read as the MCSIR Duty Operative, but when Jill answered it was Lady Bibbit on the other end of the line.

"Mantha's gone! Mantha's *gone!*" she was saying, sounding uncharacteristically panicked.

"Gone," Jill repeated, the words making no sense. "Gone where?"

"To the Devil, for all I know," Lady Bibbit said. She sounded like she was crying. Jill had never heard her so upset. "She didn't feel well after lunch, so we put her to bed. She had a fever, she threw up. I just went to check on her, and she's *gone.*"

"She isn't in the building?" Jill asked, her mind still unable to comprehend this. Mantha being sick, going missing, was a disaster—but why? She was a self-possessed girl with magical powers.

That was why this was a disaster.

"No," Lady Bibbit said. "I've searched all over. Frosty's gone too."

Jill looked down at the miserable Yell Hound crouched on her doorstep.

"Frosty's here," Jill said.

"Frosty's what?"

"Frosty is with me," Jill repeated. "In Port Austin. She just arrived. Listen, have there been any other extraordinary events in Detroit?"

"No . . . " said Lady Bibbit, almost resentfully.

"When does Lansing come on duty?"

"She's having breakfast right now," Lady Bibbit said.

"Good," said Jill, mentally clearing MCSIR from her plate of worries—which was full enough as it was. "When she comes on, tell her to make a full system check and report back to me."

"But *Mantha*—"

"Yes," said Jill. "Listen, Lady Bibbit, *do you know what Mantha is?*"

There was a miserable silence on the other end of the phone.

"She is my maker," Lady Bibbit said, eventually.

"Yes, *and?*" Jill pressed on. She invited Frosty up into the trailer, and began rerunning her data. Not the ones for Port Austin. From MCSIR. From when Mantha was living there.

"I . . . I can't describe her any better than that," Lady Bibbit said.

She had thought it was a bug, the transmuting gauges of silver. A few of the palladium ones had also been overloaded in the same way. But not consistently.

Because Mantha wasn't always in her room. And there was no gauge in her room—just at the end of her hall, by the elevators. But that was not the nearest gauge to her room. There was one in the analogous room on the floor above, and on the floor below.

Yes, those two had been the ones to transmute. Not regularly, and the level of transmutation was so variable that it had seemed like a flaw in the gauge.

Still, with six months of data, it was impossible not to see the pattern. Why hadn't Jill seen it before?

The palladium gauges went as high as 16 p-grams. From what she had seen, it appeared there was a certain amount of overhead before the element began to transmute. At least twice again as much, Jill thought, was a safe bet.

She sat back and looked at the new model, Lady Bibbit's voice a faint rattle in her ear.

"She's like . . . if you had a mother, and your mother was an inventor, and she *invented* you . . . " Lady Bibbit was saying.

Lady Bibbit, the transmuted stuffed rabbit.

"Thanks," said Jill. "That's very helpful."

"Have you been listening to a *word* I've said?" Lady Bibbit screeched.

"Some of them," said Jill. "Listen, I need to go. Thanks for calling. Keep everything buttoned up there. I think I understand."

"No, no you *don't*," Lady Bibbit yelped. "Mantha is a baby god! A baby god who never knew her parents! And if we don't find her, she might do something *terrible*. Please, *please* tell Clara! She's the only one Mantha will listen to!"

"I will," said Jill. "I promise. We'll take care of this."

"I'm coming out there," Lady Bibbit said. "I will see you soon!"

Jill's phone beeped. The call had ended. She was left with Frosty cowering in the doorway, and a veritable latticework of transmuted gauges littering her model.

Violent transdimensional events were not natural disasters. They could be anything. One *could* be a tsunami, or a volcanic eruption . . . but correlation was not causation.

Jill had had the experience of Vjor's entry through the Gateway Arch in St. Louis burned into her mind as the epitome of a violent transdimensional event. It had always been something linked to a fixed point in space and time.

It didn't have to be that way. This was *magic*, after all.

Mantha was a violent transdimensional event. She excited the ambient magic in her vicinity so much that gauges from square-yards around spontaneously transmuted. And she had, like a crafty virus, caused the people around her not to notice.

Perhaps that even extended to herself, Jill thought, remembering how Mantha had crouched in her office back at MCSIR, asking Jill for help.

Whatever else she was, Mantha was also a person.

People could be incredibly self-deluded.

Jill inhaled for the first time since Lady Bibbit had hung up, and came back to herself in a rush. Frosty was whining.

"Right," Jill wheezed. Inhaled properly. Then spoke.

"Go get Clara and Ariel. Get Chuy. I'll tell Okedo and Gadget."

Frosty thumped her tail against the wall of the trailer, and was gone in a flash of dirty white coat and red ears.

* * *

The bottom of the lake was surprisingly smooth, the silt pressed into waves as hard as concrete. Mantha's feet left no indentation on them, and she drifted across the landscape of brown and blue and green like a ghost out of place.

She was not properly in the lake. The lake had taken itself away to a place in the background. It wanted no part in this. The water arched far above her head, grown dim and black as she descended further along the path.

It was a trench now, carved in the concrete silt like the gash of a giant's claw. The dark, slippery sides rose to Mantha's waist, to her shoulders, her neck, and finally over her head.

The tunnel led down, down, down into the lake's bed. It was dark and cold and Mantha felt more alone than she had in her entire life. Just her and the dark, in the silence under the world.

The words came to her out of memory, slipping out of her mouth in a whisper of a song.

"One door leads to heaven and one door leads to hell, and the great gate in between them has secrets it won't tell . . ."

That wasn't quite right, of course. The Great Gate was all three doors, and it was one door. It was curled shut at the heart of its own nexus, and it would take more power than was even in Mantha to open.

A thousand human souls. Or half the demons in Hell. And the Spawn of Satan.

Mantha stepped out of the tunnel and into the Atrium of Earth, where the Great Gate appeared very much like it was called: a huge stone edifice made of pillars of granite and a lintel of gray marble. The aperture itself was not a gate or a door, but a shut mouth full of teeth which fit together so tightly nothing could pass through. They were long, slender teeth, almost like stone fingers, stained brown at the tips and otherwise faintly yellow. Trapped within each one, stretched almost beyond recognition, was a reflection of Mantha.

By this time she was not even disturbed to see that some of them did not look very much like herself at all. They looked more like she felt: stretched and pressed and pale; resentful, frightened, angry.

Mantha was, she realized with distant amusement, incredibly angry. Her mind had split, like an egg put through a slicer, but at the forefront of it she understood that she was a twelve-year-old girl, and she should not have to deal with—what did Jill call it?—a violent, compound, trans-dimensional event. Adventures she should have, yes, and accidents and friends and responsibilities. But bringing about the end of the world as it was known? No one should have to do that alone . . .

But you are not alone . . . said a voice in the dark.

For one mad moment Mantha thought it was the Great Gate itself that had spoken. Then she thought it was the darkness around her.

But the darkness was silent. If it judged her, it did not say what its verdict was.

Another part of her mind was horrified. Terrified. She wanted to run from that gate. Run clean away from herself. Become something innocent and innocuous like a toad or a stone.

She could still do that, she realized. But for how long? She and the Gate were linked. She would eventually find herself in the same position she was in now. Only she would be a toad.

You are not alone . . .

Finally, in the back of her mind, an ugly feeling tugged. It would be easy to open the Gate. And once she did, she wouldn't be alone anymore. She'd have friends. Lots of friends. Proper friends, who she didn't have to invent—like Lady Bibbit—or were secretly afraid of her—like Clara and Ariel.

Most of all, she would get to meet her father . . .

You are not alone . . .

Mantha's attention snapped back to the gate. The voice was coming, she realized, from *within* it. Someone was trying to speak to her from the other side.

Slowly, Mantha approached the toothy door, as if it were a sleeping tiger, and pressed her ear to a yellow, stained tooth.

It was cold against her skin, but grew quickly warm. It called out to her, like a long-forgotten memory.

A memory from thousands of years ago.

When she and the Great Gate had been one person. One thing.

But how was that possible? Mantha was twelve.

Twelve earthly years.

There was a sound from within the Gate—of countless tiny mouths gnawing and chewing. When Mantha pulled her face away to look, all she saw was her reflection, yellow and deformed. She looked so much like a flat, paper cutout of herself that she had to step back out of discomfort and look down at herself. Her real self.

She was largely still the same, she saw with satisfaction. But was there maybe a pearlescent quality to her skin that hadn't been there before? It shimmered faintly in the dark, like the belly of a fish.

How was she seeing herself, anyway? There was no light down here . . .

Except there was. There was Mantha. Mantha herself was glowing, as was the Gate—though faintly.

Mantha stood and faced the Gate. Far too young. Impossibly old. She felt like a dozen or more slices of a person pressed together into one body, and they all had their own ideas about what she should do.

Which was ridiculous, the front part of her mind realized. She was Mantha Fulgeroiu, and she could make her own decisions.

She put her glowing, pearly hand flat against the nearest yellow tooth of the Gate . . .

. . . and half the demons in Hell crowed in victory.

Port Austin
Wednesday night

A wind had whipped up that evening, contrary to the weather prediction and much to Jill's triumph. It meant that they had to stage their emergency meeting inside the trailer, but since there were only seven of them (plus Frosty), they all just about fit. Except for Clara, who filled the doorway with her worried silhouette and kept the door open to check outside.

"Why didn't I see it?" Ariel kept muttering. "Why didn't I *see* it?"

"Bro, she's an *antichrist*, they are *built* not to be recognized," Chuy said.

"None of us saw it," Clara said, her voice hollow.

"But I should have," Ariel said. "That's what I've *trained* for."

"It is possible we have caught it in time," Jill pointed out, trying to bring people back on topic. "On her own, Mantha can't have gotten here yet—even if she hijacked a car."

"She's an *antichrist*," Ariel said, emphasizing each word. "Time and space . . . the rules of physics don't apply to her. She could have been here *yesterday*."

Even Clara looked skeptical of that.

"I do not think she is that far developed," she said.

"She *could* be," Ariel sighed, dragging a hand across his face. "Sorry. I'm not being productive. Do you have a plan, boss?"

It was what Selene used to call her. Jill felt the loss keenly.

"Our objective is to avert or otherwise mitigate the event," she said. "If I understand this correctly, Mantha as an antichrist is critical to it happening or not happening."

"She is critical to the opening of the Great Gate," Clara said. "Which is the . . . transdimensional event . . . which leads to the apocalypse."

"Okay," said Jill, folding her hands tightly together. On her computer, open behind her, were two windows showing the predicted weather and the current weather side-by-side.

It was supposed to be 12° F, clear and calm.

It was currently gusting in excess of 40 mph and windchill was driving the temperature down into the negatives.

"Assuming Mantha can break the laws of physics—which I hope you realize basically makes her a godlike being"—everyone nodded—"then our best practice should be to find the local manifestation of the Great Gate . . . and wait for her there."

Everyone looked at each other in turn. They seemed ready for Jill to go on.

"You're my experts," she said, jabbing a finger at Clara, Ariel and Chuy. "Where *is* the Great Gate?"

"The Great Gate is in Heaven, Hell and Earth," Clara stated. "It regulates transfer of metaphysical properties between the three."

Jill snapped her fingers impatiently. "Okay. Where is it *on Earth*?"

Clara looked at Ariel.

Ariel looked at the ceiling of the trailer.

"That's the ten-thousand soul question, isn't it?" he sighed. "It varies, you see. The Great Gate exists within its own special bubble of reality. So it could appear anywhere *on* Earth. But as far as we're concerned, we've already found it."

Jill made a grasping motion with her hand. "Yes, *and?*"

Ariel shrugged. "It's around *here* somewhere, isn't it? All the power flowing in from Pittsburgh, Fort Wayne, Sudbury, Lake Superior? It's going to corporealize the Great Gate."

"Here," said Jill, swiveling herself around to look at her computer. She put a finger right in the center of the vortex of clouds forming over Lake Huron, just north of Port Austin. "You mean, right *there.*"

"But there's nothing on the sweeps," Chuy said.

"No," said Jill, her brow wrinkling in thought. "No, because you're sweeping for *leaked* magic. The Great Gate is sucking up all the magic. It needs magic to manifest. We need to stop it manifesting. We need to stop the magic."

"You cannot stop the magic," Clara said.

"Divert it, then," Jill said, spinning around. "Sluice it off somewhere else."

"We could tap the ley lines," Chuy suggested, looking doubtful.

Jill clapped her hands. "Yes," she said. "Yes, exactly."

"Tap them with *what?*" Ariel asked.

"Me," said Clara, her voice still hollow.

"No," said Ariel.

"What's tapping a ley line?" Jill asked.

"Sort of like tapping an artery," Chuy said. "Stick a needle in it, pipe it away."

"Only you can't let that magic spill out just anywhere," Ariel said. "It has to go *into* something, otherwise we'd be dealing with another kind of disaster."

"Which is why you should use me," Clara repeated.

"*No,*" said Ariel.

"Slow down," said Okedo, typing away on his own laptop. "Can you explain?"

"We don't have time," said Clara.

"Yes, yes we do," said Jill. She pointed the capped end of her pen at Clara. "What do you mean, 'use yourself'?"

Clara swallowed visibly, shifted from foot to foot.

"You need something to tap the ley lines, or at least one of them," she said. "Bellatrix is a magical conduit. I can use her to tap. The diverted magic needs to go *into* something. I can be that something."

"That'll kill you," Chuy said, bluntly.

Clara shrugged, as if this did not concern her. "Not necessarily," she said. "I stand a better chance of surviving than any of you."

"Why would it kill you?" Jill asked. "It's just magic, isn't it?"

478

"Raw magic," Ariel said. "Same reason getting a whole bunch of oxygen pumped into you at once would kill you. Well, maybe not *you*, but me."

"But I am more like Jill in this analogy," Clara said.

Ariel looked at her, an expression of supreme frustration on his face, when they all became aware of a persistent thumping sound coming from behind Jill's chair. Jill moved aside to reveal Frosty, lying flat on her stomach with her long snout on her outstretched paws, red ears perked, gazing up at Jill beseechingly, while her tail wagged back and forth, thumping loudly against the wall and floor of the trailer. When she saw that attention had swung to her she wagged even harder, and whined a little.

"No," said Jill.

"Frosty would actually be a better candidate," Ariel admitted.

"Why?" asked Okedo.

"We're *not* using my dog as a *test animal*," Jill said.

"She's not a dog," said a gruff voice from the back of the sofa.

Tucker, who had until then remained prudently silent, was sitting with his knees up in his chest, arms folded, looking at Frosty critically.

"She's a Yell Hound," Clara said.

"So?" asked Jill.

"Magic sticks to magic, like water sticks to water," Tucker said. "Frosty is probably the most magical of any of us. She can . . . how'd you say it? Convert the raw magic into ambient magic . . . and if she absorbs a lot at once, it won't hurt her."

"You sure?" Jill asked.

"She is," Tucker said, pointing at the hound, who had backed up onto her haunches and was sitting at attention.

Jill looked at her. "You sure?" she asked.

For answer, Frosty began to pant expectantly.

"Okay," said Jill. She paused. With surprising tenderness she reached out and petted Frosty on the head. "Okay," she said, turning around to face them. "Let's go tap a ley line."

The wind made it almost impossible. It was blowing so hard across the parking lot that if the sand hadn't been frozen, there would have been a dust storm. As it was, the air was filled with chips of frost and ice, and Tucker quickly issued them all protective glasses which they jammed on under hats to keep them from being blown off their faces.

"Have you ever raised a ley line before?" Ariel asked Clara, who was tying her glasses on with a piece of string.

"Once," she said, shouting a little to be heard above the wind. "I helped Faraday do it."

"Do you want to lead?" Ariel asked. "I know how, but I've only ever *stopped* people doing it."

Clara shrugged. They had assembled their kit in the trailer, and were now trying to lay out the pegs in the wind. They had divined the course of the nearest ley line as running northwest across the Port Austin State Harbor parking lot, and had driven Arcana and the necessary equipment around from the park.

"What's the difference between raising a ley line and tapping a ley line?" Jill asked in the roar of the wind behind them.

"Can't answer questions now!" Chuy yelled back.

"I'll do it," Clara said. "You be ready with the tap."

The tap was Frosty holding an ingot of palladium wrapped in a cotton cloth in her mouth. She was dancing around the pegs, wagging her tail and somehow still managing to bark through the weight in her mouth. The wind had blown her coat out so that she appeared half again as big, like a dog-shaped dandelion clock.

"I'll do my best," Ariel said. He reached out and touched the cuff of Clara's sleeve, where it had pulled back from her wrist. "Be careful," he said.

Clara looked at him, surprised.

"I will," she said, and pulled her left glove off. The mark on the back of her hand was already beginning to glow red around the edges. Ariel tried not to stare.

Reaching into a pocket at her belt, Clara removed a small, gray ring. Holding it between two gloved fingers she slipped it onto her bare hand—

—and at the same time, winked out of sight.

"Here it comes!" Ariel shouted.

Frosty gave a muffled *yip* and danced around his legs.

Thunder rolled across the parking lot, and around them the lights of Port Austin went out. The parking lot was illuminated moments later by a diamond of light that opened like an eye at the southeast end of the lot. It scorched the ground near it and gave every piece of debris or chip of rock a long, black shadow, and Jill could be heard gasping and covering her face.

In the gray-gold air above the door of light a giant shadow could be seen, its legs so long they straddled the door, and in its hands was an equally long sword. It brought this down into the center of the light, and the ley line spilled across the parking lot.

It looked like a serpent made of golden light, each scale a perfect diamond with gleaming facets, as it coiled its way across the concrete, which split and exploded beneath it.

Frosty bounded to meet it, her tail windmilling, and for a moment the line bent toward her.

Then a wave broke over the dock, spilling black, sparkling water across the ruined concrete. Frosty dodged to miss it, and the ley line tore past her, streaming for the shores of Lake Huron.

Something had risen from the water there. Something huge, with a flat, triangular face and curling horns, a ragged, emaciated body, and a gaping mouth.

The tapped line hit Mishipeshu full in the chest, and for a moment seemed it would force the creature back into the lake.

Then Mishipeshu rallied, the water churning around him, frothing against his sides, which were already healing. Hundreds of years worth of scars and wounds faded away, and his coat grew thick and glossy, gently spotted and striped with dots and lines of iridescent brown. He laughed, the sound echoing around the parking lot, across the lake, across the powerless town, and up to the very heavens. It filled the air, an audible storm of glee, triumph, and relief.

Mishipeshu devoured the line, his white teeth flashing against golden scales, until the door of light winked shut, and Clara stumbled out from behind it, visible only by her sword, whose blade was glowing faintly blue-white.

Frosty was growling. She had managed to catch a single scale off the ley line, for which she had dropped the bar of palladium, and was now crouched over it, gnawing fiercely.

Mishipeshu ignored her. He was bigger than Arcana now—bigger than a house, even. Ariel could see the lake water through his legs, under his coiling tail.

He lowered his great, flat face—like a cat, but also definitely not a cat—and blinked eyes that still glowed from the light of the ley line.

His voice was like his laughter: it cut the air into words and intentions. It was not like hearing a demon, or an angel. If Ariel had to describe it, he would have said it sounded like the way a rock would speak.

The way the land would speak.

It spoke to a part of him that was much older than his flesh and bones.

"Pull out my festering arrow," Mishipeshu said, and dove back into the lake.

He took the water with him. It rolled back from the loading ramp, revealing first wet concrete, and then the natural silt bed, curling and crashing over itself, the waves parting to form a canyon with walls of water leading down into the lake. The rush of it washed over the breakwater, then stopped and pounded there until the reinforced concrete barricade was reduced to rubble. Until there was nothing but open, choppy lake, and the high, peaked waves where it parted for the road into it.

For it was a road. Risen gently from the silt, it was just wide and level enough for a single car, and at the end of it—deep within the water—a dim light glimmered.

It was a grudging sort of road, made by something that did not like roads nor the things that they brought, but understood the necessity of them under the circumstances. It made Ariel's chest pound uncomfortably.

It was one thing to be ignored by natural forces, blown and buffeted by their whims and fancies. It was another thing entirely when they turned around and recognized you.

It was a terrifying thing when they *expected* something of you.

"Is that . . . it?" Jill asked. Her voice was small and uncharacteristically timid, and the only reason Ariel heard her was because the winds had stopped.

No, actually. The winds continued to roar, high above them, whipping ghostly clouds across the sky.

On the ground, beside the lake, all was still except for the perpetual crashing of the water as it flowed up, curled over, and fell back upon itself.

"That is," Clara said. She sounded a little hoarse, as if she had been yelling. When Ariel glanced at her he saw she still had her sword unsheathed, resting easy in her gloved hand, and that the blade was still glowing.

"Great," said Chuy, the sarcasm heavy in his voice. "Just *great*. Here, have a supernatural assist, and by the way, a death trap!"

"I do not believe Mishipeshu intends to kill us," Clara said.

"Maybe doesn't *intend*," Chuy said, "but what have you ever done for him?"

Clara said nothing, but Ariel remembered how she had been so careful to return the dead Mishipeshu to Devil's Lake intact.

"I don't think he likes having the Great Gate manifesting in his lake," was what he said out loud.

"So what? We should just *walk* on down there?" Chuy asked, incredulously.

"Not walk," said Jill. "We'll drive. You, Okedo, Gadget, Tucker—I want you to stay here and monitor that . . . whatever *that* is." She pointed at the parted water. "I'll drive Clara and Ariel down . . . down to the Gate."

"What about Frosty?" Ariel asked. Frosty had taken her scale and jumped up onto the bed of Arcana, where she could be heard making wet, chewing sounds.

"Frosty will go where she likes," Jill declared. "Come on, you two," she wagged a finger at Clara and Ariel. "Unless you want to set, like . . . some extra wards?"

Together they shook their heads, numbly.

There was no ward for this. Only hopes and prayers—for what good they ever did.

Then Ariel glanced at Clara, who was looking down the road with such determination she almost appeared triumphant, and thought maybe there was something worth praying to.

They climbed into the cab of Arcana—Frosty refused to budge from the back—and with a grumble of his diesel engine that was barely audible over the crash of the water, drove slowly across the parking lot, down the loading ramp, and onto the silt road.

His tires sank in the wet dirt, but only a little. Only enough to leave distinct tracks. The red of his taillights cast wild reflections in the waves to either side, and his headlights made the water sparkle and shine.

The group left behind on solid ground watched him go until his lights were swallowed up by the water.

"This isn't gonna end well," Chuy said.

None of his companions answered.

The night was silent and dark. High above them, the wind screamed. A vortex was forming in the sky.

The road was smooth and gently graded, and as long as Jill was careful to use engine braking and take what turns there were at 5 miles per hour, Arcana did not slip on the mud track. She was glad that they were driving, for the road went down a long way, winding across the bottom of Lake Huron. Always north, the compass informed her. Away from shore.

"I hope you two know what you're gonna do," she said, glancing aside at Clara and Ariel. Clara was seated next to her in the front seat, her sword laid lengthwise across the dashboard, while Ariel was in the back, methodically blessing little silver crosses.

Clara's mouth pinched in reply, and from the back Ariel gave out a dry chuckle.

"Sure," he said. "We do this every weekend."

"No," said Jill. "I hope you understand what this is really about."

"It's an apocalypse," Clara said.

They were great people, really, Jill thought. Ariel was even the kind of man she would have fallen for, in a past life. But she suspected they stood a little too close to the fire, as it were, to see what was actually burning.

"It's *Mantha*," she said.

"Yes, that too," Ariel sighed.

Jill resisted the urge to thump Arcana's steering wheel in frustration.

"No, I mean—this isn't about Mantha being the antichrist. This isn't even about the apocalypse," she said. "It's about a scared little girl who was abandoned by her parents and lost her grandma, and didn't feel *safe* confiding in the only two adults in her life who might have been able to help her!"

"What are you talking about?" Clara asked. In the back, Ariel had gone quiet.

"I mean, it was Mantha who turned me on to this," Jill said, waving her hand out the window at the solid wall of water. "Mantha *knew* this was coming. She didn't want it to happen. Imagine if you were born into something bigger than yourself, but didn't want a part of it? Imagine how *hard* it would be to stop yourself being what someone older and stronger than you wants you to be. She's got it worse even than those kids born into the mafia or whatever."

"Mantha told you this was going to happen?" Clara asked. She sounded hurt. She was entitled to, Jill supposed. She refused to feel guilty.

"She was worried it would, I think," Jill said. "I don't think she could explain what she knew, even to me."

"She went to *you* about this?" Ariel said. Now he sounded hurt as well. Great.

"I'm a *stranger*," Jill sighed. "Sometimes it's easier to talk to strangers about things than the people you really care about. Or the people who you care that they care about you. Anyway. My *point* is, this isn't about closing the Great Gate or averting this apocalypse or whatever else it seems. It's about helping Mantha."

"Helping her do what?" Clara asked, quietly.

"I . . . I don't know!" Jill said. "*Be* Mantha—whatever Mantha is—and not what her supernatural genetics are telling her to be."

Arcana hit a rock in the road, but they were going slow enough Jill was able to correct for it. They were so deep now that the night sky was lost between the towering shapes of the vertical waves. They traveled through a narrow canyon of water, which might have been a tunnel for all they could see. The water of the lake sucked up Arcana's headlights, so that only the road ahead of them was illuminated.

The Great Gate

If Mantha had thought about what she was going to do, she would have thought that she was going to knock the gate down from the outside. Push it over, like a stack of twigs. Pull down the lintel and grind it into dust.

But the Gate had been built to withstand the passage of the armies of Heaven and Hell simultaneously. Not even Mantha could put so much as a crack in it. Instead, when she put her hands upon its teeth she felt it shudder in anticipation. It recognized Mantha like a dog does its owner. It was all she could do to keep it from springing open under her palm.

That was not all the Gate, though. When she touched it from the earthly side she felt an echo of the demon from Devil's Lake. He was waiting, pushing from the other side. From the Hell side.

When she tested the Gate again, she was unnerved to feel a similar pressure from the Heaven side.

Heaven and Hell, straining eagerly at their posts, waiting for her to open the way and unleash the Apocalypse on Earth.

Which wasn't fair at all, Mantha thought. Earth had enough problems without a bunch of angels and demons fighting on and over it.

She put her hand to the teeth of the Gate, and this time it trembled. Encouraged, Mantha gathered herself for another push—

—and was nearly blown off her feet as the Gate was forced open under her hand. And—

—and a cold, wet wind whistled over the hills of Niflheim. And—

—and Mantha rallied, dredging up all the pieces of herself she kept so carefully sealed away, piling herself behind the door, and forcing it slowly shut. And—

—and—and the wind passed, but the sound of screams remained.

"If you intend to leave by the Trinity Gate," Hel said, "I suggest you do it soon."

"Someone in Midgard tried to open it," Gefiyon added. "Now they are attacking the foundations of it."

And—

—and in Midgard, Mantha stood with her shoulder braced against the Gate, her hands sinking into the face of it, as she tried to grasp what she had glimpsed in the moment it had opened.

The Great Gate was much bigger than she had first thought. If she was going to destroy it properly, she realized, she would have to pull it apart piece by piece. Scatter them wide.

She didn't have time. If she tried to do it piece by piece, the demon would stop her.

At the moment it was all she could do just to keep the thing shut.

Bottom of Lake Huron

All at once the water drew aside, and they were shot out into a dark world illuminated only by the twin beams of Arcana's headlights. These showed a structure of glossy stone, green with algae, which rose up out of the lake bottom. From what Jill could see, after she held her breath for a couple minutes, these were two pillars built out of hexagonal bricks and draped in chains.

They reminded her a little of the bridges in Purgatory, only smaller. In fact, the two pillars were so close together there was only space for one person at a time to slip between them.

From the outer side of each pillar ran a low, stone wall, and beyond that wall was the black curtain of water. There was just enough space to get Arcana turned around, at which point Jill applied the parking brake—but left the engine running, so she could keep the lights on for Clara and Ariel.

"I think this is it," she said.

Clara squinted at the twin pillars critically.

"No," she said. "Not quite. But we are close."

"Oh," said Jill, disappointed. She had not wanted to leave Arcana. Despite probable demonic possession, she still felt far safer in the vehicle than she did outside in the . . . whatever was outside.

"I think we'd better take it from here," Ariel said.

Clara gave him a look, like she was going to object, but said nothing. She turned instead to Jill, and said with a gravity that was intense even for her:

"I will remember what you said."

Then she retrieved her sword from the dashboard, opened the passenger door, and stepped out onto the lake bottom. There was a scramble of claws on metal, the sound of panting, and then Frosty was leaping up to take her place.

"Good dog," Jill said, out of habit. Frosty still had half a ley-line scale in her mouth, but she was smiling around it. "Will you be all right?" she asked Clara, who was lingering by the door.

Clara's black shoulders sagged, then rose again.

"Don't worry," Ariel said, pulling on a pair of gloves and zipping his coat all the way up. "I'll keep an eye on her."

"Just get both of you back here safely," Jill said. "And Mantha."

"Will do," he said, smiling. It was a hard smile, but warm despite it all. Jill realized she would be very sorry indeed if Ariel did not come back.

She turned herself around in her seat to watch through the rear window as the two figures approached the narrow gap between the pillars. Clara went in front, her sword drawn, while Ariel held a flashlight, which he shone over her shoulder.

Jill watched until they were eaten up between the two pillars, then began getting out her own set of gauges, vials, and sensors.

Just because she wasn't going right up to ground zero didn't mean she would waste this opportunity.

"But," she told Frosty as she set the timer on a palladium gauge, "if they're not out in two hours, we're going in after them."

Frosty, still gnawing on her scale, thumped her tail in agreement.

Outside, above them, the dark waters swirled. If Jill had cared to look closely, she might have seen a large, mantled form, with branches like antlers growing from its shoulders. It was leaning over the little bubble on the bottom of the lake, watching the proceedings with interest.

The Great Gate
The Earthly Atrium

The tight space between the pillars lasted only a couple feet, and then they emerged into a wide tunnel hewn of black rock which gleamed transparent in the beam of Ariel's flashlight when he cast it around in a broad arc.

Not rock then, but glass. The tunnel was rectangular, wider than it was tall, but only just. The floor was covered in gray sand, which when Ariel tested it with one booted toe, proved to be hardly an inch deep. Under it was more glassy rock, and a disembodied human hand. It shone pale, encased in the rock, like a dead fish.

There had been a time when seeing something like that would have caused him distress, but Ariel had learned from experience that it was not the dead things encased in rock that you needed to worry about.

You needed to worry about what had put them there.

"Hmm," he said, and when Clara turned at his voice, he indicated the hand in the rock.

"Yes," she said simply. "Past lives."

Ariel stepped carefully over the hand.

"You've heard the theory that the antichrist is reincarnated?" he asked.

"Jill would call it an hypothesis," Clara said, dryly. "And yes, I have. I do not think it is entirely correct. But they all share a connection. The Nameless God, Satan, Christ, Anti-Christ, and the Great Gate in between them."

They kept walking. Now Ariel thought to look, he saw other things trapped in the glassy rock: the wing of a bird, the branch of a tree, a new-born lamb.

A nautilus, bigger than he had ever seen, dominated a portion of the wall. Its eyes reflected back at him his flashlight, and he looked away.

Clara had drawn ahead, apparently moving by the light of her sword alone. This had not stopped glowing since she'd used it to raise the ley line, and it outlined her tall form in a black silhouette.

Ariel did not run but shuffled his feet madly in order to catch up, leaving two streaks of clear stone visible through the gray sand.

He did not have far to go. The tunnel ended in a flat wall pierced by a circle maybe eight feet in diameter, which was itself filled with a block of white marble. In the center of it was a ragged crater, as if someone had carved a chunk out of it without much care. Lying beside it, gray from the sand that lay upon it like snow, was a giant, broken chain.

Whatever guard dog had been posted there, it was now long gone.

Clara was exploring the circle with her free hand—her bare, left hand—tracing her fingertips over the seam where the white marble met the black glass.

"This is not the gate," Ariel said, just to confirm they were on the same page.

"No," Clara agreed. "It is not. I think this is the atrium door. Ordinarily the guardian beast would recognize the antichrist and open it for them, but ..."

"But no beast," Ariel said.

And no Mantha, he thought.

"No beast," Clara repeated. "No handle, no keyhole."

Ariel looked at the block of marble critically. He had a prayerbook—not the sort they left in pews at church—that held a great many esoteric and practically useless prayers. His favorite, because it was so very useless, was one which would open any door or gate sealed by magic, as long as the pray-er remained perfectly stationary. In fact, the pose one took was vital to the maintenance of the opening. He'd never used it, on account of the fact that he usually worked alone, and even when he didn't, it put both parties at such risk there had always been better alternatives.

As he watched Clara begin to test the block of marble, feeling her way into the cracks of it, he realized that now there were no better alternatives.

Now he was in a place where the risk to himself was acceptable. Now he had a partner who he knew was more capable than himself.

Most importantly, now they were both running out of time.

"I can open it," Ariel said, putting his flashlight between his teeth so he could see to open his briefcase. There were all his charms and tokens, laid out and ready for the taking. All useless.

He pulled out the false bottom and opened the accordion file this revealed, running his thumb across the spines of the books held within. Most of these had the titles worn off, and many were patched with duct tape. It didn't matter—he knew them all by feel.

Even so it took two tries to find the one he was looking for, during which time he had to whisper out loud "Don't panic," in order not to.

But there it was, two hand-stitched signatures of parchment in a leather sleeve. He pulled it out and thumbed through it until he got to the solid page of text in the back and—*yes*—his phonetic transcription which he'd typed up and printed out. Unfolding the paper across the spread of the book and holding it flat with his right hand, he took his flashlight out of his mouth with the other, and looked up at Clara.

"You go," he said, firmly telling himself as he said it that Claymore Nordstern could handle literally anything the Great Gate could throw at her.

"You go," he repeated. "I'll hold it open."

The conflict was visible on Clara's face. She seemed like she wanted to protest, but when she spoke it was with determination. A promise.

"I'll be back."

"Just bring Mantha back with you."

Clara nodded, jerkily.

Ariel smiled at her, trying to say with a look what he felt in his heart.

I believe in you, you ice-cold star.

Clara went and stood beside the circle of marble. In her black leathers, with only the light of her sword, she almost looked like a disembodied head and hand, floating in the blackness.

She stood very firm and straight—but not rigid. A creature of action at rest. Ariel tried to fix that image in his mind as he looked down at his sheet of type, and began to read the prayer.

It was a spiral prayer, the kind that repeated words without repeating patterns. Like an arcane version of the numeral Pi. You had to sit still and speak the never-ending prayer, and as long as you did, the door in front of you remained open. But once the prayer was broken, it could not be reopened.

The code in the book laid out the calculations for two hours, of which Ariel had transcribed less than a quarter. But he didn't tell Clara to hurry.

She didn't have to hurry because she would not waste time.

The first two stanzas came out rough, the words catching in his throat. But Ariel spoke through the urge to cough.

He did not look up to see if the atrium door opened. He knew it had by the way the words suddenly came easier, and by the sound of Clara's footsteps fading away. But he kept his eyes on his paper, his mouth speaking one prayer while his heart spoke another.

Within the walls of glass rock, the preserved fragments of ages past gazed at him. Cold, emotionless, and dead.

Hell

And the demons rose in columns and the demons rose in clouds. The rivers flooded, racing away uphill, and on the smoke of the fire that burned in the Forest of Despair, a white bird sailed up through the sky. The great, orange-red face of the Gate swelled to encompass the infernal firmament.

And cracked open a golden grin.

The Great Gate

Mantha felt like she was trying to hold a broken eggshell together. She could only grasp so many pieces, while the rest shattered and went everywhere. She felt the cracks all around her, like a network of cuts in her skin. In the skin of the Gate. Things were leaking through and she could not stop them. Strips of demons, hatred, and greed, they swirled around her temporarily, then went streaming off into the world.

It would take them awhile to reach the surface, but by the time they did, they would be real monsters. And Mantha couldn't stop them this time.

Clara encountered the first demon as little more than a streak of red-hot hate, which she caught on her sword and felt it sing through her arms like an electric shock. It was a weak, stripped thing—barely a fragment of a much larger demon that had been shredded by the cracks in the gate. Clara could see these once she put on her ring again, which she did the better to be able to fight the demons, which came regularly after the first.

Some of these were almost whole beings—though small ones—and they were easy to catch on her sword. They were just corporeal enough, and Bellatrix was just magic enough, that her blade worked on them as well as a butcher's cleaver worked on soft butter.

Soon the tunnel was choked with corpses, which Clara carefully threw behind her, so her way forward would not be blocked. At the same time, she tried to build up a wall of dead demons behind her. She could not afford to let a single one past, because behind her, Ariel was sitting, defenseless, speaking the endless prayer to keep the atrium door open.

It made forward progress slow going, until the most complete demon yet came barreling down the corridor, and Clara managed to wedge it sideways after cutting its head off, creating such an effective blockade that her main problem afterward was all the demons who rushed by, found their way blocked, and then circled back to take out their frustrations on her.

Clara felt the coolness on her skin where her leathers were torn by their claws, but she didn't feel if they cut her. Her marks were burning so hot they were all she could feel, and she tried to channel that energy, as her mother had once taught her.

In through your center and out through your sword.

It felt like fire running through her veins. It *hurt.* Hurt like getting flayed. Hurt like a cold knife right on a nerve.

And it hurt sweetly, like heartache. Clara concentrated on that.

It was the shape of her that hurt. She was the wrong shape. A person was not supposed to be able to do this.

And she?

She was a star made of razor-sharp blades. Her heart was solid fire. Blue fire. Cold fire.

And—

—*Yes,* a part of her said.

And—

—*This is how it goes.*

And—

—Something went *clunk* somewhere inside her veins and arteries and muscles and nerves.

It hurt, but it hurt like a joint popping back into place. It hurt like a sore muscle being relieved. In the backwash of that relief, Clara thought she understood the shape of what she should be.

It would have frightened her in any other circumstance, but the very walls of the corridor were beginning to bleed demons. Real, whole demons.

Clara had been trained her whole life to look for solutions, and no matter what the solution was—no matter how much it scared her—that solution was better taken than to be paralyzed by fear.

In through your center—

—suck in the pain on her skin, feel it turn to ice in her veins, let it flow around her heart and—

—she just had time to raise Bellatrix, sighting down her blade at a tunnel now riddled with cracks and filled with mangled, fanged, furious bodies and—

—And a hairline crack of white light appeared in the face of the Great Gate, cutting the writhing words across it into meaninglessness.

Mantha felt the heat of it on her back, heard a ringing in her ears, squeezed her eyes shut against the blinding light.

The cracks around the gate were still there, but they had been momentarily cauterized. Something had melted the edges of the gate so it bled together—and whatever had been caught in it, dissolved.

When she heard a gentle tread of footsteps behind her, Mantha dared open her eyes and twist her neck around.

The path she had taken to the Gate had narrowed to a small tunnel, out of which was presently gushing a stream of pale smoke. Wisps of ash— pieces of dead demon—fluttered pathetically to the ground.

The smoke was not so pale, and not so thick, as she first thought. There was a light in the tunnel—a cold, blue light—and it lit the dust in the air like a sunbeam. It wavered, as though the source were moving, and then it spilled out into the room.

It was Clara.

More accurately, it was Clara holding her sword, which was a solid bar of blue-white light that danced up along her arm almost to her shoulders. She walked carefully, but purposefully, and moved like she was uninjured, though there were two long cuts across her head and face—as if something with claws had made an attempt on her eyes—and the leather of her jacket was practically flayed off her shoulders. Her left hand was ungloved, and across its back rose an angry, red welt. The smoke which her sword illuminated seemed to be rising from her back.

At first Mantha was frightened. But when Clara did not appear angry, and when she lowered her sword and checked the room, Mantha was tempted to feel relief.

Clara was here. If Clara was here, things were going to be okay.

Except not necessarily. What was trying to happen was something not even Clara—not even this frightening, smoking Clara—could stop. It was all on Mantha. The only difference was, now Mantha knew she had to do it, no matter what. Because not even Clara would survive the Great Gate opening on top of her.

Clara must have known that. And yet here she was. And she wasn't even angry. She looked at Mantha, confused and concerned.

"You don't have to do what it tells you," she said.

Mantha nodded. She'd begun to cry and she couldn't stop herself.

"I know," she said.

"You can open it," Clara said. "But you can also close it."

That was what she had intended to do, Mantha wanted to explain. But that was not enough. The Gate had to be destroyed completely, otherwise people like Mantha, and demons like Jude Carson, would keep trying to open it.

And she could not destroy it, standing outside its Earthly door.

"It needs to be shut for good," she agreed. "I'm going to take care if that."

Clara nodded. "What can I do?"

Do this for me, Mantha wanted to say. *I'm too young for this. I'm too old for this.*

But only she could. It was the realization she had been avoiding ever since she'd first put her hand to the gate.

She and only she could close the gate for good.

So she shook her head. She tried to explain. Clara deserved to understand.

"I have to go inside," she said. "To shut it properly. The Gate is too strong. It needs to be taken apart from the inside."

Clara's mouth opened in shock. She looked horrified.

But she did not say *"That will destroy you, too,"* and Mantha appreciated that.

"I'll find my way back," she said. A promise to herself as much as to Clara. "To you and Ariel and Lady Bibbit. I'll find my way back."

She did not wait to see if Clara nodded, or if she moved to stop her. She had to do it now, while this strange, quiet assurance had her in its grip. While she hung in the balance of being too young, too old, temporary, and eternal.

She just had to turn herself sideways a little to step inside the gate. She thought she heard something, like the beginning of a scream, but then silence filled her ears.

It was quiet inside the Gate, filled with a warm redness that pressed in all around her. The gate was built of words, she saw. Special words that lived, so long as they were put in the right order.

The demon had spread himself throughout those words, pushing them into the order that would open the Gate. Mantha knew better than to do that herself.

She reached out between the words and plucked them apart, tore them into letters, unraveled the pattern.

It felt strangely calming and methodical, even though the demon screamed and thrashed against her. Then, like a dam giving way, the Great Gate burst apart.

Mantha held herself together long enough to see it shatter into dust, but by that point she was long ago and far away, and falling . . . falling . . . falling fast toward an uncertain world.

She realized too late that it was not the destruction of the gate that would destroy her; it was going to be the landing.

Around Selene the tiny light cracked apart and shattered across the blackness, the bird beneath her shed wings and feathers until it was only Albatross again. They clung to each other, hurtling toward the scattering window, into the blinding light.

They hit something that felt like a solid but it wasn't. The world slowed down around them, and for one confused moment Selene thought they'd gone underwater. Then she discovered she was breathing, and realized the water was air, and that it was *cold*.

Ariel had stayed focused on the paper in order to read without mistake, but he'd still noticed out of the corners of his eyes the white cracks which had shot through the clear glass walls, seen the blast of blue light from deep within the tunnel. Still, he kept speaking the prayer until the doorway was filled with white light and then with two dark bodies tumbling at him. He caught a glimpse of arms and legs flailing, and a foot struck him in the chest, sending him over backward.

Instinct took over, and he dropped the book to catch himself with his hands. He knew enough of the shape of the prayer to keep whispering it even as he hit the ground, but the book had been knocked out of arm's reach, and he faltered, coughed on the acrid smoke that had filled the chamber, and felt it slip away.

He crouched, defeated, wishing he had the luxury of denial. Somebody else was coughing, and hope flared painfully in his chest.

Someone had come through the atrium door at the last second. He pulled up a fold of his collar to cover his mouth, and squinted through the settling dust.

Two dark figures were bent over on all fours, alternately coughing and gasping. Ariel thought they were women, but neither was big enough to be Clara or small enough to be Mantha. Still, the dust was thick, and it was hard to see, and Ariel had been born to hope.

"Clara?" he called.

The nearer figure staggered to her feet, bringing her head and shoulders out of the dust. Something round glimmered at her side.

It was not Clara.

It was ...

Ariel blinked. Looked again.

It was *still* ...

It was Selene Shields.

Ariel had seen enough real ghosts in his time to know that she was not one. She was standing there, in nothing but a few scraps of cloth that might have once been clothes, her hair a wild black tangle around her head, holding what appeared to be a round shield on one arm. The face of it shimmered silver, even in the slanting light of Ariel's flashlight. She was looking around at the chamber with guarded uncertainty, and then her eyes fell on him and she sighed with relief.

"That you, Freeman?" Her voice sounded like her throat was filled with sandpaper.

"Shields?" he replied.

She coughed again. "More or less. Where on earth are we? We ..." she hesitated. "We *are* on earth?"

"Atrium of the Great Gate," he said. *How are you here?* He wanted to ask. *They said you fell. Clara saw you fall ...*

But Selene was gazing around the atrium, now more or less clear of dust, with growing apprehension. She was beginning to shiver, and no wonder. Aside from the tattered remains of her maroon work shirt, Ariel didn't think she had on any clothes at all. Quickly he turned his gaze aside and began unzipping his down jacket.

"Presently, we're at the bottom of Lake Huron. There's been an attempted apocalypse," he explained, shrugging off his coat and *damn* it was cold without it. Getting to his feet he held it up and approached Selene.

"Bottom of Lake Huron," she repeated. She sighed. "What is it with *lakes?*"

Ariel didn't know how to answer that question, but it appeared it was not directed at him. Selene had turned her head back and down, speaking to the second figure, who was still quivering on the floor. Ariel hadn't gotten a good look at them because they were the same pale color as the dust that had settled like snow over the ground, but now they sprang up—like someone literally on a spring—and he was confronted by a pale, slender young woman with feathery, white hair, and dark eyes that flashed rainbow at him.

"*You!*" she cried. She had a silky, melodious voice, and something about her face lit recognition in Ariel's mind. But he could not place her for the life of him.

Yet she seemed to know him, and was glad to see him. Ariel was not inclined to argue with that.

"Yes," he said, still holding the jacket out to Selene. "I'm me. You can have my blazer in a second."

The pale woman looked down at herself in confusion, apparently noticing for the first time that all she was wearing was a simple, sleeveless dress of knitted gray wool. She shrugged. Looked back up at him.

"I *remember!*" she exclaimed.

"Oh?" said Selene, taking Ariel's coat and wrapping it tight around her shoulders. "Remember what?"

"More and more," said the pale woman. She'd begun to hop back and forth from foot to foot. She had bare feet, but this didn't seem to bother her. She pointed excitedly at Ariel.

"You, *you*," she said. "I remember you! And if you're here, then—" she broke off, turning, for the first time, to look behind them, to where the atrium door had been.

It was shut, but broken by a star-shaped hole where the stone had cracked and shattered. The source of the dust, Ariel realized. It didn't matter that his prayer had been broken. The door had been blasted open.

"Then *what?*" Selene asked.

The pale woman turned back to them, and for a moment it looked like she wore a rainbow crown, and her shoulders were surmounted by long, white wings. She was smiling blazingly, triumphantly. And she sang, very softly:

"*Remember what the darkness said, they're not dead, they're not dead!*"

And, repeating the final three words, she climbed through the broken door and dashed off into the corridor beyond, a halo of rainbow light moving with her.

Beside him, Selene sighed—"There she goes again,"—and began hobbling after.

Ariel had just the presence of mind to snatch up his dropped book, the cheat sheet, and his briefcase, and then he was sprinting off in pursuit of the two women.

The Great Gate collapsed inward. That was the only reason Clara survived. One last gift from Mantha, though she didn't appreciate it at the time. She was left in darkness, the only light the dim glow of Bellatrix, and the pale yellow of the melted stump of stone which was all that remained of the Great Gate's Earthly door. Yet she threw herself upon it, her mind so full of screaming that no rational thought could be heard.

She was the one screaming. Quite shamefully, but she didn't care. It was the only way to drown out the quiet, evil voices she could already hear starting up in the back of her head.

You're worthless at protecting people. You're a failure. You're weak.

This was worse than Flammard, worse than Schiavona, worse than mother . . . Clara was no stranger to loss and disappointment, but familiarity with those feelings did not dull the pain. It made it worse. Because she knew what was coming.

Was this worse than Selene?

Clara wasn't sure. She felt many of the same feelings of shame and disappointment and horror. She had failed Selene, and she had failed Mantha.

Worthless.

She was throwing herself at the melted stump now. Felt it crack under the force of her body.

Strong enough to take rocks apart. Not strong enough to save the people she cared about.

All she could do was cry and scream, curled against the broken piece of rock. How pathetic. And just when she thought she'd wrung herself out, she remembered Mantha's face as she stepped into the Gate. The last time she would ever see her. And the screams started again.

For a time she became her tears and screams, a creature of pure grief, devoid of purpose.

She did not hear the footsteps in the tunnel. Did not mark the wash of rainbow light that filled the chamber. She did not notice the pale woman who came and knelt beside her until she felt the touch of cool fingers on her shoulder.

Then she stopped screaming out of pure surprise. Looked up into a round face with dark eyes in whose depths glimmered countless, unnamable colors.

"Shhh," said the woman, and Clara was so confused she also stopped crying.

"I'm so sorry," the pale woman was saying. "I didn't want to hurt you. It wasn't the Gate which shattered me, it was the impact after the fall."

Clara stared at her. She should be asking questions. But she had no heart left, and the woman went on talking, as if she was continuing a conversation they had just been having.

"It was such a huge blast," she was saying. "I must have gotten knocked backward a long time, and it took ages to get myself together again. Literally ages. But I'm glad . . . because this means it hasn't been so long for you."

The vision smiled, hopeful.

Clara was so confounded now she couldn't even sniffle. She stared at this strange, pale woman. Surely, a stranger. Yet surely, she knew her. Or she had known her sister. Or her daughter.

The face leaned in closer, the smile becoming almost conspiratorial.

"I forgot a lot of things," the pale woman whispered. "But I always *knew* them, if you know what I mean."

Somewhere in the back of Clara's throat, she found her voice.

"Who are you?"

The pale woman's smile, if possible, grew even wider.

"I am the granddaughter of the Nameless God," she said, as if this was the greatest joke of all time. "I am the white bird, the albatross. The Calamity, Destroyer of the Great Gate. I am the lightning that strikes twice."

Clara felt her mind seize up as she began to recognize the woman's voice. It was older, fuller, and she'd changed as she'd grown. The paleness made her look very different as well.

Mostly, though, it was the emotional whiplash that held her in shock. Grief did not let go its hooks so easily. She did not dare believe what was sitting, nose to nose, in front of her.

"Clara," whispered the pale woman. "I did promise, didn't I? And I *kept* my promise—even if I forgot! See? I came back, Clara. *I came back.*"

"You're not . . . Mantha?" Clara choked.

"*Mantha.*" The pale woman nodded, her smile sparkling. "Yes," she said. "That was what you called me! That was what I called myself . . . I'd forgotten that too, you see—even though I always knew. Oh, oh, and Clara—*Clara*," she said, something sparking in her eyes. "I found your moon, Clara! I found her, and even though I didn't know her, I knew she was important! I brought *her* back, too, Clara! I brought us *both* back!"

"You brought *who?*" Clara said, now truly confused. She was not sure she knew this older, pale Mantha. Though inches separated their faces, it seemed an eternity stretched between their souls.

"Your *moon*," said the new, old, pale Mantha, and gently turning her shoulder, pointed back to the tunnel opening—

—to where Selene was picking her way through the debris of broken stone and demon corpses. She was barefoot and carried a round shield with a waxing gibbous moon in burnished silver on its face. It reflected the rainbow light pouring out of Mantha's shoulders, shining like a small searchlight. She looked disgusted and a little worried, and very, very much alive.

Selene had heard the screams as soon as Albatross pushed the rotting carcass of a demon out of their way. They made her heart want to climb up into her throat. Even after literally going through Hell, she'd never heard anything like them. They made the Labyrinth of Pain sound feeble. She wanted to run faster, but the floor was slippery with demon blood and scattered with sharp chips of bone and rock that stung her feet. And whatever pain tolerance she'd developed in Hell had vanished, so that the slightest prick now made her wince and limp. It was like she was feeling everything fresh again.

Perhaps that was why she'd been struck motionless at the sight of Clara doubled up and sobbing, her sword lying, apparently forgotten, at her side. It was so outside the natural order of things it gave her momentary doubt as to whether they had actually escaped Hell or not.

But Albatross was smiling, patting Clara on the shoulder, pointing at her, and whispering in Clara's ear.

Then Clara looked at her, and nothing on Earth or in Hell could have prepared Selene for the impact of that gaze. It was shocked, desolate, disbelieving. Selene had never seen Clara so openly emotional, and it shook her to the core.

It was the same expression she had glimpsed, as she fell through the skies of Purgatory. Only this was a hundred times worse, because it did not go away.

Then she remembered how Shae had always seemed so confident, almost callous, but was secretly caring and filled with self-doubt. *Nordsterns*. She sighed.

"Hey-o," she said, waving her free hand, walking slowly over the smooth floor of the cave. It was warm under her feet, as if it had recently been in the sun. It felt . . . *nice*. As intensely nice as the shards of demon bone had hurt.

It felt *real*.

Wherever this was, it wasn't Hell. The knowledge of that made Selene smile, even though Clara still looked ready to go to pieces. Selene crossed the floor in measured steps, enjoying the feeling of each one.

"Hey," she said again, once she was closer. "You okay there?"

Clara didn't even get up, but staggered forward on her knees and threw her arms around Selene's waist. She clung there, her whole body shaking, whispering something over and over under her breath. Selene thought it was *"I'm sorry."*

"Ah, okay, that's all right," Selene said, still unsure how to deal with Clara having a meltdown. One that had been building up for some time now, by the feel of the arms around her waist. Awkwardly she draped her arms over Clara's shoulders—something had torn up her jacket, but the skin underneath looked intact—and patted the broad back through the sword's harness.

"Okay," Selene said. "Okay. Yep. Hug time. Yeah. It's all good. Wring it out, girl. This shirt has literally been through Hell, you can't possibly do anything worse to it. Sorry, was that too soon?"

Clara, at the mention of Hell, had starting sobbing against Selene's chest, choked gasps and hiccups worthy of a toddler. She was well and truly into it now. Selene wished she had some soda pop or a cookie to give her.

"It's okay," Selene repeated. "I'm okay, you're gonna be okay. We're all gonna be A-okay."

Now Clara was blubbering something about being a failure. Selene resisted the urge to roll her eyes.

"Don't even go there," Selene said, and realizing she would eventually have to tell Clara what had happened to Shae, added, "we none of us can do everything we want to."

"And you *didn't* fail me," Albatross said, leaning over and patting Clara's shoulder. "You were my ladder out."

"Hang on, you *know* her?" Selene asked.

"In another life," Albatross said, a little sadly. "Before I fell. I knew you, too," she said, looking up past Selene, who, looking behind her, saw Ariel standing by the tunnel entrance. He was casting his flashlight this way and that, systematically scanning the place for threats. Selene appreciated that, though she didn't understand why he was looking increasingly worried—there was nothing else here except them.

"Where is Mantha?" he asked, in that tense, hard way a parent asks after their child.

"Uh-oh," said Selene. But Albatross just smiled and stood up, gesturing at herself.

"I'm here," she said. "More of me than before, actually."

Ariel looked at her sideways. Then his eyes widened in recognition. "*Mantha?*" he said.

"*Who* is Mantha?" Selene asked, absentmindedly rocking Clara back and forth like she was soothing a crying baby.

"I am," said Albatross. "Or, I *was*. Mantha was the human part of me, born on Earth. A baby antichrist who did something very dangerous and very brave."

Selene nodded at her encouragingly. Albatross sighed.

"She went into the Grate Gate instead of opening it, and pulled it down around her. But she got out," she added, looking at Clara. "At the last instant, she got out. She was pulled back to Hell, to the place where she was conceived, and was broken there. Scattered. It took me a long time to put myself back together again, and in that time I grew. I think it's most accurate to say, Mantha is a part of me. The part that lives here, on Earth. I remember more and more, the longer I am here." She grinned around at all of them.

In Selene's arms, Clara had stilled, but was breathing deeply, carefully. Deliberate, calming breaths. Soon she would have her emotional armor up again, but for the moment Selene let her be.

"You were *twelve* yesterday," Ariel was saying. He sounded upset, but not angry.

Oh lily white ladies, Selene thought. *Don't let him start crying, too.*

"Yesterday to you," Albatross answered, patiently. "Time is relative, and flowed differently inside the Gate. It's been longer for me—for us—than it has for you."

Slowly, Ariel edged around in front of Selene, looking at Albatross with his head tilted sideways. He set down his briefcase.

"You destroyed the Great Gate," he said.

Albatross nodded, proudly. "When I was just Sammy," she said, "before she fell."

"You destroyed the *Great Gate*," Ariel repeated. He turned around, his eyes were shining, he looked like a man touched by grace. "The Great Gate is *gone*," he said.

Even considering everything that had happened, and everything she had just seen and learned, Selene was surprised that she had not yet realized what this meant.

"The Great Gate is *gone*," she repeated.

"No more apocalypse! No more meddling angels! *No more demons!*" Ariel said.

"Well, not from that side of things," Albatross began, but Ariel shook his head.

"Not in the way it has been," he said, and began to laugh. "The Great Gate is *gone!*" He took Albatross by the hand and hugged her, then he hugged Selene, then he hugged Clara from behind.

"No more Great Gate!" he repeated.

"No more Great Gate," Albatross declared, and came around to drape her arms across all three of them.

"Yay," said Selene. "Awkward group hug. Good job, everybody. Yay."

But under her arms, Clara had frozen. Her head moved, and she said:

"No more Great Gate. We need to get out."

"Oh," said Ariel, all the joy going out of his face in an instant. "Oh *crap*. We do."

"Jill," Clara said, getting up, shedding people as she went. In a flash she grabbed her sword and sheathed it. "We need to get back to Jill."

"Where is Jill?" asked Selene. "What's she done now?"

Clara gave her a blank look.

"We can explain later," Ariel said, picking up his briefcase again. "We need to move. Run."

"I *ain't* running through *that*," Selene declared, pointing at the tunnel and then at her bare feet.

"Of course not," agreed Clara, and scooped her up as if she were a child.

"We'll be okay," Albatross was saying, even as they hurried into the tunnel. "Mishipeshu doesn't want us trapped here anymore than we want to be. He'll keep the road open."

"Yes, but we're still in the atrium," said Clara. "And you *destroyed the Great Gate*."

Oh, thought Selene. *Well crap.*

But they made it through the tunnel before it collapsed. Clara did not pause to look back, and so Selene only heard the roar, the crash and groan of breaking rock.

Behind them, Albatross giggled. Selene wondered if she had been holding it open for them.

They were on a dark road, and all around them rose walls of black glass. These closed in around them, but at the far end was a bright red light.

Two lights.

Taillights.

The taillights of a truck.

Out through the gap between the walls, and Clara slipped a little in the soft ground. She regained her balance the next instant, and then she was sliding to a halt beside Arcana.

The driver's door opened, and Jill put her head out.

She looked exactly as Selene remembered, right down to the irritated frown.

"Clara," she began. "What happen—"

Then she saw Selene.

"Selene?" she said.

Selene wagged her shield at her. "Hi," she said. "I'm back."

"*Selene!*" Jill shouted. Shocked. Amazed. Disbelieving.

But not crying. Yet.

"Yep," said Selene. "It me."

"*Selene!*" Jill repeated. She seemed unable to get past that one word.

"Everybody in!" Ariel shouted, pulling open the rear door and climbing inside. "We gotta move!"

"Wait," said Jill. "Where's Mantha?"

"I'm here!" Albatross replied. She'd climbed into the bed of the truck, alongside a pale dog with red ears, who wagged its tail and tried to lick her face.

Jill looked. Saw Albatross. Shook her head.

"Who—what—"

"*Later!*" Clara said, opening the rear door and setting Selene on the back seat. "Drive, Jill!"

But Jill did not get back inside. She stared at Albatross, at Selene, then back at Albatross.

"Oh for f—do *I* have to drive?" Selene said. She climbed forward between the seats, shoving her shield into Ariel's lap, and dragged Jill in by her coat. "Move over," she commanded, and Jill did, all the while staring at her with wide, red eyes.

"Holy cow, you *are* back," she whispered.

"That's what I *said.*" Selene pulled the driver's door shut, put down the parking brake, and revved the engine.

The sound of Arcana roaring to life was the sweetest sound she'd heard in… well in a long time. His lights illuminated a black road in front of them. Selene didn't have to be told to know the way out was straight ahead.

No one had even been remotely tempted to follow Arcana down the impossible road into the lake, though Gadget happily went down to the point where the waves rose just over her head and took a lot of pictures with Okedo's phone. They also tested a "magic wand" tool, which was a clear plastic tube filled with flakes of silver, palladium, and platinum. Chuy didn't look close enough to see how it worked, but he gathered it was something like a fairy stone in that it could indicate when something intensely magical was happening.

Apparently it was a success, though anyone could have told you something strange was going on by the behavior of the water. It just kept going up and back on itself, keeping the road open.

Then, in the dead hours of the early morning, there was a small earthquake. Not enough to do any damage, but Chuy, who'd spent enough time in So-Cal, recognized the feeling.

The Earth shivered. A wind rushed down upon them, from the south this time. Not a wind being pushed ahead of a storm—this was air rushing in to fill a sudden void. And then the waves collapsed.

They fell together smoothly, like someone drawing up a zipper, and in less than a minute there was no road, but the clear, black, impenetrable surface of the lake.

As much as she was tempted to floor the gas pedal and rip their way out as fast as possible, Selene knew better than to try that on the wet, silty road. They seemed to be in a tunnel made of shimmering, glimmering stone that reflected Arcana's headlights in crazy ripples. Something pale moved beyond the surface, and with a jolt Selene realized it was water.

They were in a tunnel of *water.*

"Lake Huron," Ariel explained, when she asked. "The gate manifested under Lake Huron."

"But the gate collapsed," Selene said. "What's keeping this tunnel open?"

"The same thing that made it in the first place," Clara said. "Mishipeshu."

"Mishi-what now?" Selene said.

"The water panther," Ariel said.

"A *water panther?*" Selene repeated.

Water panthers were . . . what? Ojibwe? What was a water panther doing helping them?

Sudden and unbidden, a memory of Hell surfaced in her mind. The polar bear on the ice, fishing for damned souls.

There was a connection there, and in chasing it, Selene's mind wandered.

"Mind the shoulder!" Ariel shouted.

Arcana's right side had drifted close to the water wall. But so had his left side. No—the tunnel was narrowing. Selene rolled down the window and shouted out it:

"Albatross! Help!"

"Keep driving," Albatross replied, her voice seeming to come from inside the cab. Then, a moment later: "Go faster."

"Hold on, then," Selene shouted, and rolled up her window.

"Will she be all right out there?" Jill asked.

"Sure," said Selene. "What about your dog?"

"Frosty is a Yell Hound," said Clara.

"Ah," said Selene. "*Okay* then."

She revved Arcana's engine and methodically shifted up until the speedometer told her they were holding sixty.

It felt like hydroplaning. Selene didn't dare steer, just held the wheel firmly between her hands. Ahead of them Arcana's headlights made beams of yellow through a blue-green world. The sound of his engine grew soft. Like something in the distance. It became mixed with something else. The sound of hoofbeats.

Under her foot, Selene felt the gas pedal depress of its own accord. Arcana's brights came on, and the truck accelerated through the water in . . . in leaps and bounds.

It was a long, black road through an endless, black world in which huge shapes drifted; sleepy, curious. And the red truck dashed through it, leaving a stream of bubbles in its wake.

There was a storage chest mounted in the back, right behind the cab, and Frosty stood with her front paws up on it, her mouth wide open, her coat sparkling pearl and gold.

Albatross braced one foot on the bed of the truck, one foot on top of the chest, beside Frosty, and balancing there, she raised her arms.

A rainbow of light arced from one hand to the other, growing so it encompassed the whole vehicle. Ghostly shapes gathered behind it, pale dogs with red ears, leaping and wagging their tails.

And Albatross began to sing.

And inside Arcana's cab, the radio came on.

"*Ten thousand ages ago in someone else's life, I tried to believe in my god's word—now I put my faith into the turning earth!*"

And the sky opened above them. Clear, dark, and studded with countless stars. Arcana's high beams made a road of light across the surface of the lake, and he, eager and red, crowned by the rainbow, bounded gladly down it.

Lady Bibbit staggered into the parking lot, panting and clutching the stitches in her side, to find Professor Okedo arguing with their new operative, Chuy, while Tucker stood by, looking miserable.

"What's happened?" she cried, turning to Gadget as the most reliable source of information.

The goblin shrugged.

"Tunnel collapsed, didn't it," she said. "Jill and Ariel and Clara were all down there, with the truck."

"Tunnel?" said Lady Bibbit. "What tunnel?"

"Tunnel through the water," Gadget said. "They went down there to stop Mantha opening the Great Gate."

Lady Bibbit felt like crying, but she didn't have the breath. Before she could catch enough to scream even once, however, a shocked silence rolled over the parking lot.

A light had appeared in the distance, out upon the water. It cast a long streak of yellow which glimmered on the choppy waves, and as they watched, it grew steadily larger.

It appeared to bound across the surface of the water, and Lady Bibbit thought she saw, at least for a moment, the shadowy silhouette of a huge ram, his head lowered, galloping across the surface. His eyes were twin yellow headlamps and lit his path straight to the shore.

Then the vision faded, and it was just a pair of headlights, and the distant sound of a diesel engine, growing swiftly louder. And then there was the splash of wheels in shallow water, and then Arcana was driving up the boat ramp, and they scattered as he came to a screeching halt halfway down the parking lot, dripping water and rumbling happily.

Selene put on the parking brake, put the truck in first, and turned off the ignition. Almost reproachfully, the engine gurgled into silence and the radio faded out. She swallowed. There was bare, cracked pavement in front of them. There was Jill's old professor, and a small Mexican-looking man, and a goblin, and a four-foot tall rabbit in a denim dress.

"This is it," Ariel said, a little weakly. "We made it."

"We made it," Selene repeated.

"Where's Mantha?" Clara asked, twisting around in the backseat.

"Where's Frosty?" Jill said.

For answer, the pale dog with red ears pawed at the back window and barked.

But Albatross wasn't with her.

Albatross had vaulted the cab of the truck, slid down his windshield and across his nose, and gone bounding off across the pavement, where she picked up the rabbit and hugged her tightly, swinging her around in the air while the rabbit laughed and cried, and did her best to hug back.

Behind them lay the lake, dark and placidly impenetrable. Above them shone the stars. And below them, though none but perhaps Albatross could feel it, Earth turned inexorably toward morning.

I saw the moon
when I was young
and hopeful
But the years flowed past
and they took my wonder
I saw the moon
when I was lost
and I was listless
Burned by the day
And the sins of man
consumed me

Ten thousand ages ago
in someone else's life
I tried to believe in my god's word
Now I put my faith
into the turning earth.

Albatross fell asleep in the backseat, Lady Bibbit on her lap. Jill, safely ensconced in her daysuit, was disappointed.

"There'll be plenty of time for questions later," Lady Bibbit told her sharply. "She's had a hard night. Year. Century. Eternity. Whatever."

Clara drove. Arcana rumbled happily under her hands and feet. She didn't bother mentioning that his gas gauge still read as full, or that his cruise control automatically set itself to the speed limit. They would eventually have to look at him, and his increasingly opinionated behavior, but for now she had to extend all her will power to focusing on the road in front of them, otherwise she'd constantly be glancing at Mantha—and it *was* Mantha, even if she'd aged ten years and bleached her hair—in the rearview mirror, or sideways at the woman in the passenger seat, just to make sure she was still there.

Selene sat with her face pressed up against the window, staring, staring, staring at the landscape as it rolled past. Small towns and empty fields, gray skies with wispy clouds. Junkyards, gas stations, shopping malls, brief preserves of forest.

It was all so beautiful and comforting. So wonderfully, blissfully *normal.*

They'd found a pair of sweatpants and a cotton shirt for her wear, thick socks for her feet, and a pair of sunglasses, since otherwise her eyes hurt from the sunlight. It was so much brighter than she remembered.

Her work shirt, such as it was, had been wrapped around her shield, which was resting against her knees. It was still shield-sized. If anything, it was perhaps a little bigger. No one had yet asked where she had got it, or what had happened to her charm. Selene felt the matter was one for another day. A day with many intervening days between it and the present one.

They passed a billboard advertising a Christmas tree farm.

"Only a year?" she asked. "It's only been a year?"

"For us," said Clara. "Though it felt longer," she added.

"Felt longer to me, too," Selene said, and smiled.

Only a year. A real, solid, earth year. One trip around the sun, which was now threatening to burn right through the thin layer of clouds. Selene shut her eyes against the glare, and basked in the light.

> *Mother Earth*
> *and Daughter Moon*
> *part the seas of dark*
> *and the seas of death*
> *before me*
>
> *Across the plain*
> *I walk with grace*
> *And I marvel upon*
> *a magical*
> *and awe-inspiring new place*

Chuy drove behind the truck and trailer. Ariel was pensive, alternately staring out the window, then down at his hands.

"How old do you think she is now?" Chuy asked.

"Hard to say," Ariel replied. He sighed, rubbing his eyes. "Equivalent of eighteen, nineteen? But . . . not normal. She spent god-knows how much time in Hell before Selene found her, and you know how time goes screwy down there."

"So . . . basically you missed adolescent and teenage Mantha, that ain't such a bad deal!"

Ariel laughed, but there was no humor in it. He'd been that way, a little blank and hollow, ever since he came out of the tunnel.

Chuy understood. It had been a hard night, even if the outcome had been better than any of them had hoped.

No one was dead.

But something had been lost.

"She's not really Mantha anymore," Ariel said, confirming Chuy's suspicions. "She's . . . more."

"Kids do that, as they grow up," Chuy said.

"You don't have any kids," Ariel pointed out.

"Got eight nieces and three nephews," Chuy said. "Missed graduations and quinceañeras. It's always a shocker, man. Gotta be bad when you lose it in an instant."

Ariel nodded, but his smile this time was a little brighter, a little warmer.

He'd get better, with time.

"One thing I don't know if I'll get used to is all this . . . suddenly apocalypse and people coming back from Hell and flipping Native monsters showing up. Is it like this all the time with Jill?"

Ariel sighed.

"I have a feeling," he said, "that's it's gonna be like this more and more."

For the Earth is aside from our tyrants
Her laws are larger than our lives
So I turn to Earth
And with her, face the light

Okedo had briefed Lansing over the phone en route, and so the entire daytime staff of MCSIR was gathered at the front entrance when the caravan of vehicles arrived. Someone—probably Tamerlain, from how proudly they were grinning—had made a makeshift banner out of sheets of paper taped together with a letter on each one. They had hung it under the eaves, where it was difficult to read, but still discernible.

"What does that mean?" Selene asked, when they pulled up outside.

"It's the name of our organization," Jill said, voice clipped inside her daysuit.

"I thought you said your org's name was Mixer," Selene said.

"That's the acronym," Jill said. "M C S I R." She hesitated. "It's the Moonshield Center for Supernatural Investigation and Research."

Selene looked out at the banner again, uncharacteristically silent.

"Oh," she said eventually.

Then, a little while later, in a stronger voice, she said:

"Is that a *zombie?*"

"Come on," said Clara, touching her elbow. "I'll introduce you."

"Like hell," said Selene, unbuckling herself. "What the dingus have you got a zombie working for you? Jill, what have you been *doing?* I leave for *one year* and you've bought Michigan Central Station, adopted a Yell Hound, and hired a *zombie!* Jill!"

But Jill had already gotten out and had gone around the front of the truck, waving happily at the motley crew assembled on the front steps.

"Hey guys," she was saying. "Thanks for all your help! We have some exciting news, and someone *very important* I want you all to meet."

Though the Earth is aside from our tyrants
I am caught between two worlds
But I chose life
and ride the turning earth!

—With Her Face the Light/*Freud Purple*

THE LADY IN THE GRAY SUIT

Sydney, New South Wales
Australia
Late November

It was a bright, sunny November day, the first truly hot day of the season and a harbinger of summer to come. Curbing the city where it met the bay, the crescent of white-gold sand sparkled in the morning light, and the sea glimmered enticingly blue-green, except where it was interrupted by photogenic white waves, breaking elegantly on the beach. As the first rays of the morning sun touched the houses huddled on the cliff at the north end, the crescent of beach below was momentarily pristine, the wet sand at its edge reflecting the pale sky. A lone dawn runner, whose footprints faded after her passing with the wash of the surf, was the only sign of human life upon the shore. Then with a grumble and a cough a four-wheeler emerged from under the squat, round tower which dominated the center of the beach, towing behind it a trailer loaded with surfboards and poles with flags on the end. Methodically it made its way down the beach, stopping at intervals so the people driving it—they were both men—could get out and set up poles with red-and-yellow flags, or lay out a surfboard, or both. They greeted the runner as the two parties passed, waving and smiling. They were in a good mood. It was early, the beach was empty, it was going to be a beautiful day. Anything could happen.

Anything could happen, but one could live in hope.

The four-wheeler reached the south end of the crescent, where the water was darker and smoother from the current of spent surf running off the shore. The vehicle stopped. The men got out and began setting up surfboards—big, blue things with white rope handles on the edges—on little stands which held them in such a way that someone could grab them by the handles as they ran past at full speed into the water. They set up poles which held, not flags, but big rectangular signs that said, in letters and in pictures "DANGEROUS CURRENT: NO SWIMMING."

They were mostly looking at what they were doing. But they were lifeguards—it said so in big, dark blue letters across the backs of their light blue rash guards—and a lifeguard can never really stop looking at the water. Not as long as there is water to look at. Something about always wanting to check: Is it clear? Is it normal? Can I see through that spot of glare *now?*

Even so, neither of them noticed the dark shape that moved in, slicing down the edge of the rip like it could smell the current, until its dorsal fin broke a small wave and a combination of training and instinct made both men stop what they were doing and turn to look.

So they were both watching when the shark, huge and gray-green and shining wetly in the early sun, drove itself out of the waves and onto the beach, thrashing sand and flailing.

"*Jesus*, Mary and—" said the older man, who had had a lot of practice carefully not swearing, but he was cut off by his younger partner shouting a word which, had they been on television, would have gotten him a long, loud, BLEEP.

"What's it *doing?*" he asked.

"That's a *shark*," said the older one, as if he had to say the words to believe what he was seeing.

"It's *on the beach*," said the younger one.

It was a shark. And it was on the beach. It had barely gotten clear of the wave which had brought it to shore, and now it was lying, belly down, tail still thrashing, as if it would swim right up the sand to them.

If it had been a dolphin, or a whale, or even just a smaller shark, the men would probably have tried to get it back in the water. As it was, it was nearly four meters of powerful finned body lying in the sand. Even if it hadn't had an open mouth full of sharp, serrated teeth, they would have been hard pressed to get its bulk back into the surf on their own.

The older man, who was only older by relative standards—his hair was still mostly blond and even with his collection of crow's feet wrinkles he would have compared favorably in appearance to men ten years younger— went over to the four-wheeler and took out the radio, while his partner—a downright boyish twenty-three whose powerful shoulders looked to be in danger of stretching his uniform top beyond repair—danced around the shark, failing to get a grip on its tail but succeeding admirably in giving a vocabulary lesson in local New South Wales cursing.

"Rhino One to Tower," said the older guard into the radio. "We have a . . . a shark just leapt outta the water at Backpacker's."

"Copy, Rhino One," came the crackling reply. There was a beat. "You said a *what* came out of the water?"

"A shark," said the lifeguard, carefully separating the two words. "I . . . I think it's a great white, maybe a tiger. It's still alive so if you could, I dunno, bring the Jet Ski down here maybe we can tow it off?"

There was another beat, probably as Cornflake got out his binoculars to see for himself.

Anyone else would have demanded more explanations, would have had to spend at least ten minutes exclaiming at the improbability of the event, might have even denied it happening.

But Cornflake hadn't been a Team Leader with the Waverley Council Lifeguards for five seasons for nothing. After about two seconds his voice came through again, his tone hardly changed except that now he sounded properly awake.

"Yeah, I see you Bugs. We'll get the Jet Ski down there with some rope but I don't know if we'll make it in time."

"Copy, thanks Tower," said Bugs, and clipped the radio to the waistband of his board shorts to go help Pebbles splash water over the shark.

The crowd of early morning beachgoers were temporarily halted in their progress down to the surf by the appearance of a second four-wheeler, this one towing a trailer with a Jet Ski mounted on the back, as it ran down the beach at top speed. It arrived at the south end where, with some quick backing and filling that left deep trenches in the sand, it got the trailer down to the surf's edge, and its driver got out to launch the Jet Ski.

The Jet Ski, big and heavy with the floating sledge trailing behind it, threatened to topple over multiple times while the three men figured out a rope-and-carabiner arrangement that they could attach to the shark's tail (now flopping weekly) and to the Jet Ski in such a way that Vanna, who was riding the thing, could let go very quickly if the shark recovered once it was back in the water.

Which, Bugs was unsurprised to realize, he *did* want it to recover. Far, far away from him, yes, but he held no personal animosity toward sharks—not even the man-eaters. In the back of his mind he was already thinking: *we can't let people in the water until it's out past the nets. If it dies, we'll have to call the rangers. We should probably call the rangers, anyway.*

But that was Cornflake's job. All he had to worry about was not getting his feet bitten off while he helped Pebbles throw a loop of rope around the shark's tail. They'd tied a carabiner to the end of it and ran the rope through itself, so that once pulled tight it wouldn't slip off, but when whoever was holding the other end let go, it would go loose and (hopefully) release the shark.

In the end Pebbles had to climb on the back of the Jet Ski to manage the rope while Vanna drove them off the beach and into the rip, using the current to help move them past the breakers and the impact zone, out to the relative calm of the bay.

Bugs stood on the beach, at the head of the trench left by the shark as it had been dragged, still flailing, into the water. The surf was washing it clean with each new wave, and soon there would be no sign that anything untoward had happened, except for the nervous lifeguard standing at attention, sand kicked up all over his uniform shorts and rash guard, clutching the radio to his neck like it was a lifeline.

Squinting into the sun, Bugs saw the Jet Ski turn, saw motion as Pebbles waved the rope back and forth, then dropped the rope in a hurry and scrambled up onto the Jet Ski behind Vanna so quickly he nearly brought them over.

"Jet Ski, can you give us an update?" Cornflake asked over the radio.

"No worries," said Vanna, who even at that moment was in danger of being smothered by the much-larger Pebbles. "It's swum away."

"Uh . . . copy that, Jet Ski. Which way was it swimming?"

"It's just . . . uh . . . " Bugs saw Vanna's torso twist this way and that. "Actually it's . . . it's sort of swimming around us. But . . . but not well. It looks confused."

Only Vanna, all of five feet tall and 45 kilos soaking wet, could sound that calm while astride a Jet Ski, a nervous Pebbles clutching his shoulders, while a shark circled him in open water. But that was Vanna for you, and one of the reasons he'd been hired straight out of his traineeship the minute he'd turned eighteen.

"Tower, I'm gonna try to herd it out to sea," Vanna said over the radio. "But you should probably try to keep people out of the water until then."

"Right," said Cornflake, heavily. "Copy that, Jet Ski. Uh . . . good luck."

He wasn't just wishing Vanna good luck, Bugs knew. The morning was growing hotter by the minute and the crowds up on the parade, and in the carpark, and on the ramps, were moving steadily and purposefully toward the enticing waters of the sea. There was very little they could do to stop them, short of sounding the shark alarm, which—Bugs checked his watch—it wasn't even 8 a.m. yet.

In the moment he had looked down, a gaggle of tourists had dumped their backpacks at the foot of the DANGEROUS CURRENT: NO SWIMMING sign, kicked off their shoes, and when he looked up they were frolicking fully clothed in the frothing white waves inches from where the shark had beached.

Bugs sighed and went to work.

It took Vanna almost two hours to herd the shark out into open water, by which time they had sounded the alarm twice and then, as the day progressed into true heat, gave up and started allowing swimmers in a limited area at the north end. It made for crowded water, full of bobbing bodies and heads and waving arms, which made Bugs's blood pressure go up. It was almost a relief to do the inevitable Rhino runs down to the south end to paddle out and fetch in people from Backpacker's.

"There was a *shark*, right *here*," he told his latest patient, once he had her on the sand.

She was a tourist—of course she was—but at least she spoke English. American English, no less. She glared at him from under her ridiculous yellow sunhat, now limp and floppy from having been doused in saltwater, and put her hands on her hips.

She was about sixty, wearing an old-fashioned onesie with loud orange and purple horizontal stripes, white-out sunblock on her substantial nose, and blue mesh water slippers. She had also been wearing a mask and snorkel but this had come off in the rescue, and now it was dangling by the strap looped around one arm.

"Yes," she said, somehow managing to stare down her white nose at him even though she was barely taller than Vanna. "I *know*."

"Then why were you in the water?" *You daft old sheila,* Bugs did not add, because he was a professional and wanted to stay one.

"Because," the woman said, and then stopped. Threw up her hands. "Never mind. You boys wouldn't understand."

The superiority in her tone annoyed Bugs, but he had spent the better part of his adult life working with people who annoyed him. He'd learned not to let it show.

The important thing wasn't that you made them see the error of their ways.

The *important thing* was that they walked away from the beach, breathing on their own.

He swung an arm out, pointing at the DANGEROUS CURRENT: NO SWIMMING sign, and then north, up the beach, where Drover was living up to his nickname, corralling beachgoers and keeping them on the north end with a combination of the megaphone and his blindingly white smile.

"Please don't swim here," he said. "There's a dangerous current, *and* we had a shark *on the beach* this morning. We are *trying* to keep people safe. *Please* swim up there, between the red-and-yellow flags."

The woman looked. Narrowed her eyes. She reached into the pocket of her soaking swimsuit and pulled out a pair of sunglasses which had somehow survived her aborted swim and the board ride back to shore. She shook the water off them, put them on, and peered up the beach.

Then suddenly she smiled.

"Yes," she said. "Oh yes, you're right, that's *much* better."

She took a step up the beach, and then stopped. She looked from Bugs to the Rhino and back again.

"Can you give us a lift, lifeguard?"

Bugs sighed. *Well, it'll get her away from Backpacker's.*

As soon as they were in the Rhino Bugs regretted his decision, because the woman started pestering him with questions.

"A shark, you say?" "What kind of shark?" "What happened to it?" "Where is it now?"

"Yes, a shark." "I dunno, a big one. Like a great white or a tiger or maybe a bull shark." "We dragged it off the beach."

To answer the last question Bugs stopped the Rhino and pointed out to sea, where Vanna was just visible out beyond the breakers, almost clear of Mackenzies Point, still with Pebbles clinging to his back.

"What are they doing with it?" the woman asked.

As if in answer to her question the radio came on and Vanna, now beginning to sound a little annoyed, said, "Jet Ski to Tower. Can you send the other ski out to Mackenzies? Our friend doesn't want to go out to sea and we need a break."

"Uh, yeah copy that Jet Ski," said the voice of Haitchbee, who had apparently relieved Cornflake but was still being briefed on the early morning events. "You'll also see air patrol pretty soon. They're just gonna come and help get us a visual."

"Copy that, Tower."

Bugs was about to start the engine again when Pebbles, apparently leaning over Vanna's shoulder to speak breathily into the radio, said: "Boss we need like a shark whisperer or something. This guy is . . . he's not well. He keeps trying to breach. But he's not going for the sledge or us or anything. It's too weird."

Beside Bugs, in the passenger seat of the Rhino, the woman tensed. Her lips pursed. But she said nothing. She reached into the pocket of her suit and pulled out a pair of binoculars and raised them to her face.

Bugs barely had time to wonder at the depth of that swimsuit pocket, which hadn't looked big enough to hold a set of keys let alone a pair of binos, when they were engulfed by a flock of gulls.

There was a confused minute of flapping, crying, yellow beaks and feet and an ominous *splatting* sound on the roof of the Rhino, and the woman standing up and raising her hand and speaking to the gulls in a croaking, guttural language, and then they were gone, beating off into the sky in a white-and-gray profusion of wings.

The woman sat down and tapped the steering wheel with her binos.

"You know where this other Jet Ski is going to be," she said. It wasn't a question. "I need to be on it."

It was a bright, sunny, hot day at the beach. Campbell Parade was clogged with traffic both motorized and pedestrian, and the cast of characters making their way down the ramps to the sand were as varied as they were numerous. Fat white tour buses disgorged meandering groups all in sunglasses with white sun hats; municipal buses let loose rangy people in flip-flops and jeans shorts. Skateboarders wove in and out through the crowd. An old man sat busking beside the second ramp, and countless families with children in tow walked, laden with chairs and coolers and umbrellas and inflatable toys, across the sand to stake out territory as near the water as they could. This meant spreading out the length of the beach, much to the consternation of the lifeguard in the ATV who seemed possessed of the notion that he could keep people at the north end through the power of his voice amplified by a megaphone. But his was only one voice in thousands chatting, laughing, crying, singing, and already several squatters had laid claim to the southern half of the beach, and defiant surfers were dancing darkly on the white-water off shore.

The lady in the gray suit watched them from behind the railings on Campbell Parade, elbows in gray linen resting on the top bar, while a foot, incongruously bare, hooked toes with sky-blue painted nails over the bottom. In one hand she held a large plastic cup, slightly battered, from which she sucked bright orange crushed ice through a straw, and in the other a fidget spinner. Both things she had pulled out of the trash bin just ten feet away. Really. The junk people threw in the ocean had nothing on the trash they put in actual bins.

The lady in the gray suit sucked leftover slushie and fiddled the spinner idly as she watched the press of brightly colored bodies moving down the sand to the water. She had straight brown hair and pale skin and was wearing dark sunglasses and dark gray lipstick. At least, everyone who looked assumed it was lipstick. And when a young man smelling strongly of alcohol flopped on the rail next to her and told her in slurred but loud speech that she was the best—the *best*—dressed lady in the *entire city* and that she should really follow him because his cousin had a home distillery and they could drink *for free* those lips parted and she smiled at him. Wide. Wider than was normal, or usually possible for a human face. And her teeth gleamed, fresh and white as a baby's teeth, but far, far too sharp.

"Aw, babe, you're a *treat*," said the young man, laughing fumes at her. He was about to say more when a voice as sharp as the woman's smile cut between them like a knife.

"*Excuse me* is everything all right here?" it said. It was high and keen and far, far too sweet to be innocent. Both parties turned to look, and were confronted by a young woman carrying a surfboard longer than she was tall. She was wearing board shorts with loud pink flowers on them, a black Body Glove rash guard, and her legs looked odd. Mismatched, somehow.

The man laughed, but not in a nice way.

"Oh yeah," he said. "We're all good. Good. Yeah. Just *havin' a conversation.*"

The young woman looked at him. She had shiny black hair that had been pulled up in a loose bun behind her head, and very dark brown eyes that nevertheless seemed to blaze as she said: "Go *away*. Go away *now*."

The man jerked himself off the rail, affronted, but too uncoordinated to do anything more. He looked between the two women, turning his entire body as he did so, and then, like a cat who has been shouted at to get off the counter, he sauntered with exaggerated casualness away down the parade, pausing only to vomit over the railing to the sand below.

The lady in the gray suit turned to look at the interloper, who rolled her eyes.

"I could have taken him," said the lady in the gray suit.

A proper smile, soft and warm and a little apologetic. It made the young woman's face bunch up into a heart shape, pink at the cheeks.

"Oh, I'm *sure* you coulda," said the woman. "It's just . . . you know, the *principle* of the thing." A hand, light brown with fingers like little sausages, was thrust at the lady in the gray suit. "I'm Tom."

The lady looked at the hand for a moment, licked her lips with a thin, pale tongue, and then gave herself a little shake and took the brown hand with one of her white, blue-nailed ones.

"Call me . . . Tiger," she said.

Tom grinned. She had the slightest gap between her two front teeth. "Cool. Tiger. You just visiting Bondi or . . . ?"

"Just visiting," said Tiger. "I'm only here for today." Her face was implacable under the dark shades, but she seemed to be looking Tom over as though something confused her.

"You are going surfing?"

Tom sighed, looked over her shoulder at the beach. The lifeguards appeared to be in the process of launching a second Jet Ski, but there was some confusion about who was going to be on it. Among the tall, blue-clad men there was a much smaller figure in a yellow hat who seemed to be causing them trouble.

"I *was*," she said. "But there was a shark sighting this morning. I guess it's still inside the nets."

Tiger nodded at the surfers already out in the waves. "That doesn't seem to be stopping them," she remarked.

Tom's eyes narrowed. She had very nice eyes—almond-shaped, and the irises were so dark they looked almost like they were all pupil. She wrinkled her nose.

"That's on them," she said. Then she looked at Tiger. "You don't sound like you're from around here." Clearly she wanted to change the subject.

"Not exactly," said Tiger.

"I'm not, either," said Tom, smiling again. "I'm from Hawaii originally. I've been here almost a year, though. I could show you around the beach, if you like."

Tiger sucked on her slushie. It was almost empty. But then, the parade was lined with trash bins. Surely, there was more where it came from.

"I think I would like that very much," she said, and smiled.

Bugs's erstwhile patient was becoming an issue. Namely, that she would not go away.

"You don't *understand*," she was telling Stubsy as he tried to launch the second Jet Ski. "There's something *very wrong* with that shark. She needs *help*. You're just going to scare her on that thing."

"Ma'am, we're know what we're doing. We don't want to hurt the shark," Stubsy was saying, soft and polite and utterly ineffectual.

"Just because you don't *want* to doesn't mean you *won't*," she said.

"Ma'am," said Bugs. "You really need to let us do our job."

"No," said the old woman. "*You* need to let me do *mine*."

"Haitchbee," said Stubsy out of the corner of his mouth and into his radio. "We might need some help with this one."

"Yeah, Stubsy," said Haitchbee out of the radio. "Got a coupla officers on their way."

"Lady," said Bugs, trying very hard to hide his mounting annoyance. "I don't know what you think your job is, but—"

He broke off, because Cornflake had just come on the radio, saying words which lit up all sorts of warning signs inside Bugs's head.

"Boys, ah, we just had word of a missing person. Adult, female, last seen this morning at Ben Buckler. She was supposed to be swimming across the bay but she's not been seen since. So, ah, we've got that on our radar now."

Bugs was lifting his radio to respond when the woman, moving like a striking snake, snatched the radio from his hand and answered:

"What was her *name?*" she demanded.

A pause.

"Yeah, um," said Cornflake. "Who is this?"

Bugs moved for the radio. Stubsy moved for the radio. Somehow, neither of them could reach it before the woman said:

"This is Faraday. I need to know the missing woman's name. *And* I need a ride out to that shark."

"Ma'am, please give that radio back to the lifeguard," said Haitchbee, from the radio. "As it is you're obstructing emergency personnel and you could be arrested."

Even as the words emanated from the radio, two stout women in light blue shirts bedecked with gear came shuffling through the sand, but they stopped dead at sight of the old woman in the yellow sun hat.

"Oh . . . no," said one.

"They already *tried* that," said the old woman. She jerked her nose at the cops. "Ladies, I need to use this Jet Ski. It is a matter of life and death." She clicked on the radio. "Now, *what is the missing woman's name?*"

Five minutes later Bugs was standing on the shore of North Bondi, watching the second Jet Ski jumping the waves out to sea, Stubsy driving with Farah Day clutching his waist with one arm, the other held up to secure her hat.

He wasn't quite sure how it had happened. He looked, open-mouthed and speechless, at the two officers, who shrugged. Then a small child reached up and tugged the hem of his shorts and said something in tearful Mandarin that he nevertheless understood to mean that his parents had been misplaced.

"Here," he said, handing the child to the nearest officer. "Find his mum." And before they could do anything else he stomped over to the Rhino, which was in danger of being commandeered by a group of teenage boys.

The sun beat down on the sand, on the surf, and on the growing crowds which flocked to both, spilled past the designated swimming area, and soon the entire beach was covered in a buzzing mass as thousands of humans threw down towels, set up umbrellas, got out drinks, and went splashing in the surf.

Up in the lifeguard tower, Cornflake rested his face gently in his hands and groaned loudly. "I've never wished for a bluebottle storm," he muttered through his fingers. "But that's all we need right now."

"Haha," said Haitchbee. "Have you had your lunch yet?"

"No," groaned Cornflake.

Haitchbee, gazing out the windows at the beach like some sort of man-shaped surveillance turret, said: "Go take your lunch, Flake."

"We're short enough as it is," Cornflake protested.

"Cutlet is coming in," said Haitchbee, still with his eyes on the beach. "Should be here any minute."

Cutlet was their resident Iron Man, soft-sand running, surf swimming, bicycle-commuting superhero, who had returned to lifeguarding since to him it counted as relaxing. He came in the back door to the tower just as Cornflake was leaving by it, still in his cycling cap, the only blemish in his otherwise perfect golden tan being the white patches around his eyes from his near-constant use of sunglasses. They stood together by the door while Haitchbee scanned the beach and Cornflake briefed Cutlet on the morning's events.

"A shark *on* the beach?" Cutlet said.

"Yeah," said Cornflake. "But there's more."

He told Cutlet about the missing person. Karly Simmons, a local no less, had been missed from her rendezvous at Ben Buckler that morning.

"And now there's a shark in the bay," Cutlet said, his face falling.

"It gets worse," Cornflake began.

"Flake, *lunch, go,*" said Haitchbee.

"I'm going," said Cornflake, slapped Cutlet on the shoulder, and skidded out the door.

On the beach, Tom and Tiger walked down the thin strip of relatively clear sand just below the parade wall, the former carrying her giant board, the latter chewing the straw of her vanquished slushie.

"Most of the families go swimming up at the north end," Tom was explaining. "There's a kiddie pool up there, and Flat Rock, which'll cut you up nasty if you're unlucky but people still jump. You see the flags—the red-and-yellow ones—those mark safe swimming areas. The lifeguards set them up each day. They don't like people swimming down at the south end, because there's almost always a rip there. People who don't know the ocean see the water with no waves, think it's calm, get in, and the next second they're getting pulled off shore. They panic, and then they need to get rescued. Also, because it's closer to the bus stop, they get a lot of tourists who don't know the ocean, or how to swim very well. That's why they call it Backpacker's Rip."

"We appear to be walking toward it," Tiger observed, chewing thoughtfully on her straw.

"They don't like people *swimming* in it," Tom said. "So there's less swimmers. Which makes it better for *surfing.*"

"You're not afraid of being sucked off shore?"

Tom laughed. "I'm Hawaiian," she said, as if this explained everything. When Tiger raised a thin brown eyebrow she elaborated: "I've been swimming in the ocean since I was four. I used to go for rip rides for fun. See, it won't sweep you out to sea—well, it kinda will—but all you have to do is swim *sideways*, across the current, and you get back in the incoming water. Sometimes it's just a matter of a couple feet and then you're on a sandbank. The ocean is bigger and stronger than all of us, but if you respect it, it won't kill you. Most of the time."

They were approaching the south end, where a tall pole held a sign warning swimmers not to. There was a little stand holding a blue surfboard even longer than Tom's, and she set hers down a little ways from it.

Tiger tilted her head and peered over the tops of her sunglasses at Tom. "You're afraid of it," she said.

"Of course I'm afraid of it," Tom said, as if this were obvious. She sighed. "But I love it." She sat down in the sand next to her board and stretched out her mismatched legs. Tiger noticed that while one foot's toes spread and wiggled in the sand, the other's seemed fused together.

Tiger took the straw out of her mouth. It was an inch shorter than it had been. She fiddled with the spinner.

"How do you love something you're afraid of?" she asked, folding herself up to sit next to Tom, pushing her blue toenails into the sand.

Tom laughed, a short, breathy sigh.

"It's not that hard. Like . . . I can recognize that there are legitimate things to be afraid of, but I can still appreciate the beauty and the serenity and . . . and the *joy* I experience from it."

She paused, looking down at her feet.

"It's like how I can still love sharks," she said.

Tiger looked down at Tom, her mouth a thin gray line under her black glasses.

"Why wouldn't you love sharks?" she asked in a voice as thin as her mouth.

Tom gave her a quizzical look.

"You really haven't noticed? I've seen you looking at my leg."

Tiger glanced down. Yes, still two legs. One a slightly different shade of brown than the other, with fused toes. Only, now, from this angle, Tiger saw how that one had a strange band across it, just under the knee, and behind the knee, a weird gap. A gap where there should have been flesh but instead there was a little hollow with something black and shiny inside.

"When I was thirteen," Tom said, voice very calm and even, "a shark bit it off."

"Oh," said Tiger. Spun the spinner. "What were you doing?"

"Surfing," said Tom. "Just like any other day. Caught a wave. A shark came out of it. Took my leg and a chunk of my board." She made a face. Somewhere between annoyance and amusement. "Four *weeks* out of the water. Worst month of my life." Then she smiled. "I got really into sharks after that. I wanted to understand them. See them. Help them. Sharks are really important, you know, and most of them aren't even a threat to humans. *We're* the ones going into their territory and messing things up. Littering, polluting, overfishing. It's just awful."

"Yes, it is," agreed Tiger, but her voice sounded distant.

"I mean, *shark fin soup?* It's hideous. It's just . . . status," Tom went on. "And people are so shallow. They watch *Jaws* and then it's all 'oooh sharks are all scary man-eaters and bad!' People kill more sharks than sharks kill people. People kill more *people* than sharks do."

"Humans," said Tiger, still in that distant voice. "Humans kill more sharks than sharks kill humans."

"Yes," said Tom. "That's what I said. Are you all right?"

Tiger was looking out to sea, beyond the surf, where the two Jet Skis had converged and were circling each other, slowly.

"Where . . . where was this?" she asked. "Where did you lose your leg?"

"Kauai," said Tom, matter-of-factly. "Lumaha'i Beach."

Tiger frowned. "Which beach is that?"

"North shore, off 56," said Tom, squinting up at her. "You've been to Kauai?"

"Remind me which island it is," said Tiger.

"It's north of O'ahu," said Tom. "The one at the top."

Tiger's face cleared. "I don't think I got that far north," she admitted. "It was a while ago."

"You've traveled a lot?"

"Oh, oh yes," said Tiger, but she seemed disinclined to talk about herself. She wanted to hear more about what Tom thought of sharks, and since she was content to actually sit and listen and not argue with Tom's opinions, Tom liked this just fine. She was on the point of asking Tiger out to lunch, when there was a disruption in the sea.

One of the Jet Skis was tearing toward shore, looking for all the world like it was headed straight for them. At the same time there was a honking up the beach and a lifeguard in an ATV could be seen navigating the crowds, heading south.

Both women stood up, but while Tiger looked around curiously, Tom looked at the water. Specifically, she looked at the water where the Jet Ski was aiming.

"*Oh,*" she said, quiet but harsh, and then she had grabbed her board and was running down the sand, into the water, skipping a little to get over the smaller waves, and then she was on the board chest down, paddling, mismatched feet kicking the air behind her, to a dark shape fifty meters off shore.

The surfer reached the flailing swimmer—who was on the brink of becoming a non-swimmer—before the Jet Ski, but only just. Handing him off to the guard on the rescue sledge to get towed to shore, she coasted in behind the Jet Ski, catching a wave almost as an afterthought.

They were greeted by the guard in the ATV, who helped the man up onto the sand where he sat down and was shortly besieged by his family— wife and two kids—and they began laughing in that nervous, hysterical way of people who are scared and embarrassed and don't know what else to do. The lifeguard began patiently explaining about rips, and not swimming in them, and telling the man to seek medical attention if he developed a persistent cough or had any difficulty breathing.

"If this nice lady hadn't gotten to you, you'd probably be *dead*," he said, pointing at Tom. Then he actually looked at her. "Thanks for that, by the way. It was a good catch."

Tom shrugged. Ordinarily assisting in a rescue would have been the highlight of her day, and she'd been looking forward to seeing Tiger's reaction, but now they were back at the beach, Tiger was nowhere to be seen. The sand by the sign and the rescue board was empty. Not even the battered slushie cup remained.

Out beyond the breakers, on the second Jet Ski, Stubsy was quickly learning what Bugs and the police officers had already known: that Farah Day was the most impossible person to deal with.

She kept giving orders as if she expected them to be followed, and worse, somehow they *were* followed, even though Stubsy was quite sure he never agreed to taking her on the Jet Ski—she wasn't even wearing a wetsuit, let alone a PFD—and yet, here she was, clutching his waist from behind as they bounced gaily out to meet Vanna and Pebbles.

She wouldn't stop asking questions: Had they hurt the shark? When had she first been seen? Had she spoken to them?

She kept referring to the shark as female, like it was a lost child she was intent on finding. And she wouldn't answer any of *his* questions: Who was she? What was she doing here? Did she have a relative or a caregiver they could call?

She did chuckle at that last one, but only said: "Calling Tesla won't do you any good. Can this thing go any faster?"

But they were already almost to Vanna, and Stubsy coasted up alongside them with relief that, if he had to suffer Farah Day, he wouldn't have to suffer *alone*.

"Who is this?" asked Vanna, gazing at the woman in consternation.

"I'm Faraday," said the woman, saying her name like it was one word. "I'm here to help, believe it or not."

"Who *is* she?" Vanna asked Stubsy, dismayed.

He had been out on the Jet Ski, Stubsy knew, almost since dawn. Had to be dying to use a bathroom. Probably dehydrated. And yet he appeared as calm and collected as ever, if a little irritated.

"No idea," said Stubsy. "I don't even know how she got on my Jet Ski. Where's the shark?"

Pebbles, who was sitting astride behind Vanna, pointed seaward. "It keeps trying to make a break for shore," he said. "Be *careful*."

"She," Farah-Day corrected.

"You're a shark expert?" Vanna asked.

"Something like that," Farah-Day said evasively, and might have said more but both radios went off at the same time.

"Mates," said Cutlet on the radio. "We got someone out the back in Backpacker's. Black shirt. He's waving but he's not going anywhere, and he looks tired."

"*Exciting,*" said Vanna, in tones that suggested he felt exactly the opposite.

"Looks like Drover is going for a paddle but he's coming from the north end," said Cutlet from the radio. "Can I get a Jet Ski down there?"

"This is Jet Ski One," Vanna said. "I'm on my way." And just like that he was off, Stubsy thought, with some relief.

Then he was alone with Farah-Day. And the shark.

He could see it—her—now, as a dark gray shape distressingly close to the surface. Easily three meters long, she snaked slowly through the water with a kind of thoughtless grace that, despite the situation, was beautiful and alluring. As he watched, her dorsal fin broke the surface, raising the tiniest of white waves, before receding, and he remembered what Pebbles had said earlier.

She kept trying to breach.

Sharks weren't built to breach, like dolphins, but that didn't mean they couldn't propel themselves out of the water if they were properly motivated.

He tucked his knees further up into the Jet Ski, which had never before felt so precarious.

Pressure was released from his waist and twisting his head sideways he saw, to his horror, that Farah-Day had climbed down onto the rescue sledge and was lying with her face inches from the water.

"Lady—Ma'am—don't—" he began.

"Get me *closer,*" snapped Farah-Day. "I need to *talk* to her."

"I—*what?*" said Stubsy.

"I need to *talk* to her," Farah-Day repeated, taking off her sunglasses the better to glare at him. "She's scared and confused, and you would be, too."

"Ma'am," said Stubsy, reining in his temper like it was an overactive dog. "She's a *shark.* She's not going to listen to you."

To his surprise this actually stopped Farah-Day. She blinked. Put her glasses back on. Glanced at the water. The shark had moved—*damn* the shark had *moved.*

"Hold on," said Stubsy, and hastily scooted the Jet Ski along so it was once again between the shark and the shore.

"You're right," Farah-Day said suddenly from behind his ear. "She won't listen to *me.* But she might listen to *you.* Given the right circumstances."

Stubsy decided he didn't like where this conversation was going. At all.

"Ma'am," he began, but stopped when a scrawny brown hand grabbed his upper arm, nails digging into his wetsuit.

"*Listen,*" hissed Farah-Day, in a voice so intense it overpowered all other sound. The slosh of the water and the whistle of the wind and the rumble of the engine faded away, and all that remained was that voice, saying: "We've got to get her to shore. If the magic wears off and she's out here, it'll be so much worse. You have a protected area of bay on the north end of the beach. We'll bring her there. *You* will bring her there. She'll listen to you—and she won't hurt you, I'll make *sure* of it."

"Ma'am," said Stubsy, weakly. "How am I supposed to talk to a *shark?*"

"Her name is Karly," said Farah-Day.

Stubsy opened his mouth in exasperation, and something metal the size and shape of a quarter was shoved neatly between his teeth.

He tried to spit it out. He couldn't. He felt dizzy. The world was a big, confused, blue whirl. He was tipping over sideways and realized he was going in the water a moment before he hit the surface. He was aware of Farah-Day's face above him, backlit against the blazing sky, and around her was a storm of white wings. Gulls, coming to roost on her shoulders.

Then he was in the water, and things got very confusing indeed.

First it felt like every part of his body—including his brain—turned numb, and then came back as pins and needles. When these faded they left his body in a completely different shape than it had been.

He felt . . . expansive. His feet—and they weren't feet anymore, but tail flukes—were much, much farther away than they had been. His arms were not arms, but fins, and even though he was underwater and holding his breath, that felt . . . fine. Like he could go for twenty minutes and not need a breath.

The Jet Ski was a tiny, dark object floating above his right eyebrow—or what passed for his right eyebrow now. Did whales even have eyebrows?

"Sorry, that was abrupt," said Farah-Day's voice inside his head. "But I had to do *something* and it's easier to change other people than it is to change myself. Now go get Karly."

He was a whale. A *big* whale, by the feel of it. That should have been impossible. Should have made him panic.

But whales are not built to panic, and Stubsy discovered that, in his whale body, he felt unaccountably calm and serene. Almost elated.

The shark was a small gray shape a little to his left. She'd swum away from him when he'd hit the water—as any sensible creature would had done—but he only needed to twitch his tail and suddenly he was beside her.

"Who are you? Where did you come from? What are you *doing?*" she was asking, in her shark voice. It was not at all a human voice. It involved fin movement and electrical pulses and some smells, but Stubsy understood her perfectly. Better still, he understood how to answer.

Falling back to the familiar words that had been drilled into him over hours and hours of training, he said, in deep whines and motions of his flippers and a little burst of bubbles:

"Hi, I'm a lifeguard, I'm here to help."

*　*　*

It was a little after 2 p.m. The sand was hot, the sun had begun descending to the west, the water was cool and blue and inviting, and for the third time that day the shark siren blared out across Bondi Beach, driving bathers from the water and surfers to shore. They gathered there, dripping, squinting, some confused and frightened, others annoyed and impatient. No sooner had feet hit the sand than Drover was pelted with questions asking when they would be allowed back into the water.

Drover looked at the crowded beach, then out to sea where the Jet Skis were making their way carefully around Flat Rock toward the kiddie pool. Vanna, exhausted but in denial about it, had been replaced by Cutlet, who was now escorting the second Jet Ski and—and this was the part that Drover was having trouble with—the shark and *whale* to shore.

"A *whale?*" he'd said.

"Looks like a gray, or a blue," said Cornflake, back from lunch and sounding like he'd swallowed a ball of styrofoam.

"Why . . . why are they bringing them in?" Drover asked. It made no logical sense.

"Because that's where they're going," Cutlet said. "And Farah Day says we can't stop them. She says . . . " he broke off to listen to a high-pitched voice over the roar of engine and ocean. "She says they know what they're doing."

He sounded shaken. He sounded like he'd just made a body retrieval. And, Drover felt this was perhaps the most urgent issue, there was no sign of Stubsy.

"Jet Ski, where is Stubsy?" he asked.

"Stubsy's here, mate," said Cutlet. "He's the whale."

On the beach, and on the knoll, and on the cliffs of Ben Buckler and on Campbell Parade and the car park and the skate bowl and just about everywhere there was a view of the water, crowds formed. People had stormed from the water at the alarm, but now they turned and watched, stunned into silence at the sight of the enormous, graceful, overpowering presence of the *whale* as it coasted serenely out of the ocean and into the surf. Next to it, the blue-green shark swam under its flipper, like a new calf, barely noticed until the pair reached the relative calm of the shallow waters beside the kiddie pool.

The crowd had become nervous by then, worried for the whale which would surely be beached if it kept on its current course. But when it got to waters too shallow for its bulk, it suddenly vanished.

At least, it appeared to vanish to the people watching from a distance. To Bugs, who had been in charge of clearing the kiddie pool area and was standing over it, he clearly saw the whale shimmer, turn to blue foam, and then condense suddenly in on itself until all that remained was the shark, floating serenely in the shallow water, and Stubsy, swimming in a desperate crawl away from it. He swam until his arms struck sand, got up, tried to walk, and fell over in the little waves. He sat there, the water sloshing around his waist, and looked back at the shark.

It hadn't moved. It was still floating, calm and effectively still, apparently most interested in the sand directly below it.

Training took over Bugs's legs and, heedless of the shark, he trotted into the water and grabbed Stubsy under the armpits.

"'M okay," Stubsy said, a little thickly. He spat something out into his hand. Something the size of a quarter, but browner, with a hole in the middle. "Legs are just weird, that's all. Where's the Jet Ski?"

At that moment Cutlet was still a little way out past the shark, while the second was beaching just south of them. Bugs stared as Farah Day hopped off the machine and went marching right back into the water toward shark.

It was suddenly overwhelmingly too much.

"Mate," said Bugs. "You were a *whale*."

"Yeah," laughed Stubsy, a little hysterically.

"Mate," said Bugs, and couldn't go on.

You heard—you always *heard*—about things going on. Weird things. People would say and do the wildest things to get attention. And there was always *something* spooky going on in America these days. But . . . *but* . . .

"How the heck were you a *whale?*"

Stubsy shrugged expressively. "I think Farah-Day is a witch," he said.

Which brought Bugs's attention back to the woman, standing in the gentle surf next to the shark, who was swimming languidly back and forth next to the kiddie pool. She'd put her mask and snorkel back on, and was intermittently putting her face in the water and gesticulating with her hands.

"What's she trying to do?" Bugs asked.

"Probably talk to her," said Stubsy.

"*Talk* to her?"

"Yeah." Stubsy looked down at the coin in his hand. "I think that's Karly Simmons. The missing swimmer."

First, Bugs felt a flood of automatic relief. *No body retrieval.* Then he realized. "But that's a *shark*."

"Mate," said Stubsy. "I was a *whale*."

Bugs swallowed. Half his brain was in a whirl. The other half—the lifeguard half—told him gently that he should get somewhere out of the sun and sit down.

He settled for sitting on the retaining wall of the kiddie pool, where he could keep an eye on Farah Day and the shark and the beach.

"Mate," he said. "What's going on?"

As if she'd heard, Farah Day popped up out of the water and came sloshing through the gentle waves toward them. Pulling off her mask she stuffed it into her pocket—and really, that pocket had to be bigger on the inside or something—and took out a bag of lollies, which she thrust at Stubsy.

"Eat that, thank me later," she said, as Stubsy took the bag, nonplussed. She peered over at Bugs from under the brim of her hat. "This is a tough one," she said. "I can't change her *back* because she's got a mutually exclusive link to whoever laid the transformation spell on her. But I managed to explain as much to her, and she understands now more or less what's going on, and to stay in the shallow water and not bite anyone. She is hungry, though, so if you've got any spare meat lying around I'm sure she'd appreciate it."

Bugs nodded, as if what the woman was saying was perfectly reasonable. It was the only thing he could do. That or scream.

"You can let people back in the water, though. Not right here, of course, but farther down the beach."

"Uh . . . " said Bugs, glancing at the shadow which was all he could see of the shark.

"She's not really a shark, you understand," Farah Day said, perfectly serious. "She's a transformed human. She won't hurt anyone."

Bugs stared at her. Beside him, Stubsy had succumbed to temptation and ripped open the miraculously dry bag of lollies. They looked like Tim Tams. Bugs faintly envied him.

"The thing we need to worry about," said Farah Day, "is that mutually exclusive link."

"How's that?" asked Bugs, dourly.

"Because, she's a *shark*," said Farah Day. "A human who got turned into a shark through a form-swapping spell. Which means, somewhere nearby, there's a shark who's been turned into a *human*."

Tom had all but despaired of catching any proper waves when the alarm sounded again: the blessed, brief blare of the all-clear. Though the lifeguards were keeping people away from the north end for some reason, that made little difference to her, and all in all she managed a decent afternoon of surfing the gentle swell and emerged around 5, wet and hungry, and began the trek up the beach to her car.

There was still a crowd up at the north end, and Tom could see a couple park rangers along with a TV crew. It was because of this distraction, she later decided, that she didn't see the drunk angling to block her way up the ramp.

When she did, warning bells went off in her head, and she began assessing her surfboard as a potential weapon. There was just something about the way he was standing, casual and yet confrontative, that made her feel intensely unsafe.

She turned. Made for the next ramp. To her dismay, he hopped down onto the sand and followed her.

"Hey, *hey*," he was saying, trotting to keep up. "I just wanted to *apologize*, you gotta let a bloke *apologize*."

Tom didn't even look at him, although she did tilt her head to keep his shape in her peripheral vision. There were a few other people on the beach up here, but they were studiously ignoring the man. Lucky them.

"Hey, hey *I'm talkin' to ya*," said the man, coming up on her left. Tom switched the board so it was between them. "What's wrong with you?" he said, on the other side of her board. "Why you gotta be like that?"

She was almost to the next ramp. She picked up her pace to keep ahead of the man. And to give herself momentum. The parade was crowded, at least. She wanted to get up into that crowd.

The man caught her at the top of the ramp, blocking her way.

"*Bitch* I'm *talking* to you," he said, laughing, but not in a happy way, and grabbed her board.

A wave of people went past behind him. From where she stood, Tom clearly saw the lady in the gray suit slip between the bodies, lunging out of the crowd with her head held strangely and stiffly forward, her mouth opened much wider than should have been possible.

She latched onto the man's shoulder, still moving, so that he was pulled sharply around in a tight circle, and then she was gone, striding off into the crowd with something trailing from her mouth.

The man collapsed, dazed, in front of Tom. His shoulder was a mess of ripped cotton, skin, and blood, and he cursed after Tiger almost reflexively before the pain got through to his inebriated brain and he began to scream.

Tom wanted to run. But there was nowhere she *could* run except back down the ramp. So she put her board down and stripped off her rashie. People were stopping on the parade, staring.

"Someone, call an ambulance," Tom shouted at them. "Or get a lifeguard—or both!"

The man was curled on the ground now, crying, clutching his shoulder, which was dripping blood at an alarming rate.

Dripping, Tom reminded herself. Not spurting. There was that, at least. She was trying to get her rashie over the worst of it and apply pressure when the lifeguard from earlier appeared, already with gloves on, and gently took over.

"Mate, I'm a lifeguard, I'm here to help. Can you tell me what happened?"

When the man just shook and cried, he glanced over his shoulder at Tom. "Did you see what happened?"

Tom, beginning to shake herself, nodded. Then she said what she knew was impossible, and yet what she knew, deep down, was true:

"He got bit by a shark."

Bugs arrived at the tower just after the patient and the girl, Farah Day close on his heel. He took one look at the ragged wound on the man's shoulder. It could have been from a shark. A very small shark.

"It wasn't Karly," he said. "We've been watching her the whole time."

"I found them at the top of the third ramp," Drover said. "Miss Tomiko here says he was harassing her, and some woman came out of the crowd and bit him."

Bugs felt a sharp jab at his waist and instinctively moved aside. Farah Day pushed past him and over to Tomiko, who'd been wrapped in a towel and set up in a chair next to surveillance.

"You saw the shark," she said, harsh and direct. But the girl seemed to revive at the words.

"Yes," said said, her voice hollow.

"What did it look like?"

She blinked. "She looks like a woman. A woman in a gray suit—like a business suit—but she's barefoot. She has . . . blue toenails. Brown hair. Her name's Tiger."

Farah Day leaned backward to glance into the first-aid area.

"Was he bothering you?" she asked, briskly.

The girl shuddered. "*Was,*" she said. "Earlier, he was bothering Tiger. So I told him to get lost. He found me coming off the beach. Wouldn't leave me alone. Tiger came out of the crowd. She bit him."

She lifted her face, gazing at Farah Day with wide black eyes. "What's *happening?*"

"Magic," said Farah Day, sounding disgusted. She reached into her pocket and pulled out another bag of Tim Tams, which she thrust at the girl. "Eat those," she said and marched out of the tower.

Bugs followed her. She was leaning on the rail overlooking the beach, which was even more crowded as the heat of the afternoon swelled—one last hurrah before sunset. There was a gull perched on the rail next to her, and it eyed Bugs as he came to stand behind the woman.

"You got that," Farah Day was muttering to the gull. "This has gone on long enough." She tossed it what looked like a witchetty grub, and the gull flew off in a flurry of white and gray feathers. It left Farah Day peering at Bugs keenly.

"You need anything?" she said.

Bugs sighed. It was just going to be one of those days. "Have you got any more of those Tim Tams?" he asked.

The sun sank low over the suburbs of Sydney, casting long shadows across the beach, which slowly cleared of people—but not entirely. Surfers still cut the waves at the south end, and up north, a small crowd had gathered. Reporters and two men with cameras were interviewing Haitchbee, while Cornflake walked the makeshift perimeter of stretched-out caution tape, shooing those who crossed it back to the other side. Stubsy, technically off duty but still in his uniform, sat on the retaining wall of the kiddie pool, where he could keep an eye on Karly.

They had given her an entire tuna, which she had eaten almost delicately, and now she was swimming back and forth beside the pool, apparently oblivious to the activity on the beach.

Movement on the sand made Stubsy look up. Cutlet was out in the Rhino, collecting flags, signs and surfboards and announcing to what remained of the public that the lifeguards were ending their service for the day, and that they continued to swim at their own risk. But that wasn't what had caught his attention. It was the gulls.

A huge flock of gulls had arrived on the parade, whirling and squawking and appearing to drive something in their midst down toward the beach.

They continued moving, in a tumbling, whirling flock, across the sand to where Farah-Day stood, hands on her hips, and there they dissipated, revealing a somewhat harried woman in a light gray linen suit, sunglasses and bare feet.

The two women stood talking, Farah-Day standing very straight and indignant, the woman in gray linen picking feathers out of her hair. Eventually they both turned and walked up the beach together.

Stubsy felt a strange prickle creep up his arms as they approached. There was something not quite right about the lady in the gray suit, but he couldn't put his finger on it.

She had a dark smear around her mouth, and when she smiled at Haitchbee and the cameras her teeth looked far too sharp.

She walked past the caution tape—Cornflake stopped dead at the sight of her—and across the sand to the edge of the water. Then she paused, and lifting her shades up her forehead, she looked back down the beach to the tower, where a girl wrapped in a towel had come out to stand on the balcony.

The lady in the gray suit made a quick salute, and then she strode into the shallow water, sending little splashes up around her bare feet as she went.

Then she turned darker all over, foam rising around her legs, and at the same time Karly came swimming at her, fast and hard.

Shark and woman met. There was a burst of white-water and foam. And then the shark was swimming out to sea, its dorsal fin a retreating black triangle against the darkening water, and it was a different woman entirely who stood up on the beach, panting and pale, but very much alive.

Karly Simmons was easily six feet tall and stood in the slight S-curve of someone who could move very fast through water even when she wasn't in the shape of a shark. She wore a gray onesie and a blue cap and tinted goggles which she tore off her head as she looked around, blinking water out of her eyes. She was quickly surrounded by a concerned huddle of lifeguards, but she pushed them away. She seemed more annoyed than anything. She walked a little shakily over to the retaining wall where Stubsy was still sitting, and sat down next to him.

"Why," she asked, wringing her hair out, "do they call you *Stubsy?*"

Stubsy felt his ears heating up.

"My last name is Stubbs," he said. "Also, 'cause I'm kinda short."

Karly frowned at him.

"I'm shorter than *you*," he said. He wasn't about to stand up to prove it. Even sitting, Karly towered over him. Leaner, maybe, but obviously taller.

Karly waved her hand dismissively. "Lots of people are shorter than me," she said. She looked at him expectantly.

"Well," Stubsy admitted. "My real name's Andrew."

"Andrew," said Karly, smiling. "That's nice. You made a good whale, Andrew."

"Thanks," said Stubsy, still feeling hot around his ears.

Karly's face froze, still in that faint half-smile. "I was a *shark*," she said, as if she was only just realizing it. She stood up in a hurry, wobbled, and then sat back down again. "Where's that witch?" she demanded. "I've got lots of questions for her!"

Stubsy looked around, and sighed. Of course now that they actually wanted to see Farah-Day, that impossible woman was nowhere to be found. Beyond the crowd of lifeguards and the reporter and the handful of curious surfers, the sand was cast in cool purply shadow.

The sun had set on Bondi Beach. The day was over.

Sunlight hit the café on Campbell Parade just as the old woman sat creakily down with her tray of breakfast. She glared at it, and put on her shades as she sipped coffee and began slicing into her French toast.

Faraday was actually feeling her age this morning. Something about dealing with sharks—oh, and that Hamilton fool had called in the middle of the night. That was it. Talking to Jill always gave her a headache. And there was probably going to be another apocalypse before she got back to America. She sighed. She ate her toast.

She was just beginning to feel better when a shadow crossed in front of her, and to her consternation a second tray appeared on the table and a young woman sat down across from her.

Not just any young woman. The young woman from yesterday. Black hair. Black eyes. No towel this time and looking a lot better than when she'd been huddled in the lifeguard tower.

"So," said Tom, digging into her omelet. "Explain how it all works."

"How did you find me?" Faraday demanded, sour.

"Honestly I was just passing and saw you going in," said Tom around a bite of omelet.

"You shouldn't have seen me," said Faraday, nose to her toast.

"Because you're a witch?" said Tom.

Faraday humphed.

"So, explain," said Tom.

Faraday sighed. She did so *hate* explaining things.

"It wasn't transformation. It was form swapping," she said, and took a big sip of coffee.

"Mm," said Tom. "So, like, the shark got to be a woman because a woman got to be a shark?"

"Very basically," said Faraday. "Yes."

Another shadow. Another tray joined theirs on the table. Steak and eggs. Hands with blue painted nails. Tom let out a strangled gasp.

"I'm still new at this," said the lady in the gray suit, stealing a chair from a nearby table and sitting in it. "But you were right, what you said yesterday. And it's irresponsible to let a human loose in the ocean like that." She put the entire steak into her mouth at once, chewed twice, and swallowed.

Faraday chanced a glance at her companions. Tom was staring at the woman, a forkful of omelet frozen halfway to her mouth. The lady in the gray suit was maneuvering her first egg onto a piece of toast.

"Who did you grab this time?" Faraday asked.

The woman—shark—looked at her, all wide-eyed marine innocence.

"No one," she said. "As I said, it'd be *irresponsible*. This is all me. Just me." The toast and its accompanying egg disappeared into her maw.

And tomorrow it would be the sea snakes and the crabs and the jellyfish and good *grief* she wouldn't be getting back to America anytime soon, Faraday thought.

The woman looked seriously over her plate at Tom.

"I'm not ... *sorry*," she said. "About what happened to you. But ... you didn't *deserve* it."

Tom shivered. Then she shrugged. Put the bite of omelet in her mouth at last. Chewed. Swallowed. Then she frowned.

"You *bit* that man," she said reproachfully.

"Oh," said the woman airily. "I knew you could handle him, but it's the *principle* of the thing." She smiled. Very wide. Full of teeth. And yet ... friendly?

Tom narrowed her eyes.

"Aren't you gonna ask if he's okay?"

"Nope," said the woman, going for her second egg.

"But you can't just go around taking chunks out of people," said Tom. "That's not ... that's not how *humans* do it."

"And I should do things like humans do?" said the woman, devouring her second egg on toast.

"If you're shaped like a human, being around humans, then ... *yes*," said Tom.

The woman smiled at her. Bright and sunny as the morning.

"Maybe, if I had someone to show me how humans did things ... ?" she trailed off suggestively.

Tom's mouth came open in astonishment.

Faraday took her plate of toast and the opportunity to escape. Neither of them noticed her go.

"I'm not going to be your *babysitter*," Tom said, eating her omelet with a vengeance.

"See, I don't even know what a babysitter *is*," said the lady in the gray suit. "I'm completely helpless, really."

Tom snorted with laughter.

"Please?" said the shark-woman, quietly. "The whole point of this is . . . I want to understand. Human-people. It's a lot of trouble, actually, putting myself into this shape."

Tom looked over her omelet at the woman. At the shark. Her face was blank. Then she sighed.

"Let me finish this," she said, and took a big bite of omelet.

"I can help," offered the shark, grinning.

"No," said Tom, but she was smiling.

She finished her omelet. The shark chewed on her plastic fork. They looked around for the witch, but she had already gone. So they stacked the empty trays in the receptacle, and then, side by side, the young woman and the shark-woman crossed the parade and walked down the ramp to the crowded beach.

It was a beautiful day, and anything could happen.

THE SAGA CONTINUES . . .

Jill, Selene, and Clara
and the staff of MCSIR
will return in

THE SOUND
OF WINGS

DRIVING
W H E E L 4
ARCANA

Apocalypse Paused · Half Arcana
White Noise · A Bloody Breeze · Ghost Ocean
The Sound of Wings · Under the Midnight Sun
Loki is Alive and Well and Living in New Orleans
Beyond Ragnarök

ABOUT THE AUTHOR

Goldeen Ogawa is a self-taught author, illustrator and cartoonist. She works primarily in watercolor, colored and graphite pencil, subverted tropes and under-represented narrative voices in the genres of fantasy and science fiction. Her other works of fiction include *The Adventures of Bouragner Felpz* and *Professor Odd,* and her artwork can be found online at **goldeenogawa.com.** Born and raised in California, she currently lives in Bend, Oregon.

TEXT AND DESIGN

The body of this book was typeset using LaTeX in Skema Pro Livro.

Cover art and book design by the author.

www.ingramcontent.com/pod-product-compliance
Lightning Source LLC
Chambersburg PA
CBHW050839030726
47503CB00007BA/2244